MW01070605

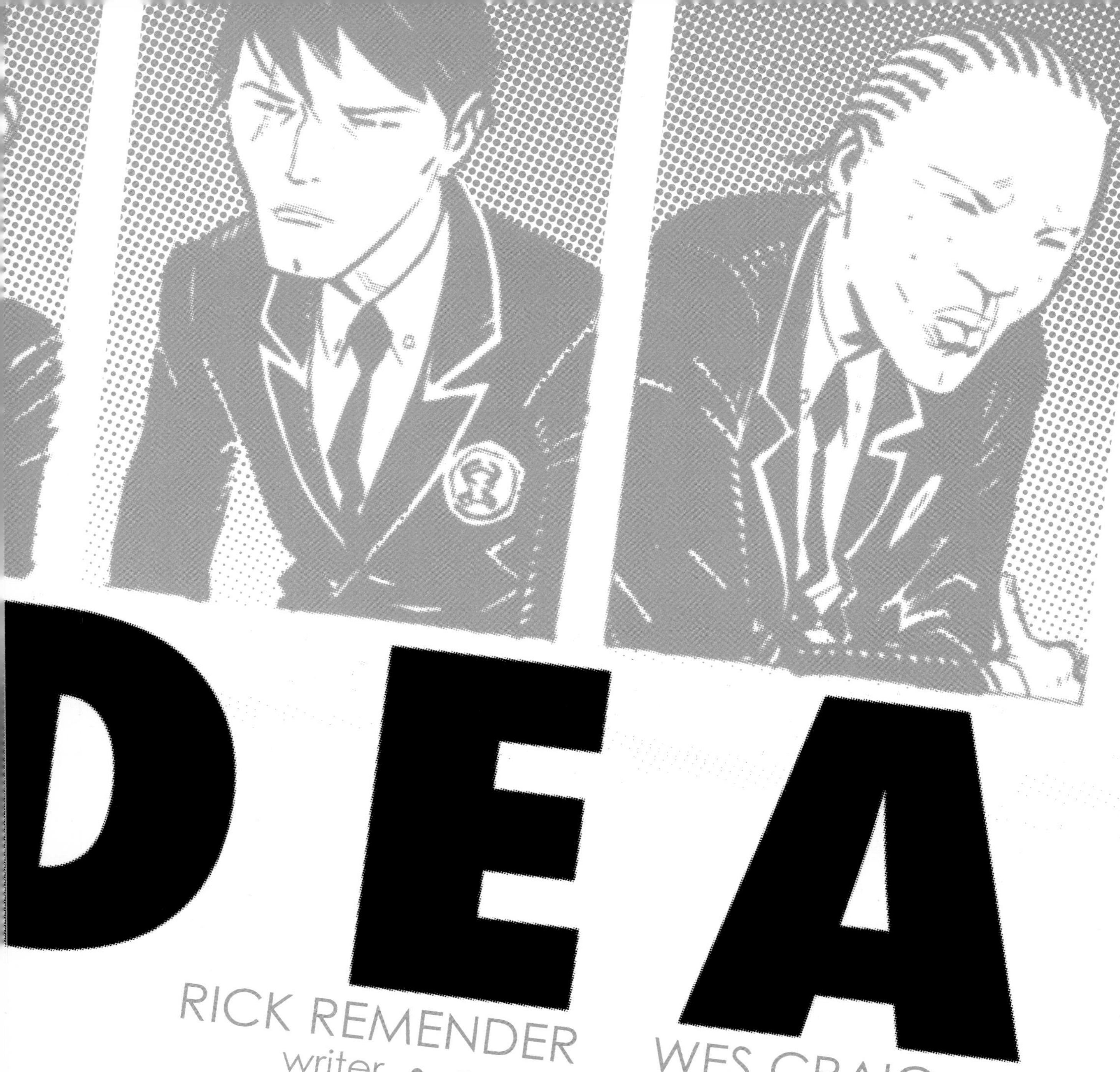

DEA

RICK REMENDER
writer • co-creators • artist
WES CRAIG

CL

BOOK 3
TEEN AGE RIOT

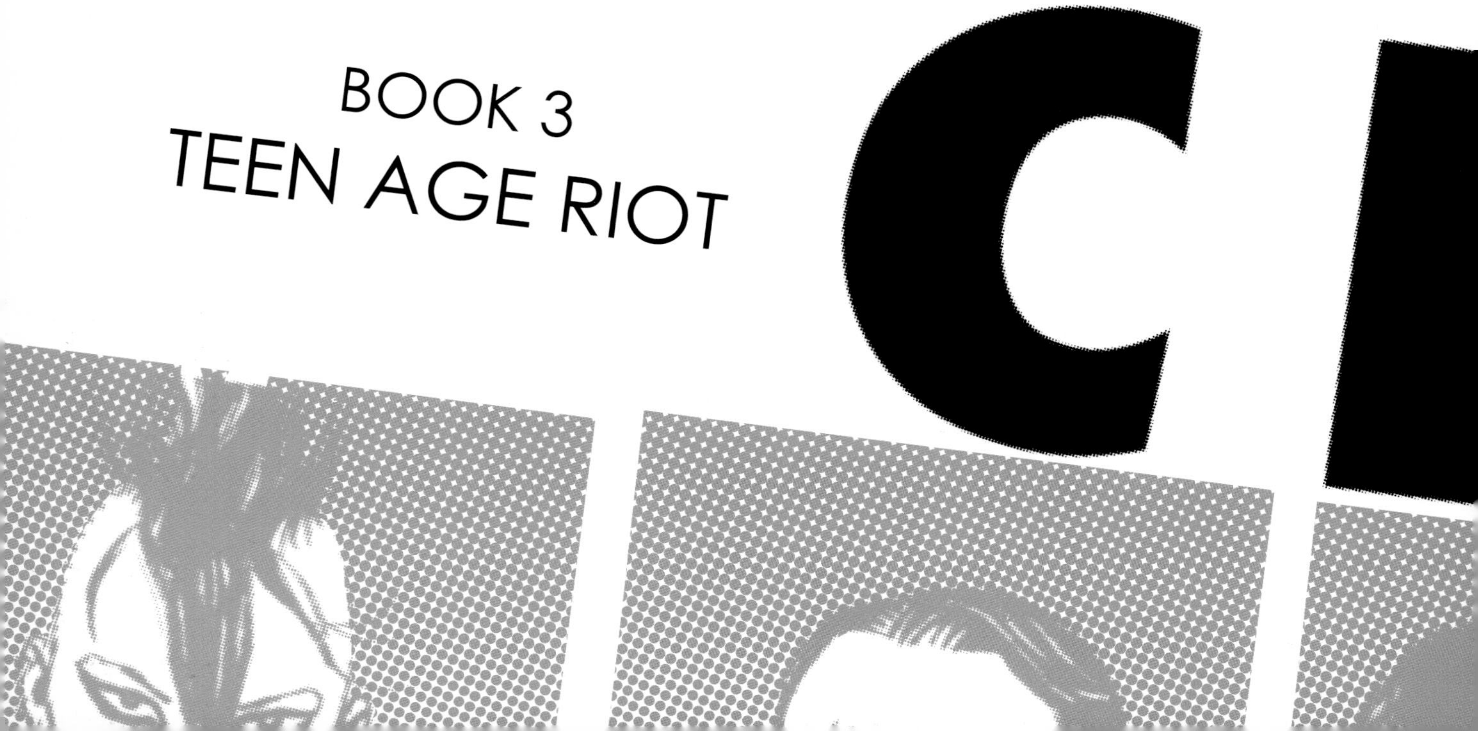

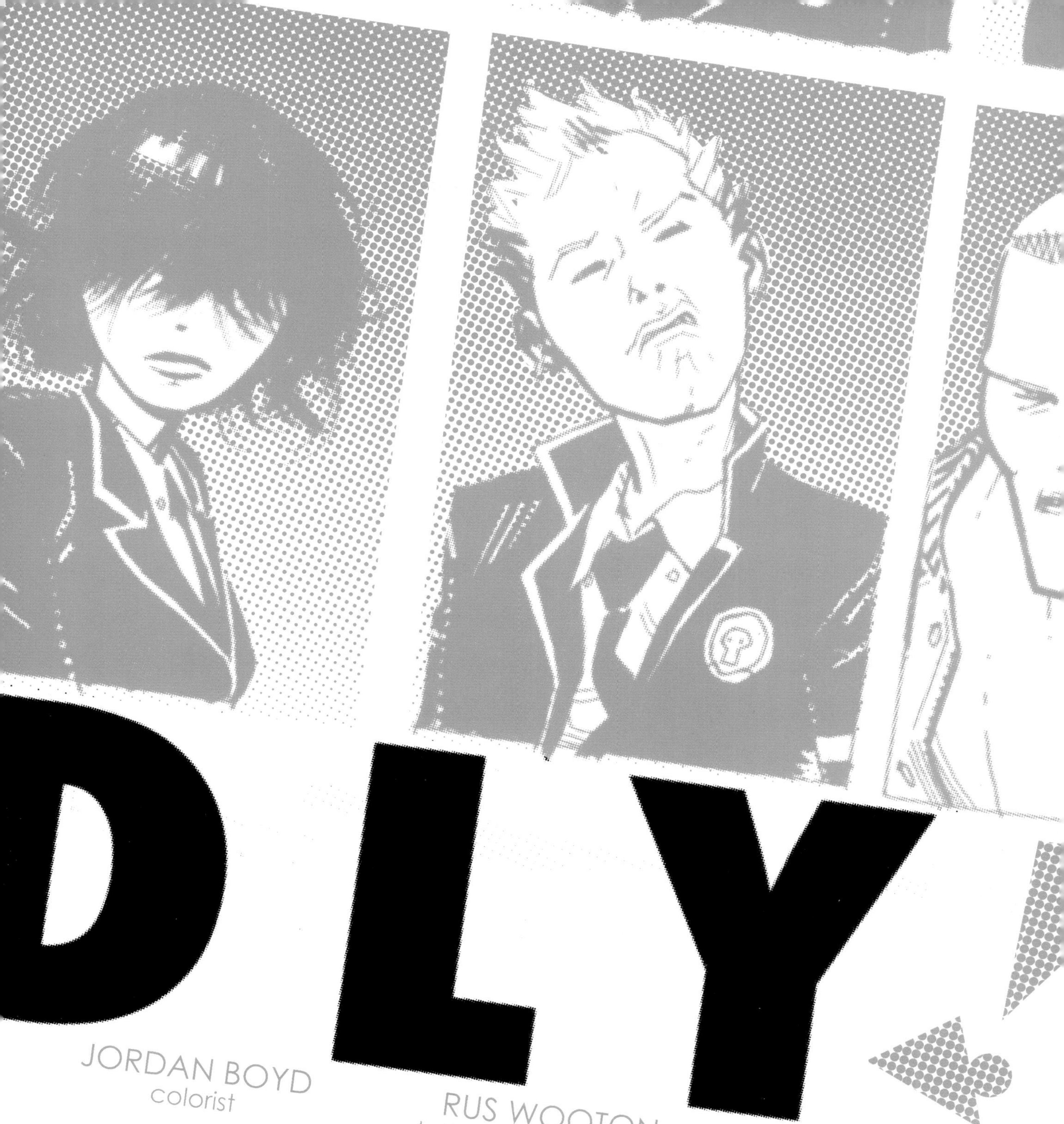

JORDAN BOYD
colorist

RUS WOOTON
letterer • logo design

SEBASTIAN GIRNER,
BRIAH SKELLY &
WILL DENNIS
editors

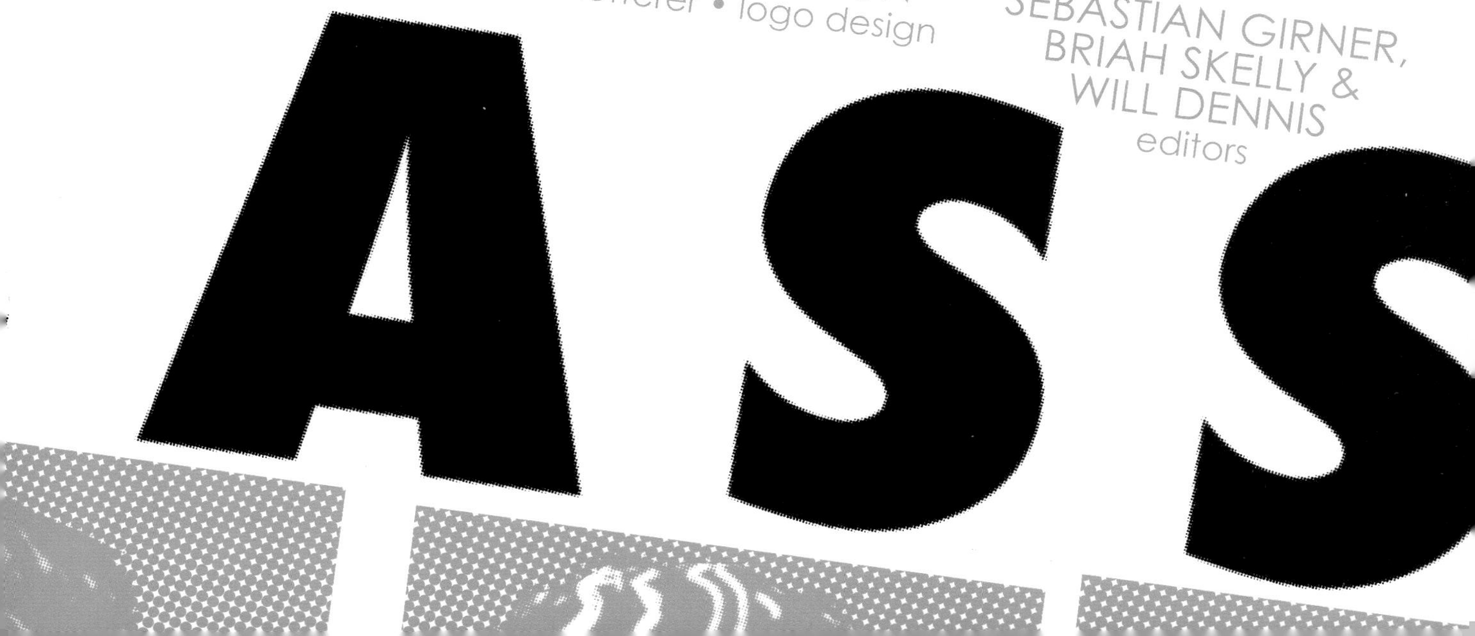

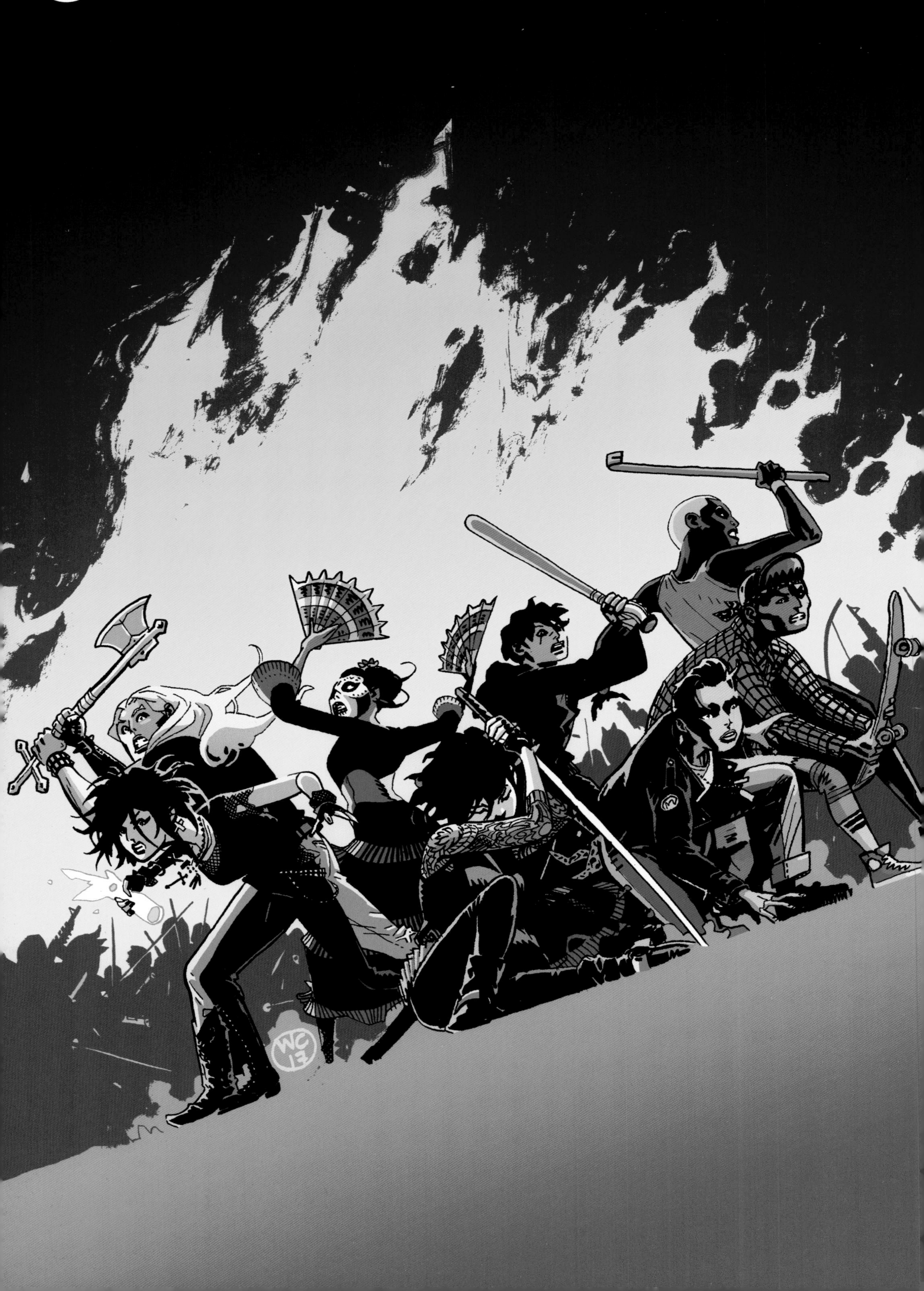

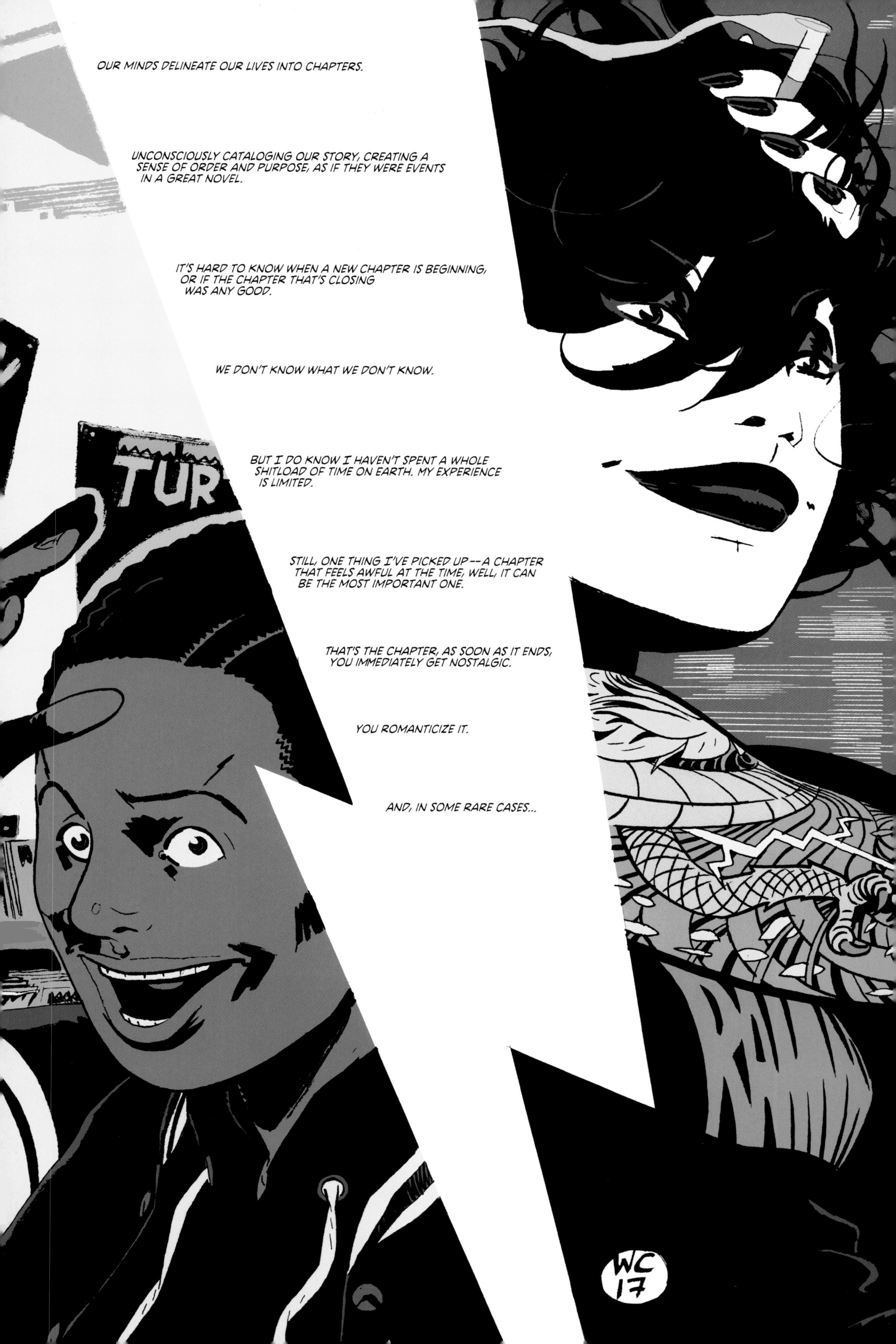
OUR MINDS DELINEATE OUR LIVES INTO CHAPTERS.
UNCONSCIOUSLY CATALOGING OUR STORY, CREATING A SENSE OF ORDER AND PURPOSE, AS IF THEY WERE EVENTS IN A GREAT NOVEL.
IT'S HARD TO KNOW WHEN A NEW CHAPTER IS BEGINNING, OR IF THE CHAPTER THAT'S CLOSING WAS ANY GOOD.
WE DON'T KNOW WHAT WE DON'T KNOW.
BUT I DO KNOW I HAVEN'T SPENT A WHOLE SHITLOAD OF TIME ON EARTH. MY EXPERIENCE IS LIMITED.
STILL, ONE THING I'VE PICKED UP--A CHAPTER THAT FEELS AWFUL AT THE TIME, WELL, IT CAN BE THE MOST IMPORTANT ONE.
THAT'S THE CHAPTER, AS SOON AS IT ENDS, YOU IMMEDIATELY GET NOSTALGIC.
YOU ROMANTICIZE IT.
AND, IN SOME RARE CASES...
WC 17

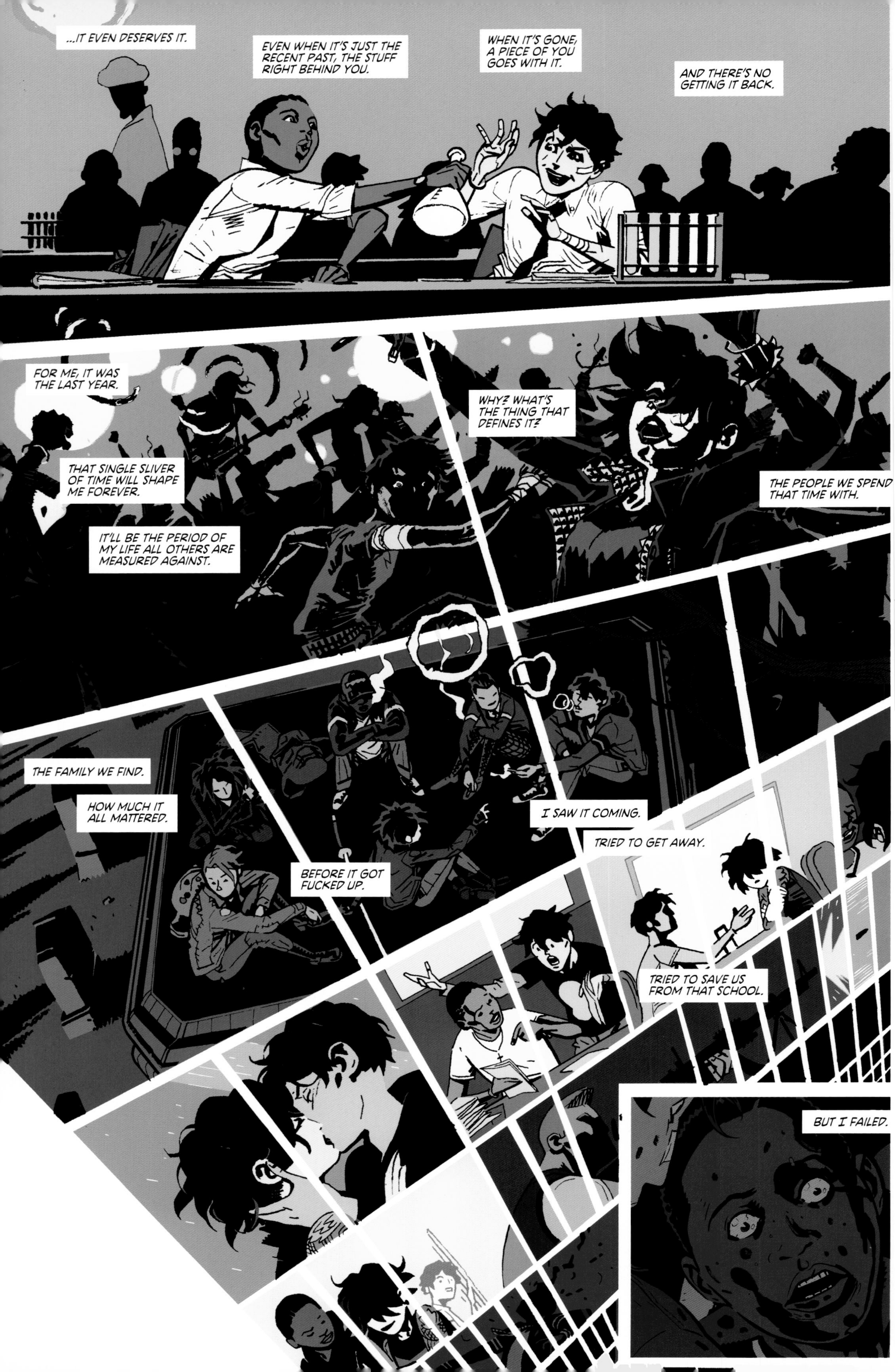
...IT EVEN DESERVES IT.
EVEN WHEN IT'S JUST THE RECENT PAST, THE STUFF RIGHT BEHIND YOU.
WHEN IT'S GONE, A PIECE OF YOU GOES WITH IT.
AND THERE'S NO GETTING IT BACK.
FOR ME, IT WAS THE LAST YEAR.
THAT SINGLE SLIVER OF TIME WILL SHAPE ME FOREVER.
IT'LL BE THE PERIOD OF MY LIFE ALL OTHERS ARE MEASURED AGAINST.
WHY? WHAT'S THE THING THAT DEFINES IT?
THE PEOPLE WE SPEND THAT TIME WITH.
THE FAMILY WE FIND.
HOW MUCH IT ALL MATTERED.
BEFORE IT GOT FUCKED UP.
I SAW IT COMING.
TRIED TO GET AWAY.
TRIED TO SAVE US FROM THAT SCHOOL.
BUT I FAILED.

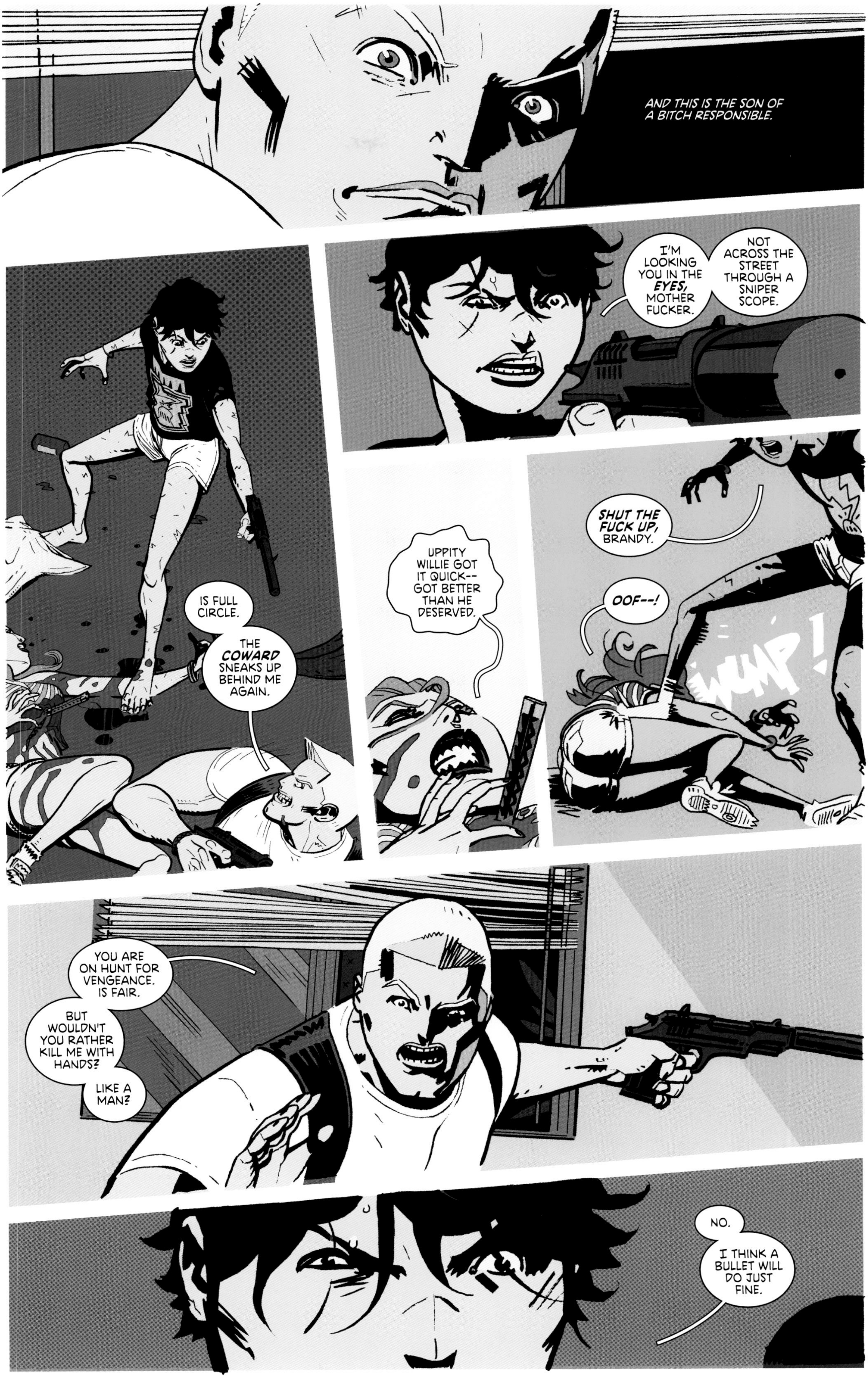
AND THIS IS THE SON OF A BITCH RESPONSIBLE.
I'M LOOKING YOU IN THE EYES, MOTHER FUCKER.
NOT ACROSS THE STREET THROUGH A SNIPER SCOPE.
IS FULL CIRCLE.
THE COWARD SNEAKS UP BEHIND ME AGAIN.
UPPITY WILLIE GOT IT QUICK-- GOT BETTER THAN HE DESERVED.
SHUT THE FUCK UP, BRANDY.
OOF--!
WUMP!
YOU ARE ON HUNT FOR VENGEANCE. IS FAIR.
BUT WOULDN'T YOU RATHER KILL ME WITH HANDS?
LIKE A MAN?
NO.
I THINK A BULLET WILL DO JUST FINE.

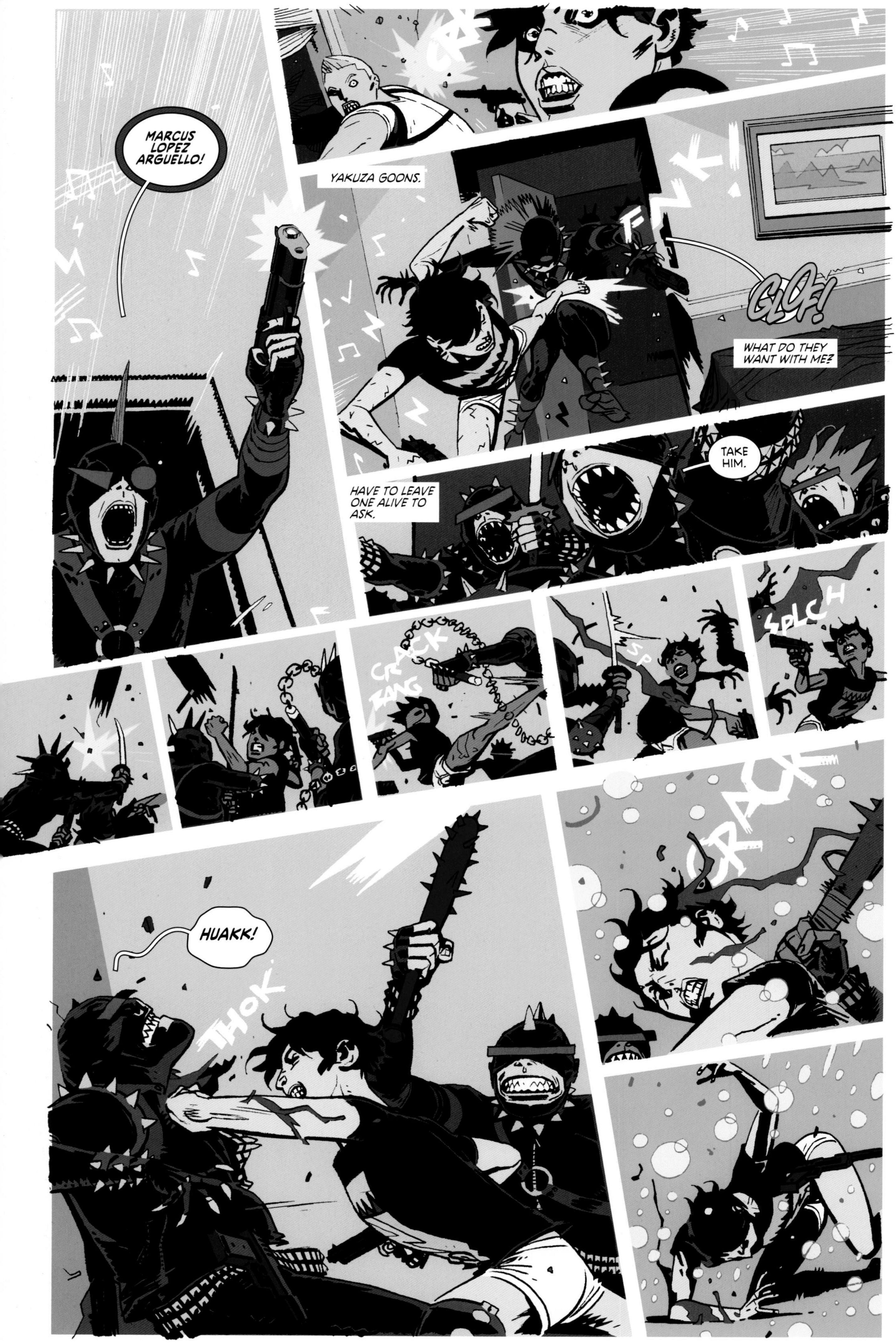
CR
MARCUS LOPEZ ARGUELLO!
YAKUZA GOONS.
FNK!
GLOF!
WHAT DO THEY WANT WITH ME?
HAVE TO LEAVE ONE ALIVE TO ASK.
TAKE HIM.
CRACK
CRACK
BANG
SP
SPLCH
CRACK
HUAKK!
THOK

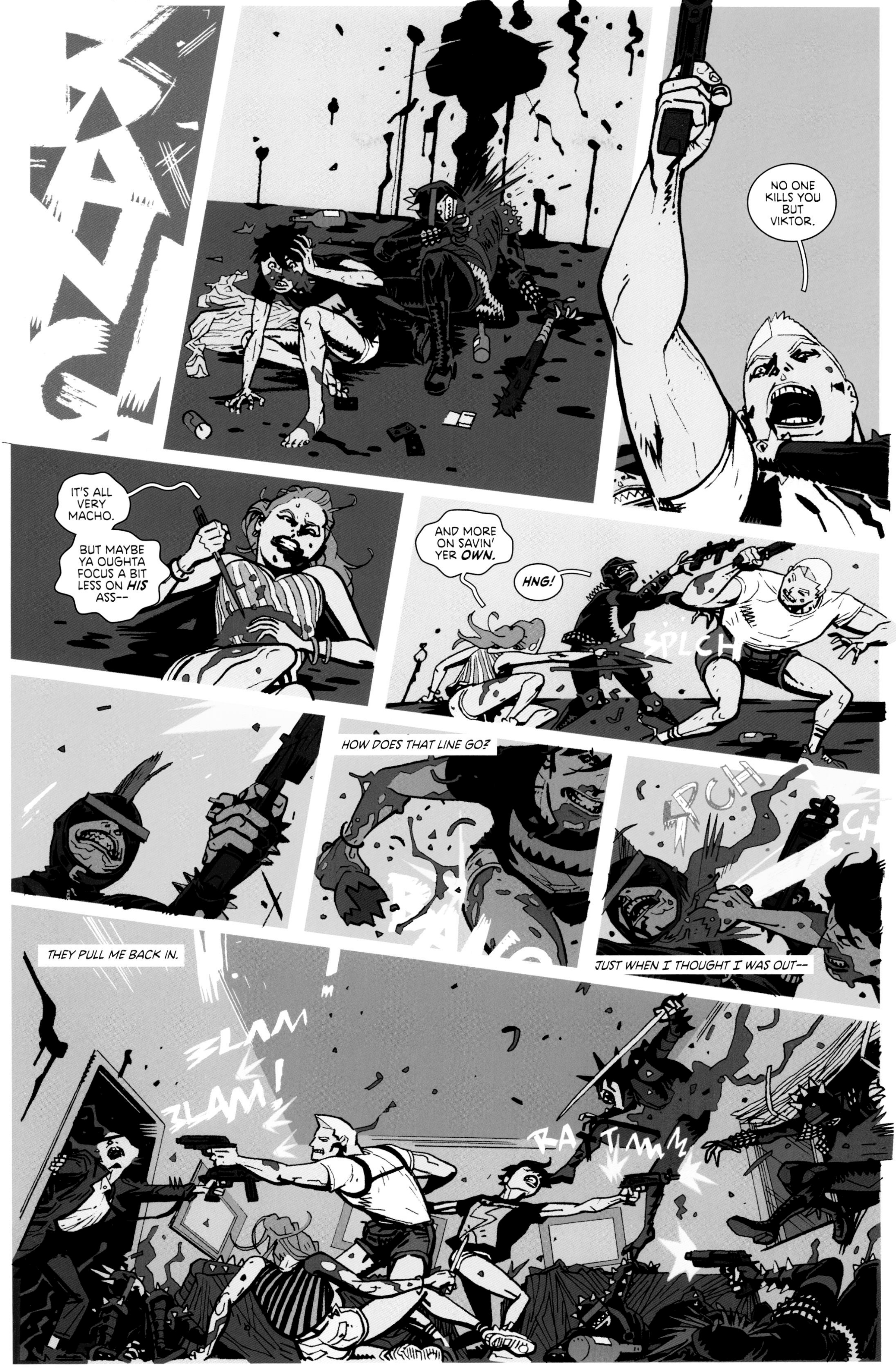

NO ONE KILLS YOU BUT VIKTOR.
IT'S ALL VERY MACHO.
BUT MAYBE YA OUGHTA FOCUS A BIT LESS ON *HIS* ASS--
AND MORE ON SAVIN' YER *OWN.*
HNG!
HOW DOES THAT LINE GO?
JUST WHEN I THOUGHT I WAS OUT--
THEY PULL ME BACK IN.

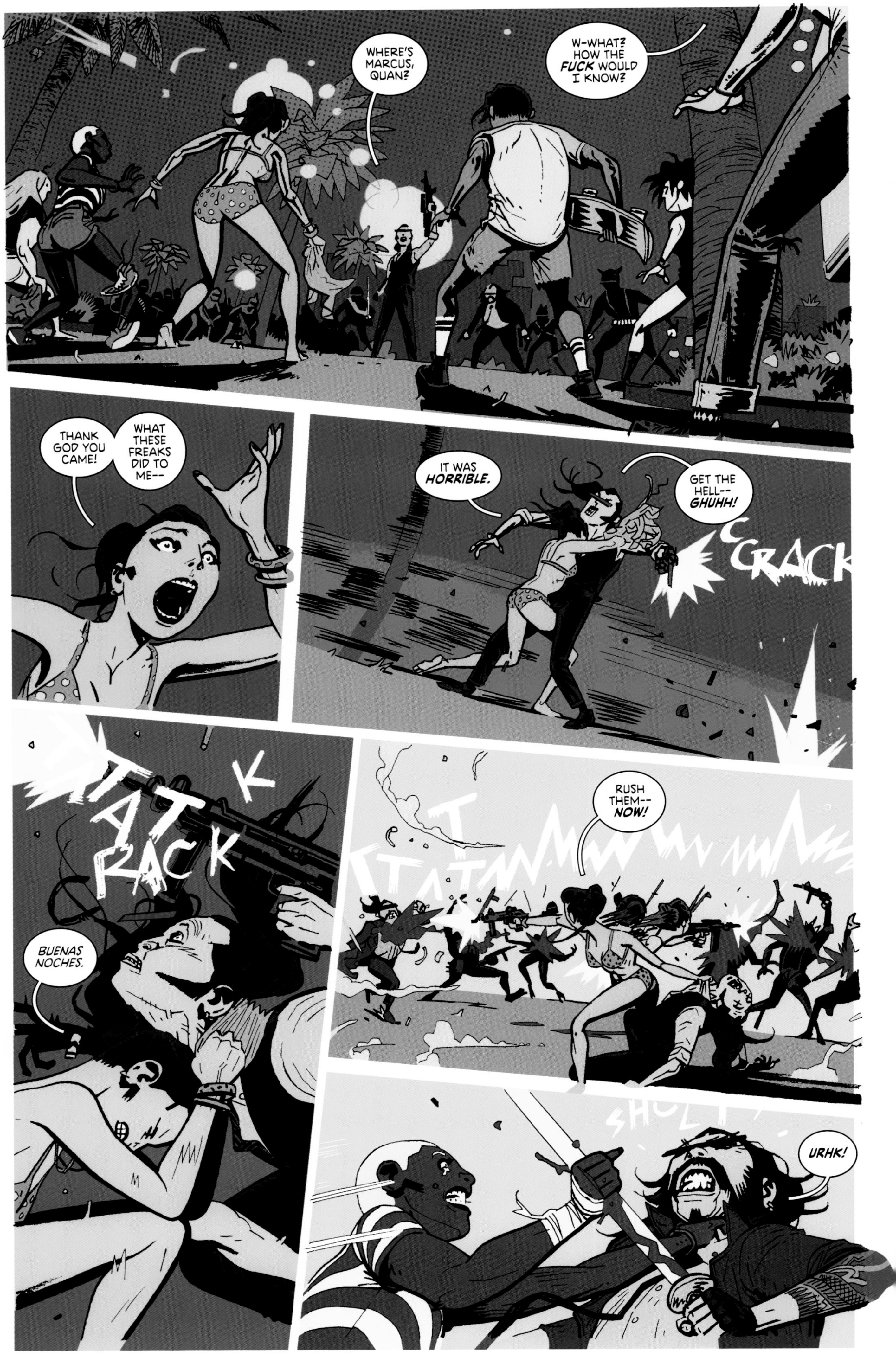
WHERE'S MARCUS, QUAN?
W-WHAT? HOW THE FUCK WOULD I KNOW?
THANK GOD YOU CAME!
WHAT THESE FREAKS DID TO ME--
IT WAS HORRIBLE.
GET THE HELL-- GHUHH!
CCRACK
TAT K
TAT RACK
BUENAS NOCHES.
RUSH THEM-- NOW!
URHK!

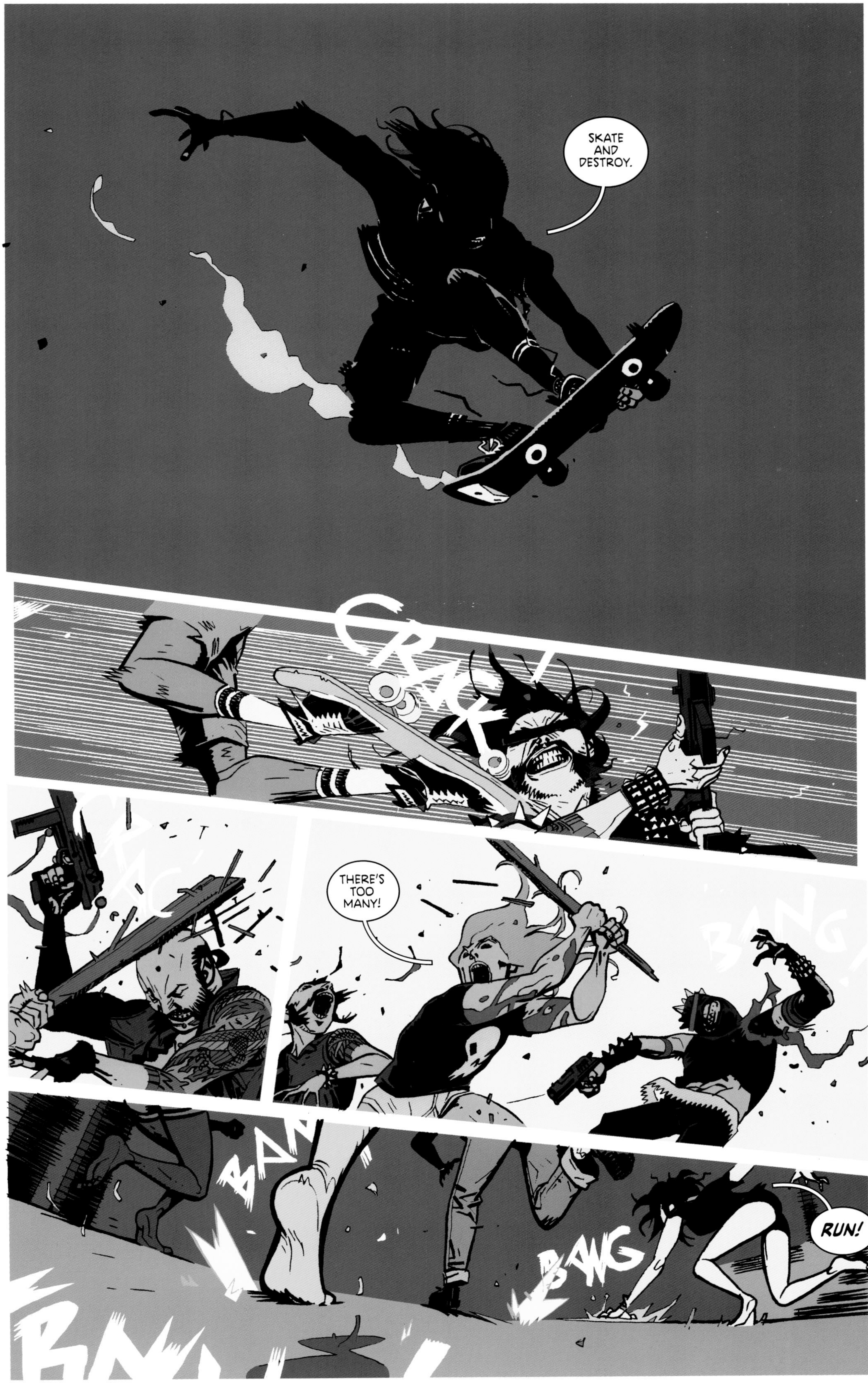
SKATE AND DESTROY.
CRACK!
THERE'S TOO MANY!
BANG!
BANG
BANG
RUN!

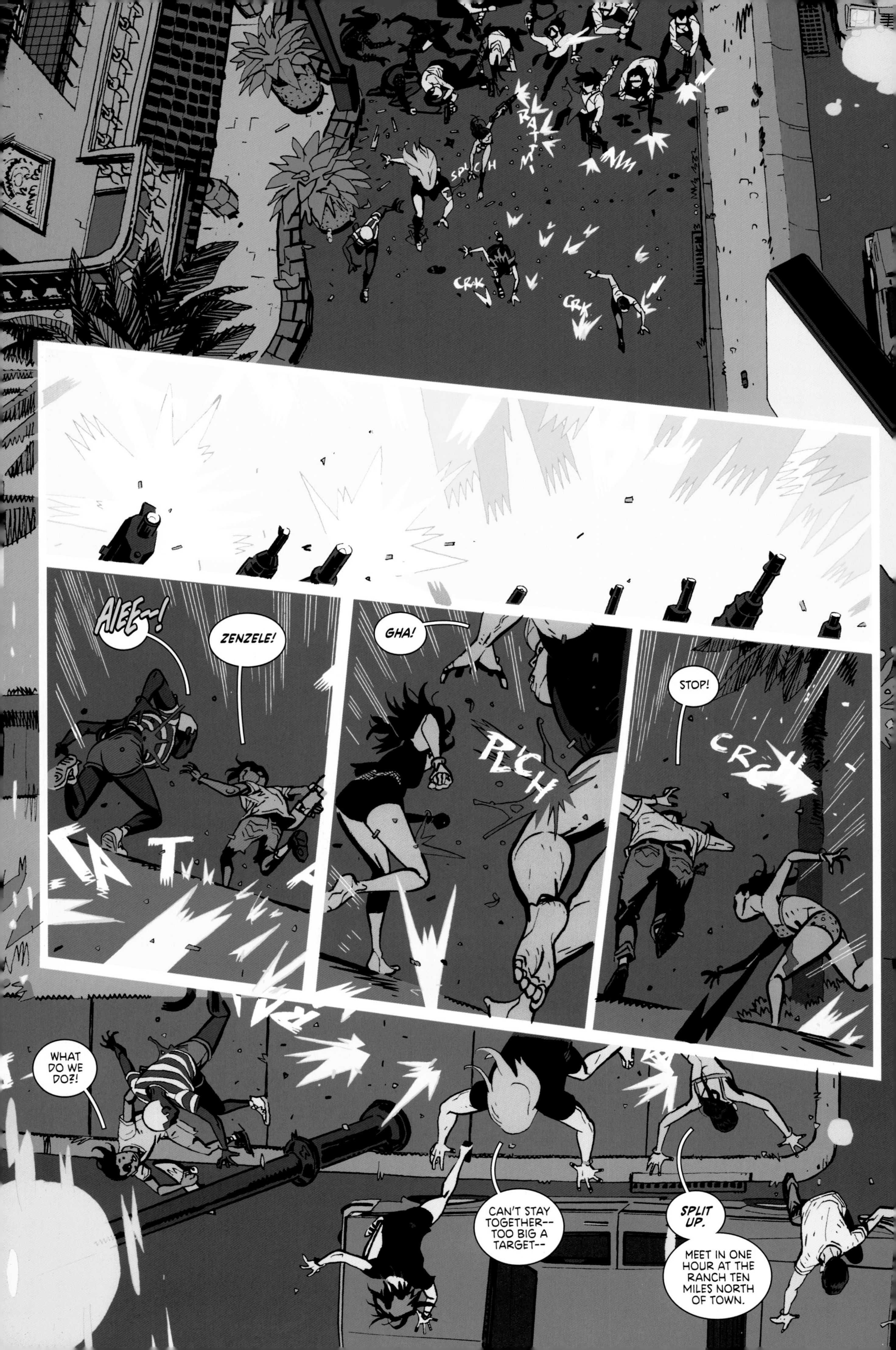
SPLCH
CRK
CRK
AIEE--!
ZENZELE!
GHA!
PLCH
STOP!
WHAT DO WE DO?!
CAN'T STAY TOGETHER-- TOO BIG A TARGET--
SPLIT UP.
MEET IN ONE HOUR AT THE RANCH TEN MILES NORTH OF TOWN.

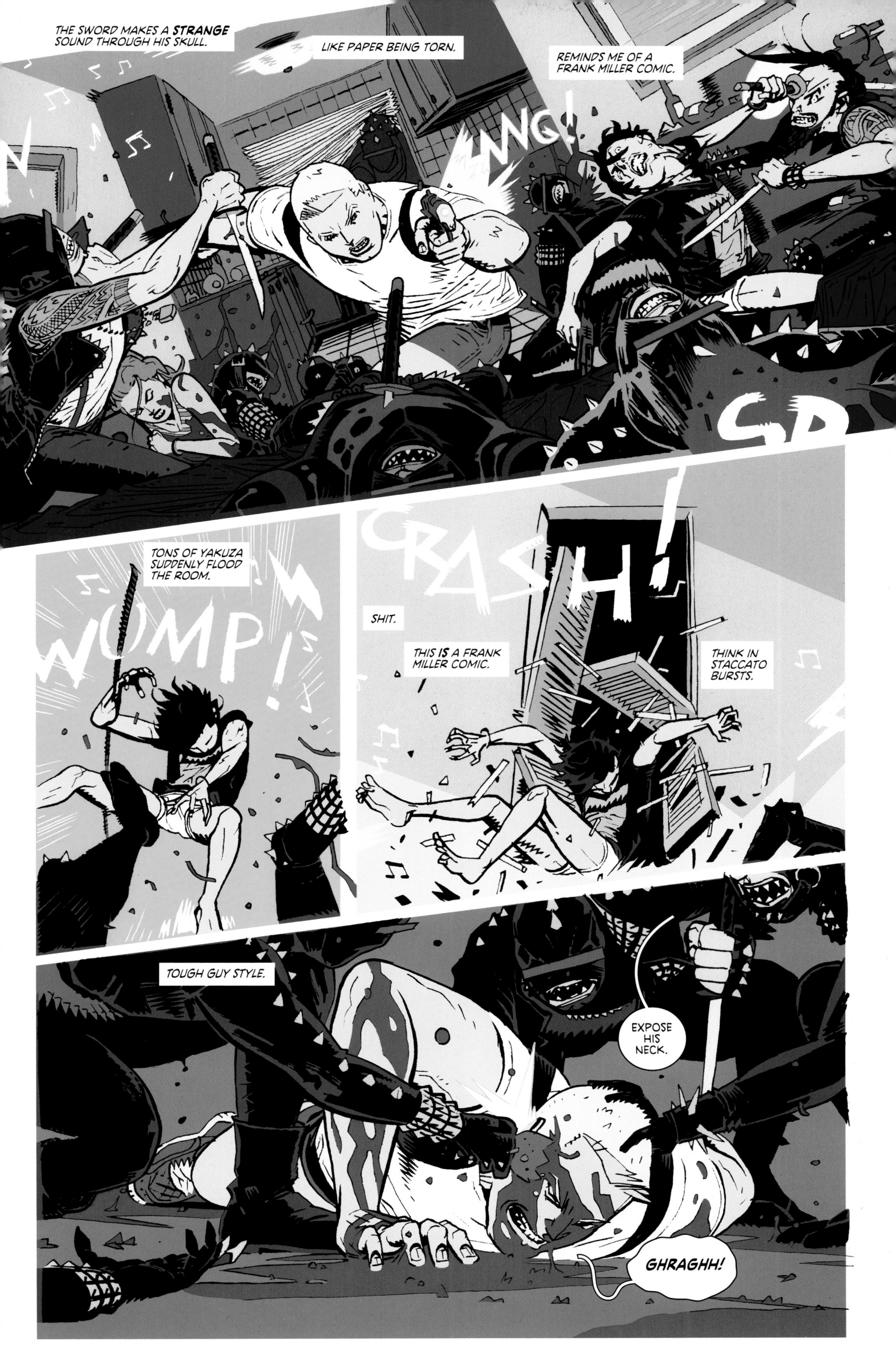
THE SWORD MAKES A **STRANGE** SOUND THROUGH HIS SKULL.
LIKE PAPER BEING TORN.
REMINDS ME OF A FRANK MILLER COMIC.
NNG!
TONS OF YAKUZA SUDDENLY FLOOD THE ROOM.
WOMP!
CRASH!
SHIT.
THIS **IS** A FRANK MILLER COMIC.
THINK IN STACCATO BURSTS.
TOUGH GUY STYLE.
EXPOSE HIS NECK.
GHRAGHH!

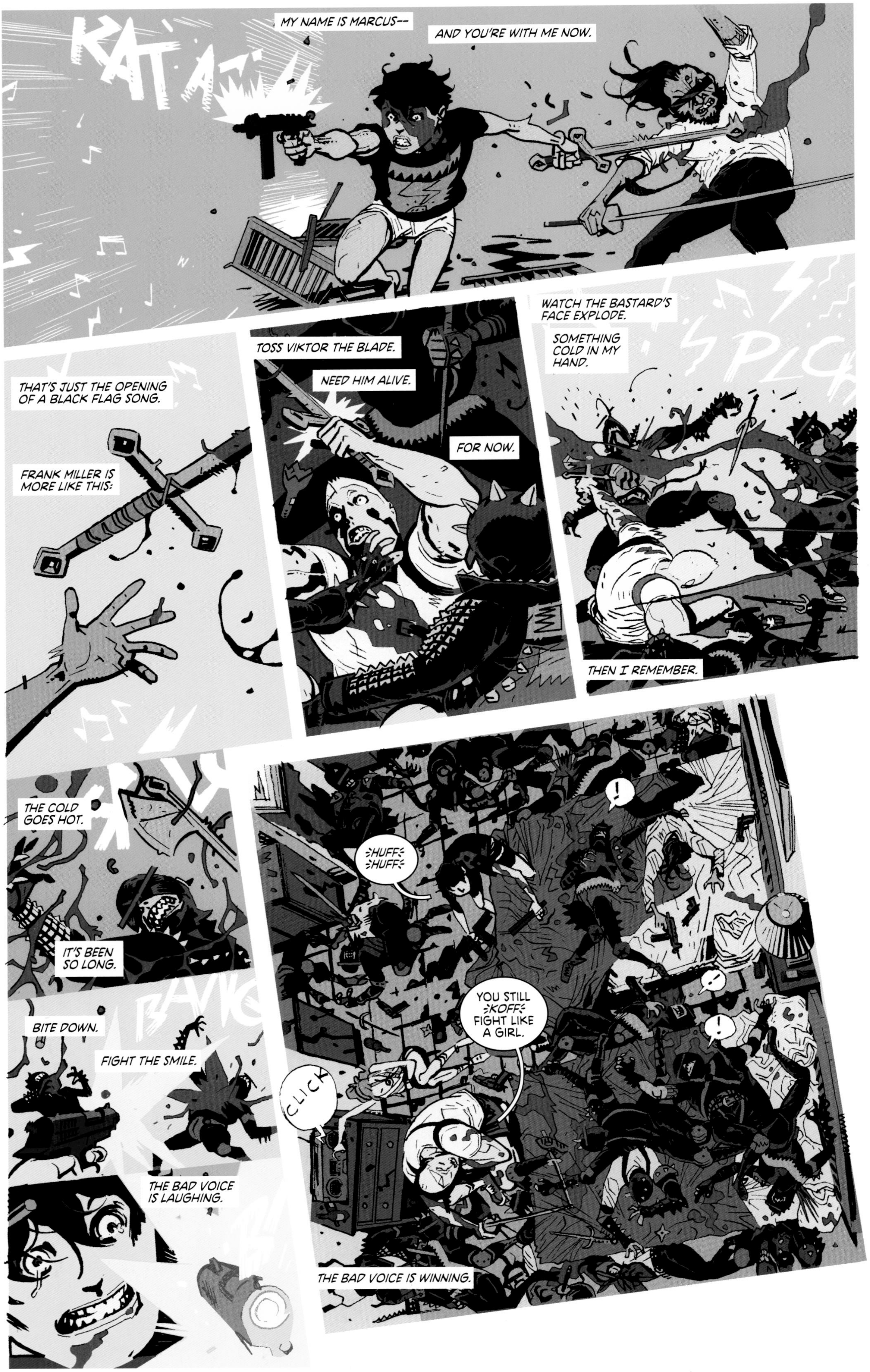
KAT A--
MY NAME IS MARCUS--
AND YOU'RE WITH ME NOW.
THAT'S JUST THE OPENING OF A BLACK FLAG SONG.
FRANK MILLER IS MORE LIKE THIS:
TOSS VIKTOR THE BLADE.
NEED HIM ALIVE.
FOR NOW.
WATCH THE BASTARD'S FACE EXPLODE.
SOMETHING COLD IN MY HAND.
SPLCH
THEN I REMEMBER.
THE COLD GOES HOT.
IT'S BEEN SO LONG.
BITE DOWN.
FIGHT THE SMILE.
THE BAD VOICE IS LAUGHING.
HUFF HUFF
!
YOU STILL KOFF FIGHT LIKE A GIRL.
CLICK
!
THE BAD VOICE IS WINNING.

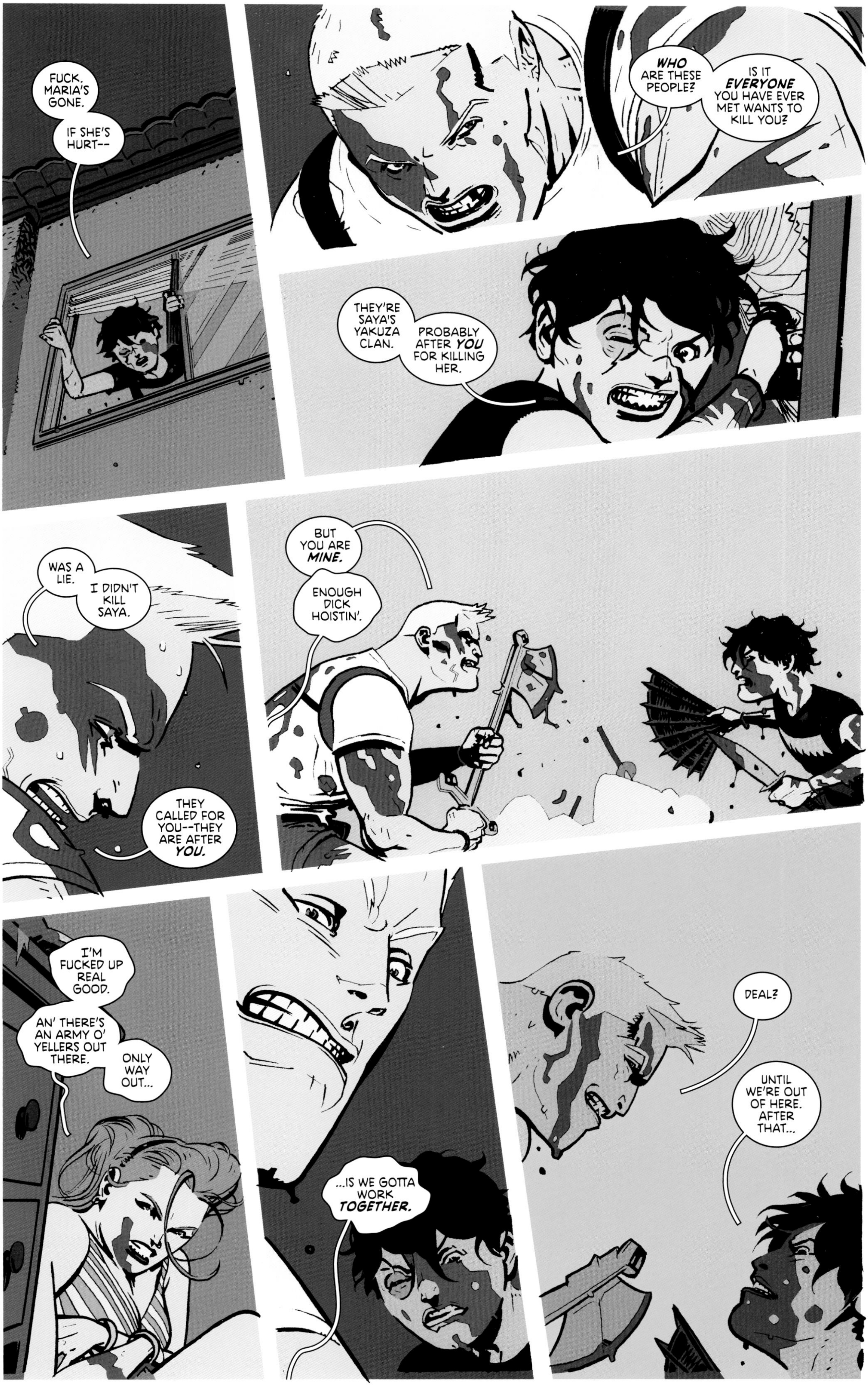
FUCK. MARIA'S GONE.
IF SHE'S HURT--
WHO ARE THESE PEOPLE?
IS IT EVERYONE YOU HAVE EVER MET WANTS TO KILL YOU?
THEY'RE SAYA'S YAKUZA CLAN.
PROBABLY AFTER YOU FOR KILLING HER.
WAS A LIE.
I DIDN'T KILL SAYA.
THEY CALLED FOR YOU--THEY ARE AFTER YOU.
BUT YOU ARE MINE.
ENOUGH DICK HOISTIN'.
I'M FUCKED UP REAL GOOD.
AN' THERE'S AN ARMY O' YELLERS OUT THERE.
ONLY WAY OUT...
...IS WE GOTTA WORK TOGETHER.
DEAL?
UNTIL WE'RE OUT OF HERE. AFTER THAT...

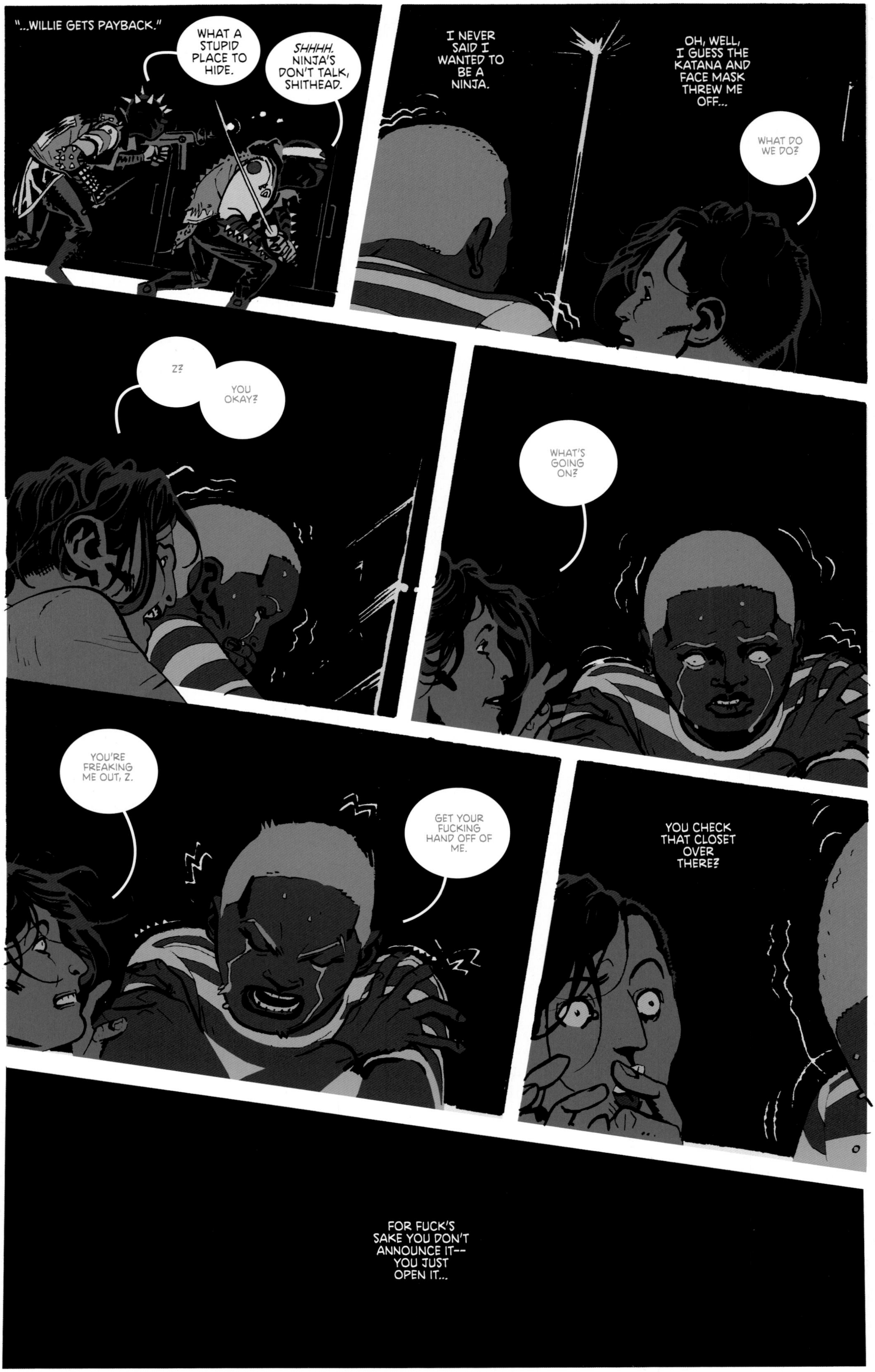
"...WILLIE GETS PAYBACK."
WHAT A STUPID PLACE TO HIDE.
SHHHH. NINJA'S DON'T TALK, SHITHEAD.
I NEVER SAID I WANTED TO BE A NINJA.
OH, WELL, I GUESS THE KATANA AND FACE MASK THREW ME OFF...
WHAT DO WE DO?
Z?
YOU OKAY?
WHAT'S GOING ON?
YOU'RE FREAKING ME OUT, Z.
GET YOUR FUCKING HAND OFF OF ME.
YOU CHECK THAT CLOSET OVER THERE?
FOR FUCK'S SAKE YOU DON'T ANNOUNCE IT-- YOU JUST OPEN IT...

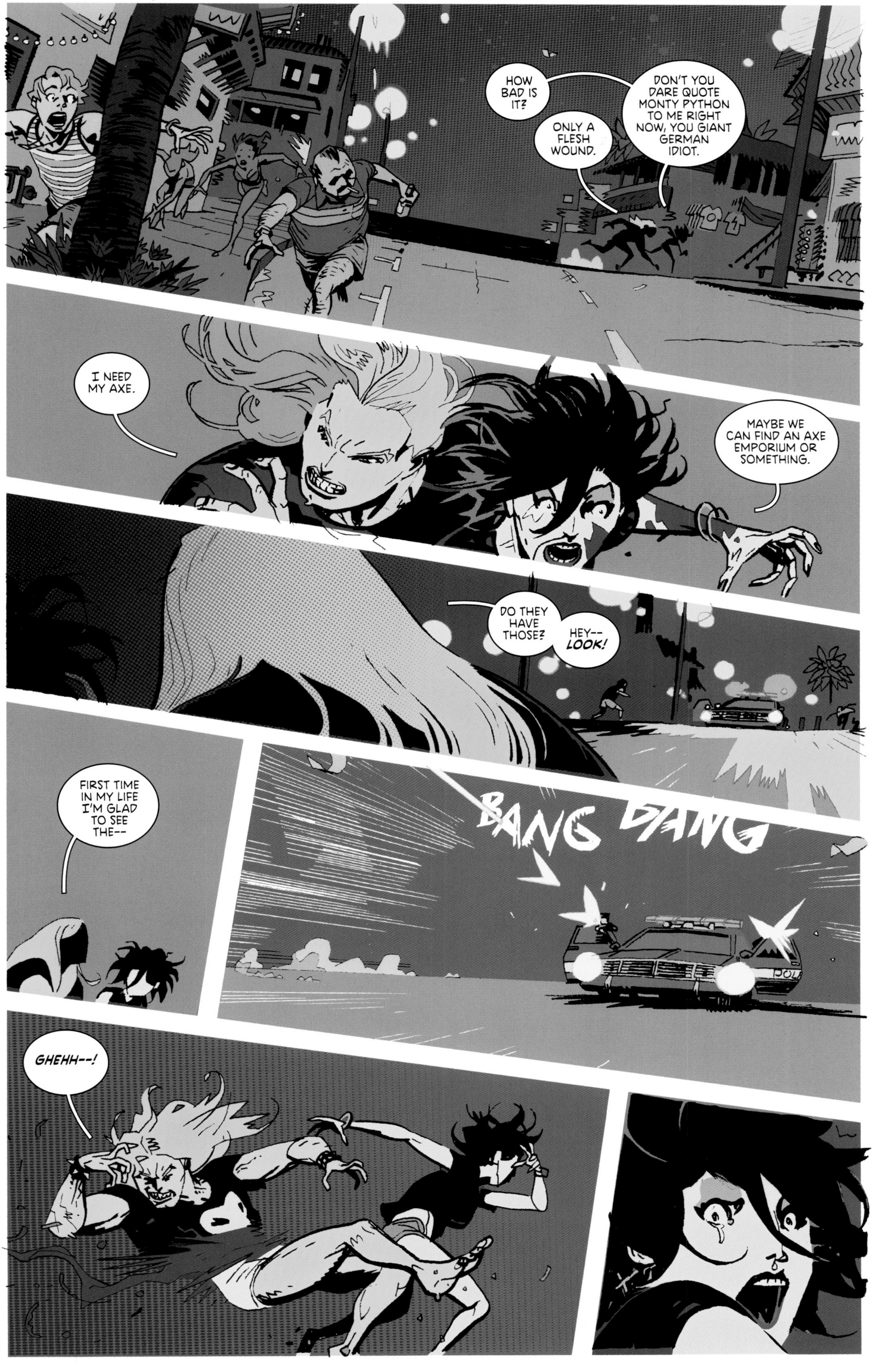
HOW BAD IS IT?
ONLY A FLESH WOUND.
DON'T YOU DARE QUOTE MONTY PYTHON TO ME RIGHT NOW, YOU GIANT GERMAN IDIOT.
I NEED MY AXE.
MAYBE WE CAN FIND AN AXE EMPORIUM OR SOMETHING.
DO THEY HAVE THOSE?
HEY-- LOOK!
FIRST TIME IN MY LIFE I'M GLAD TO SEE THE--
BANG BANG
GHEHH--!

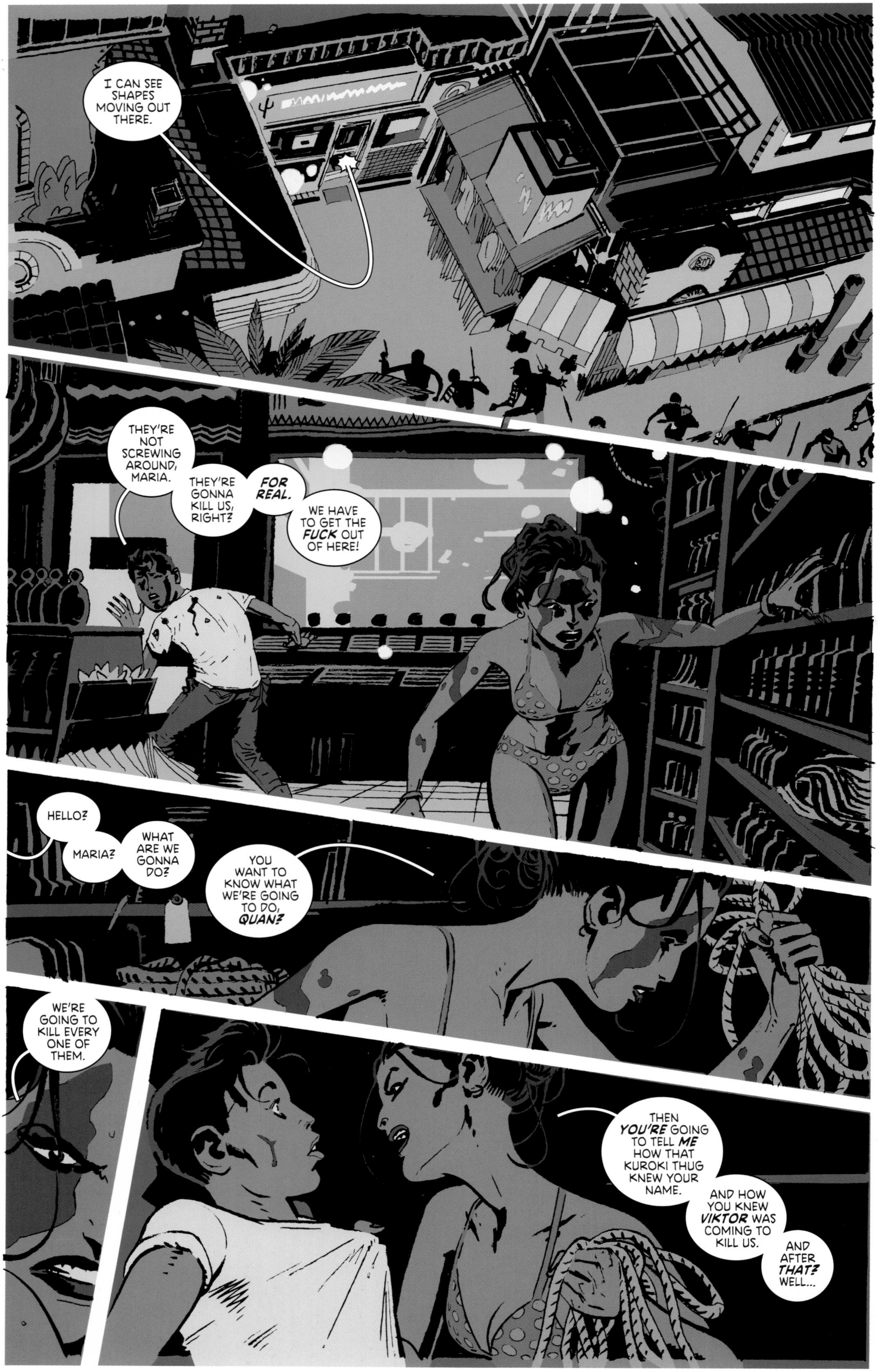
I CAN SEE SHAPES MOVING OUT THERE.
THEY'RE NOT SCREWING AROUND, MARIA.
THEY'RE GONNA KILL US, RIGHT?
FOR REAL.
WE HAVE TO GET THE FUCK OUT OF HERE!
HELLO?
MARIA?
WHAT ARE WE GONNA DO?
YOU WANT TO KNOW WHAT WE'RE GOING TO DO, QUAN?
WE'RE GOING TO KILL EVERY ONE OF THEM.
THEN YOU'RE GOING TO TELL ME HOW THAT KUROKI THUG KNEW YOUR NAME.
AND HOW YOU KNEW VIKTOR WAS COMING TO KILL US.
AND AFTER THAT? WELL...

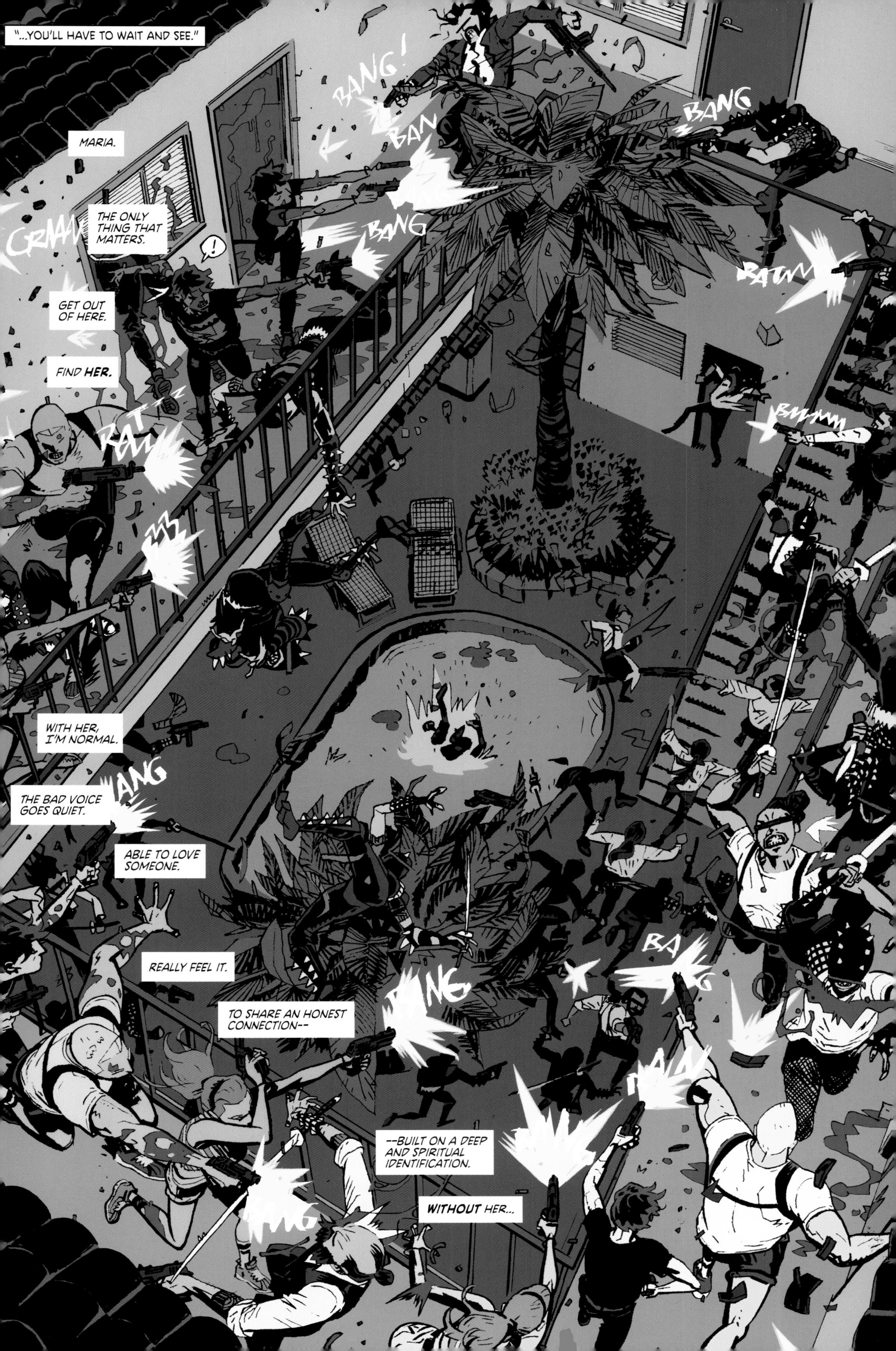
"...YOU'LL HAVE TO WAIT AND SEE."
BANG!
BAN
BANG
MARIA.
BANG
THE ONLY THING THAT MATTERS.
!
GET OUT OF HERE.
FIND HER.
WITH HER, I'M NORMAL.
THE BAD VOICE GOES QUIET.
ABLE TO LOVE SOMEONE.
REALLY FEEL IT.
TO SHARE AN HONEST CONNECTION--
--BUILT ON A DEEP AND SPIRITUAL IDENTIFICATION.
WITHOUT HER...

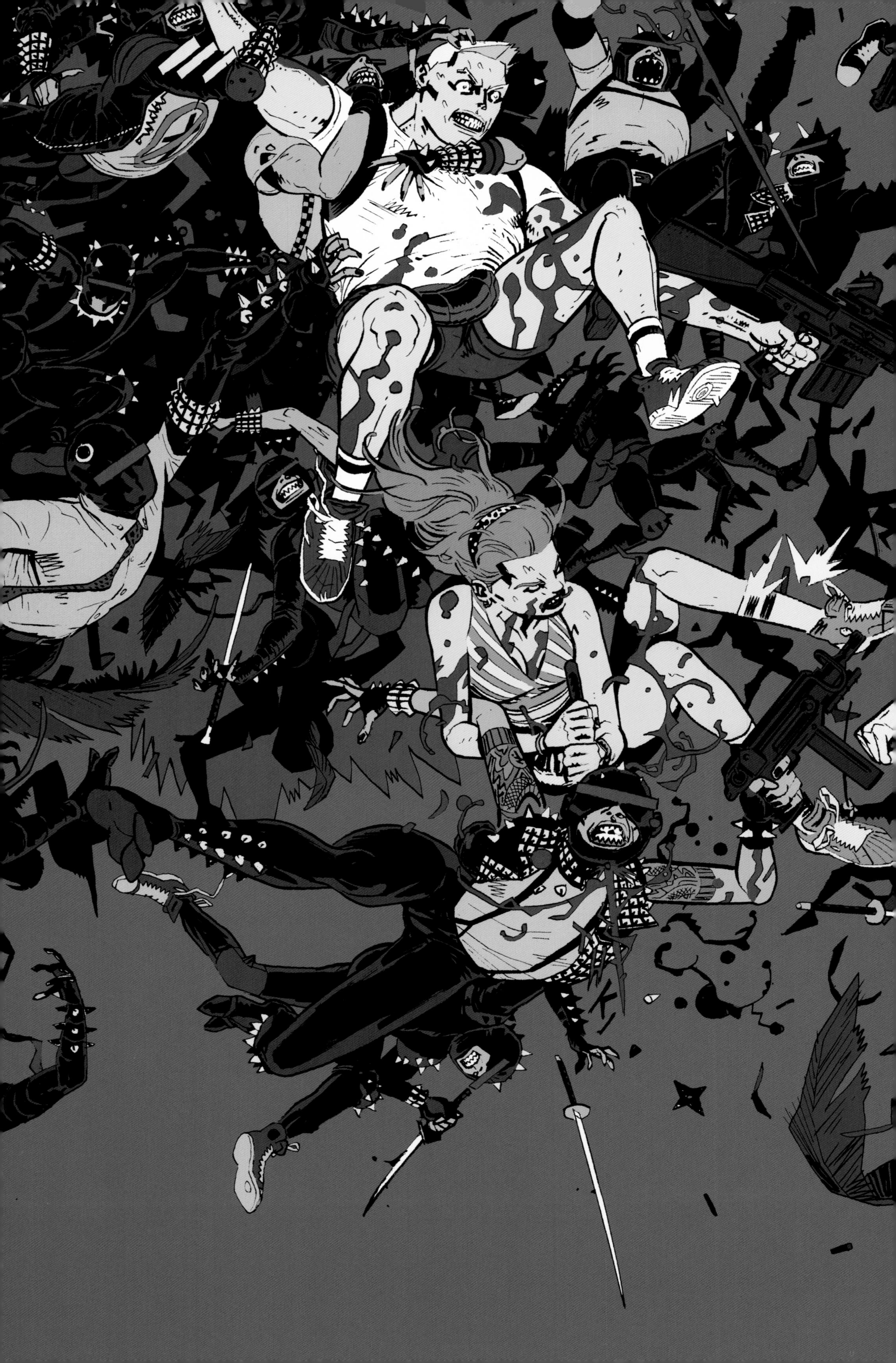

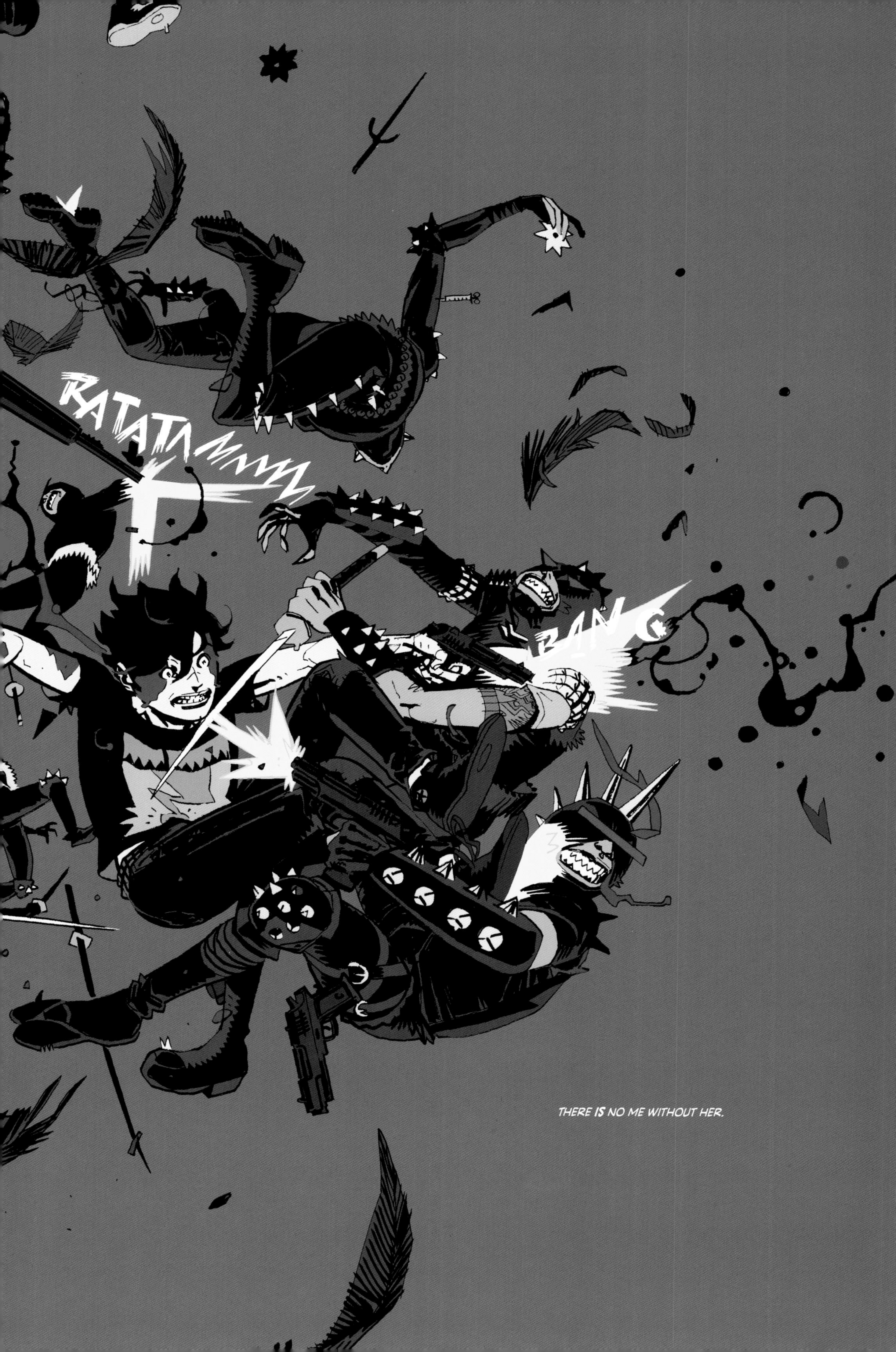
RATATAMMMM
BANG

THERE **IS** NO ME WITHOUT HER.

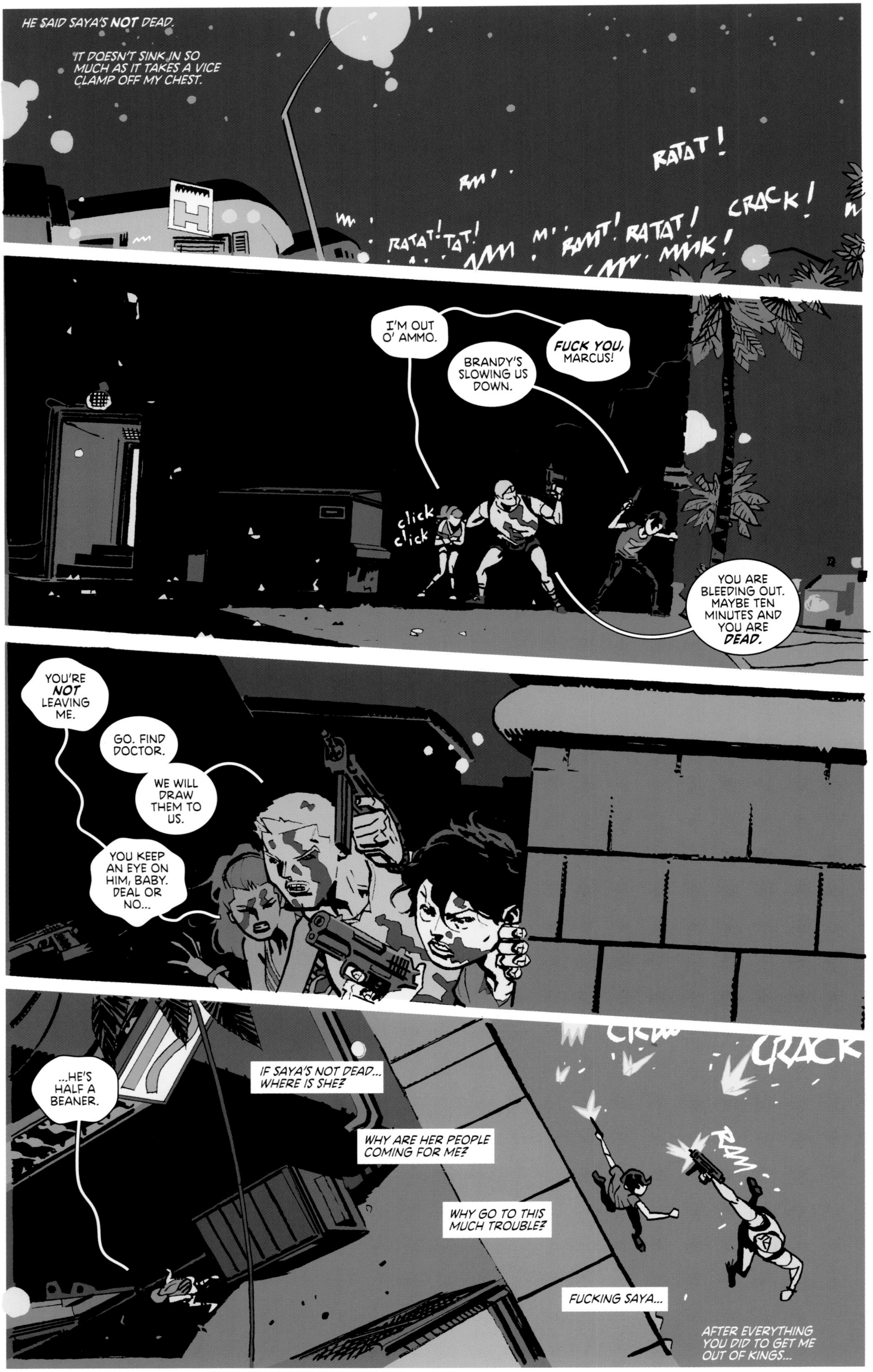
HE SAID SAYA'S NOT DEAD.
IT DOESN'T SINK IN SO MUCH AS IT TAKES A VICE CLAMP OFF MY CHEST.
RATAT!
RATAT! TAT!
RATAT!
CRACK!
I'M OUT O' AMMO.
BRANDY'S SLOWING US DOWN.
FUCK YOU, MARCUS!
click click
YOU ARE BLEEDING OUT. MAYBE TEN MINUTES AND YOU ARE DEAD.
YOU'RE NOT LEAVING ME.
GO. FIND DOCTOR.
WE WILL DRAW THEM TO US.
YOU KEEP AN EYE ON HIM, BABY. DEAL OR NO...
...HE'S HALF A BEANER.
IF SAYA'S NOT DEAD... WHERE IS SHE?
WHY ARE HER PEOPLE COMING FOR ME?
WHY GO TO THIS MUCH TROUBLE?
CRACK
FUCKING SAYA...
AFTER EVERYTHING YOU DID TO GET ME OUT OF KINGS...

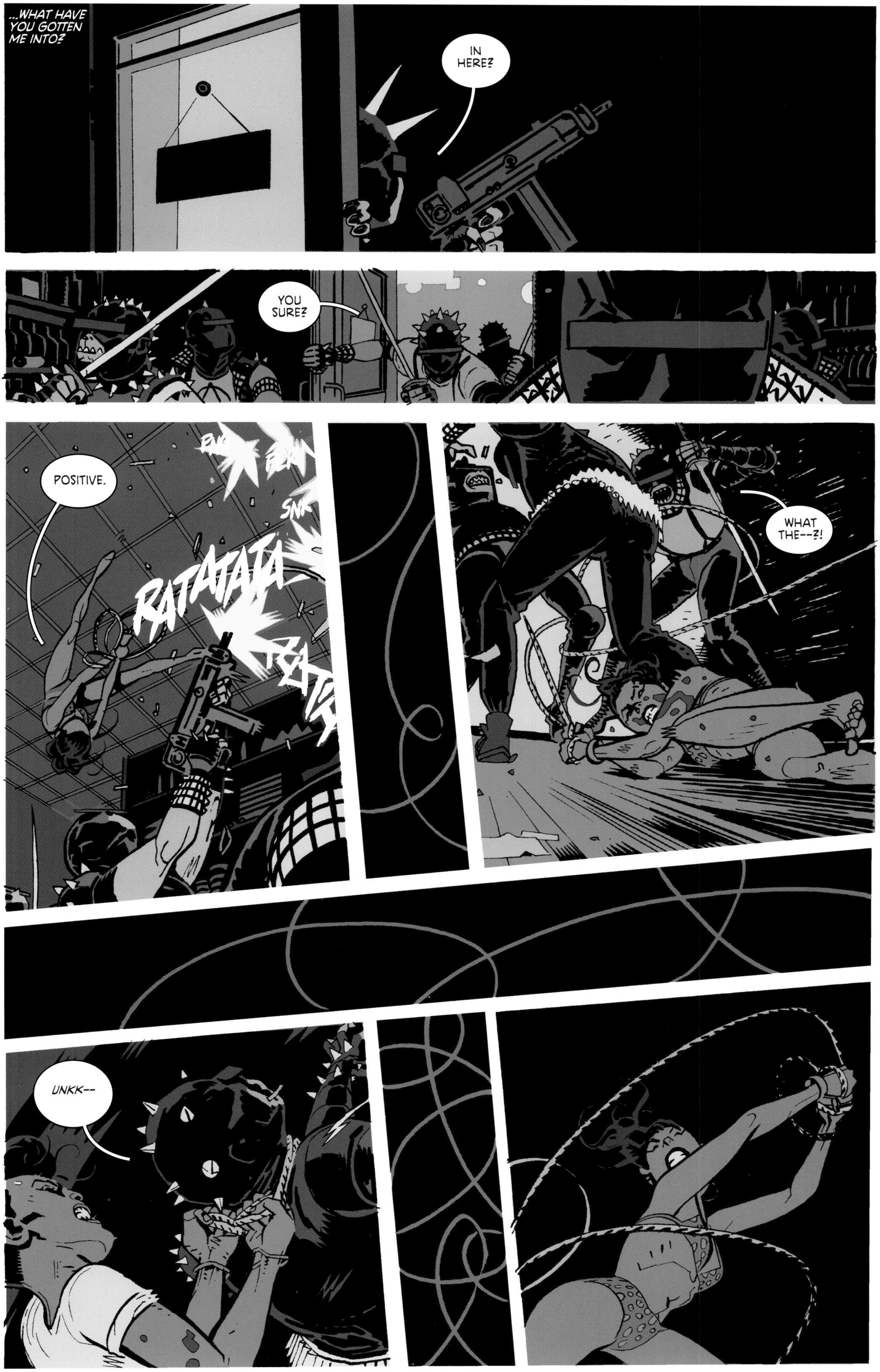
...WHAT HAVE YOU GOTTEN ME INTO?
IN HERE?
YOU SURE?
POSITIVE.
RATATATA
WHAT THE--?!
UNKK--

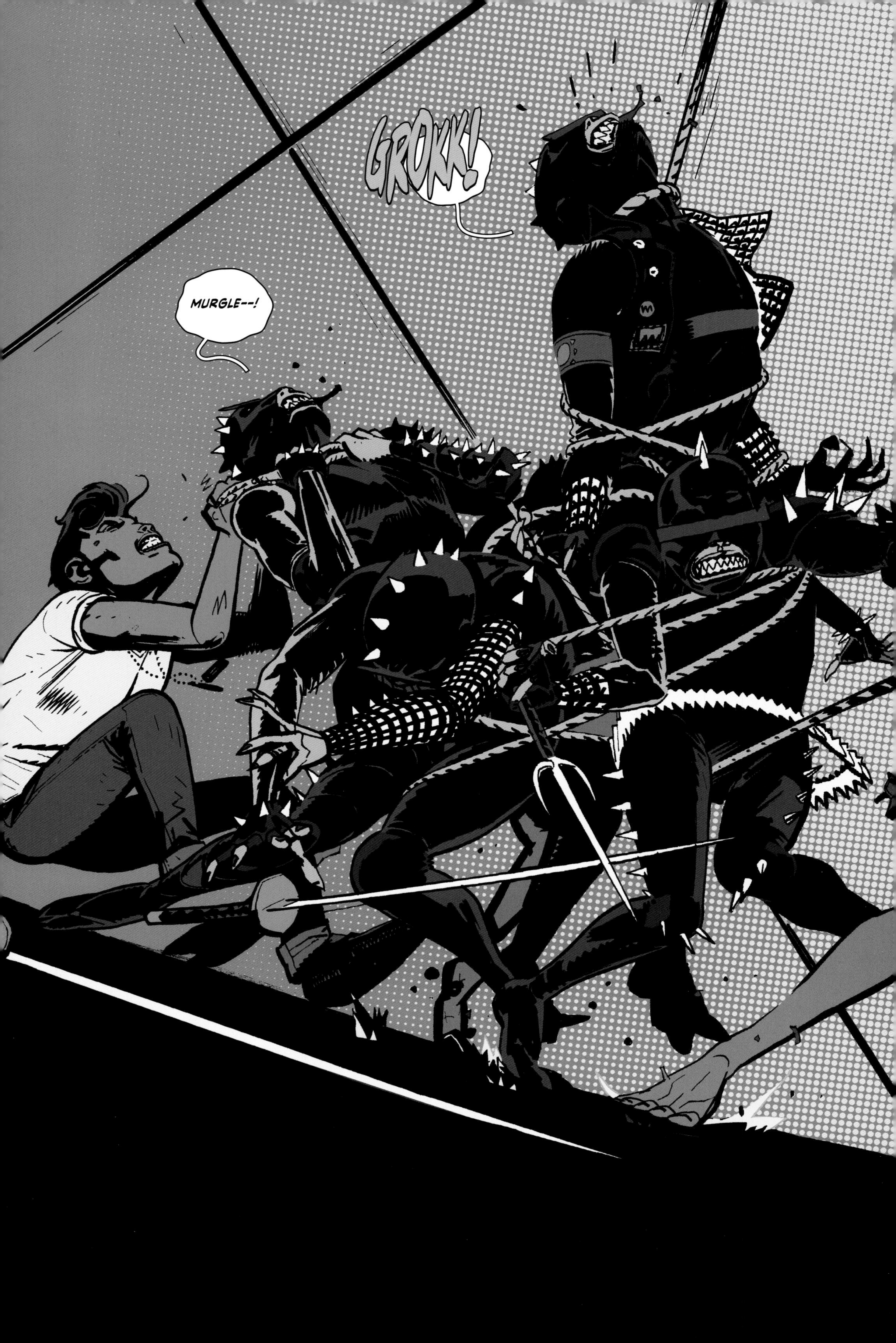
GROKK!
MURGLE--!

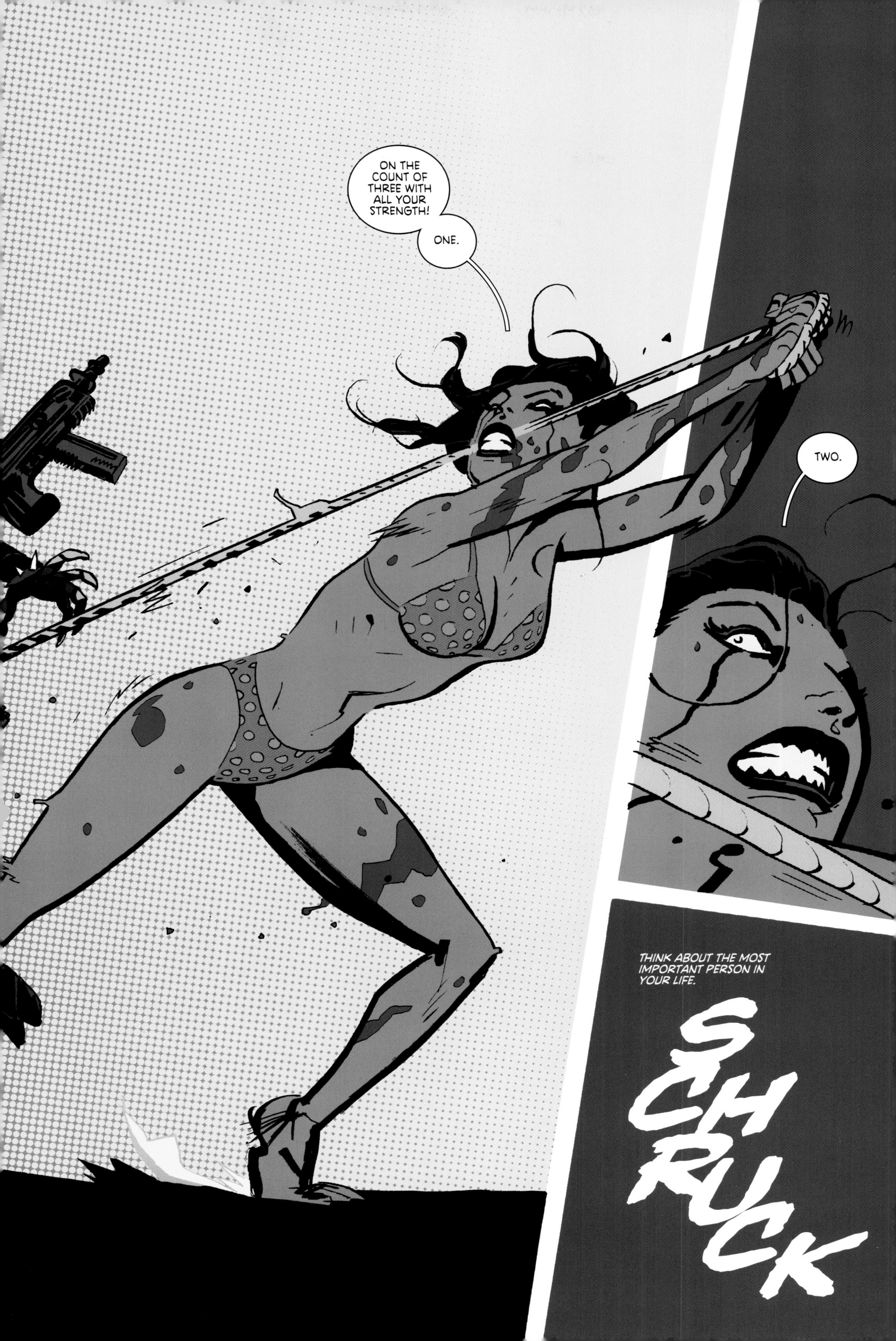
ON THE COUNT OF THREE WITH ALL YOUR STRENGTH!
ONE.
TWO.
THINK ABOUT THE MOST IMPORTANT PERSON IN YOUR LIFE.
SCHRUCK

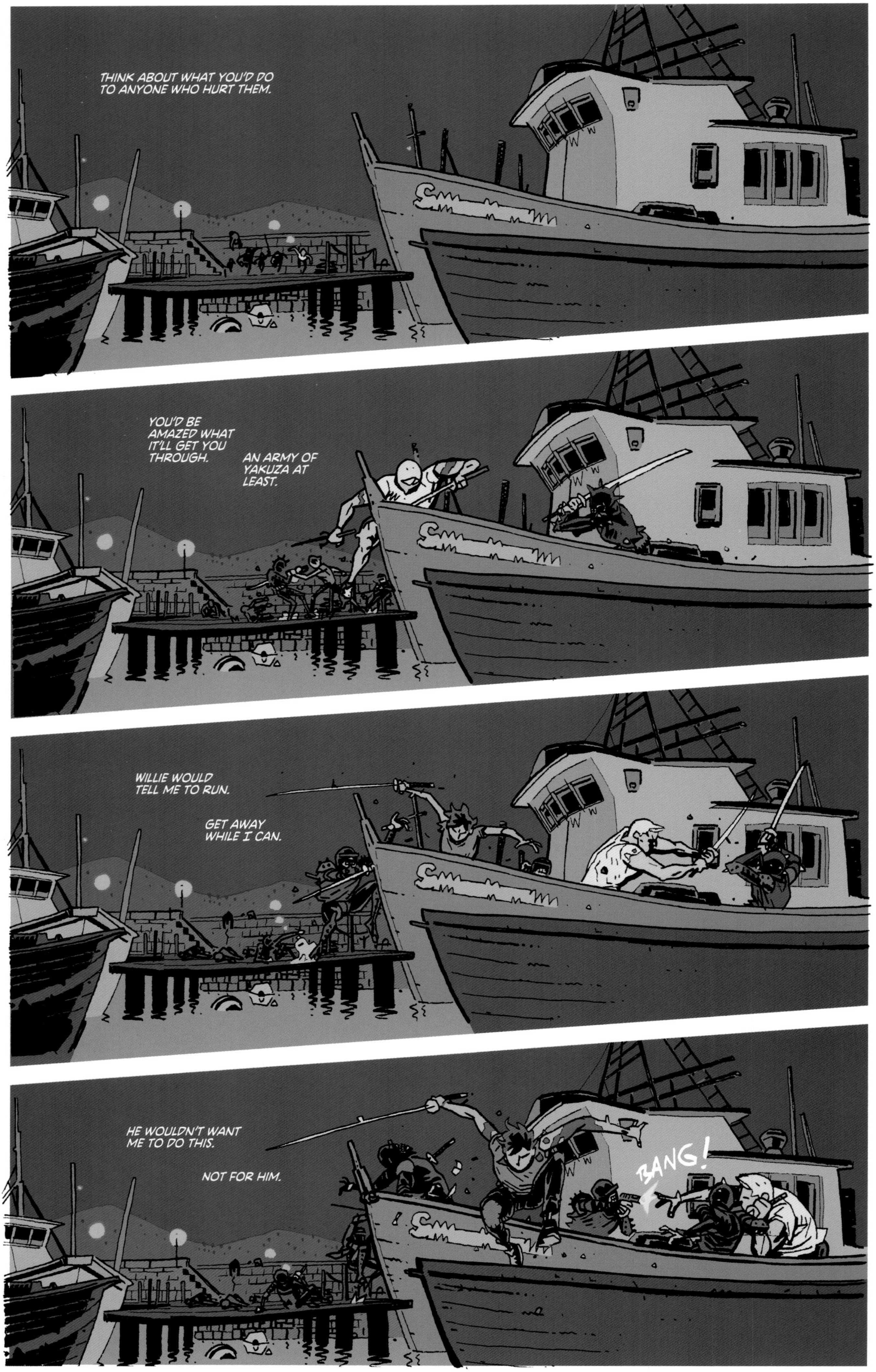
THINK ABOUT WHAT YOU'D DO TO ANYONE WHO HURT THEM.
YOU'D BE AMAZED WHAT IT'LL GET YOU THROUGH.
AN ARMY OF YAKUZA AT LEAST.
WILLIE WOULD TELL ME TO RUN.
GET AWAY WHILE I CAN.
HE WOULDN'T WANT ME TO DO THIS.
NOT FOR HIM.
BANG!

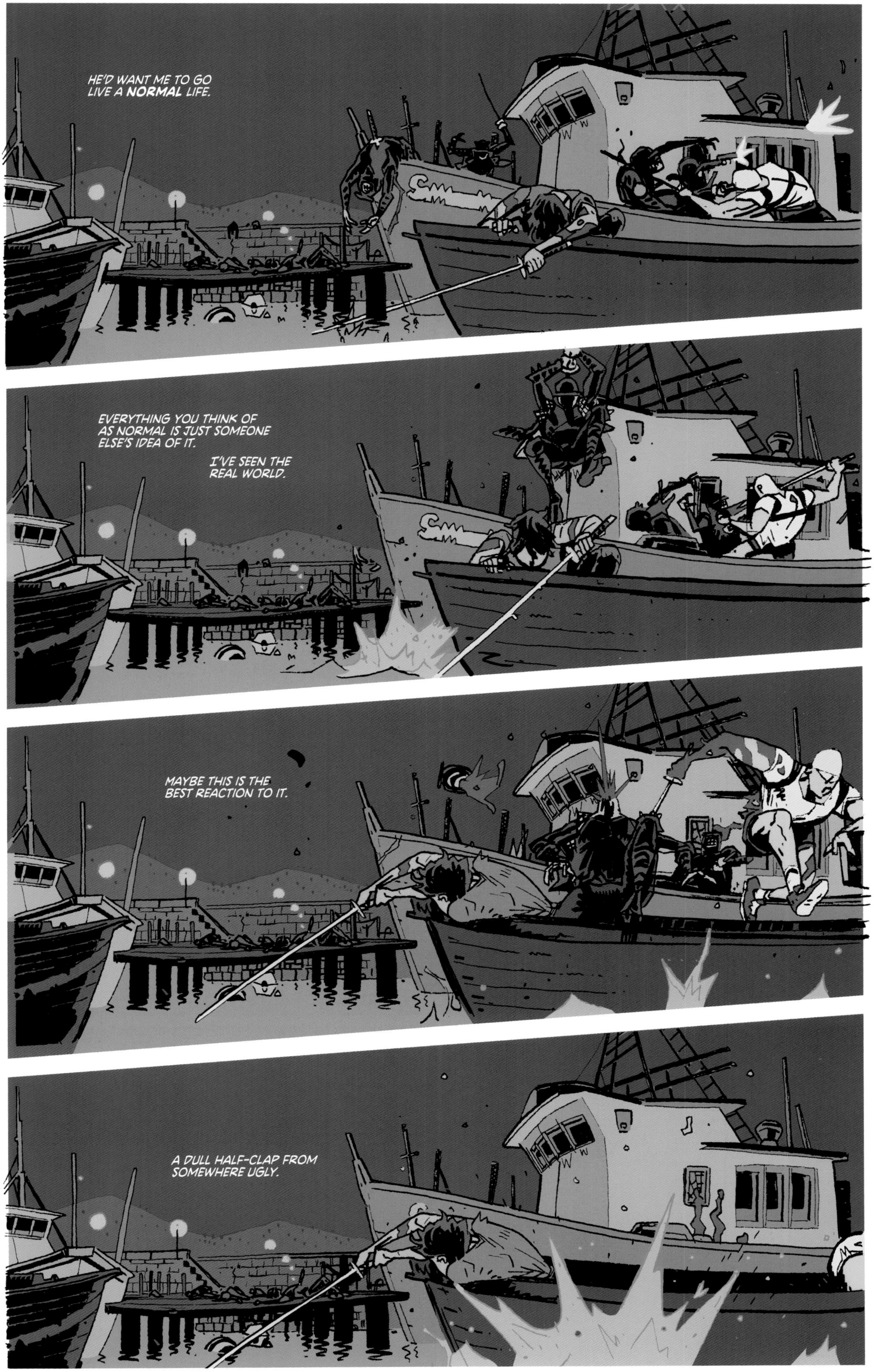
HE'D WANT ME TO GO LIVE A NORMAL LIFE.
EVERYTHING YOU THINK OF AS NORMAL IS JUST SOMEONE ELSE'S IDEA OF IT.
I'VE SEEN THE REAL WORLD.
MAYBE THIS IS THE BEST REACTION TO IT.
A DULL HALF-CLAP FROM SOMEWHERE UGLY.

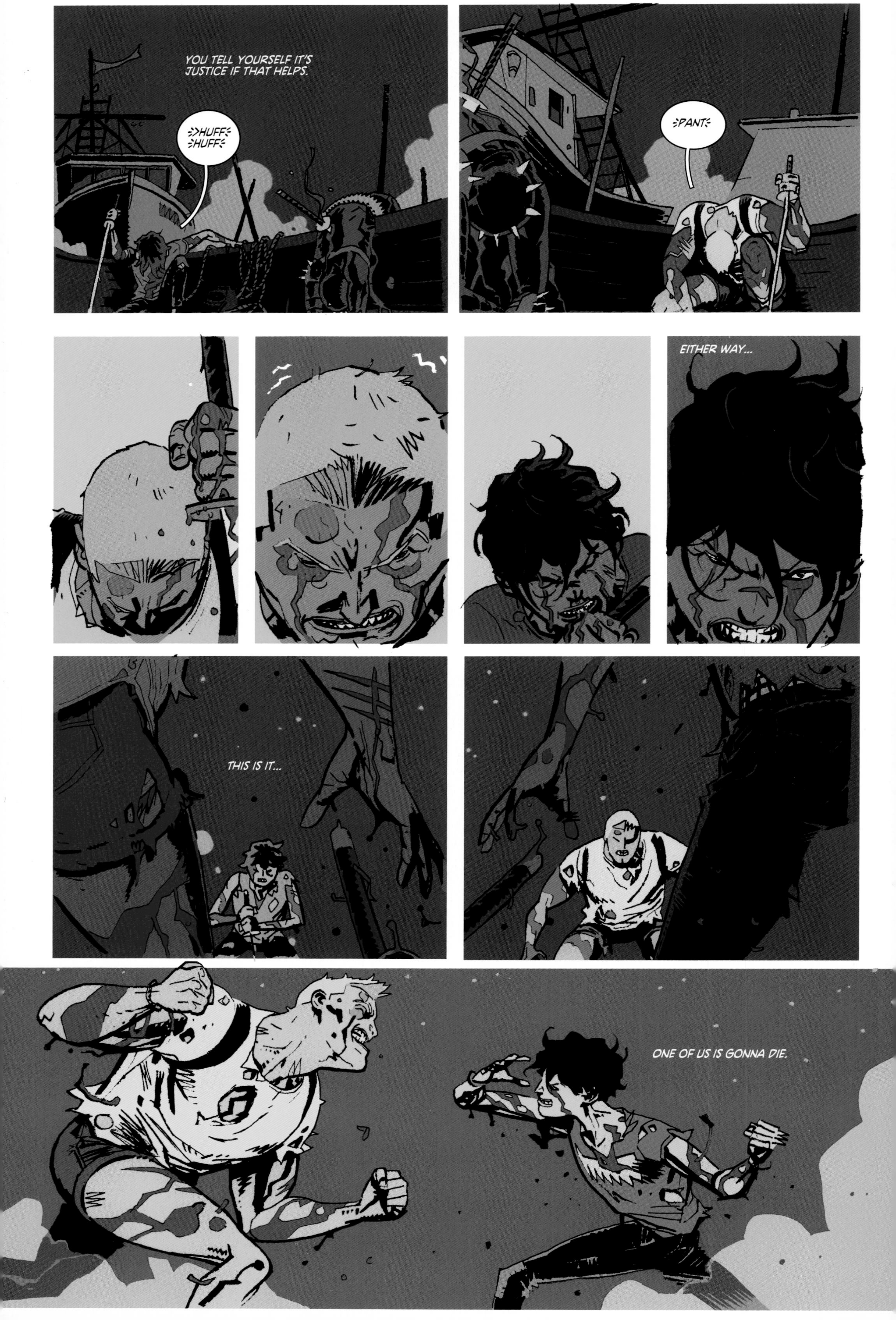
YOU TELL YOURSELF IT'S JUSTICE IF THAT HELPS.
HUFF HUFF
PANT
EITHER WAY...
THIS IS IT...
ONE OF US IS GONNA DIE.

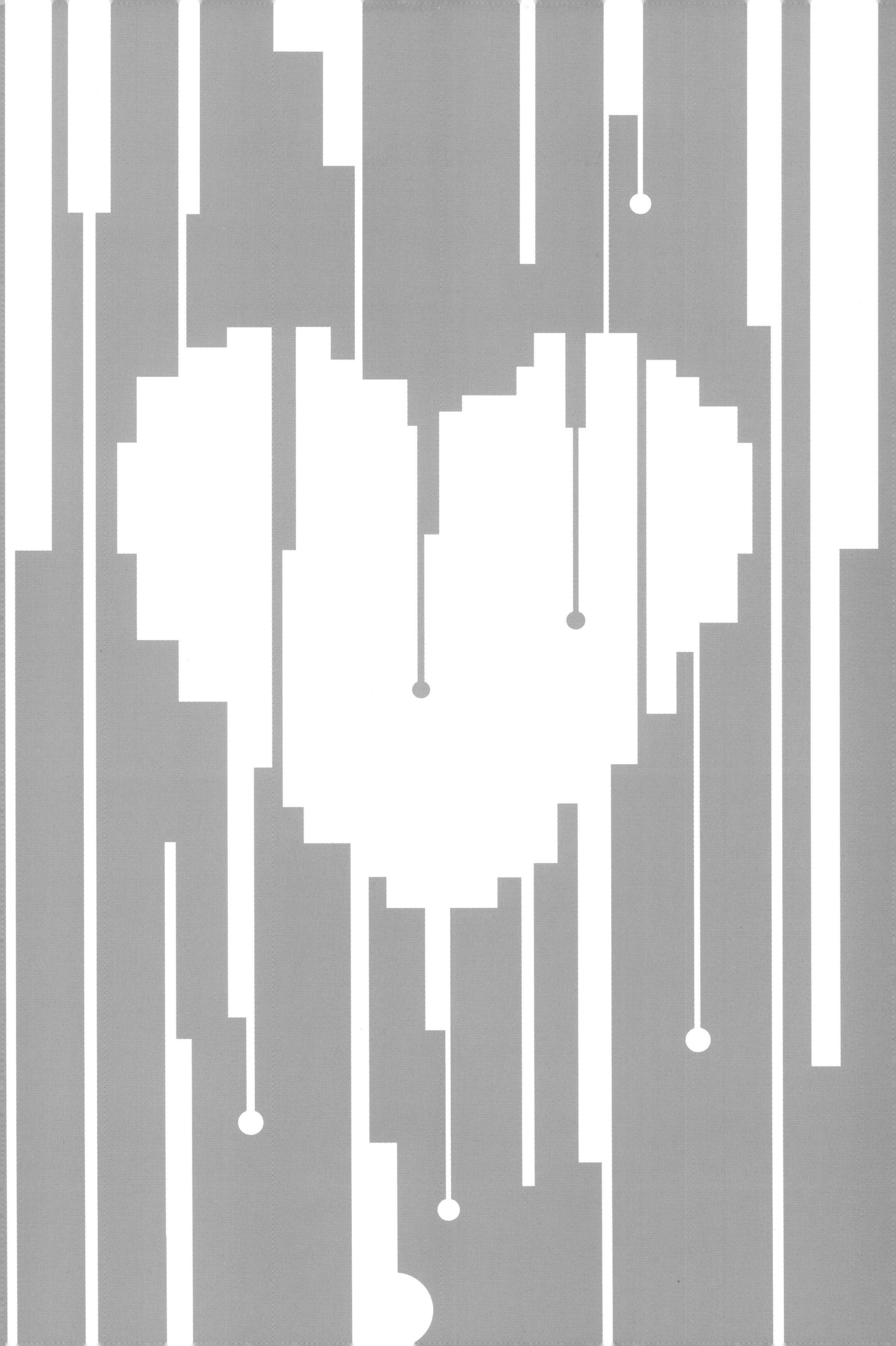

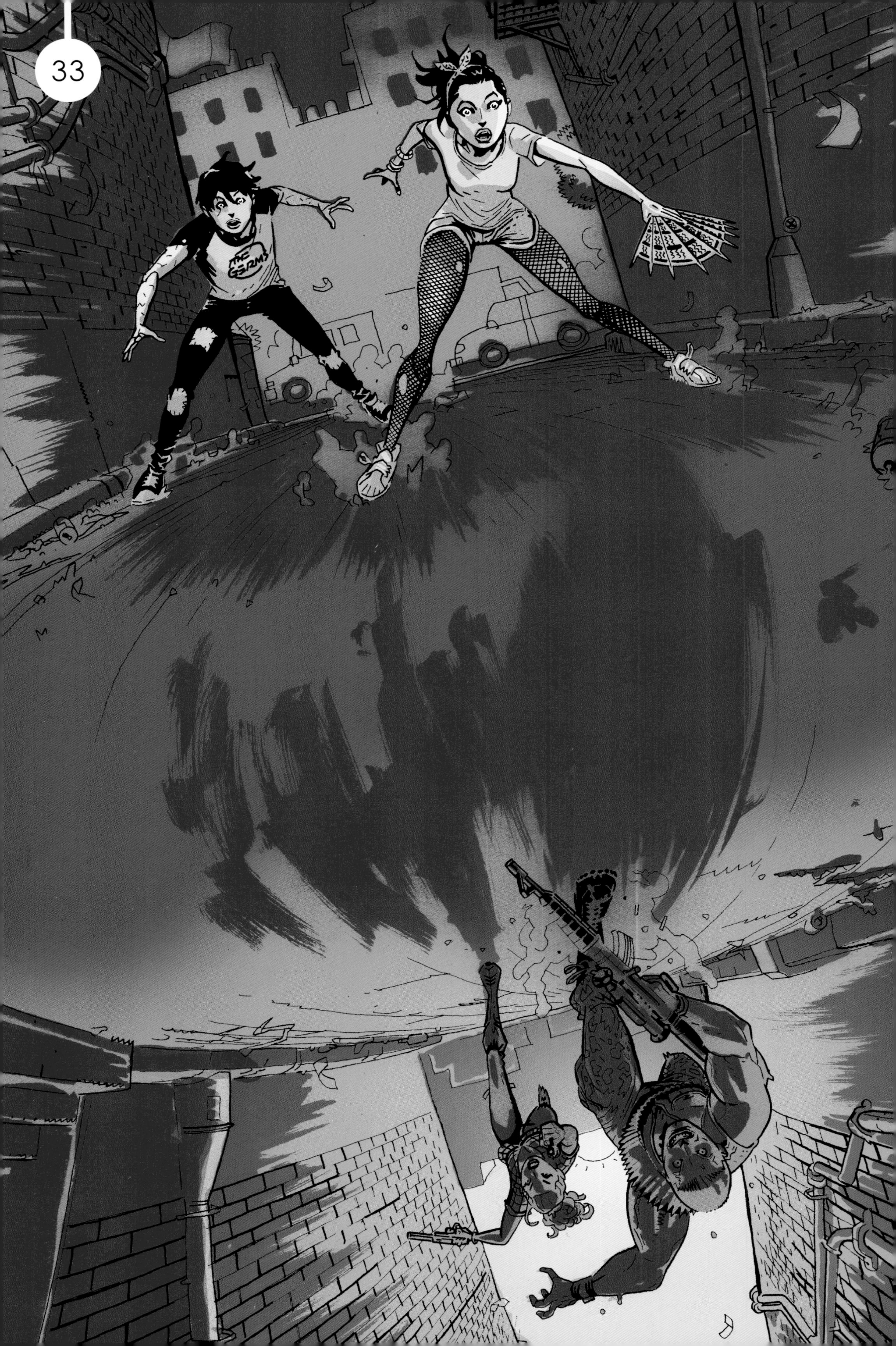
THE GERMS

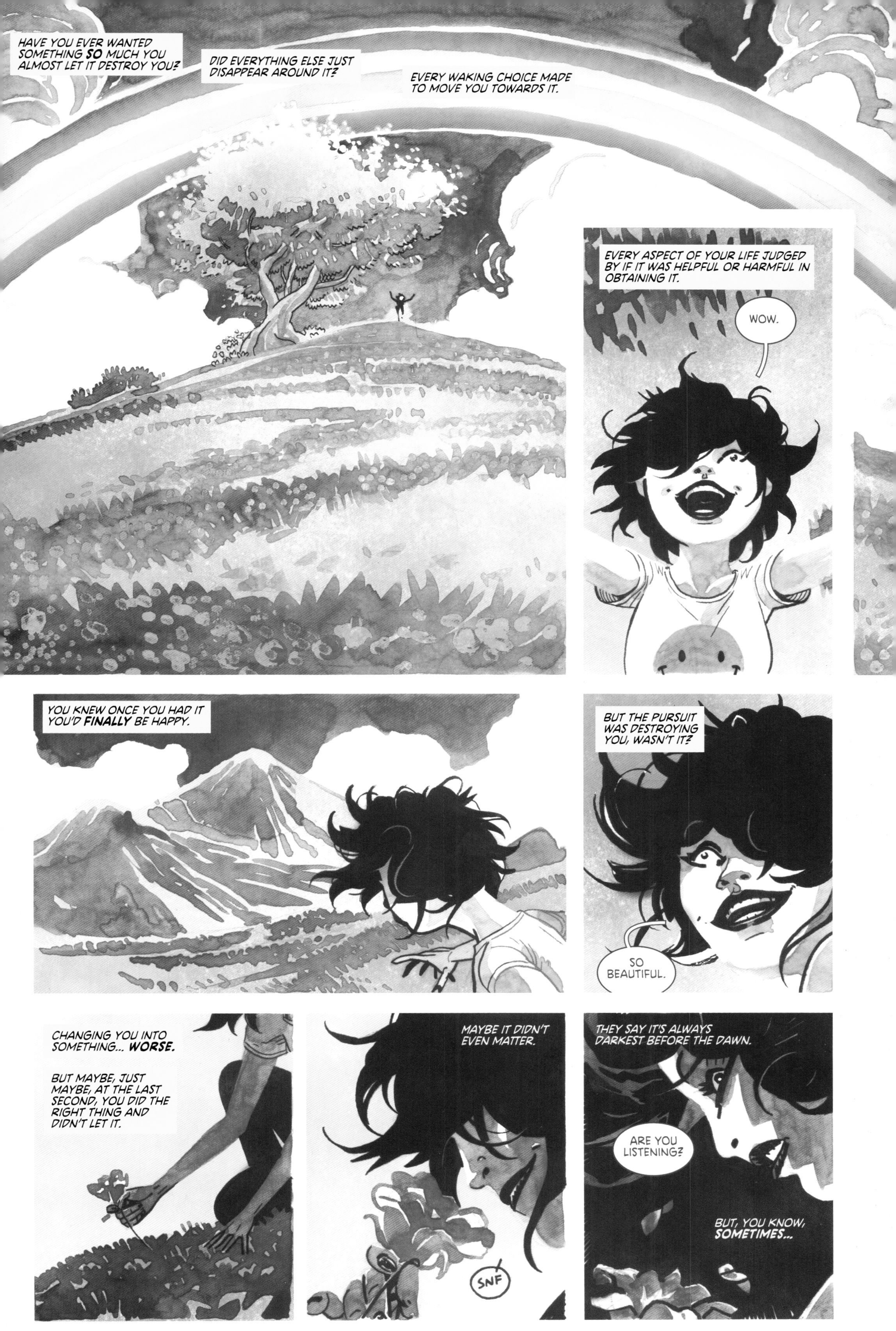
HAVE YOU EVER WANTED SOMETHING SO MUCH YOU ALMOST LET IT DESTROY YOU?
DID EVERYTHING ELSE JUST DISAPPEAR AROUND IT?
EVERY WAKING CHOICE MADE TO MOVE YOU TOWARDS IT.
EVERY ASPECT OF YOUR LIFE JUDGED BY IF IT WAS HELPFUL OR HARMFUL IN OBTAINING IT.
WOW.
YOU KNEW ONCE YOU HAD IT YOU'D FINALLY BE HAPPY.
BUT THE PURSUIT WAS DESTROYING YOU, WASN'T IT?
SO BEAUTIFUL.
CHANGING YOU INTO SOMETHING... WORSE.
BUT MAYBE, JUST MAYBE, AT THE LAST SECOND, YOU DID THE RIGHT THING AND DIDN'T LET IT.
MAYBE IT DIDN'T EVEN MATTER.
SNF
THEY SAY IT'S ALWAYS DARKEST BEFORE THE DAWN.
ARE YOU LISTENING?
BUT, YOU KNOW, SOMETIMES...

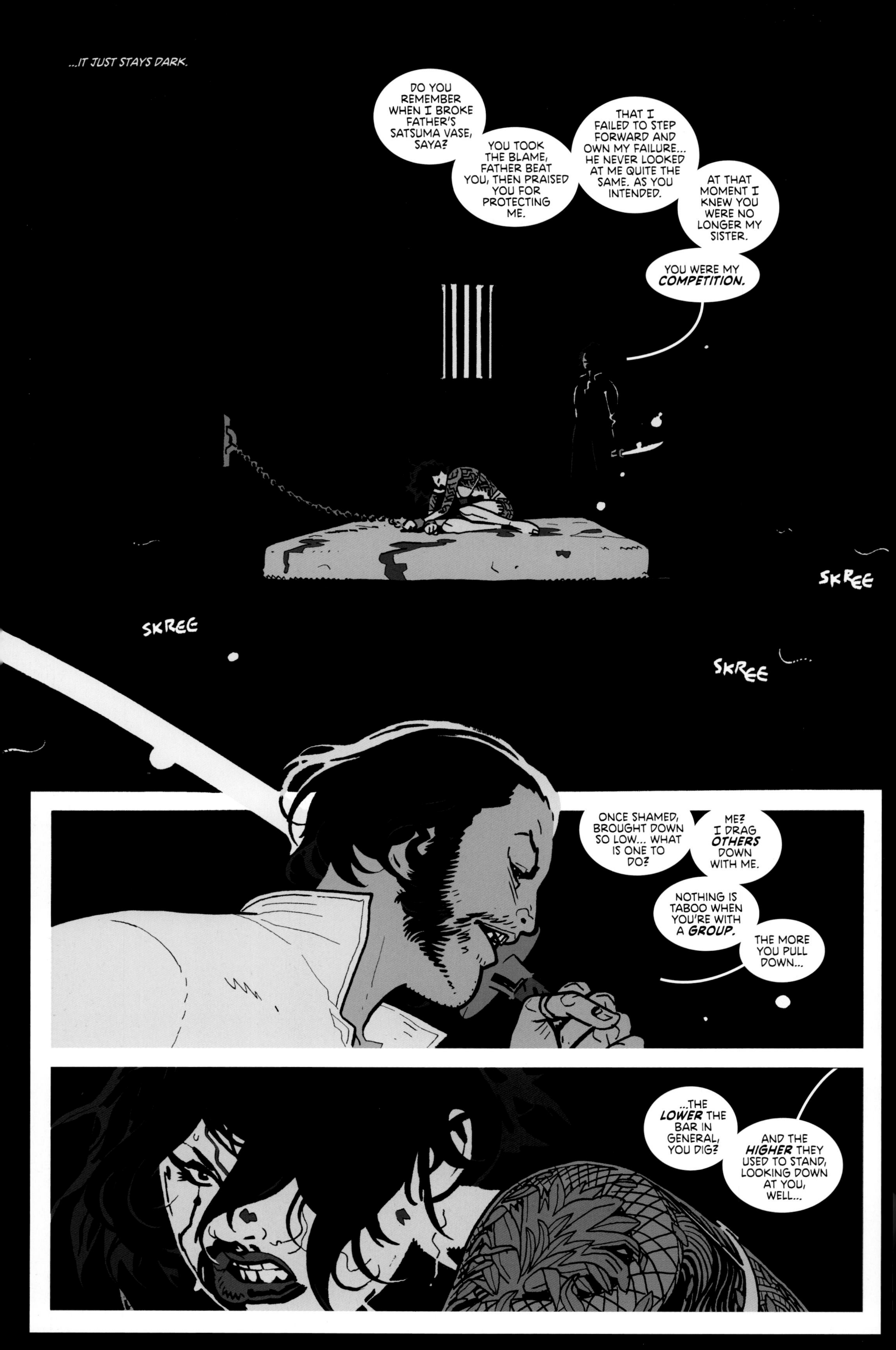
...IT JUST STAYS DARK.
DO YOU REMEMBER WHEN I BROKE FATHER'S SATSUMA VASE, SAYA?
YOU TOOK THE BLAME, FATHER BEAT YOU, THEN PRAISED YOU FOR PROTECTING ME.
THAT I FAILED TO STEP FORWARD AND OWN MY FAILURE... HE NEVER LOOKED AT ME QUITE THE SAME. AS YOU INTENDED.
AT THAT MOMENT I KNEW YOU WERE NO LONGER MY SISTER.
YOU WERE MY *COMPETITION.*
SKREE
SKREE
SKREE
ONCE SHAMED, BROUGHT DOWN SO LOW... WHAT IS ONE TO DO?
ME? I DRAG *OTHERS* DOWN WITH ME.
NOTHING IS TABOO WHEN YOU'RE WITH A *GROUP.*
THE MORE YOU PULL DOWN...
...THE *LOWER* THE BAR IN GENERAL, YOU DIG?
AND THE *HIGHER* THEY USED TO STAND, LOOKING DOWN AT YOU, WELL...

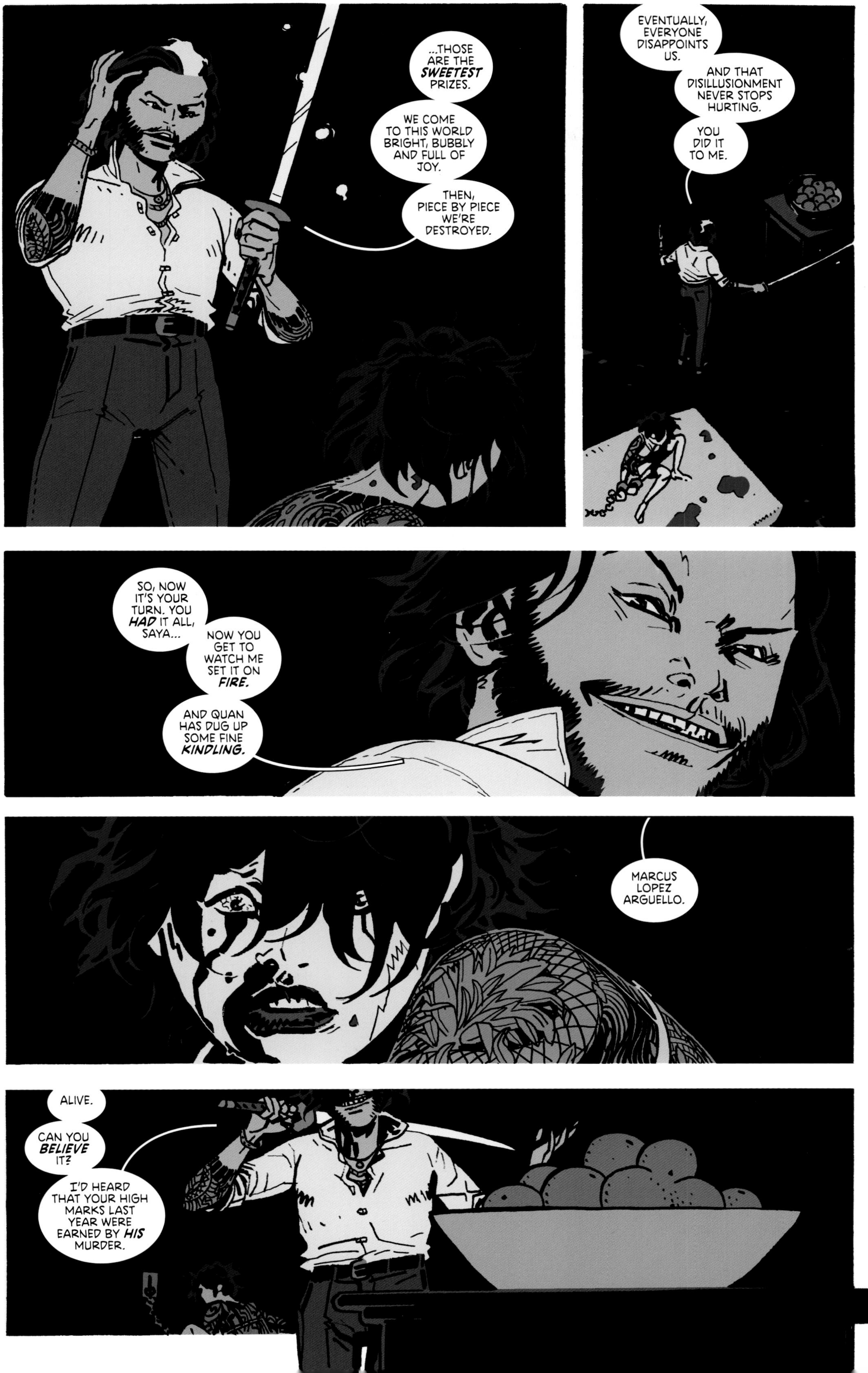
...THOSE ARE THE SWEETEST PRIZES.
WE COME TO THIS WORLD BRIGHT, BUBBLY AND FULL OF JOY.
THEN, PIECE BY PIECE WE'RE DESTROYED.
EVENTUALLY, EVERYONE DISAPPOINTS US.
AND THAT DISILLUSIONMENT NEVER STOPS HURTING.
YOU DID IT TO ME.
SO, NOW IT'S YOUR TURN. YOU HAD IT ALL, SAYA...
NOW YOU GET TO WATCH ME SET IT ON FIRE.
AND QUAN HAS DUG UP SOME FINE KINDLING.
MARCUS LOPEZ ARGUELLO.
ALIVE.
CAN YOU BELIEVE IT?
I'D HEARD THAT YOUR HIGH MARKS LAST YEAR WERE EARNED BY HIS MURDER.

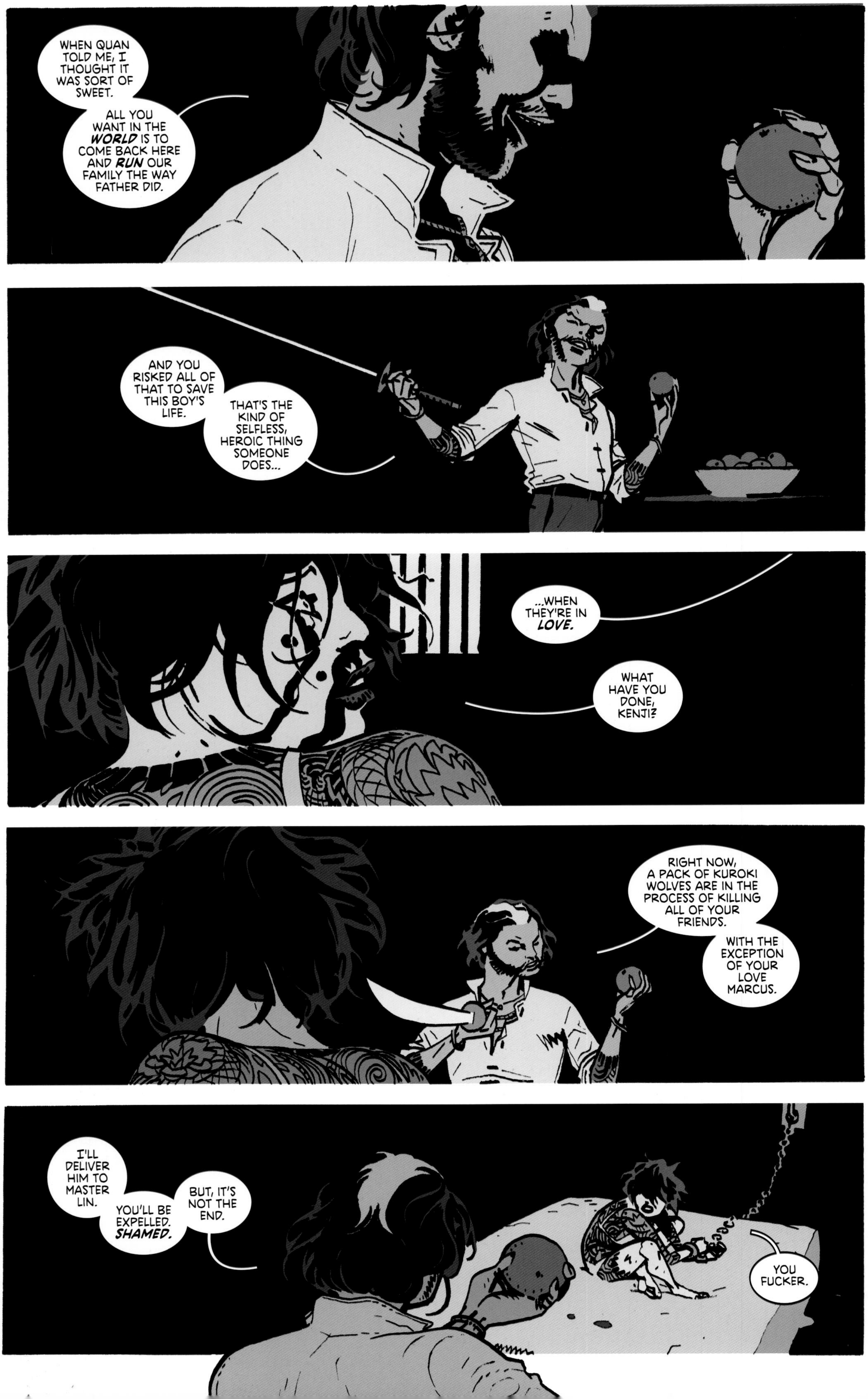
WHEN QUAN TOLD ME, I THOUGHT IT WAS SORT OF SWEET.
ALL YOU WANT IN THE *WORLD* IS TO COME BACK HERE AND *RUN* OUR FAMILY THE WAY FATHER DID.
AND YOU RISKED ALL OF THAT TO SAVE THIS BOY'S LIFE.
THAT'S THE KIND OF SELFLESS, HEROIC THING SOMEONE DOES...
...WHEN THEY'RE IN *LOVE.*
WHAT HAVE YOU DONE, KENJI?
RIGHT NOW, A PACK OF KUROKI WOLVES ARE IN THE PROCESS OF KILLING ALL OF YOUR FRIENDS.
WITH THE EXCEPTION OF YOUR LOVE MARCUS.
I'LL DELIVER HIM TO MASTER LIN.
YOU'LL BE EXPELLED. *SHAMED.*
BUT, IT'S NOT THE END.
YOU FUCKER.

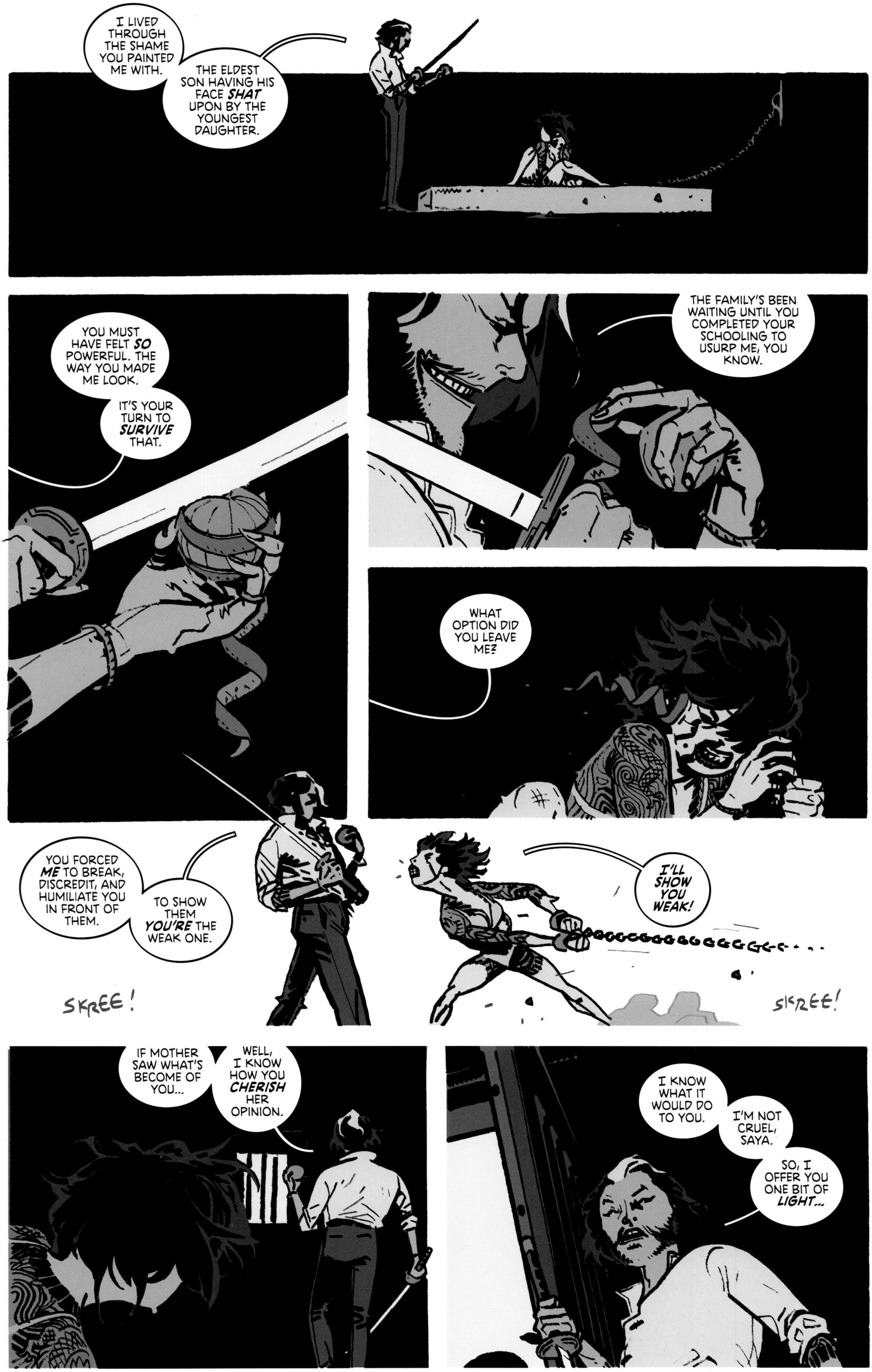
I LIVED THROUGH THE SHAME YOU PAINTED ME WITH.
THE ELDEST SON HAVING HIS FACE SHAT UPON BY THE YOUNGEST DAUGHTER.
YOU MUST HAVE FELT SO POWERFUL. THE WAY YOU MADE ME LOOK.
IT'S YOUR TURN TO SURVIVE THAT.
THE FAMILY'S BEEN WAITING UNTIL YOU COMPLETED YOUR SCHOOLING TO USURP ME, YOU KNOW.
WHAT OPTION DID YOU LEAVE ME?
YOU FORCED ME TO BREAK, DISCREDIT, AND HUMILIATE YOU IN FRONT OF THEM.
TO SHOW THEM YOU'RE THE WEAK ONE.
I'LL SHOW YOU WEAK!
SKREE!
SKREE!
IF MOTHER SAW WHAT'S BECOME OF YOU...
WELL, I KNOW HOW YOU CHERISH HER OPINION.
I KNOW WHAT IT WOULD DO TO YOU.
I'M NOT CRUEL, SAYA.
SO, I OFFER YOU ONE BIT OF LIGHT...

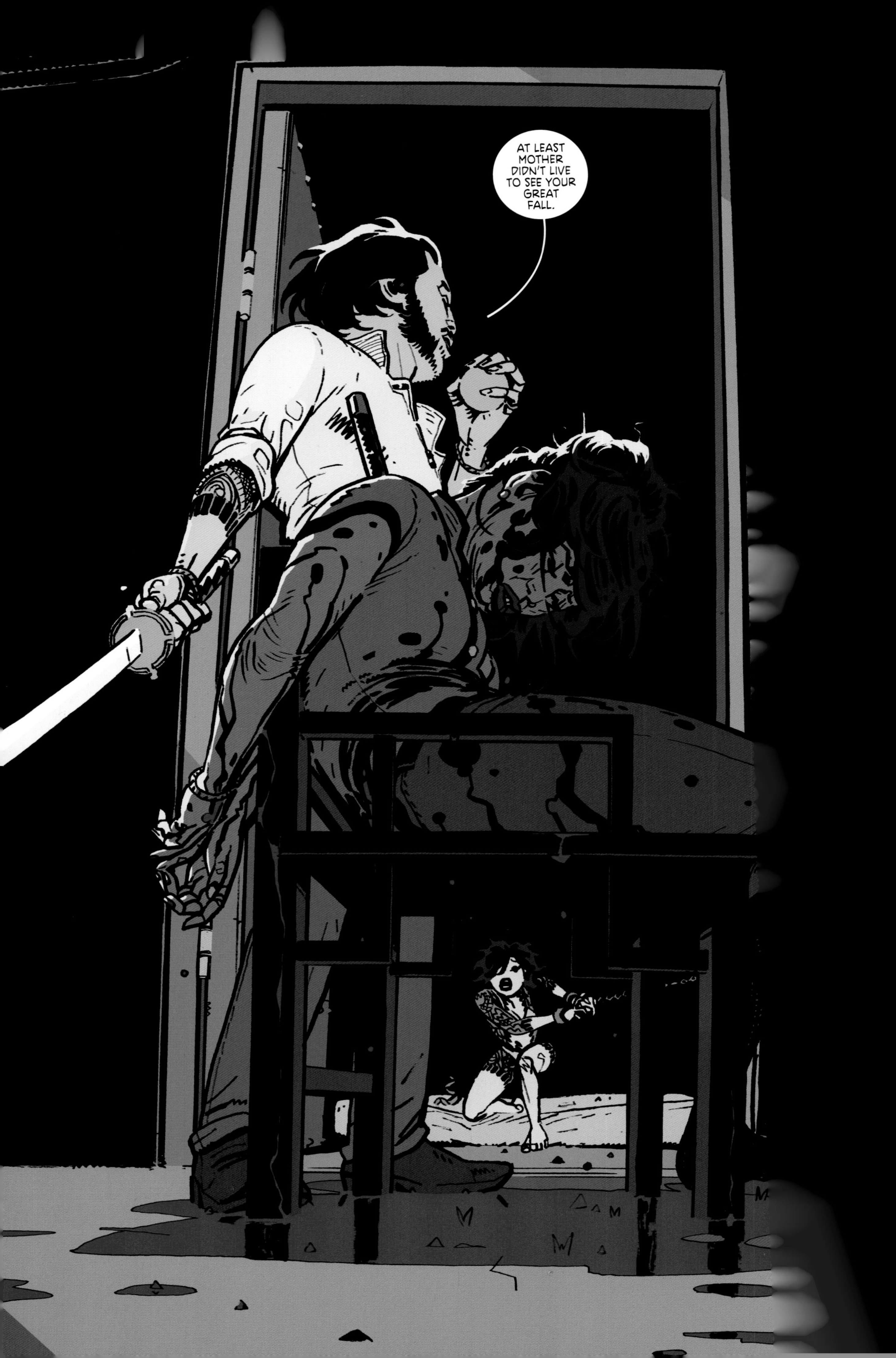
AT LEAST MOTHER DIDN'T LIVE TO SEE YOUR GREAT FALL.

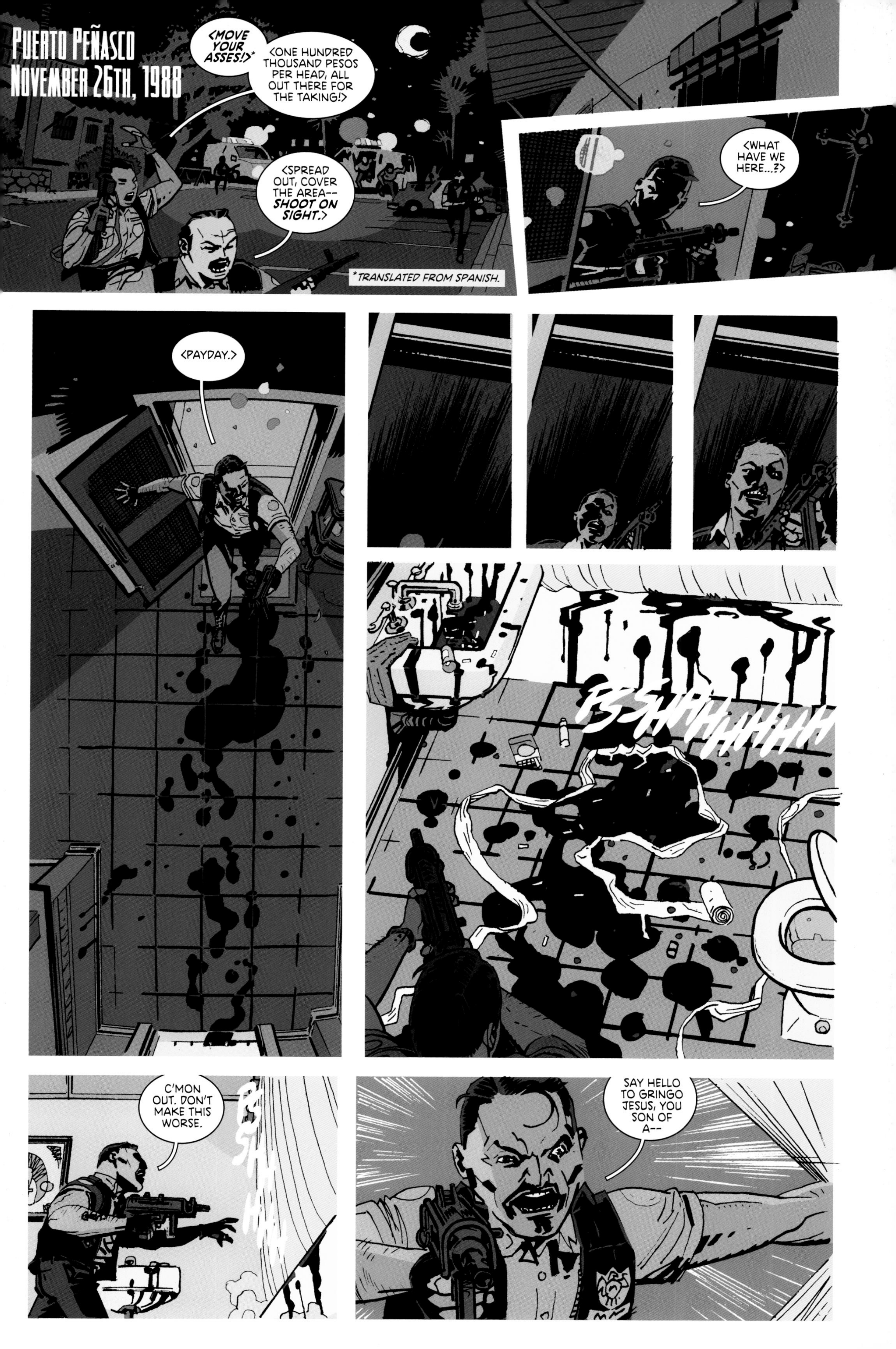

Puerto Peñasco
November 26th, 1988
<MOVE YOUR ASSES!>*
<ONE HUNDRED THOUSAND PESOS PER HEAD, ALL OUT THERE FOR THE TAKING!>
<SPREAD OUT, COVER THE AREA-- SHOOT ON SIGHT.>
*TRANSLATED FROM SPANISH.
<WHAT HAVE WE HERE...?>
<PAYDAY.>
PSSHHHHHHHHHH
C'MON OUT. DON'T MAKE THIS WORSE.
PSSHHHHH
SAY HELLO TO GRINGO JESUS, YOU SON OF A--

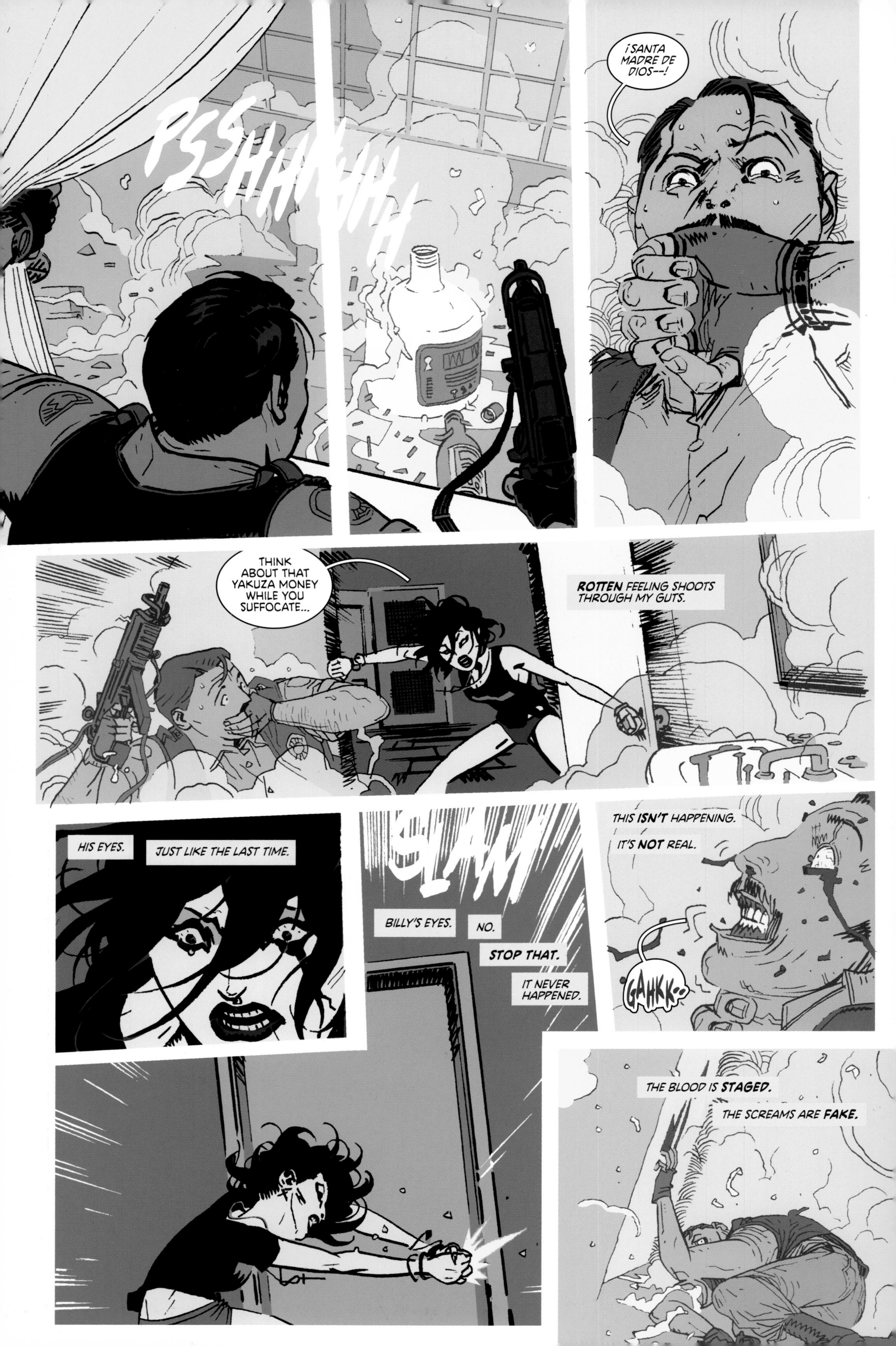
PSSHHHHHHH
¡SANTA MADRE DE DIOS--!
THINK ABOUT THAT YAKUZA MONEY WHILE YOU SUFFOCATE...
ROTTEN FEELING SHOOTS THROUGH MY GUTS.
HIS EYES.
JUST LIKE THE LAST TIME.
SLAM
BILLY'S EYES.
NO.
STOP THAT.
IT NEVER HAPPENED.
THIS ISN'T HAPPENING.
IT'S NOT REAL.
GAHKK..
THE BLOOD IS STAGED.
THE SCREAMS ARE FAKE.

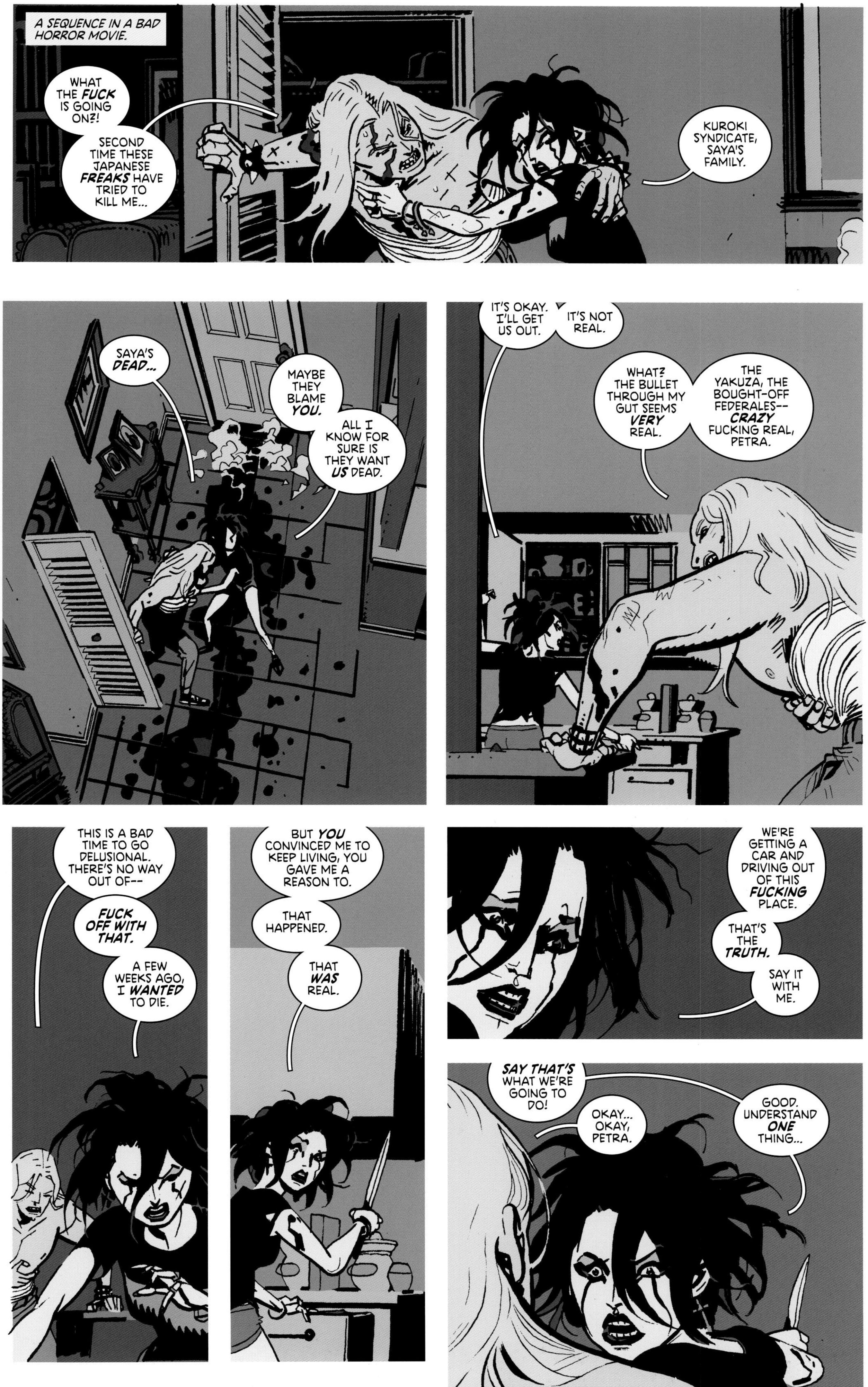
A SEQUENCE IN A BAD HORROR MOVIE.
WHAT THE FUCK IS GOING ON?!
SECOND TIME THESE JAPANESE FREAKS HAVE TRIED TO KILL ME...
KUROKI SYNDICATE, SAYA'S FAMILY.
SAYA'S DEAD...
MAYBE THEY BLAME YOU.
ALL I KNOW FOR SURE IS THEY WANT US DEAD.
IT'S OKAY. I'LL GET US OUT.
IT'S NOT REAL.
WHAT? THE BULLET THROUGH MY GUT SEEMS VERY REAL.
THE YAKUZA, THE BOUGHT-OFF FEDERALES-- CRAZY FUCKING REAL, PETRA.
THIS IS A BAD TIME TO GO DELUSIONAL. THERE'S NO WAY OUT OF--
FUCK OFF WITH THAT.
A FEW WEEKS AGO, I WANTED TO DIE.
BUT YOU CONVINCED ME TO KEEP LIVING, YOU GAVE ME A REASON TO.
THAT HAPPENED.
THAT WAS REAL.
WE'RE GETTING A CAR AND DRIVING OUT OF THIS FUCKING PLACE.
THAT'S THE TRUTH.
SAY IT WITH ME.
SAY THAT'S WHAT WE'RE GOING TO DO!
OKAY... OKAY, PETRA.
GOOD. UNDERSTAND ONE THING...

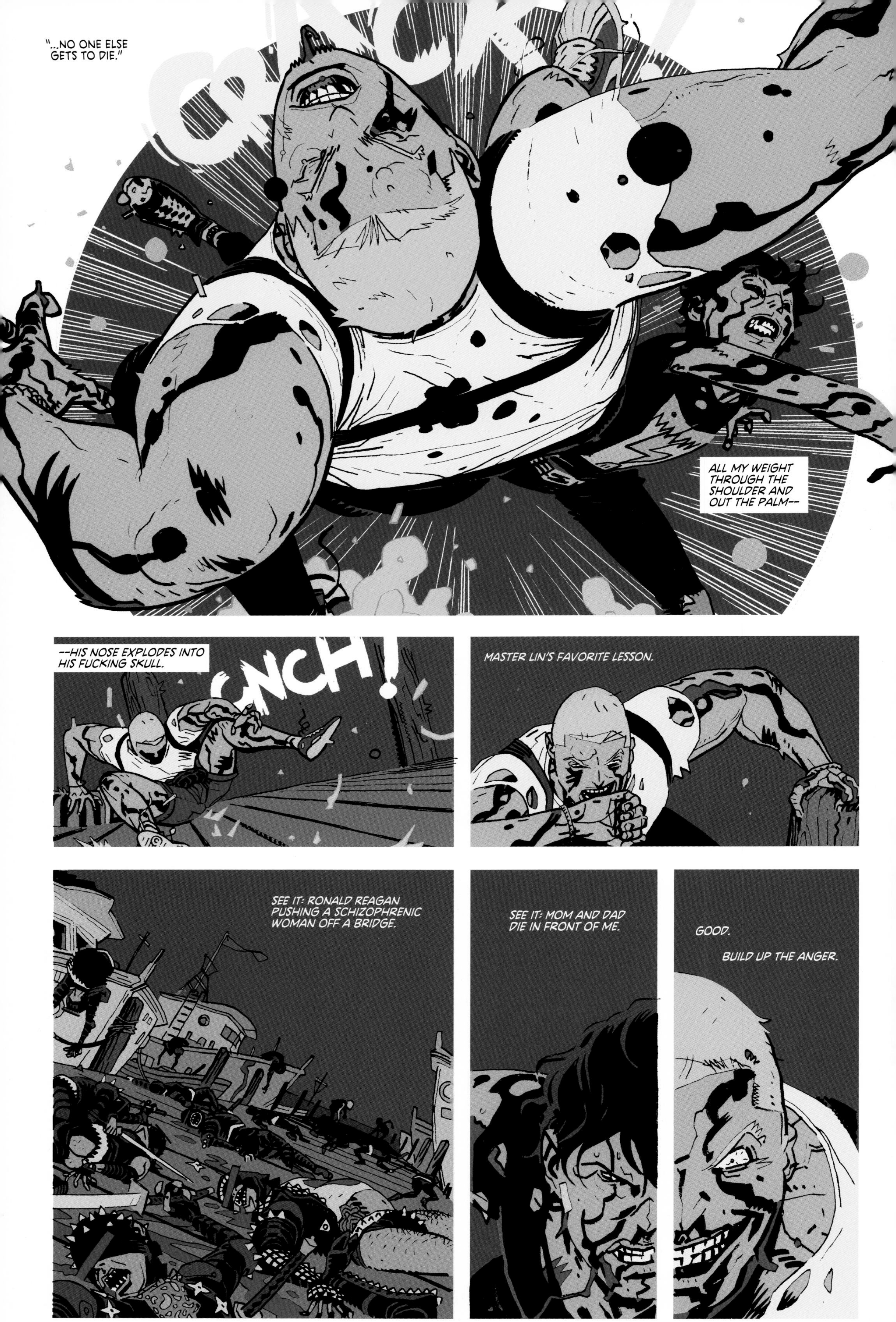
"...NO ONE ELSE GETS TO DIE."
ALL MY WEIGHT THROUGH THE SHOULDER AND OUT THE PALM--
--HIS NOSE EXPLODES INTO HIS FUCKING SKULL.
MASTER LIN'S FAVORITE LESSON.
SEE IT: RONALD REAGAN PUSHING A SCHIZOPHRENIC WOMAN OFF A BRIDGE.
SEE IT: MOM AND DAD DIE IN FRONT OF ME.
GOOD.
BUILD UP THE ANGER.

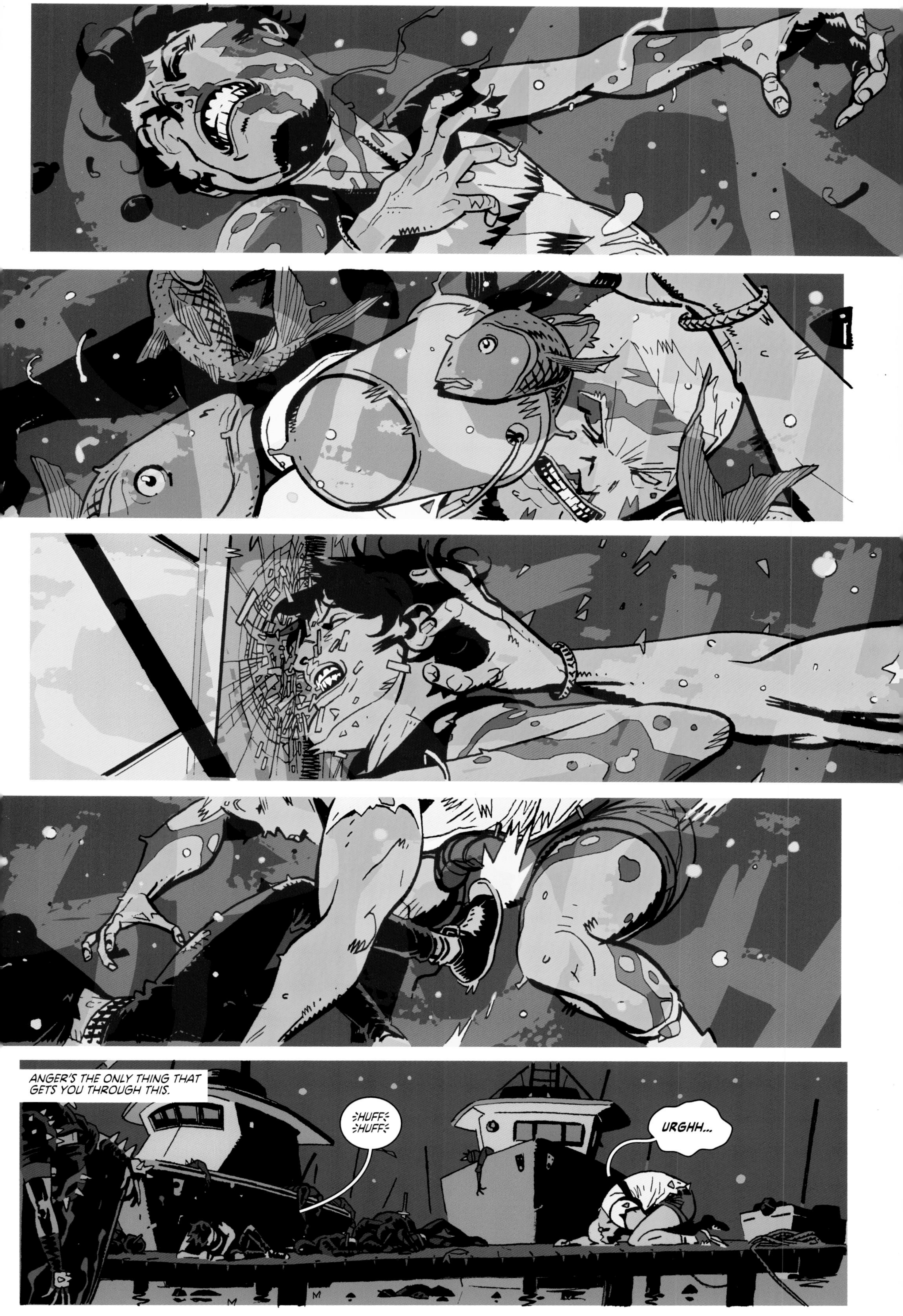
ANGER'S THE ONLY THING THAT GETS YOU THROUGH THIS.
HUFF HUFF
URGHH...

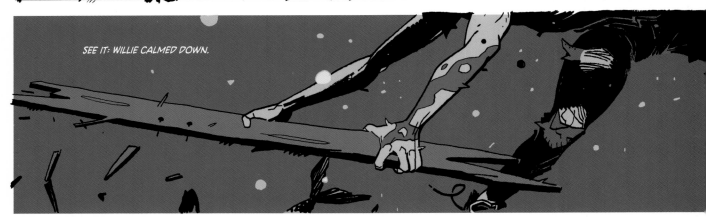

SEE IT: WILLIE CALMED DOWN.

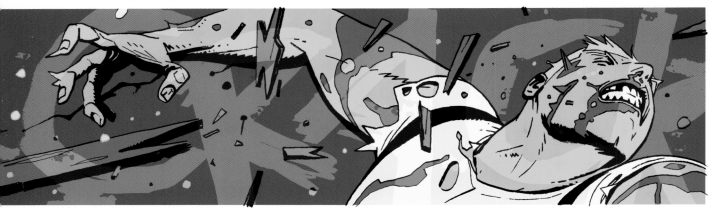

SEE HIM: READY TO RUN AWAY WITH ME.

REMEMBER.

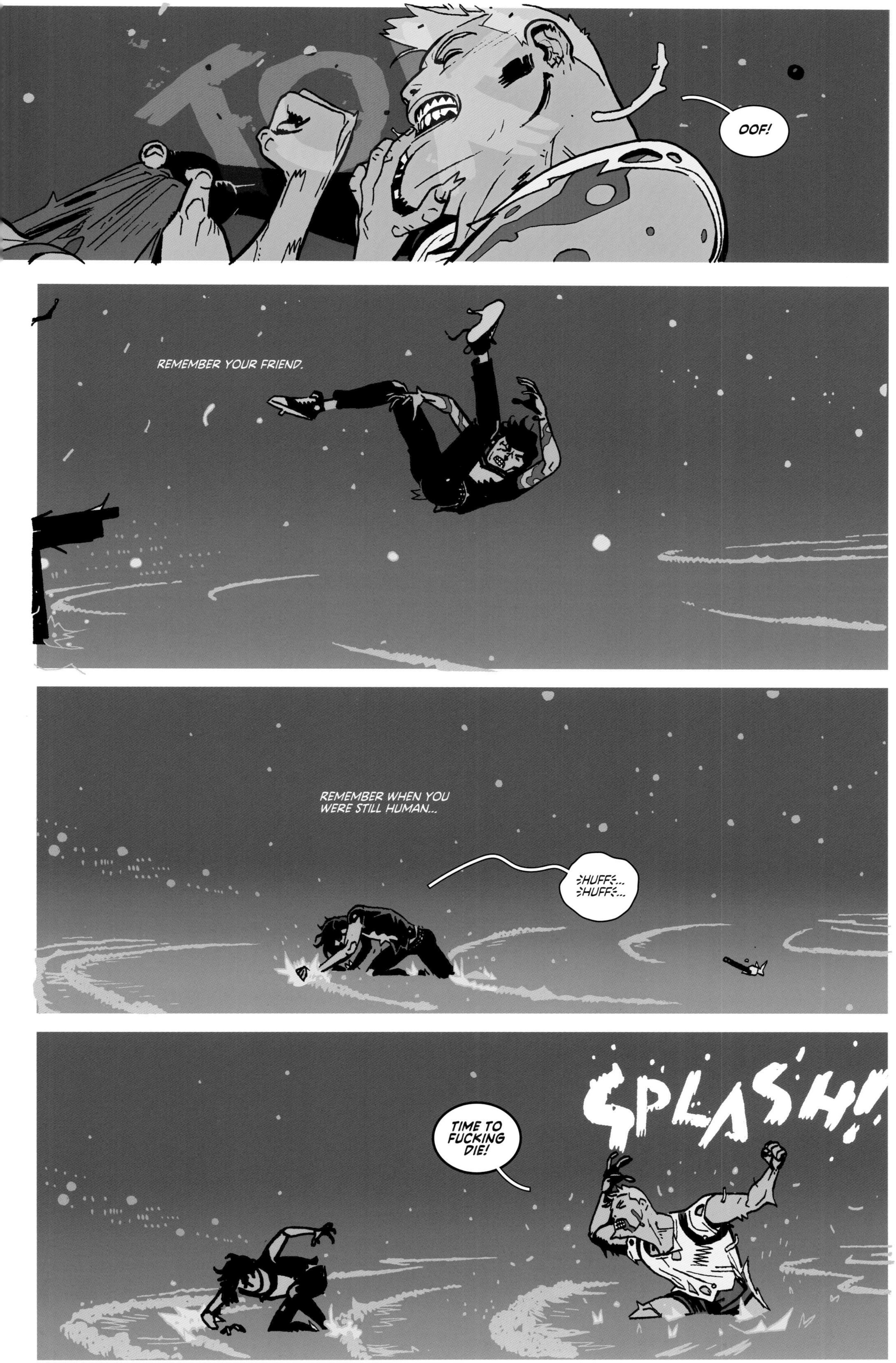
OOF!
REMEMBER YOUR FRIEND.
REMEMBER WHEN YOU WERE STILL HUMAN...
HUFF... HUFF...
TIME TO FUCKING DIE!
SPLASH!!

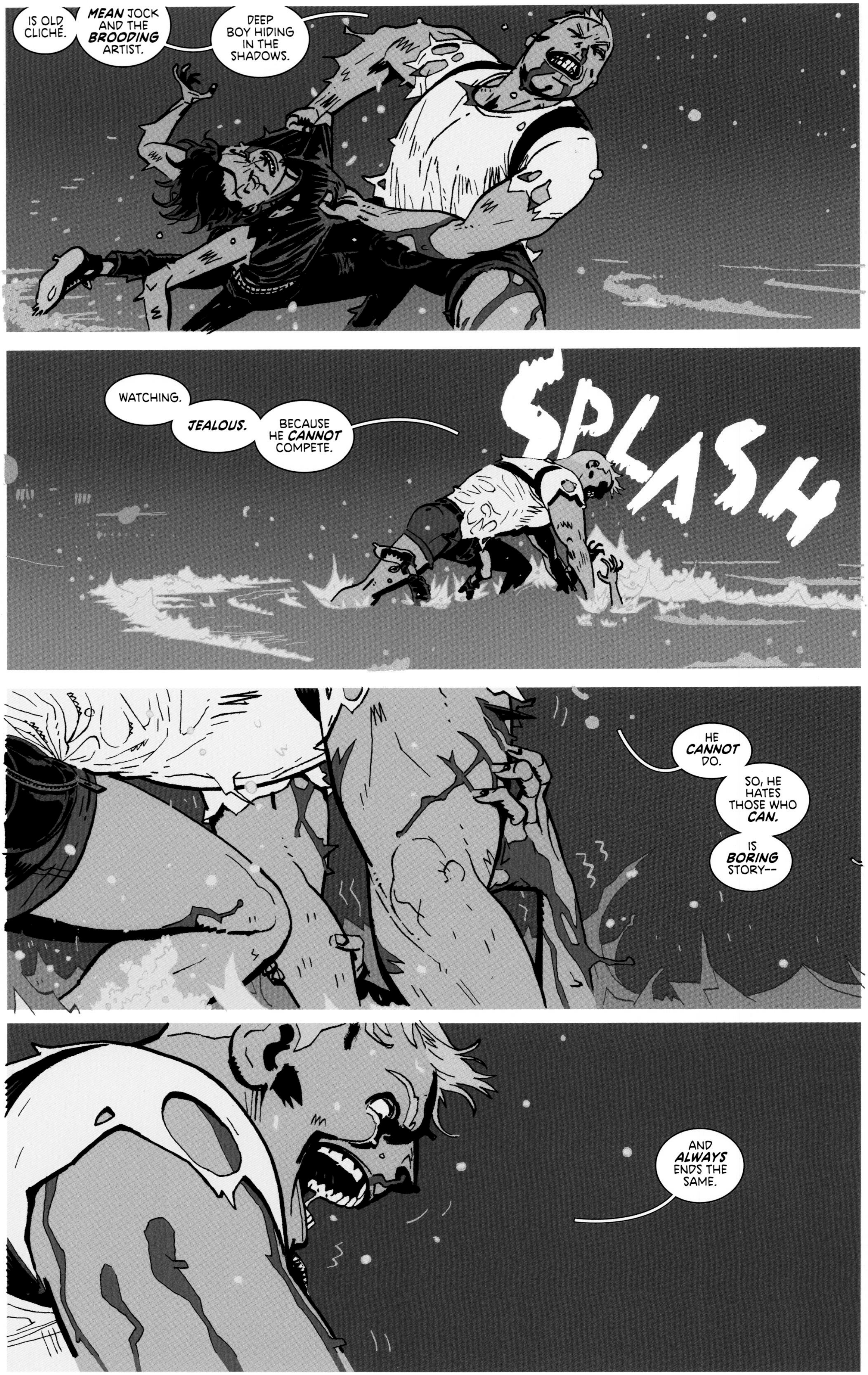
IS OLD CLICHÉ.
MEAN JOCK AND THE *BROODING* ARTIST.
DEEP BOY HIDING IN THE SHADOWS.
WATCHING.
JEALOUS.
BECAUSE HE *CANNOT* COMPETE.
SPLASH
HE *CANNOT* DO.
SO, HE HATES THOSE WHO *CAN.*
IS *BORING* STORY--
AND *ALWAYS* ENDS THE SAME.

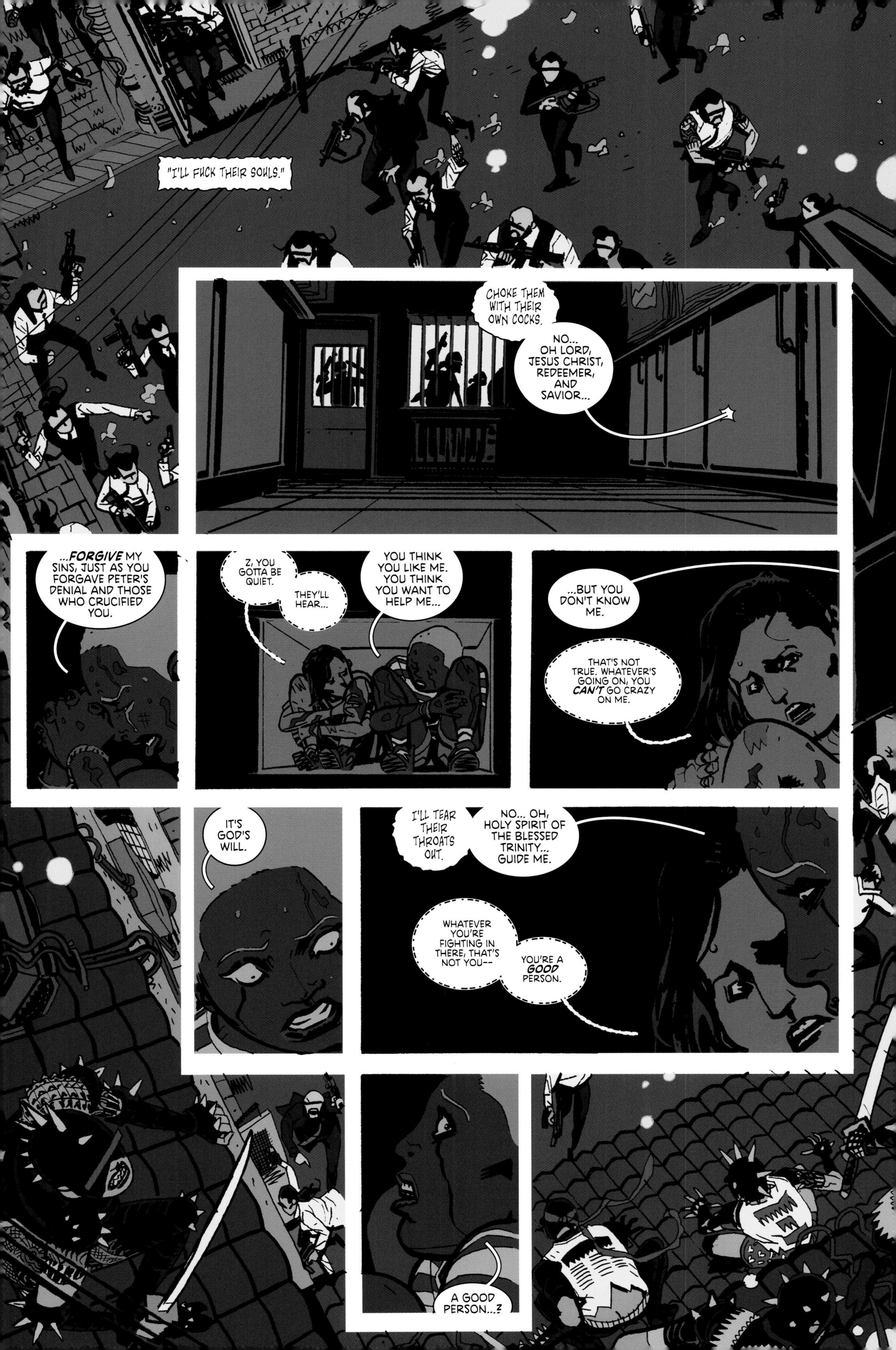
"I'LL FUCK THEIR SOULS."
CHOKE THEM WITH THEIR OWN COCKS.
NO... OH LORD, JESUS CHRIST, REDEEMER, AND SAVIOR...
...FORGIVE MY SINS, JUST AS YOU FORGAVE PETER'S DENIAL AND THOSE WHO CRUCIFIED YOU.
Z, YOU GOTTA BE QUIET.
THEY'LL HEAR...
YOU THINK YOU LIKE ME. YOU THINK YOU WANT TO HELP ME...
...BUT YOU DON'T KNOW ME.
THAT'S NOT TRUE. WHATEVER'S GOING ON, YOU CAN'T GO CRAZY ON ME.
IT'S GOD'S WILL.
I'LL TEAR THEIR THROATS OUT.
NO... OH, HOLY SPIRIT OF THE BLESSED TRINITY... GUIDE ME.
WHATEVER YOU'RE FIGHTING IN THERE, THAT'S NOT YOU--
YOU'RE A GOOD PERSON.
A GOOD PERSON...?

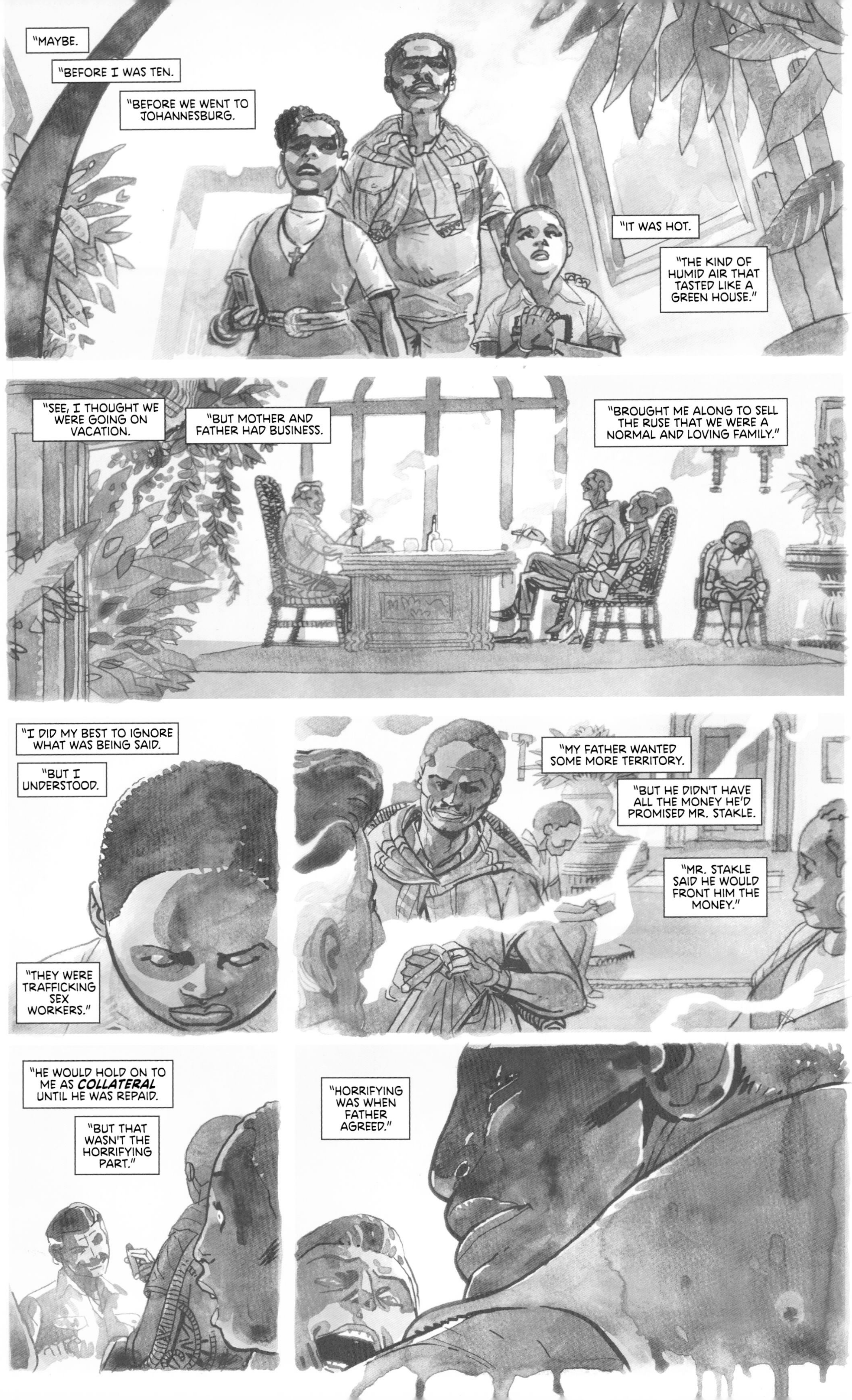
"MAYBE.
"BEFORE I WAS TEN.
"BEFORE WE WENT TO JOHANNESBURG.
"IT WAS HOT.
"THE KIND OF HUMID AIR THAT TASTED LIKE A GREEN HOUSE."
"SEE, I THOUGHT WE WERE GOING ON VACATION.
"BUT MOTHER AND FATHER HAD BUSINESS.
"BROUGHT ME ALONG TO SELL THE RUSE THAT WE WERE A NORMAL AND LOVING FAMILY."
"I DID MY BEST TO IGNORE WHAT WAS BEING SAID.
"BUT I UNDERSTOOD.
"THEY WERE TRAFFICKING SEX WORKERS."
"MY FATHER WANTED SOME MORE TERRITORY.
"BUT HE DIDN'T HAVE ALL THE MONEY HE'D PROMISED MR. STAKLE.
"MR. STAKLE SAID HE WOULD FRONT HIM THE MONEY."
"HE WOULD HOLD ON TO ME AS COLLATERAL UNTIL HE WAS REPAID.
"BUT THAT WASN'T THE HORRIFYING PART."
"HORRIFYING WAS WHEN FATHER AGREED."

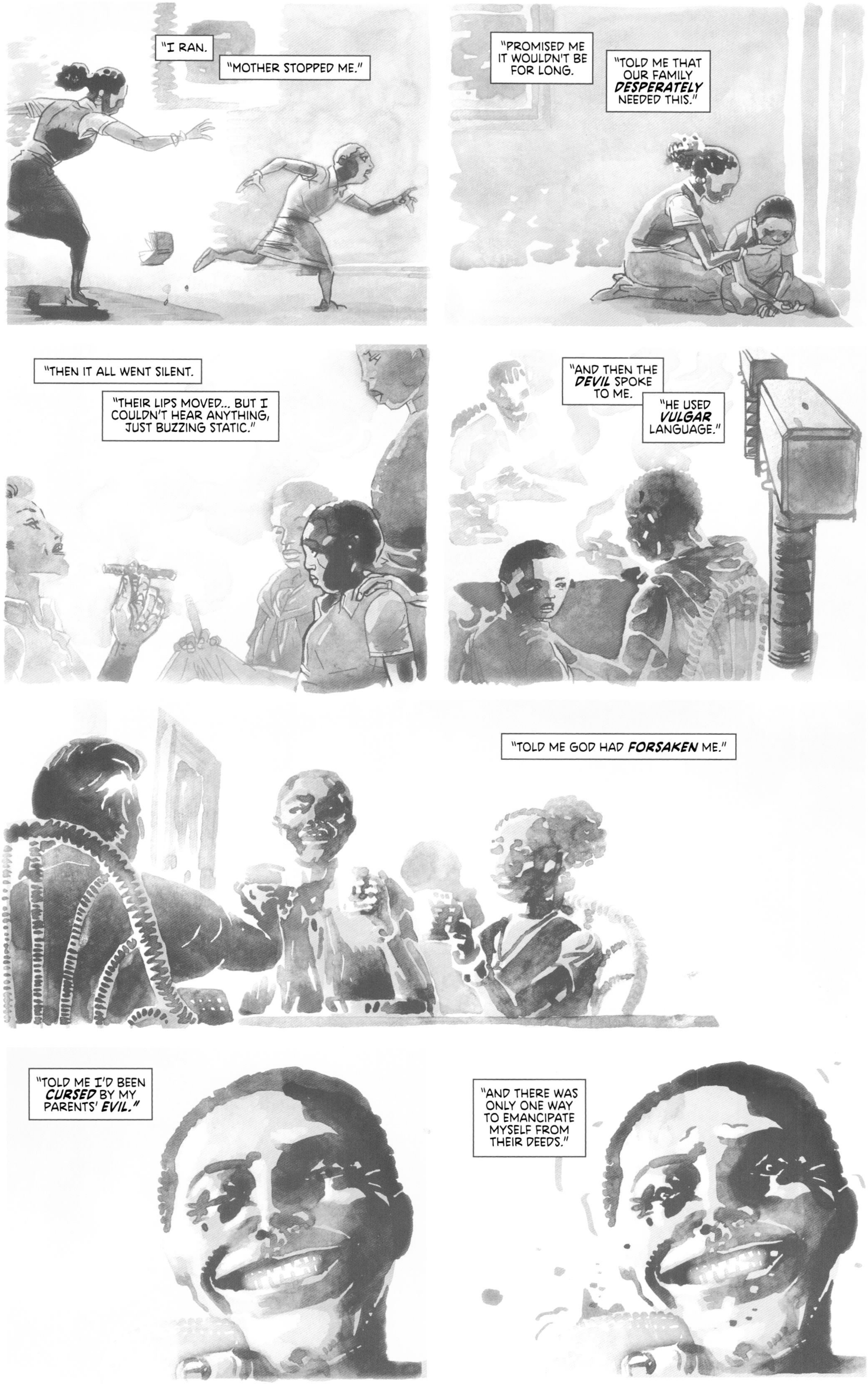
"I RAN.
"MOTHER STOPPED ME."
"PROMISED ME IT WOULDN'T BE FOR LONG.
"TOLD ME THAT OUR FAMILY **DESPERATELY** NEEDED THIS."
"THEN IT ALL WENT SILENT.
"THEIR LIPS MOVED... BUT I COULDN'T HEAR ANYTHING, JUST BUZZING STATIC."
"AND THEN THE **DEVIL** SPOKE TO ME.
"HE USED **VULGAR** LANGUAGE."
"TOLD ME GOD HAD **FORSAKEN** ME."
"TOLD ME I'D BEEN **CURSED** BY MY PARENTS' **EVIL.**"
"AND THERE WAS ONLY ONE WAY TO EMANCIPATE MYSELF FROM THEIR DEEDS."

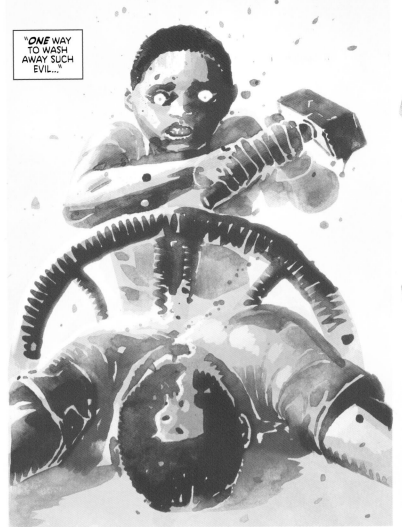

"*ONE* WAY TO WASH AWAY SUCH EVIL..."

"...WITH *MORE* EVIL."

I ENDED UP LIVING WITH MR. STAKLE.

HE SAW THE DEVIL IN ME.

WANTED ME TRAINED TO USE IT, TO BECOME HIS PERFECT BODYGUARD.

SENT ME TO KINGS DOMINION.

AND I WENT. YOU SEE, TOSAHWI...

I AM *NOT* GOOD.

I AM A VESSEL OF SATAN.

STOP IT.

THE ROTTEN SHIT PEOPLE DO IS WHY THEY MADE EVERYONE BELIEVE IN GOD.

SOME KIND OF HOPE THERE'S AS MUCH GOOD AS--

HEY, AKI!

YOU CHECK IN HERE?

DOOR TO THIS KITCHEN IS UNLOCKED.

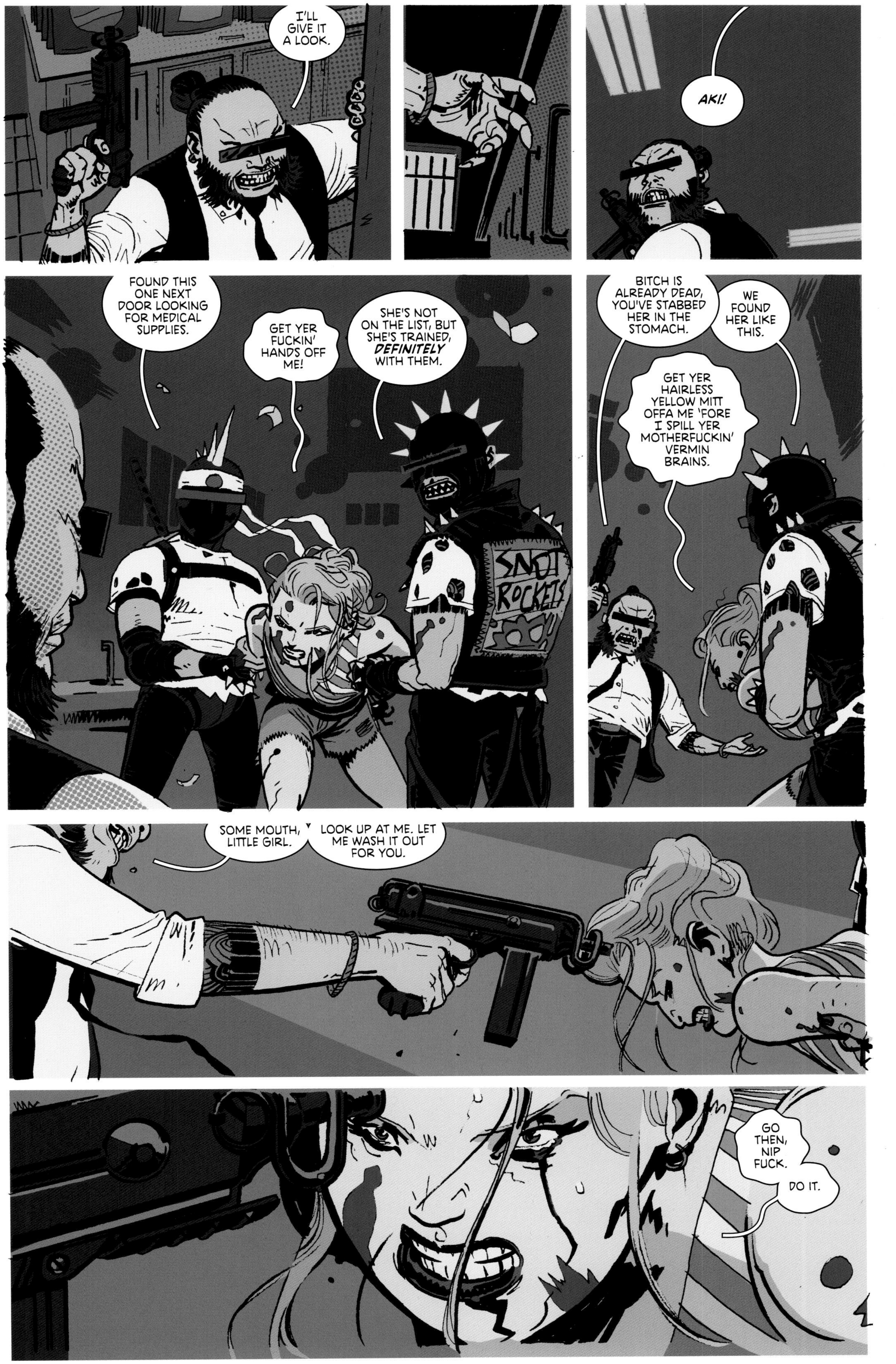

I'LL GIVE IT A LOOK.
AKI!
FOUND THIS ONE NEXT DOOR LOOKING FOR MEDICAL SUPPLIES.
GET YER FUCKIN' HANDS OFF ME!
SHE'S NOT ON THE LIST, BUT SHE'S TRAINED, DEFINITELY WITH THEM.
SNOT ROCKETS
BITCH IS ALREADY DEAD, YOU'VE STABBED HER IN THE STOMACH.
WE FOUND HER LIKE THIS.
GET YER HAIRLESS YELLOW MITT OFFA ME 'FORE I SPILL YER MOTHERFUCKIN' VERMIN BRAINS.
SOME MOUTH, LITTLE GIRL.
LOOK UP AT ME. LET ME WASH IT OUT FOR YOU.
GO THEN, NIP FUCK.
DO IT.

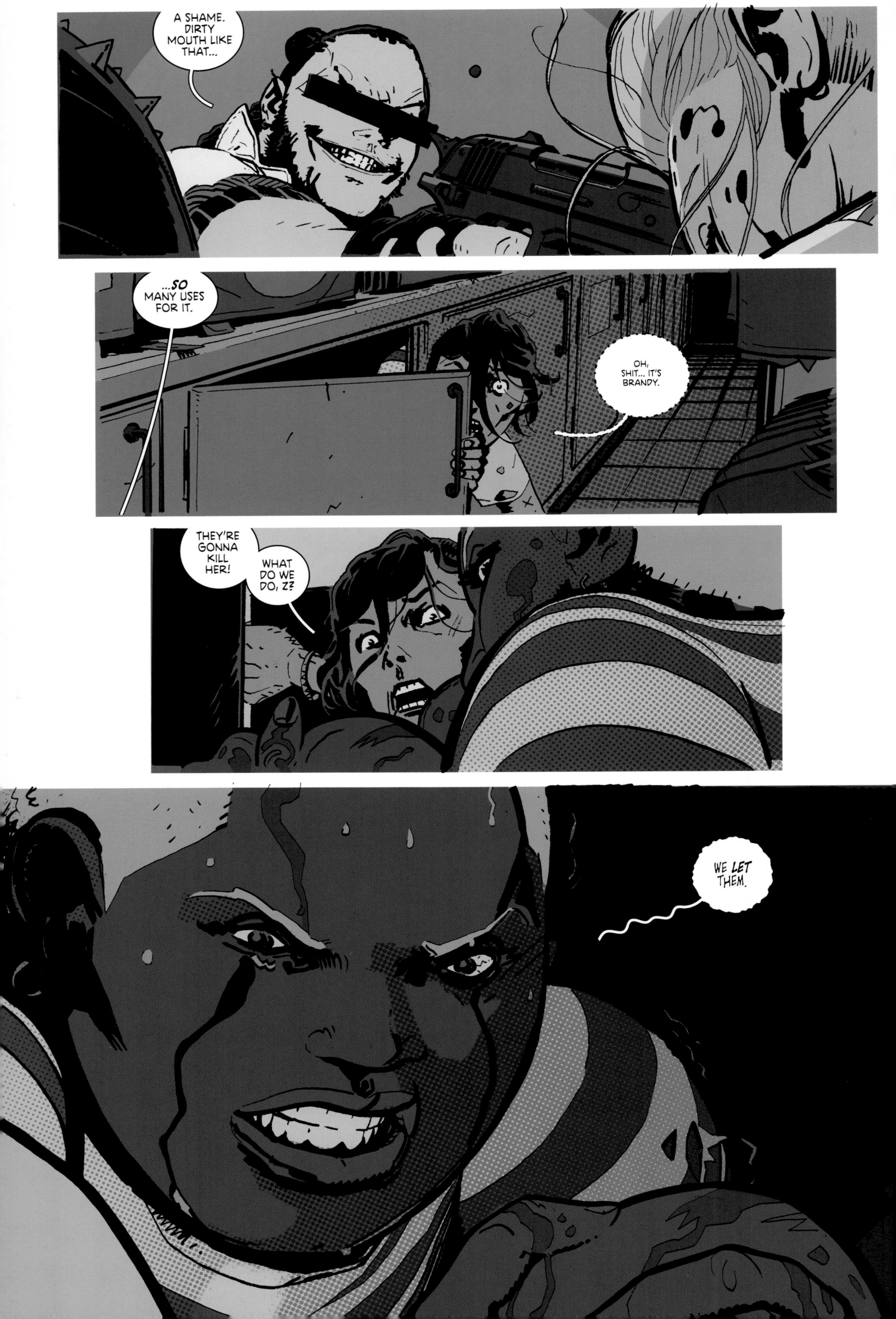
A SHAME. DIRTY MOUTH LIKE THAT...
...SO MANY USES FOR IT.
OH, SHIT... IT'S BRANDY.
THEY'RE GONNA KILL HER!
WHAT DO WE DO, Z?
WE LET THEM.

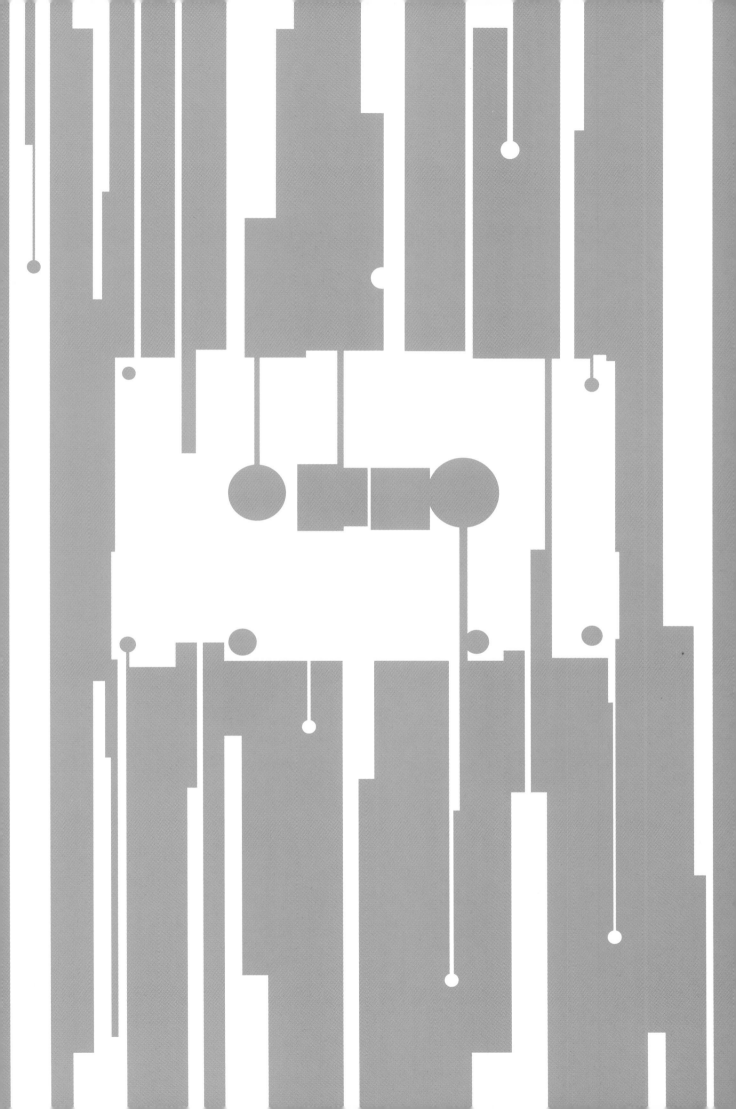

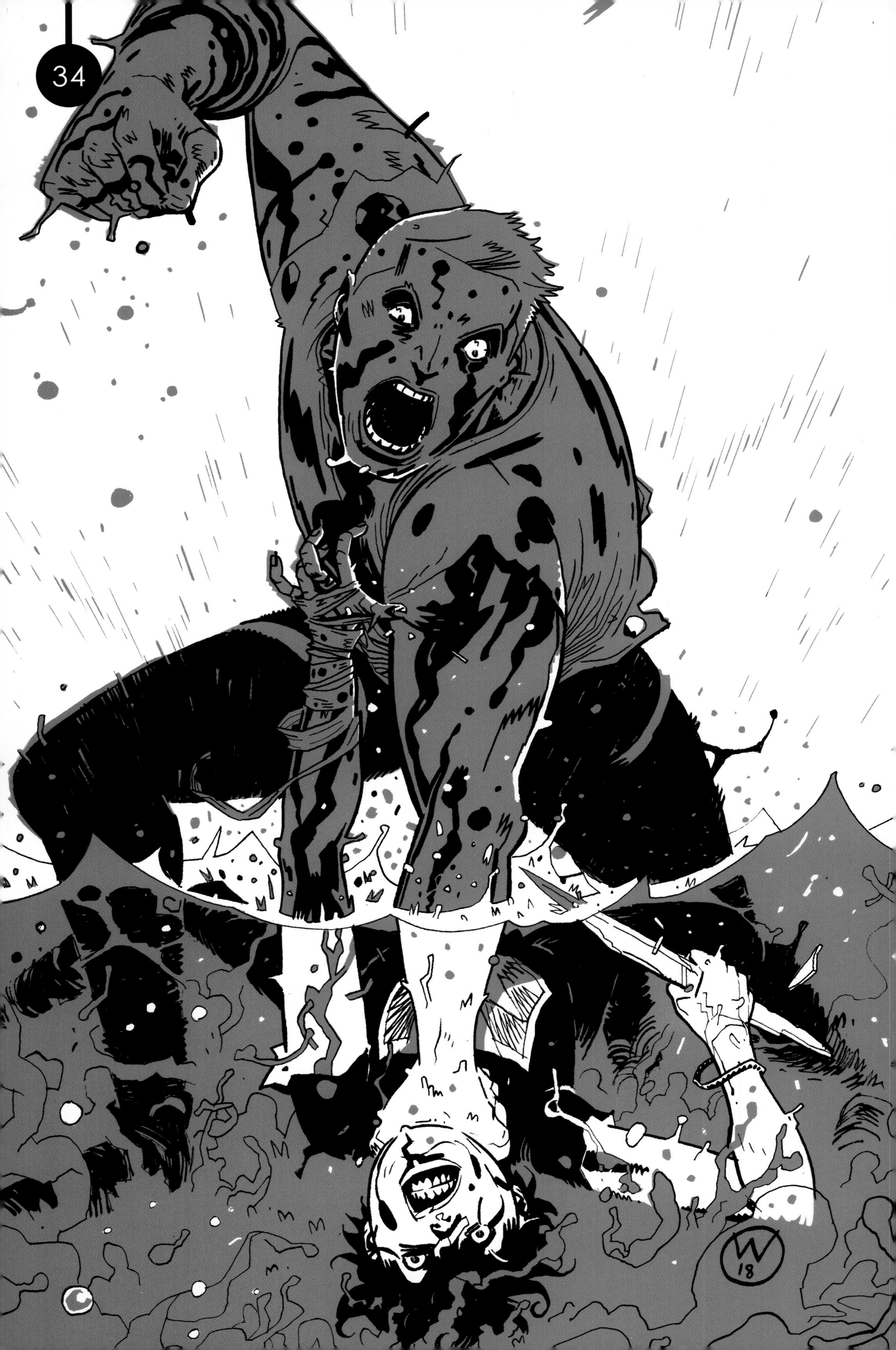

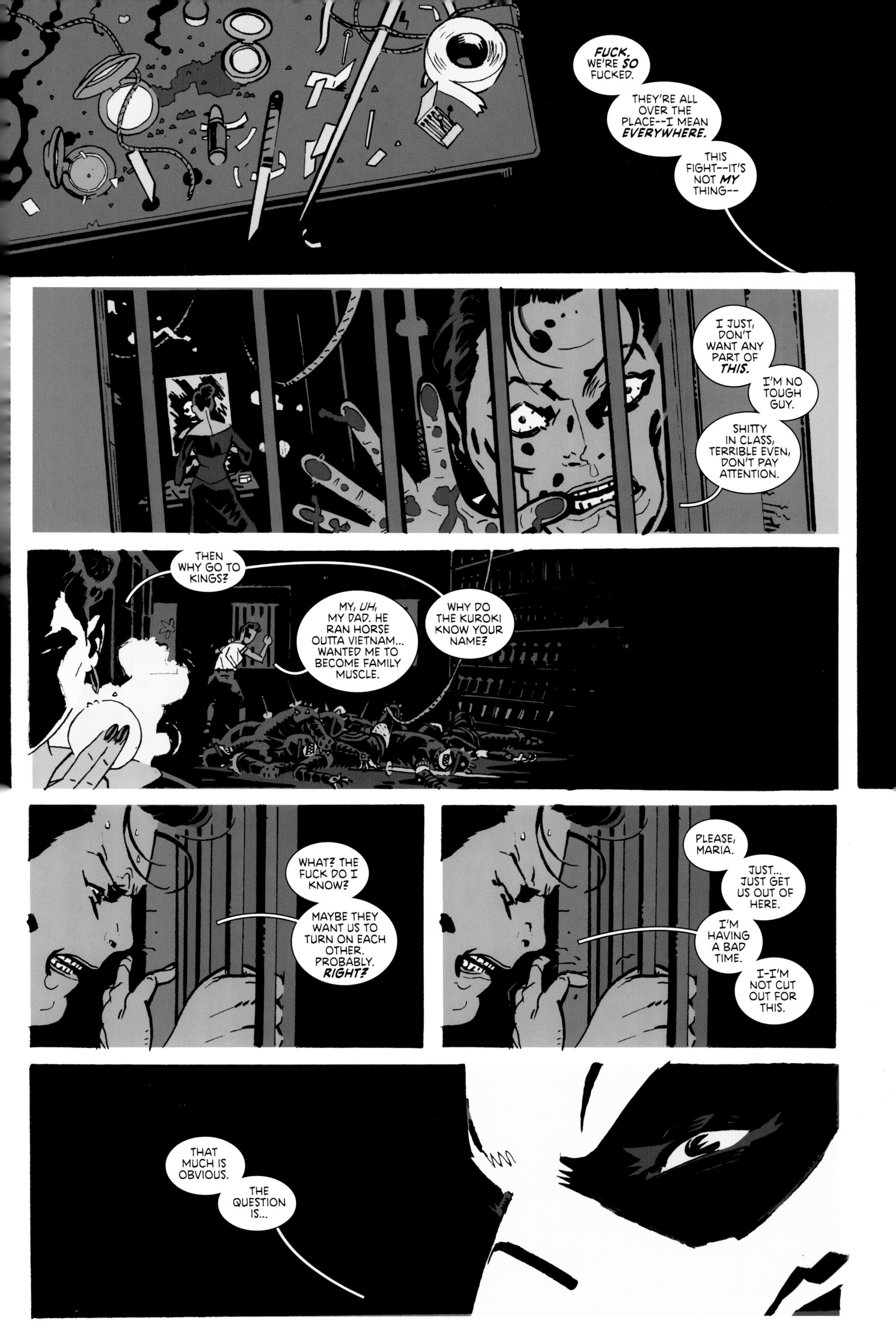
FUCK. WE'RE SO FUCKED.
THEY'RE ALL OVER THE PLACE--I MEAN EVERYWHERE.
THIS FIGHT--IT'S NOT MY THING--
I JUST, DON'T WANT ANY PART OF THIS.
I'M NO TOUGH GUY.
SHITTY IN CLASS, TERRIBLE EVEN, DON'T PAY ATTENTION.
THEN WHY GO TO KINGS?
MY, UH, MY DAD. HE RAN HORSE OUTTA VIETNAM... WANTED ME TO BECOME FAMILY MUSCLE.
WHY DO THE KUROKI KNOW YOUR NAME?
WHAT? THE FUCK DO I KNOW?
MAYBE THEY WANT US TO TURN ON EACH OTHER. PROBABLY. RIGHT?
PLEASE, MARIA.
JUST... JUST GET US OUT OF HERE.
I'M HAVING A BAD TIME.
I-I'M NOT CUT OUT FOR THIS.
THAT MUCH IS OBVIOUS.
THE QUESTION IS...

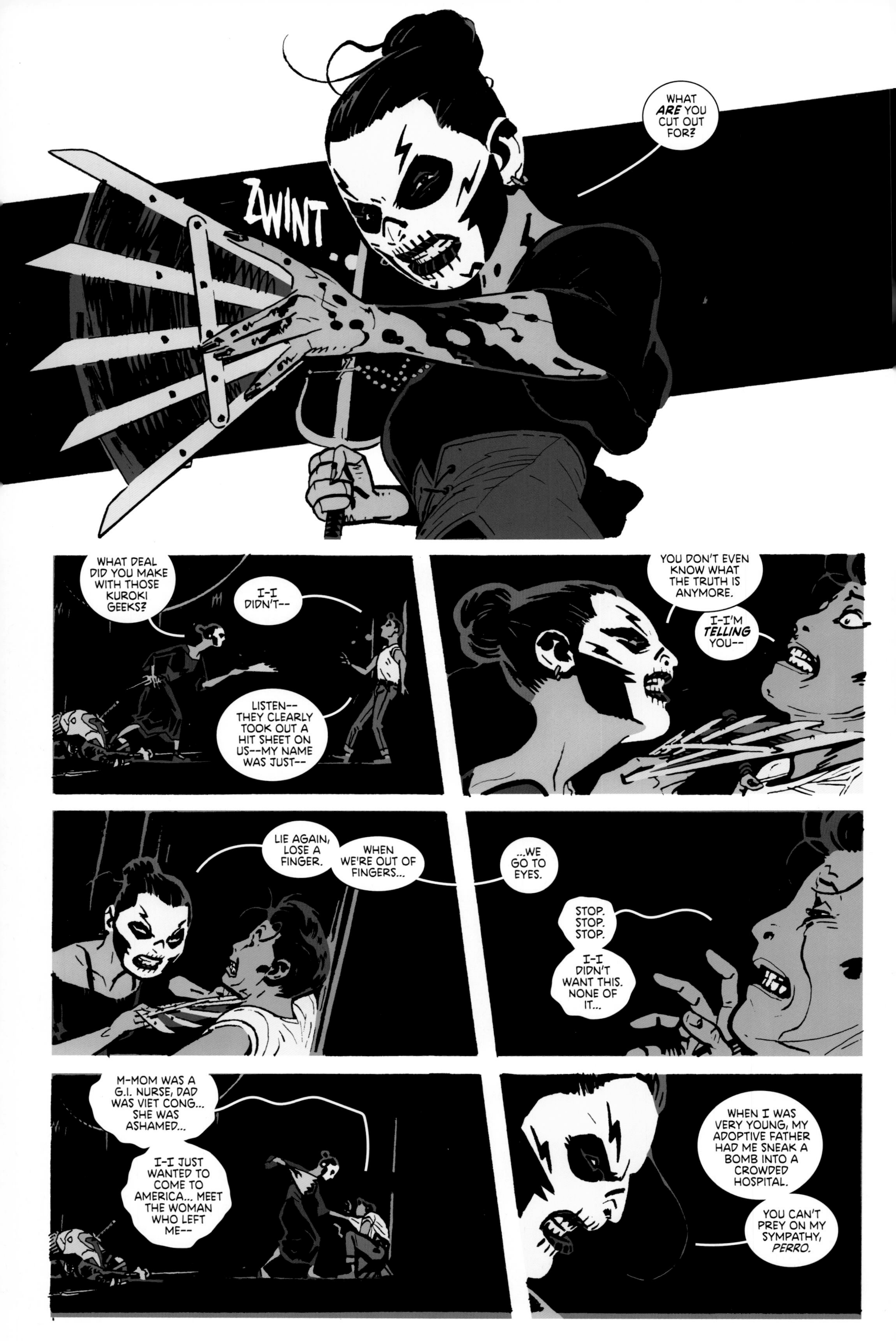
WHAT ARE YOU CUT OUT FOR?
ZWINT
WHAT DEAL DID YOU MAKE WITH THOSE KUROKI GEEKS?
I-I DIDN'T--
LISTEN-- THEY CLEARLY TOOK OUT A HIT SHEET ON US--MY NAME WAS JUST--
YOU DON'T EVEN KNOW WHAT THE TRUTH IS ANYMORE.
I-I'M TELLING YOU--
LIE AGAIN, LOSE A FINGER.
WHEN WE'RE OUT OF FINGERS...
...WE GO TO EYES.
STOP. STOP. STOP.
I-I DIDN'T WANT THIS. NONE OF IT...
M-MOM WAS A G.I. NURSE, DAD WAS VIET CONG... SHE WAS ASHAMED...
I-I JUST WANTED TO COME TO AMERICA... MEET THE WOMAN WHO LEFT ME--
WHEN I WAS VERY YOUNG, MY ADOPTIVE FATHER HAD ME SNEAK A BOMB INTO A CROWDED HOSPITAL.
YOU CAN'T PREY ON MY SYMPATHY, PERRO.

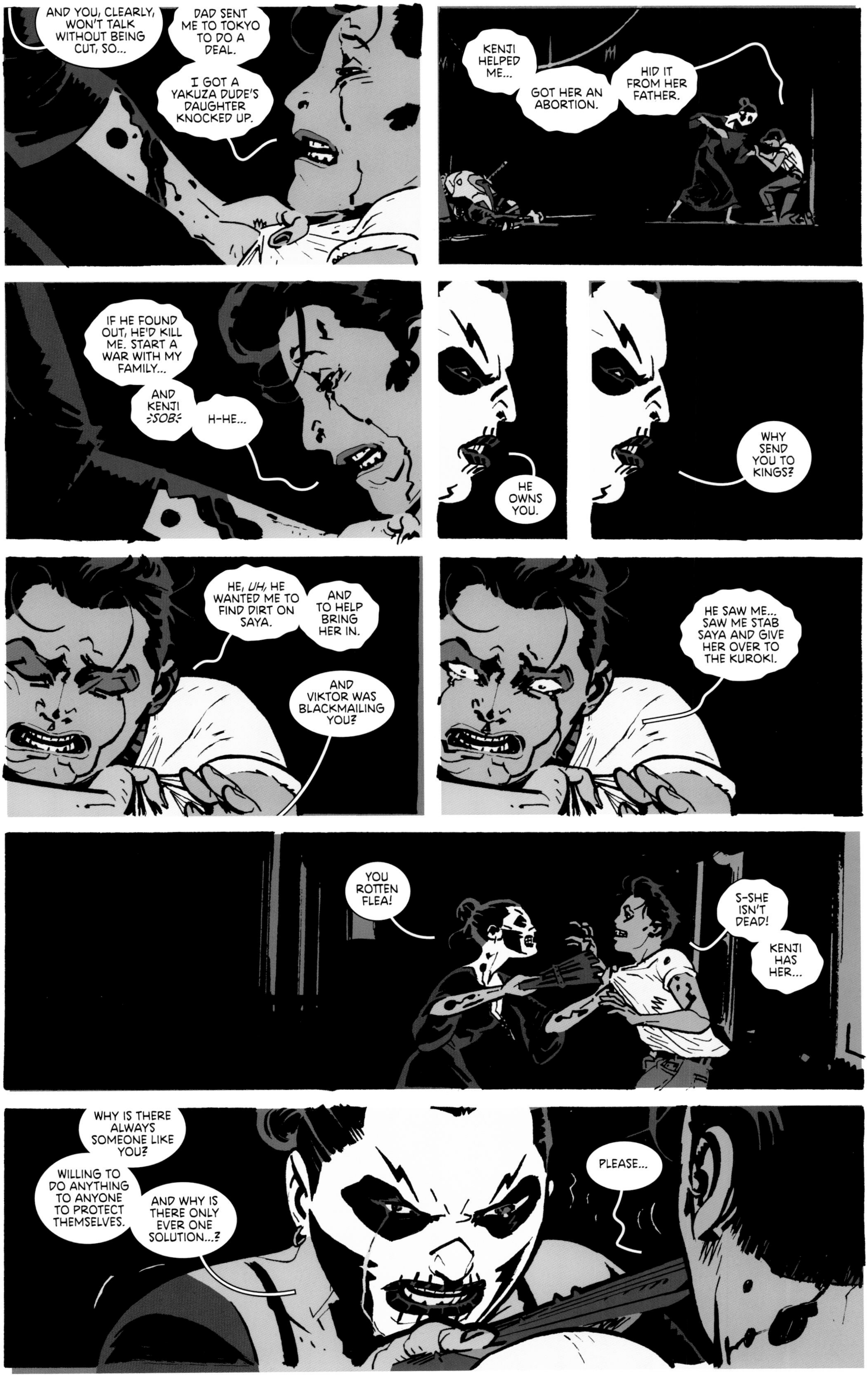
AND YOU, CLEARLY, WON'T TALK WITHOUT BEING CUT, SO...
DAD SENT ME TO TOKYO TO DO A DEAL.
I GOT A YAKUZA DUDE'S DAUGHTER KNOCKED UP.
KENJI HELPED ME...
GOT HER AN ABORTION.
HID IT FROM HER FATHER.
IF HE FOUND OUT, HE'D KILL ME. START A WAR WITH MY FAMILY...
AND KENJI *SOB*
H-HE...
HE OWNS YOU.
WHY SEND YOU TO KINGS?
HE, *UH*, HE WANTED ME TO FIND DIRT ON SAYA.
AND TO HELP BRING HER IN.
AND VIKTOR WAS BLACKMAILING YOU?
HE SAW ME... SAW ME STAB SAYA AND GIVE HER OVER TO THE KUROKI.
YOU ROTTEN FLEA!
S-SHE ISN'T DEAD!
KENJI HAS HER...
WHY IS THERE ALWAYS SOMEONE LIKE YOU?
WILLING TO DO ANYTHING TO ANYONE TO PROTECT THEMSELVES.
AND WHY IS THERE ONLY EVER ONE SOLUTION...?
PLEASE...

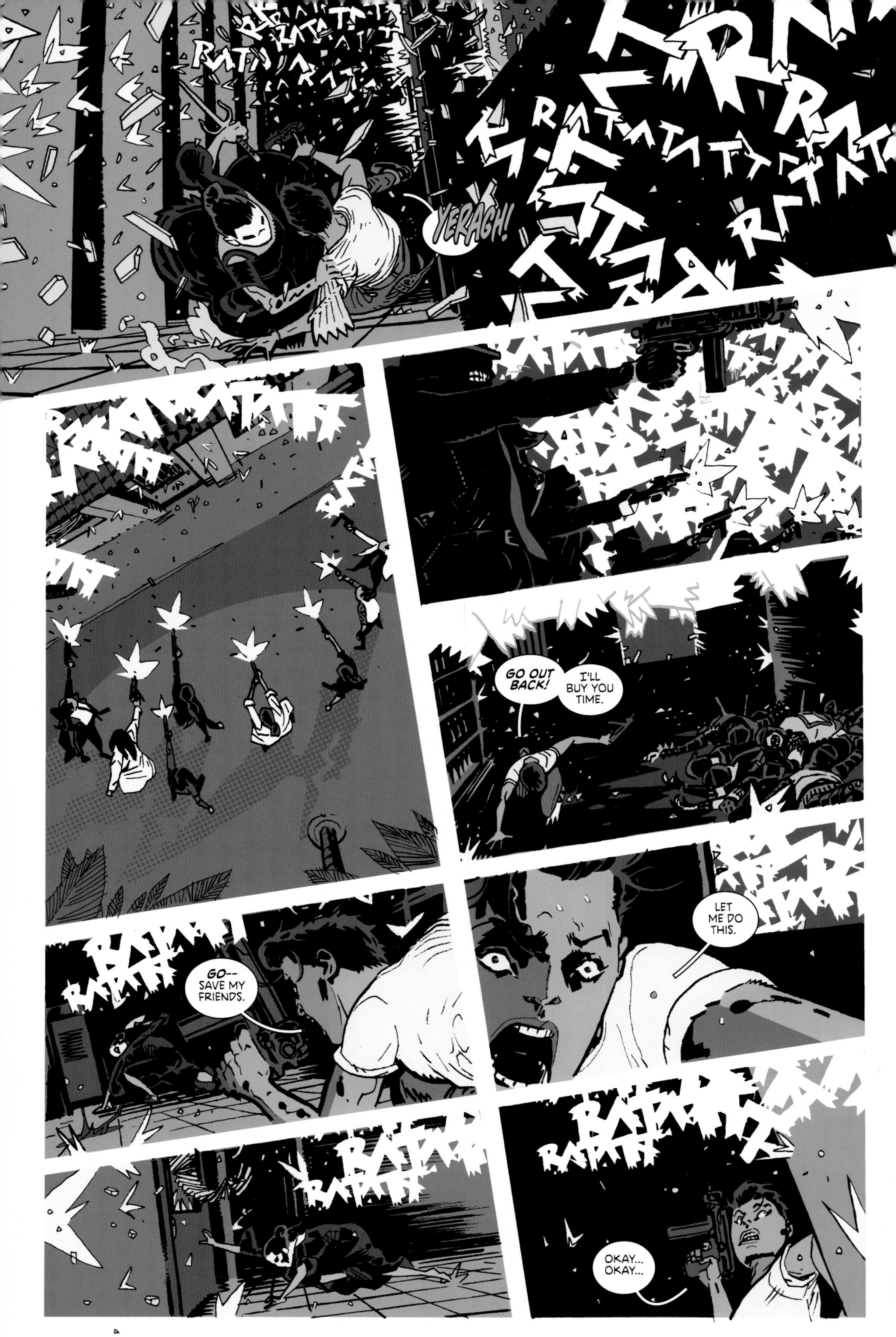
YERAGH!
GO OUT BACK!
I'LL BUY YOU TIME.
GO-- SAVE MY FRIENDS.
LET ME DO THIS.
OKAY... OKAY...

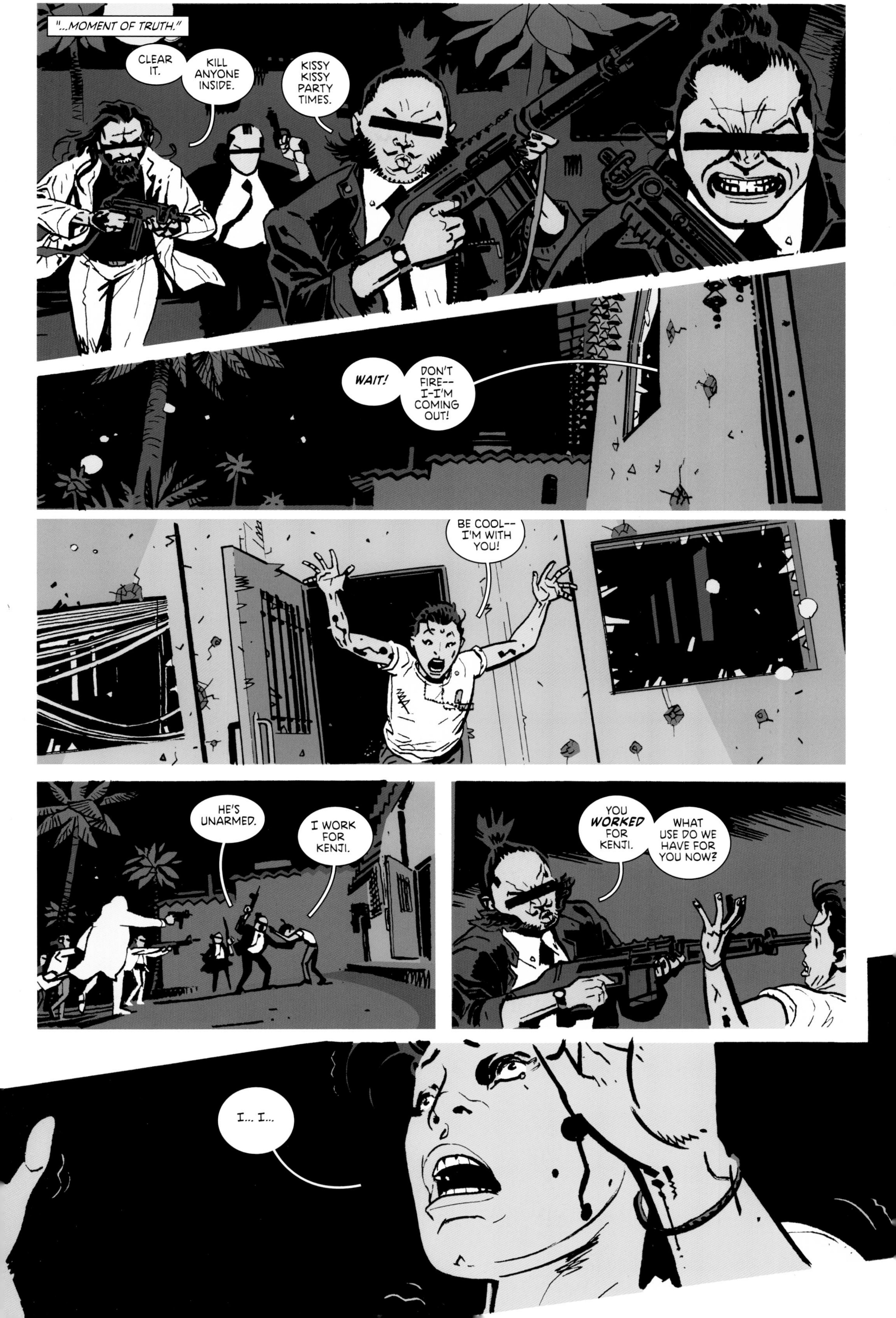
"...MOMENT OF TRUTH."
CLEAR IT.
KILL ANYONE INSIDE.
KISSY KISSY PARTY TIMES.
WAIT!
DON'T FIRE-- I-I'M COMING OUT!
BE COOL-- I'M WITH YOU!
HE'S UNARMED.
I WORK FOR KENJI.
YOU *WORKED* FOR KENJI.
WHAT USE DO WE HAVE FOR YOU NOW?
I... I...

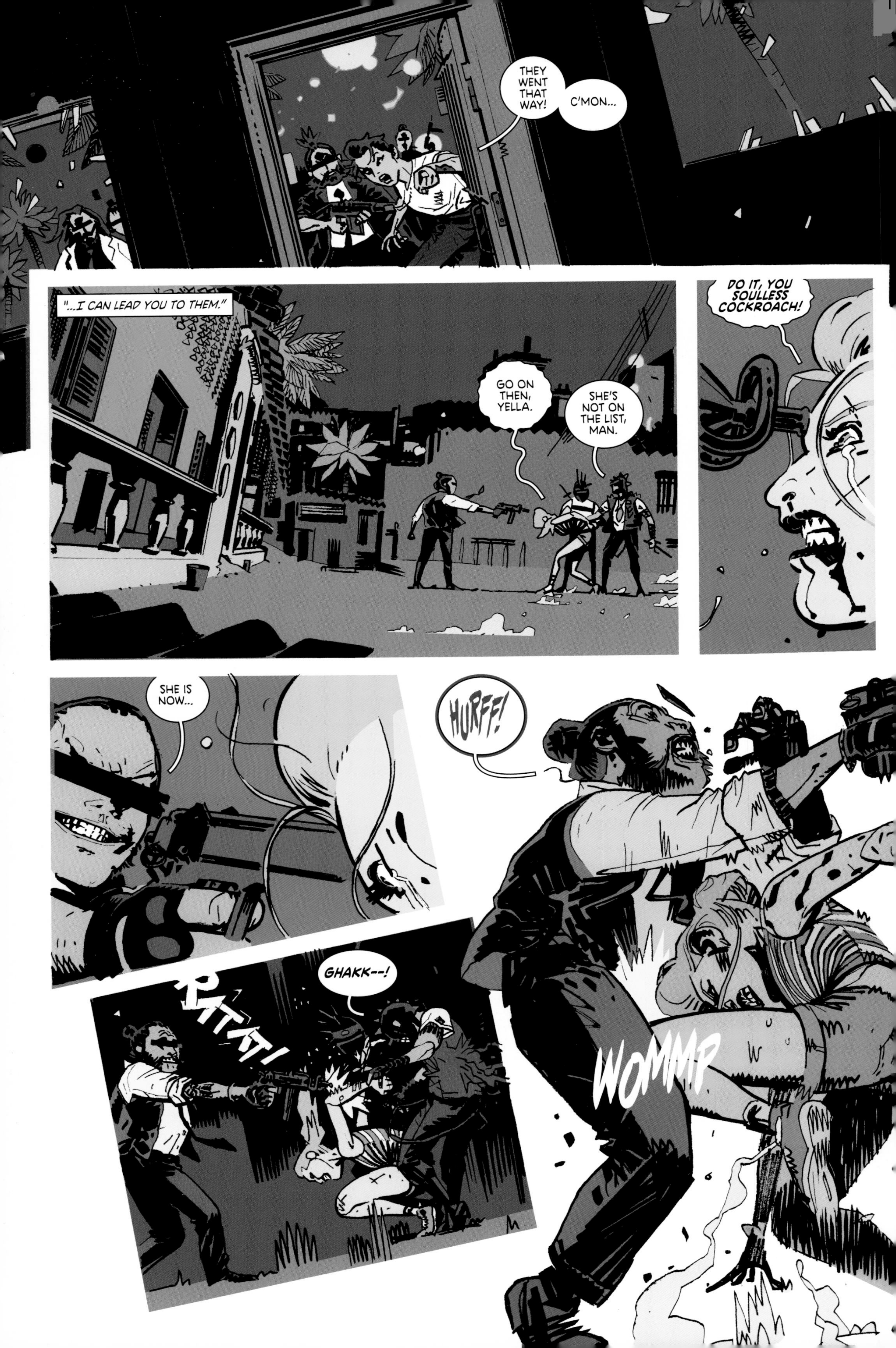
THEY WENT THAT WAY!
C'MON...
"...I CAN LEAD YOU TO THEM."
GO ON THEN, YELLA.
SHE'S NOT ON THE LIST, MAN.
DO IT, YOU SOULLESS COCKROACH!
SHE IS NOW...
HURFF!
RATATAT!
GHAKK--!
WOMMP

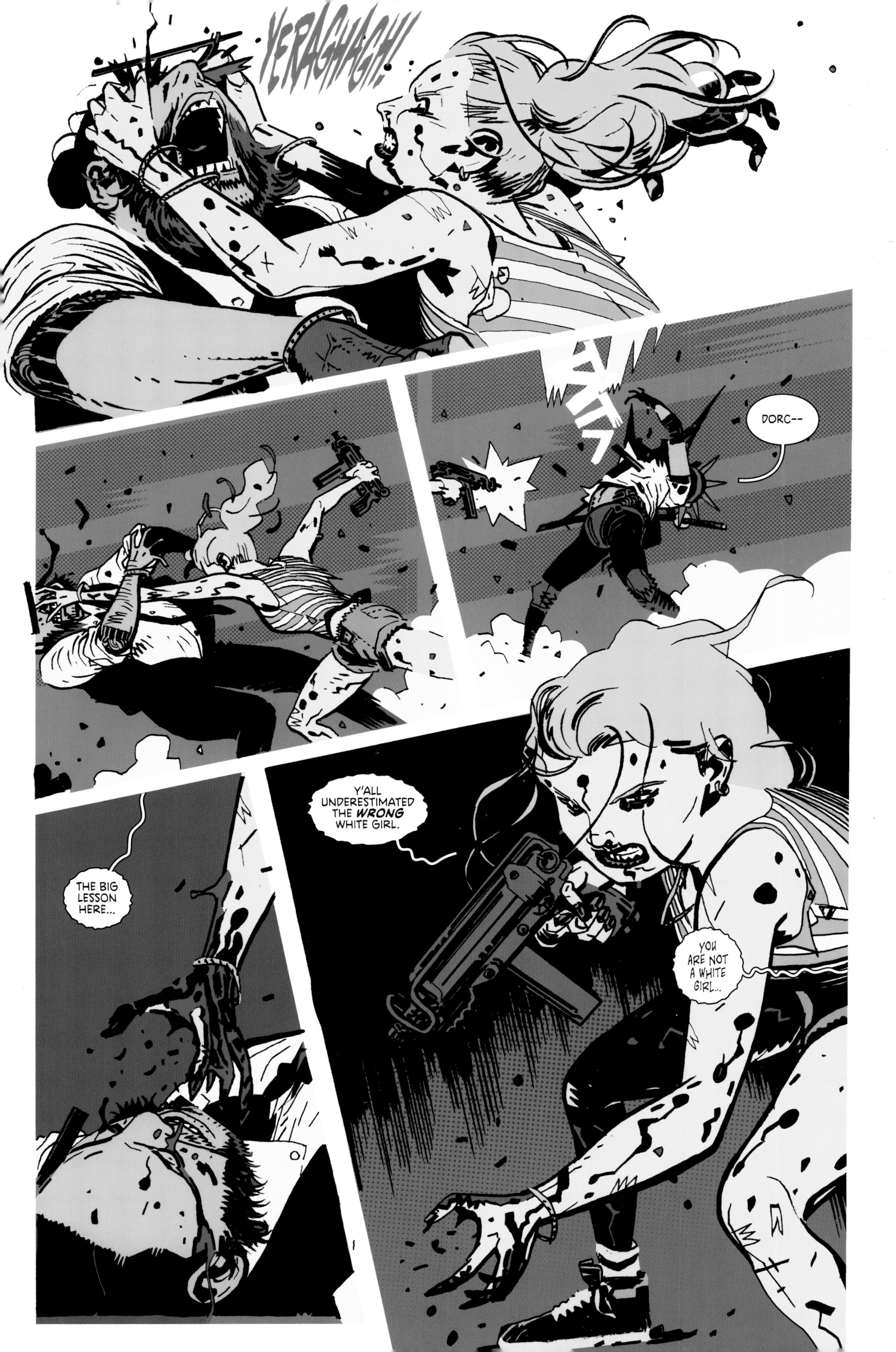
YERAGHAGH!
TATTA
DORC--
THE BIG LESSON HERE...
Y'ALL UNDERESTIMATED THE *WRONG* WHITE GIRL.
YOU ARE NOT A WHITE GIRL...

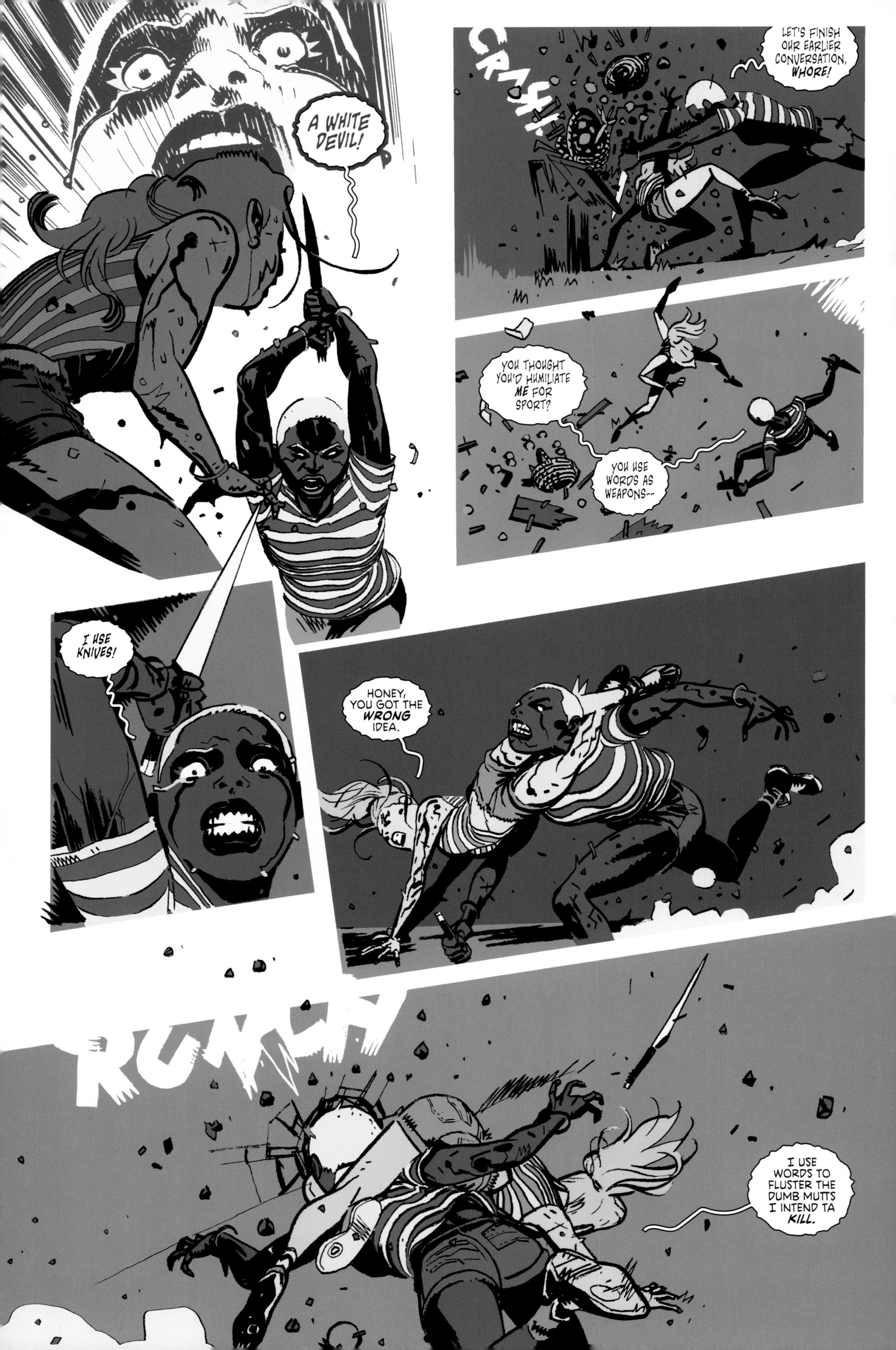
A WHITE DEVIL!
CRASH!
LET'S FINISH OUR EARLIER CONVERSATION, WHORE!
YOU THOUGHT YOU'D HUMILIATE ME FOR SPORT?
YOU USE WORDS AS WEAPONS--
I USE KNIVES!
HONEY, YOU GOT THE WRONG IDEA.
I USE WORDS TO FLUSTER THE DUMB MUTTS I INTEND TA KILL.

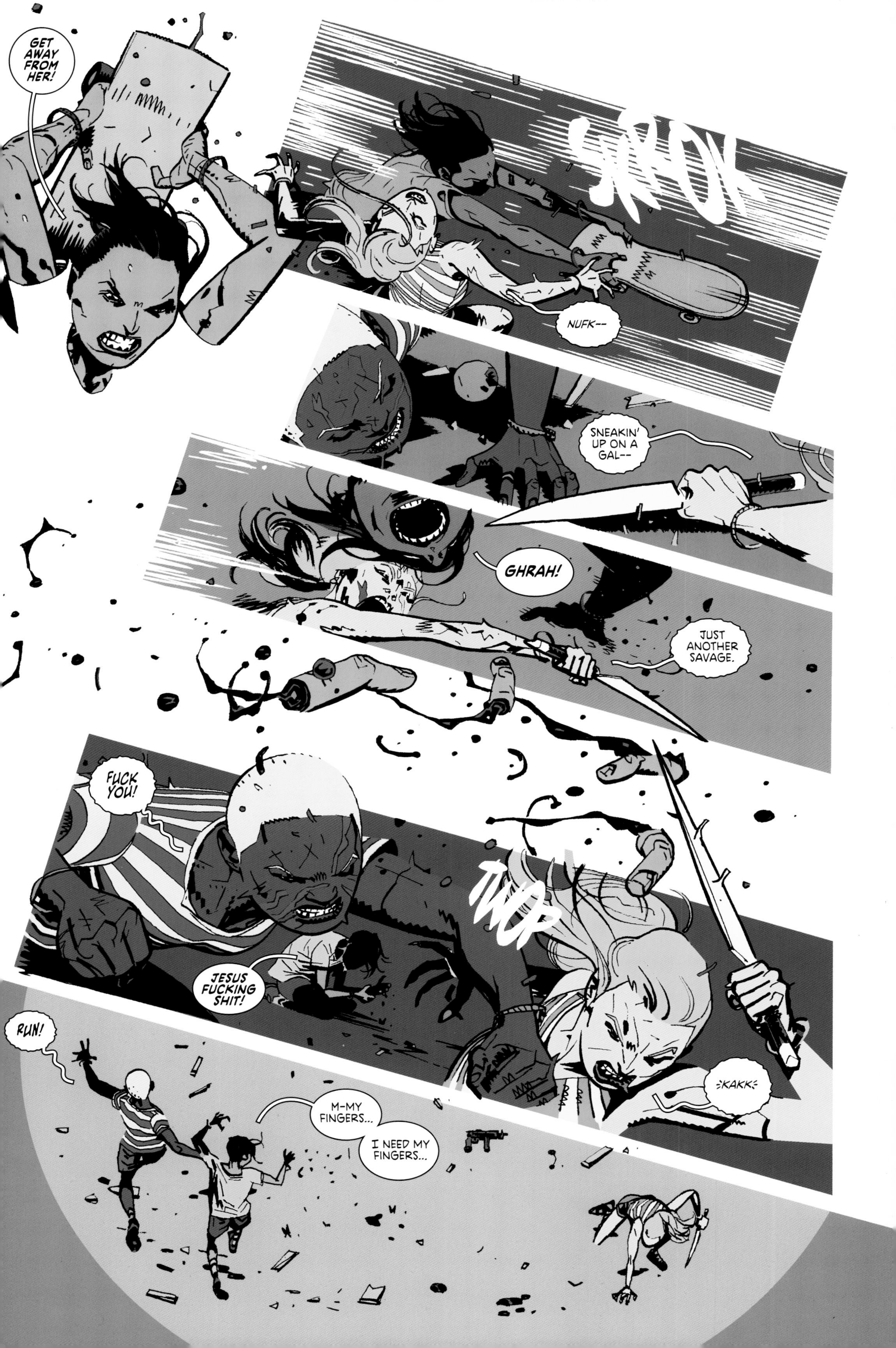
GET AWAY FROM HER!
NUFK--
SNEAKIN' UP ON A GAL--
GHRAH!
JUST ANOTHER SAVAGE.
FUCK YOU!
TWOP
JESUS FUCKING SHIT!
KAKK
RUN!
M-MY FINGERS...
I NEED MY FINGERS...

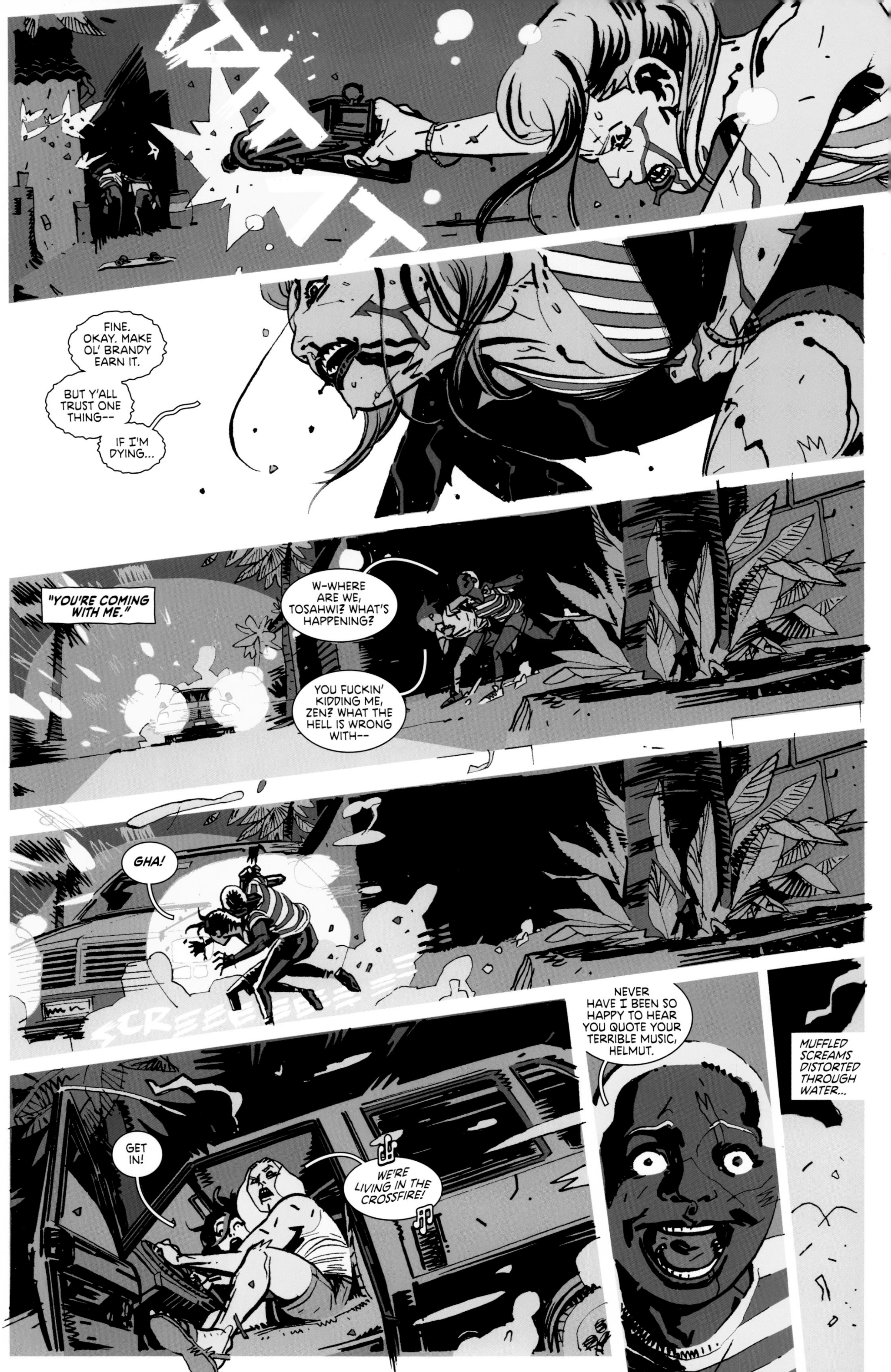
FINE. OKAY. MAKE OL' BRANDY EARN IT.
BUT Y'ALL TRUST ONE THING--
IF I'M DYING...
"YOU'RE COMING WITH ME."
W-WHERE ARE WE, TOSAHWI? WHAT'S HAPPENING?
YOU FUCKIN' KIDDING ME, ZEN? WHAT THE HELL IS WRONG WITH--
GHA!
SCREEEEEEEEEE
GET IN!
WE'RE LIVING IN THE CROSSFIRE!
NEVER HAVE I BEEN SO HAPPY TO HEAR YOU QUOTE YOUR TERRIBLE MUSIC, HELMUT.
MUFFLED SCREAMS DISTORTED THROUGH WATER...

...GLAD I DON'T SPEAK RUSSIAN.

DON'T HAVE TO HEAR IT.

WINDPIPE COMPRESSING IN.

BURNING LUNGS BEG ME TO BREATHE IN WATER.

AND I'M *SO* TIRED...

TAKE AIR INSTINCTIVELY.

PROLONG MY OWN TORTURE.

DASVIDANIYA, SOFT BOY.

THING IS, I DON'T MIND DYING HERE.

ON THE BEACH, I USED TO WATCH YOU SURF, PAPA.

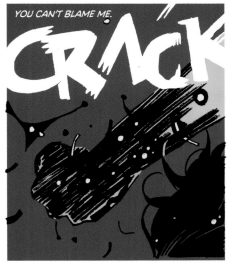

YOU CAN'T BLAME ME.

CRACK

I'M BORED.

BORED OF THE EFFORT.

BORED OF FAILING.

BORED OF PAIN.

BORED OF LOSING PEOPLE I LOVE.

THERE IT IS. THE SPIRIT LEAVES. THE BODY QUITS ITS FUTILE STRUGGLE.

AND, TO TELL THE TRUTH...

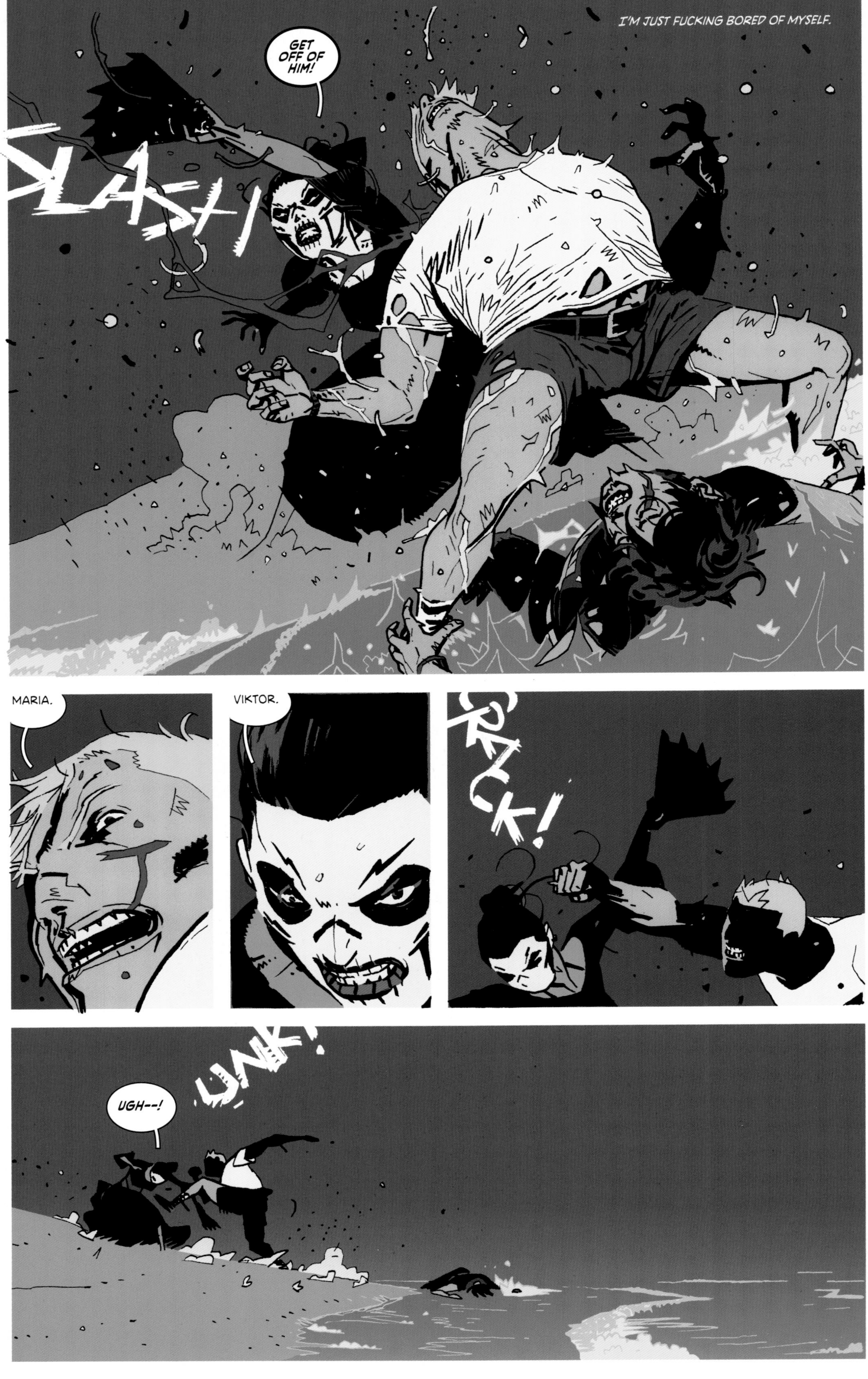
I'M JUST FUCKING BORED OF MYSELF.
GET OFF OF HIM!
MARIA.
VIKTOR.
CRACK!
UGH--!

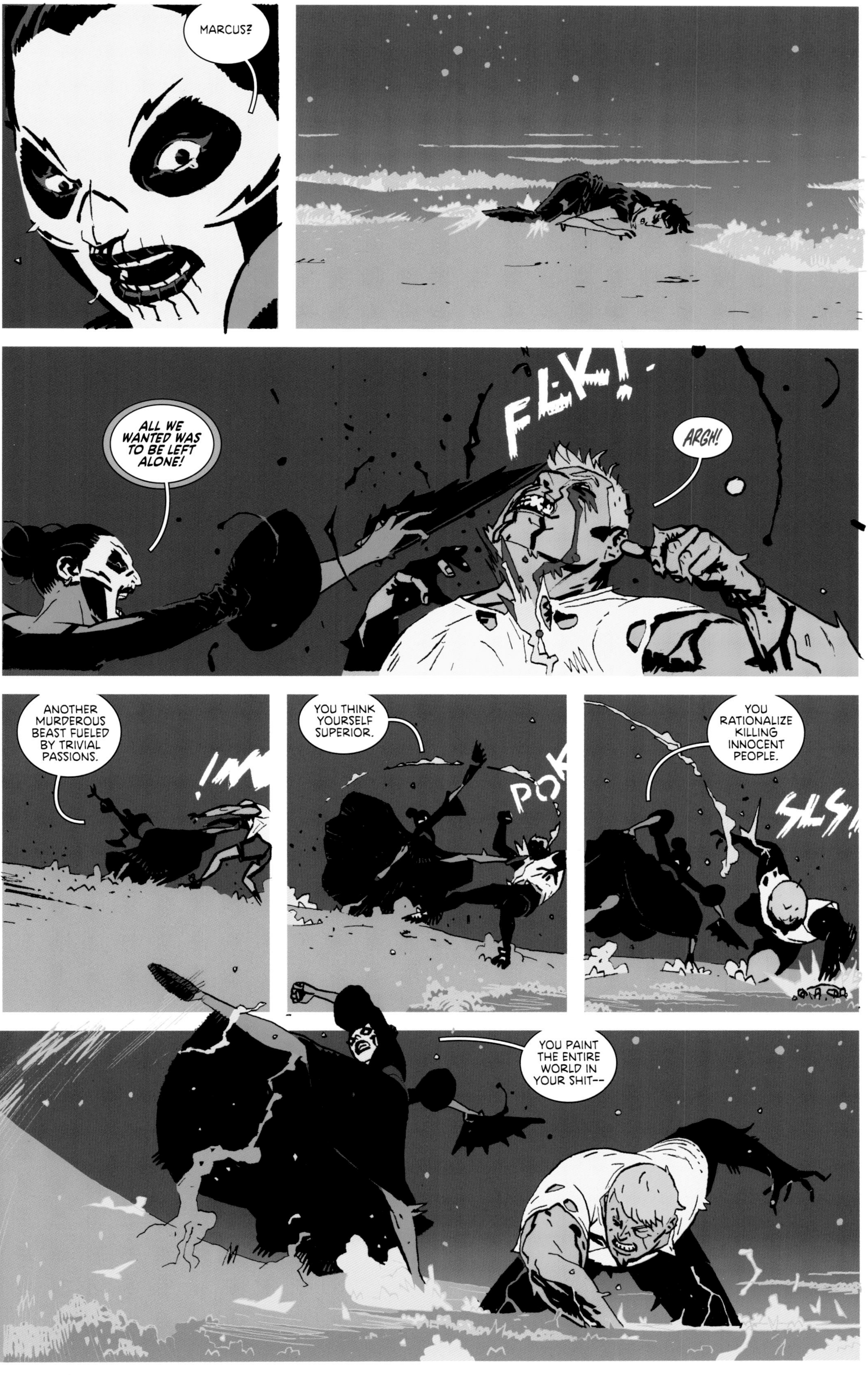
MARCUS?
ALL WE WANTED WAS TO BE LEFT ALONE!
FLK!
ARGH!
ANOTHER MURDEROUS BEAST FUELED BY TRIVIAL PASSIONS.
YOU THINK YOURSELF SUPERIOR.
POK
YOU RATIONALIZE KILLING INNOCENT PEOPLE.
YOU PAINT THE ENTIRE WORLD IN YOUR SHIT--

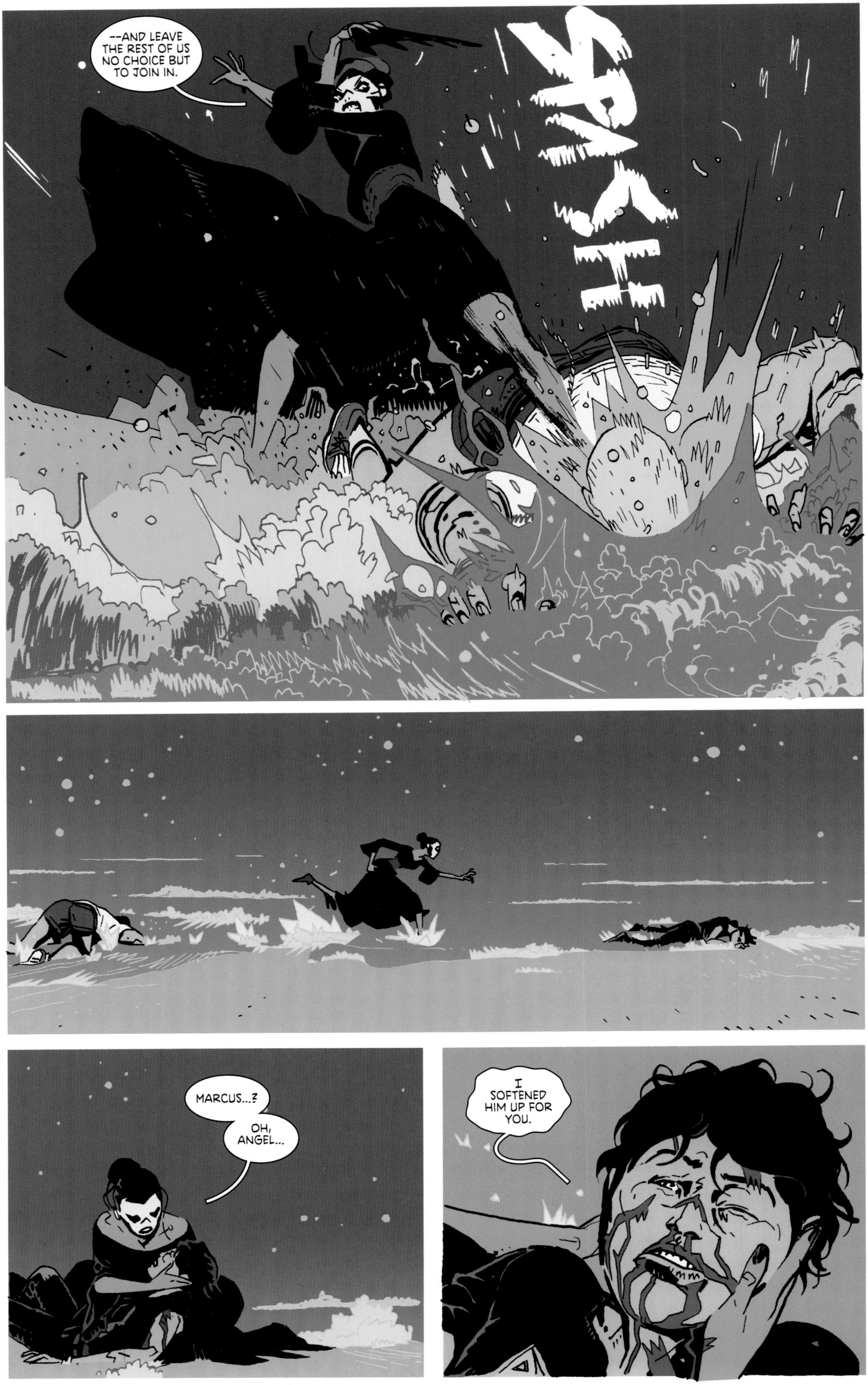
--AND LEAVE THE REST OF US NO CHOICE BUT TO JOIN IN.
MARCUS...?
OH, ANGEL...
I SOFTENED HIM UP FOR YOU.

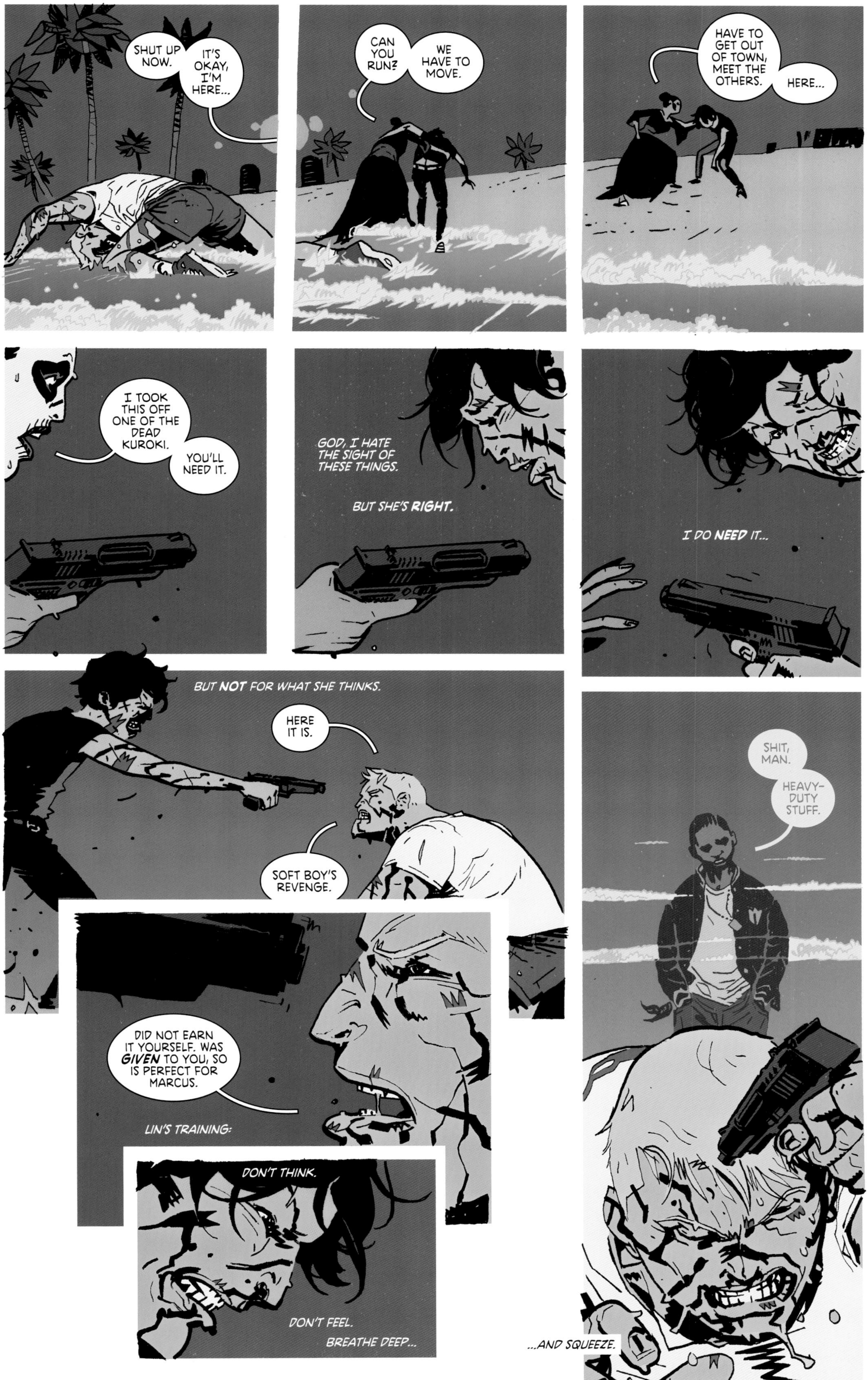
SHUT UP NOW.
IT'S OKAY, I'M HERE...
CAN YOU RUN?
WE HAVE TO MOVE.
HAVE TO GET OUT OF TOWN, MEET THE OTHERS.
HERE...
I TOOK THIS OFF ONE OF THE DEAD KUROKI.
YOU'LL NEED IT.
GOD, I HATE THE SIGHT OF THESE THINGS.
BUT SHE'S RIGHT.
I DO NEED IT...
BUT NOT FOR WHAT SHE THINKS.
HERE IT IS.
SOFT BOY'S REVENGE.
SHIT, MAN.
HEAVY-DUTY STUFF.
DID NOT EARN IT YOURSELF. WAS GIVEN TO YOU, SO IS PERFECT FOR MARCUS.
LIN'S TRAINING:
DON'T THINK.
DON'T FEEL.
BREATHE DEEP...
...AND SQUEEZE.

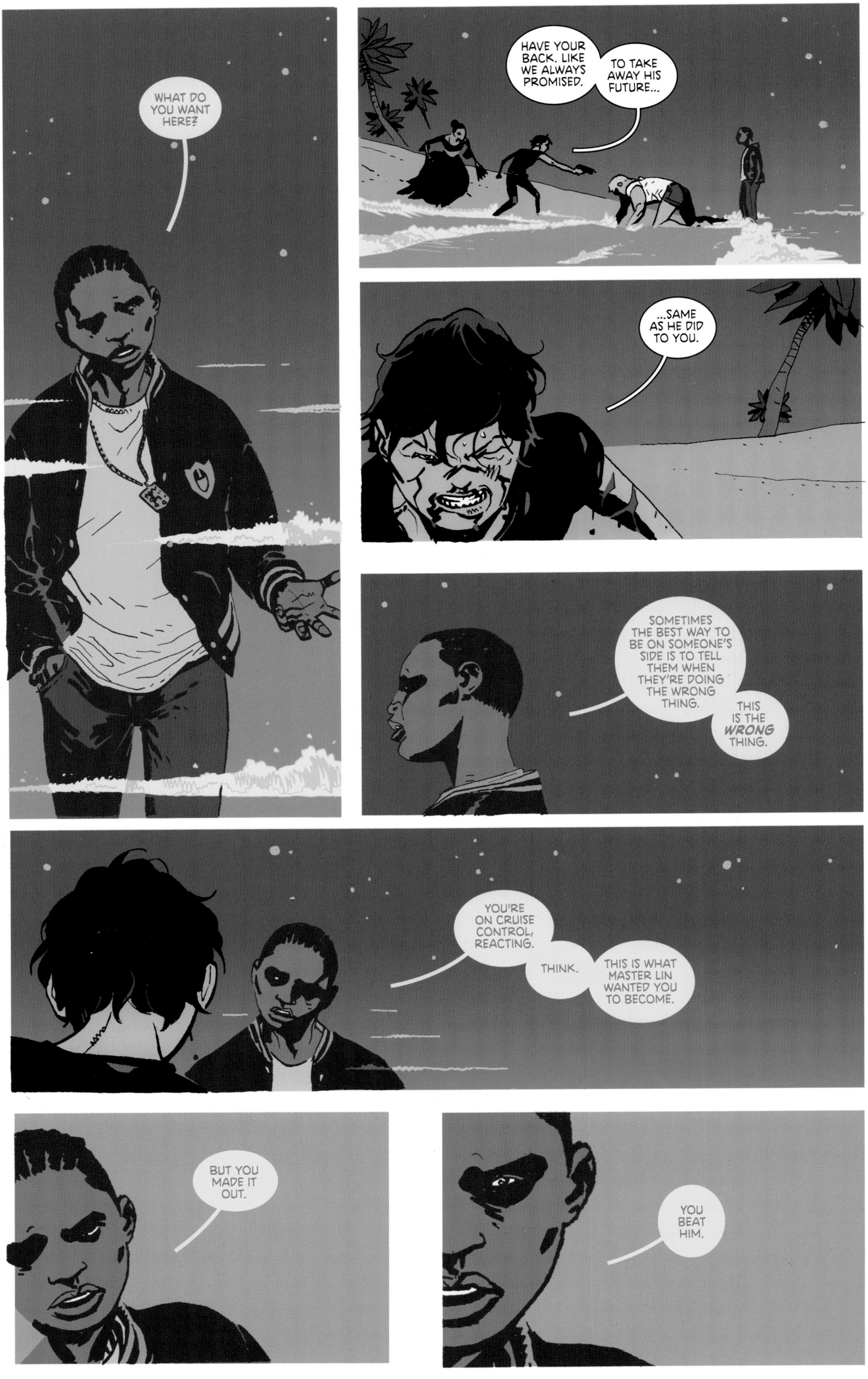
WHAT DO YOU WANT HERE?
HAVE YOUR BACK. LIKE WE ALWAYS PROMISED.
TO TAKE AWAY HIS FUTURE...
...SAME AS HE DID TO YOU.
SOMETIMES THE BEST WAY TO BE ON SOMEONE'S SIDE IS TO TELL THEM WHEN THEY'RE DOING THE WRONG THING.
THIS IS THE *WRONG* THING.
YOU'RE ON CRUISE CONTROL, REACTING.
THINK.
THIS IS WHAT MASTER LIN WANTED YOU TO BECOME.
BUT YOU MADE IT OUT.
YOU BEAT HIM.

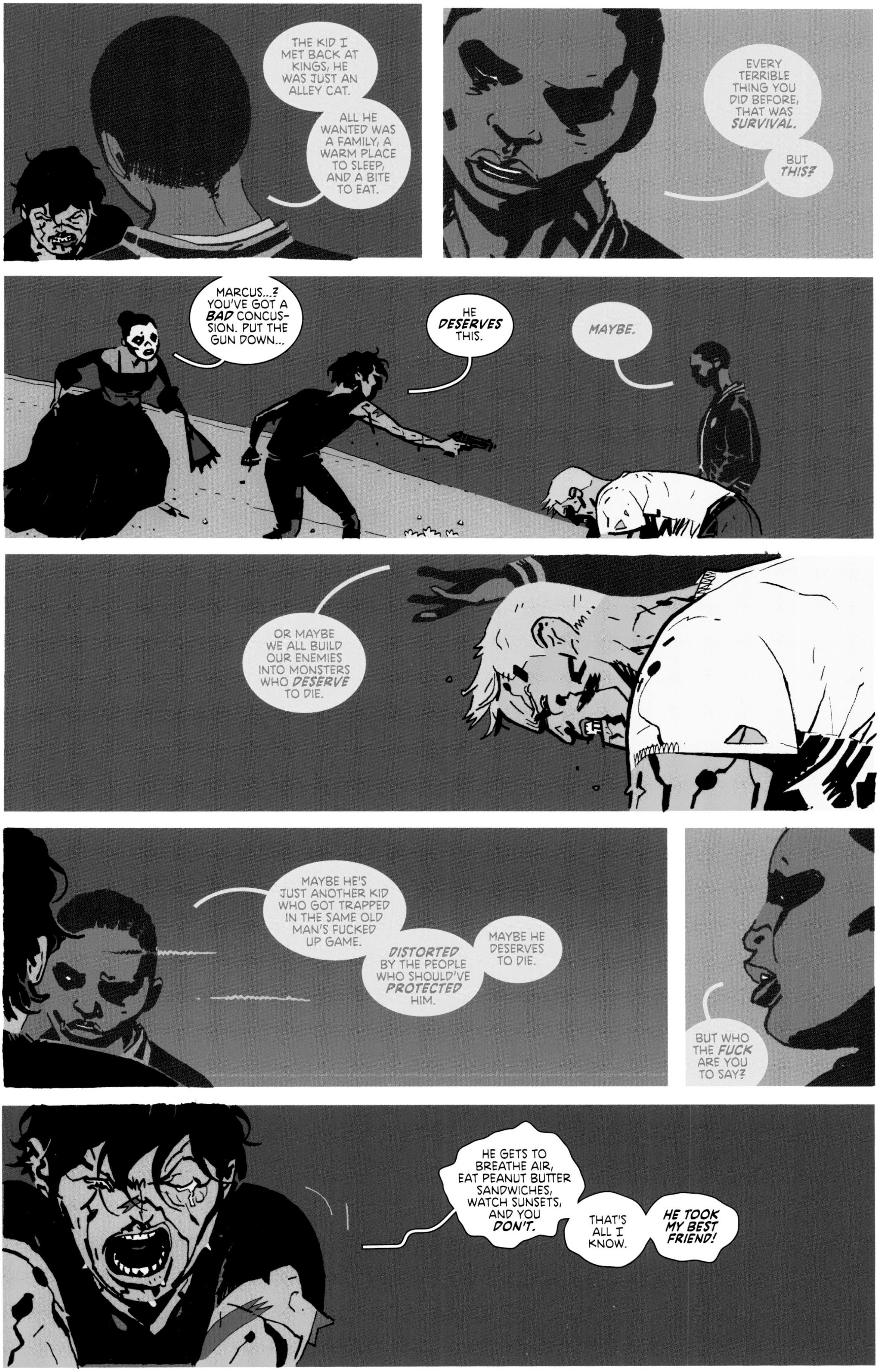
THE KID I MET BACK AT KINGS, HE WAS JUST AN ALLEY CAT.
ALL HE WANTED WAS A FAMILY, A WARM PLACE TO SLEEP, AND A BITE TO EAT.
EVERY TERRIBLE THING YOU DID BEFORE, THAT WAS *SURVIVAL.*
BUT *THIS?*
MARCUS...? YOU'VE GOT A *BAD* CONCUSSION. PUT THE GUN DOWN...
HE *DESERVES* THIS.
MAYBE.
OR MAYBE WE ALL BUILD OUR ENEMIES INTO MONSTERS WHO *DESERVE* TO DIE.
MAYBE HE'S JUST ANOTHER KID WHO GOT TRAPPED IN THE SAME OLD MAN'S FUCKED UP GAME.
DISTORTED BY THE PEOPLE WHO SHOULD'VE *PROTECTED* HIM.
MAYBE HE DESERVES TO DIE.
BUT WHO THE *FUCK* ARE YOU TO SAY?
HE GETS TO BREATHE AIR, EAT PEANUT BUTTER SANDWICHES, WATCH SUNSETS, AND YOU *DON'T.*
THAT'S ALL I KNOW.
HE TOOK MY BEST FRIEND!

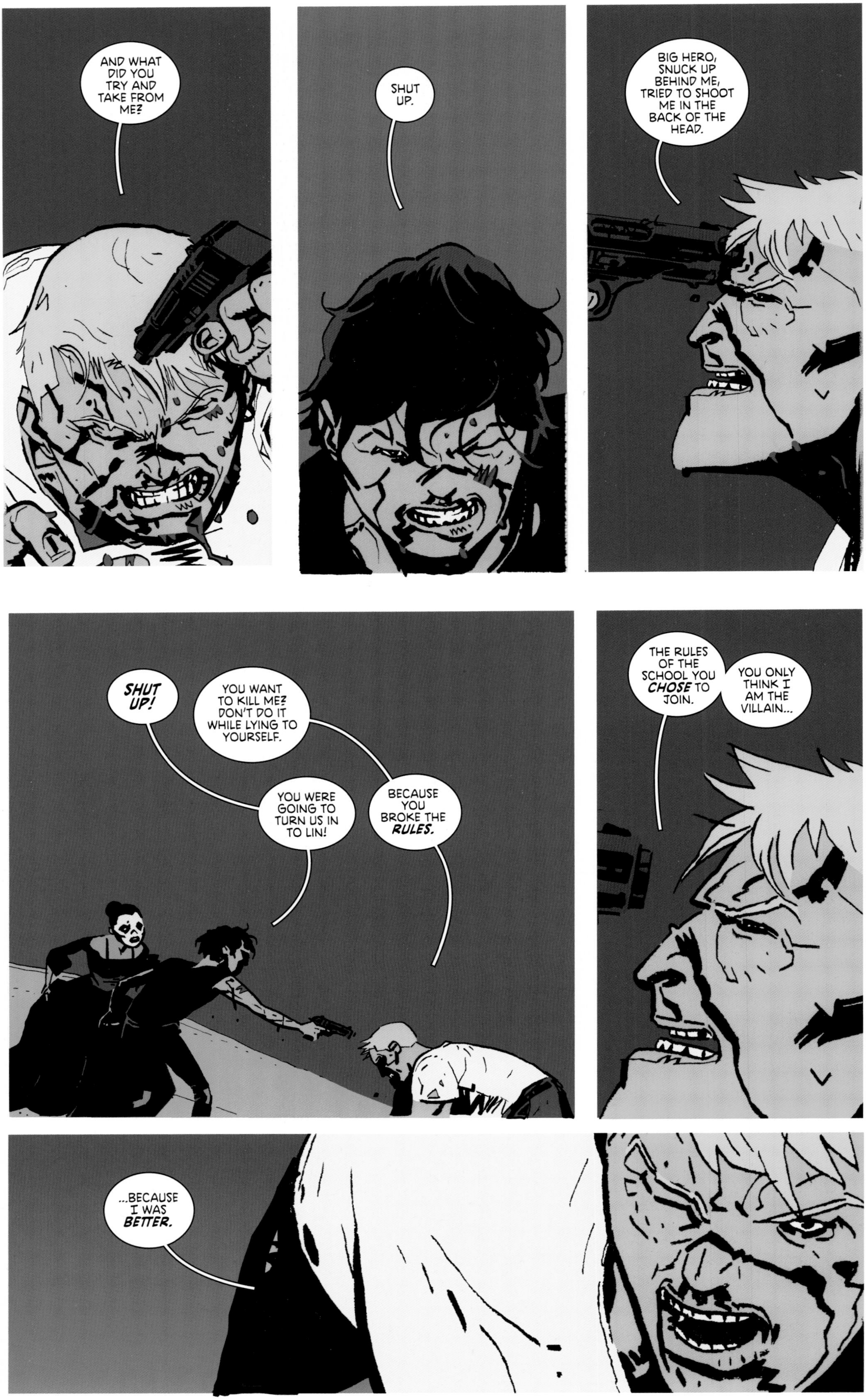
AND WHAT DID YOU TRY AND TAKE FROM ME?
SHUT UP.
BIG HERO, SNUCK UP BEHIND ME, TRIED TO SHOOT ME IN THE BACK OF THE HEAD.
SHUT UP!
YOU WANT TO KILL ME? DON'T DO IT WHILE LYING TO YOURSELF.
YOU WERE GOING TO TURN US IN TO LIN!
BECAUSE YOU BROKE THE RULES.
THE RULES OF THE SCHOOL YOU CHOSE TO JOIN.
YOU ONLY THINK I AM THE VILLAIN...
...BECAUSE I WAS BETTER.

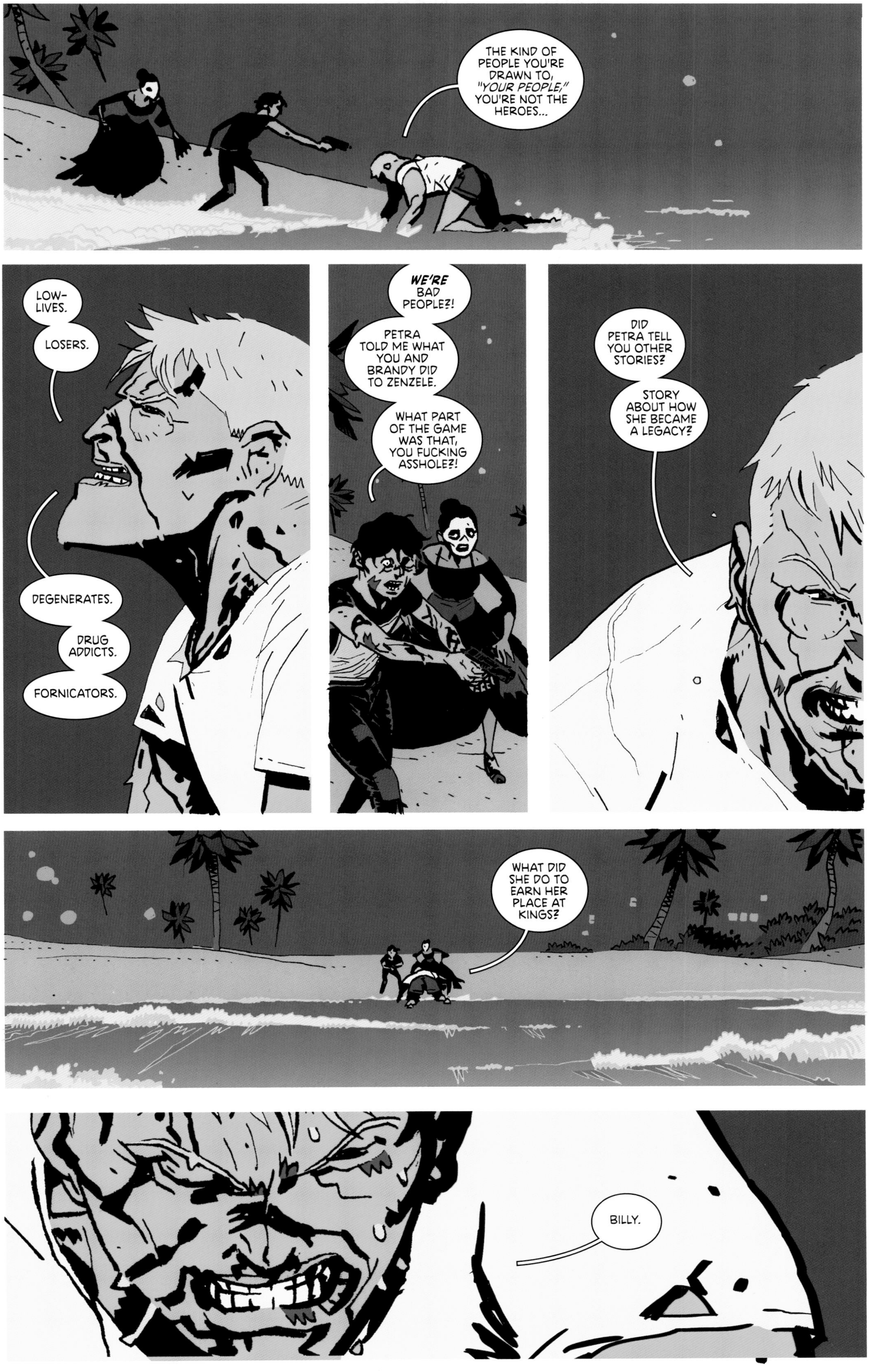
THE KIND OF PEOPLE YOU'RE DRAWN TO, "YOUR PEOPLE," YOU'RE NOT THE HEROES...
LOW-LIVES.
LOSERS.
DEGENERATES.
DRUG ADDICTS.
FORNICATORS.
WE'RE BAD PEOPLE?!
PETRA TOLD ME WHAT YOU AND BRANDY DID TO ZENZELE.
WHAT PART OF THE GAME WAS THAT, YOU FUCKING ASSHOLE?!
DID PETRA TELL YOU OTHER STORIES?
STORY ABOUT HOW SHE BECAME A LEGACY?
WHAT DID SHE DO TO EARN HER PLACE AT KINGS?
BILLY.

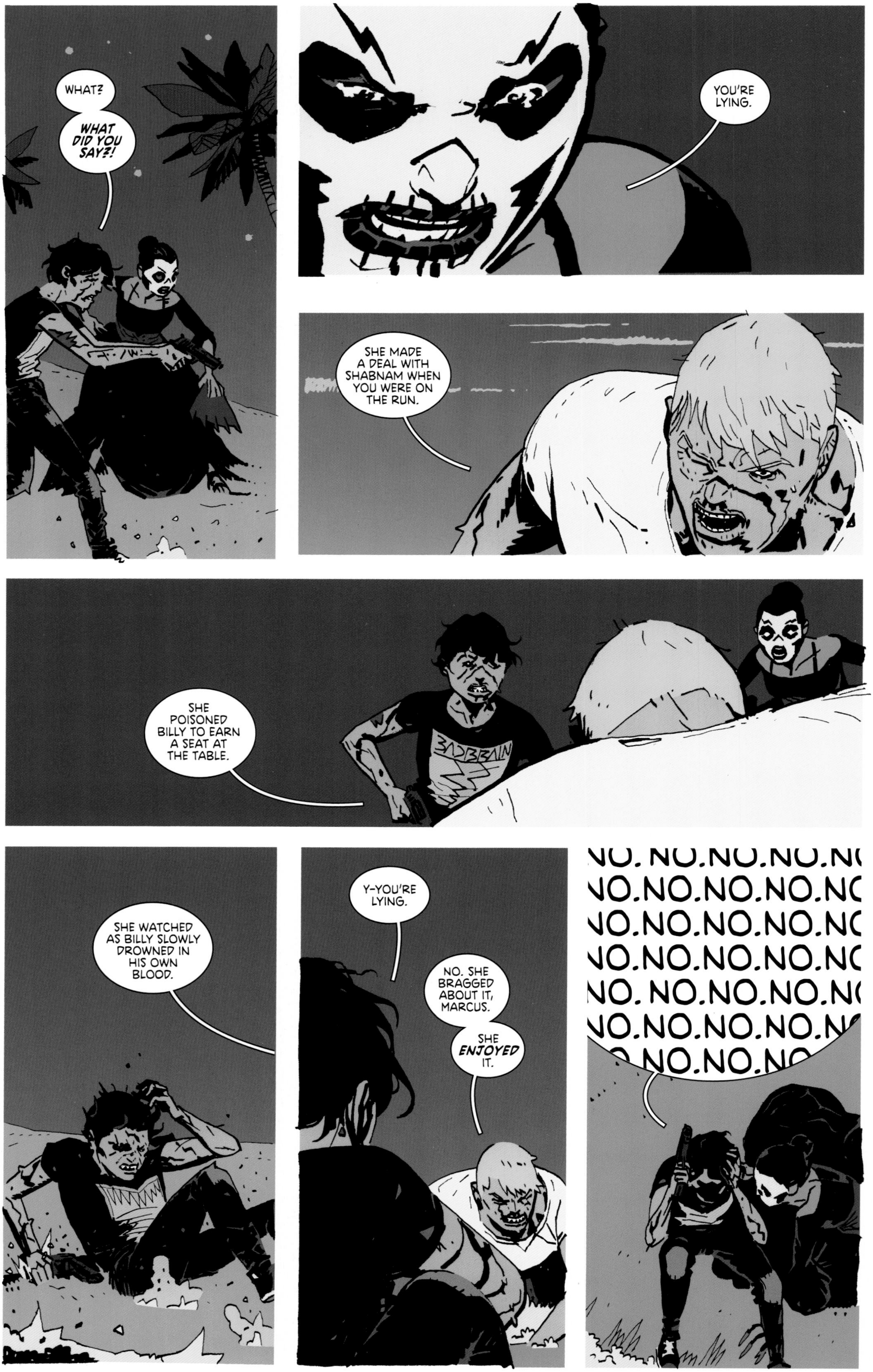
WHAT?
WHAT DID YOU SAY?!
YOU'RE LYING.
SHE MADE A DEAL WITH SHABNAM WHEN YOU WERE ON THE RUN.
SHE POISONED BILLY TO EARN A SEAT AT THE TABLE.
BADBRAIN
SHE WATCHED AS BILLY SLOWLY DROWNED IN HIS OWN BLOOD.
Y-YOU'RE LYING.
NO. SHE BRAGGED ABOUT IT, MARCUS.
SHE ENJOYED IT.
NO. NO.NO.NO.NO.
NO.NO.NO.NO.NO.
NO.NO.NO.NO.NO.
NO.NO.NO.NO.NO.
NO. NO.NO.NO.NO.
NO.NO.NO.NO.NO.
NO.NO.NO.

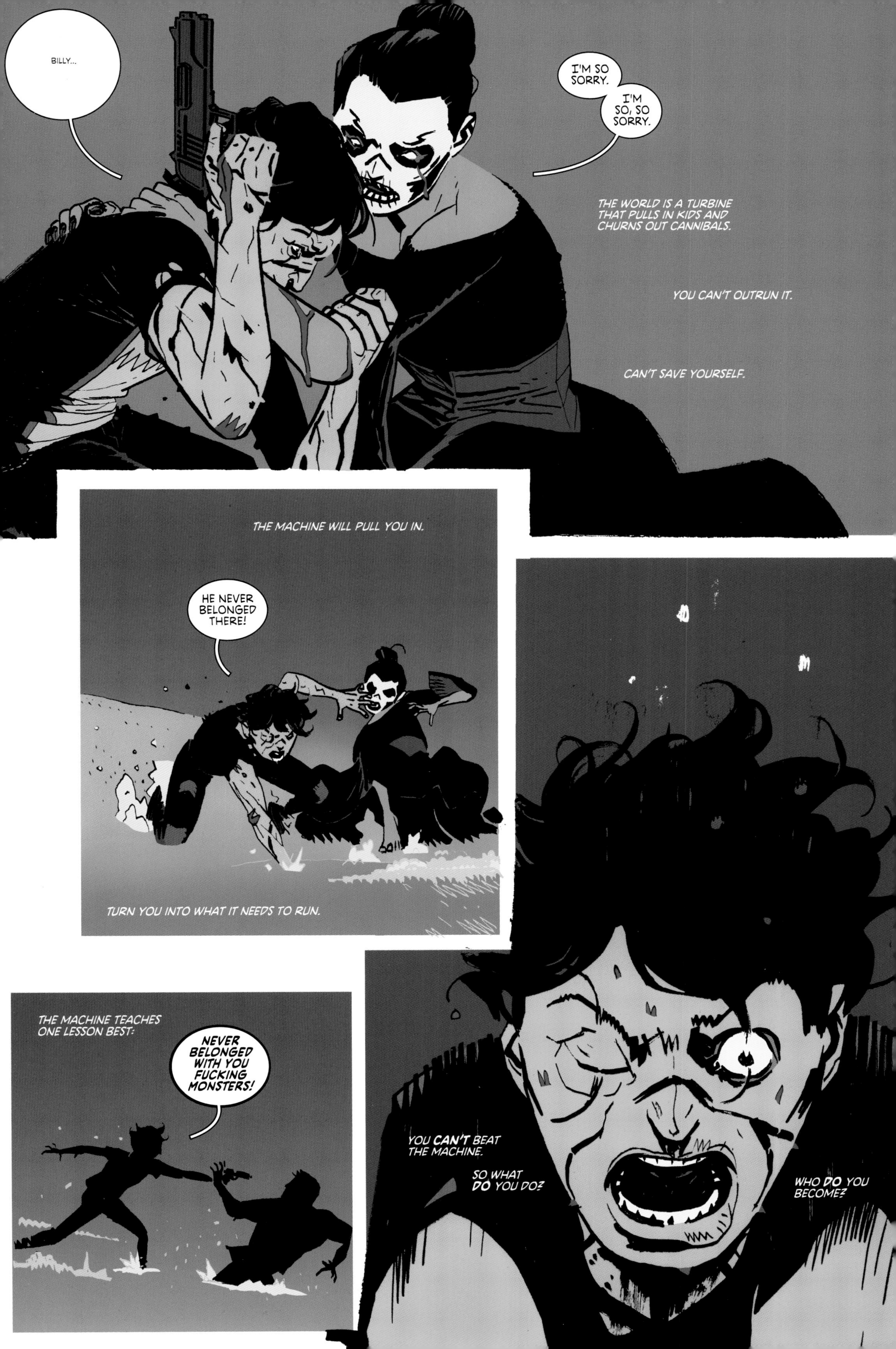

BILLY...
I'M SO SORRY.
I'M SO, SO SORRY.
THE WORLD IS A TURBINE THAT PULLS IN KIDS AND CHURNS OUT CANNIBALS.
YOU CAN'T OUTRUN IT.
CAN'T SAVE YOURSELF.
THE MACHINE WILL PULL YOU IN.
HE NEVER BELONGED THERE!
TURN YOU INTO WHAT IT NEEDS TO RUN.
THE MACHINE TEACHES ONE LESSON BEST:
NEVER BELONGED WITH YOU FUCKING MONSTERS!
YOU CAN'T BEAT THE MACHINE.
SO WHAT DO YOU DO?
WHO DO YOU BECOME?

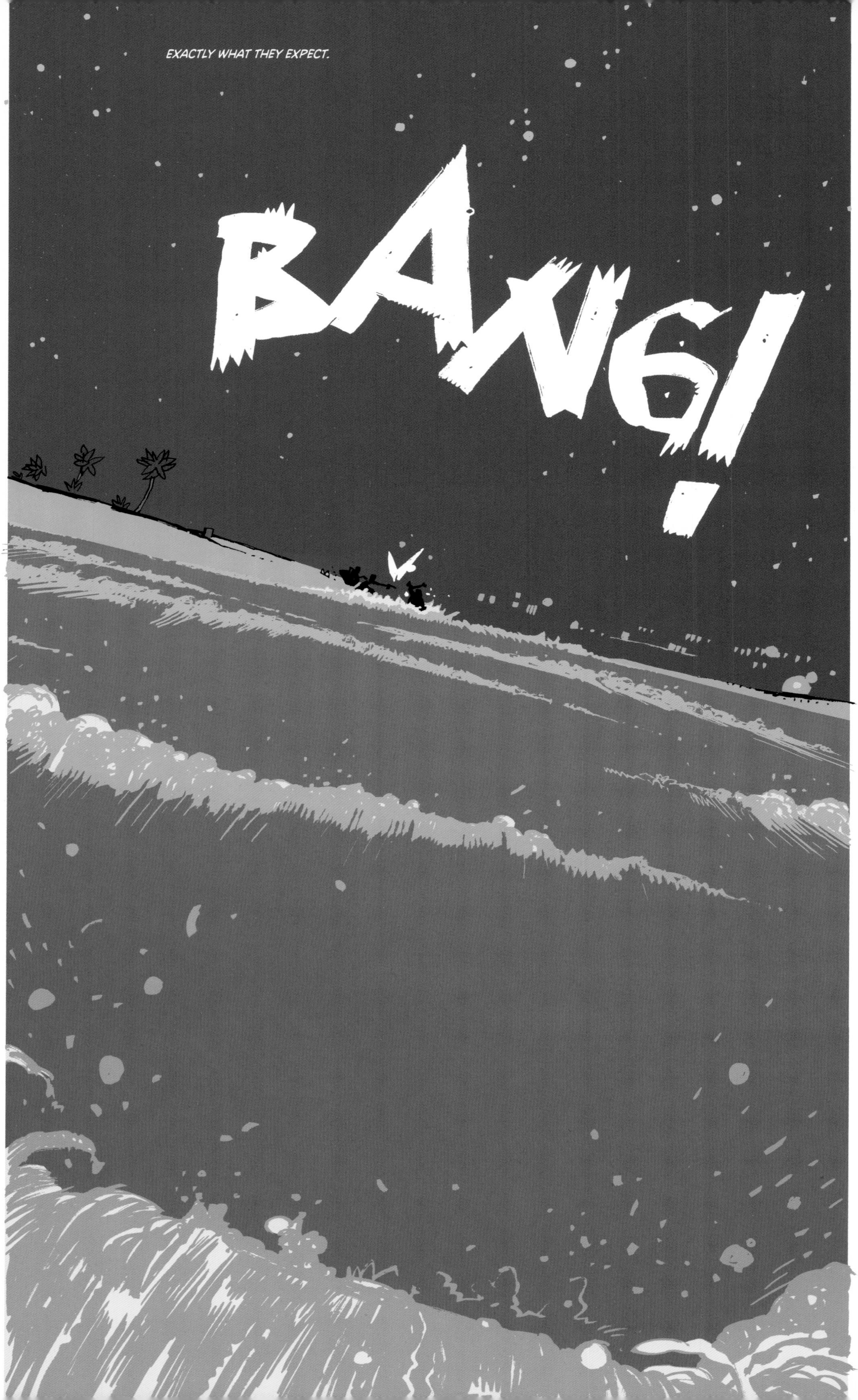
EXACTLY WHAT THEY EXPECT.
BANG!

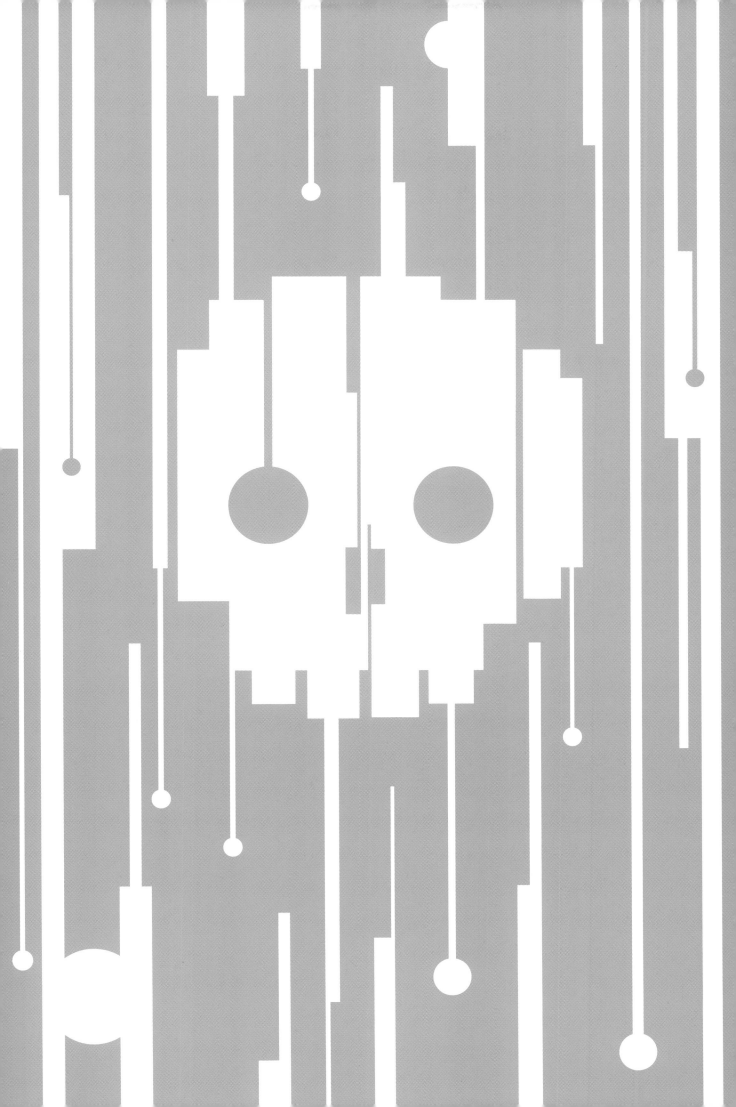

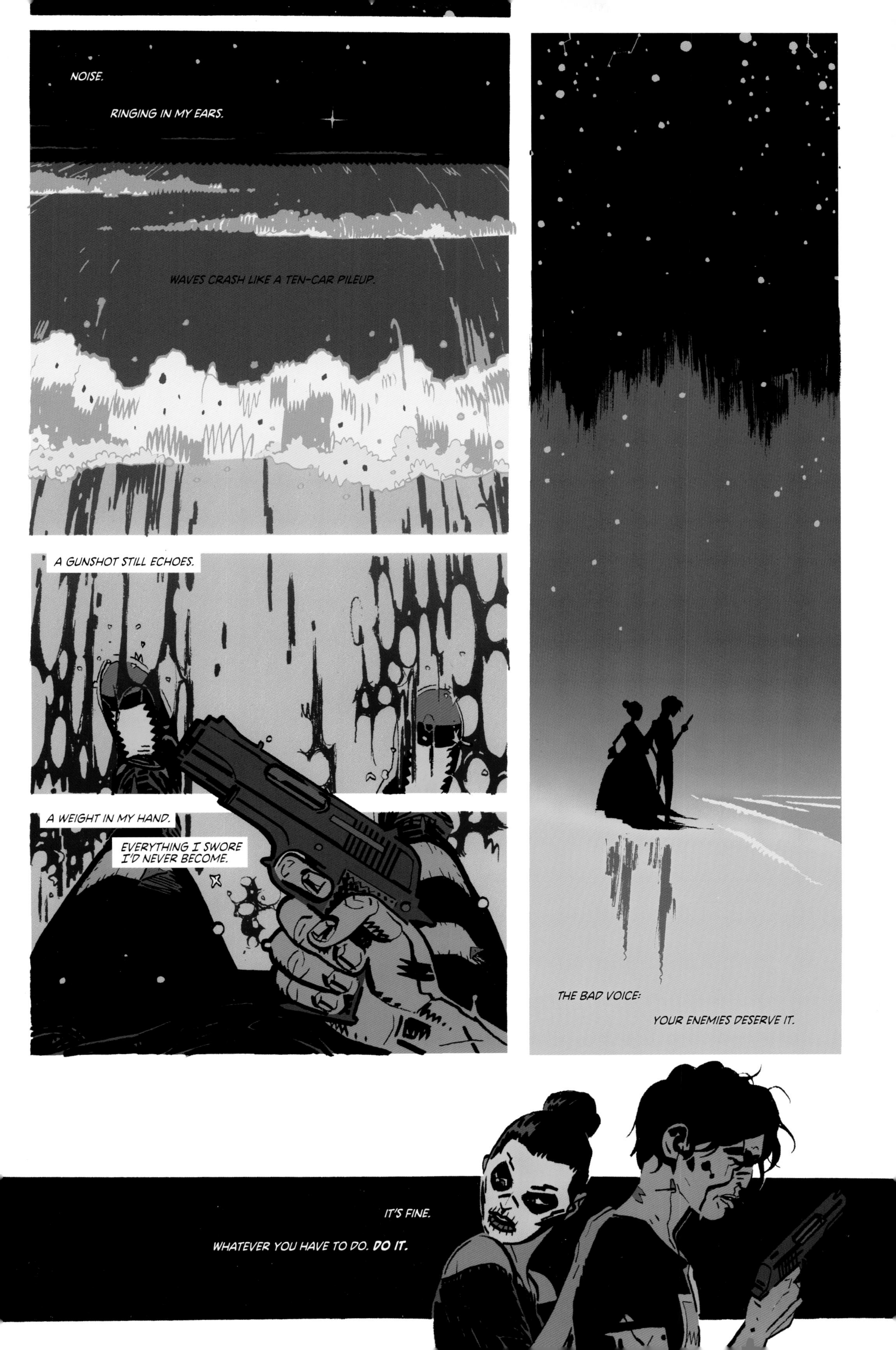
NOISE.
RINGING IN MY EARS.
WAVES CRASH LIKE A TEN-CAR PILEUP.
A GUNSHOT STILL ECHOES.
A WEIGHT IN MY HAND.
EVERYTHING I SWORE I'D NEVER BECOME.
THE BAD VOICE:
YOUR ENEMIES DESERVE IT.
IT'S FINE.
WHATEVER YOU HAVE TO DO. DO IT.

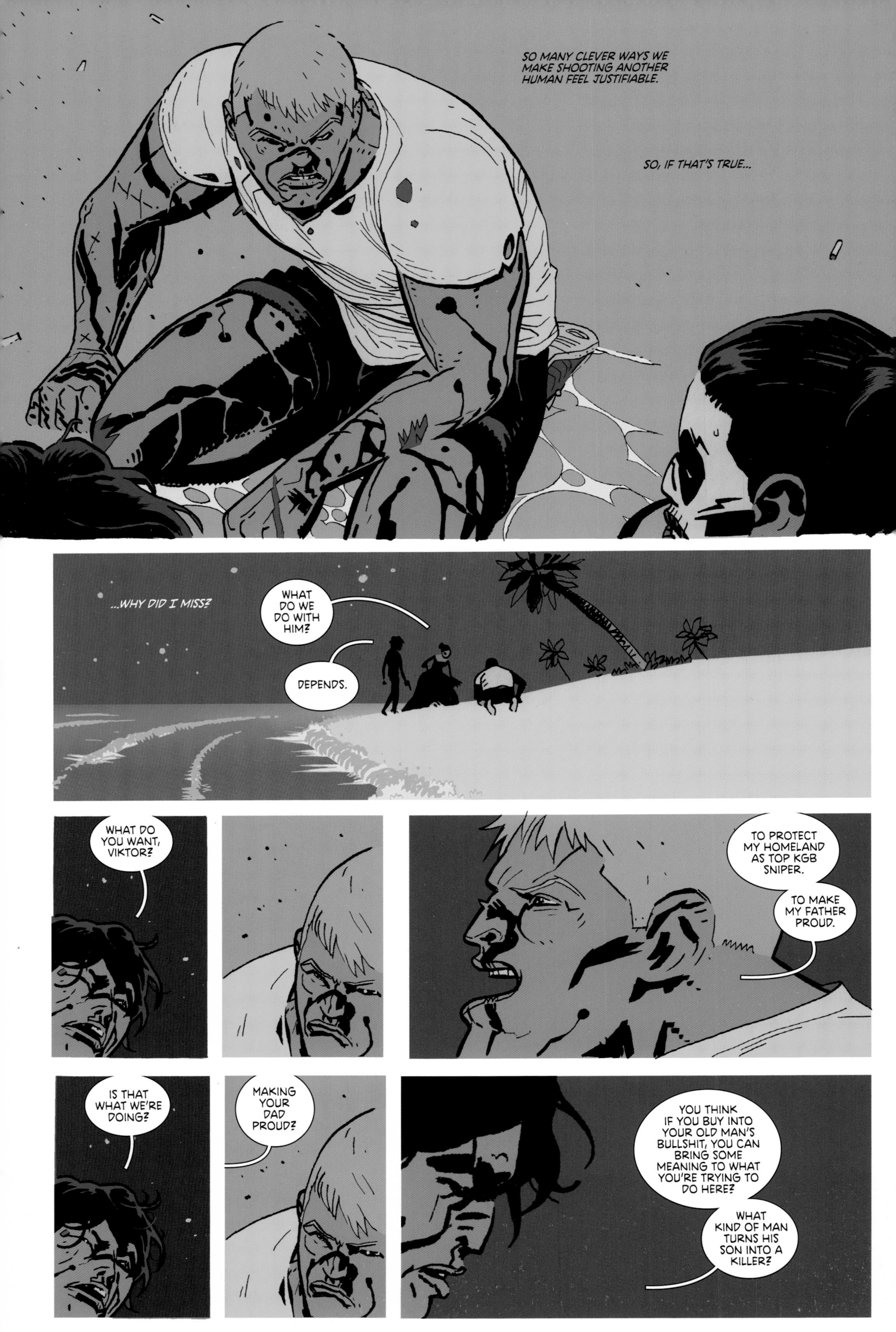
SO MANY CLEVER WAYS WE MAKE SHOOTING ANOTHER HUMAN FEEL JUSTIFIABLE.
SO, IF THAT'S TRUE...
...WHY DID I MISS?
WHAT DO WE DO WITH HIM?
DEPENDS.
WHAT DO YOU WANT, VIKTOR?
TO PROTECT MY HOMELAND AS TOP KGB SNIPER.
TO MAKE MY FATHER PROUD.
IS THAT WHAT WE'RE DOING?
MAKING YOUR DAD PROUD?
YOU THINK IF YOU BUY INTO YOUR OLD MAN'S BULLSHIT, YOU CAN BRING SOME MEANING TO WHAT YOU'RE TRYING TO DO HERE?
WHAT KIND OF MAN TURNS HIS SON INTO A KILLER?

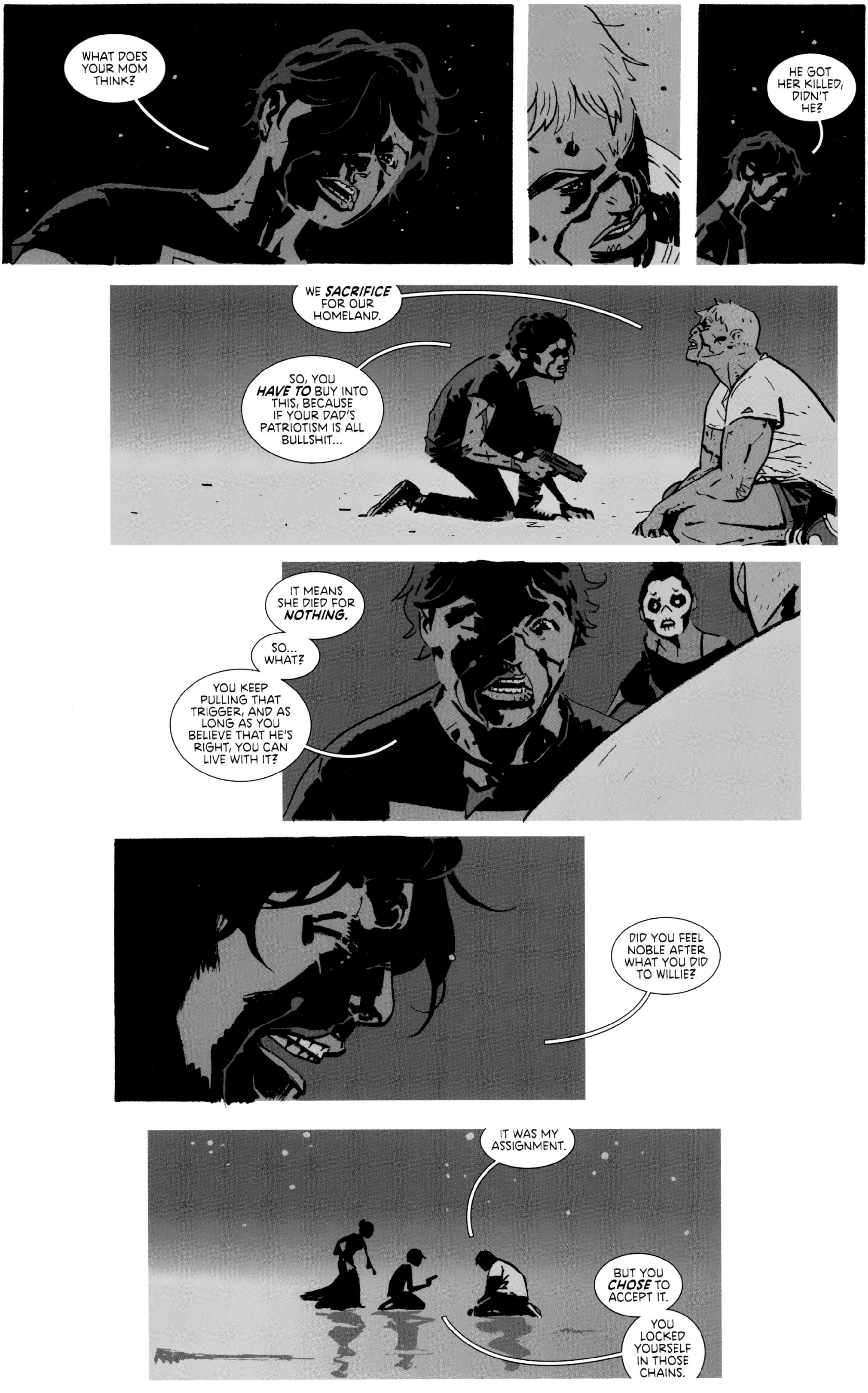
WHAT DOES YOUR MOM THINK?
HE GOT HER KILLED, DIDN'T HE?
WE SACRIFICE FOR OUR HOMELAND.
SO, YOU HAVE TO BUY INTO THIS, BECAUSE IF YOUR DAD'S PATRIOTISM IS ALL BULLSHIT...
IT MEANS SHE DIED FOR NOTHING.
SO... WHAT?
YOU KEEP PULLING THAT TRIGGER, AND AS LONG AS YOU BELIEVE THAT HE'S RIGHT, YOU CAN LIVE WITH IT?
DID YOU FEEL NOBLE AFTER WHAT YOU DID TO WILLIE?
IT WAS MY ASSIGNMENT.
BUT YOU CHOSE TO ACCEPT IT.
YOU LOCKED YOURSELF IN THOSE CHAINS.

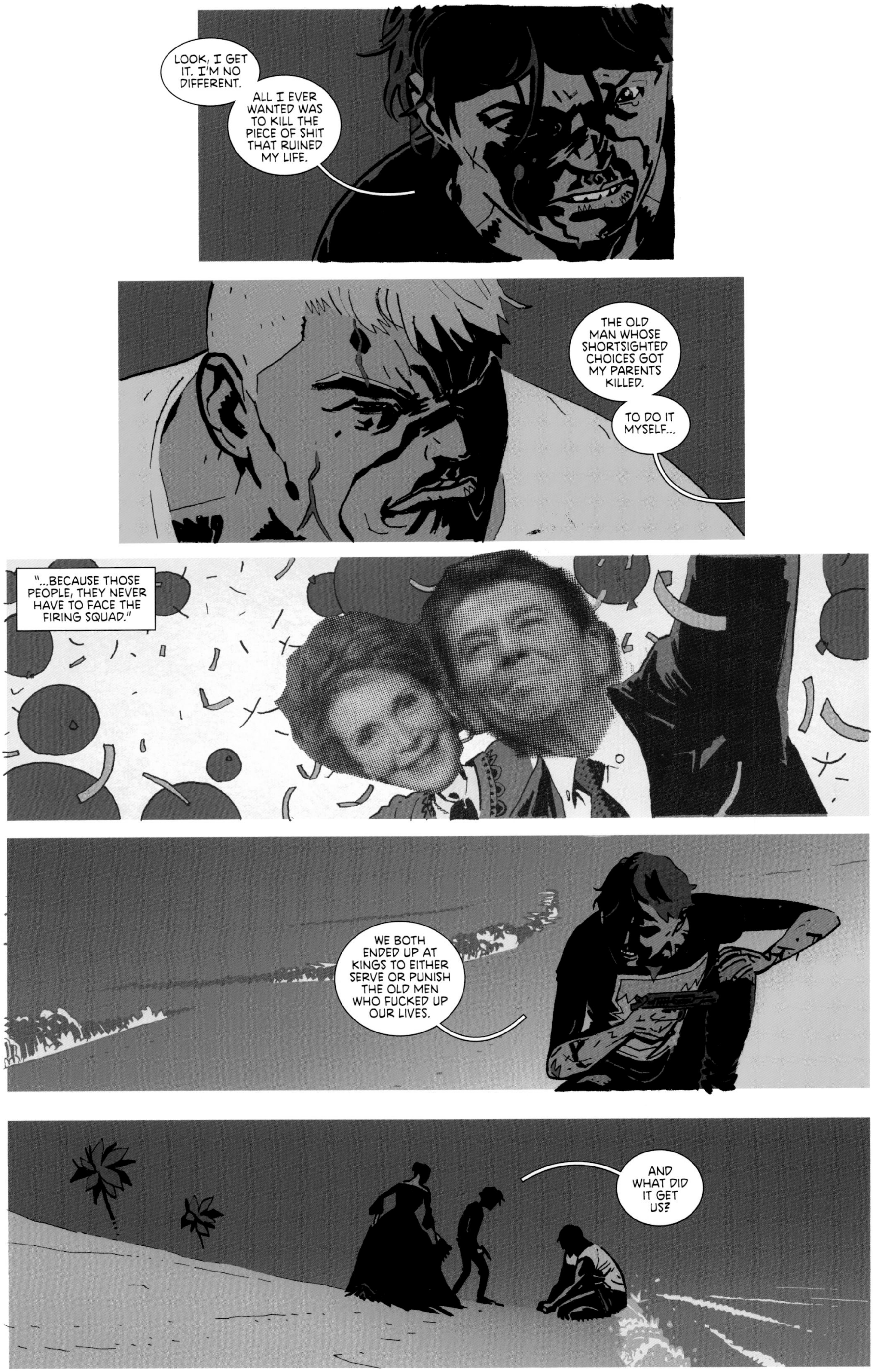
LOOK, I GET IT. I'M NO DIFFERENT.
ALL I EVER WANTED WAS TO KILL THE PIECE OF SHIT THAT RUINED MY LIFE.
THE OLD MAN WHOSE SHORTSIGHTED CHOICES GOT MY PARENTS KILLED.
TO DO IT MYSELF...
"...BECAUSE THOSE PEOPLE, THEY NEVER HAVE TO FACE THE FIRING SQUAD."
WE BOTH ENDED UP AT KINGS TO EITHER SERVE OR PUNISH THE OLD MEN WHO FUCKED UP OUR LIVES.
AND WHAT DID IT GET US?

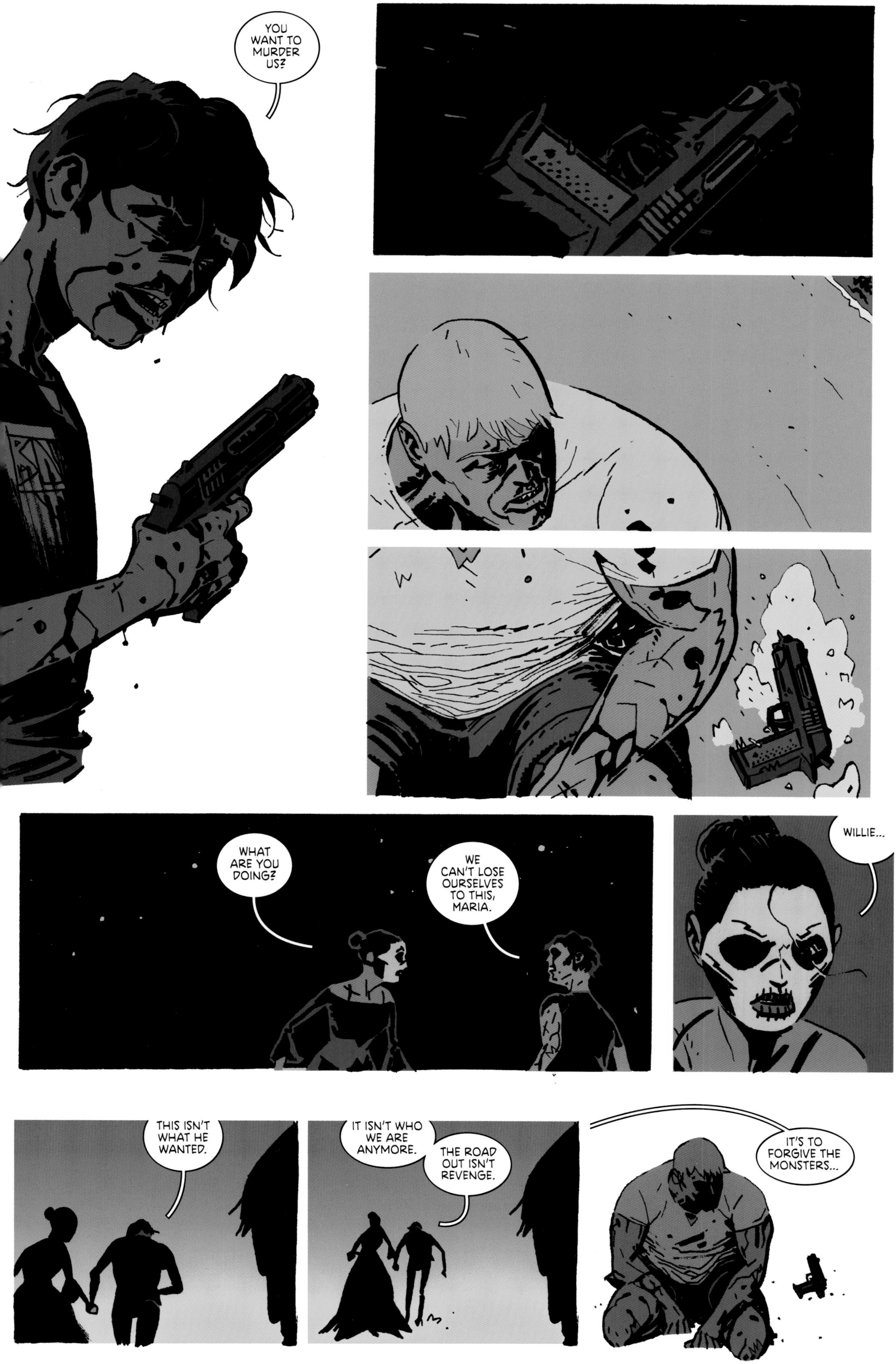
YOU WANT TO MURDER US?
WHAT ARE YOU DOING?
WE CAN'T LOSE OURSELVES TO THIS, MARIA.
WILLIE...
THIS ISN'T WHAT HE WANTED.
IT ISN'T WHO WE ARE ANYMORE.
THE ROAD OUT ISN'T REVENGE.
IT'S TO FORGIVE THE MONSTERS...

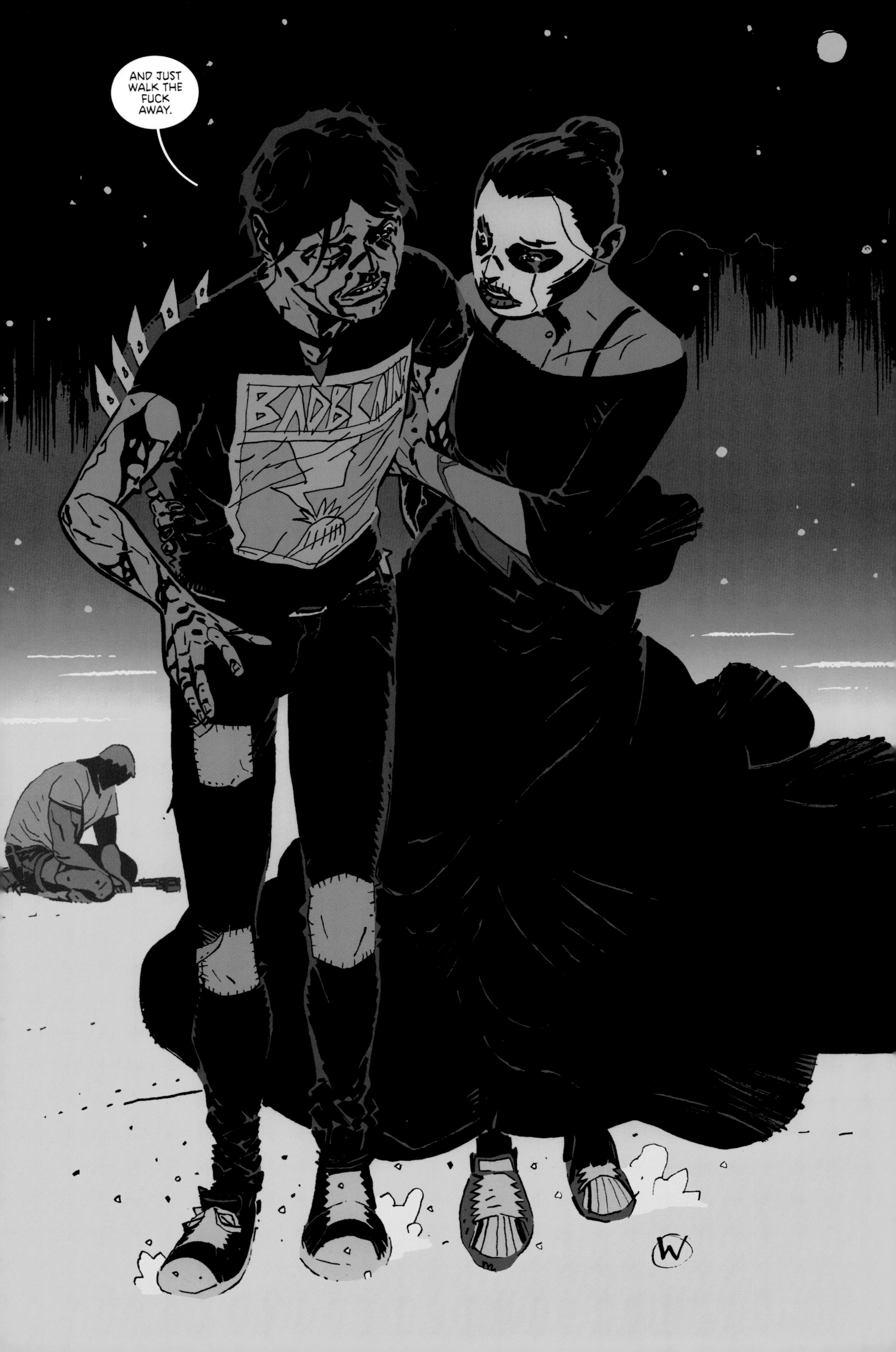
AND JUST WALK THE FUCK AWAY.

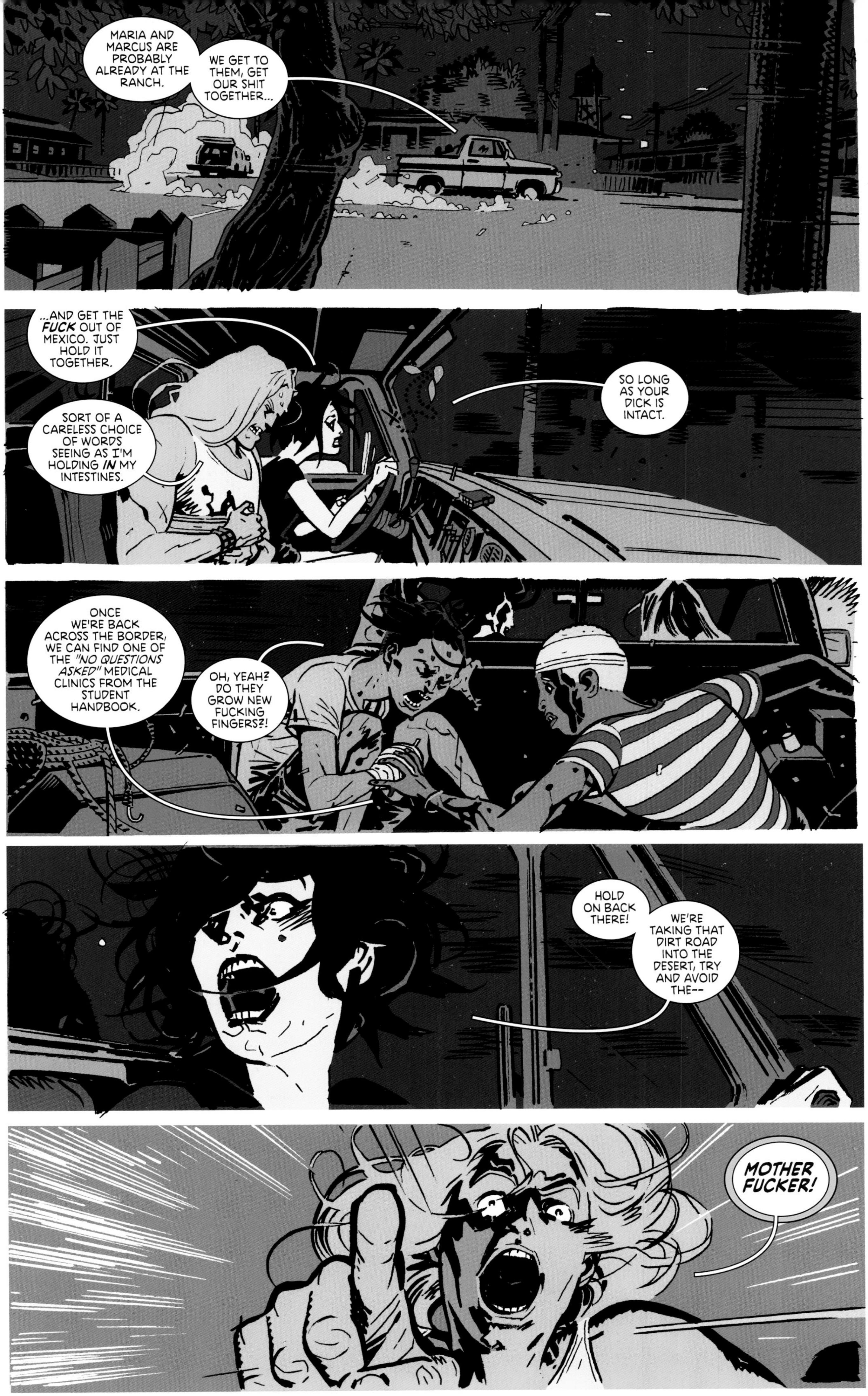
MARIA AND MARCUS ARE PROBABLY ALREADY AT THE RANCH.
WE GET TO THEM, GET OUR SHIT TOGETHER...
...AND GET THE FUCK OUT OF MEXICO. JUST HOLD IT TOGETHER.
SORT OF A CARELESS CHOICE OF WORDS SEEING AS I'M HOLDING IN MY INTESTINES.
SO LONG AS YOUR DICK IS INTACT.
ONCE WE'RE BACK ACROSS THE BORDER, WE CAN FIND ONE OF THE "NO QUESTIONS ASKED" MEDICAL CLINICS FROM THE STUDENT HANDBOOK.
OH, YEAH? DO THEY GROW NEW FUCKING FINGERS?!
HOLD ON BACK THERE!
WE'RE TAKING THAT DIRT ROAD INTO THE DESERT, TRY AND AVOID THE--
MOTHER FUCKER!

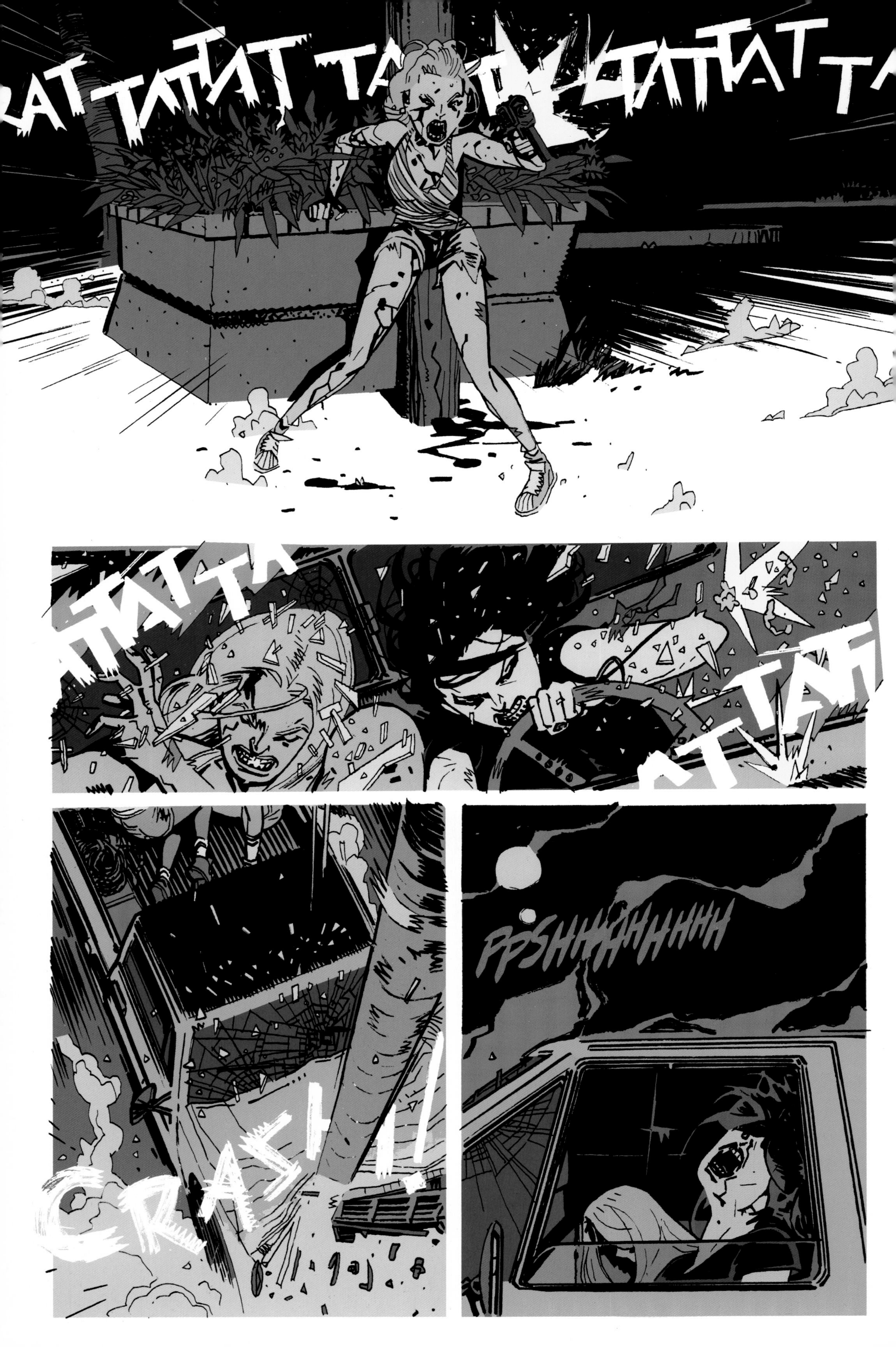
RAT-TATTAT TA TA TATTAT TA
TATTAT TA
TAT TAT
CRASH!!
PPSHHHHHHHHHH

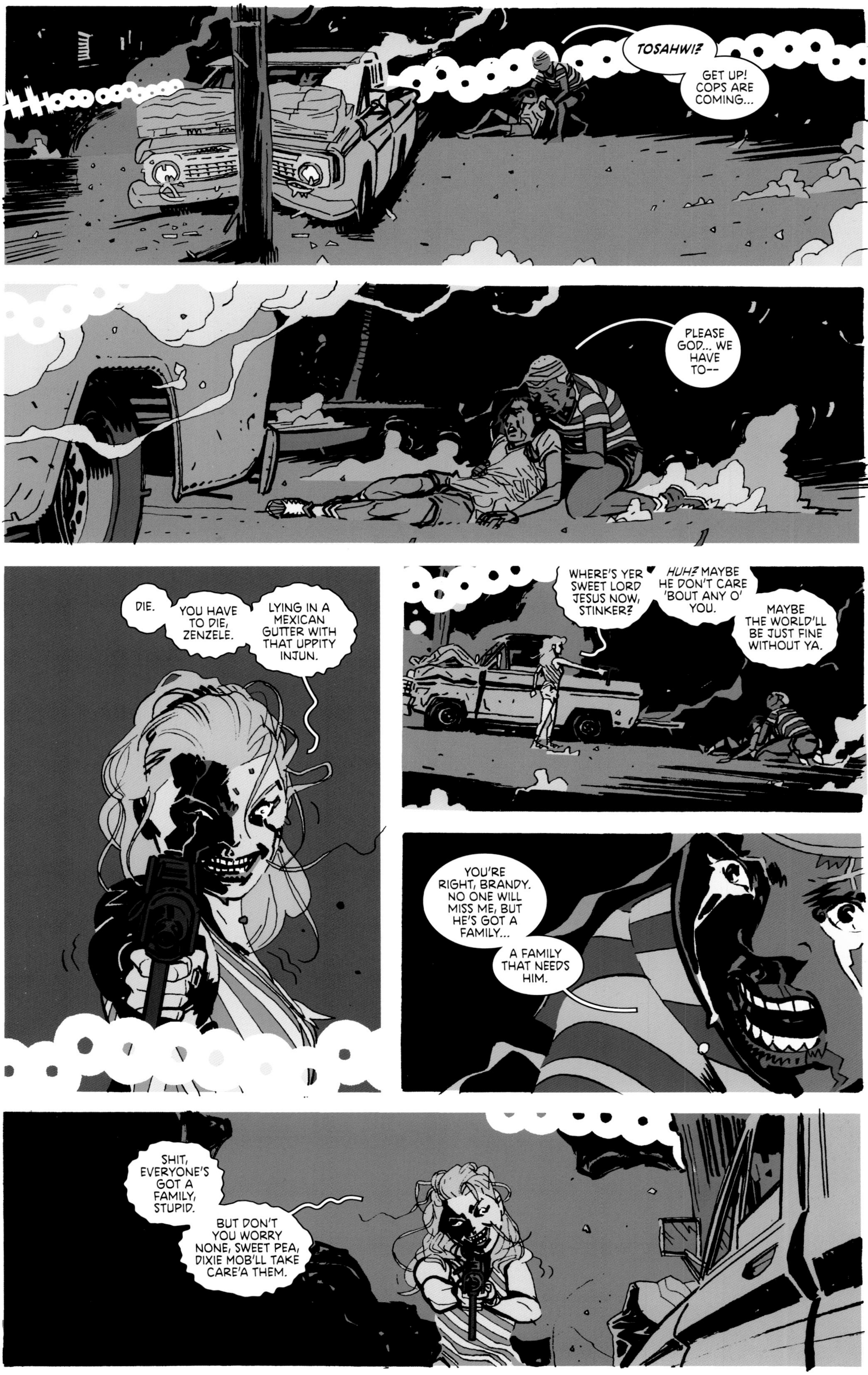
TOSAHWI?
GET UP! COPS ARE COMING...
PLEASE GOD... WE HAVE TO--
DIE.
YOU HAVE TO DIE, ZENZELE.
LYING IN A MEXICAN GUTTER WITH THAT UPPITY INJUN.
WHERE'S YER SWEET LORD JESUS NOW, STINKER?
HUH? MAYBE HE DON'T CARE 'BOUT ANY O' YOU.
MAYBE THE WORLD'LL BE JUST FINE WITHOUT YA.
YOU'RE RIGHT, BRANDY. NO ONE WILL MISS ME, BUT HE'S GOT A FAMILY...
A FAMILY THAT NEEDS HIM.
SHIT, EVERYONE'S GOT A FAMILY, STUPID.
BUT DON'T YOU WORRY NONE, SWEET PEA, DIXIE MOB'LL TAKE CARE'A THEM.

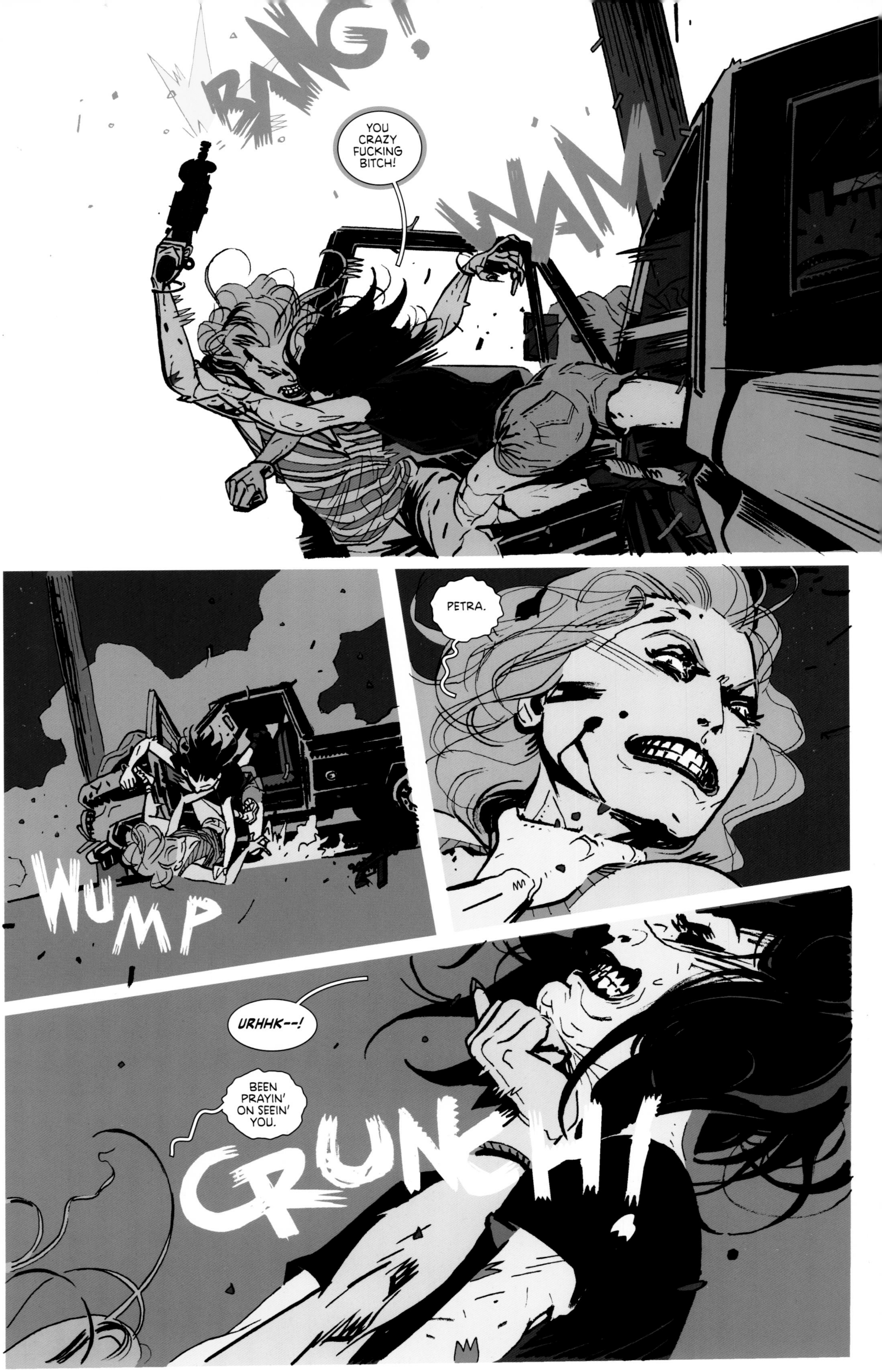
BANG!
YOU CRAZY FUCKING BITCH!
WAM
WUMP
PETRA.
URHHK--!
BEEN PRAYIN' ON SEEIN' YOU.
CRUNCH!

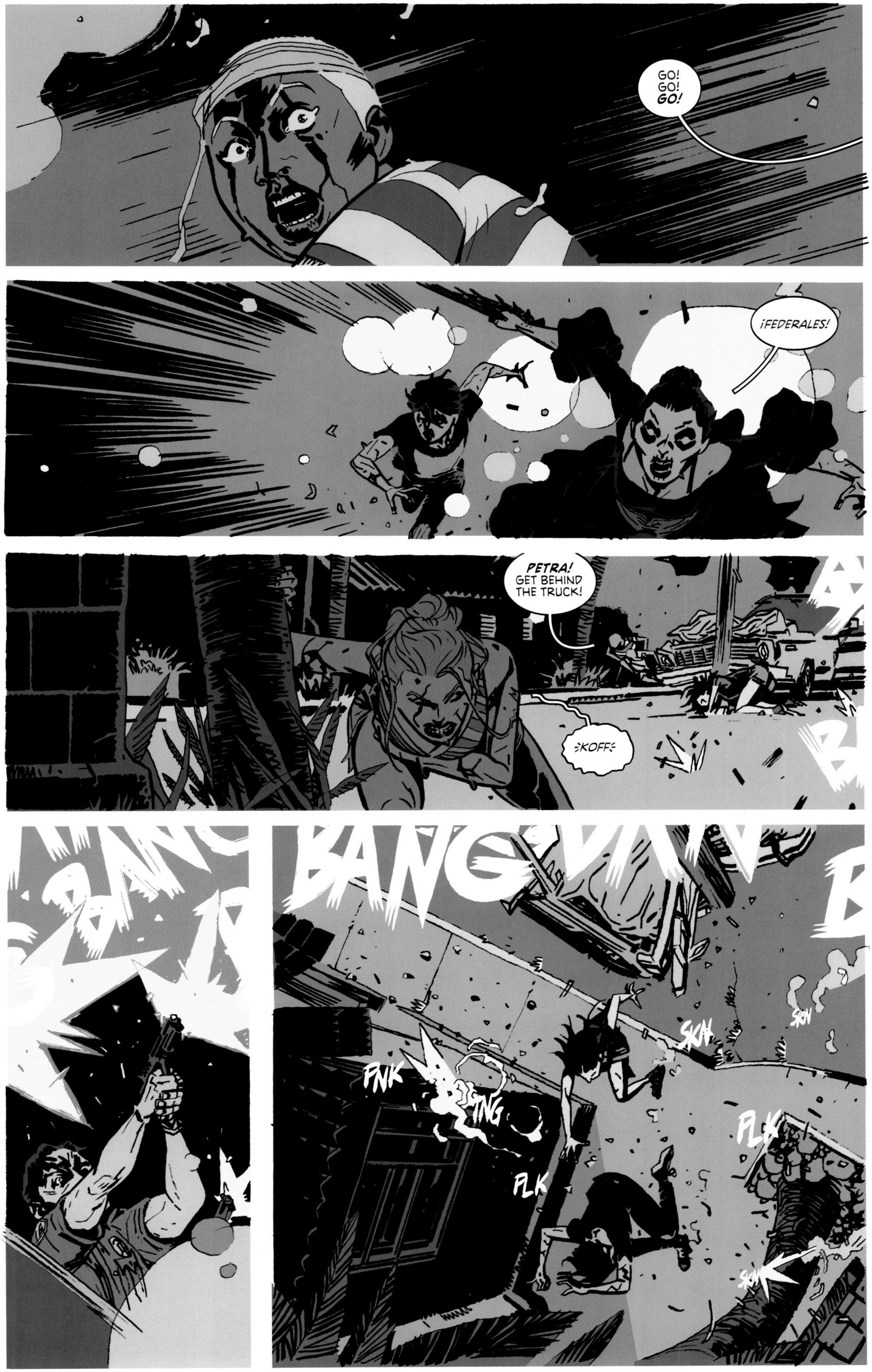

GO! GO! GO!
¡FEDERALES!
PETRA! GET BEHIND THE TRUCK!
KOFF
BANG
PNK
TING
PLK
PLK

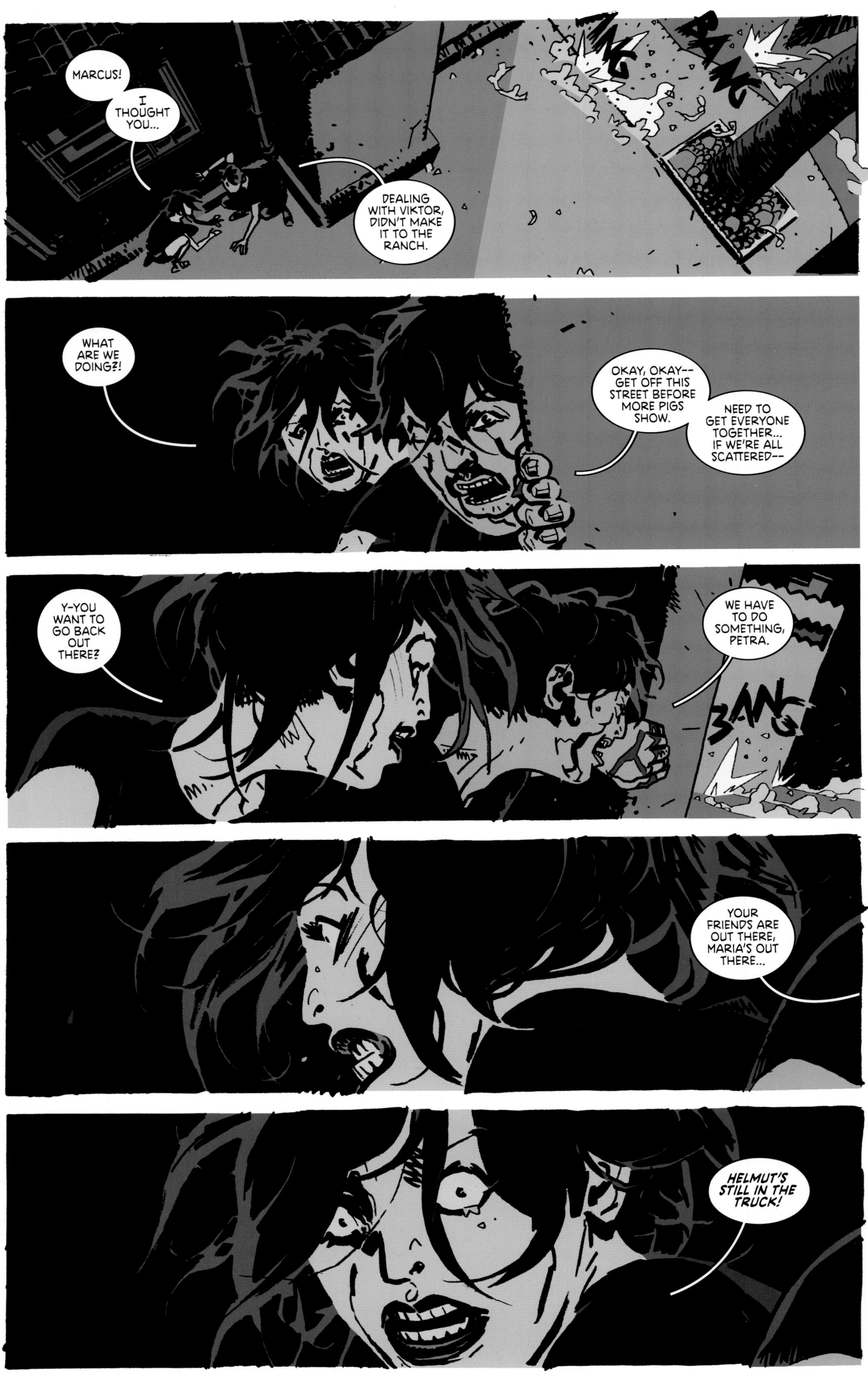
MARCUS!
I THOUGHT YOU...
DEALING WITH VIKTOR, DIDN'T MAKE IT TO THE RANCH.
BANG
WHAT ARE WE DOING?!
OKAY, OKAY-- GET OFF THIS STREET BEFORE MORE PIGS SHOW.
NEED TO GET EVERYONE TOGETHER... IF WE'RE ALL SCATTERED--
Y-YOU WANT TO GO BACK OUT THERE?
WE HAVE TO DO SOMETHING, PETRA.
BANG
YOUR FRIENDS ARE OUT THERE, MARIA'S OUT THERE...
HELMUT'S STILL IN THE TRUCK!

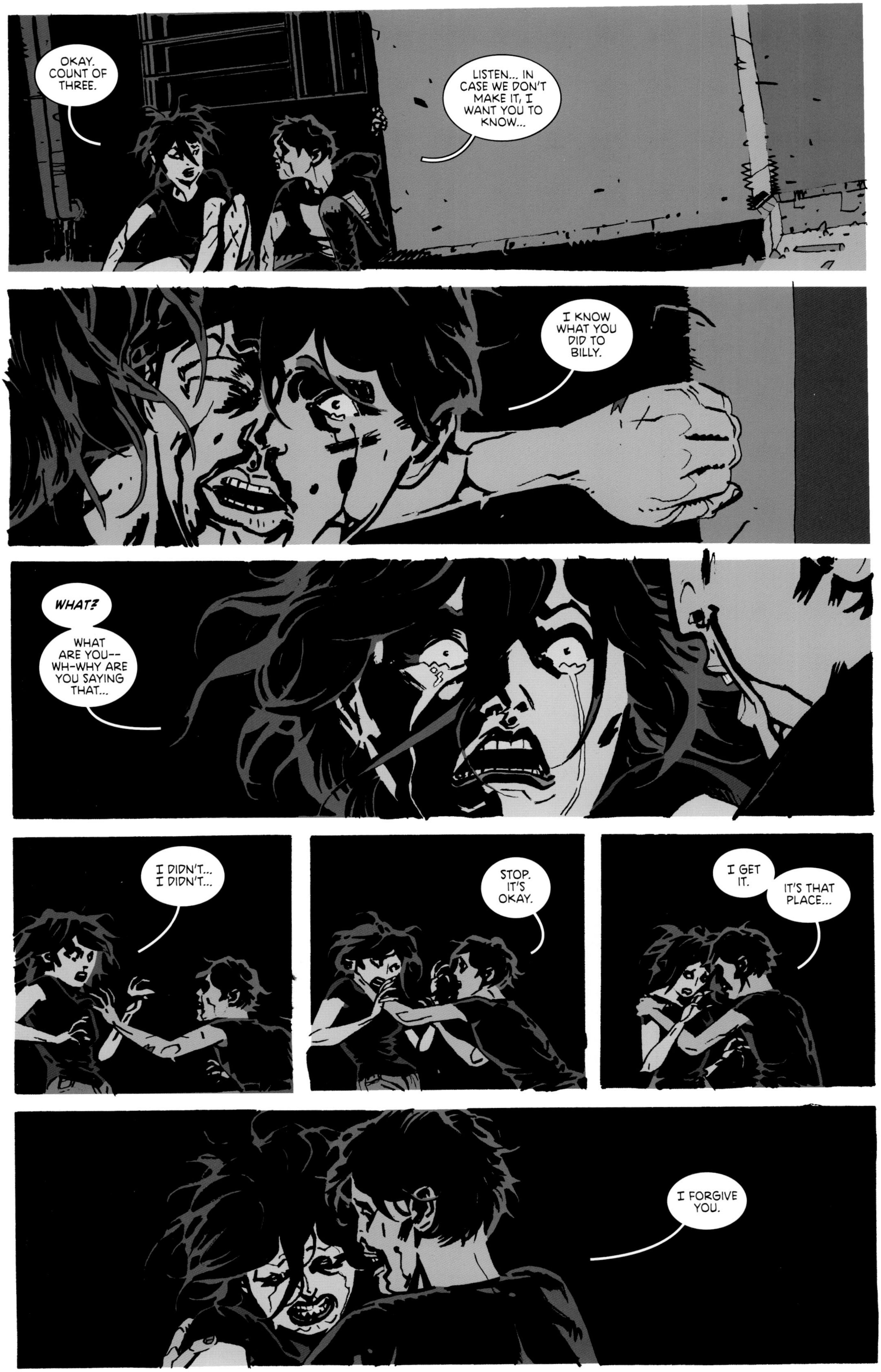

OKAY. COUNT OF THREE.
LISTEN... IN CASE WE DON'T MAKE IT, I WANT YOU TO KNOW...
I KNOW WHAT YOU DID TO BILLY.
WHAT?
WHAT ARE YOU-- WH-WHY ARE YOU SAYING THAT...
I DIDN'T... I DIDN'T...
STOP. IT'S OKAY.
I GET IT.
IT'S THAT PLACE...
I FORGIVE YOU.

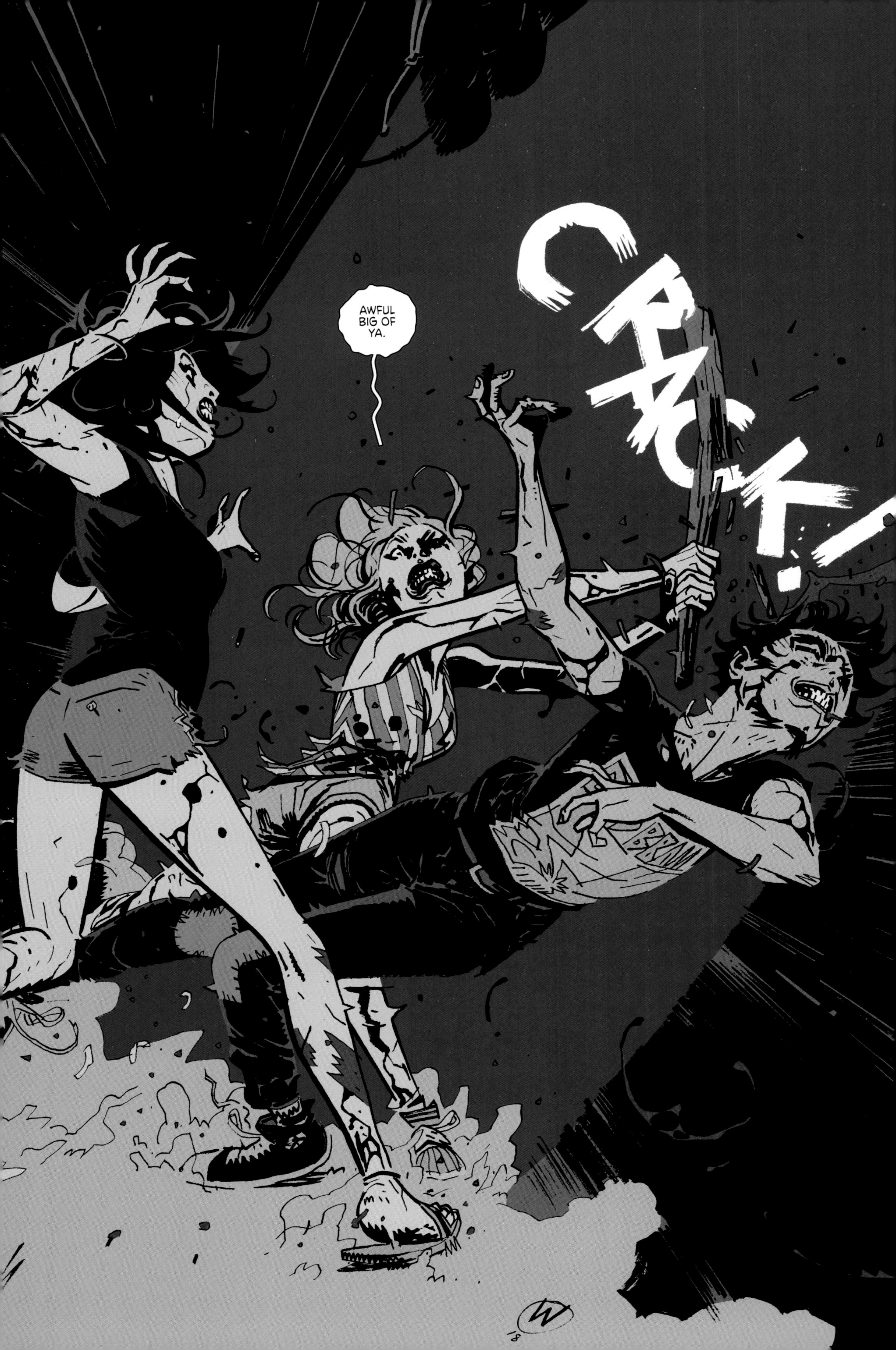
AWFUL BIG OF YA.
CRACK!

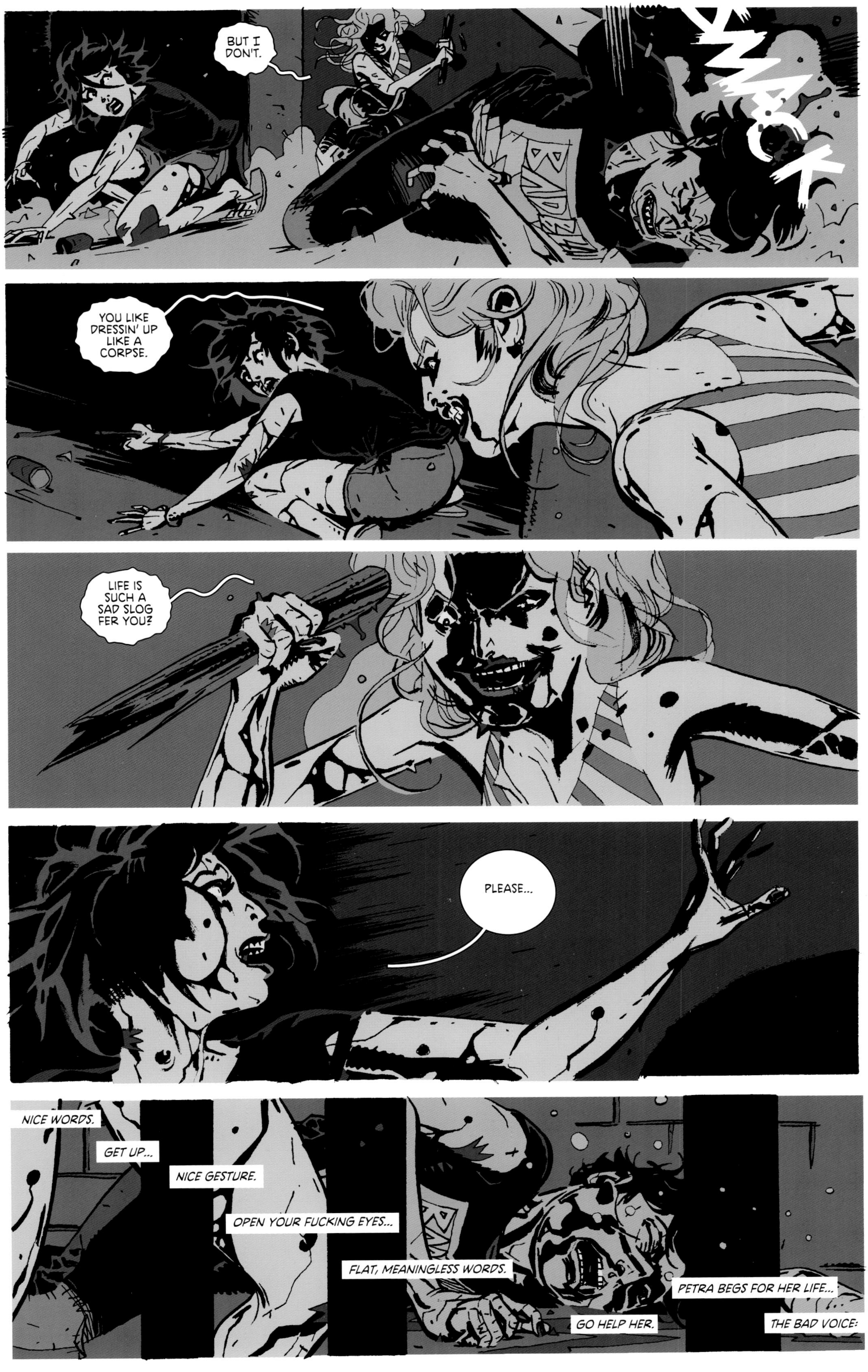
BUT I DON'T.
YOU LIKE DRESSIN' UP LIKE A CORPSE.
LIFE IS SUCH A SAD SLOG FER YOU?
PLEASE...
NICE WORDS.
GET UP...
NICE GESTURE.
OPEN YOUR FUCKING EYES...
FLAT, MEANINGLESS WORDS.
PETRA BEGS FOR HER LIFE...
GO HELP HER.
THE BAD VOICE:

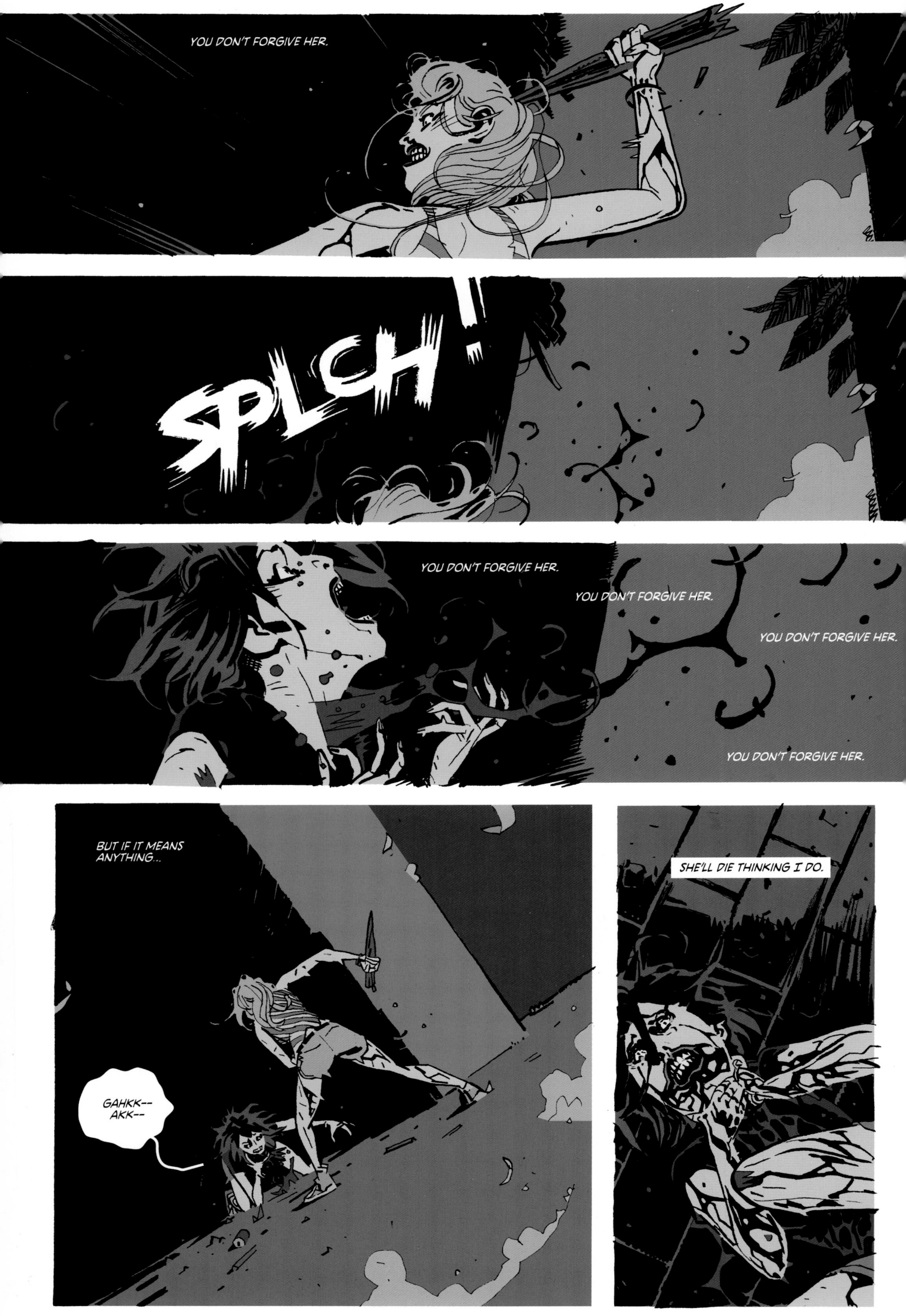
YOU DON'T FORGIVE HER.
SPLCH!
YOU DON'T FORGIVE HER.
YOU DON'T FORGIVE HER.
YOU DON'T FORGIVE HER.
YOU DON'T FORGIVE HER.
BUT IF IT MEANS ANYTHING...
GAHKK-- AKK--
SHE'LL DIE THINKING I DO.

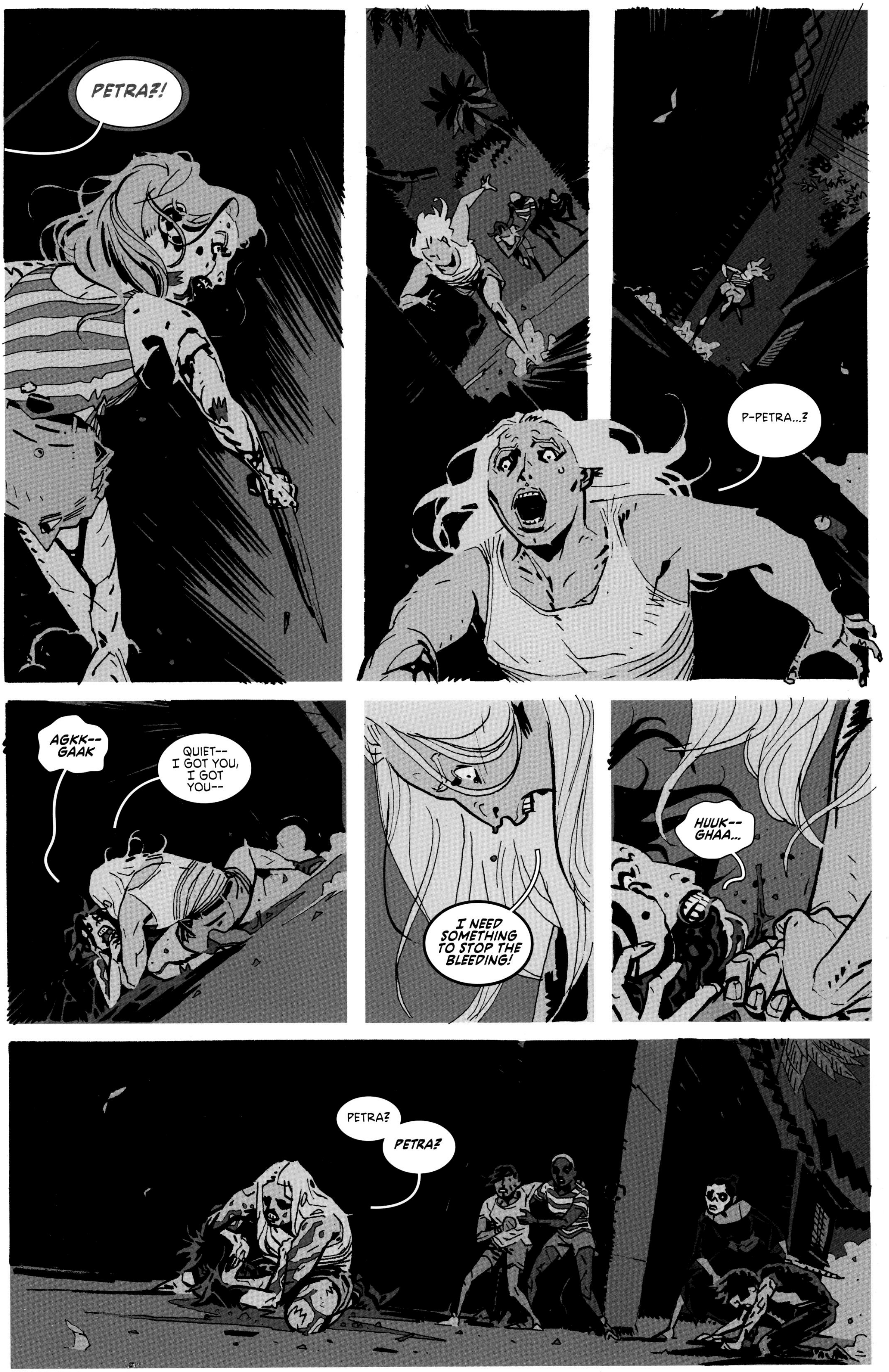
PETRA?!
P-PETRA...?
AGKK--GAAK
QUIET-- I GOT YOU, I GOT YOU--
I NEED SOMETHING TO STOP THE BLEEDING!
HUUK--GHAA...
PETRA?
PETRA?

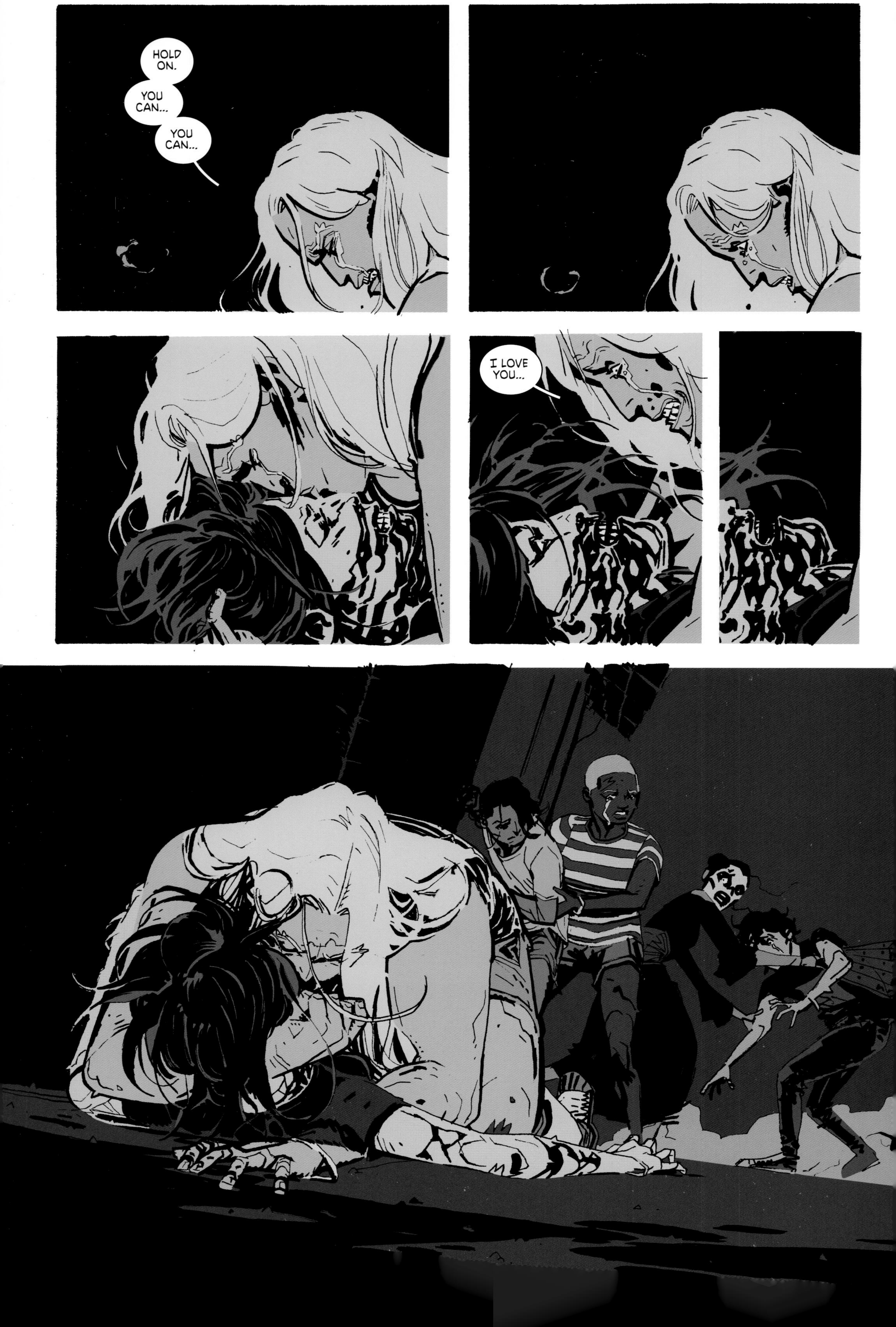
HOLD ON.
YOU CAN...
YOU CAN...
I LOVE YOU...

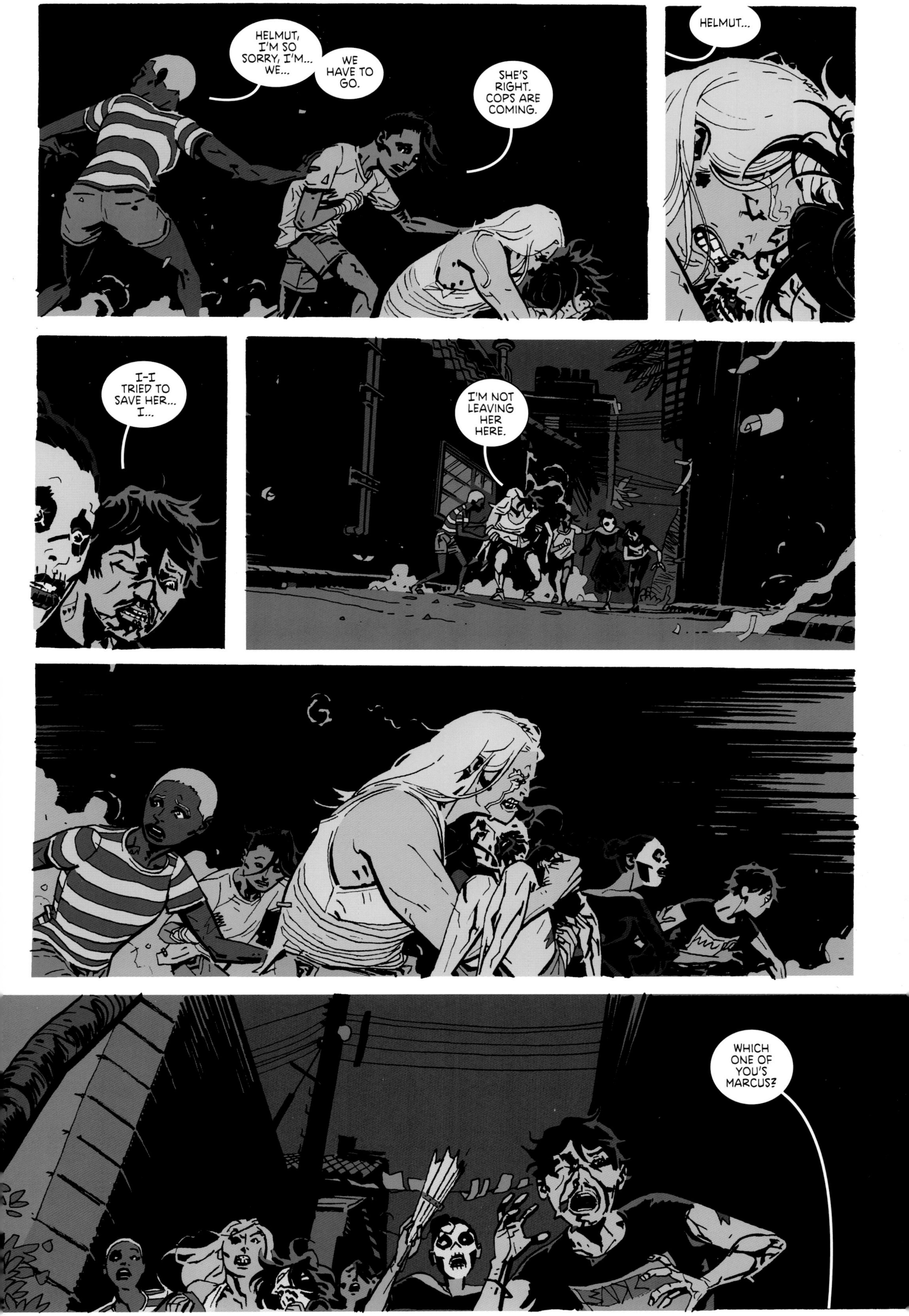
HELMUT, I'M SO SORRY, I'M... WE...
WE HAVE TO GO.
SHE'S RIGHT. COPS ARE COMING.
HELMUT...
I-I TRIED TO SAVE HER... I...
I'M NOT LEAVING HER HERE.
WHICH ONE OF YOU'S MARCUS?

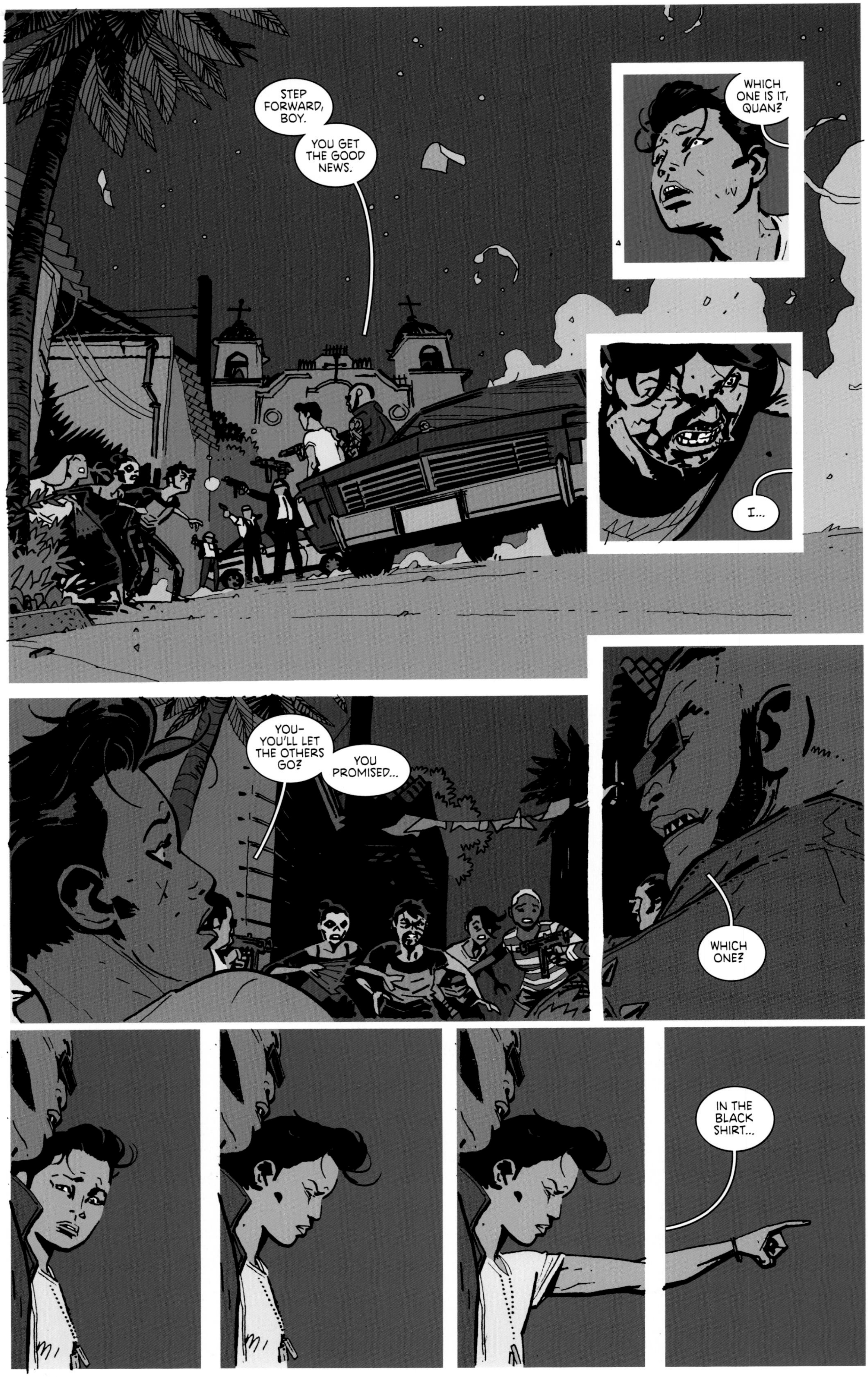
STEP FORWARD, BOY.
YOU GET THE GOOD NEWS.
WHICH ONE IS IT, QUAN?
I...
YOU-YOU'LL LET THE OTHERS GO?
YOU PROMISED...
WHICH ONE?
IN THE BLACK SHIRT...

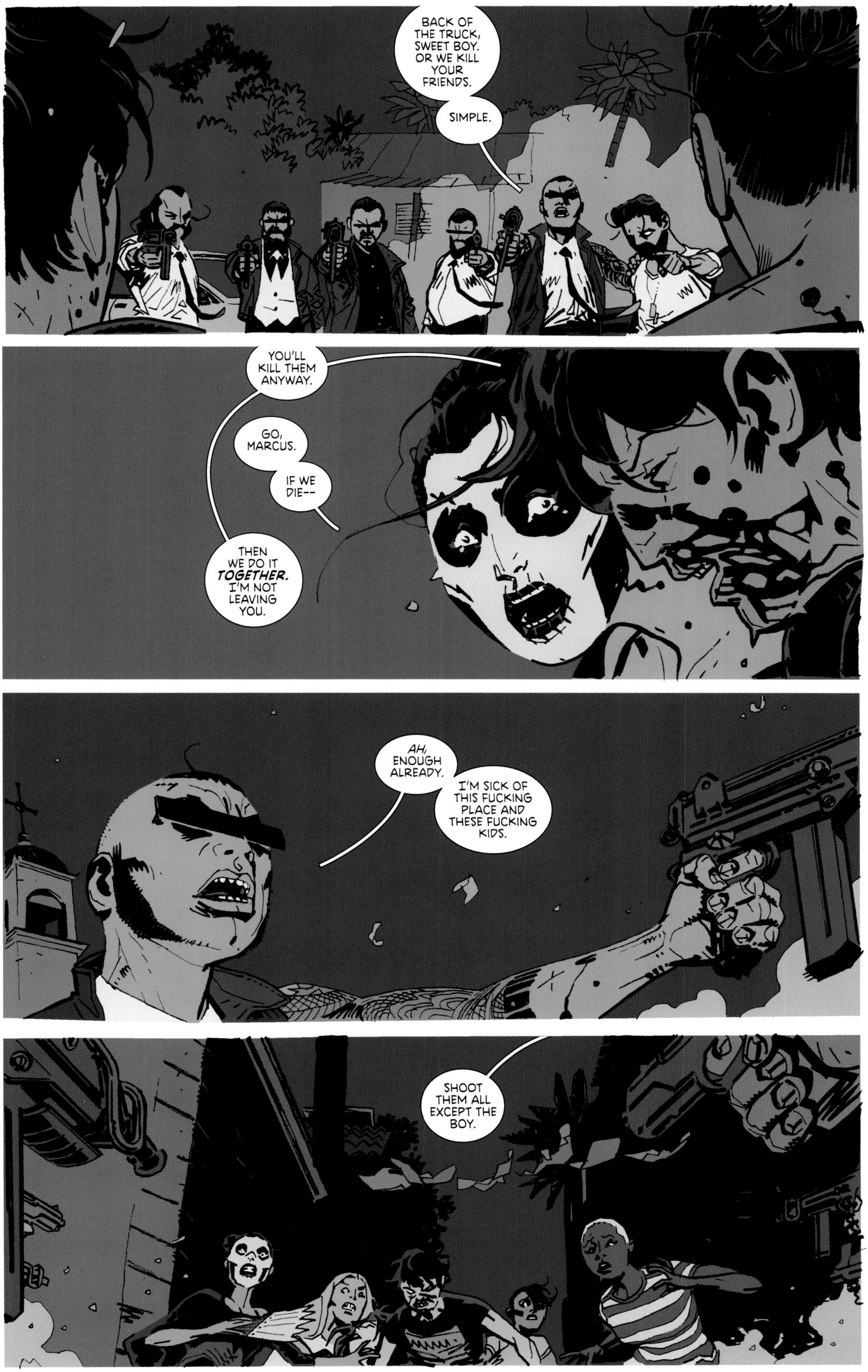
BACK OF THE TRUCK, SWEET BOY. OR WE KILL YOUR FRIENDS.
SIMPLE.
YOU'LL KILL THEM ANYWAY.
GO, MARCUS.
IF WE DIE--
THEN WE DO IT *TOGETHER.* I'M NOT LEAVING YOU.
AH, ENOUGH ALREADY.
I'M SICK OF THIS FUCKING PLACE AND THESE FUCKING KIDS.
SHOOT THEM ALL EXCEPT THE BOY.

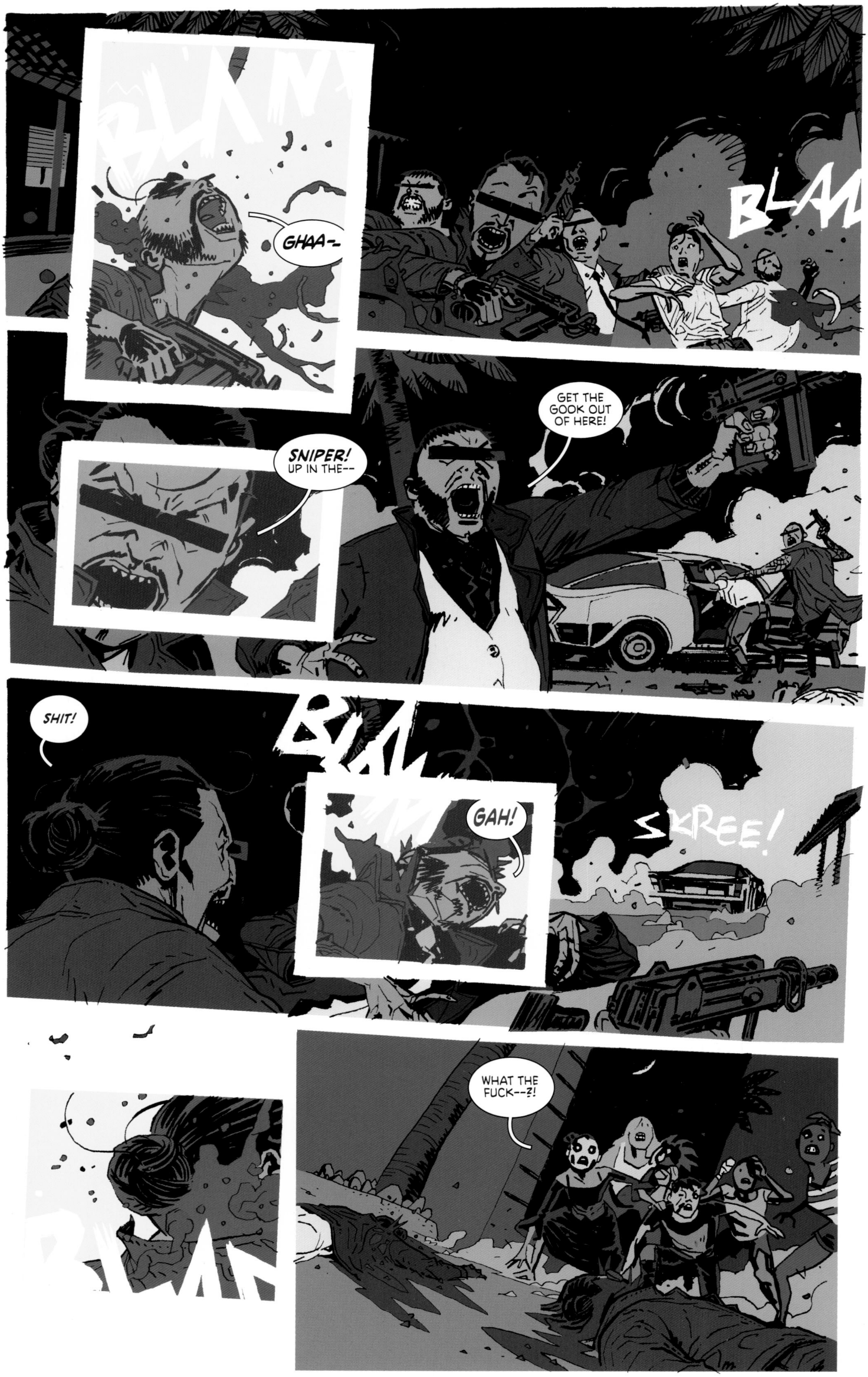
GHAA--
SNIPER! UP IN THE--
GET THE GOOK OUT OF HERE!
SHIT!
GAH!
SKREE!
WHAT THE FUCK--?!

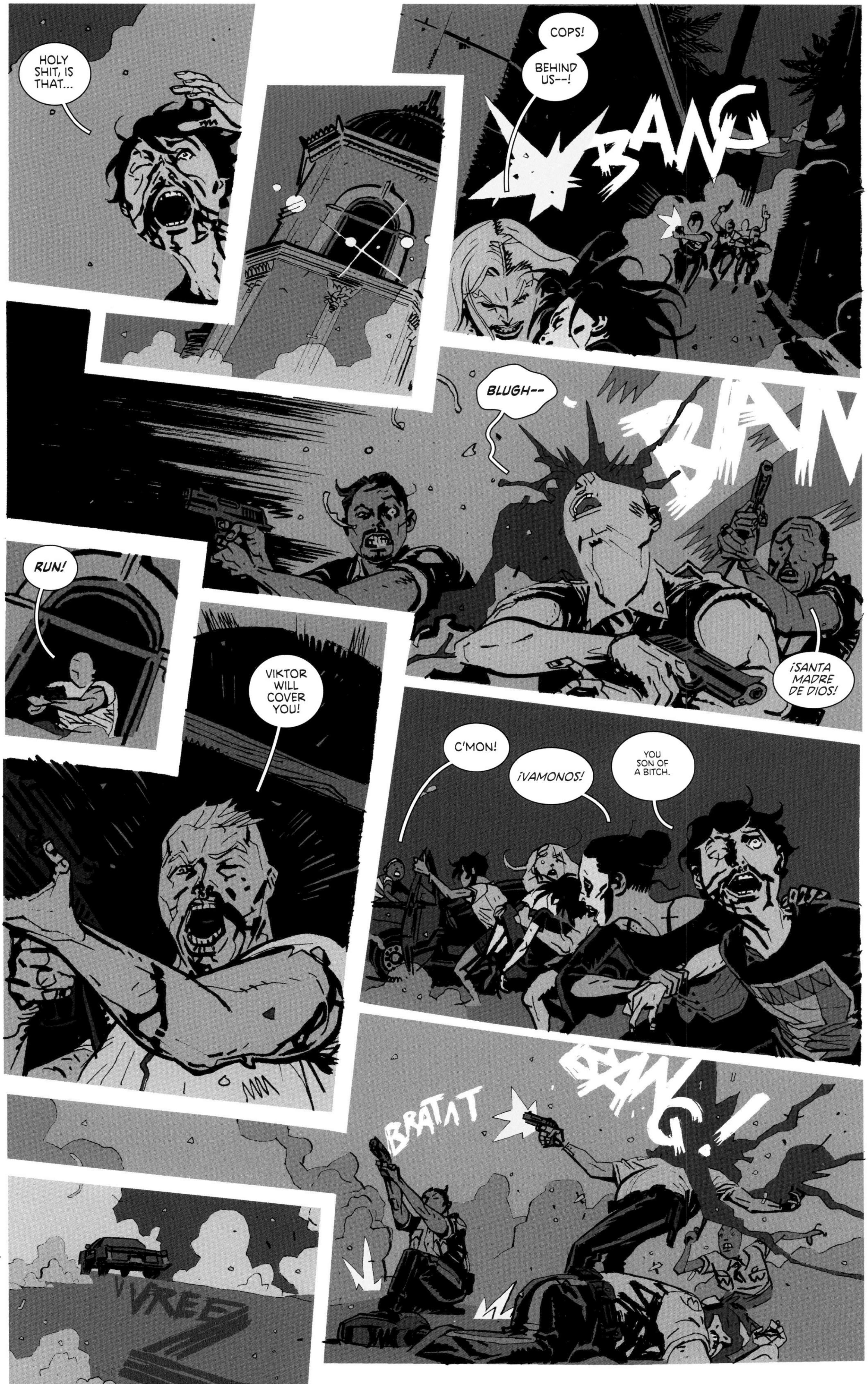
HOLY SHIT, IS THAT...
COPS!
BEHIND US--!
BANG
BLUGH--
BAM
¡SANTA MADRE DE DIOS!
RUN!
VIKTOR WILL COVER YOU!
C'MON!
¡VAMONOS!
YOU SON OF A BITCH.
BRATATAT
BANG
VVREE

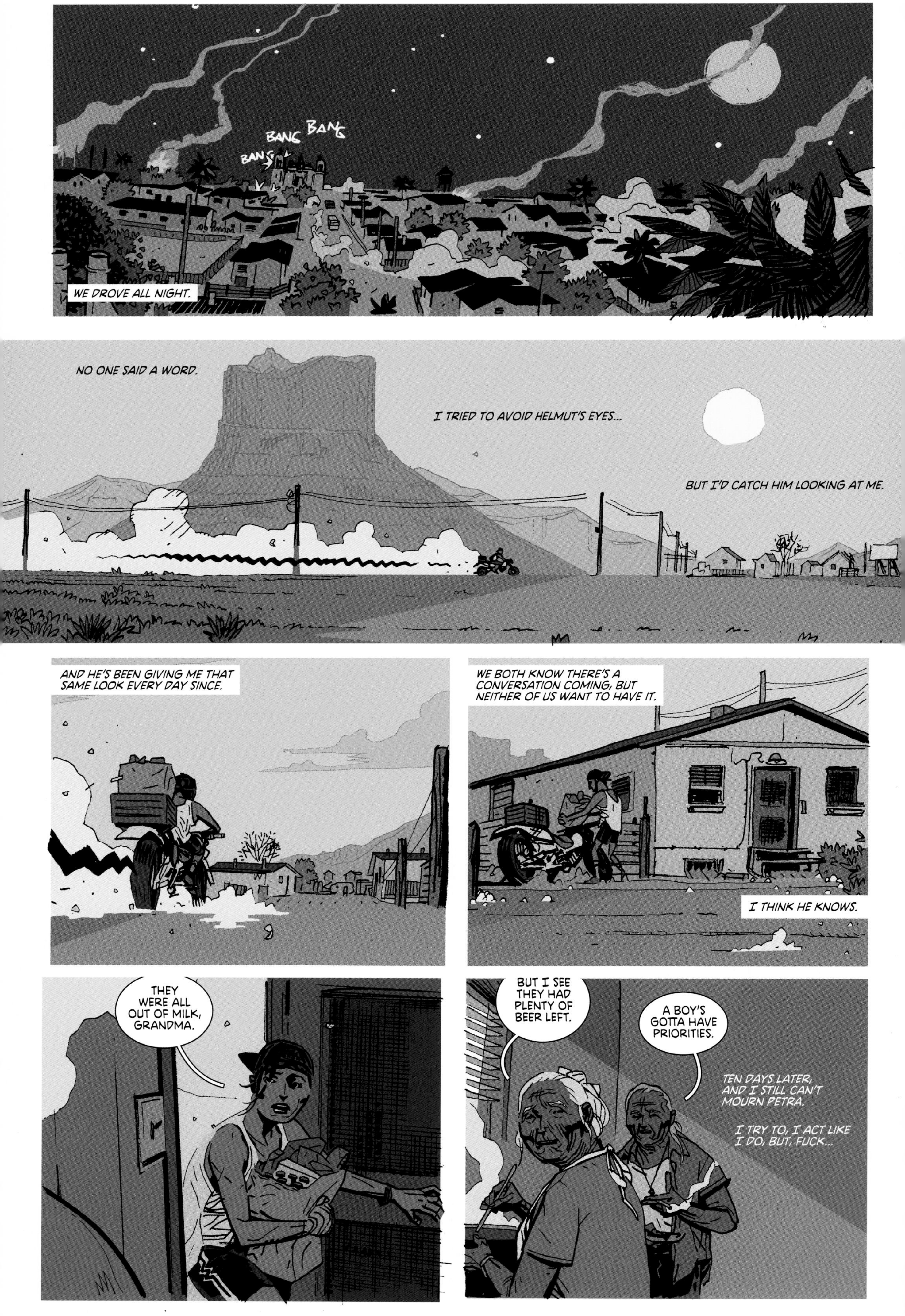
BANG
BANG
BANG
WE DROVE ALL NIGHT.
NO ONE SAID A WORD.
I TRIED TO AVOID HELMUT'S EYES...
BUT I'D CATCH HIM LOOKING AT ME.
AND HE'S BEEN GIVING ME THAT SAME LOOK EVERY DAY SINCE.
WE BOTH KNOW THERE'S A CONVERSATION COMING, BUT NEITHER OF US WANT TO HAVE IT.
I THINK HE KNOWS.
THEY WERE ALL OUT OF MILK, GRANDMA.
BUT I SEE THEY HAD PLENTY OF BEER LEFT.
A BOY'S GOTTA HAVE PRIORITIES.
TEN DAYS LATER, AND I STILL CAN'T MOURN PETRA.
I TRY TO, I ACT LIKE I DO, BUT, FUCK...

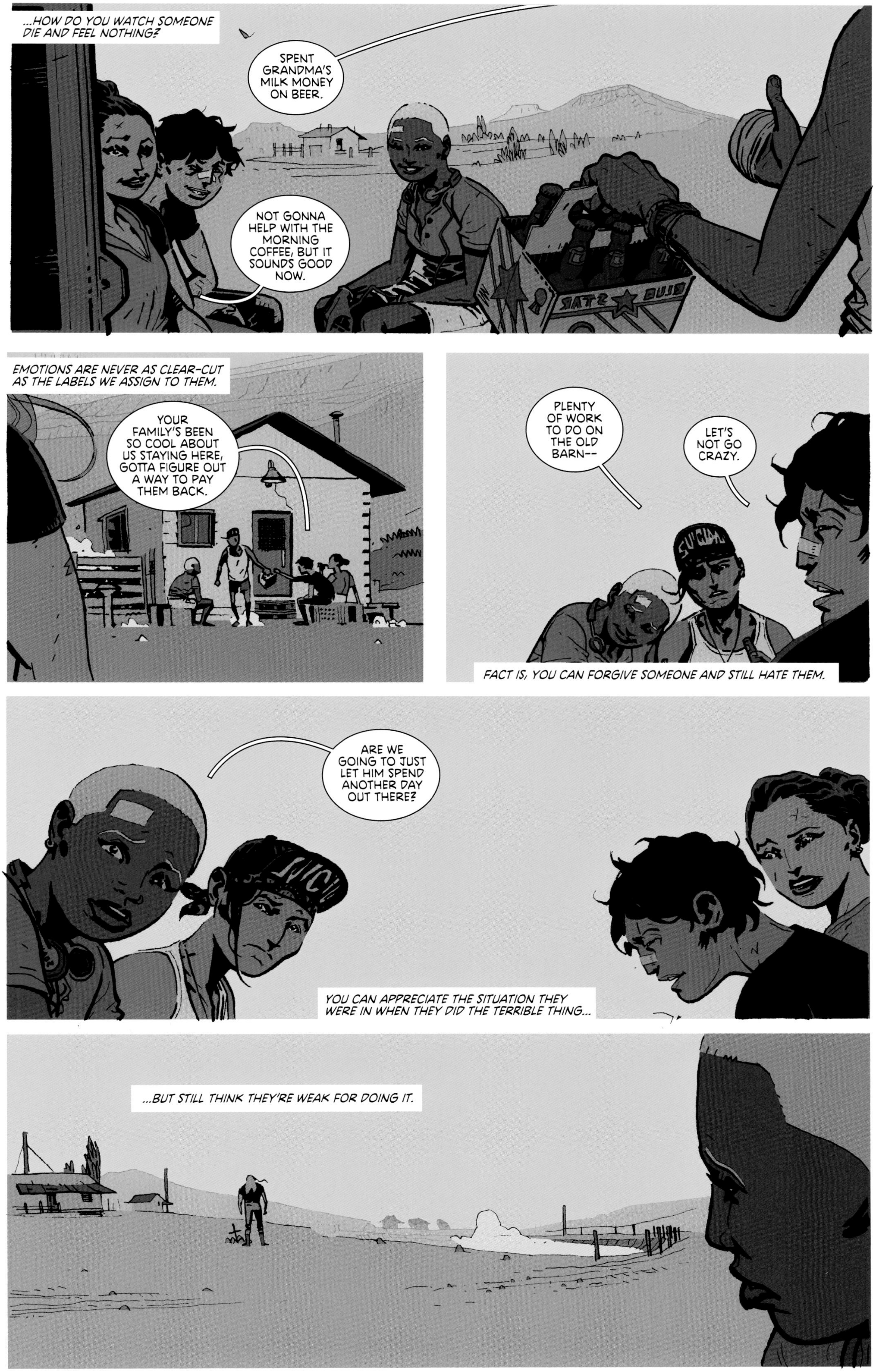
...HOW DO YOU WATCH SOMEONE DIE AND FEEL NOTHING?
SPENT GRANDMA'S MILK MONEY ON BEER.
NOT GONNA HELP WITH THE MORNING COFFEE, BUT IT SOUNDS GOOD NOW.
EMOTIONS ARE NEVER AS CLEAR-CUT AS THE LABELS WE ASSIGN TO THEM.
YOUR FAMILY'S BEEN SO COOL ABOUT US STAYING HERE, GOTTA FIGURE OUT A WAY TO PAY THEM BACK.
PLENTY OF WORK TO DO ON THE OLD BARN--
LET'S NOT GO CRAZY.
FACT IS, YOU CAN FORGIVE SOMEONE AND STILL HATE THEM.
ARE WE GOING TO JUST LET HIM SPEND ANOTHER DAY OUT THERE?
YOU CAN APPRECIATE THE SITUATION THEY WERE IN WHEN THEY DID THE TERRIBLE THING...
...BUT STILL THINK THEY'RE WEAK FOR DOING IT.

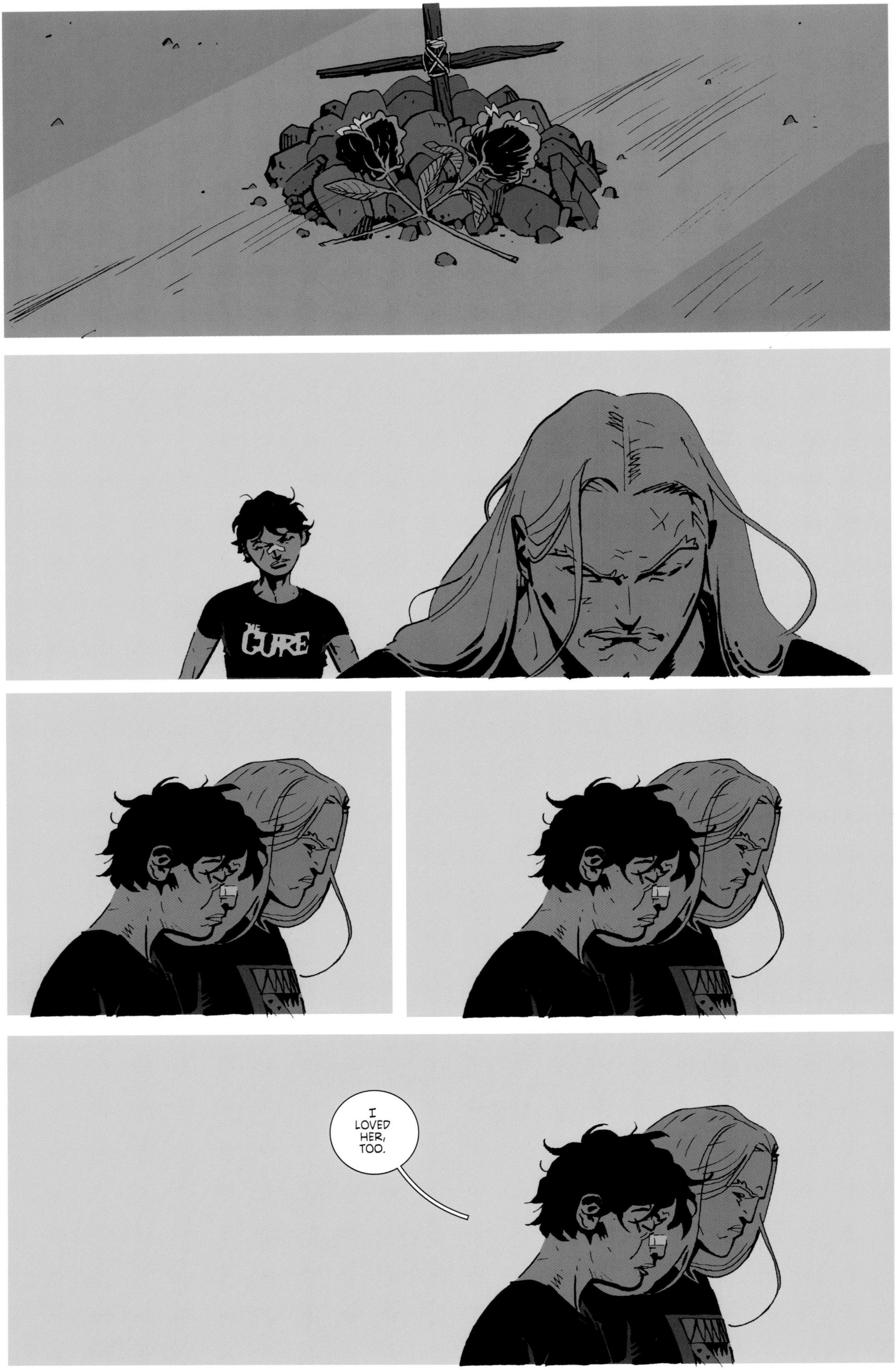
THE CURE
I LOVED HER, TOO.

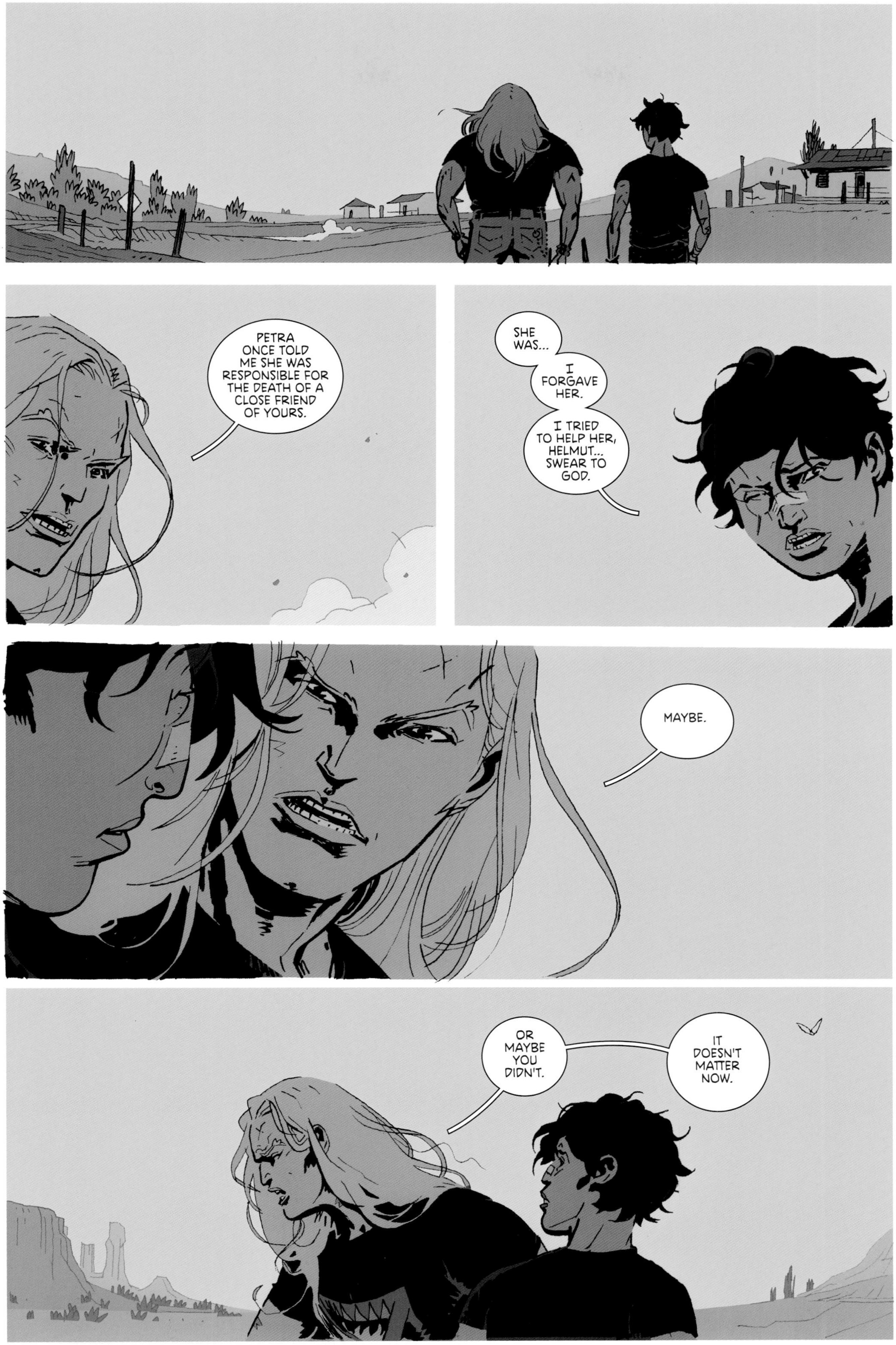
PETRA ONCE TOLD ME SHE WAS RESPONSIBLE FOR THE DEATH OF A CLOSE FRIEND OF YOURS.
SHE WAS...
I FORGAVE HER.
I TRIED TO HELP HER, HELMUT... SWEAR TO GOD.
MAYBE.
OR MAYBE YOU DIDN'T.
IT DOESN'T MATTER NOW.

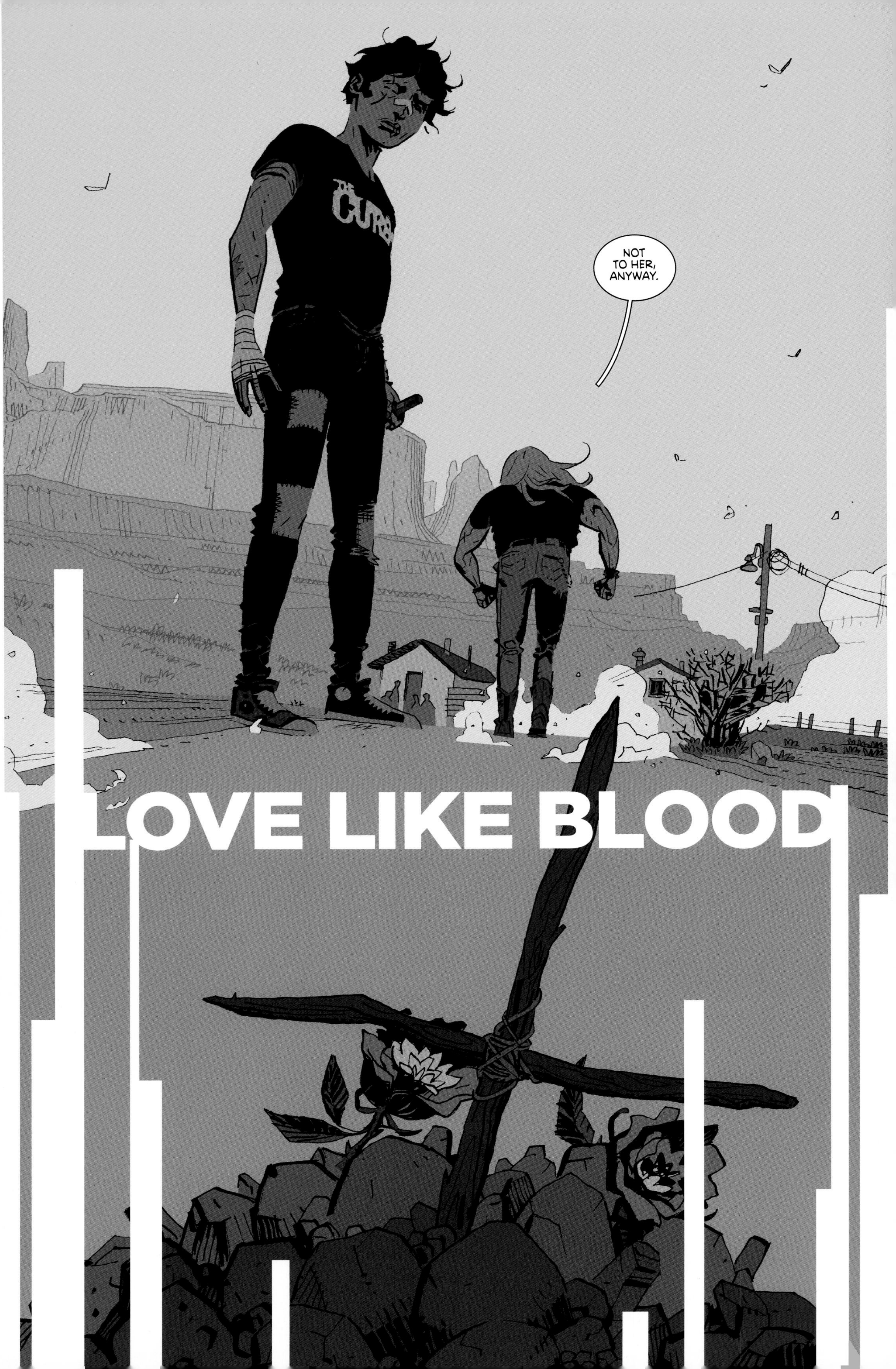
NOT TO HER, ANYWAY.
LOVE LIKE BLOOD

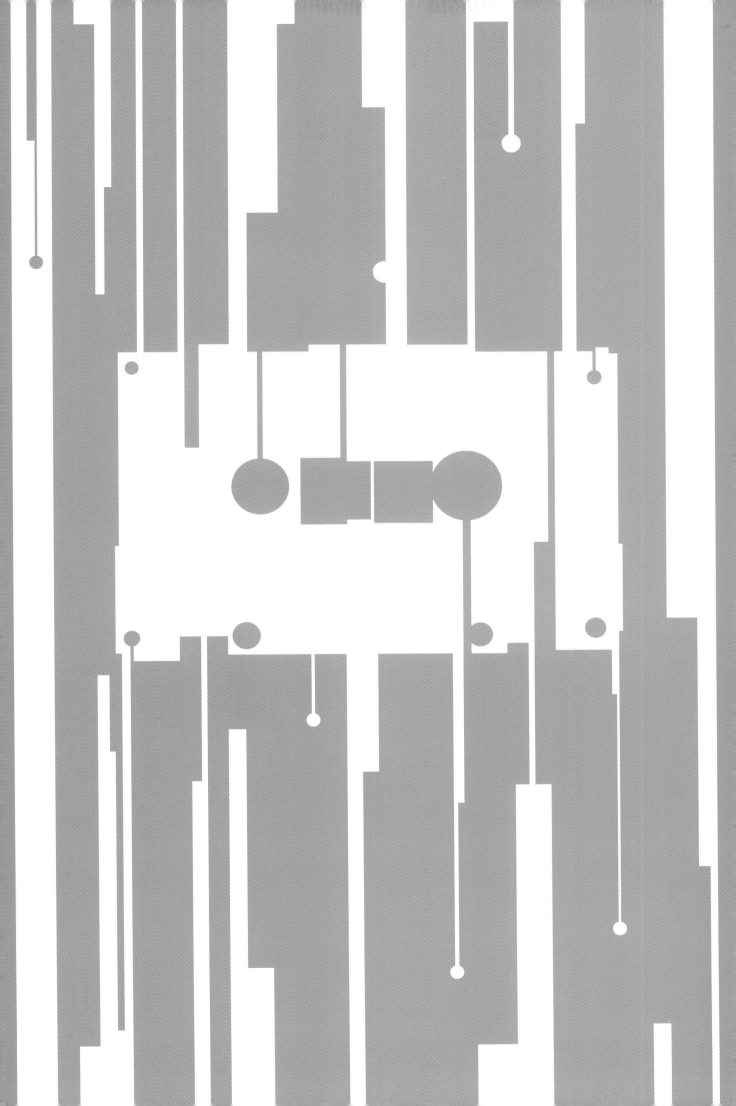

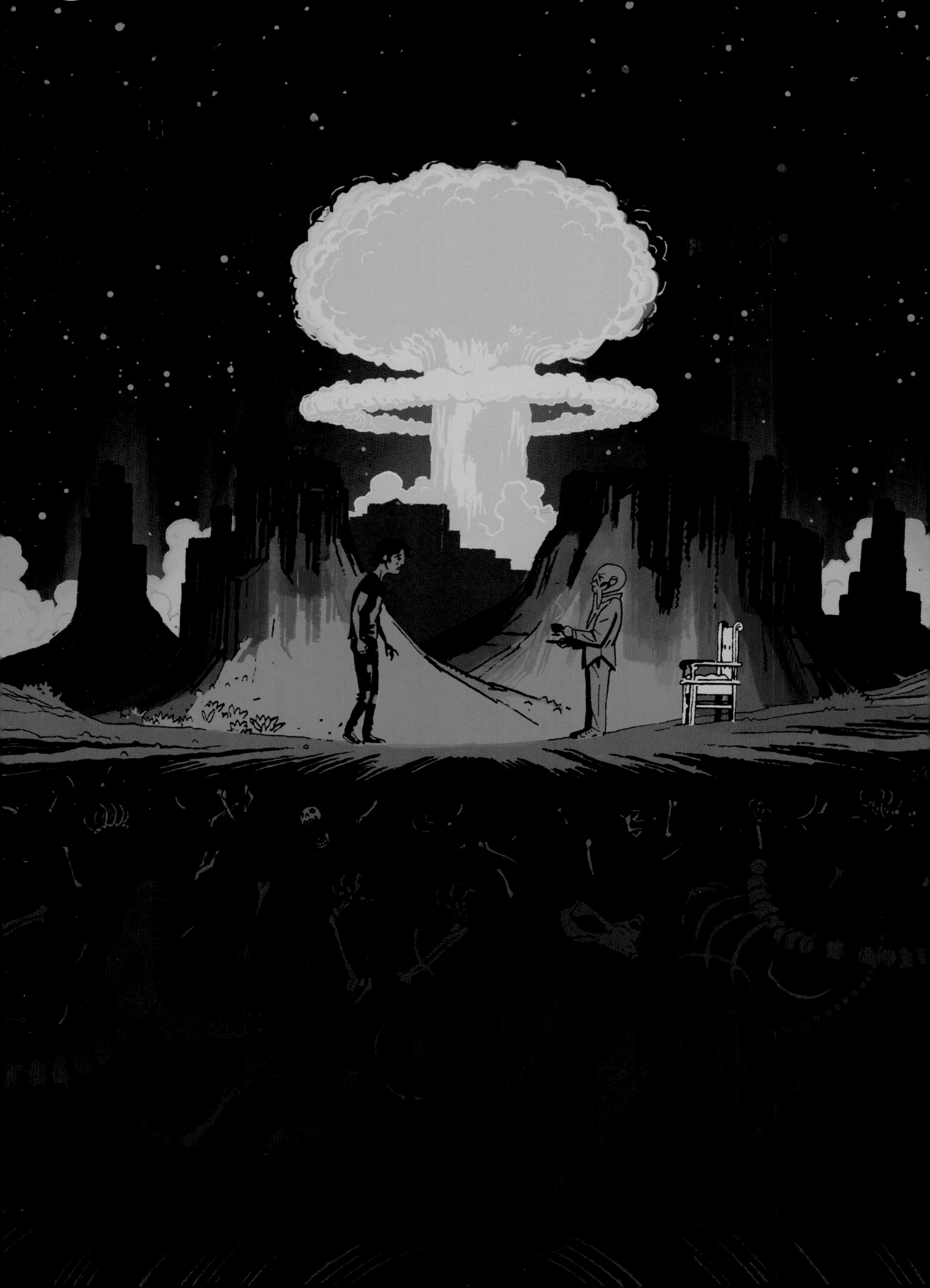

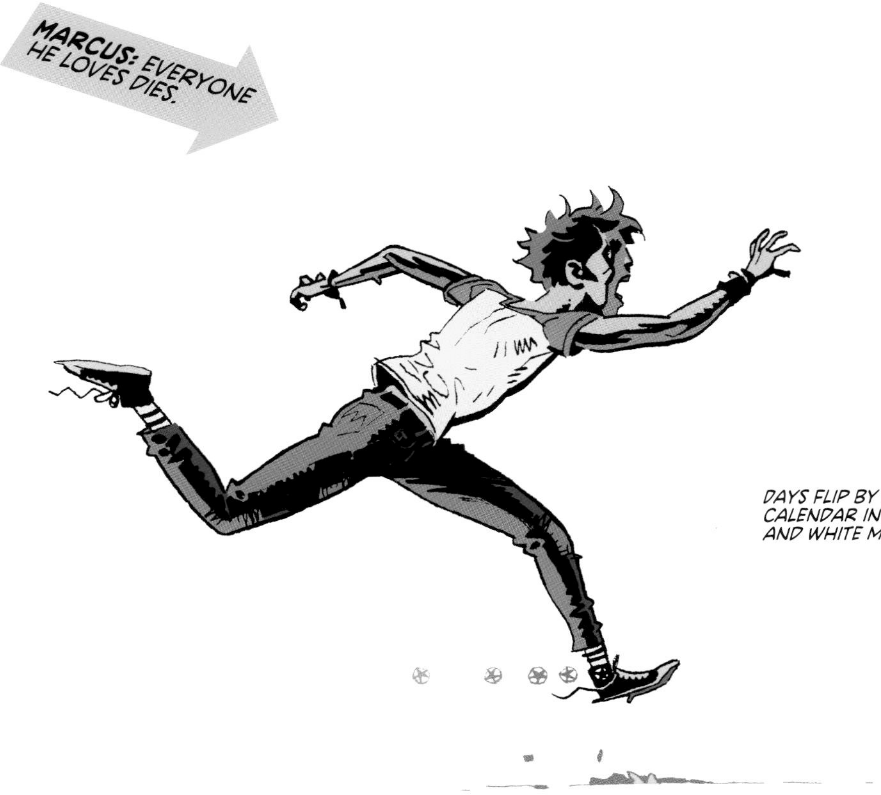
MARCUS: EVERYONE HE LOVES DIES.

DAYS FLIP BY LIKE AN OLD CALENDAR IN A BLACK AND WHITE MONTAGE.

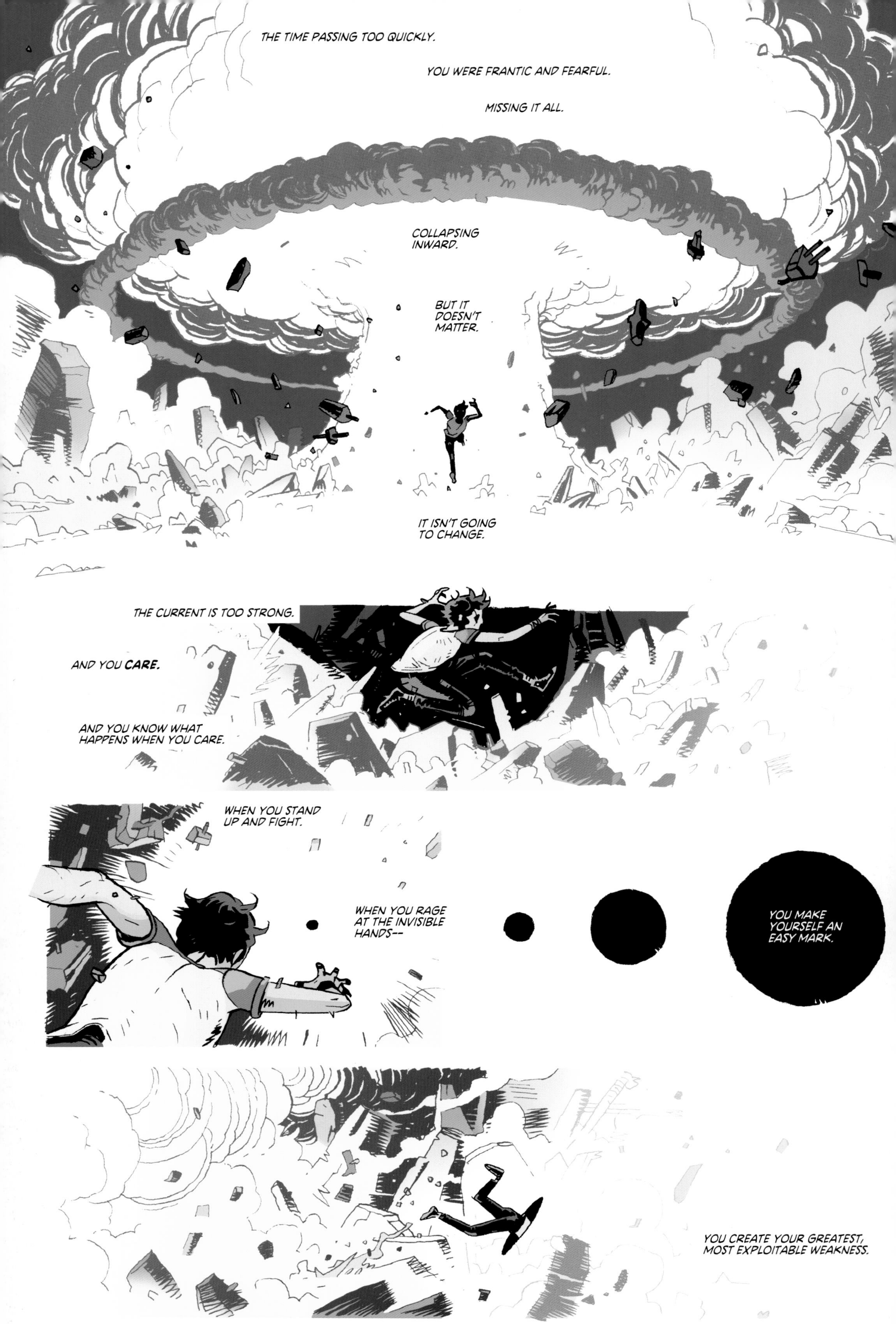
THE TIME PASSING TOO QUICKLY.
YOU WERE FRANTIC AND FEARFUL.
MISSING IT ALL.
COLLAPSING INWARD.
BUT IT DOESN'T MATTER.
IT ISN'T GOING TO CHANGE.
THE CURRENT IS TOO STRONG.
AND YOU **CARE.**
AND YOU KNOW WHAT HAPPENS WHEN YOU CARE.
WHEN YOU STAND UP AND FIGHT.
WHEN YOU RAGE AT THE INVISIBLE HANDS--
YOU MAKE YOURSELF AN EASY MARK.
YOU CREATE YOUR GREATEST, MOST EXPLOITABLE WEAKNESS.

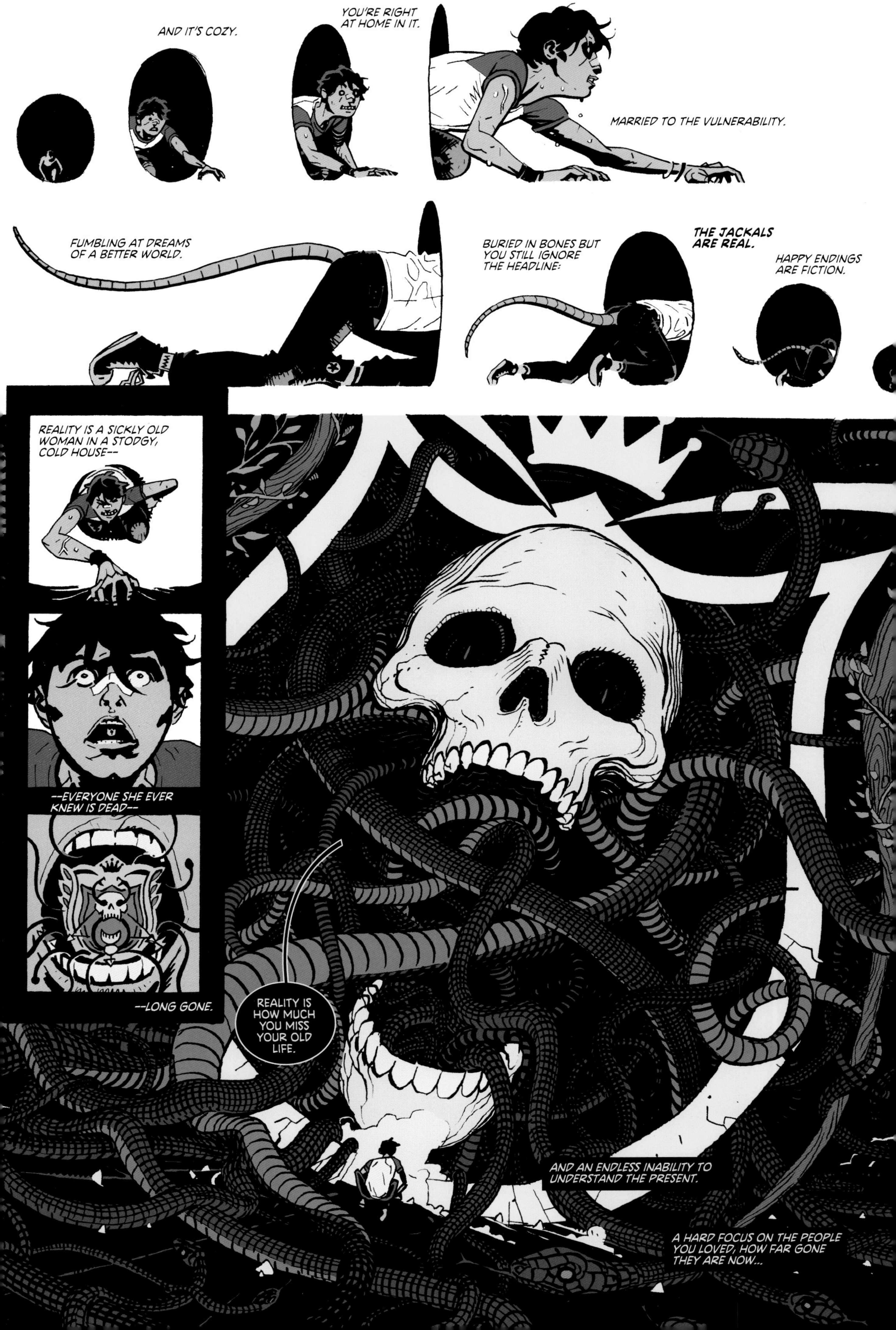

AND IT'S COZY.
YOU'RE RIGHT AT HOME IN IT.
MARRIED TO THE VULNERABILITY.
FUMBLING AT DREAMS OF A BETTER WORLD.
BURIED IN BONES BUT YOU STILL IGNORE THE HEADLINE:
THE JACKALS ARE REAL.
HAPPY ENDINGS ARE FICTION.
REALITY IS A SICKLY OLD WOMAN IN A STODGY, COLD HOUSE--
--EVERYONE SHE EVER KNEW IS DEAD--
--LONG GONE.
REALITY IS HOW MUCH YOU MISS YOUR OLD LIFE.
AND AN ENDLESS INABILITY TO UNDERSTAND THE PRESENT.
A HARD FOCUS ON THE PEOPLE YOU LOVED, HOW FAR GONE THEY ARE NOW...

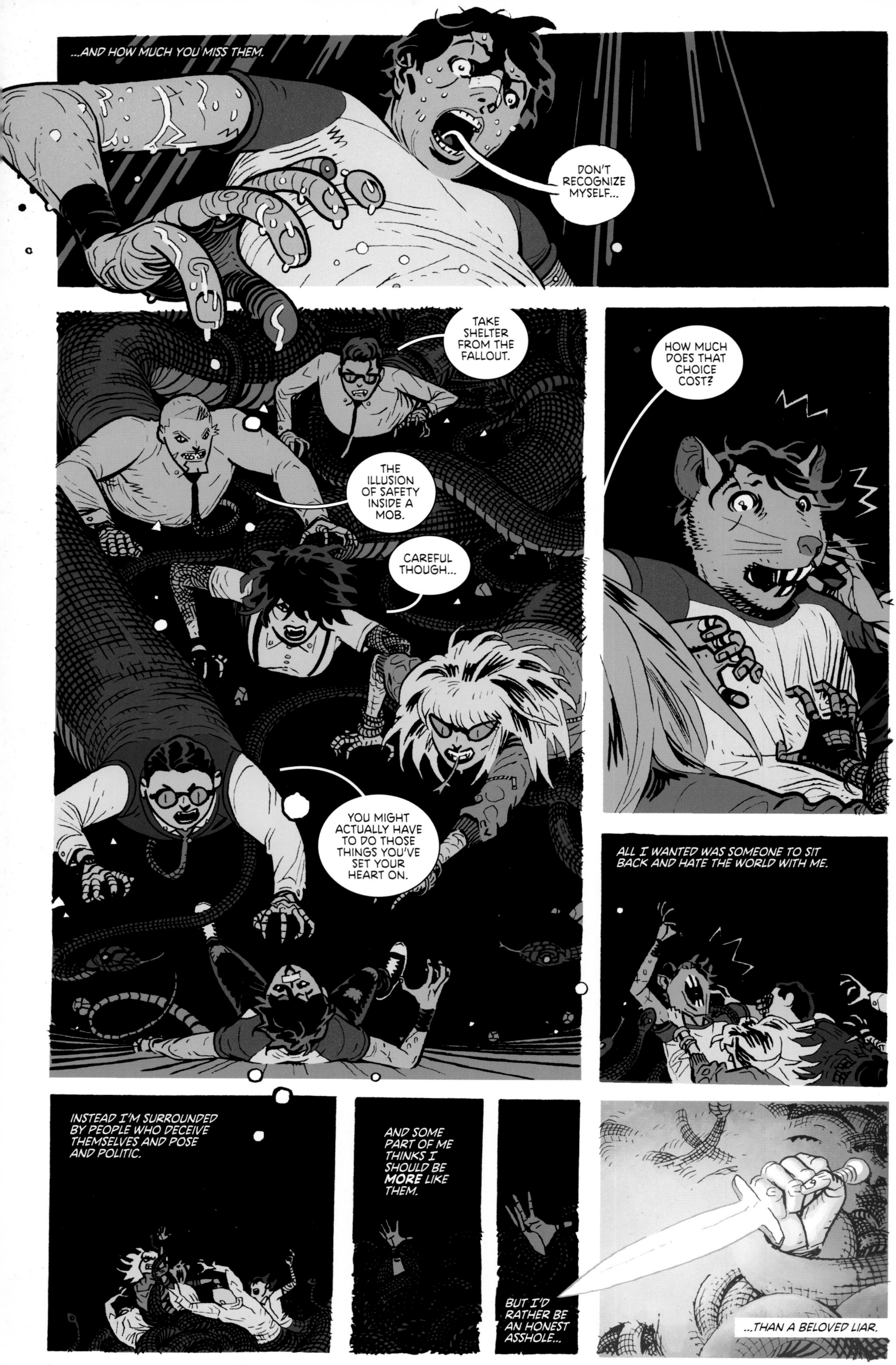
...AND HOW MUCH YOU MISS THEM.
DON'T RECOGNIZE MYSELF...
TAKE SHELTER FROM THE FALLOUT.
THE ILLUSION OF SAFETY INSIDE A MOB.
CAREFUL THOUGH...
YOU MIGHT ACTUALLY HAVE TO DO THOSE THINGS YOU'VE SET YOUR HEART ON.
HOW MUCH DOES THAT CHOICE COST?
ALL I WANTED WAS SOMEONE TO SIT BACK AND HATE THE WORLD WITH ME.
INSTEAD I'M SURROUNDED BY PEOPLE WHO DECEIVE THEMSELVES AND POSE AND POLITIC.
AND SOME PART OF ME THINKS I SHOULD BE MORE LIKE THEM.
BUT I'D RATHER BE AN HONEST ASSHOLE...
...THAN A BELOVED LIAR.

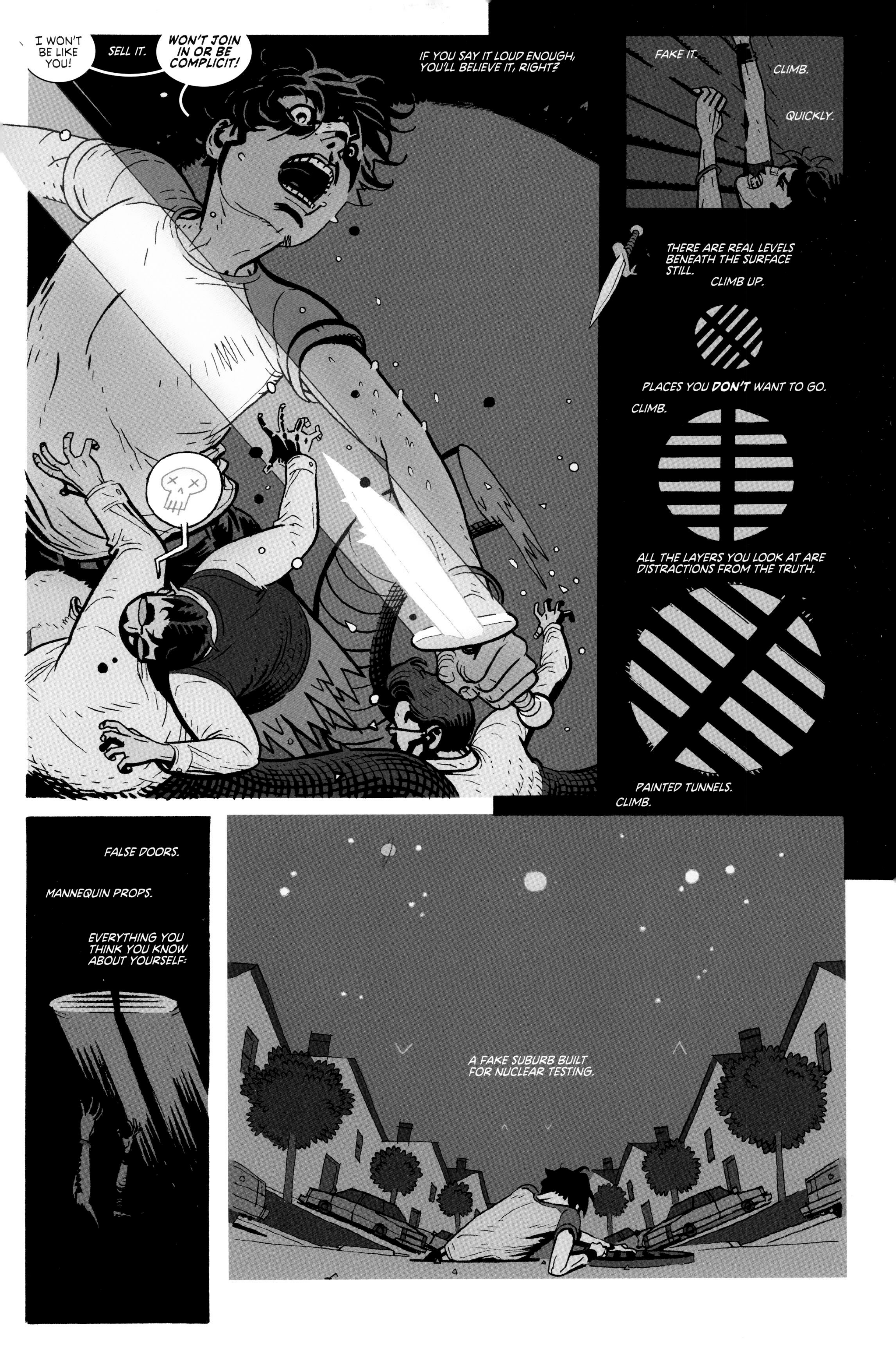
I WON'T BE LIKE YOU!
SELL IT.
WON'T JOIN IN OR BE COMPLICIT!
IF YOU SAY IT LOUD ENOUGH, YOU'LL BELIEVE IT, RIGHT?
FAKE IT.
CLIMB.
QUICKLY.
THERE ARE REAL LEVELS BENEATH THE SURFACE STILL.
CLIMB UP.
PLACES YOU DON'T WANT TO GO.
CLIMB.
ALL THE LAYERS YOU LOOK AT ARE DISTRACTIONS FROM THE TRUTH.
PAINTED TUNNELS.
CLIMB.
FALSE DOORS.
MANNEQUIN PROPS.
EVERYTHING YOU THINK YOU KNOW ABOUT YOURSELF:
A FAKE SUBURB BUILT FOR NUCLEAR TESTING.

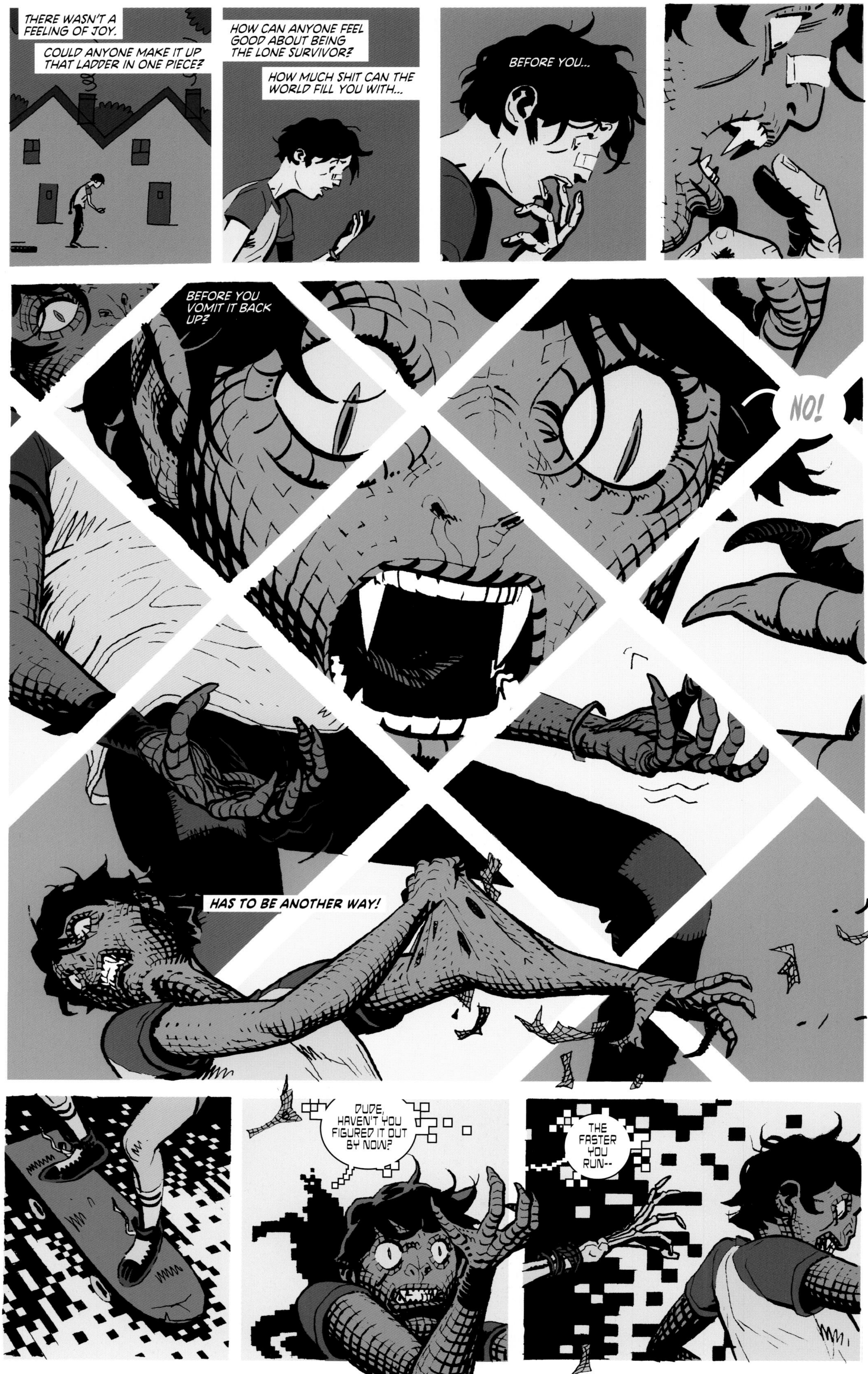
THERE WASN'T A FEELING OF JOY.
COULD ANYONE MAKE IT UP THAT LADDER IN ONE PIECE?
HOW CAN ANYONE FEEL GOOD ABOUT BEING THE LONE SURVIVOR?
HOW MUCH SHIT CAN THE WORLD FILL YOU WITH...
BEFORE YOU...
BEFORE YOU VOMIT IT BACK UP?
NO!
HAS TO BE ANOTHER WAY!
DUDE, HAVEN'T YOU FIGURED IT OUT BY NOW?
THE FASTER YOU RUN--

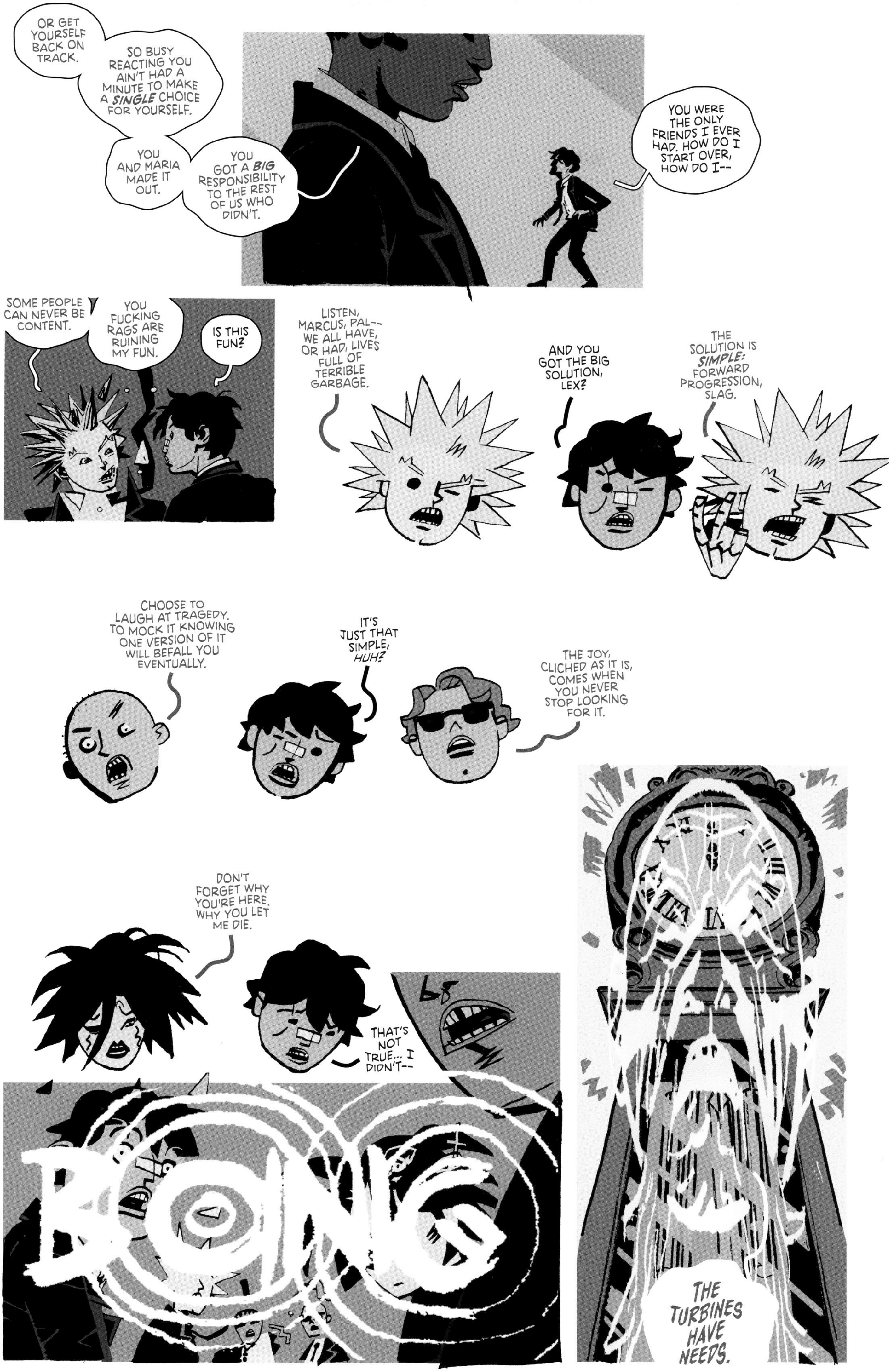
OR GET YOURSELF BACK ON TRACK.
SO BUSY REACTING YOU AIN'T HAD A MINUTE TO MAKE A SINGLE CHOICE FOR YOURSELF.
YOU AND MARIA MADE IT OUT.
YOU GOT A BIG RESPONSIBILITY TO THE REST OF US WHO DIDN'T.
YOU WERE THE ONLY FRIENDS I EVER HAD. HOW DO I START OVER, HOW DO I--
SOME PEOPLE CAN NEVER BE CONTENT.
YOU FUCKING RAGS ARE RUINING MY FUN.
IS THIS FUN?
LISTEN, MARCUS, PAL-- WE ALL HAVE, OR HAD, LIVES FULL OF TERRIBLE GARBAGE.
AND YOU GOT THE BIG SOLUTION, LEX?
THE SOLUTION IS SIMPLE: FORWARD PROGRESSION, SLAG.
CHOOSE TO LAUGH AT TRAGEDY. TO MOCK IT KNOWING ONE VERSION OF IT WILL BEFALL YOU EVENTUALLY.
IT'S JUST THAT SIMPLE, HUH?
THE JOY, CLICHED AS IT IS, COMES WHEN YOU NEVER STOP LOOKING FOR IT.
DON'T FORGET WHY YOU'RE HERE. WHY YOU LET ME DIE.
THAT'S NOT TRUE... I DIDN'T--
BONG
THE TURBINES HAVE NEEDS.

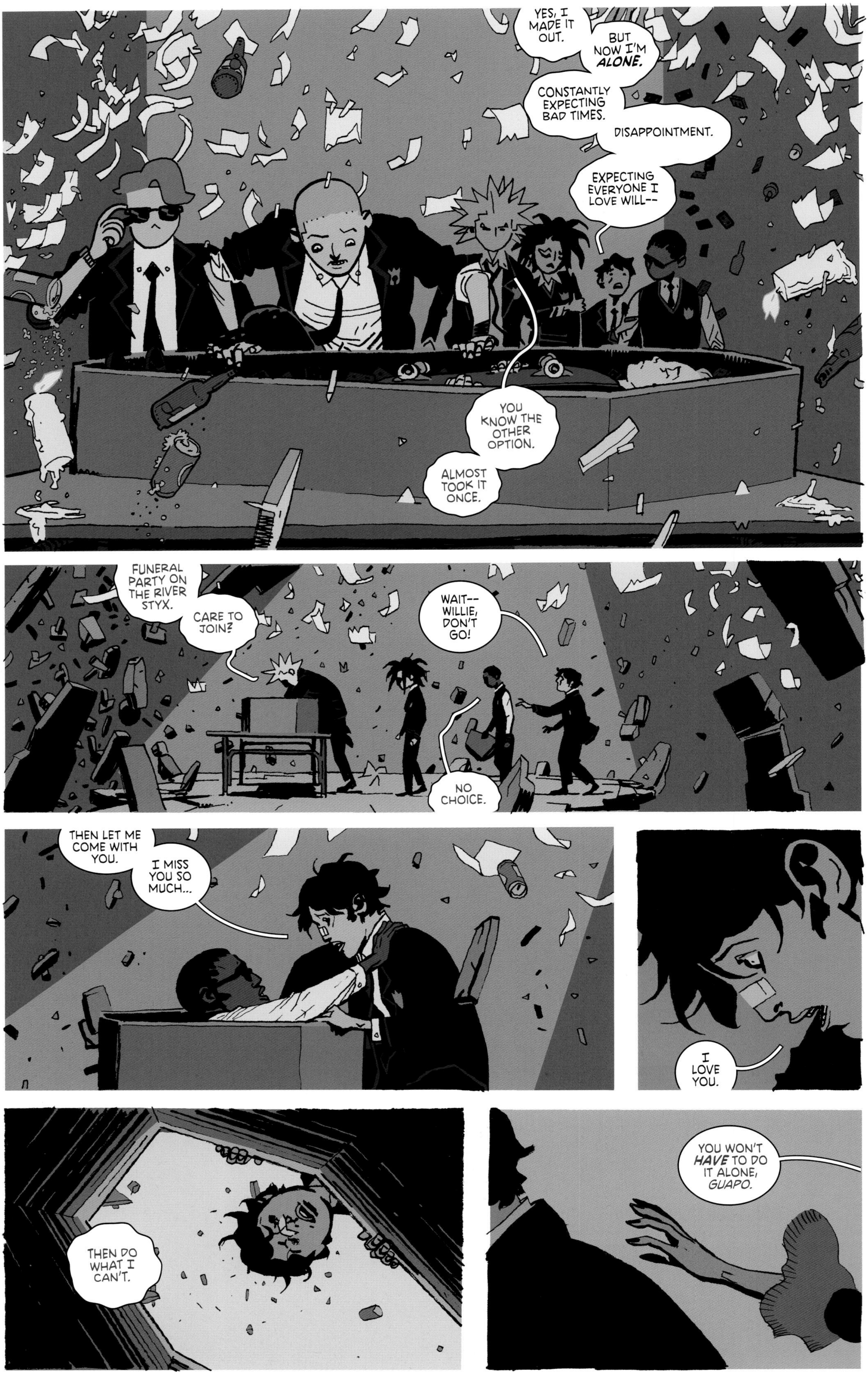
YES, I MADE IT OUT.
BUT NOW I'M ***ALONE.***
CONSTANTLY EXPECTING BAD TIMES.
DISAPPOINTMENT.
EXPECTING EVERYONE I LOVE WILL--
YOU KNOW THE OTHER OPTION.
ALMOST TOOK IT ONCE.
FUNERAL PARTY ON THE RIVER STYX.
CARE TO JOIN?
WAIT-- WILLIE, DON'T GO!
NO CHOICE.
THEN LET ME COME WITH YOU.
I MISS YOU SO MUCH...
I LOVE YOU.
THEN DO WHAT I CAN'T.
YOU WON'T ***HAVE*** TO DO IT ALONE, *GUAPO.*

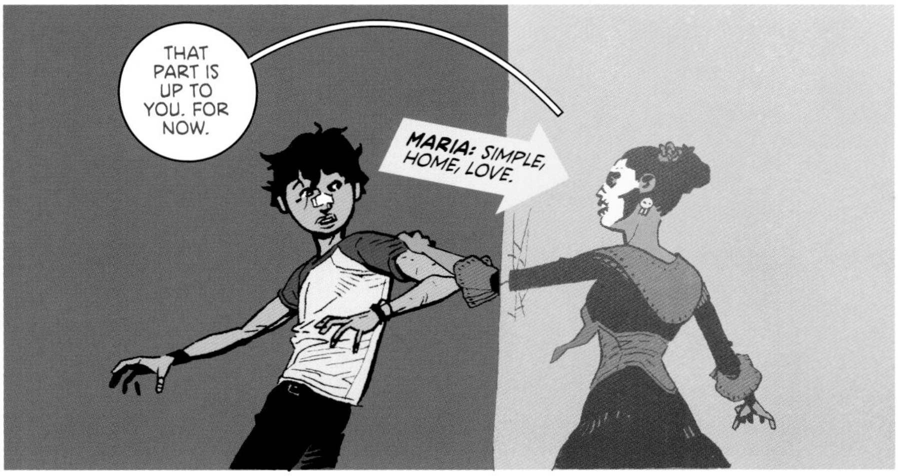
THAT PART IS UP TO YOU. FOR NOW.
MARIA: SIMPLE, HOME, LOVE.

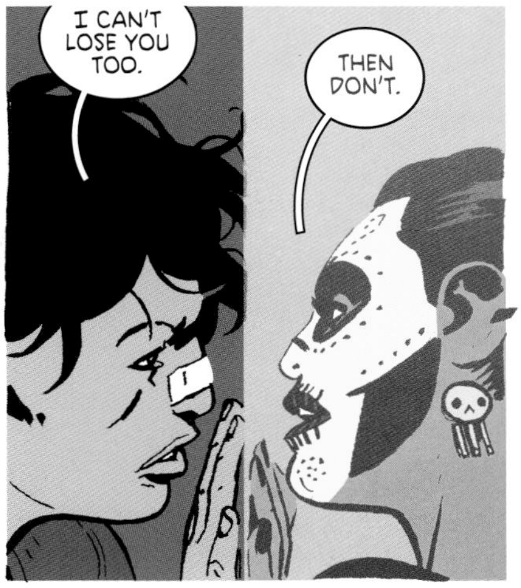
I CAN'T LOSE YOU TOO.
THEN DON'T.

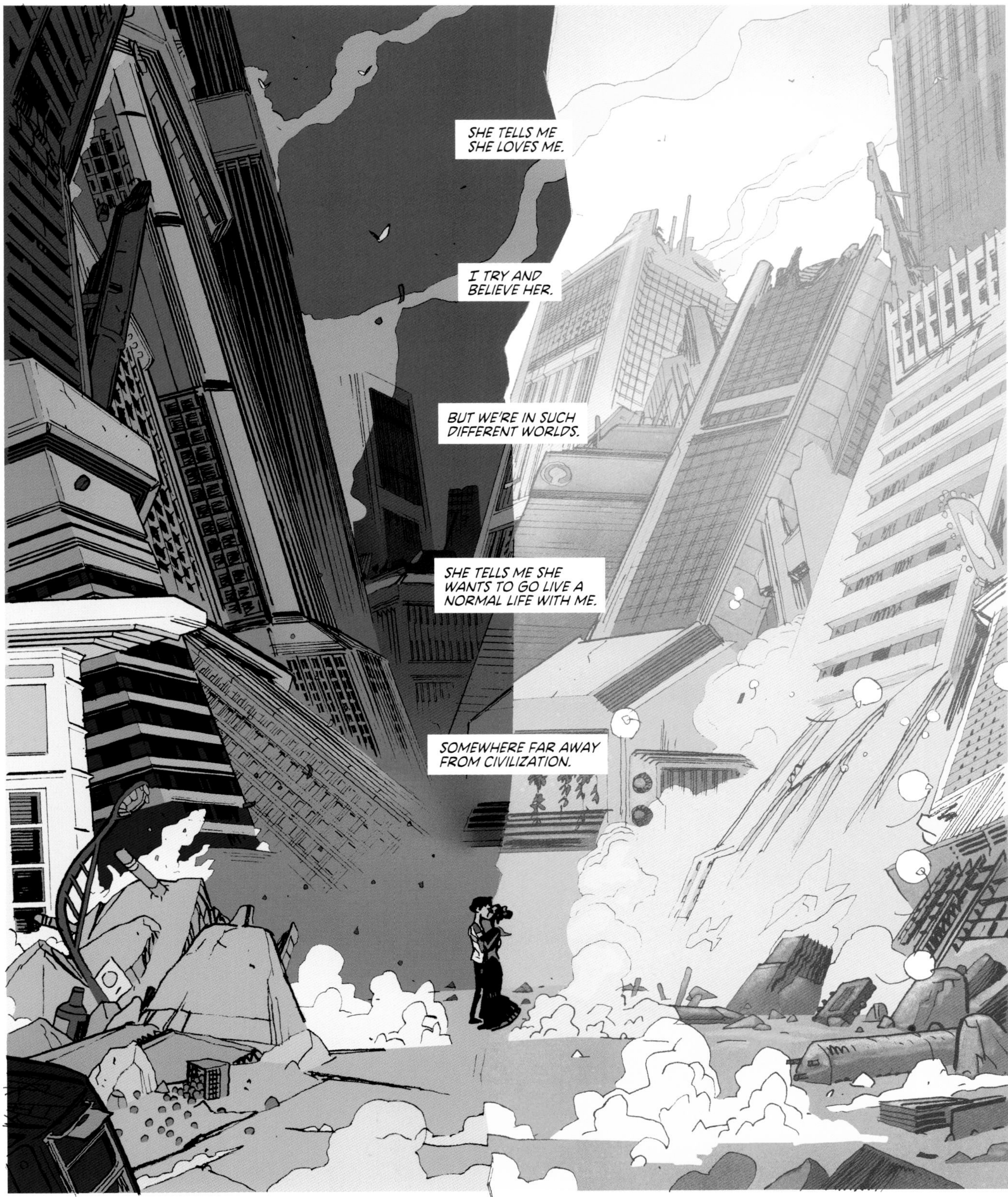
SHE TELLS ME SHE LOVES ME.
I TRY AND BELIEVE HER.
BUT WE'RE IN SUCH DIFFERENT WORLDS.
SHE TELLS ME SHE WANTS TO GO LIVE A NORMAL LIFE WITH ME.
SOMEWHERE FAR AWAY FROM CIVILIZATION.

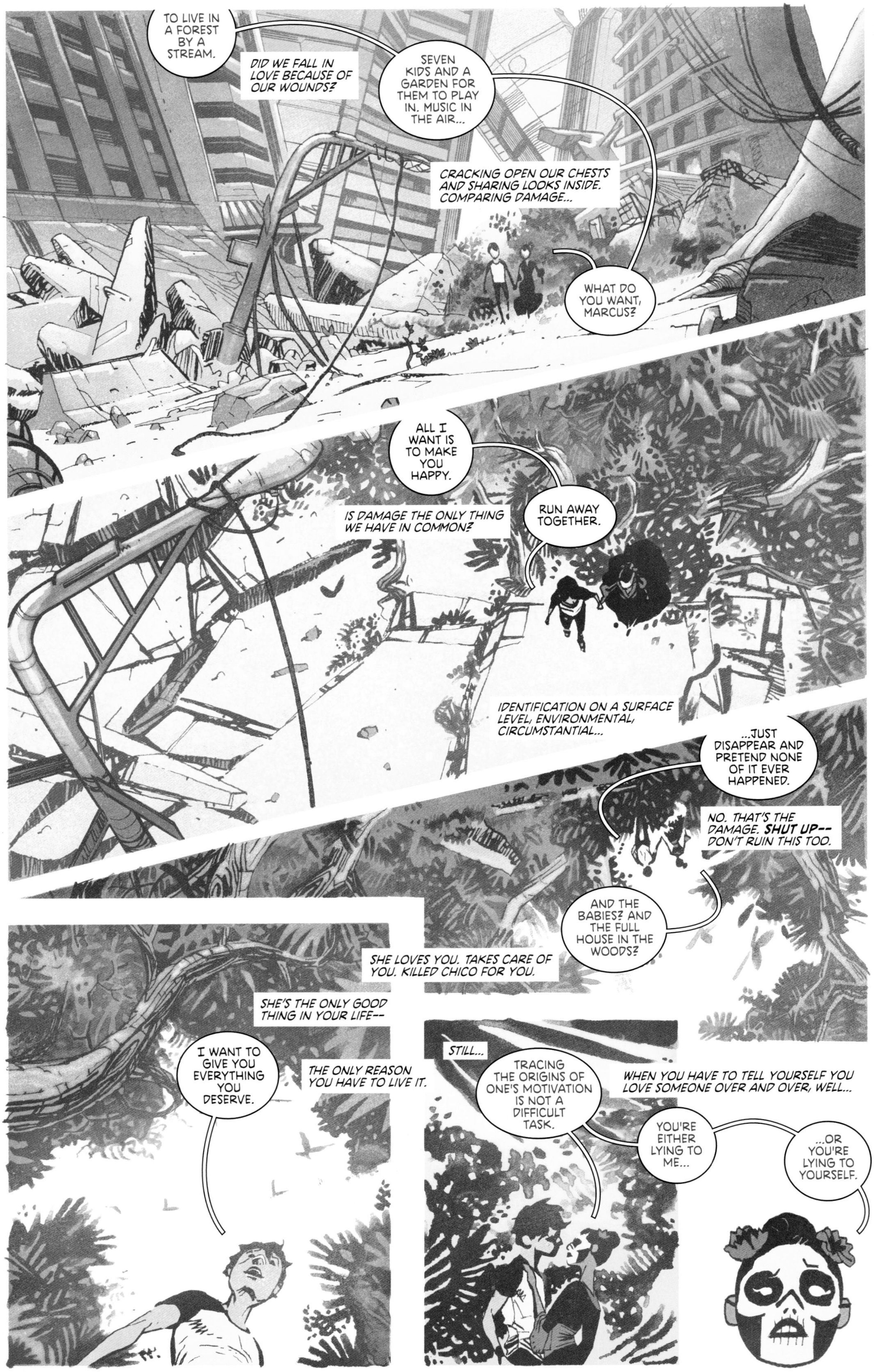
TO LIVE IN A FOREST BY A STREAM.
DID WE FALL IN LOVE BECAUSE OF OUR WOUNDS?
SEVEN KIDS AND A GARDEN FOR THEM TO PLAY IN. MUSIC IN THE AIR...
CRACKING OPEN OUR CHESTS AND SHARING LOOKS INSIDE. COMPARING DAMAGE...
WHAT DO YOU WANT, MARCUS?
ALL I WANT IS TO MAKE YOU HAPPY.
IS DAMAGE THE ONLY THING WE HAVE IN COMMON?
RUN AWAY TOGETHER.
IDENTIFICATION ON A SURFACE LEVEL, ENVIRONMENTAL, CIRCUMSTANTIAL...
...JUST DISAPPEAR AND PRETEND NONE OF IT EVER HAPPENED.
NO. THAT'S THE DAMAGE. SHUT UP-- DON'T RUIN THIS TOO.
AND THE BABIES? AND THE FULL HOUSE IN THE WOODS?
SHE LOVES YOU. TAKES CARE OF YOU. KILLED CHICO FOR YOU.
SHE'S THE ONLY GOOD THING IN YOUR LIFE--
I WANT TO GIVE YOU EVERYTHING YOU DESERVE.
THE ONLY REASON YOU HAVE TO LIVE IT.
STILL...
TRACING THE ORIGINS OF ONE'S MOTIVATION IS NOT A DIFFICULT TASK.
WHEN YOU HAVE TO TELL YOURSELF YOU LOVE SOMEONE OVER AND OVER, WELL...
YOU'RE EITHER LYING TO ME...
...OR YOU'RE LYING TO YOURSELF.

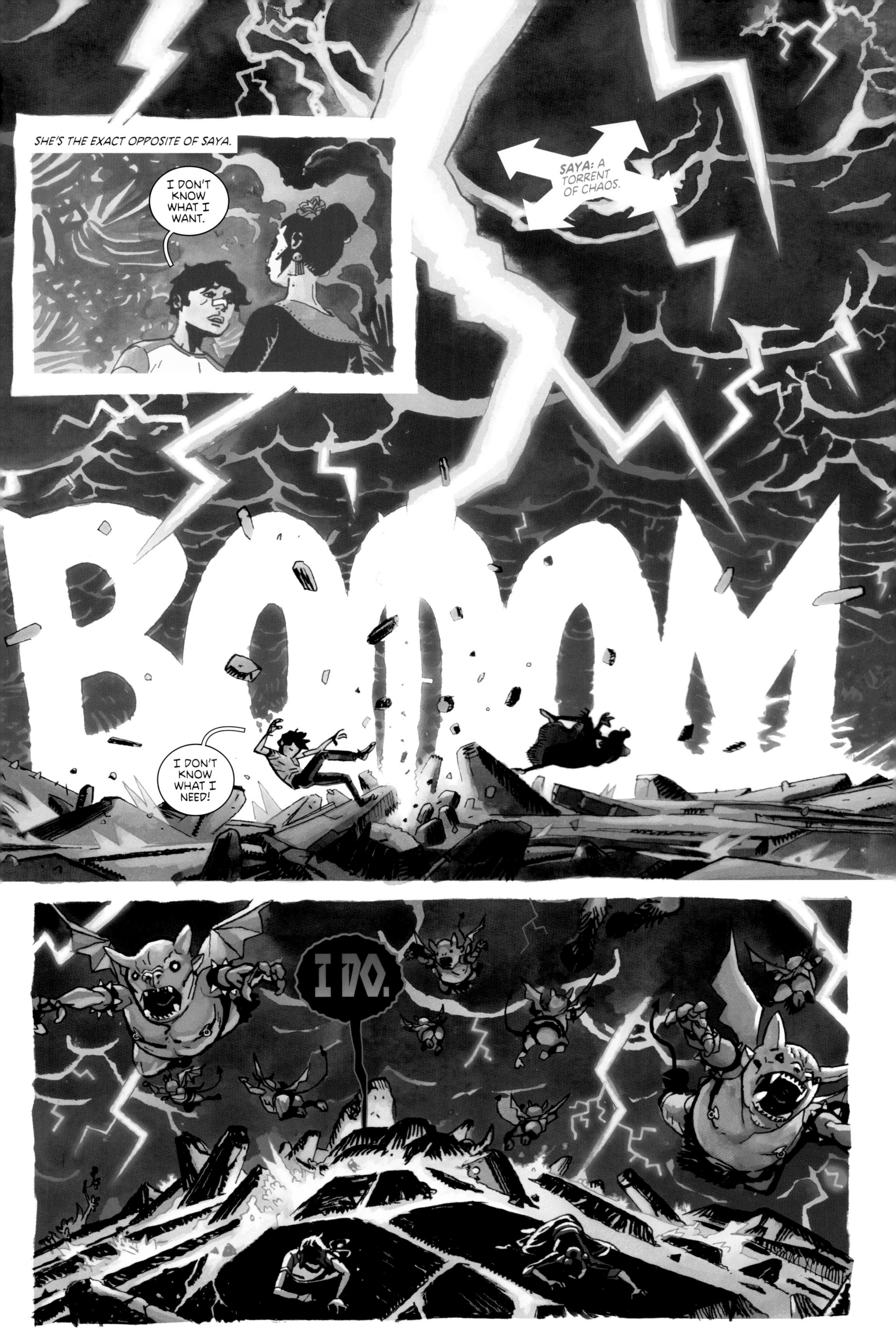
SHE'S THE EXACT OPPOSITE OF SAYA.
I DON'T KNOW WHAT I WANT.
SAYA: A TORRENT OF CHAOS.
BOOOM
I DON'T KNOW WHAT I NEED!
I DO.

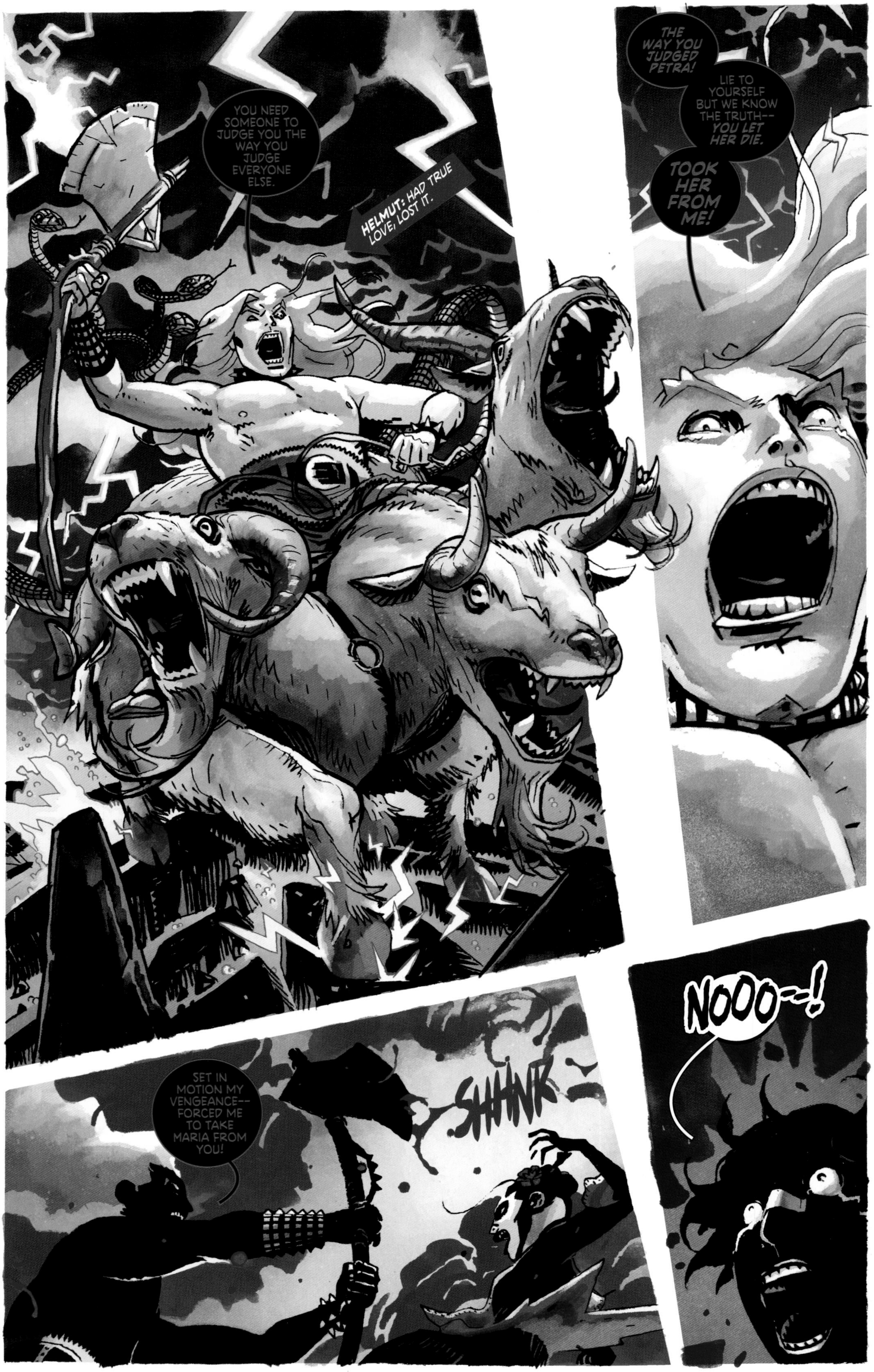
YOU NEED SOMEONE TO JUDGE YOU THE WAY YOU JUDGE EVERYONE ELSE.
HELMUT: HAD TRUE LOVE, LOST IT.
THE WAY YOU JUDGED PETRA!
LIE TO YOURSELF BUT WE KNOW THE TRUTH-- YOU LET HER DIE.
TOOK HER FROM ME!
SET IN MOTION MY VENGEANCE-- FORCED ME TO TAKE MARIA FROM YOU!
SHHNK
NOOO--!

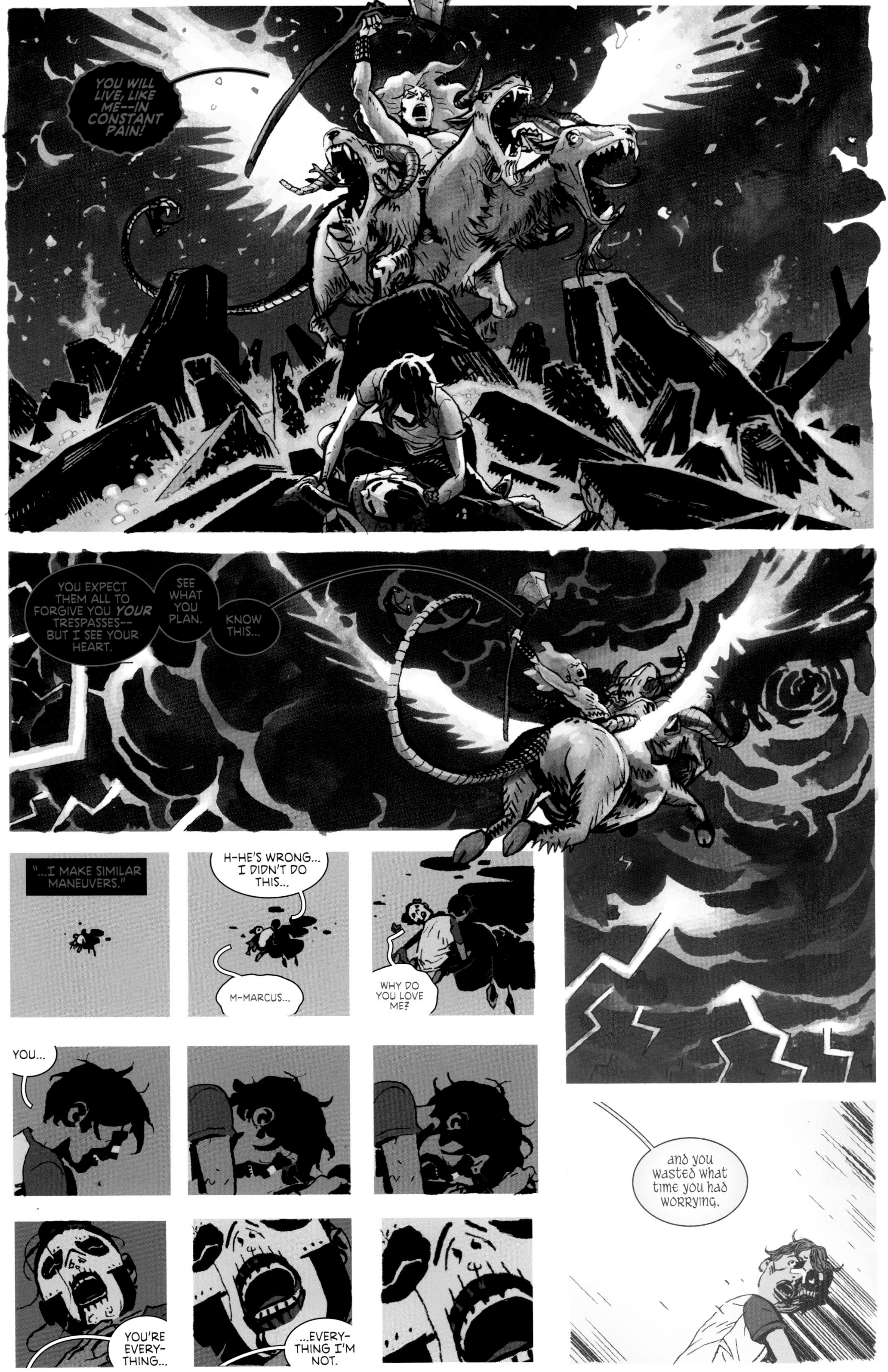
YOU WILL LIVE, LIKE ME--IN CONSTANT PAIN!
YOU EXPECT THEM ALL TO FORGIVE YOU YOUR TRESPASSES-- BUT I SEE YOUR HEART.
SEE WHAT YOU PLAN.
KNOW THIS...
"...I MAKE SIMILAR MANEUVERS."
H-HE'S WRONG... I DIDN'T DO THIS...
M-MARCUS...
WHY DO YOU LOVE ME?
YOU...
YOU'RE EVERY-THING...
...EVERY-THING I'M NOT.
and you wasted what time you had worrying.

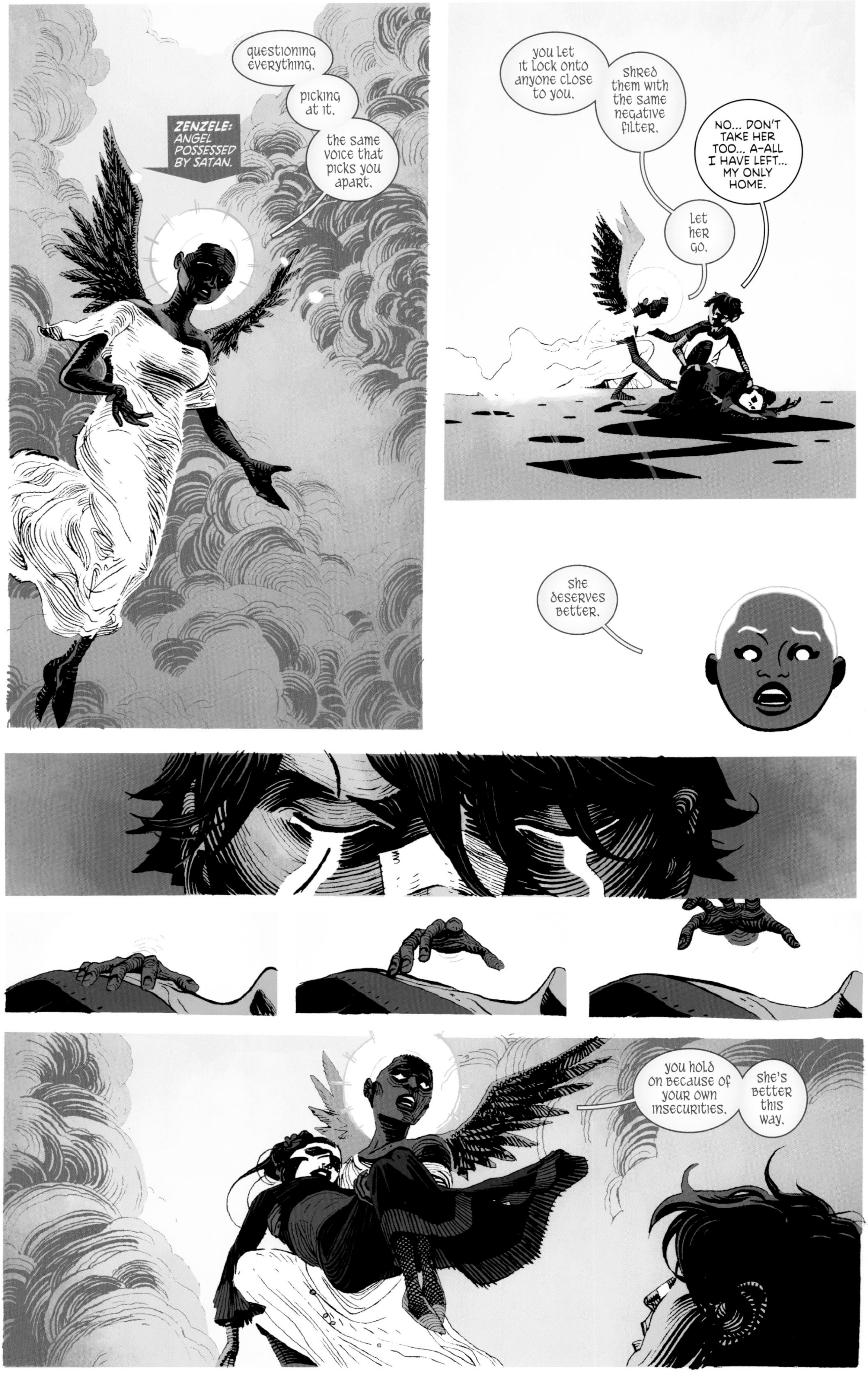
ZENZELE: ANGEL POSSESSED BY SATAN.
questioning everything.
picking at it.
the same voice that picks you apart.
you let it lock onto anyone close to you.
shred them with the same negative filter.
let her go.
NO... DON'T TAKE HER TOO... A-ALL I HAVE LEFT... MY ONLY HOME.
she deserves better.
you hold on because of your own insecurities.
she's better this way.

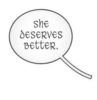

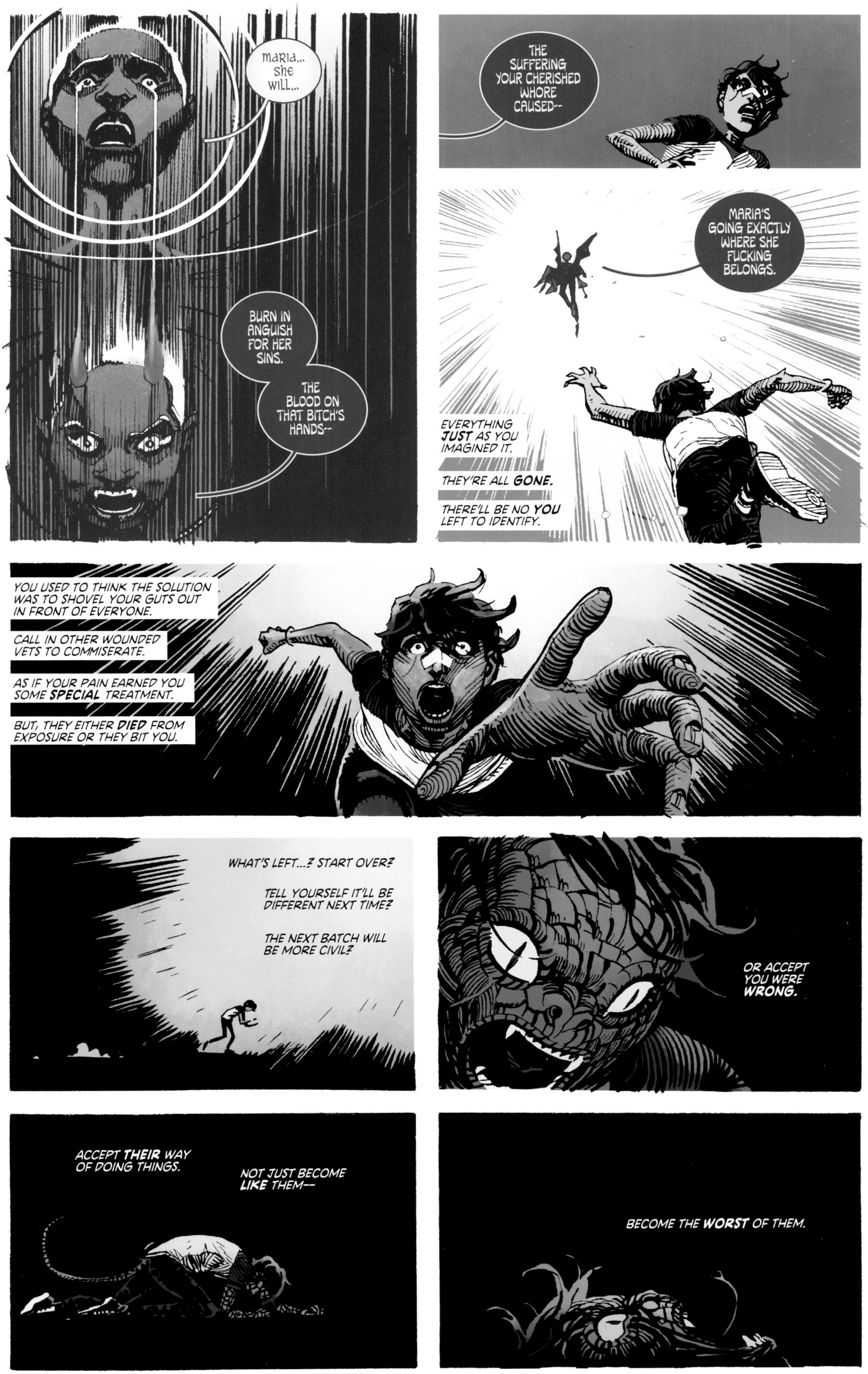

MARIA... SHE WILL...
BURN IN ANGUISH FOR HER SINS.
THE BLOOD ON THAT BITCH'S HANDS--
THE SUFFERING YOUR CHERISHED WHORE CAUSED--
MARIA'S GOING EXACTLY WHERE SHE FUCKING BELONGS.
EVERYTHING JUST AS YOU IMAGINED IT.
THEY'RE ALL GONE.
THERE'LL BE NO YOU LEFT TO IDENTIFY.
YOU USED TO THINK THE SOLUTION WAS TO SHOVEL YOUR GUTS OUT IN FRONT OF EVERYONE.
CALL IN OTHER WOUNDED VETS TO COMMISERATE.
AS IF YOUR PAIN EARNED YOU SOME SPECIAL TREATMENT.
BUT, THEY EITHER DIED FROM EXPOSURE OR THEY BIT YOU.
WHAT'S LEFT...? START OVER?
TELL YOURSELF IT'LL BE DIFFERENT NEXT TIME?
THE NEXT BATCH WILL BE MORE CIVIL?
OR ACCEPT YOU WERE WRONG.
ACCEPT THEIR WAY OF DOING THINGS.
NOT JUST BECOME LIKE THEM--
BECOME THE WORST OF THEM.

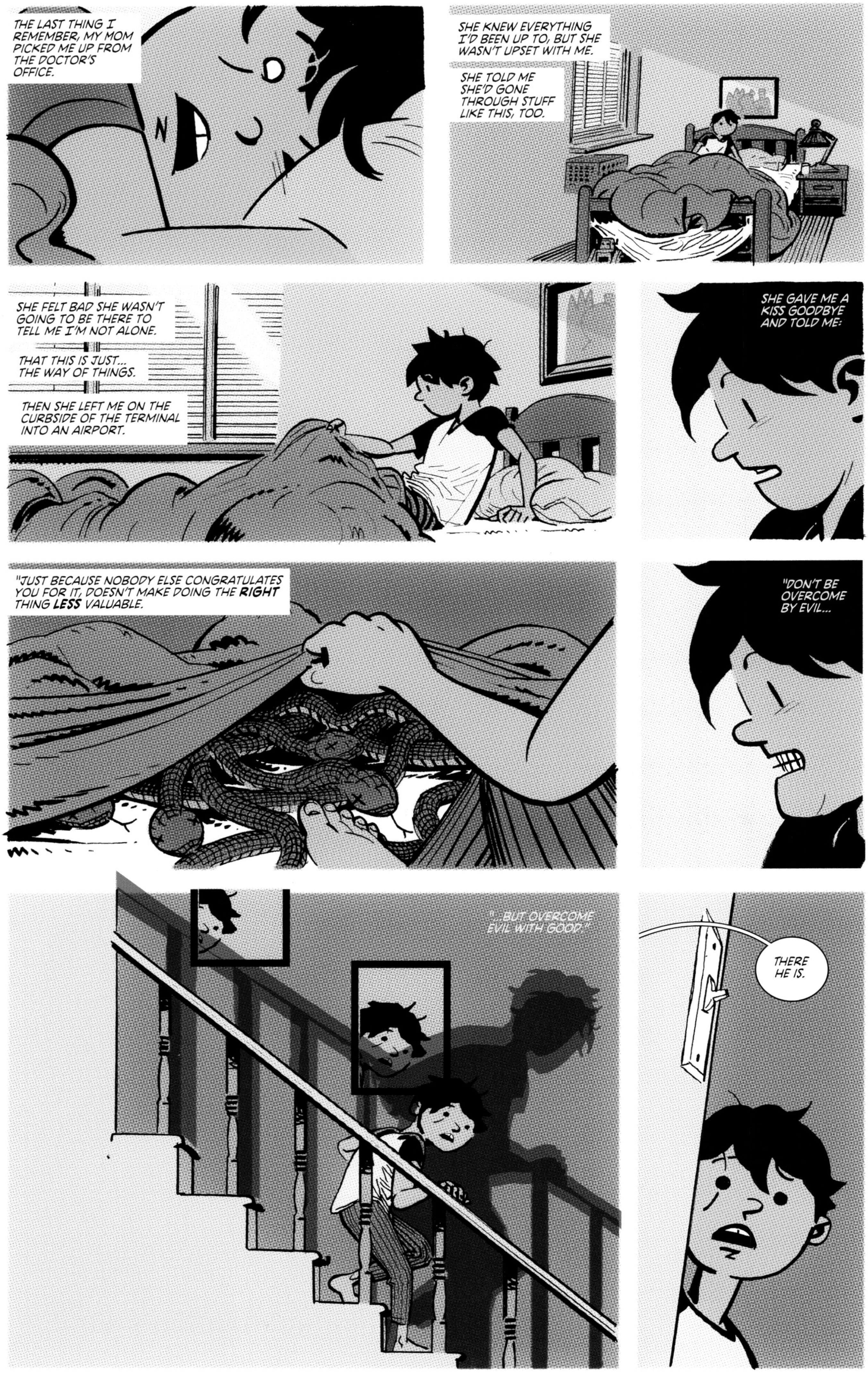
THE LAST THING I REMEMBER, MY MOM PICKED ME UP FROM THE DOCTOR'S OFFICE.
SHE KNEW EVERYTHING I'D BEEN UP TO, BUT SHE WASN'T UPSET WITH ME.
SHE TOLD ME SHE'D GONE THROUGH STUFF LIKE THIS, TOO.
SHE FELT BAD SHE WASN'T GOING TO BE THERE TO TELL ME I'M NOT ALONE.
THAT THIS IS JUST... THE WAY OF THINGS.
THEN SHE LEFT ME ON THE CURBSIDE OF THE TERMINAL INTO AN AIRPORT.
SHE GAVE ME A KISS GOODBYE AND TOLD ME:
"JUST BECAUSE NOBODY ELSE CONGRATULATES YOU FOR IT, DOESN'T MAKE DOING THE **RIGHT** THING **LESS** VALUABLE.
"DON'T BE OVERCOME BY EVIL...
"...BUT OVERCOME EVIL WITH GOOD."
THERE HE IS.

THE OLD KITCHEN.

LIKE LOOKING AT AN OLD PHOTO ALBUM.

HOW'D YOU SLEEP, SWEETHEART? WAS IT ALL ABOUT YOU, YOU, YOU?

HEH... YOUR FOLKS MUST'VE BEEN OVERLY NURTURING BECAUSE YOU HAVE A *TOTALLY* OVERDEVELOPED SENSE OF SELF-WORTH.

MY SWEET, SPECIAL BOY.

AND SEEING YOURSELF IN A PICTURE.

THAT YOU HAVE NO MEMORY OF.

HIT THE PARK TODAY, BUD?

YAY!

WE'LL SEE THE SWANS.

AND WE'VE GOT A *SPECIAL GUEST!*

VOTE FOR ME AND I'LL SET YOU FREE!

≶CANNED APPLAUSE≷

HEARD THROUGH THE LOSER GRAPEVINE THAT MARIA ASKED YOU WHAT YOU WANTED, WHERE YOU SEE YOURSELF IN THE FUTURE.

YOU GAVE HER SOME BULLSHIT ANSWER, THAT'S THE RIGHT MOVE.

IF YOU TELL THE TRUTH YOU'LL *JINX* IT!

NO, MOM--

STOP! DON'T FOLLOW HIM!

THINKING ABOUT THE FUTURE IS A LUXURY FOR RICH KIDS.

BUT WHAT DOES THAT MEAN FOR OUR BABY?

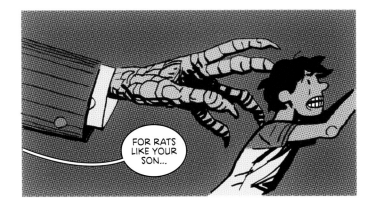

FOR RATS LIKE YOUR SON...

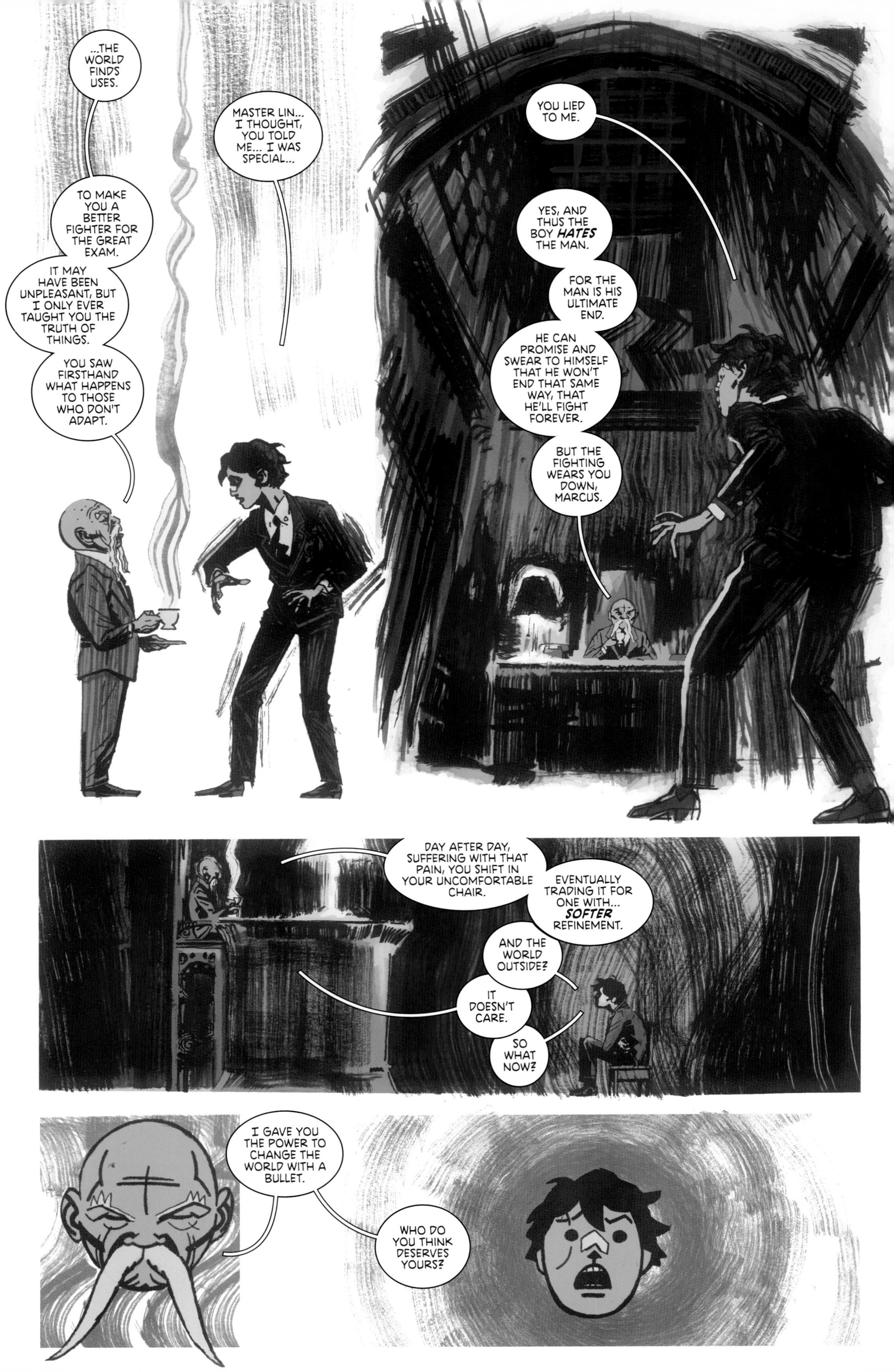
...THE WORLD FINDS USES.
TO MAKE YOU A BETTER FIGHTER FOR THE GREAT EXAM.
IT MAY HAVE BEEN UNPLEASANT, BUT I ONLY EVER TAUGHT YOU THE TRUTH OF THINGS.
YOU SAW FIRSTHAND WHAT HAPPENS TO THOSE WHO DON'T ADAPT.
MASTER LIN... I THOUGHT, YOU TOLD ME... I WAS SPECIAL...
YOU LIED TO ME.
YES, AND THUS THE BOY HATES THE MAN.
FOR THE MAN IS HIS ULTIMATE END.
HE CAN PROMISE AND SWEAR TO HIMSELF THAT HE WON'T END THAT SAME WAY, THAT HE'LL FIGHT FOREVER.
BUT THE FIGHTING WEARS YOU DOWN, MARCUS.
DAY AFTER DAY, SUFFERING WITH THAT PAIN, YOU SHIFT IN YOUR UNCOMFORTABLE CHAIR.
EVENTUALLY TRADING IT FOR ONE WITH... SOFTER REFINEMENT.
AND THE WORLD OUTSIDE?
IT DOESN'T CARE.
SO WHAT NOW?
I GAVE YOU THE POWER TO CHANGE THE WORLD WITH A BULLET.
WHO DO YOU THINK DESERVES YOURS?

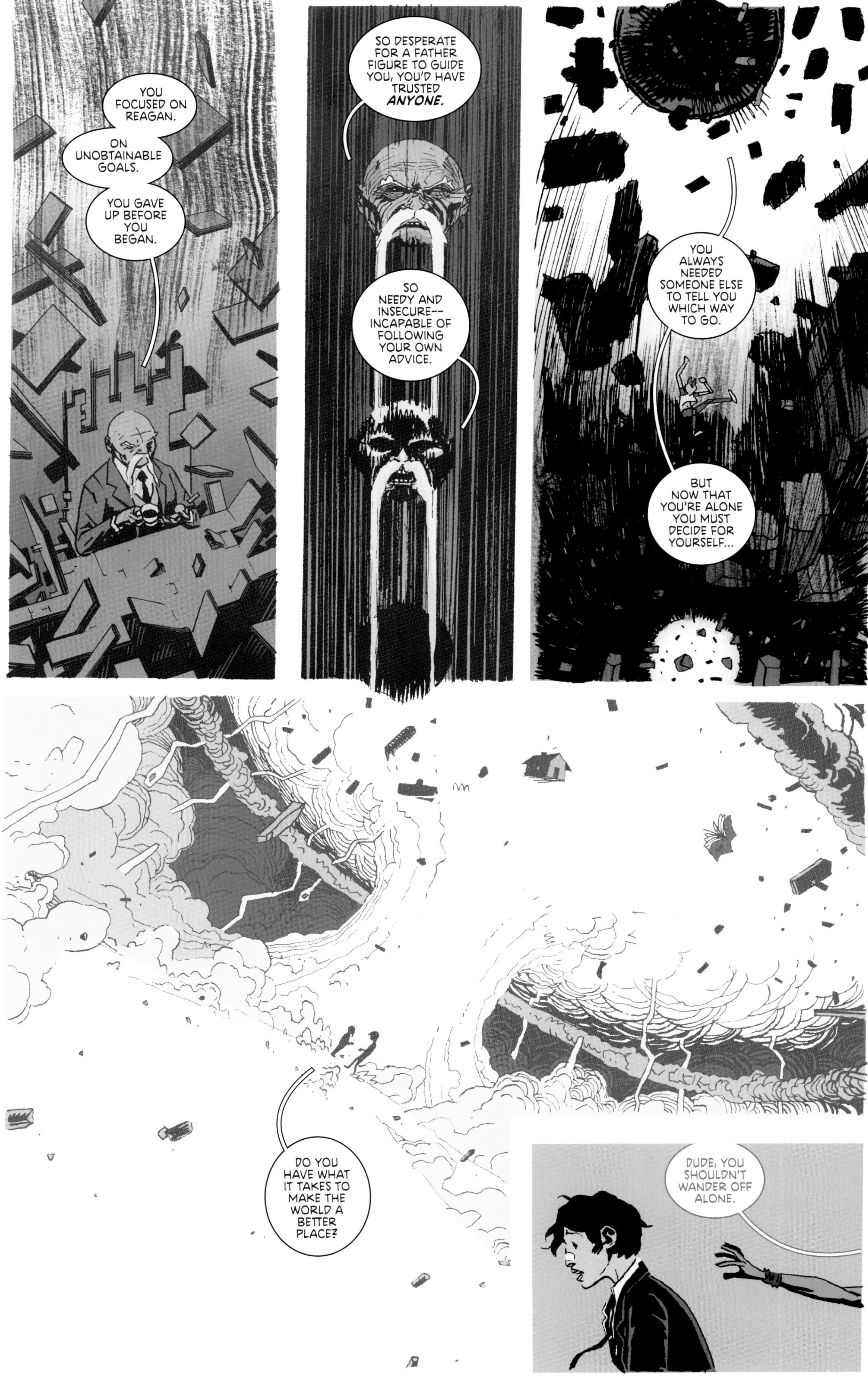
YOU FOCUSED ON REAGAN.
ON UNOBTAINABLE GOALS.
YOU GAVE UP BEFORE YOU BEGAN.
SO DESPERATE FOR A FATHER FIGURE TO GUIDE YOU, YOU'D HAVE TRUSTED *ANYONE.*
SO NEEDY AND INSECURE-- INCAPABLE OF FOLLOWING YOUR OWN ADVICE.
YOU ALWAYS NEEDED SOMEONE ELSE TO TELL YOU WHICH WAY TO GO.
BUT NOW THAT YOU'RE ALONE YOU MUST DECIDE FOR YOURSELF...
DO YOU HAVE WHAT IT TAKES TO MAKE THE WORLD A BETTER PLACE?
DUDE, YOU SHOULDN'T WANDER OFF ALONE.

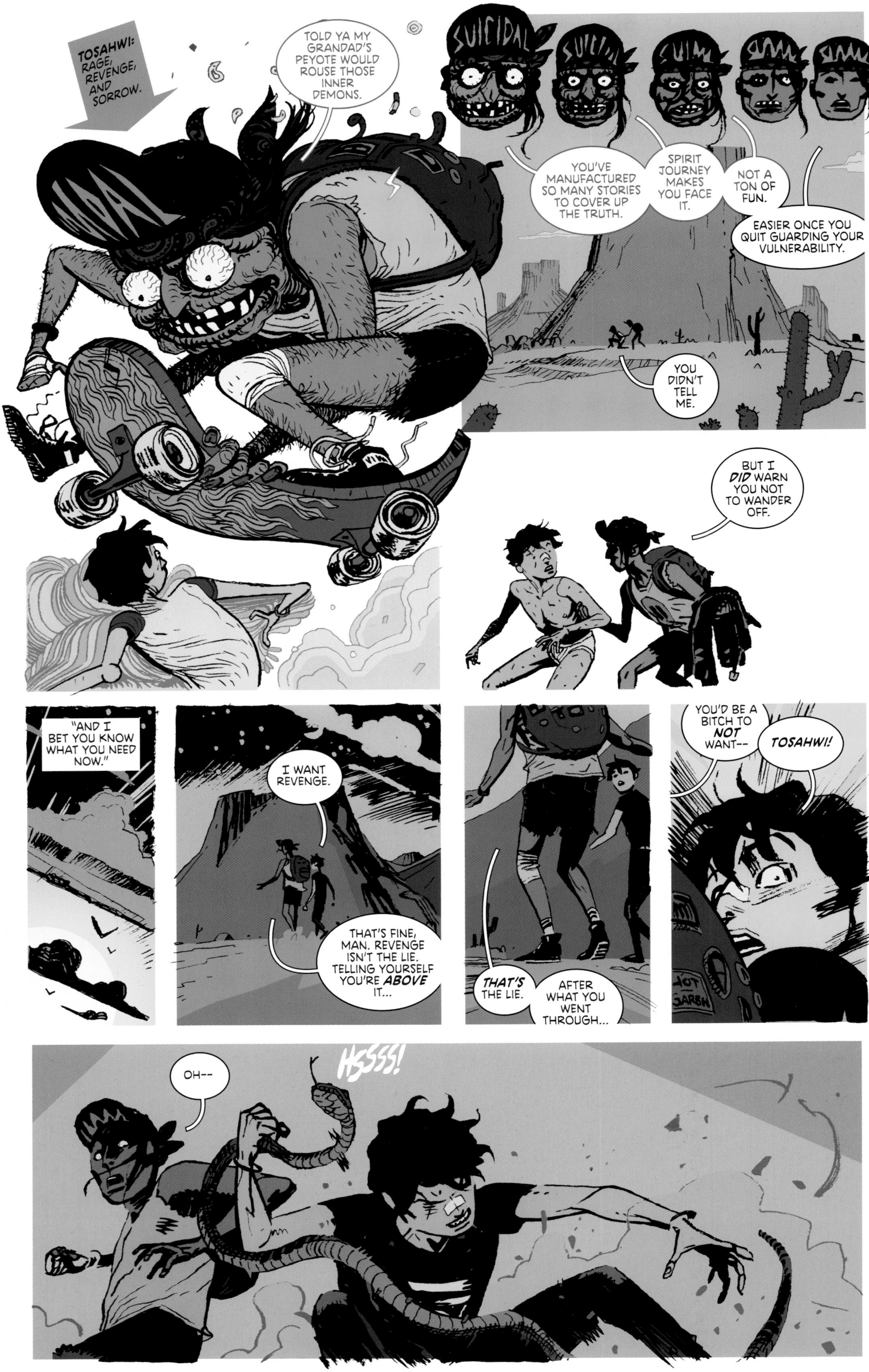
TOSAHWI: RAGE, REVENGE, AND SORROW.
TOLD YA MY GRANDAD'S PEYOTE WOULD ROUSE THOSE INNER DEMONS.
SUICIDAL
YOU'VE MANUFACTURED SO MANY STORIES TO COVER UP THE TRUTH.
SPIRIT JOURNEY MAKES YOU FACE IT.
NOT A TON OF FUN.
EASIER ONCE YOU QUIT GUARDING YOUR VULNERABILITY.
YOU DIDN'T TELL ME.
BUT I DID WARN YOU NOT TO WANDER OFF.
"AND I BET YOU KNOW WHAT YOU NEED NOW."
I WANT REVENGE.
THAT'S FINE, MAN. REVENGE ISN'T THE LIE. TELLING YOURSELF YOU'RE ABOVE IT...
THAT'S THE LIE.
AFTER WHAT YOU WENT THROUGH...
YOU'D BE A BITCH TO NOT WANT--
TOSAHWI!
OH--
HSSSS!

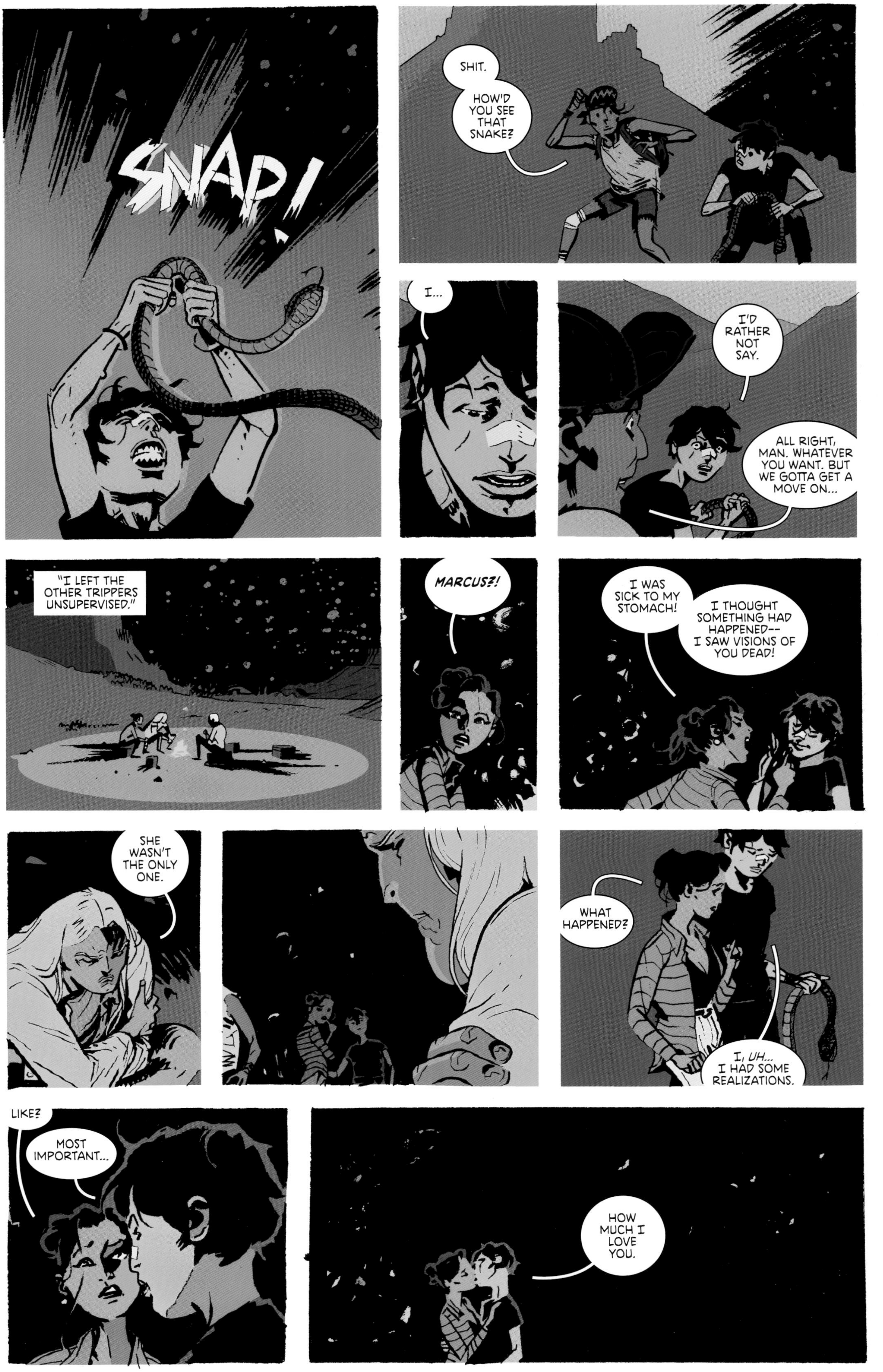

SNAP!
SHIT.
HOW'D YOU SEE THAT SNAKE?
I...
I'D RATHER NOT SAY.
ALL RIGHT, MAN. WHATEVER YOU WANT. BUT WE GOTTA GET A MOVE ON...
"I LEFT THE OTHER TRIPPERS UNSUPERVISED."
MARCUS?!
I WAS SICK TO MY STOMACH!
I THOUGHT SOMETHING HAD HAPPENED-- I SAW VISIONS OF YOU DEAD!
SHE WASN'T THE ONLY ONE.
WHAT HAPPENED?
I, UH... I HAD SOME REALIZATIONS.
LIKE?
MOST IMPORTANT...
HOW MUCH I LOVE YOU.

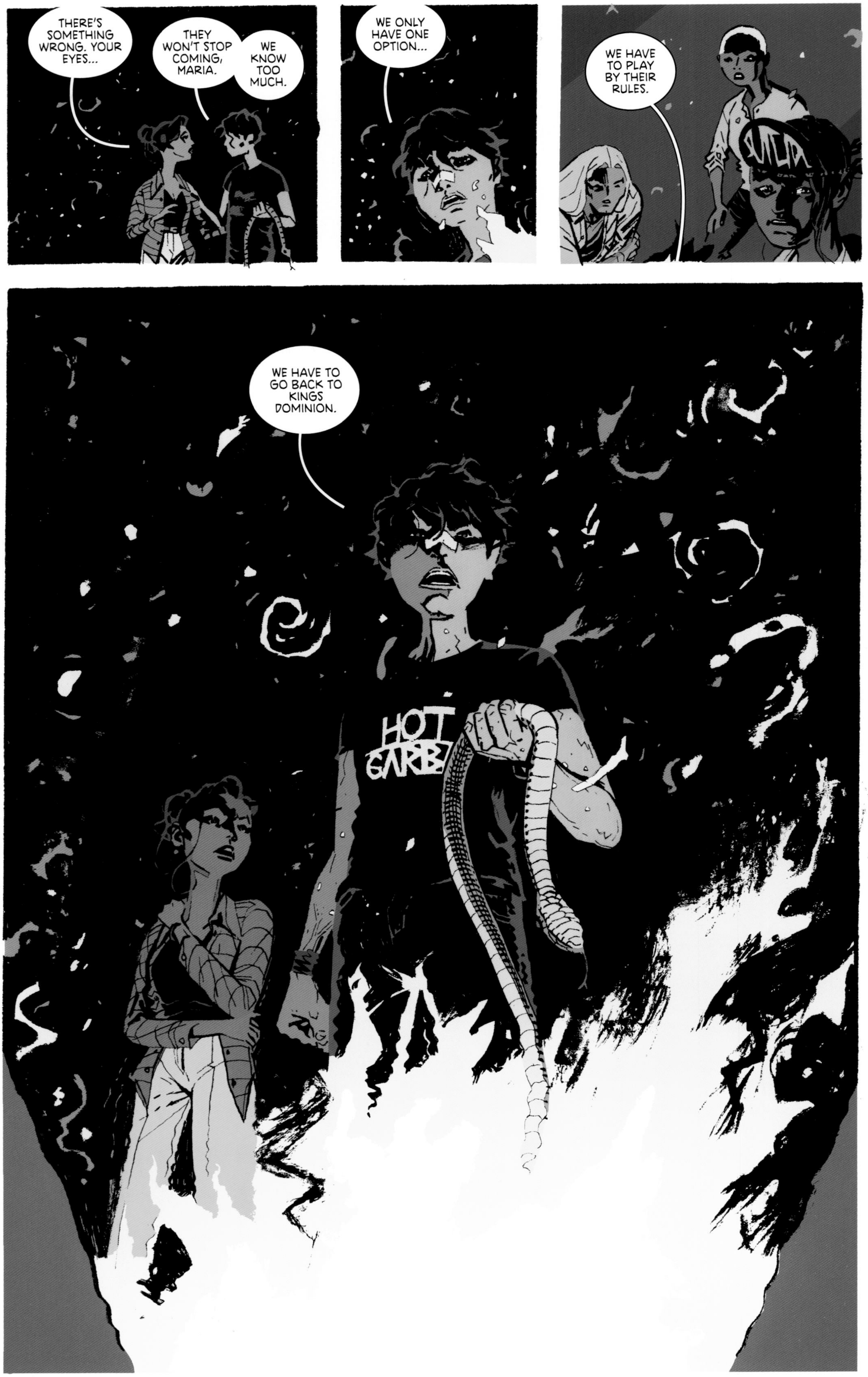
THERE'S SOMETHING WRONG. YOUR EYES...
THEY WON'T STOP COMING, MARIA.
WE KNOW TOO MUCH.
WE ONLY HAVE ONE OPTION...
WE HAVE TO PLAY BY THEIR RULES.
WE HAVE TO GO BACK TO KINGS DOMINION.
HOT GARB

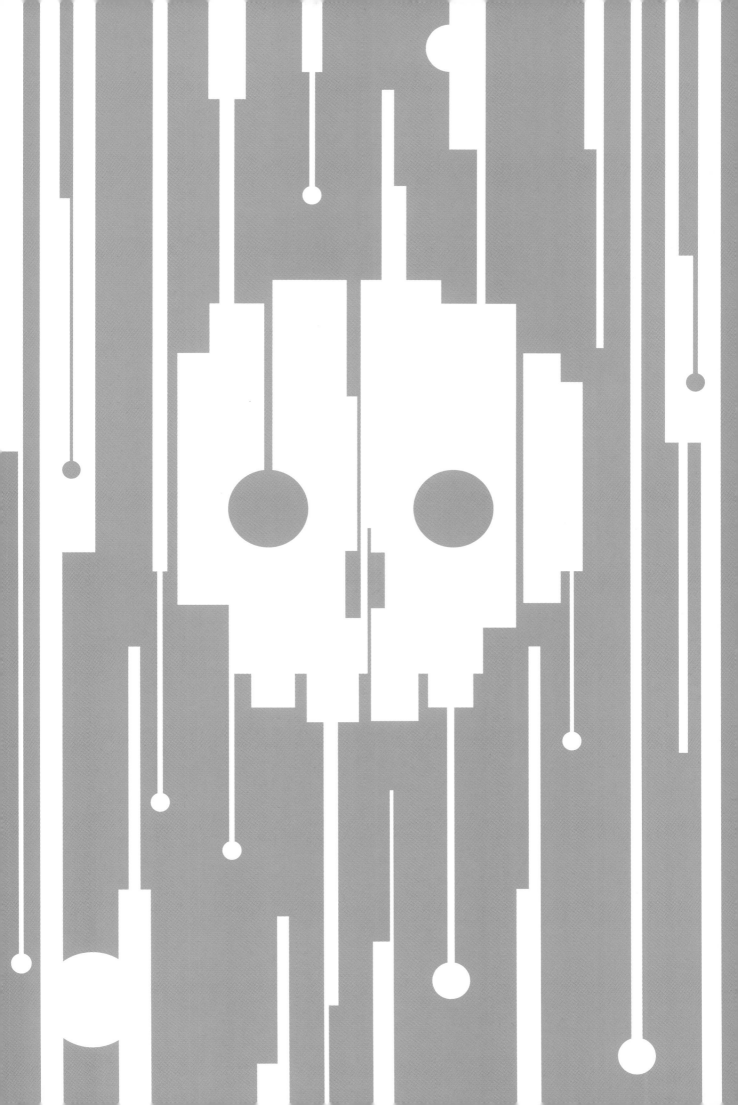

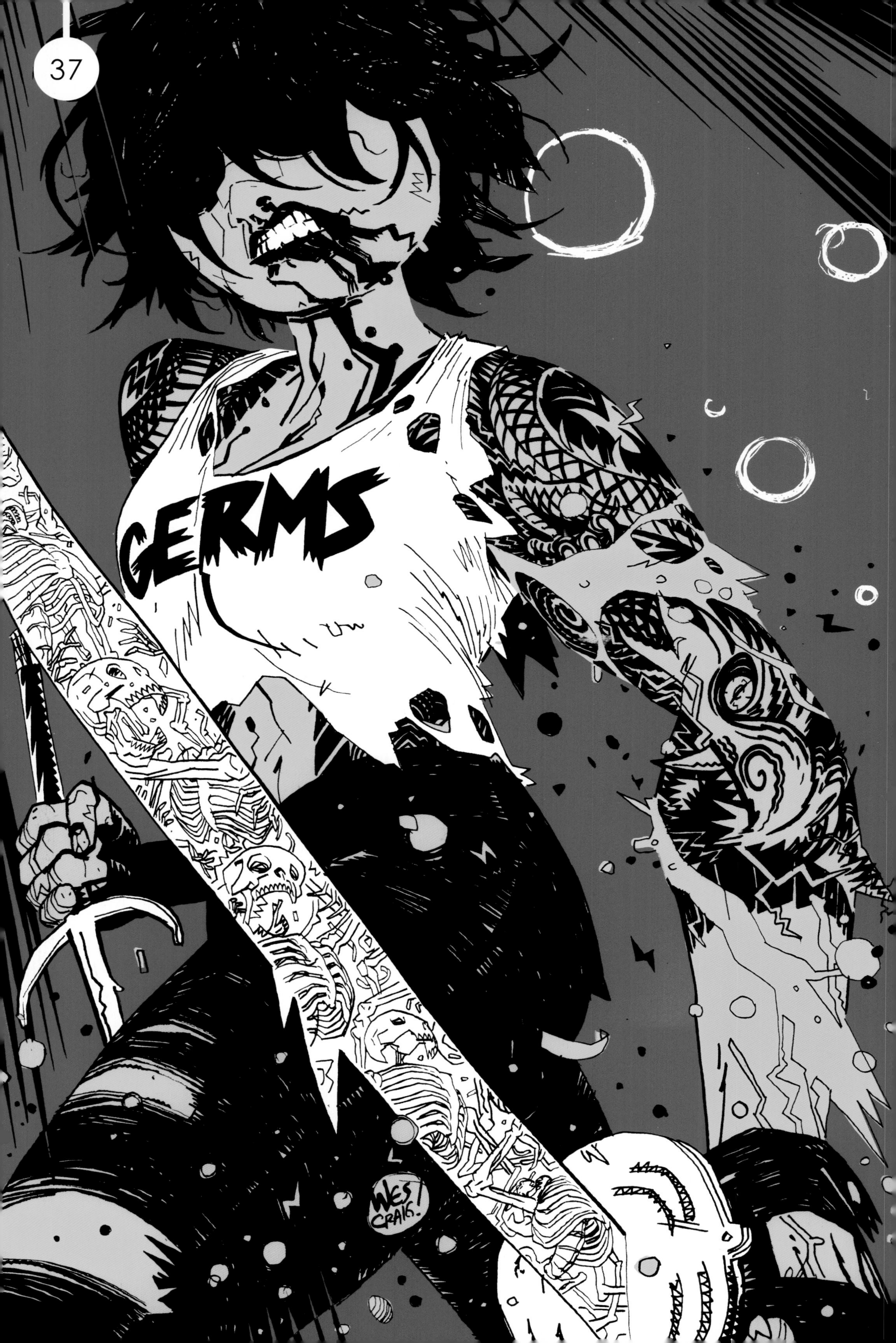
GERMS
WES CRAIG!

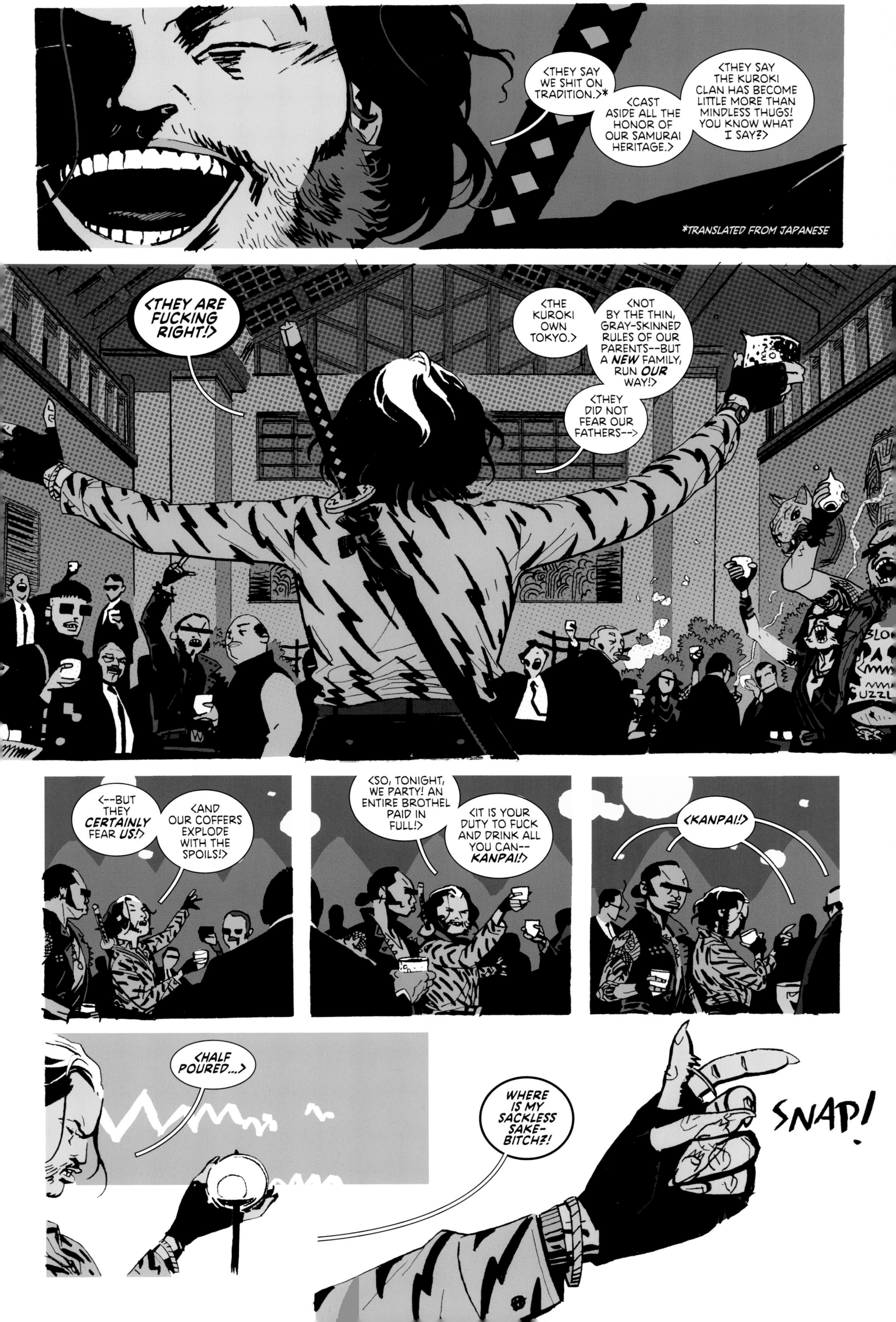

<THEY SAY WE SHIT ON TRADITION.>*
<CAST ASIDE ALL THE HONOR OF OUR SAMURAI HERITAGE.>
<THEY SAY THE KUROKI CLAN HAS BECOME LITTLE MORE THAN MINDLESS THUGS! YOU KNOW WHAT I SAY?>
*TRANSLATED FROM JAPANESE
<THEY ARE FUCKING RIGHT!>
<THE KUROKI OWN TOKYO.>
<NOT BY THE THIN, GRAY-SKINNED RULES OF OUR PARENTS--BUT A NEW FAMILY, RUN OUR WAY!>
<THEY DID NOT FEAR OUR FATHERS-->
<--BUT THEY CERTAINLY FEAR US!>
<AND OUR COFFERS EXPLODE WITH THE SPOILS!>
<SO, TONIGHT, WE PARTY! AN ENTIRE BROTHEL PAID IN FULL!>
<IT IS YOUR DUTY TO FUCK AND DRINK ALL YOU CAN--KANPAI!>
<KANPAI!>
<HALF POURED...>
WHERE IS MY SACKLESS SAKE-BITCH?!
SNAP!

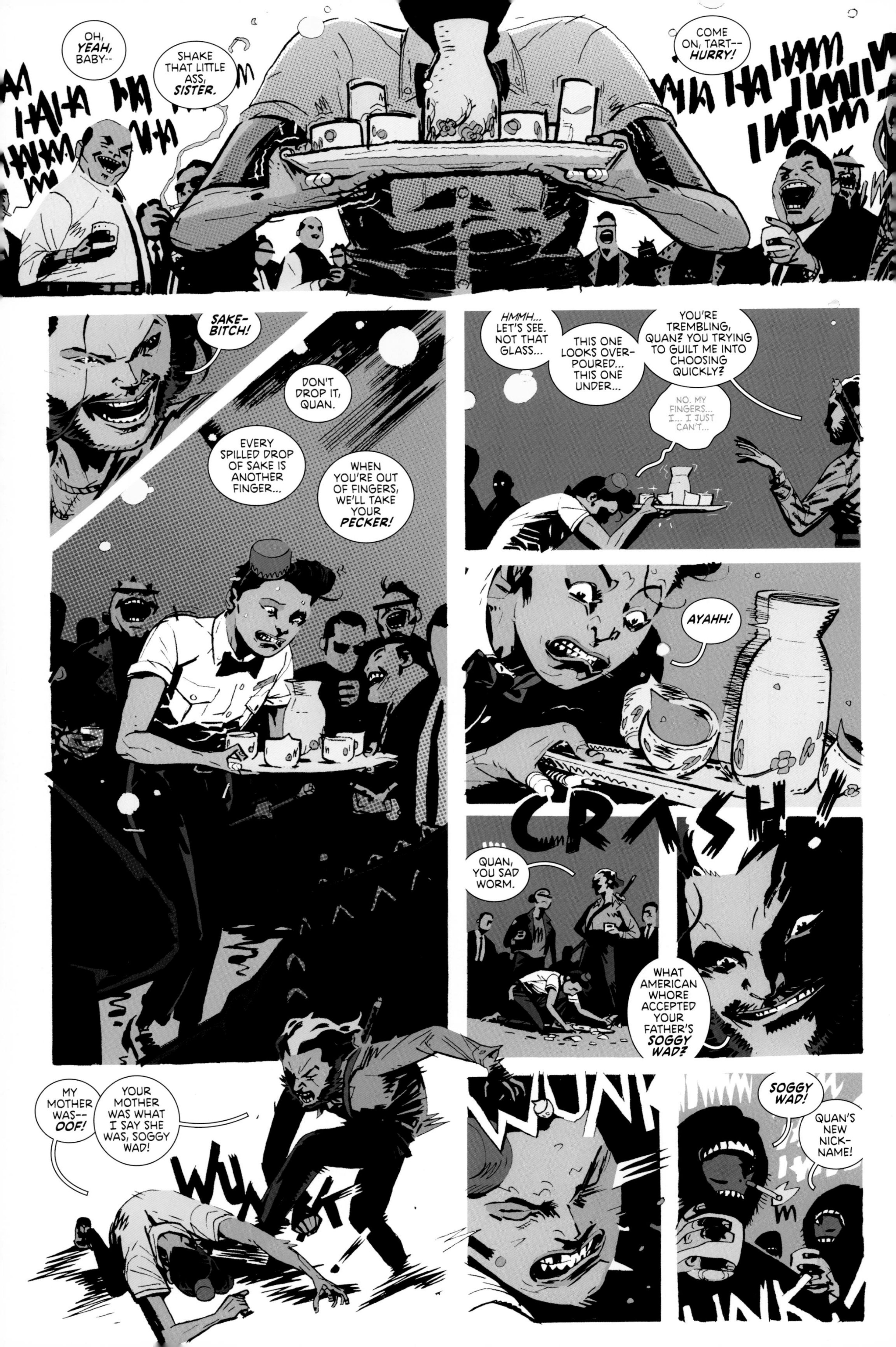

OH, YEAH, BABY--
SHAKE THAT LITTLE ASS, SISTER.
COME ON, TART-- HURRY!
SAKE-BITCH!
DON'T DROP IT, QUAN.
EVERY SPILLED DROP OF SAKE IS ANOTHER FINGER...
WHEN YOU'RE OUT OF FINGERS, WE'LL TAKE YOUR PECKER!
HMMH... LET'S SEE. NOT THAT GLASS...
THIS ONE LOOKS OVER-POURED... THIS ONE UNDER...
YOU'RE TREMBLING, QUAN? YOU TRYING TO GUILT ME INTO CHOOSING QUICKLY?
NO. MY FINGERS... I... I JUST CAN'T...
AYAHH!
CRASH!
QUAN, YOU SAD WORM.
WHAT AMERICAN WHORE ACCEPTED YOUR FATHER'S SOGGY WAD?
MY MOTHER WAS-- OOF!
YOUR MOTHER WAS WHAT I SAY SHE WAS, SOGGY WAD!
WUNK
SOGGY WAD!
QUAN'S NEW NICK-NAME!

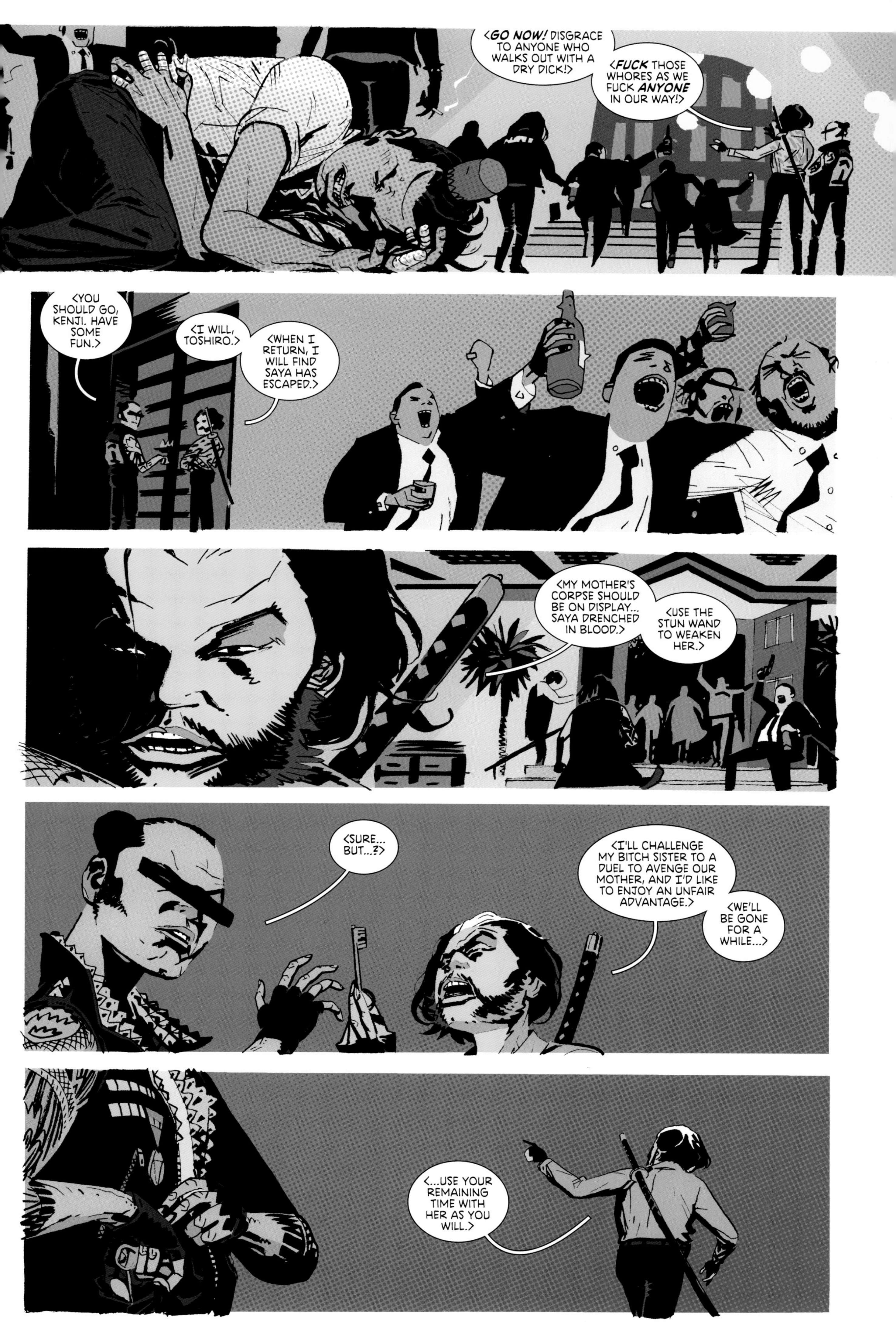
<GO NOW! DISGRACE TO ANYONE WHO WALKS OUT WITH A DRY DICK!>
<FUCK THOSE WHORES AS WE FUCK ANYONE IN OUR WAY!>
<YOU SHOULD GO, KENJI. HAVE SOME FUN.>
<I WILL, TOSHIRO.>
<WHEN I RETURN, I WILL FIND SAYA HAS ESCAPED.>
<MY MOTHER'S CORPSE SHOULD BE ON DISPLAY... SAYA DRENCHED IN BLOOD.>
<USE THE STUN WAND TO WEAKEN HER.>
<SURE... BUT...?>
<I'LL CHALLENGE MY BITCH SISTER TO A DUEL TO AVENGE OUR MOTHER, AND I'D LIKE TO ENJOY AN UNFAIR ADVANTAGE.>
<WE'LL BE GONE FOR A WHILE...>
<...USE YOUR REMAINING TIME WITH HER AS YOU WILL.>

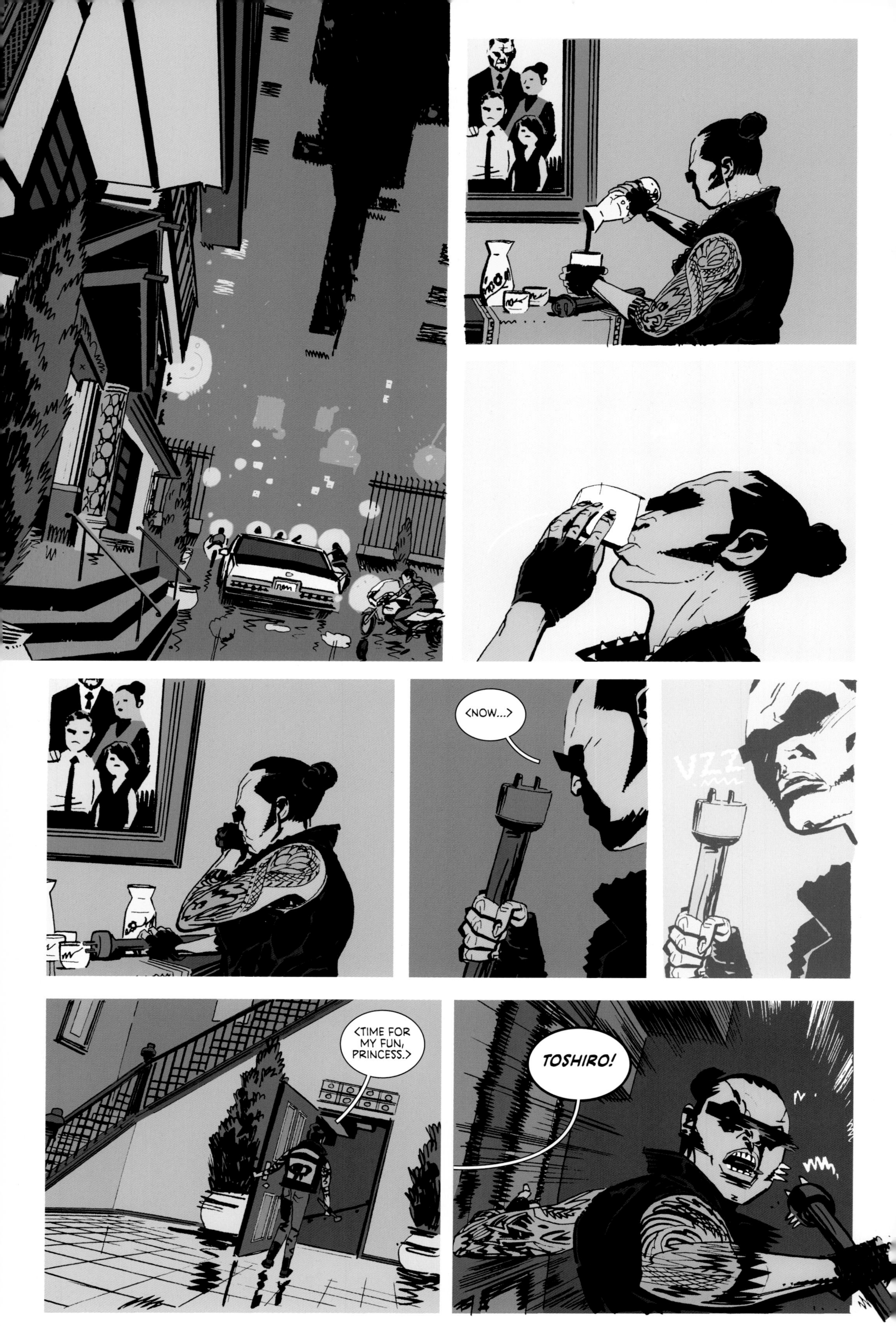
<NOW...>
VZZ
<TIME FOR MY FUN, PRINCESS.>
TOSHIRO!

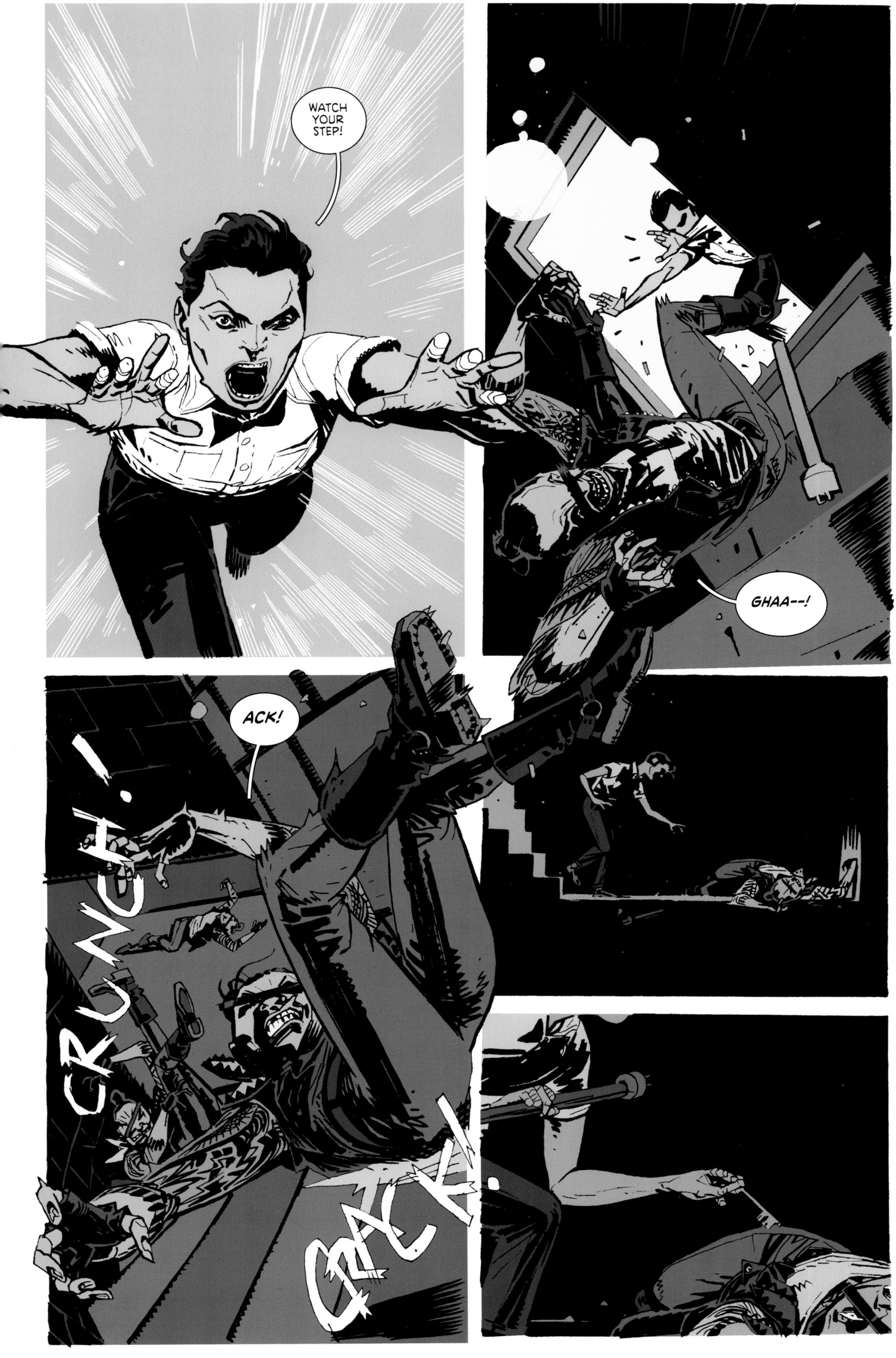
WATCH YOUR STEP!
GHAA--!
ACK!
CRUNCH!
CRACK!

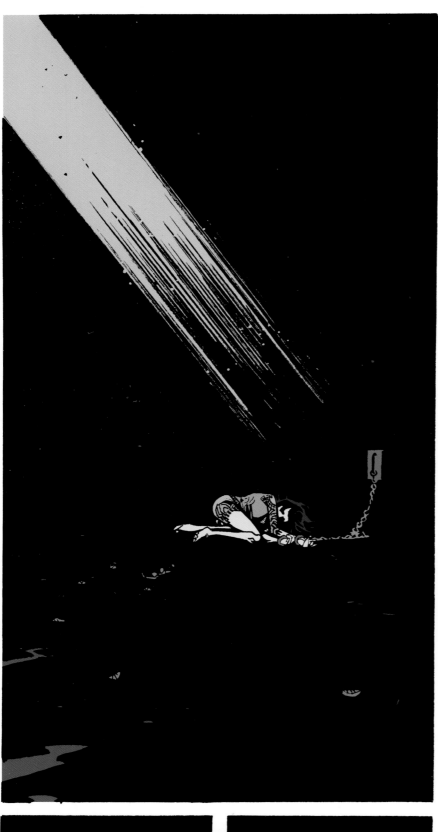

click

SAYA...?

I-I BROUGHT THE KEY...

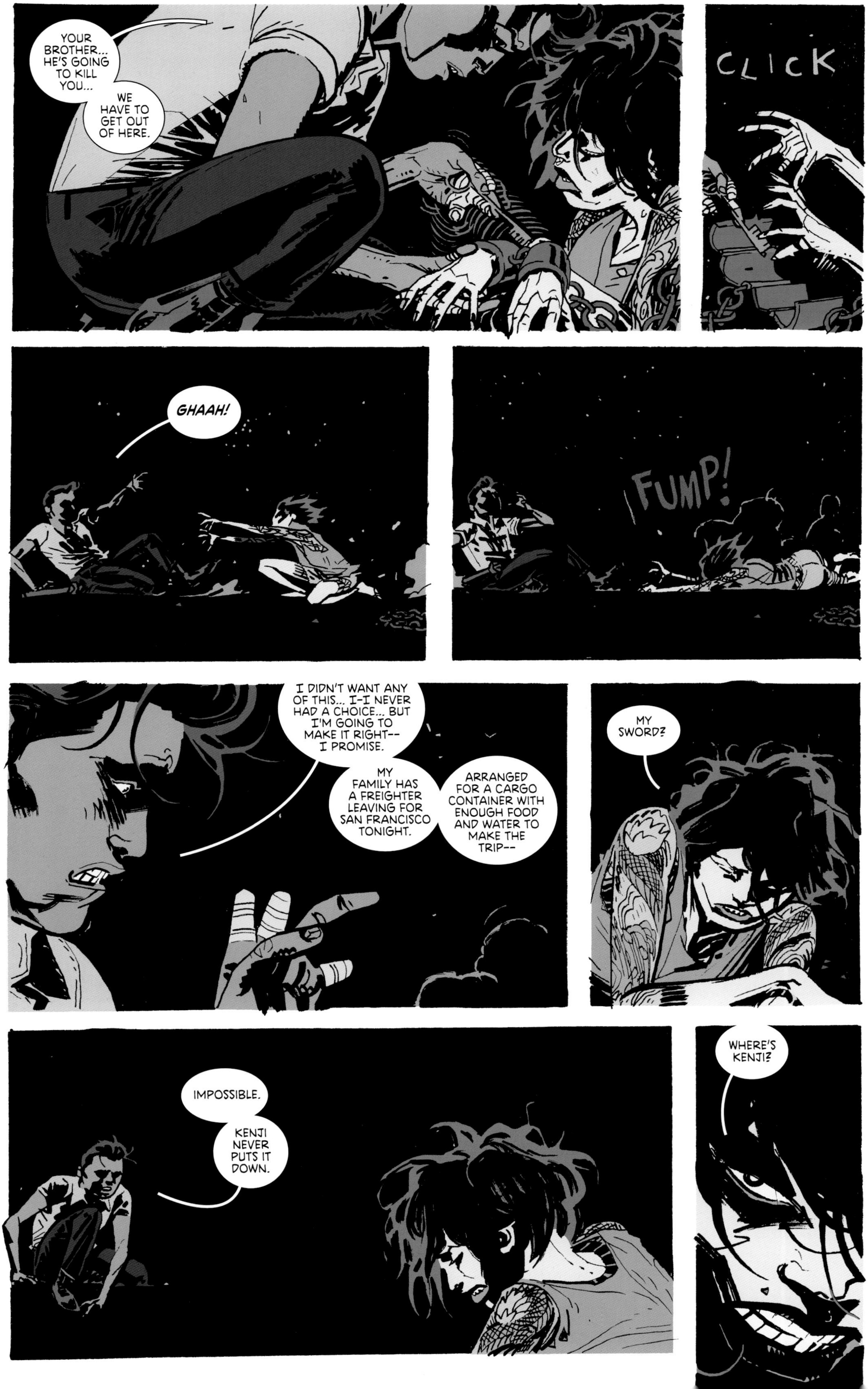
YOUR BROTHER... HE'S GOING TO KILL YOU...
WE HAVE TO GET OUT OF HERE.
CLICK
GHAAH!
FUMP!
I DIDN'T WANT ANY OF THIS... I-I NEVER HAD A CHOICE... BUT I'M GOING TO MAKE IT RIGHT-- I PROMISE.
MY FAMILY HAS A FREIGHTER LEAVING FOR SAN FRANCISCO TONIGHT.
ARRANGED FOR A CARGO CONTAINER WITH ENOUGH FOOD AND WATER TO MAKE THE TRIP--
MY SWORD?
IMPOSSIBLE.
KENJI NEVER PUTS IT DOWN.
WHERE'S KENJI?

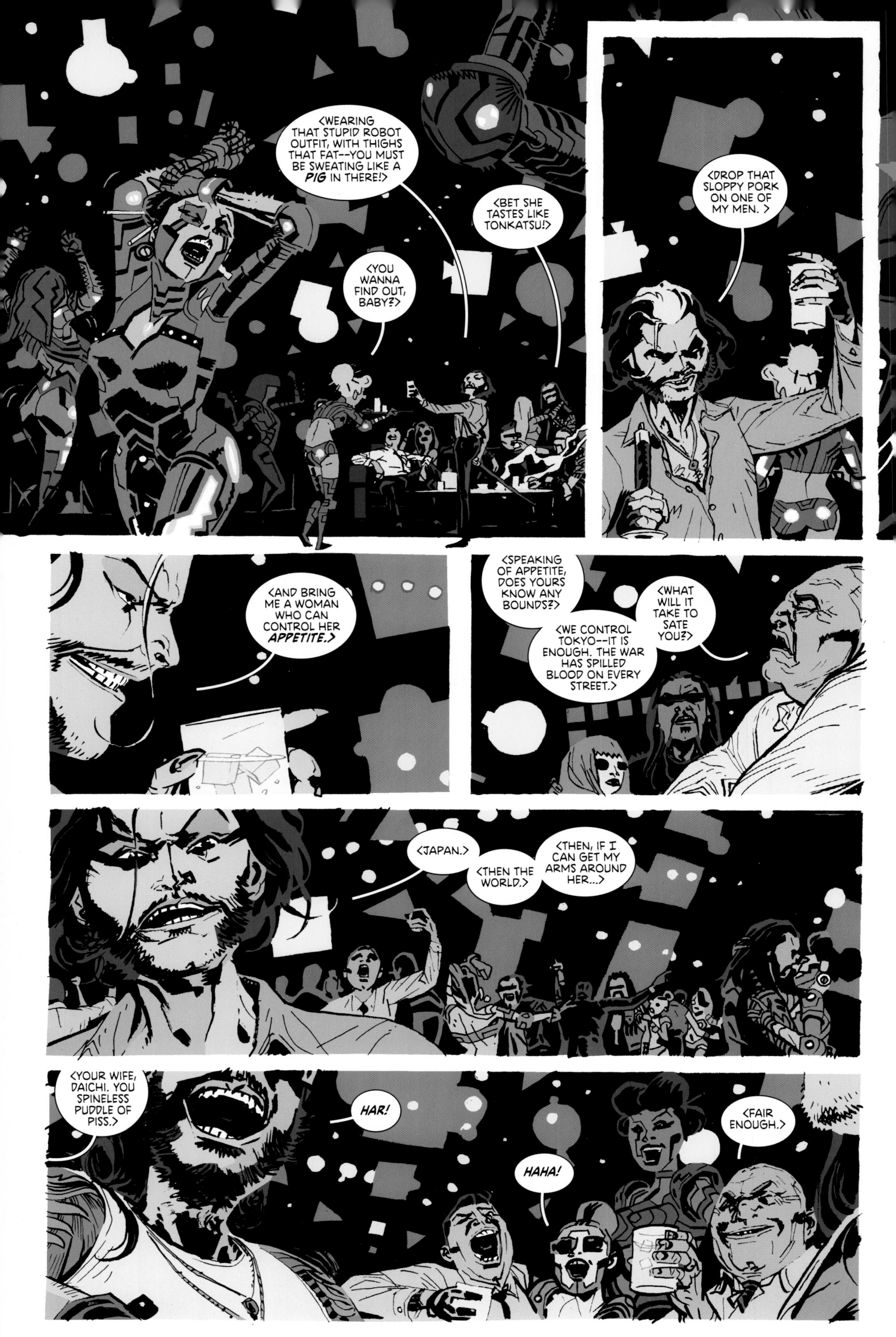
<WEARING THAT STUPID ROBOT OUTFIT, WITH THIGHS THAT FAT--YOU MUST BE SWEATING LIKE A *PIG* IN THERE!>
<YOU WANNA FIND OUT, BABY?>
<BET SHE TASTES LIKE TONKATSU!>
<DROP THAT SLOPPY PORK ON ONE OF MY MEN. >
<AND BRING ME A WOMAN WHO CAN CONTROL HER *APPETITE.*>
<SPEAKING OF APPETITE, DOES YOURS KNOW ANY BOUNDS?>
<WE CONTROL TOKYO--IT IS ENOUGH. THE WAR HAS SPILLED BLOOD ON EVERY STREET.>
<WHAT WILL IT TAKE TO SATE YOU?>
<JAPAN.>
<THEN THE WORLD.>
<THEN, IF I CAN GET MY ARMS AROUND HER...>
<YOUR WIFE, DAICHI. YOU SPINELESS PUDDLE OF PISS.>
HAR!
HAHA!
<FAIR ENOUGH.>

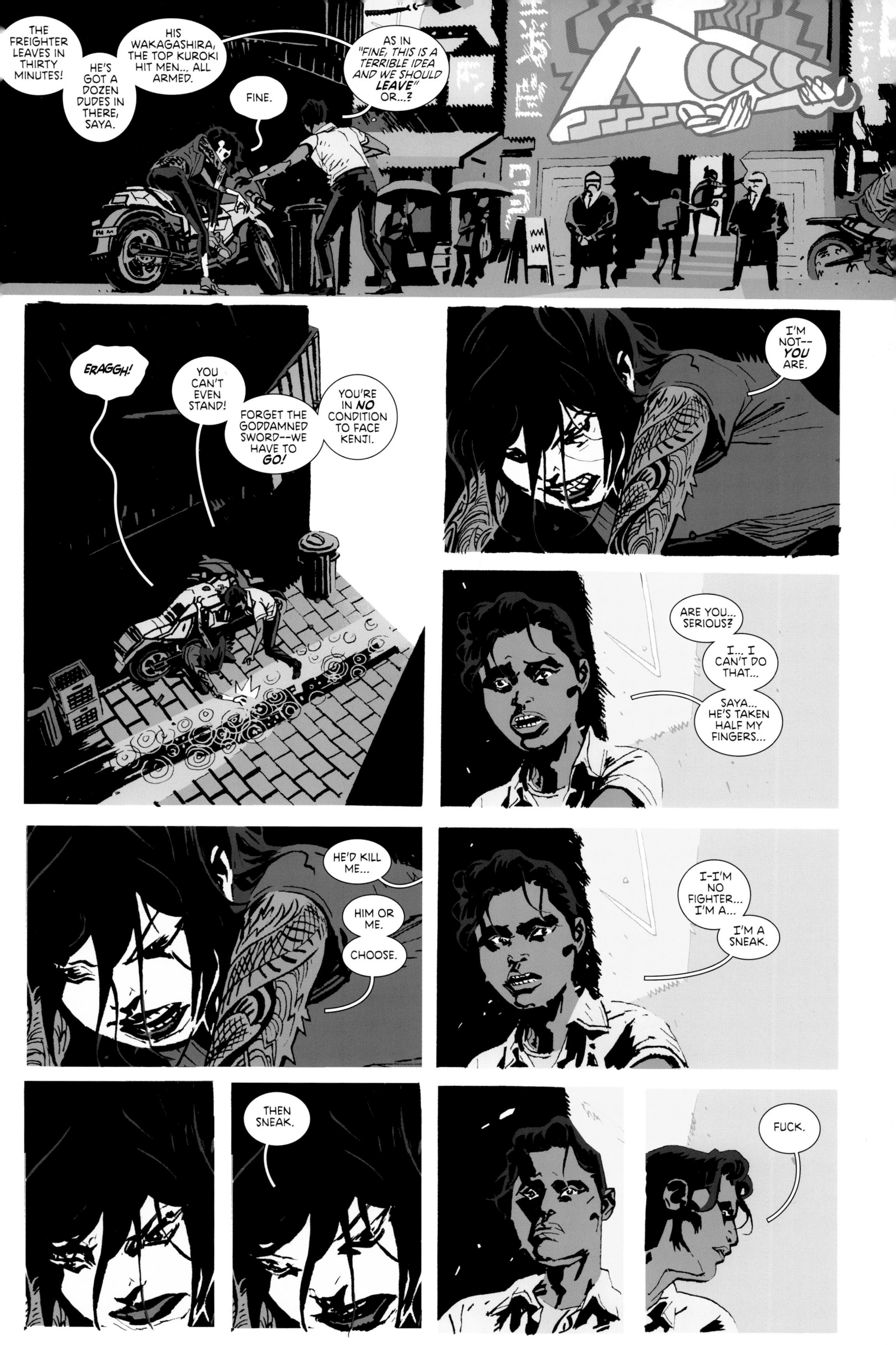
THE FREIGHTER LEAVES IN THIRTY MINUTES!
HE'S GOT A DOZEN DUDES IN THERE, SAYA.
HIS WAKAGASHIRA, THE TOP KUROKI HIT MEN... ALL ARMED.
FINE.
AS IN "FINE, THIS IS A TERRIBLE IDEA AND WE SHOULD LEAVE" OR...?
ERAGGH!
YOU CAN'T EVEN STAND!
FORGET THE GODDAMNED SWORD--WE HAVE TO GO!
YOU'RE IN NO CONDITION TO FACE KENJI.
I'M NOT-- YOU ARE.
ARE YOU... SERIOUS?
I... I CAN'T DO THAT...
SAYA... HE'S TAKEN HALF MY FINGERS...
HE'D KILL ME...
HIM OR ME.
CHOOSE.
I-I'M NO FIGHTER... I'M A...
I'M A SNEAK.
THEN SNEAK.
FUCK.

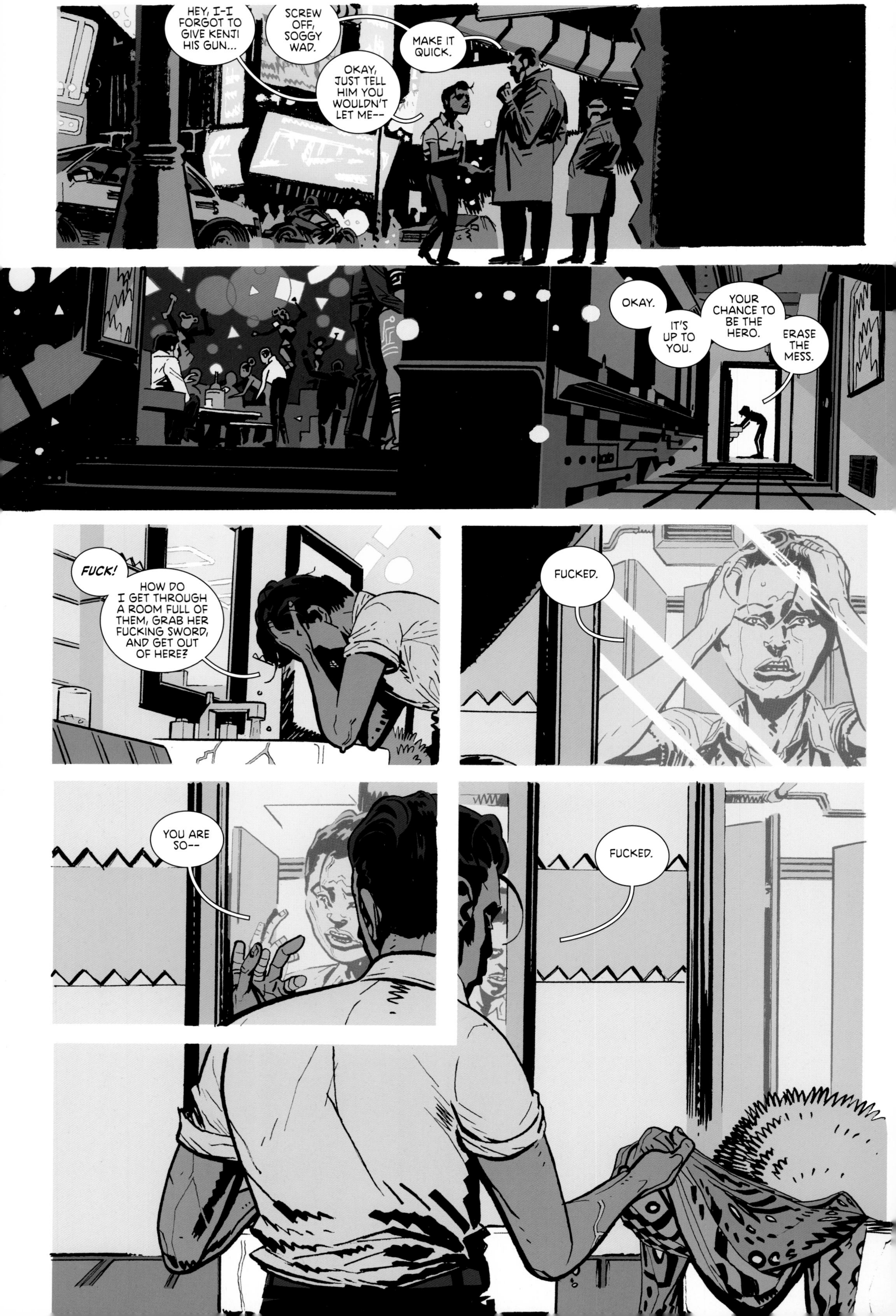
HEY, I-I FORGOT TO GIVE KENJI HIS GUN...
SCREW OFF, SOGGY WAD.
MAKE IT QUICK.
OKAY, JUST TELL HIM YOU WOULDN'T LET ME--
OKAY.
IT'S UP TO YOU.
YOUR CHANCE TO BE THE HERO.
ERASE THE MESS.
FUCK!
HOW DO I GET THROUGH A ROOM FULL OF THEM, GRAB HER FUCKING SWORD, AND GET OUT OF HERE?
FUCKED.
YOU ARE SO--
FUCKED.

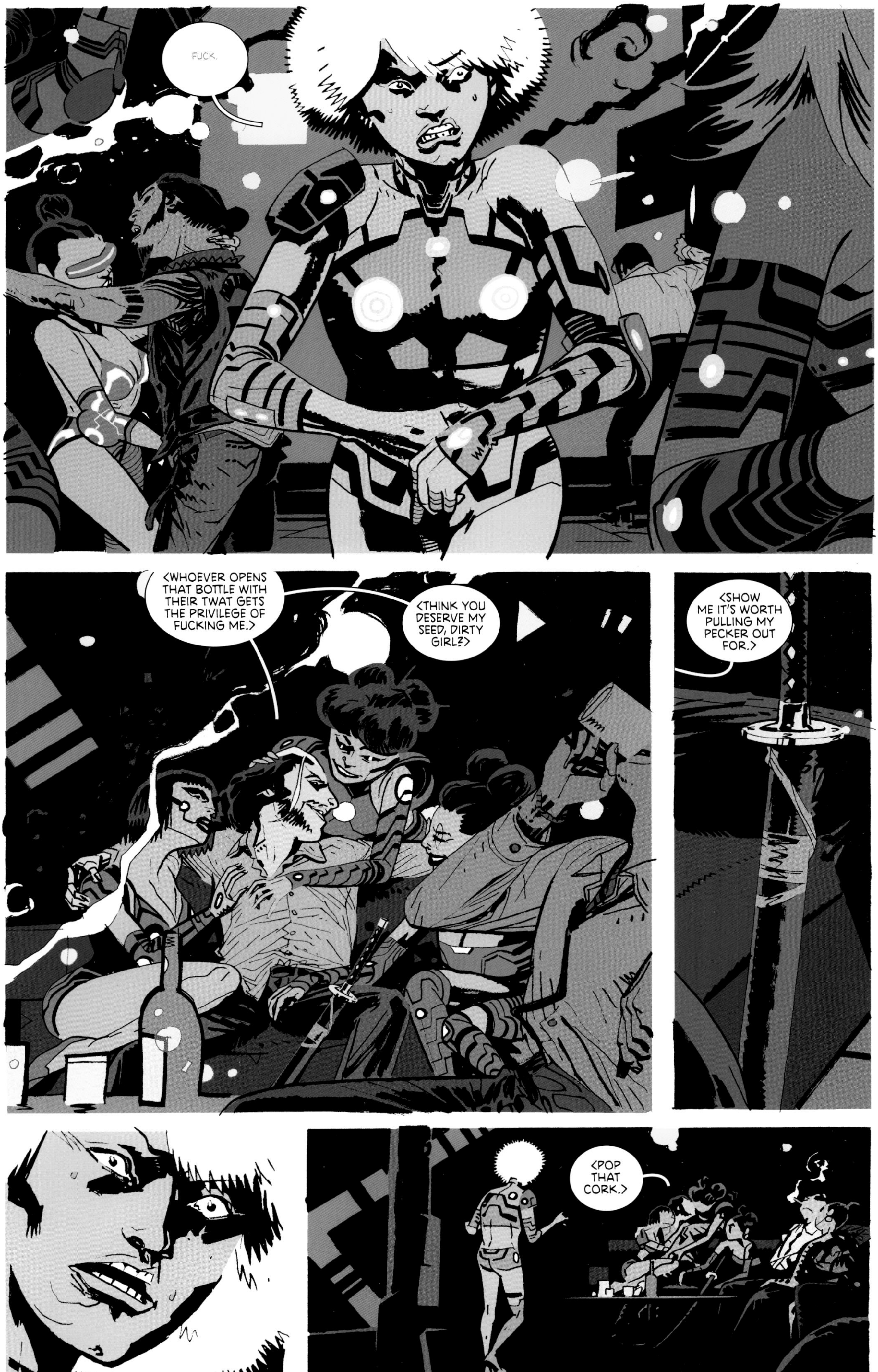
FUCK.
<WHOEVER OPENS THAT BOTTLE WITH THEIR TWAT GETS THE PRIVILEGE OF FUCKING ME.>
<THINK YOU DESERVE MY SEED, DIRTY GIRL?>
<SHOW ME IT'S WORTH PULLING MY PECKER OUT FOR.>
<POP THAT CORK.>

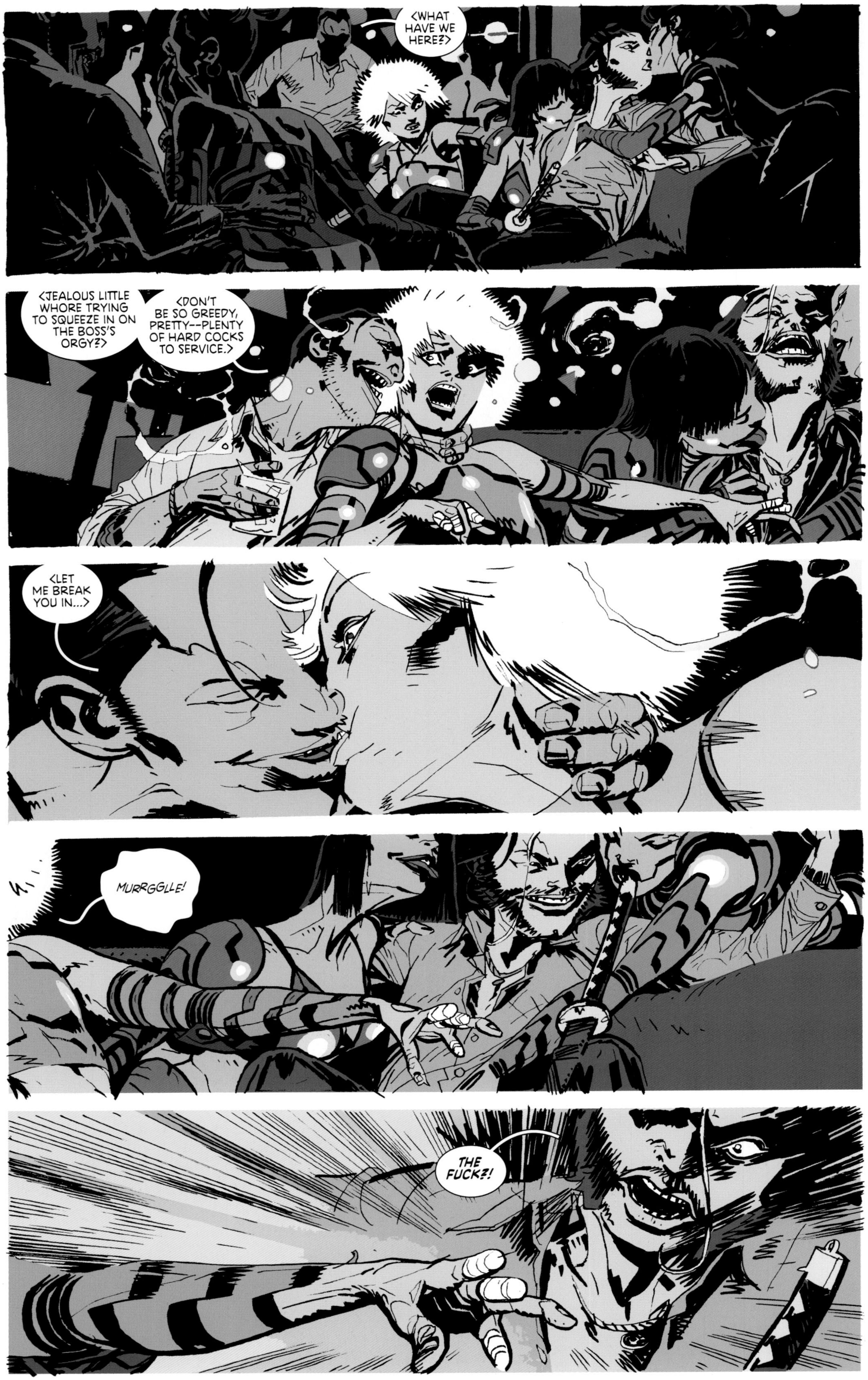
<WHAT HAVE WE HERE?>
<JEALOUS LITTLE WHORE TRYING TO SQUEEZE IN ON THE BOSS'S ORGY?>
<DON'T BE SO GREEDY, PRETTY--PLENTY OF HARD COCKS TO SERVICE.>
<LET ME BREAK YOU IN...>
MURRGGLLE!
THE FUCK?!

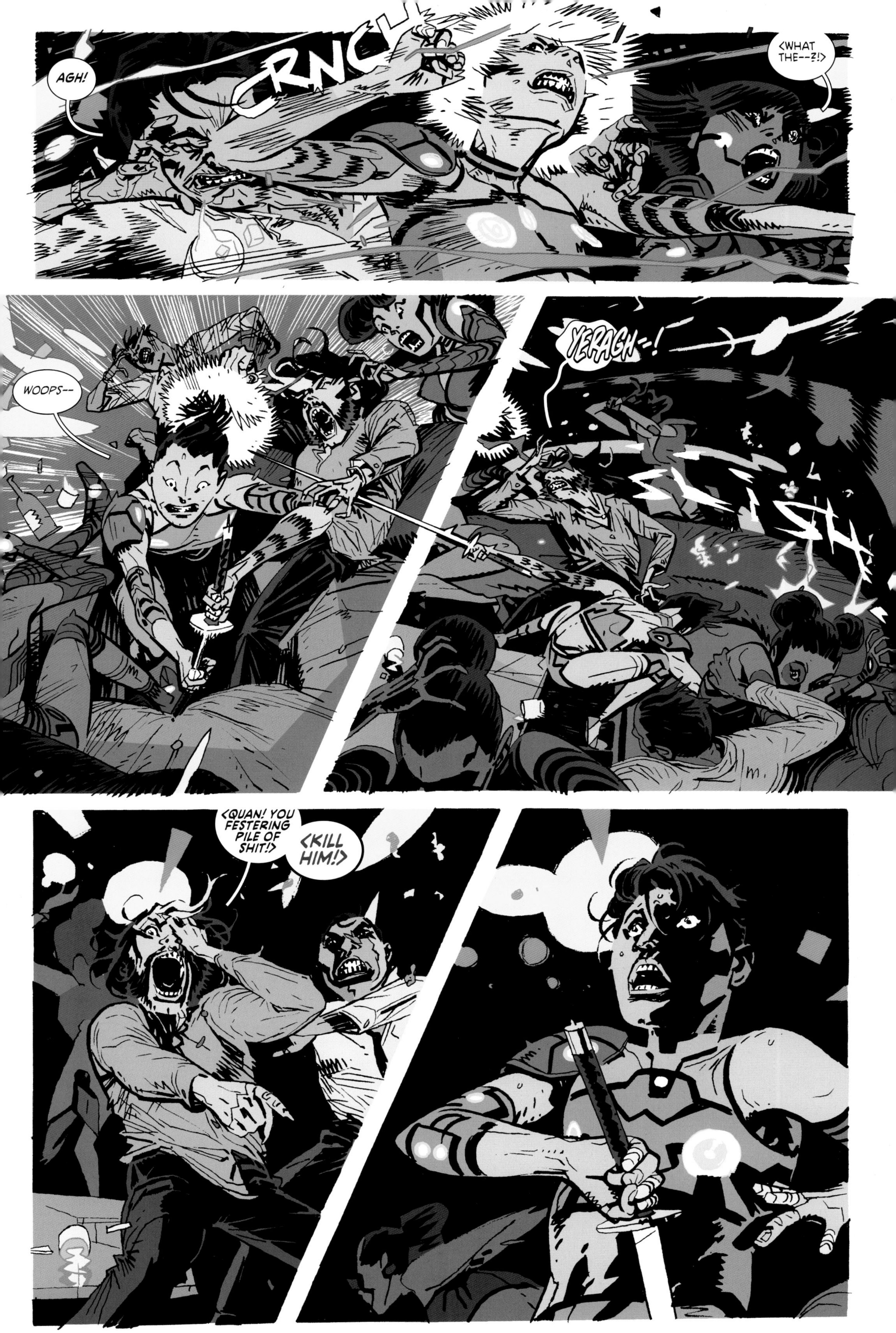
AGH!
CRNCH
<WHAT THE--?!>
WOOPS--
YERAGH--!
SHISH
<QUAN! YOU FESTERING PILE OF SHIT!>
<KILL HIM!>

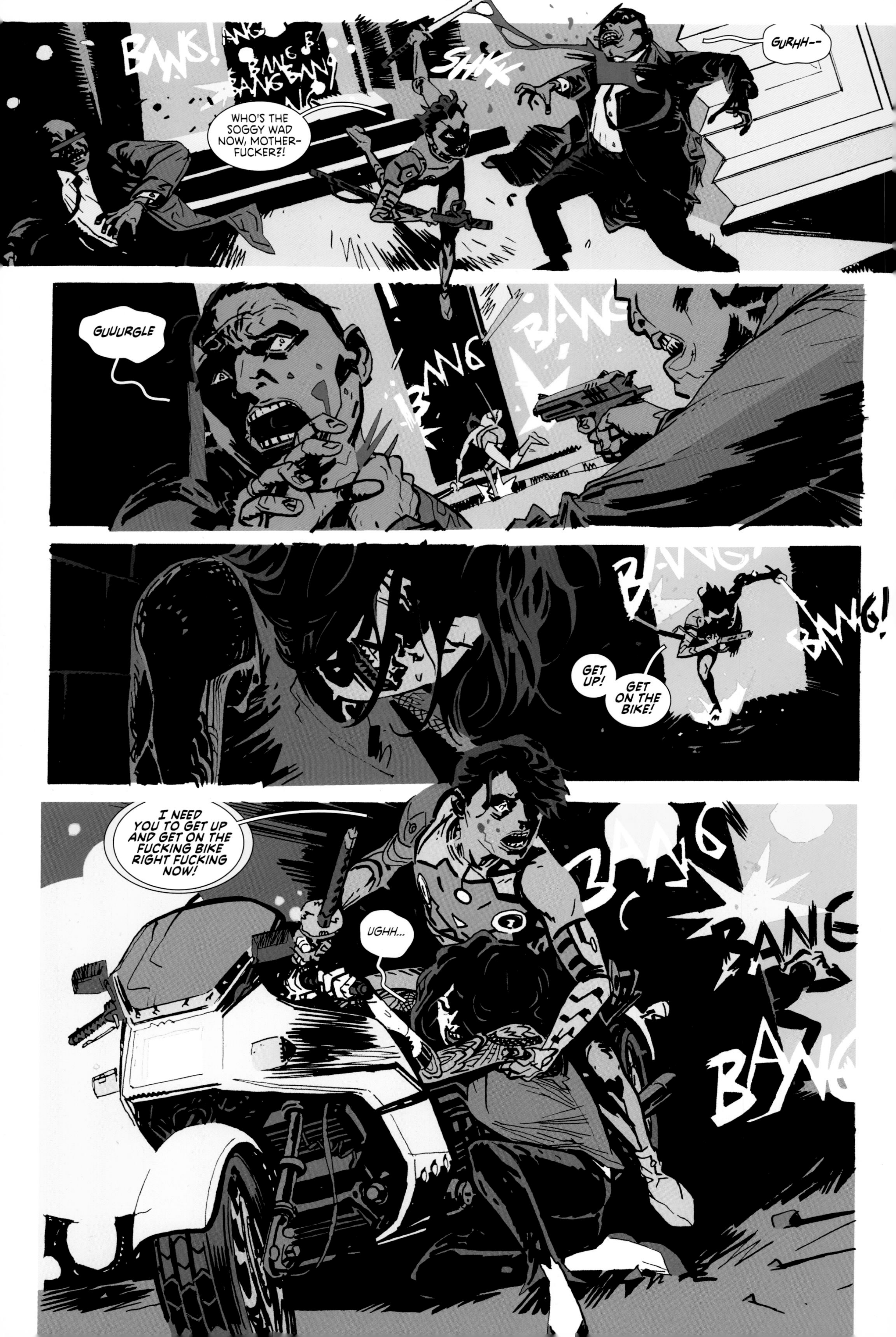
BANG!
WHO'S THE SOGGY WAD NOW, MOTHER-FUCKER?!
GURHH--
GUURGLE
BANG
BANG
BANG!
BANG!
GET UP!
GET ON THE BIKE!
I NEED YOU TO GET UP AND GET ON THE FUCKING BIKE RIGHT FUCKING NOW!
UGHH...
BANG
BANG
BANG

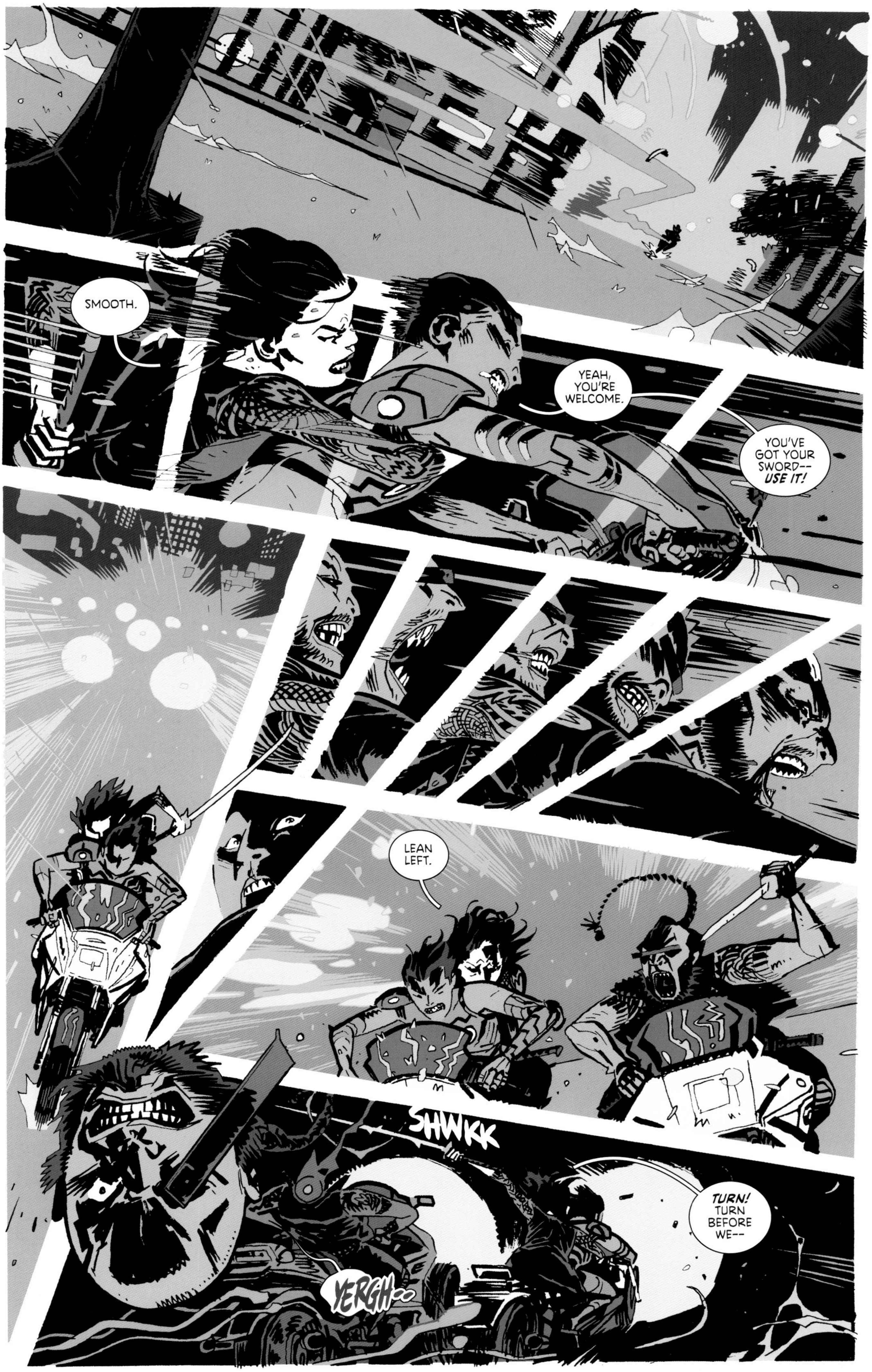
SMOOTH.
YEAH, YOU'RE WELCOME.
YOU'VE GOT YOUR SWORD-- *USE IT!*
LEAN LEFT.
SHWKK
TURN! TURN BEFORE WE--
YERGH..

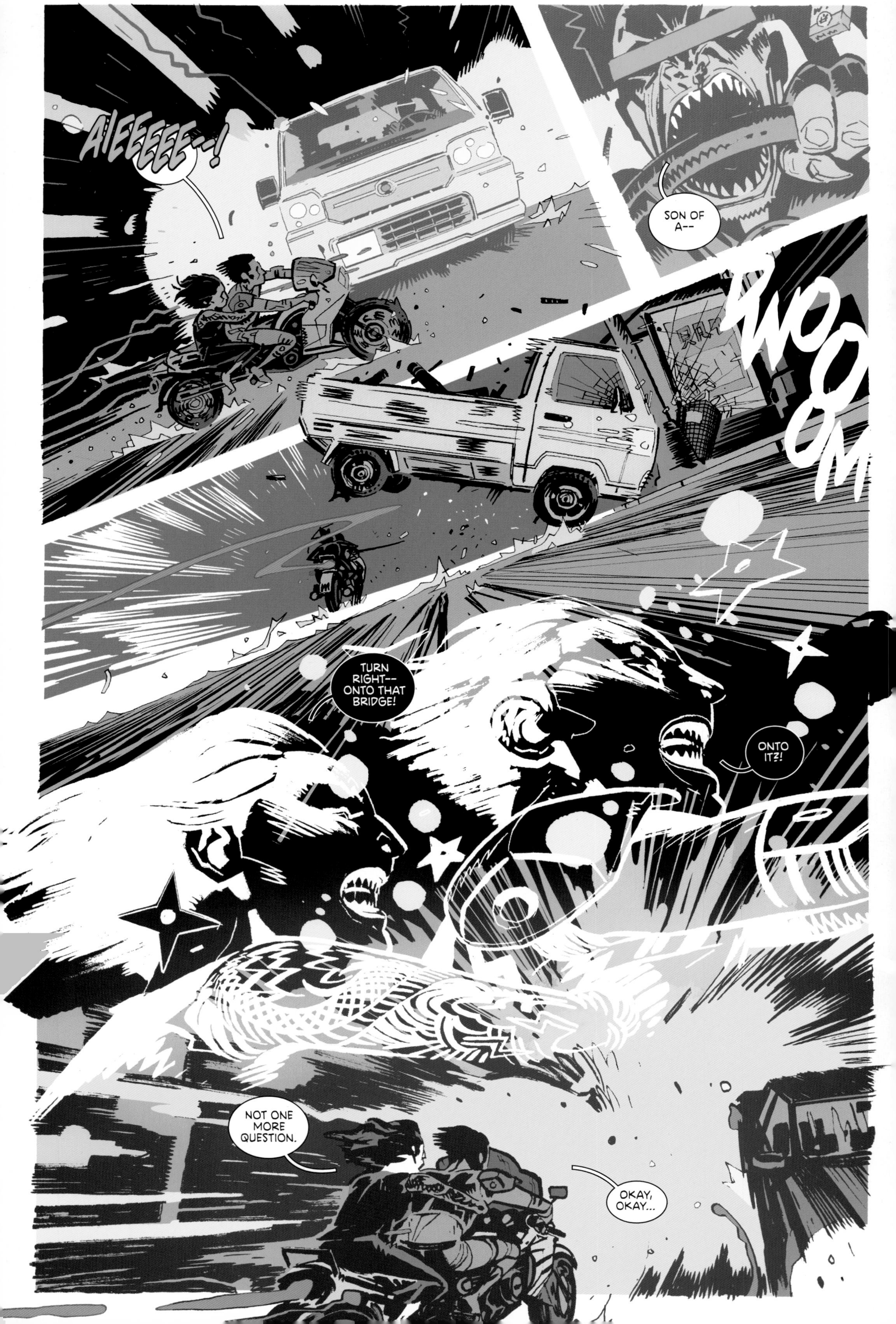
AIEEEEEE--!
SON OF A--
WOOOM
TURN RIGHT--ONTO THAT BRIDGE!
ONTO IT?!
NOT ONE MORE QUESTION.
OKAY, OKAY...

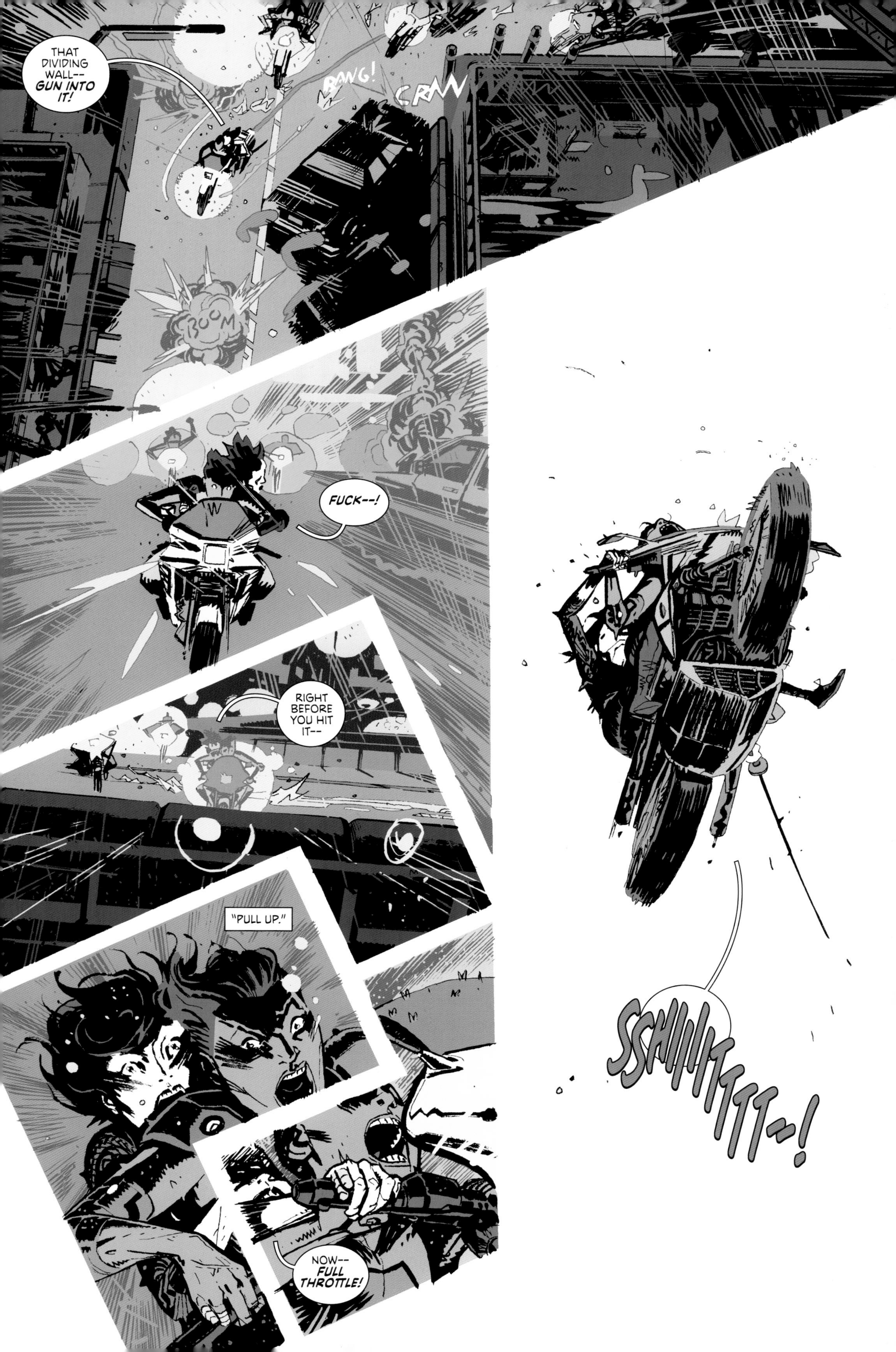
THAT DIVIDING WALL-- GUN INTO IT!
BANG!
CRNN
BOOM
FUCK--!
RIGHT BEFORE YOU HIT IT--
"PULL UP."
NOW-- FULL THROTTLE!
SSHIIIITTTT--!

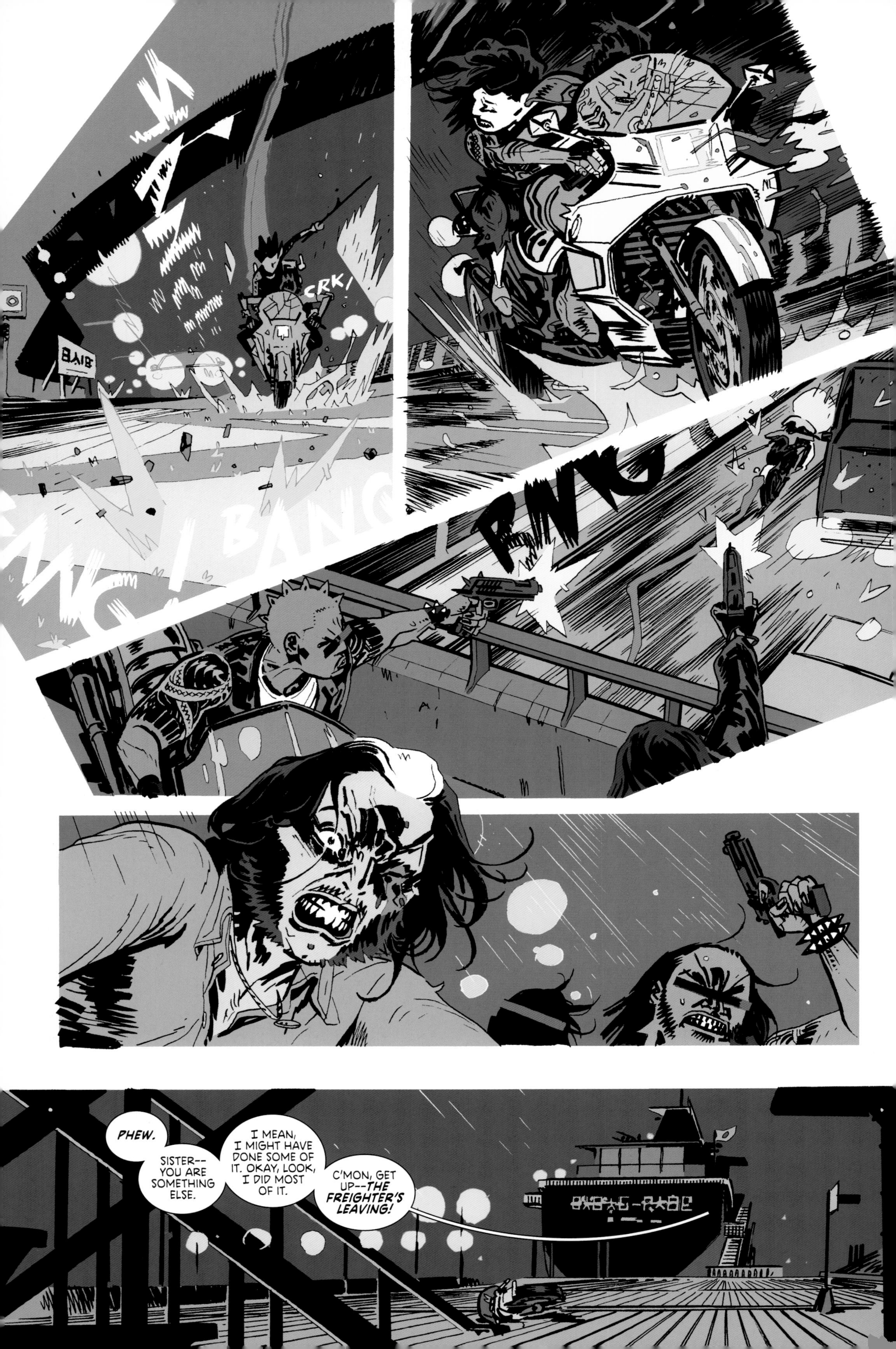
CRK!
BANG
BANG
RNG
PHEW.
SISTER-- YOU ARE SOMETHING ELSE.
I MEAN, I MIGHT HAVE DONE SOME OF IT. OKAY, LOOK, I DID MOST OF IT.
C'MON, GET UP--THE FREIGHTER'S LEAVING!

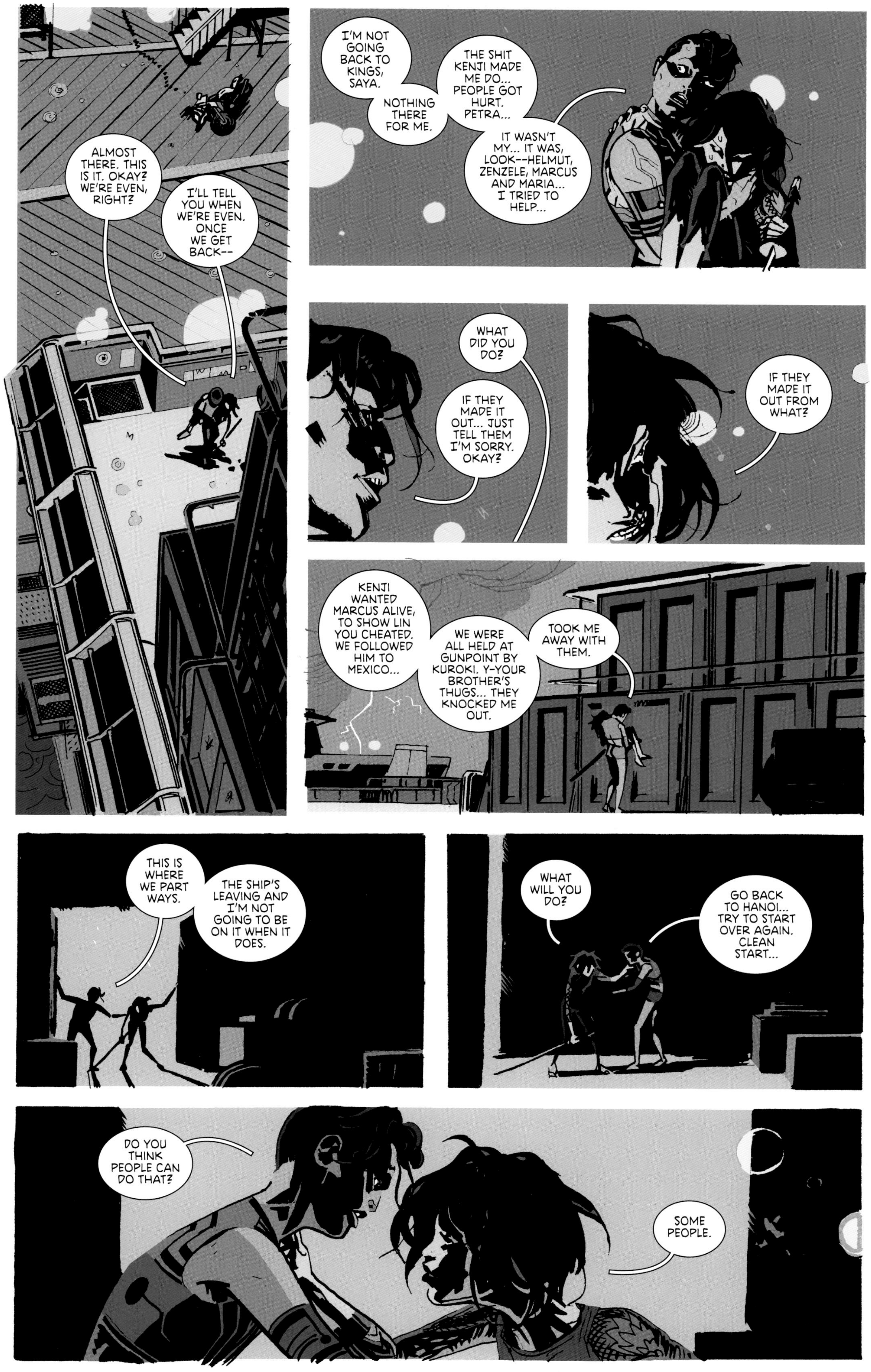
ALMOST THERE. THIS IS IT. OKAY? WE'RE EVEN, RIGHT?
I'LL TELL YOU WHEN WE'RE EVEN. ONCE WE GET BACK--
I'M NOT GOING BACK TO KINGS, SAYA.
NOTHING THERE FOR ME.
THE SHIT KENJI MADE ME DO... PEOPLE GOT HURT. PETRA...
IT WASN'T MY... IT WAS, LOOK--HELMUT, ZENZELE, MARCUS AND MARIA... I TRIED TO HELP...
WHAT DID YOU DO?
IF THEY MADE IT OUT... JUST TELL THEM I'M SORRY. OKAY?
IF THEY MADE IT OUT FROM WHAT?
KENJI WANTED MARCUS ALIVE, TO SHOW LIN YOU CHEATED. WE FOLLOWED HIM TO MEXICO...
WE WERE ALL HELD AT GUNPOINT BY KUROKI. Y-YOUR BROTHER'S THUGS... THEY KNOCKED ME OUT.
TOOK ME AWAY WITH THEM.
THIS IS WHERE WE PART WAYS.
THE SHIP'S LEAVING AND I'M NOT GOING TO BE ON IT WHEN IT DOES.
WHAT WILL YOU DO?
GO BACK TO HANOI... TRY TO START OVER AGAIN. CLEAN START...
DO YOU THINK PEOPLE CAN DO THAT?
SOME PEOPLE.

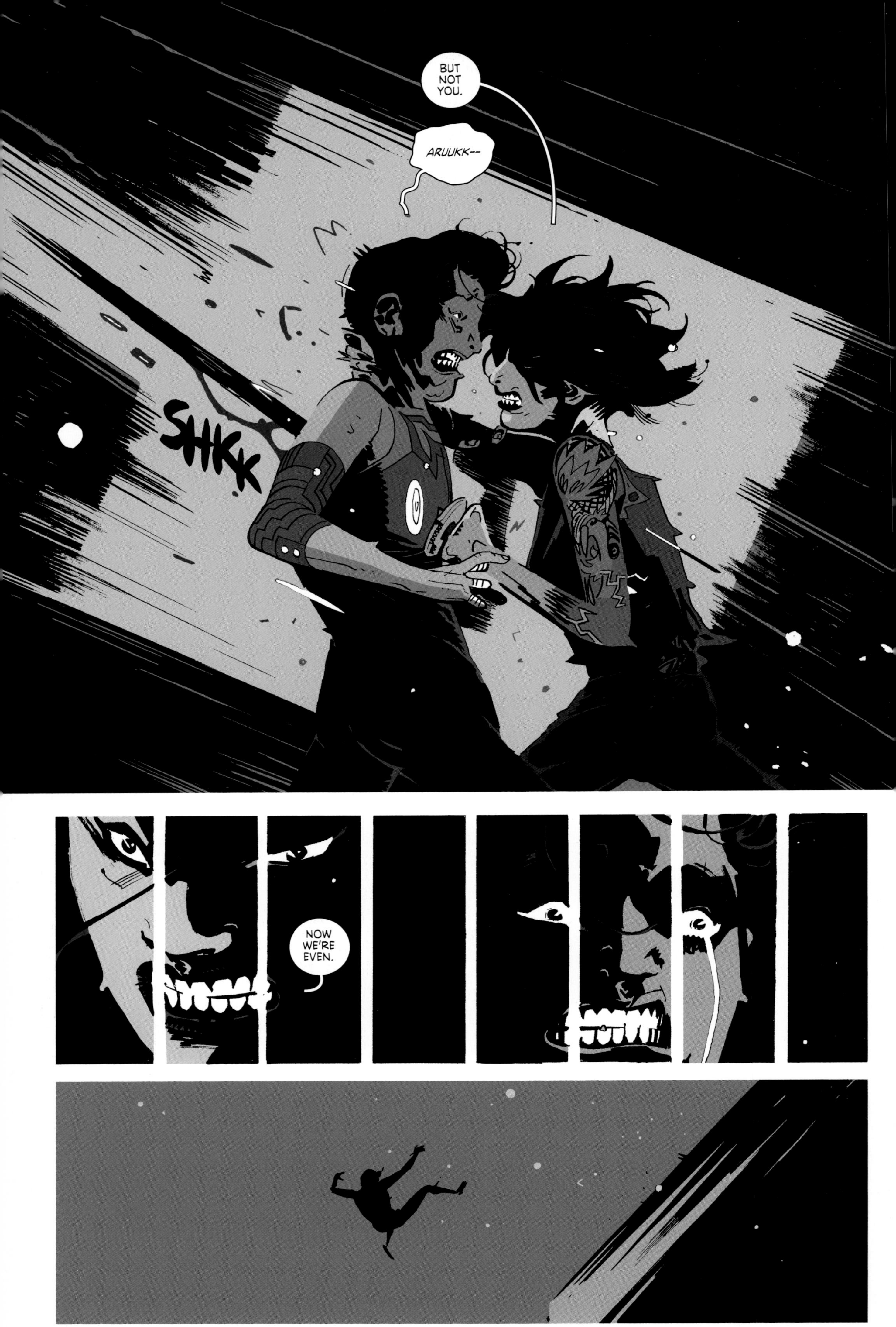
BUT NOT YOU.
ARUUKK--
SHKK
NOW WE'RE EVEN.

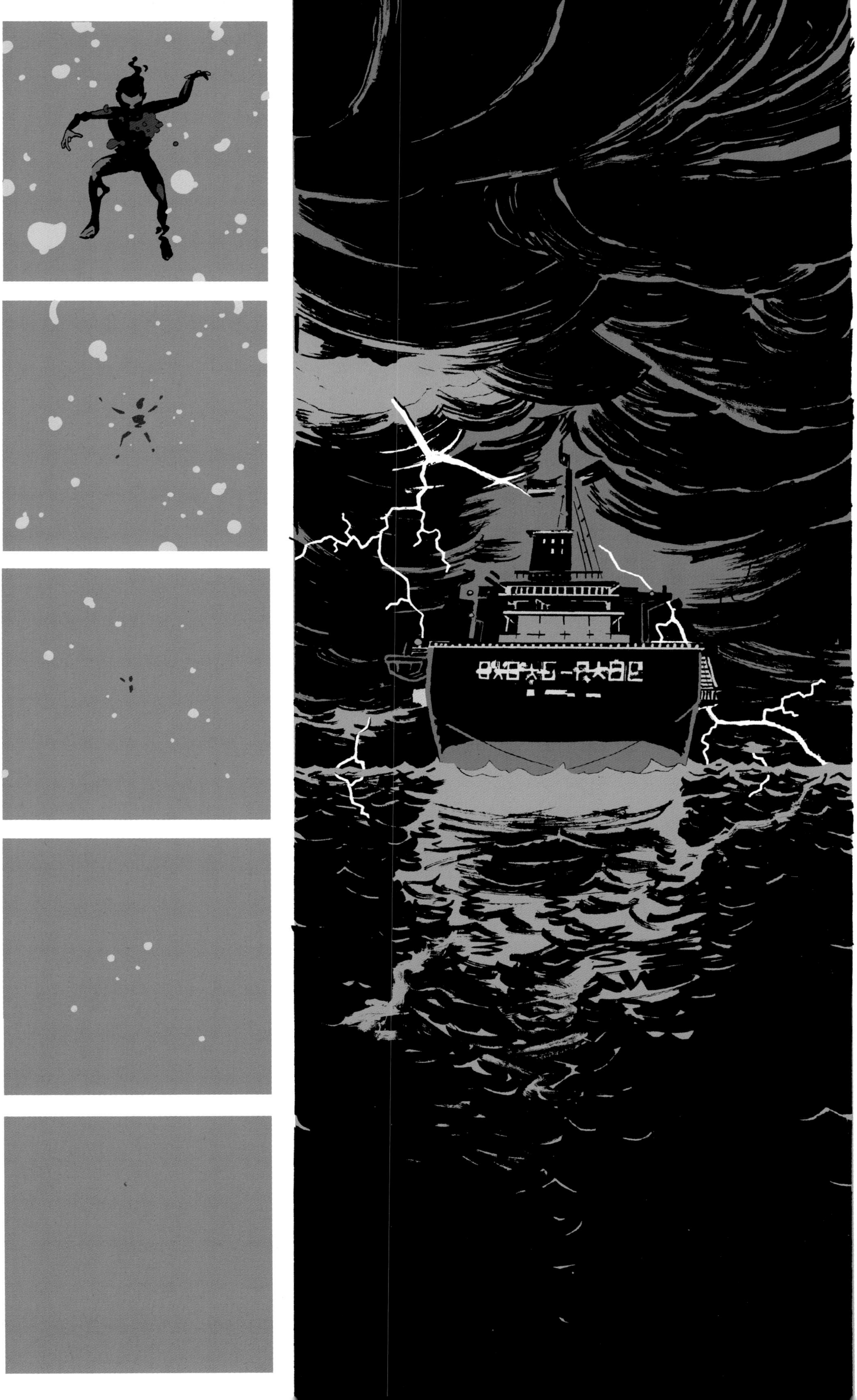

38

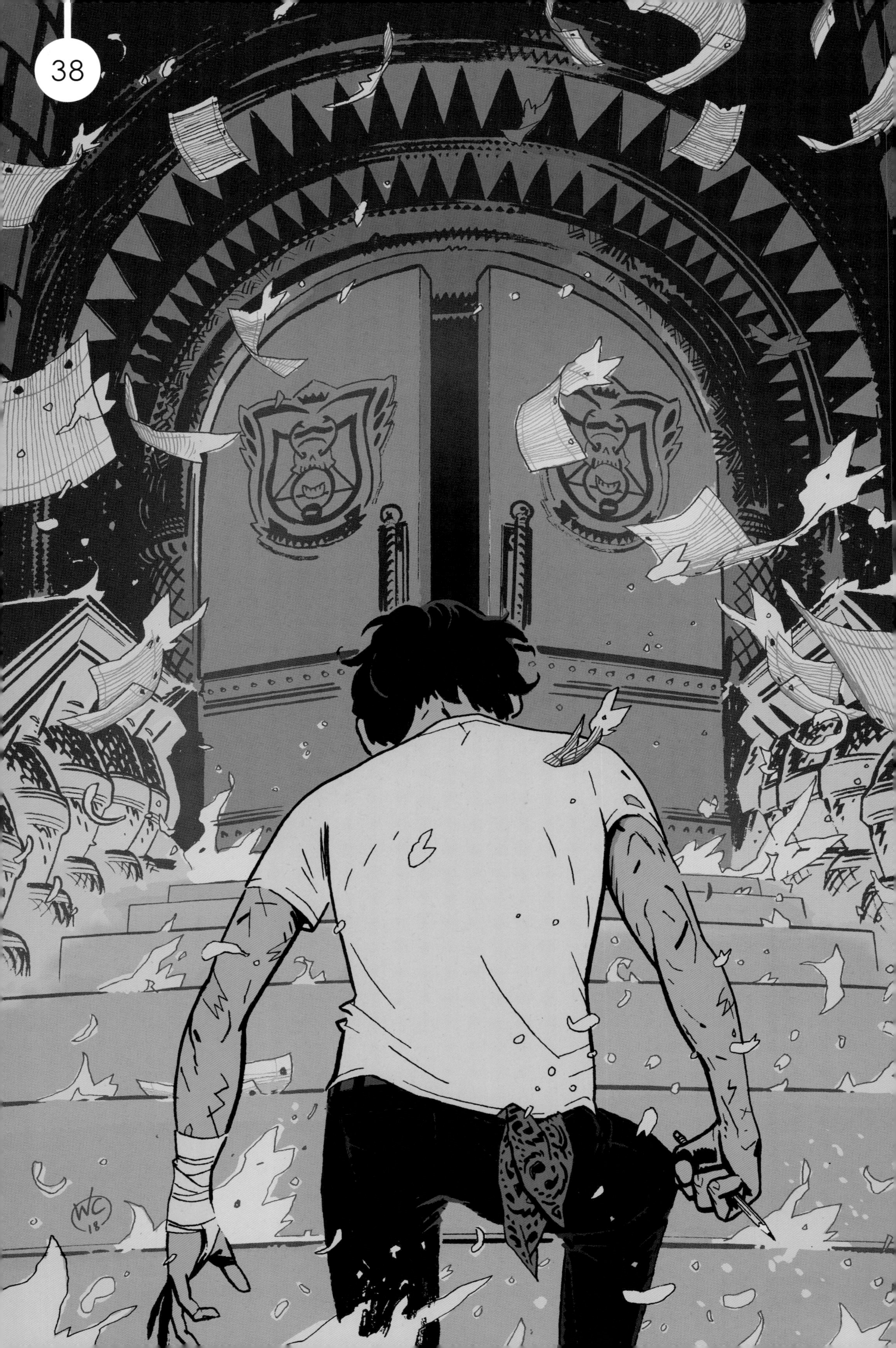

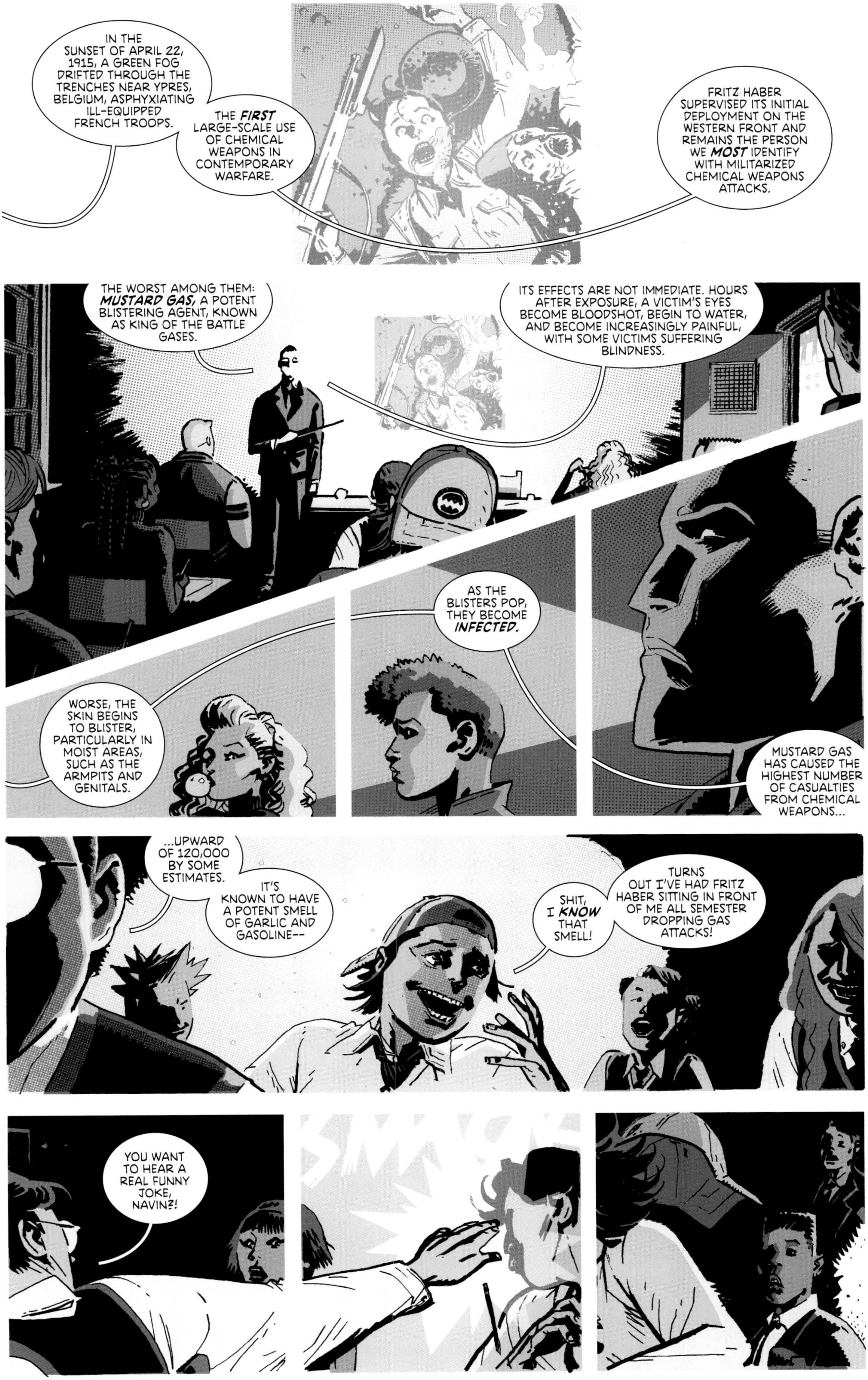
IN THE SUNSET OF APRIL 22, 1915, A GREEN FOG DRIFTED THROUGH THE TRENCHES NEAR YPRES, BELGIUM, ASPHYXIATING ILL-EQUIPPED FRENCH TROOPS.
THE **FIRST** LARGE-SCALE USE OF CHEMICAL WEAPONS IN CONTEMPORARY WARFARE.
FRITZ HABER SUPERVISED ITS INITIAL DEPLOYMENT ON THE WESTERN FRONT AND REMAINS THE PERSON WE **MOST** IDENTIFY WITH MILITARIZED CHEMICAL WEAPONS ATTACKS.
THE WORST AMONG THEM: **MUSTARD GAS,** A POTENT BLISTERING AGENT, KNOWN AS KING OF THE BATTLE GASES.
ITS EFFECTS ARE NOT IMMEDIATE. HOURS AFTER EXPOSURE, A VICTIM'S EYES BECOME BLOODSHOT, BEGIN TO WATER, AND BECOME INCREASINGLY PAINFUL, WITH SOME VICTIMS SUFFERING BLINDNESS.
WORSE, THE SKIN BEGINS TO BLISTER, PARTICULARLY IN MOIST AREAS, SUCH AS THE ARMPITS AND GENITALS.
AS THE BLISTERS POP, THEY BECOME **INFECTED.**
MUSTARD GAS HAS CAUSED THE HIGHEST NUMBER OF CASUALTIES FROM CHEMICAL WEAPONS...
...UPWARD OF 120,000 BY SOME ESTIMATES.
IT'S KNOWN TO HAVE A POTENT SMELL OF GARLIC AND GASOLINE--
SHIT, I **KNOW** THAT SMELL!
TURNS OUT I'VE HAD FRITZ HABER SITTING IN FRONT OF ME ALL SEMESTER DROPPING GAS ATTACKS!
YOU WANT TO HEAR A REAL FUNNY JOKE, NAVIN?!

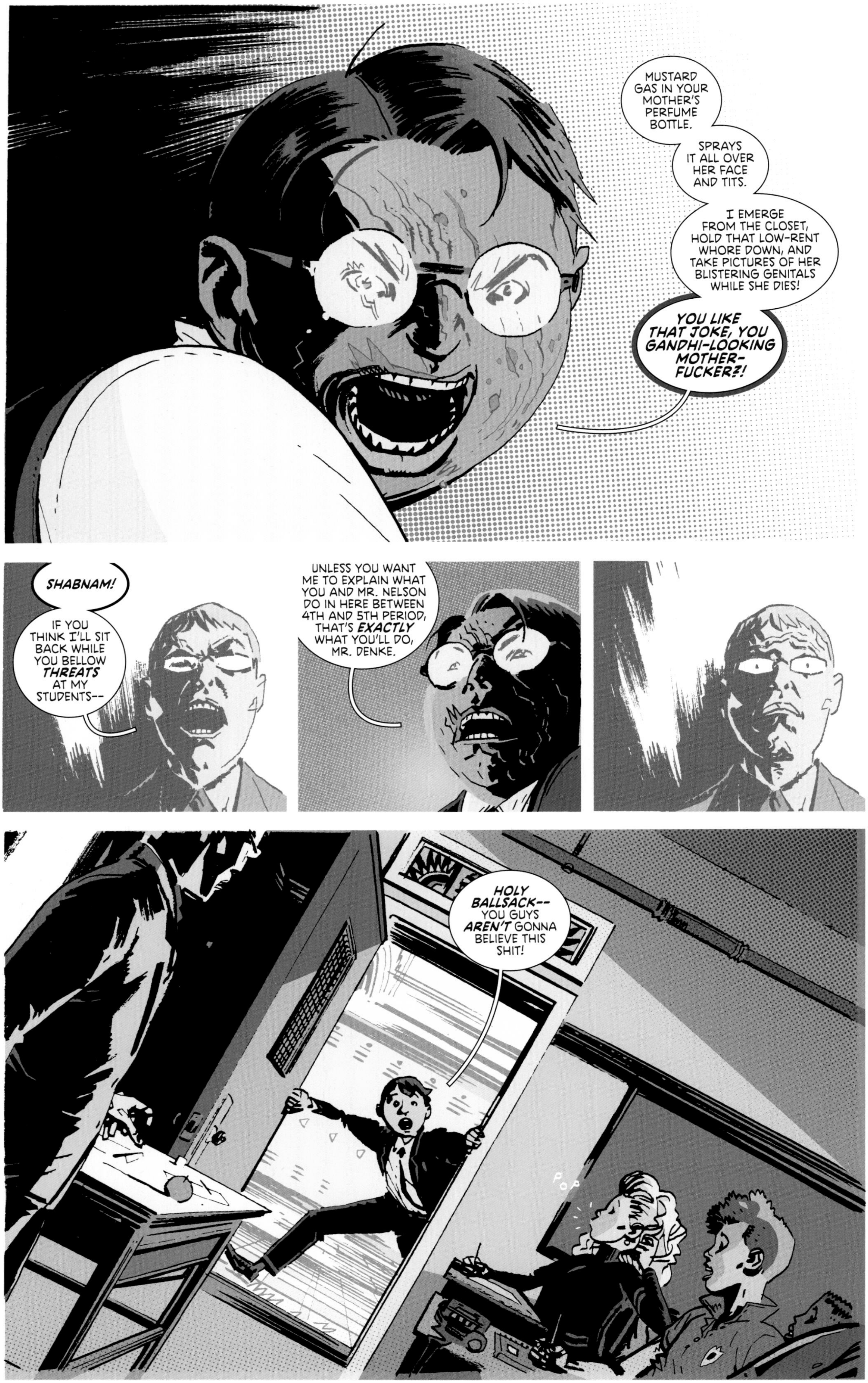
MUSTARD GAS IN YOUR MOTHER'S PERFUME BOTTLE.
SPRAYS IT ALL OVER HER FACE AND TITS.
I EMERGE FROM THE CLOSET, HOLD THAT LOW-RENT WHORE DOWN, AND TAKE PICTURES OF HER BLISTERING GENITALS WHILE SHE DIES!
YOU LIKE THAT JOKE, YOU GANDHI-LOOKING MOTHER-FUCKER?!
SHABNAM!
IF YOU THINK I'LL SIT BACK WHILE YOU BELLOW THREATS AT MY STUDENTS--
UNLESS YOU WANT ME TO EXPLAIN WHAT YOU AND MR. NELSON DO IN HERE BETWEEN 4TH AND 5TH PERIOD, THAT'S EXACTLY WHAT YOU'LL DO, MR. DENKE.
HOLY BALLSACK-- YOU GUYS AREN'T GONNA BELIEVE THIS SHIT!
POP

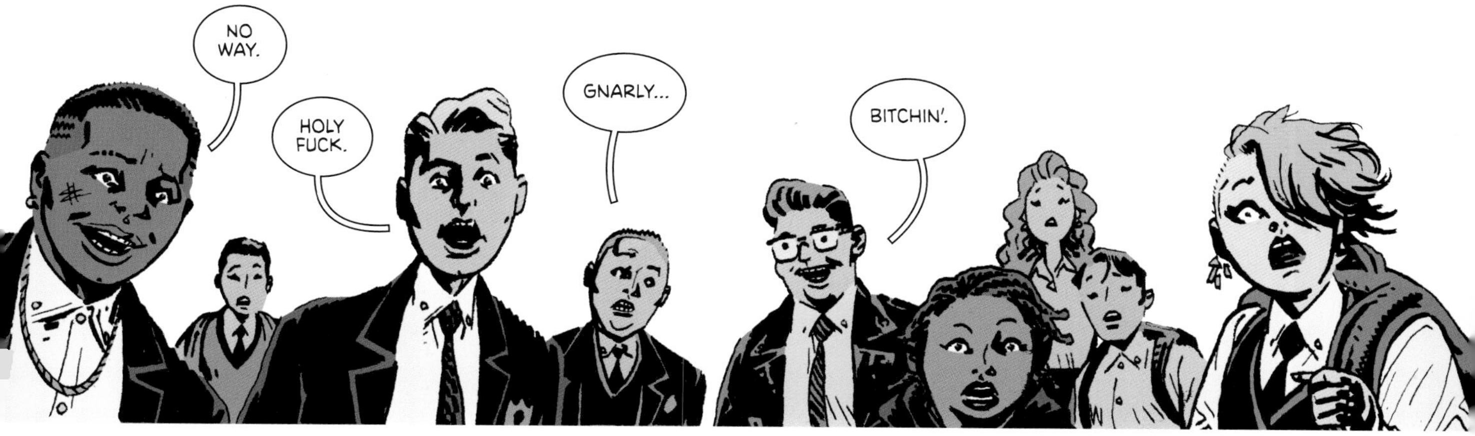
NO WAY.
HOLY FUCK.
GNARLY...
BITCHIN'.

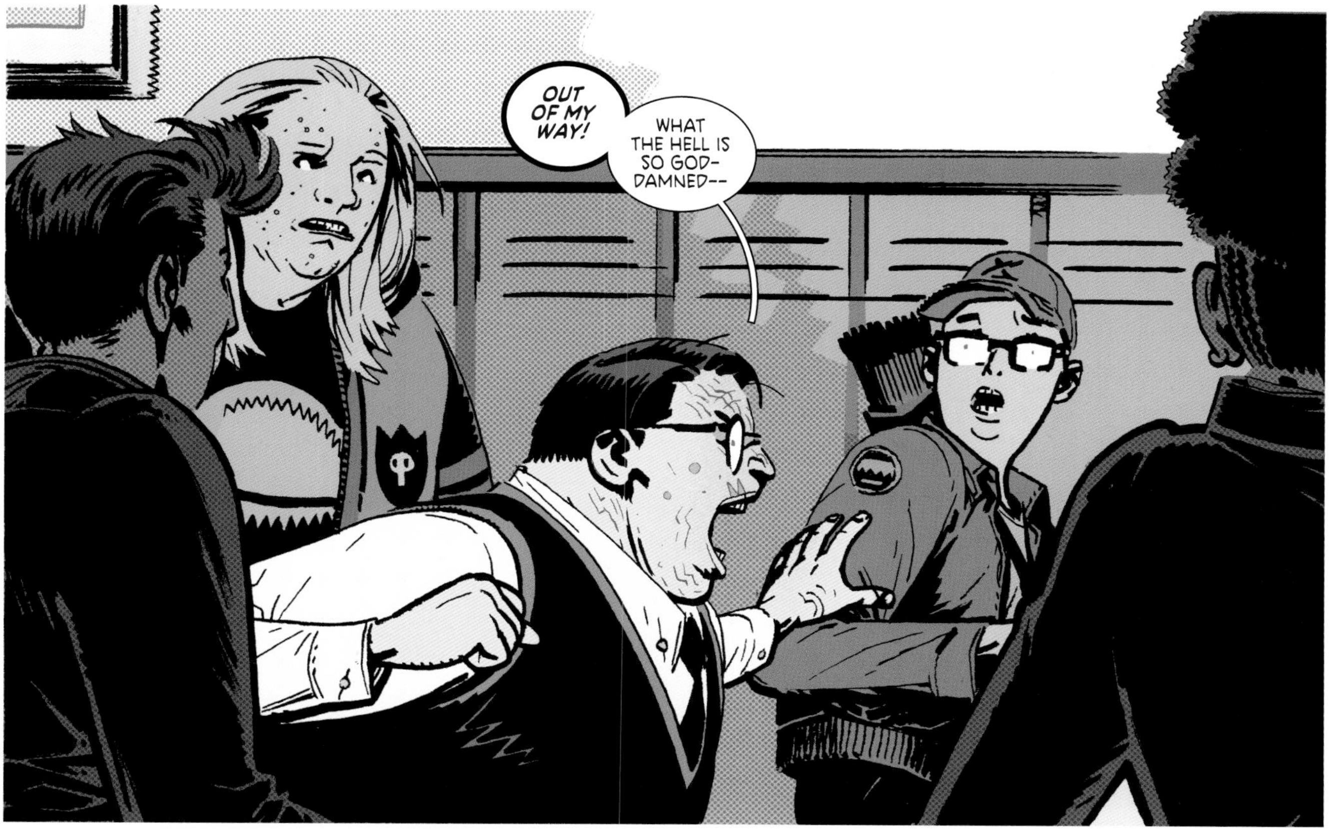
OUT OF MY WAY!
WHAT THE HELL IS SO GOD-DAMNED--

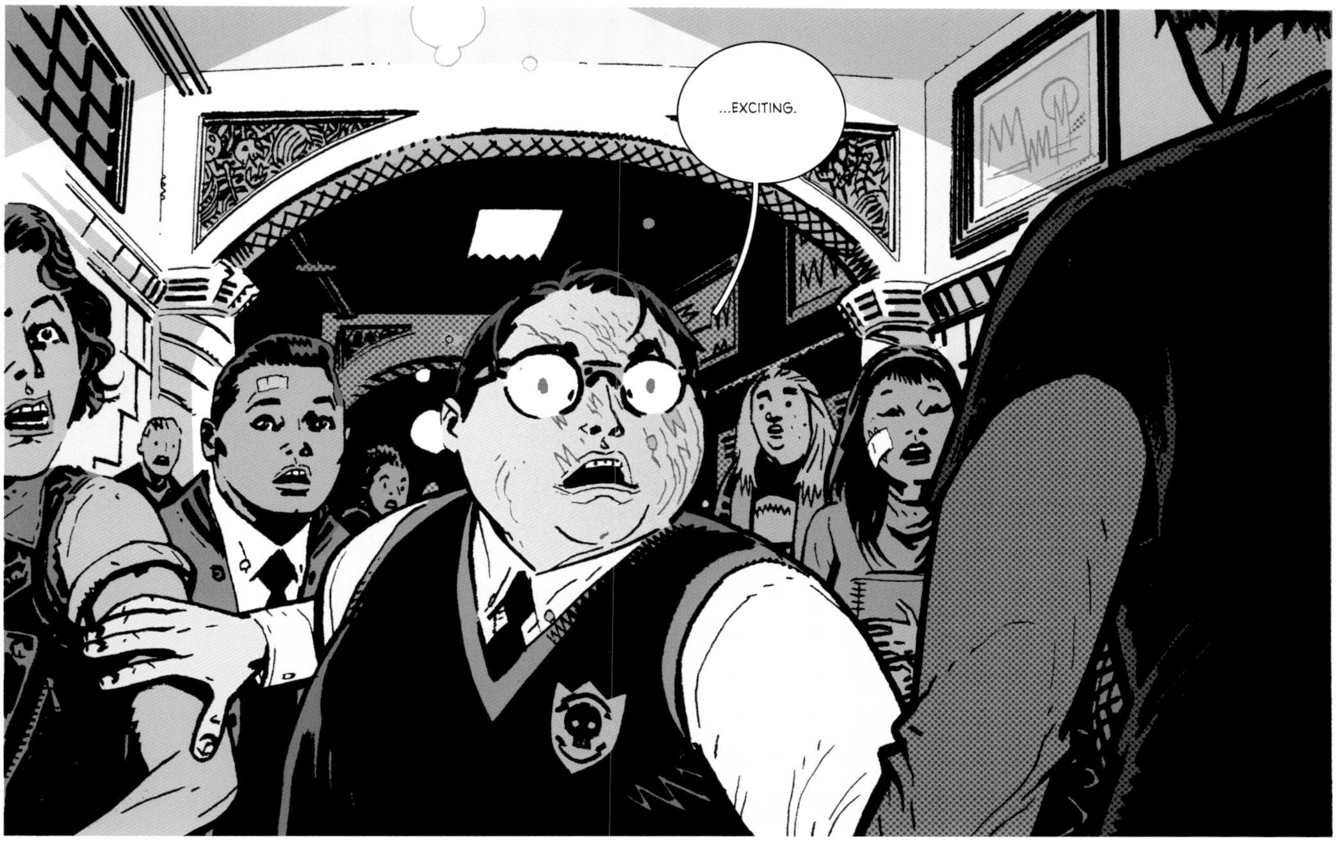
...EXCITING.

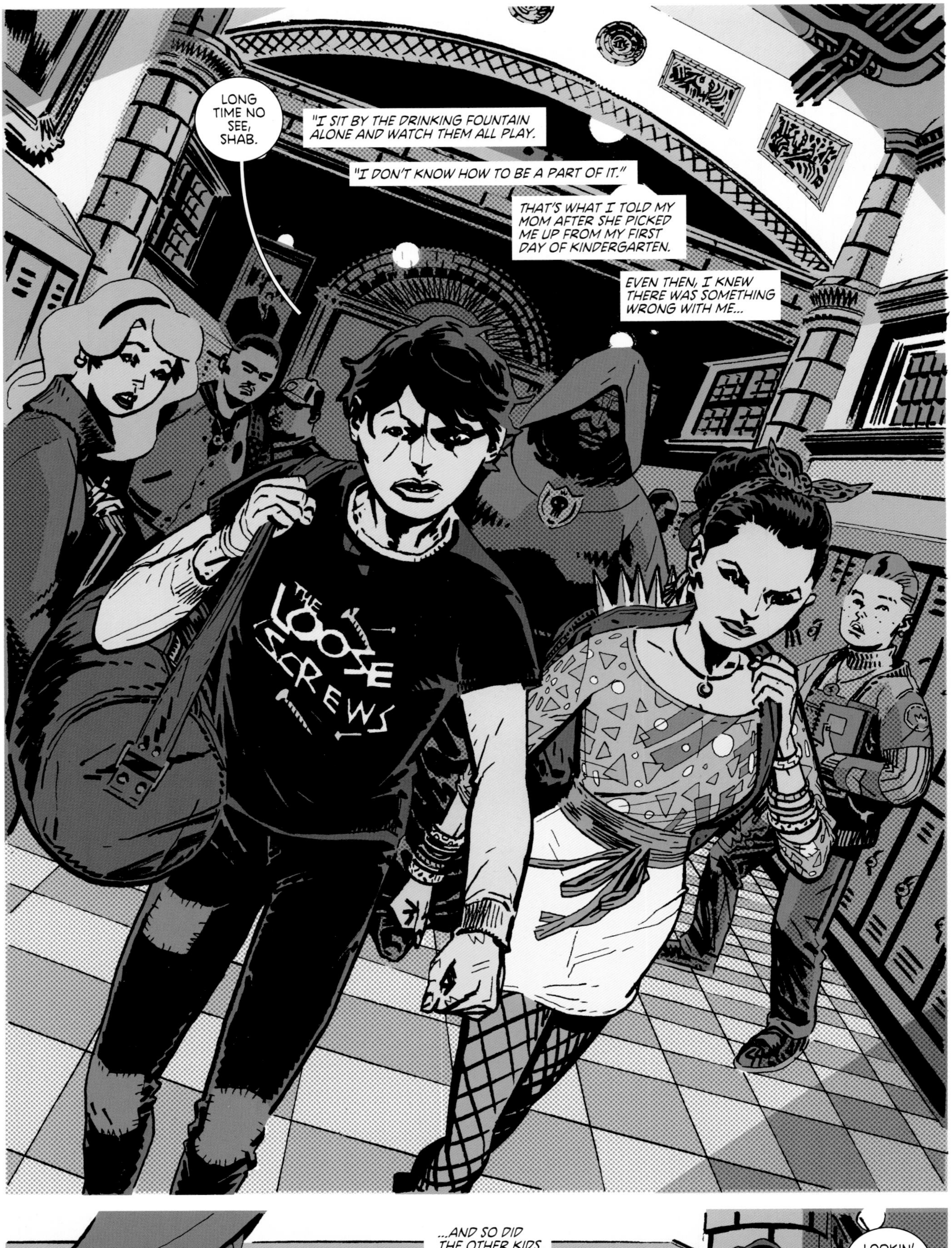
LONG TIME NO SEE, SHAB.
"I SIT BY THE DRINKING FOUNTAIN ALONE AND WATCH THEM ALL PLAY.
"I DON'T KNOW HOW TO BE A PART OF IT."
THAT'S WHAT I TOLD MY MOM AFTER SHE PICKED ME UP FROM MY FIRST DAY OF KINDERGARTEN.
EVEN THEN, I KNEW THERE WAS SOMETHING WRONG WITH ME...
THE LOOSE SCREWS
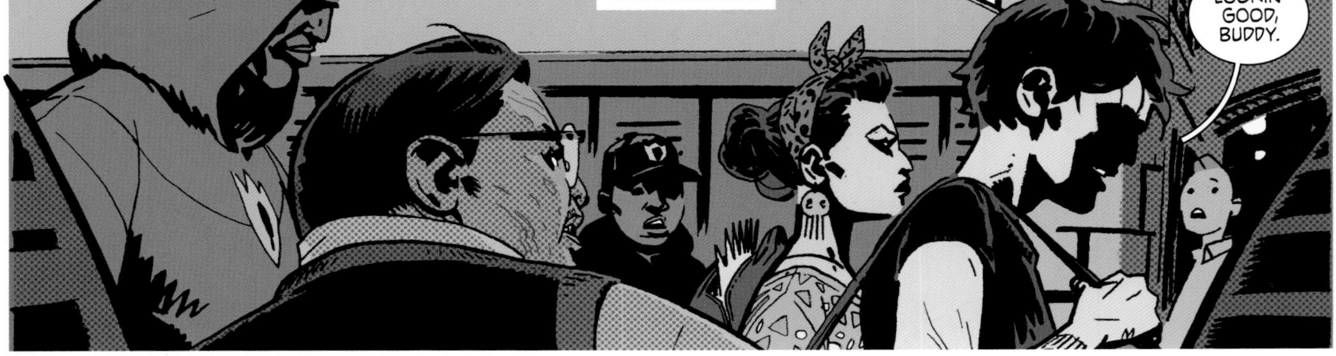
...AND SO DID THE OTHER KIDS.
LOOKIN' GOOD, BUDDY.

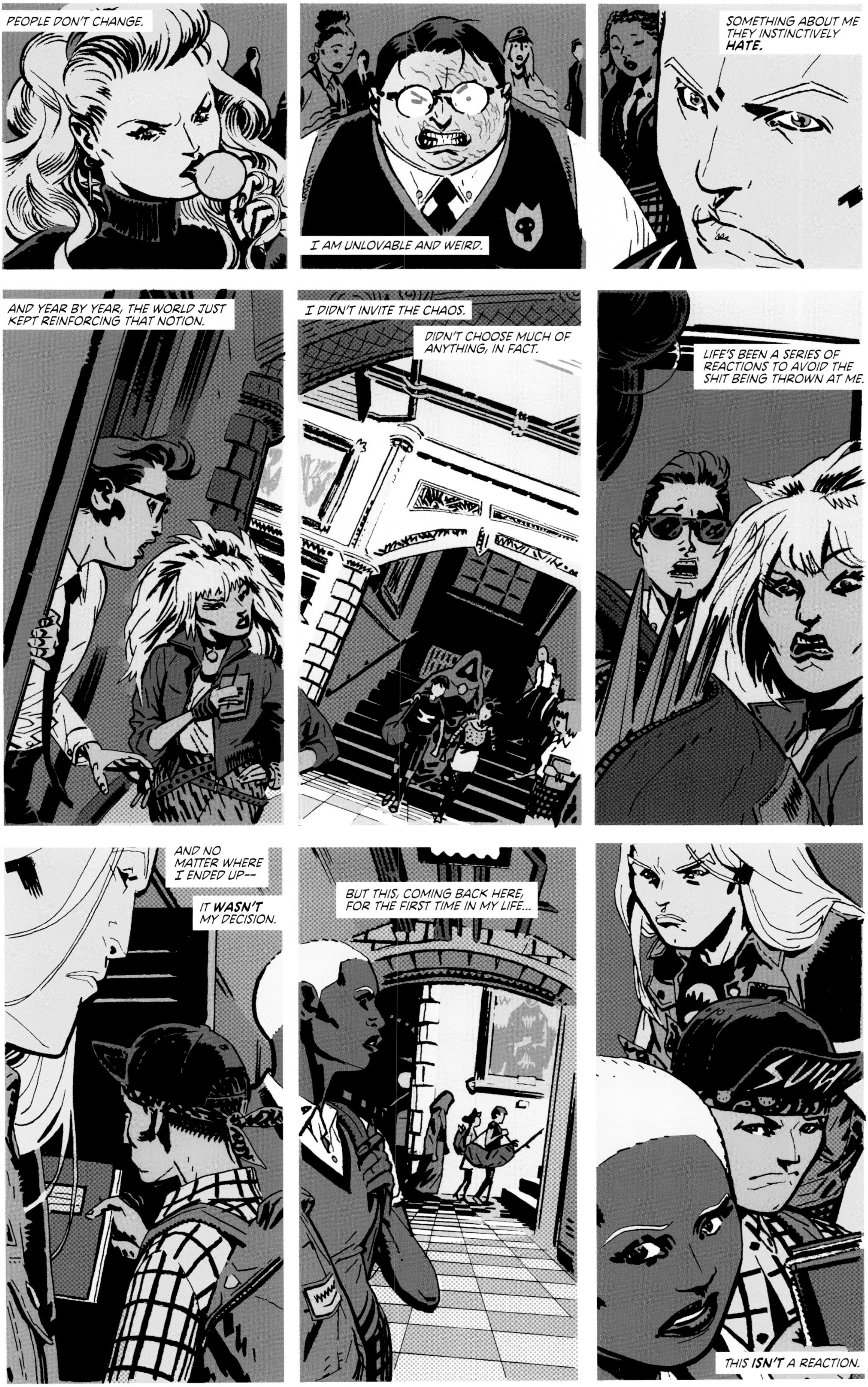
PEOPLE DON'T CHANGE.
I AM UNLOVABLE AND WEIRD.
SOMETHING ABOUT ME THEY INSTINCTIVELY **HATE.**
AND YEAR BY YEAR, THE WORLD JUST KEPT REINFORCING THAT NOTION.
I DIDN'T INVITE THE CHAOS.
DIDN'T CHOOSE MUCH OF ANYTHING, IN FACT.
LIFE'S BEEN A SERIES OF REACTIONS TO AVOID THE SHIT BEING THROWN AT ME.
AND NO MATTER WHERE I ENDED UP--
IT **WASN'T** MY DECISION.
BUT THIS, COMING BACK HERE, FOR THE FIRST TIME IN MY LIFE...
THIS **ISN'T** A REACTION.

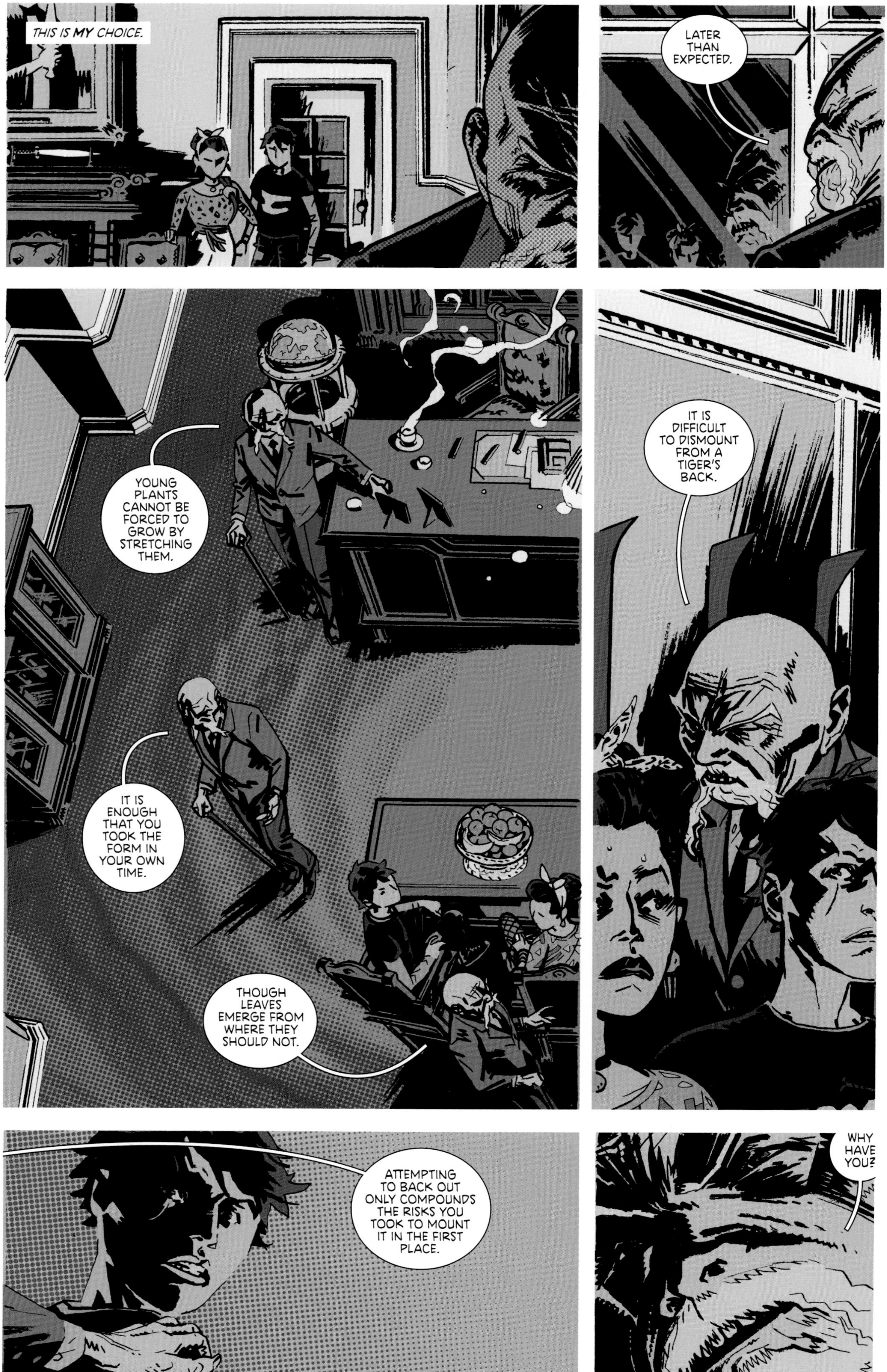
THIS IS MY CHOICE.
LATER THAN EXPECTED.
YOUNG PLANTS CANNOT BE FORCED TO GROW BY STRETCHING THEM.
IT IS ENOUGH THAT YOU TOOK THE FORM IN YOUR OWN TIME.
THOUGH LEAVES EMERGE FROM WHERE THEY SHOULD NOT.
IT IS DIFFICULT TO DISMOUNT FROM A TIGER'S BACK.
ATTEMPTING TO BACK OUT ONLY COMPOUNDS THE RISKS YOU TOOK TO MOUNT IT IN THE FIRST PLACE.
WHY HAVE YOU?

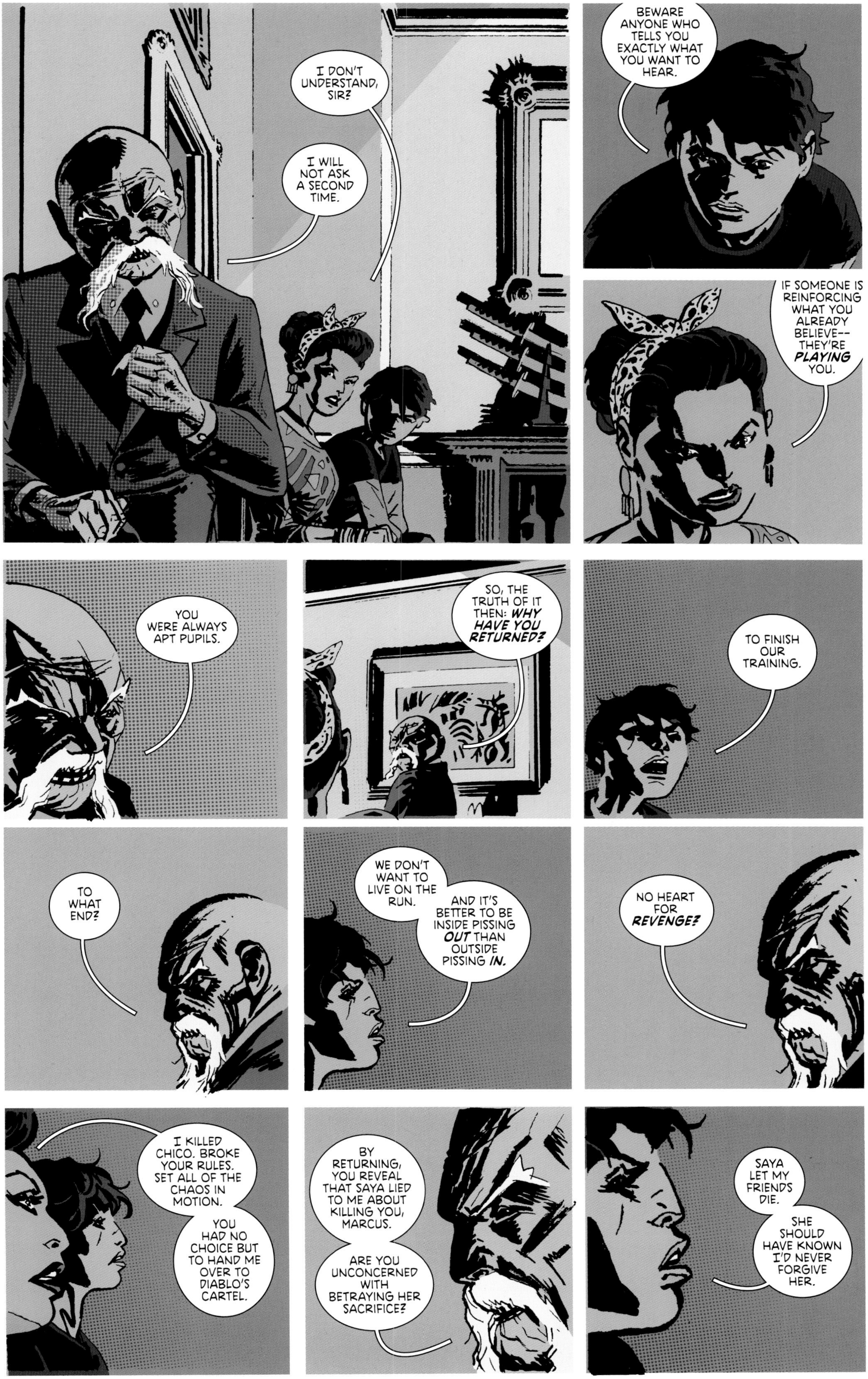
I DON'T UNDERSTAND, SIR?
I WILL NOT ASK A SECOND TIME.
BEWARE ANYONE WHO TELLS YOU EXACTLY WHAT YOU WANT TO HEAR.
IF SOMEONE IS REINFORCING WHAT YOU ALREADY BELIEVE-- THEY'RE *PLAYING* YOU.
YOU WERE ALWAYS APT PUPILS.
SO, THE TRUTH OF IT THEN: *WHY HAVE YOU RETURNED?*
TO FINISH OUR TRAINING.
TO WHAT END?
WE DON'T WANT TO LIVE ON THE RUN.
AND IT'S BETTER TO BE INSIDE PISSING *OUT* THAN OUTSIDE PISSING *IN.*
NO HEART FOR *REVENGE?*
I KILLED CHICO. BROKE YOUR RULES. SET ALL OF THE CHAOS IN MOTION.
YOU HAD NO CHOICE BUT TO HAND ME OVER TO DIABLO'S CARTEL.
BY RETURNING, YOU REVEAL THAT SAYA LIED TO ME ABOUT KILLING YOU, MARCUS.
ARE YOU UNCONCERNED WITH BETRAYING HER SACRIFICE?
SAYA LET MY FRIENDS DIE.
SHE SHOULD HAVE KNOWN I'D NEVER FORGIVE HER.

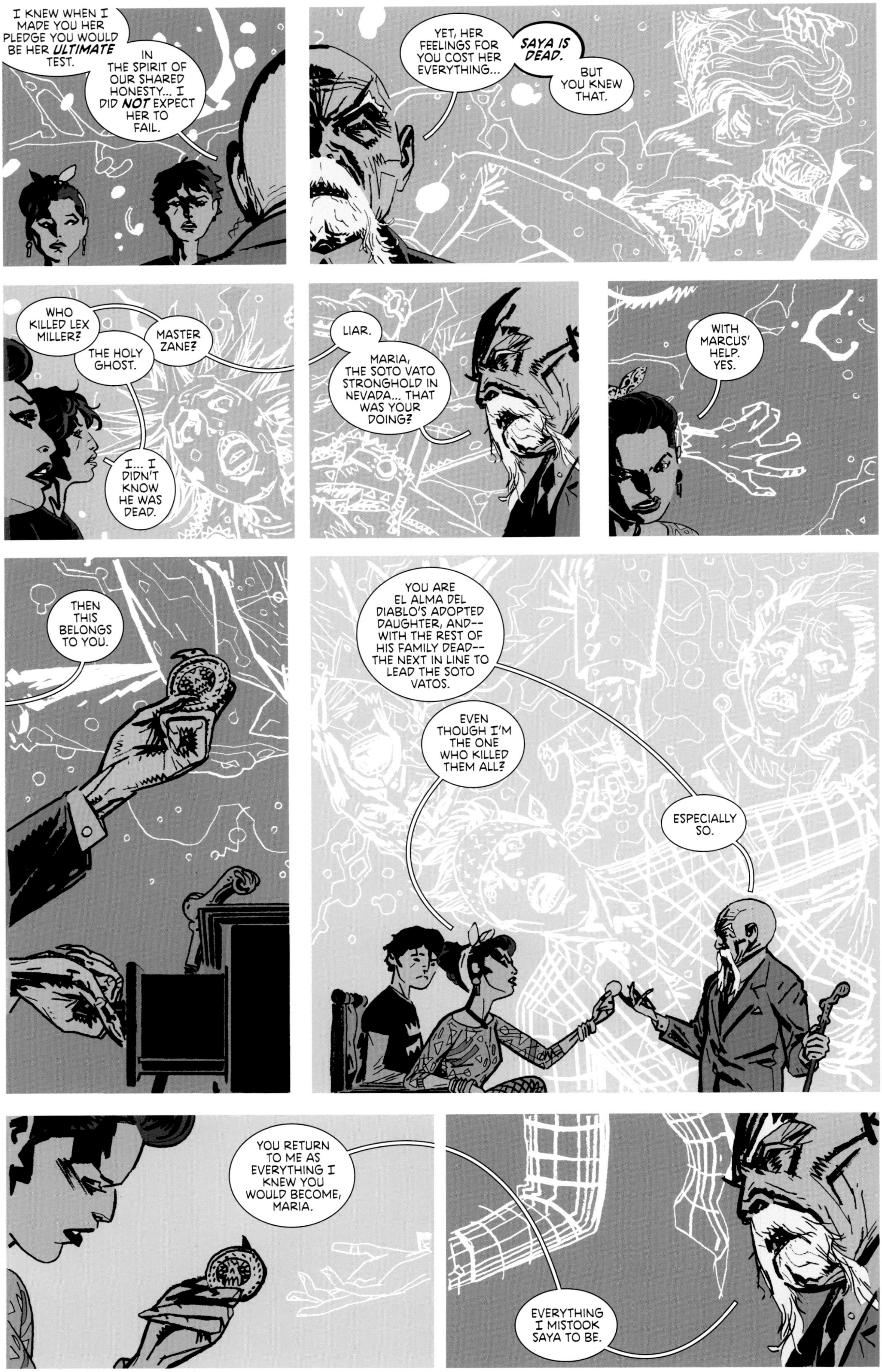
I KNEW WHEN I MADE YOU HER PLEDGE YOU WOULD BE HER *ULTIMATE* TEST.
IN THE SPIRIT OF OUR SHARED HONESTY... I DID *NOT* EXPECT HER TO FAIL.
YET, HER FEELINGS FOR YOU COST HER EVERYTHING...
SAYA IS DEAD.
BUT YOU KNEW THAT.
WHO KILLED LEX MILLER?
THE HOLY GHOST.
MASTER ZANE?
I... I DIDN'T KNOW HE WAS DEAD.
LIAR.
MARIA, THE SOTO VATO STRONGHOLD IN NEVADA... THAT WAS YOUR DOING?
WITH MARCUS' HELP. YES.
THEN THIS BELONGS TO YOU.
YOU ARE EL ALMA DEL DIABLO'S ADOPTED DAUGHTER, AND-- WITH THE REST OF HIS FAMILY DEAD-- THE NEXT IN LINE TO LEAD THE SOTO VATOS.
EVEN THOUGH I'M THE ONE WHO KILLED THEM ALL?
ESPECIALLY SO.
YOU RETURN TO ME AS EVERYTHING I KNEW YOU WOULD BECOME, MARIA.
EVERYTHING I MISTOOK SAYA TO BE.

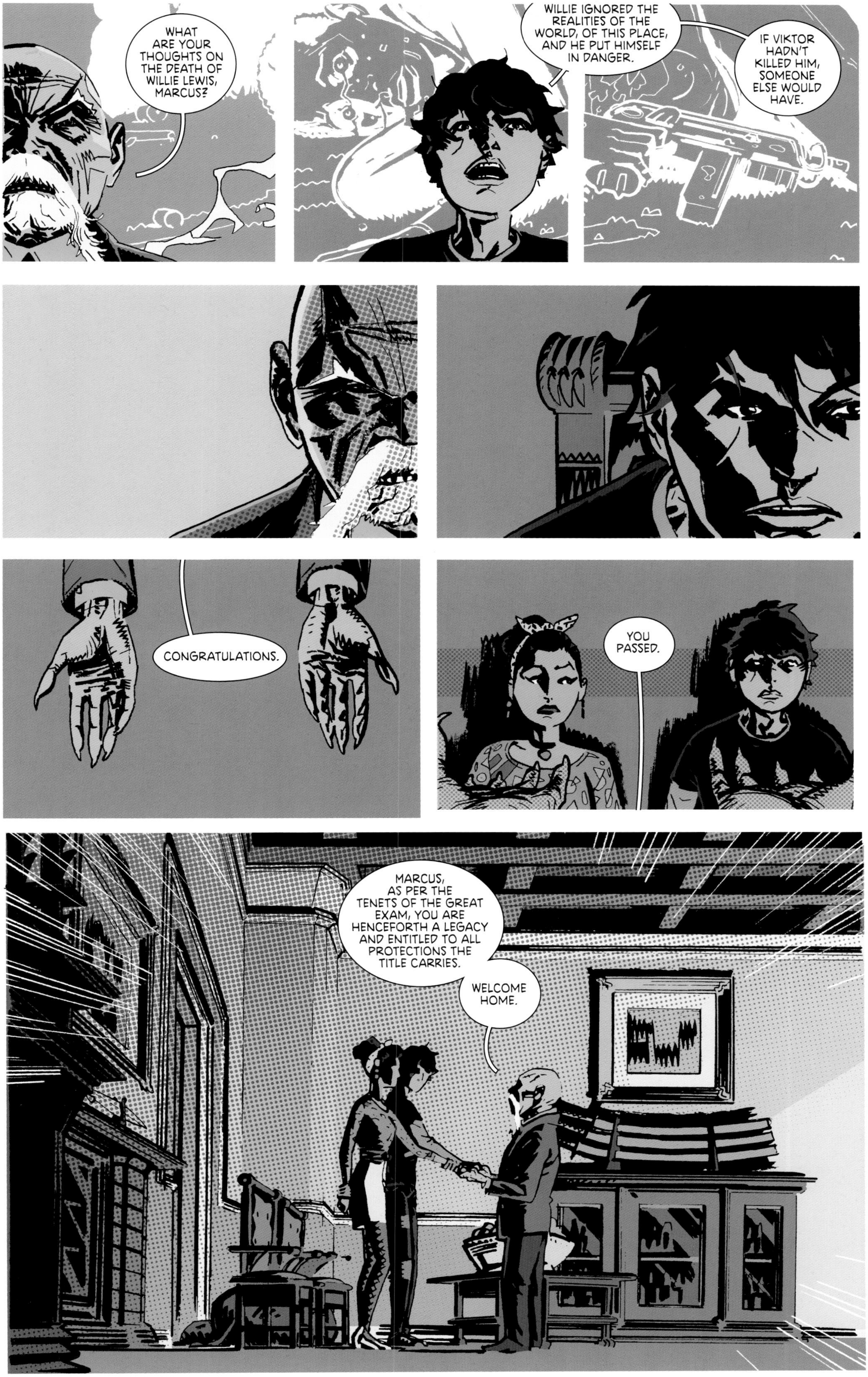
WHAT ARE YOUR THOUGHTS ON THE DEATH OF WILLIE LEWIS, MARCUS?
WILLIE IGNORED THE REALITIES OF THE WORLD, OF THIS PLACE, AND HE PUT HIMSELF IN DANGER.
IF VIKTOR HADN'T KILLED HIM, SOMEONE ELSE WOULD HAVE.
CONGRATULATIONS.
YOU PASSED.
MARCUS, AS PER THE TENETS OF THE GREAT EXAM, YOU ARE HENCEFORTH A LEGACY AND ENTITLED TO ALL PROTECTIONS THE TITLE CARRIES.
WELCOME HOME.

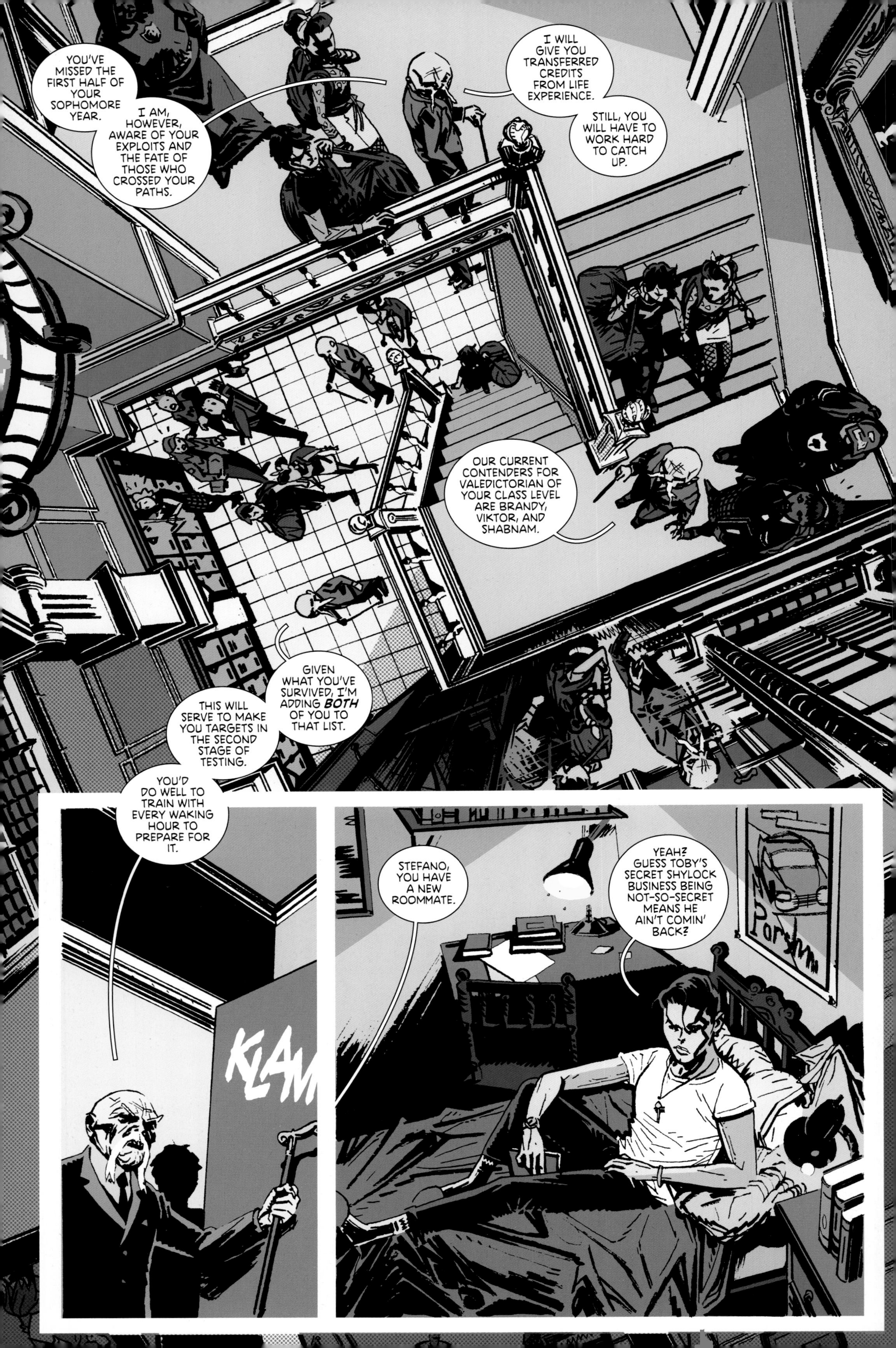
YOU'VE MISSED THE FIRST HALF OF YOUR SOPHOMORE YEAR.
I AM, HOWEVER, AWARE OF YOUR EXPLOITS AND THE FATE OF THOSE WHO CROSSED YOUR PATHS.
I WILL GIVE YOU TRANSFERRED CREDITS FROM LIFE EXPERIENCE.
STILL, YOU WILL HAVE TO WORK HARD TO CATCH UP.
OUR CURRENT CONTENDERS FOR VALEDICTORIAN OF YOUR CLASS LEVEL ARE BRANDY, VIKTOR, AND SHABNAM.
GIVEN WHAT YOU'VE SURVIVED, I'M ADDING **BOTH** OF YOU TO THAT LIST.
THIS WILL SERVE TO MAKE YOU TARGETS IN THE SECOND STAGE OF TESTING.
YOU'D DO WELL TO TRAIN WITH EVERY WAKING HOUR TO PREPARE FOR IT.
KLAM
STEFANO, YOU HAVE A NEW ROOMMATE.
YEAH? GUESS TOBY'S SECRET SHYLOCK BUSINESS BEING NOT-SO-SECRET MEANS HE AIN'T COMIN' BACK?

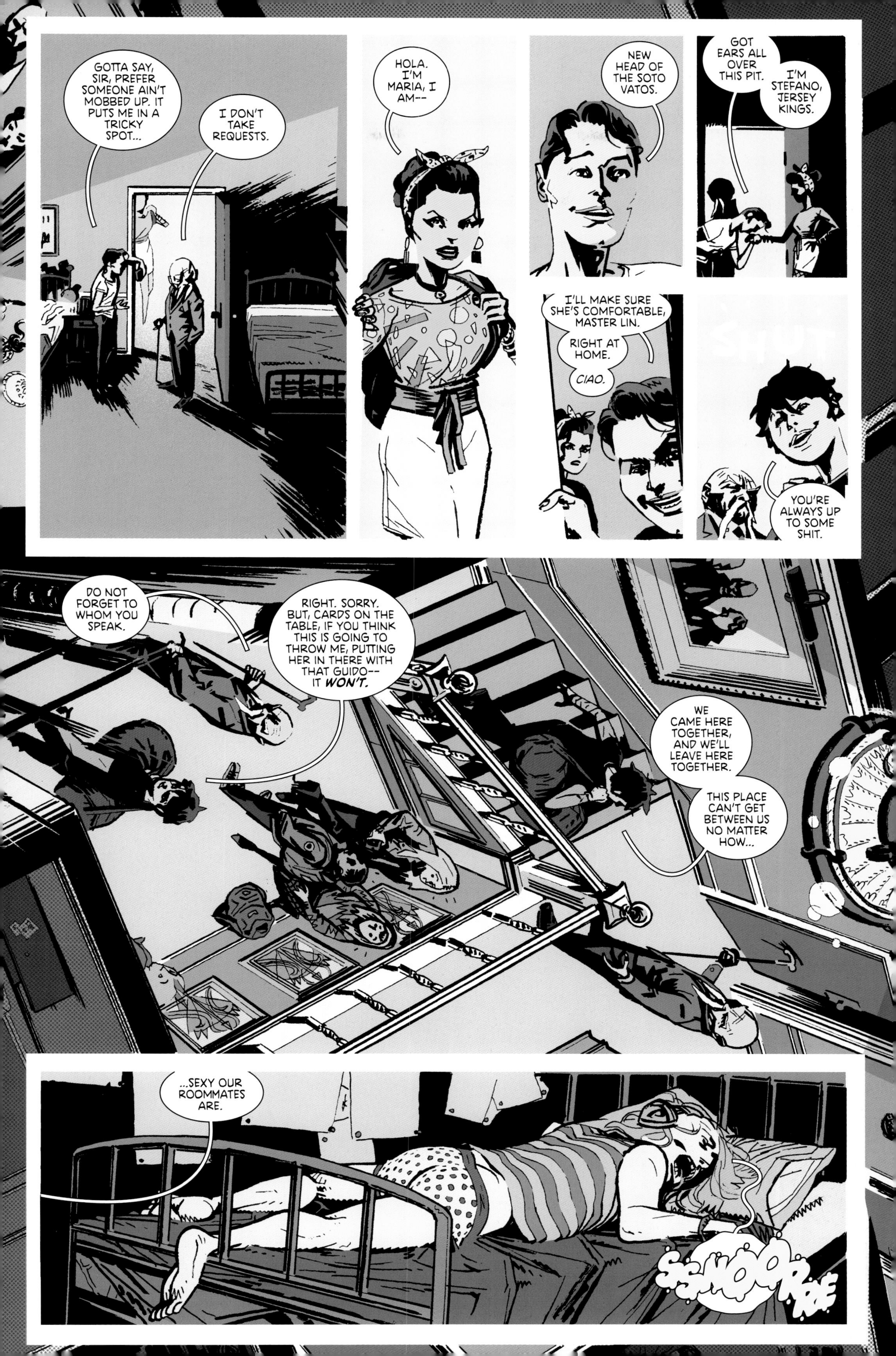
GOTTA SAY, SIR, PREFER SOMEONE AIN'T MOBBED UP. IT PUTS ME IN A TRICKY SPOT...
I DON'T TAKE REQUESTS.
HOLA. I'M MARIA, I AM--
NEW HEAD OF THE SOTO VATOS.
GOT EARS ALL OVER THIS PIT.
I'M STEFANO, JERSEY KINGS.
I'LL MAKE SURE SHE'S COMFORTABLE, MASTER LIN.
RIGHT AT HOME.
CIAO.
YOU'RE ALWAYS UP TO SOME SHIT.
DO NOT FORGET TO WHOM YOU SPEAK.
RIGHT. SORRY. BUT, CARDS ON THE TABLE, IF YOU THINK THIS IS GOING TO THROW ME, PUTTING HER IN THERE WITH THAT GUIDO-- IT *WON'T.*
WE CAME HERE TOGETHER, AND WE'LL LEAVE HERE TOGETHER.
THIS PLACE CAN'T GET BETWEEN US NO MATTER HOW...
...SEXY OUR ROOMMATES ARE.
SSNOORRE

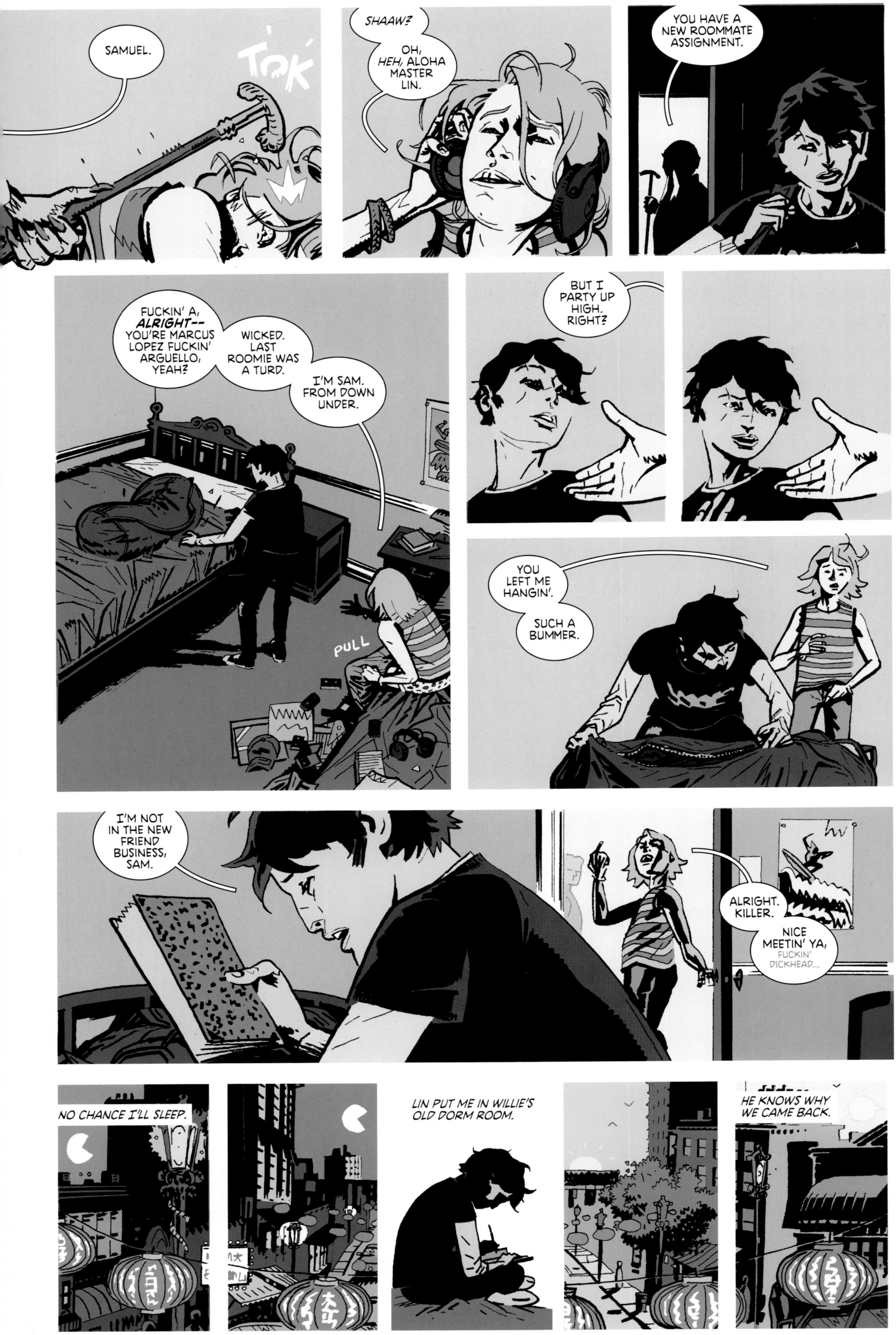
SAMUEL.
TOK
SHAAW?
OH, HEH, ALOHA MASTER LIN.
YOU HAVE A NEW ROOMMATE ASSIGNMENT.
FUCKIN' A, ALRIGHT-- YOU'RE MARCUS LOPEZ FUCKIN' ARGUELLO, YEAH?
WICKED. LAST ROOMIE WAS A TURD.
I'M SAM. FROM DOWN UNDER.
PULL
BUT I PARTY UP HIGH. RIGHT?
YOU LEFT ME HANGIN'.
SUCH A BUMMER.
I'M NOT IN THE NEW FRIEND BUSINESS, SAM.
ALRIGHT. KILLER.
NICE MEETIN' YA, FUCKIN' DICKHEAD...
NO CHANCE I'LL SLEEP.
LIN PUT ME IN WILLIE'S OLD DORM ROOM.
HE KNOWS WHY WE CAME BACK.

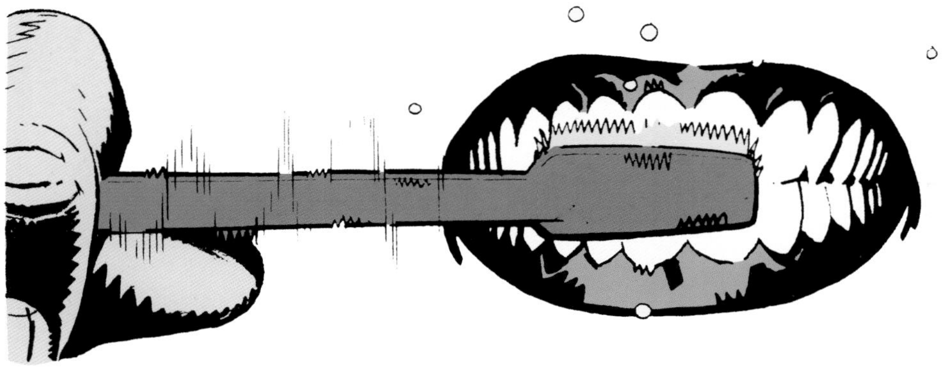

EVERYTHING IS **WRONG.**
OFF-BALANCE.

CAN YOU FEEL IT?

I **SHOULDN'T** BE HERE.
I SHOULDN'T BE ALIVE.

ENDED UP IN A STRANGE ALTERNATE DIMENSION WHERE EVERYTHING IS ON THE WRONG AXIS.

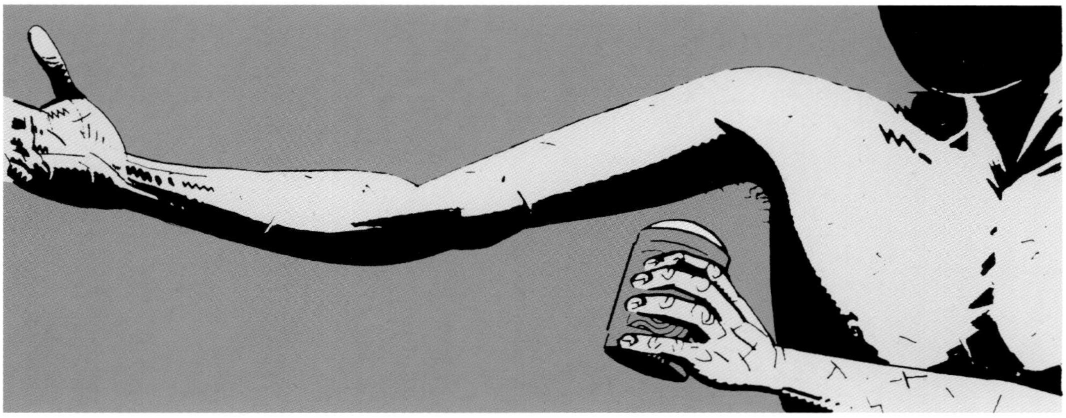

THE AIR RADIATES **REJECTION.**

THE SMELL OF THIS PLACE... WET EARTH, MOLD, SAGE... FORCED MEMORY FLASHES:

THE LAST NIGHT I SLEPT HERE.

HIGH ON METH.

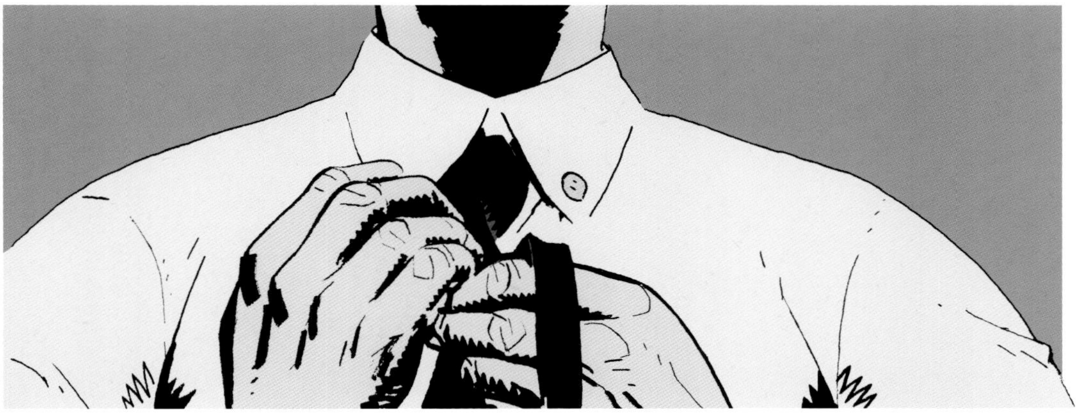

STRESSED MUSCLES TENSE UP INVOLUNTARILY.

FWO WAS GOING AFTER WILLIE BECAUSE OF WHAT I TOLD THEM.

SAYA WAS GOING TO **KILL** ME FOR BETRAYING HIM.

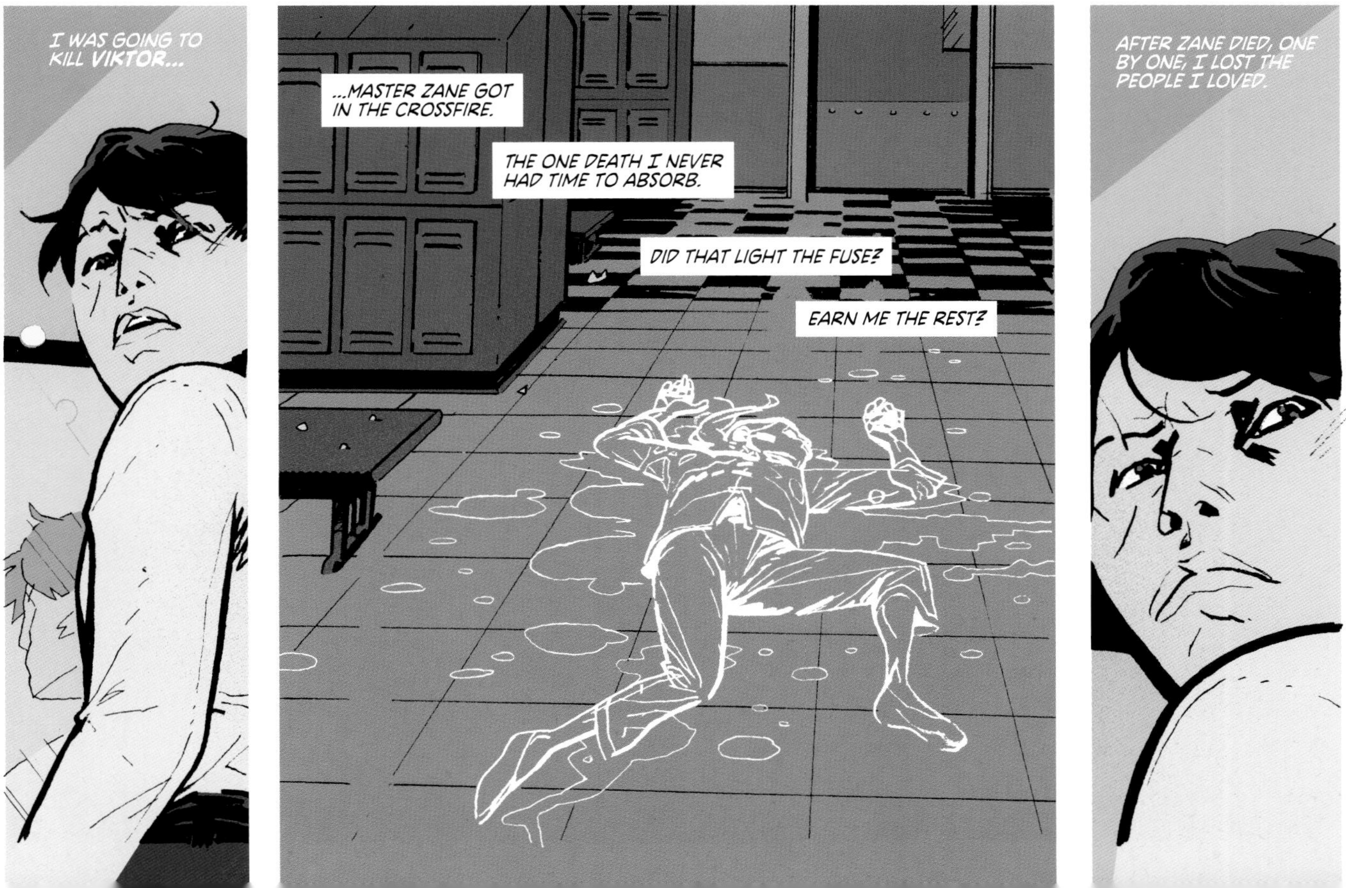
I WAS GOING TO KILL **VIKTOR...**
...MASTER ZANE GOT IN THE CROSSFIRE.
THE ONE DEATH I NEVER HAD TIME TO ABSORB.
DID THAT LIGHT THE FUSE?
EARN ME THE REST?
AFTER ZANE DIED, ONE BY ONE, I LOST THE PEOPLE I LOVED.

HAD A DREAM LAST NIGHT THAT I PUT HEROIN IN THE FANGS OF SNAKES AND LAY IN A BED WITH THEM.

I HELD THE BEDPOST TIGHT AS THEY BIT ME OVER AND OVER.

BILLY WAS HIDING IN THE CORNER. HE TOLD ME I HAD A VICTIM COMPLEX. THAT I FIXATED ON WHO HAD DONE WRONG BY ME INSTEAD OF WHO HAD DONE **RIGHT.**

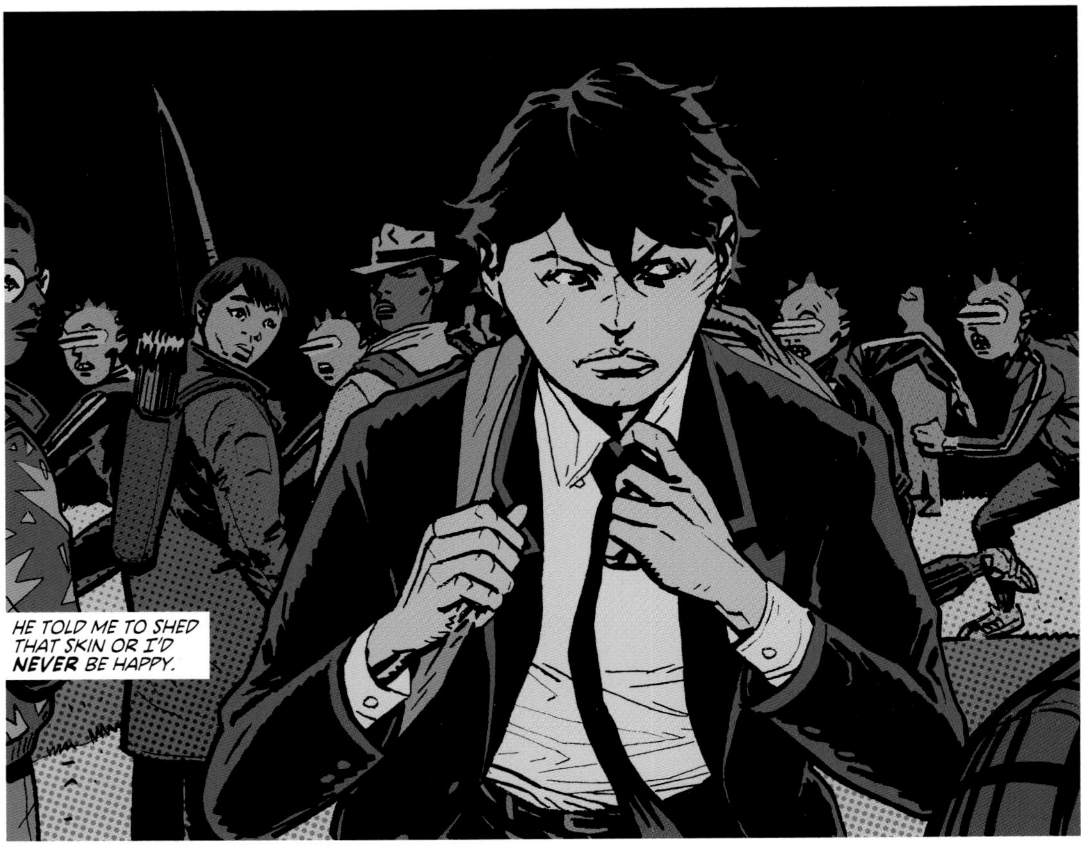
HE TOLD ME TO SHED THAT SKIN OR I'D **NEVER** BE HAPPY.

I DON'T RECOGNIZE MYSELF ANYMORE.

MAYBE WILLIE WAS RIGHT.

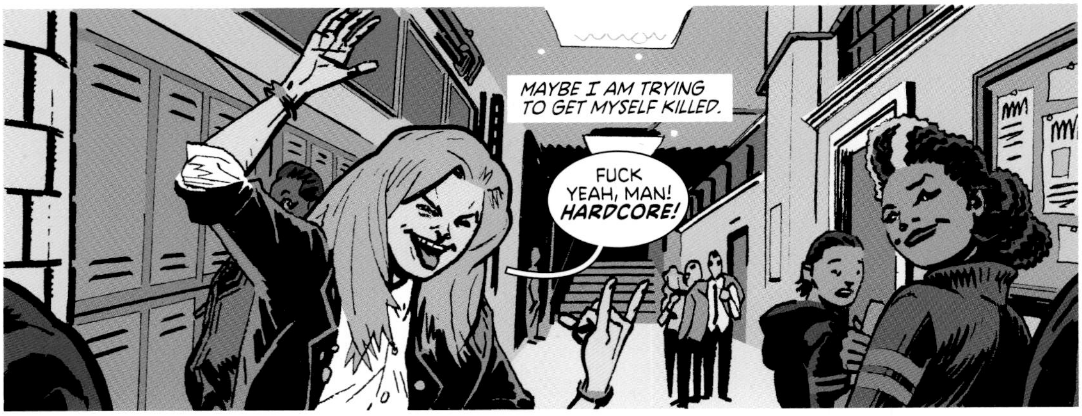
MAYBE I AM TRYING TO GET MYSELF KILLED.
FUCK YEAH, MAN! **HARDCORE!**

NOTHING LIKE WHAT I IMAGINED.

THEY SMILE. THEY WAVE. THEY FLIRT.

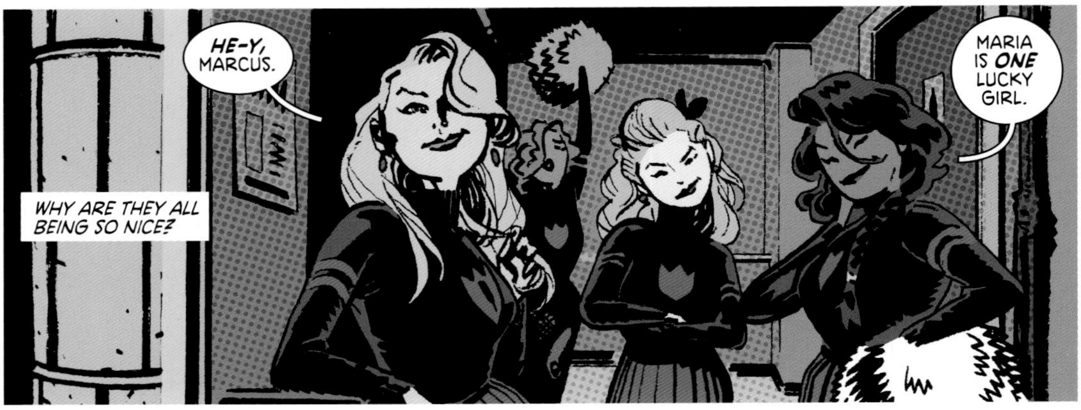
HE-Y, MARCUS.
WHY ARE THEY ALL BEING SO NICE?
MARIA IS **ONE** LUCKY GIRL.

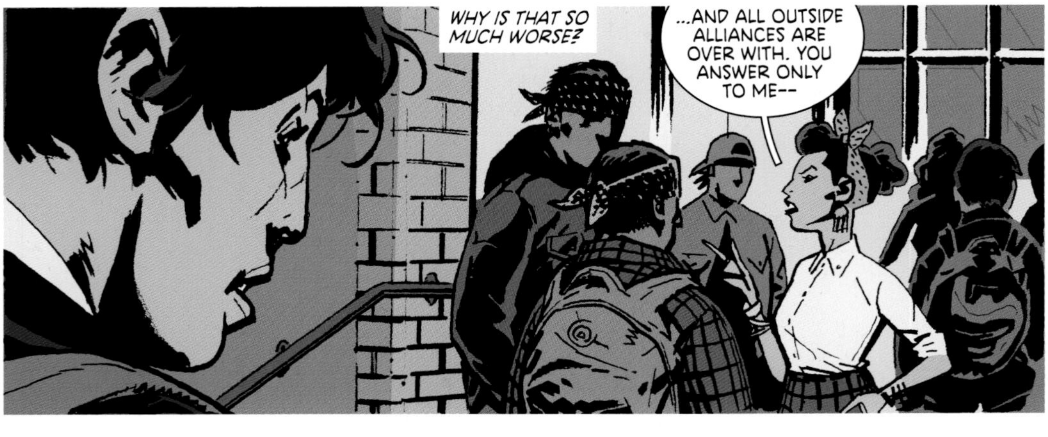
WHY IS THAT SO MUCH WORSE?
...AND ALL OUTSIDE ALLIANCES ARE OVER WITH. YOU ANSWER ONLY TO ME--

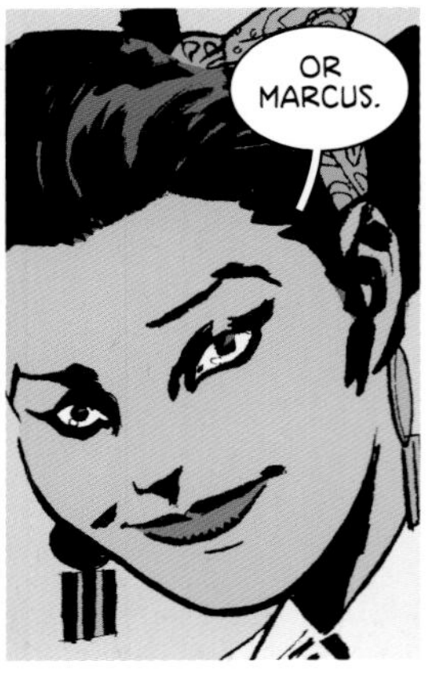
OR MARCUS.

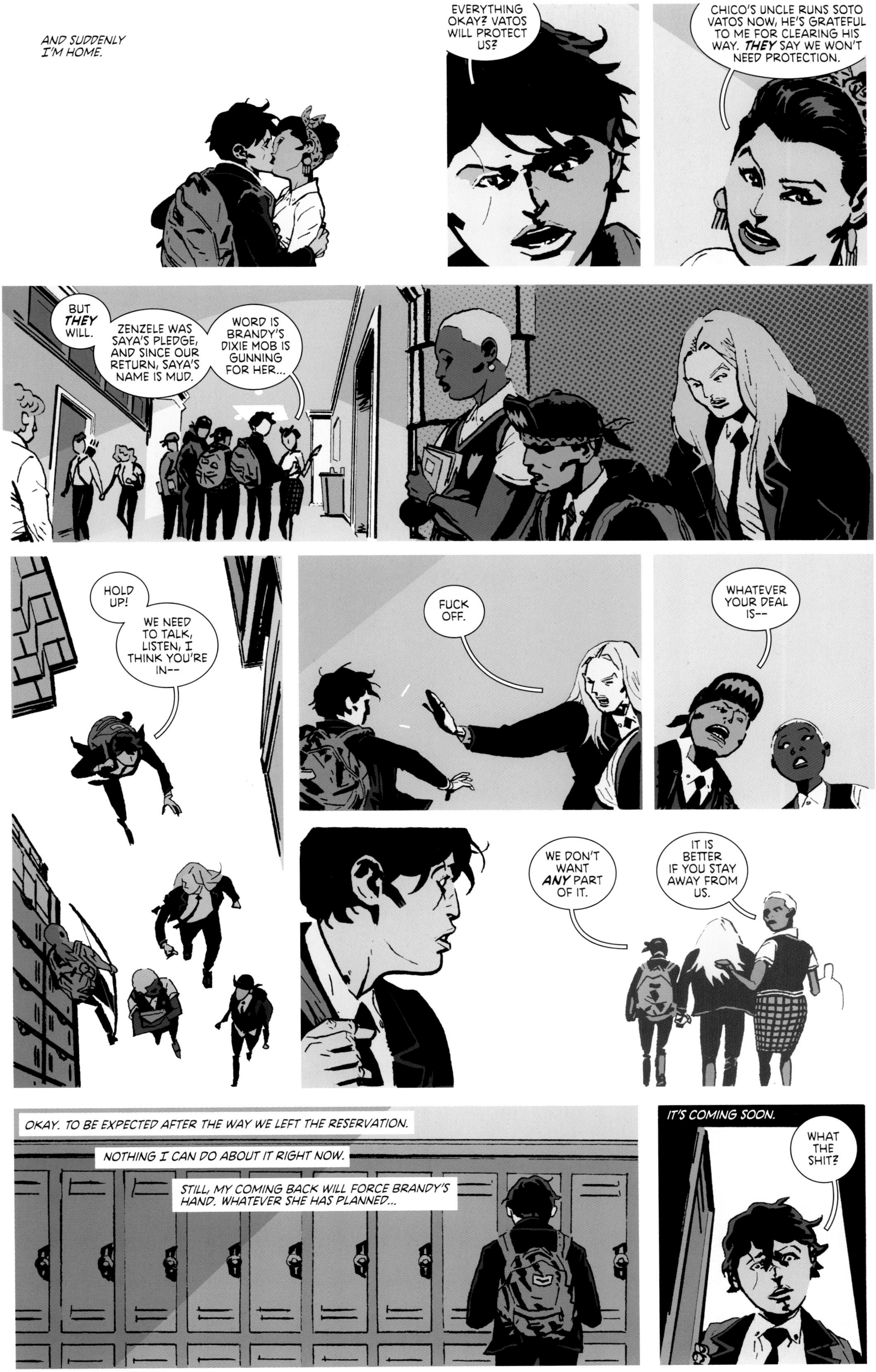
AND SUDDENLY I'M HOME.
EVERYTHING OKAY? VATOS WILL PROTECT US?
CHICO'S UNCLE RUNS SOTO VATOS NOW, HE'S GRATEFUL TO ME FOR CLEARING HIS WAY. THEY SAY WE WON'T NEED PROTECTION.
BUT THEY WILL.
ZENZELE WAS SAYA'S PLEDGE, AND SINCE OUR RETURN, SAYA'S NAME IS MUD.
WORD IS BRANDY'S DIXIE MOB IS GUNNING FOR HER...
HOLD UP!
WE NEED TO TALK, LISTEN, I THINK YOU'RE IN--
FUCK OFF.
WHATEVER YOUR DEAL IS--
WE DON'T WANT ANY PART OF IT.
IT IS BETTER IF YOU STAY AWAY FROM US.
OKAY. TO BE EXPECTED AFTER THE WAY WE LEFT THE RESERVATION.
NOTHING I CAN DO ABOUT IT RIGHT NOW.
STILL, MY COMING BACK WILL FORCE BRANDY'S HAND. WHATEVER SHE HAS PLANNED...
IT'S COMING SOON.
WHAT THE SHIT?

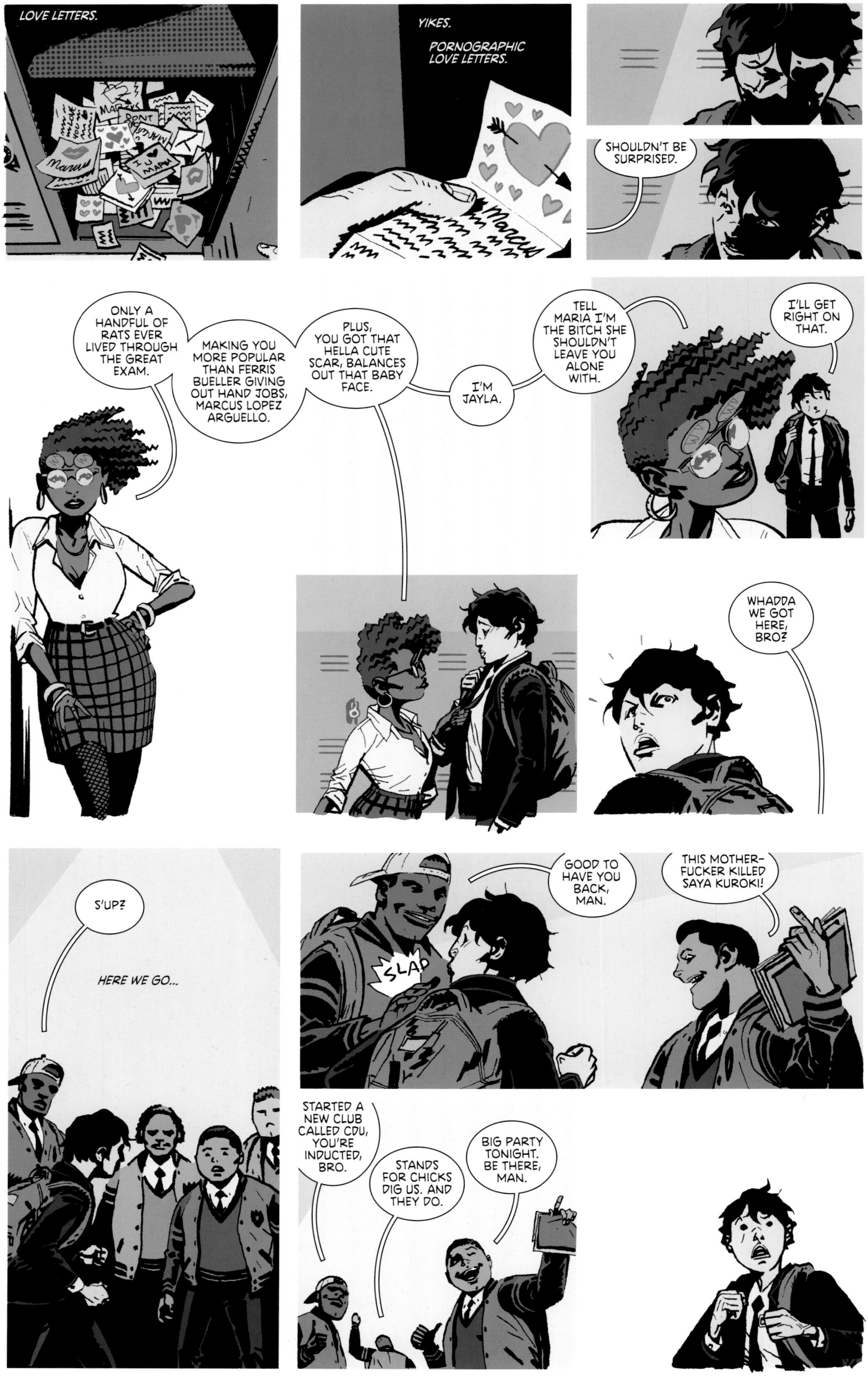
LOVE LETTERS.
YIKES.
PORNOGRAPHIC LOVE LETTERS.
SHOULDN'T BE SURPRISED.
ONLY A HANDFUL OF RATS EVER LIVED THROUGH THE GREAT EXAM.
MAKING YOU MORE POPULAR THAN FERRIS BUELLER GIVING OUT HAND JOBS, MARCUS LOPEZ ARGUELLO.
PLUS, YOU GOT THAT HELLA CUTE SCAR, BALANCES OUT THAT BABY FACE.
I'M JAYLA.
TELL MARIA I'M THE BITCH SHE SHOULDN'T LEAVE YOU ALONE WITH.
I'LL GET RIGHT ON THAT.
WHADDA WE GOT HERE, BRO?
S'UP?
HERE WE GO...
SLAP
GOOD TO HAVE YOU BACK, MAN.
THIS MOTHER-FUCKER KILLED SAYA KUROKI!
STARTED A NEW CLUB CALLED CDU, YOU'RE INDUCTED, BRO.
STANDS FOR CHICKS DIG US. AND THEY DO.
BIG PARTY TONIGHT. BE THERE, MAN.

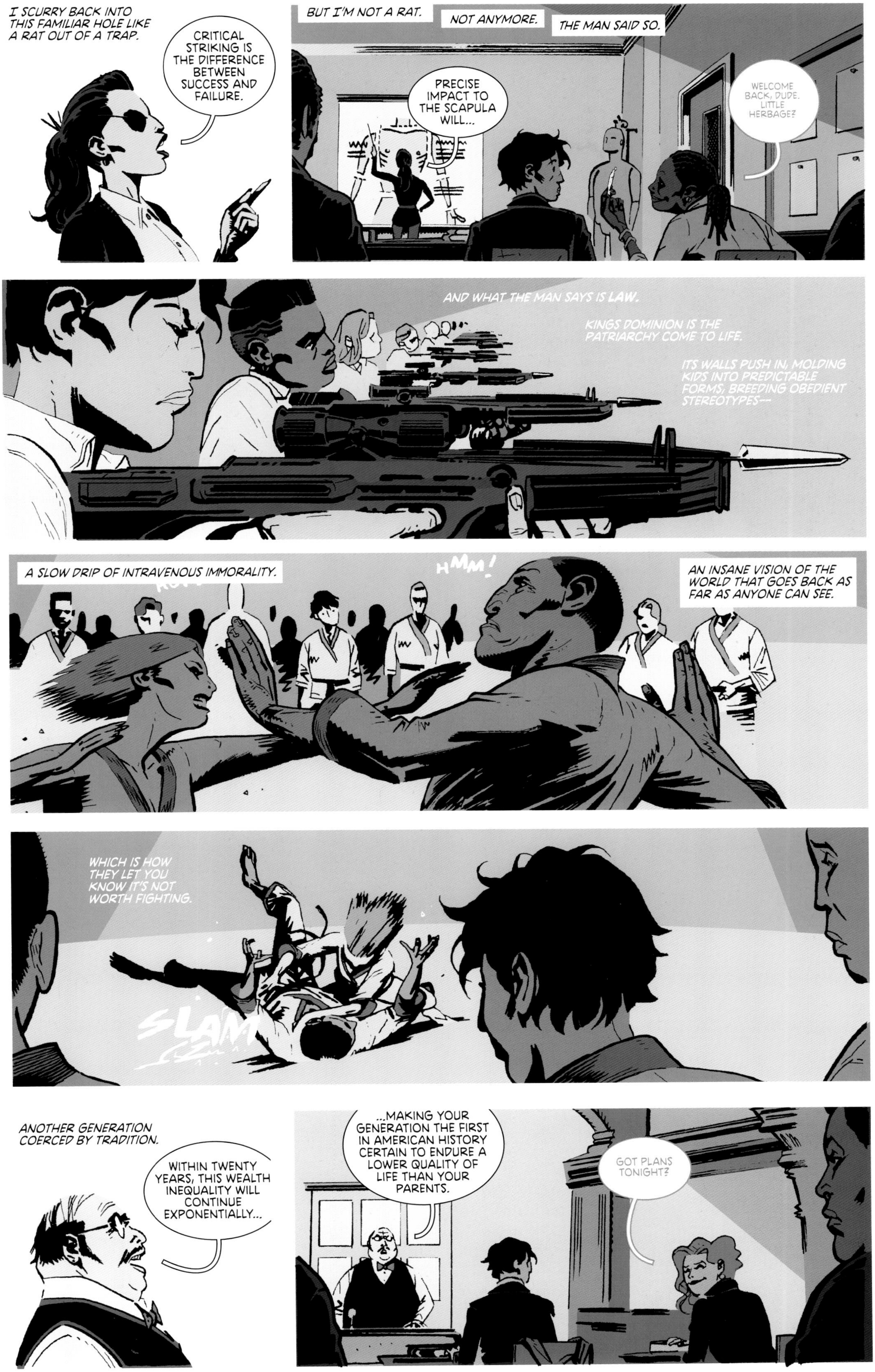
I SCURRY BACK INTO THIS FAMILIAR HOLE LIKE A RAT OUT OF A TRAP.
CRITICAL STRIKING IS THE DIFFERENCE BETWEEN SUCCESS AND FAILURE.
BUT I'M NOT A RAT.
NOT ANYMORE.
THE MAN SAID SO.
PRECISE IMPACT TO THE SCAPULA WILL...
WELCOME BACK, DUDE. LITTLE HERBAGE?
AND WHAT THE MAN SAYS IS LAW.
KINGS DOMINION IS THE PATRIARCHY COME TO LIFE.
ITS WALLS PUSH IN, MOLDING KIDS INTO PREDICTABLE FORMS, BREEDING OBEDIENT STEREOTYPES--
A SLOW DRIP OF INTRAVENOUS IMMORALITY.
HMM!
AN INSANE VISION OF THE WORLD THAT GOES BACK AS FAR AS ANYONE CAN SEE.
WHICH IS HOW THEY LET YOU KNOW IT'S NOT WORTH FIGHTING.
SLAM
ANOTHER GENERATION COERCED BY TRADITION.
WITHIN TWENTY YEARS, THIS WEALTH INEQUALITY WILL CONTINUE EXPONENTIALLY...
...MAKING YOUR GENERATION THE FIRST IN AMERICAN HISTORY CERTAIN TO ENDURE A LOWER QUALITY OF LIFE THAN YOUR PARENTS.
GOT PLANS TONIGHT?

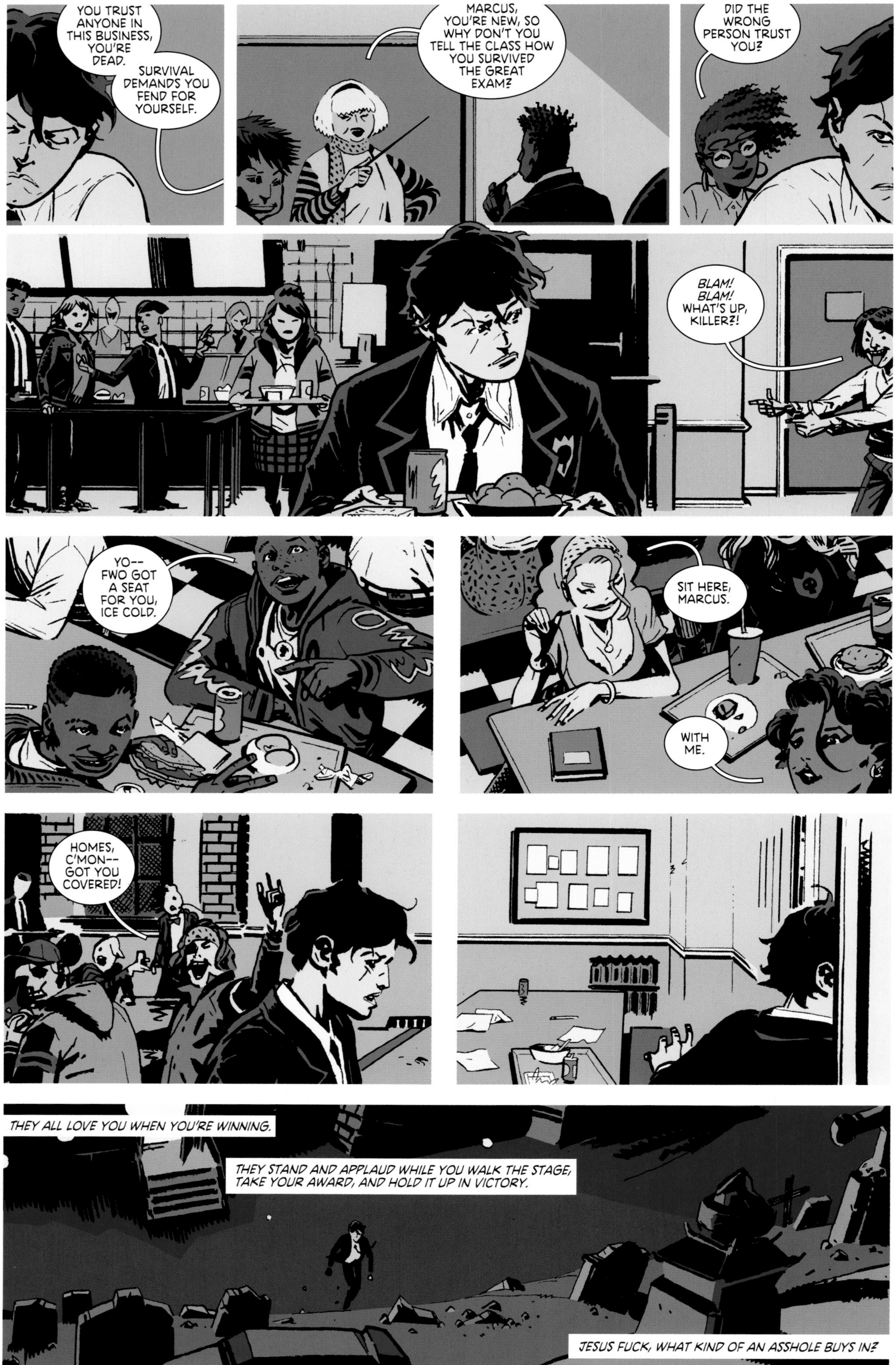
YOU TRUST ANYONE IN THIS BUSINESS, YOU'RE DEAD.
SURVIVAL DEMANDS YOU FEND FOR YOURSELF.
MARCUS, YOU'RE NEW, SO WHY DON'T YOU TELL THE CLASS HOW YOU SURVIVED THE GREAT EXAM?
DID THE WRONG PERSON TRUST YOU?
BLAM! BLAM! WHAT'S UP, KILLER?!
YO-- FWO GOT A SEAT FOR YOU, ICE COLD.
SIT HERE, MARCUS.
WITH ME.
HOMES, C'MON-- GOT YOU COVERED!
THEY ALL LOVE YOU WHEN YOU'RE WINNING.
THEY STAND AND APPLAUD WHILE YOU WALK THE STAGE, TAKE YOUR AWARD, AND HOLD IT UP IN VICTORY.
JESUS FUCK, WHAT KIND OF AN ASSHOLE BUYS IN?

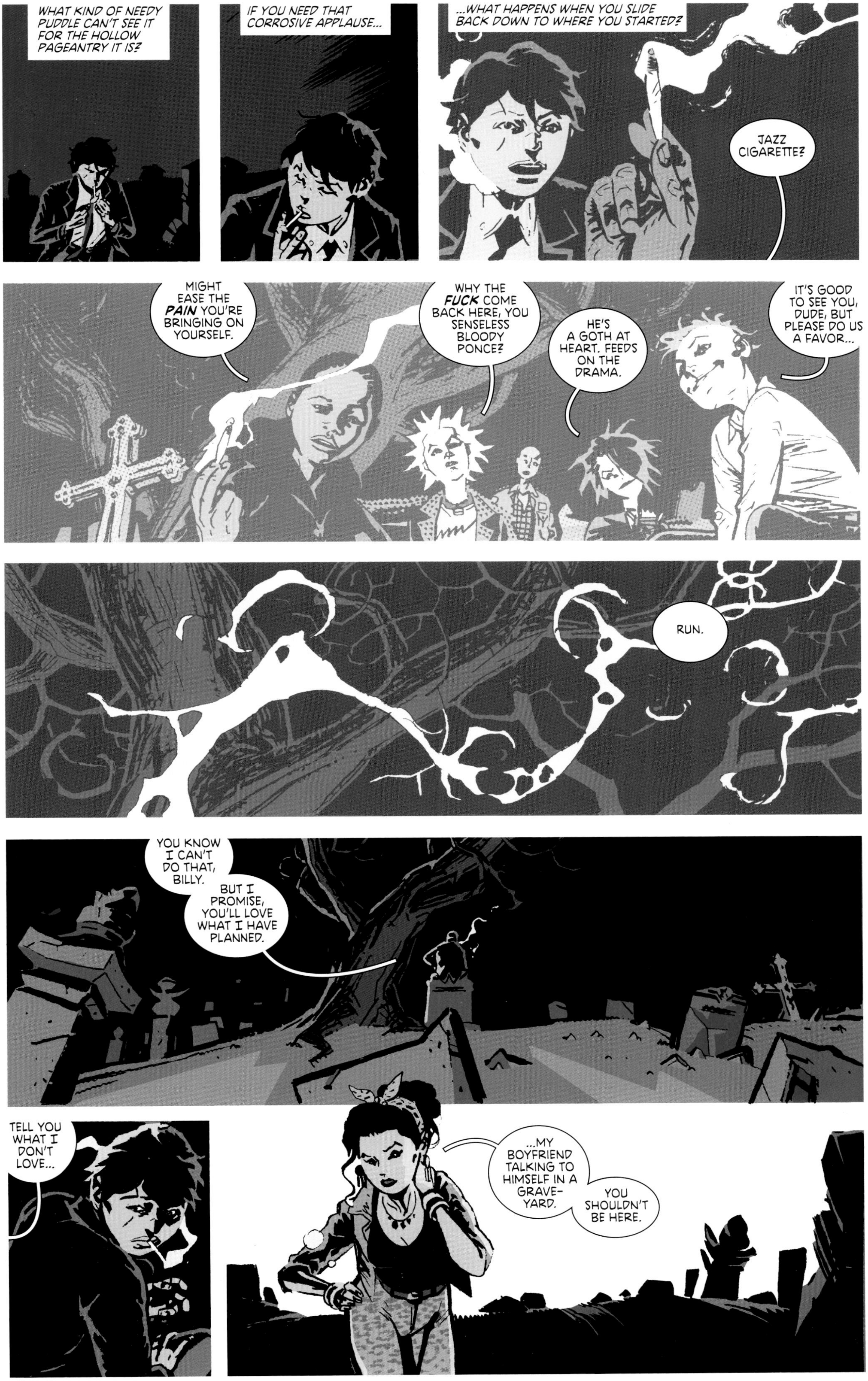
WHAT KIND OF NEEDY PUDDLE CAN'T SEE IT FOR THE HOLLOW PAGEANTRY IT IS?
IF YOU NEED THAT CORROSIVE APPLAUSE...
...WHAT HAPPENS WHEN YOU SLIDE BACK DOWN TO WHERE YOU STARTED?
JAZZ CIGARETTE?
MIGHT EASE THE PAIN YOU'RE BRINGING ON YOURSELF.
WHY THE FUCK COME BACK HERE, YOU SENSELESS BLOODY PONCE?
HE'S A GOTH AT HEART. FEEDS ON THE DRAMA.
IT'S GOOD TO SEE YOU, DUDE, BUT PLEASE DO US A FAVOR...
RUN.
YOU KNOW I CAN'T DO THAT, BILLY.
BUT I PROMISE, YOU'LL LOVE WHAT I HAVE PLANNED.
TELL YOU WHAT I DON'T LOVE...
...MY BOYFRIEND TALKING TO HIMSELF IN A GRAVE-YARD.
YOU SHOULDN'T BE HERE.

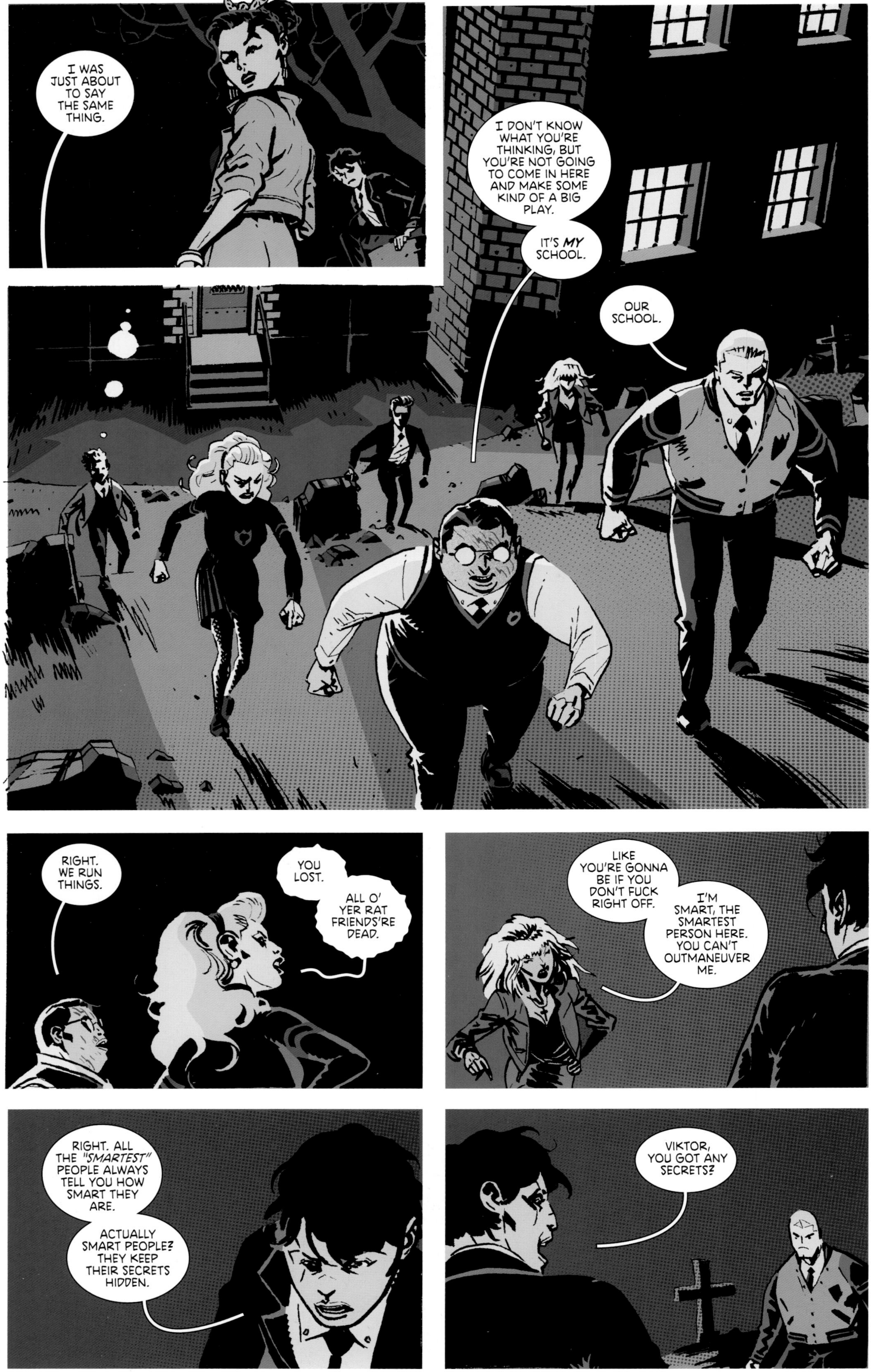
I WAS JUST ABOUT TO SAY THE SAME THING.
I DON'T KNOW WHAT YOU'RE THINKING, BUT YOU'RE NOT GOING TO COME IN HERE AND MAKE SOME KIND OF A BIG PLAY.
IT'S *MY* SCHOOL.
OUR SCHOOL.
RIGHT. WE RUN THINGS.
YOU LOST.
ALL O' YER RAT FRIENDS'RE DEAD.
LIKE YOU'RE GONNA BE IF YOU DON'T FUCK RIGHT OFF.
I'M SMART, THE SMARTEST PERSON HERE. YOU CAN'T OUTMANEUVER ME.
RIGHT. ALL THE *"SMARTEST"* PEOPLE ALWAYS TELL YOU HOW SMART THEY ARE.
ACTUALLY SMART PEOPLE? THEY KEEP THEIR SECRETS HIDDEN.
VIKTOR, YOU GOT ANY SECRETS?

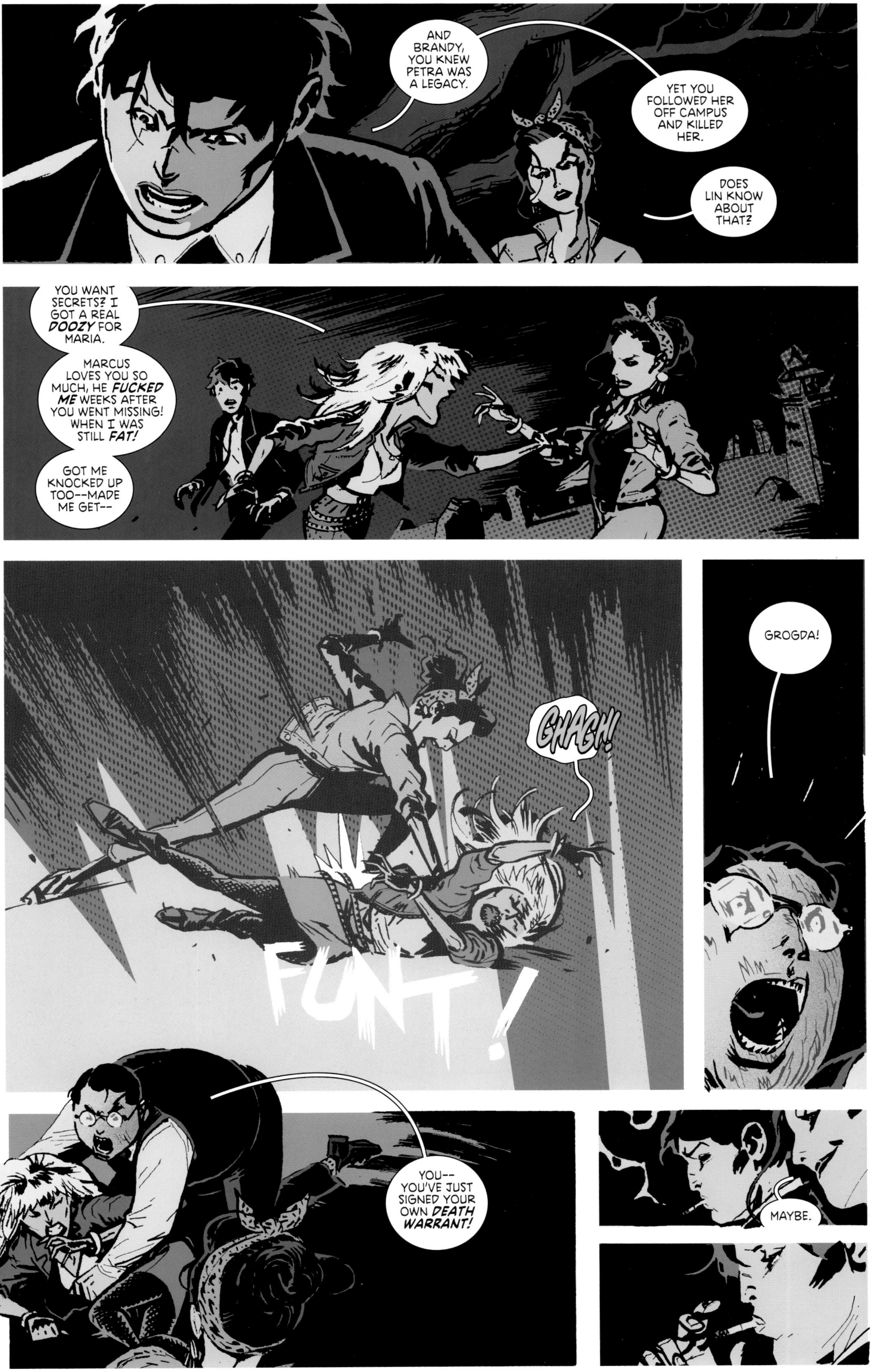
AND BRANDY, YOU KNEW PETRA WAS A LEGACY.
YET YOU FOLLOWED HER OFF CAMPUS AND KILLED HER.
DOES LIN KNOW ABOUT THAT?
YOU WANT SECRETS? I GOT A REAL DOOZY FOR MARIA.
MARCUS LOVES YOU SO MUCH, HE FUCKED ME WEEKS AFTER YOU WENT MISSING! WHEN I WAS STILL FAT!
GOT ME KNOCKED UP TOO--MADE ME GET--
GHAGH!
FUNT!
GROGDA!
YOU-- YOU'VE JUST SIGNED YOUR OWN DEATH WARRANT!
MAYBE.

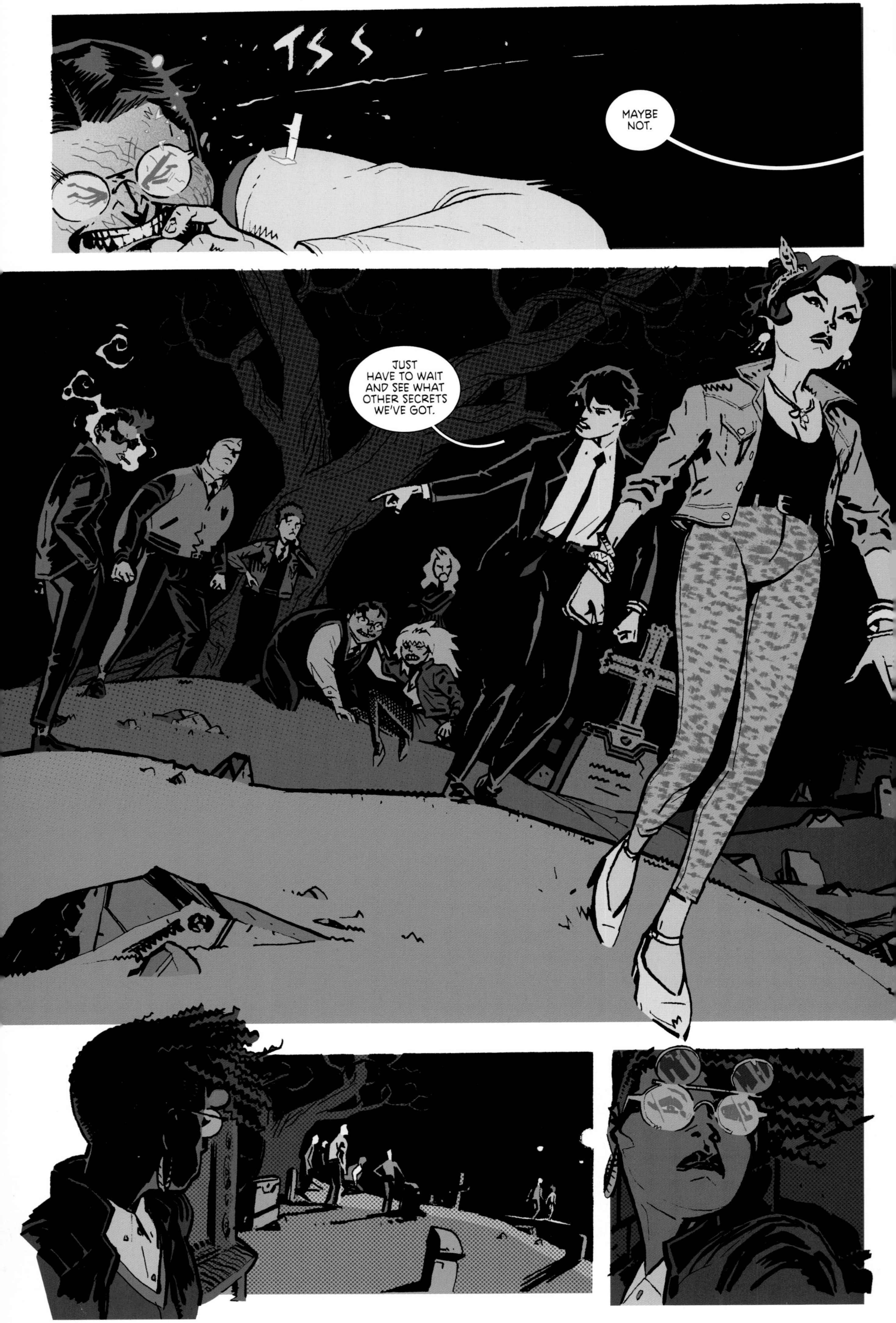
TSS
MAYBE NOT.
JUST HAVE TO WAIT AND SEE WHAT OTHER SECRETS WE'VE GOT.

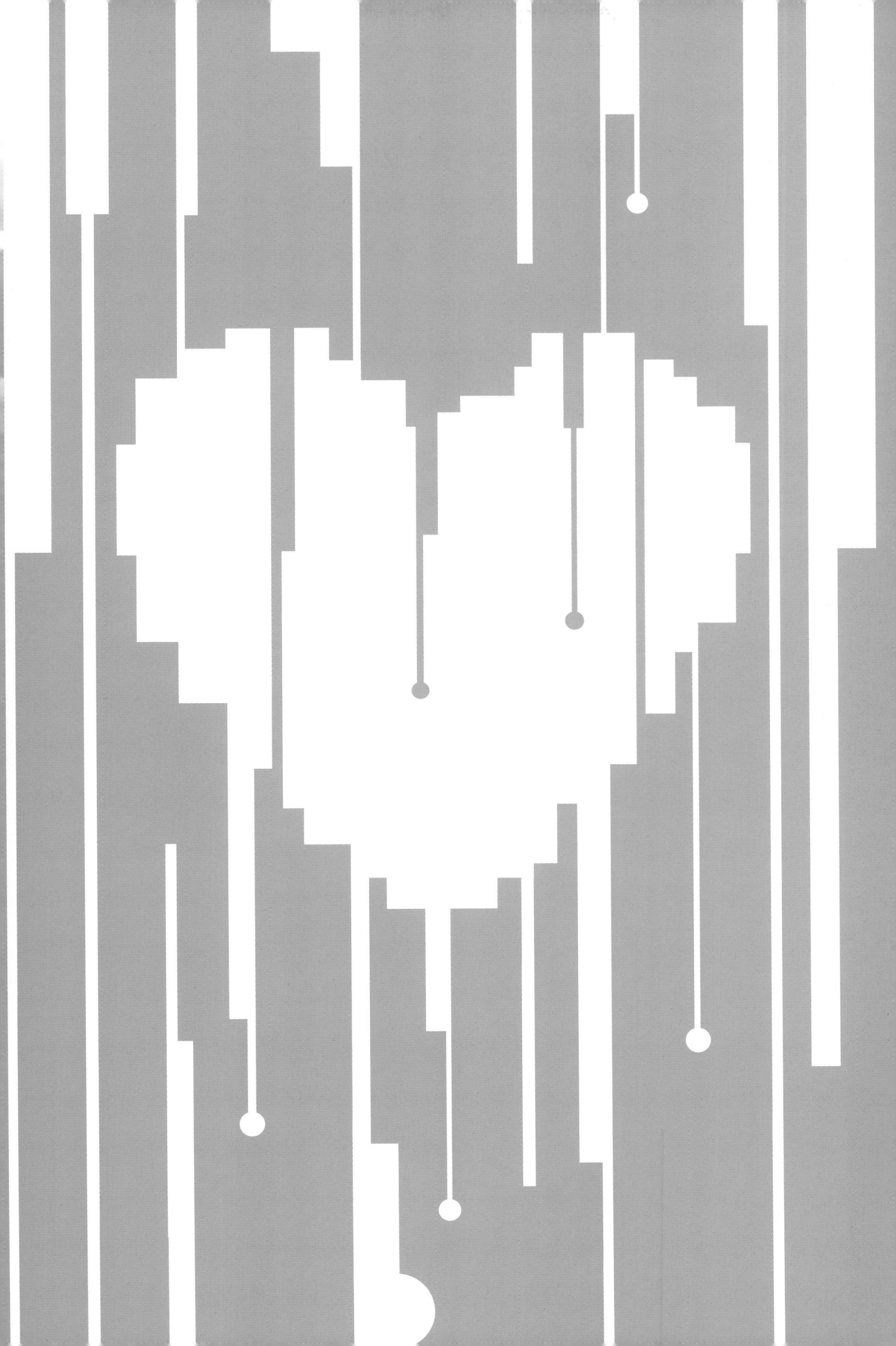

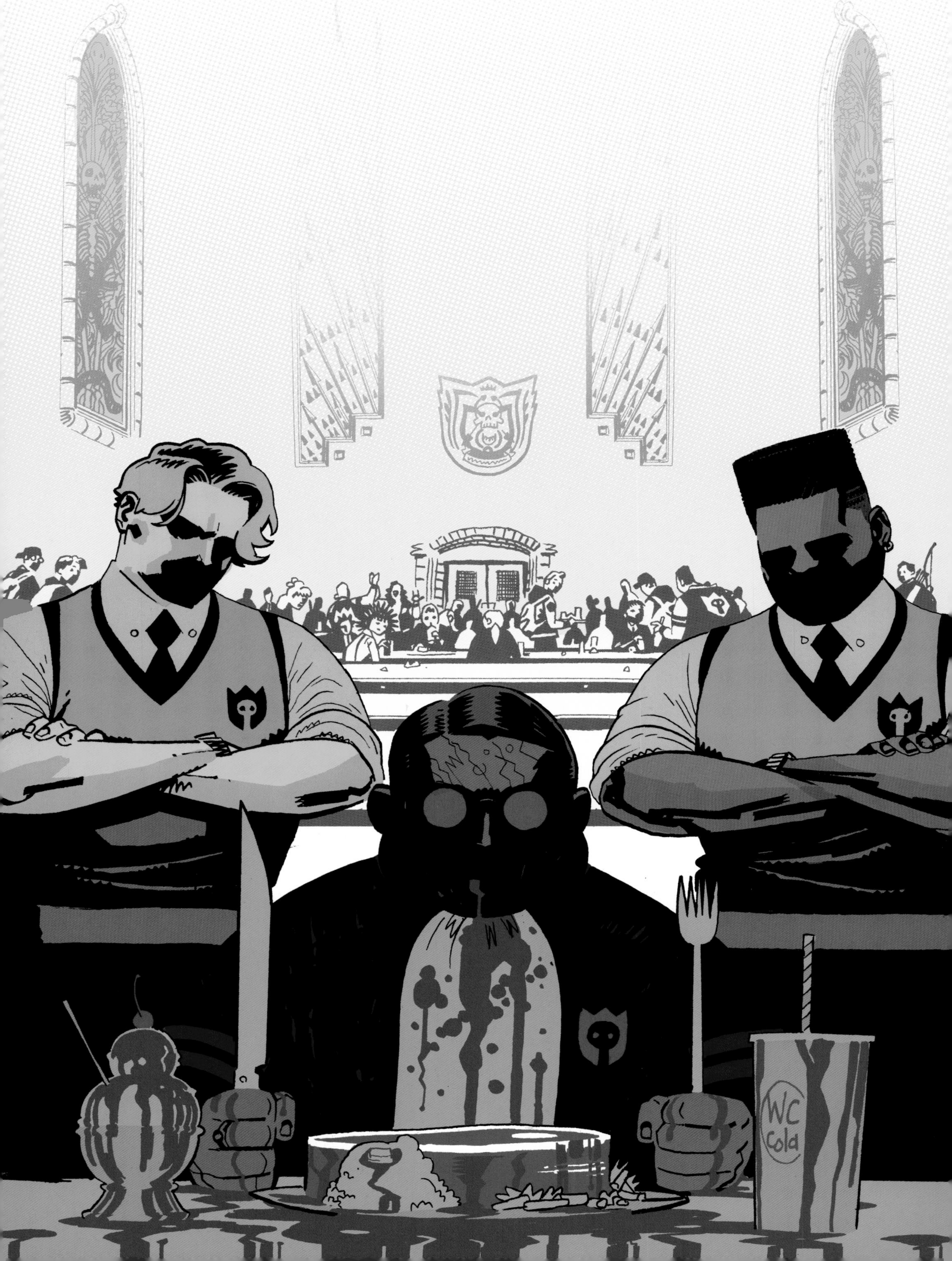
WC
Cola

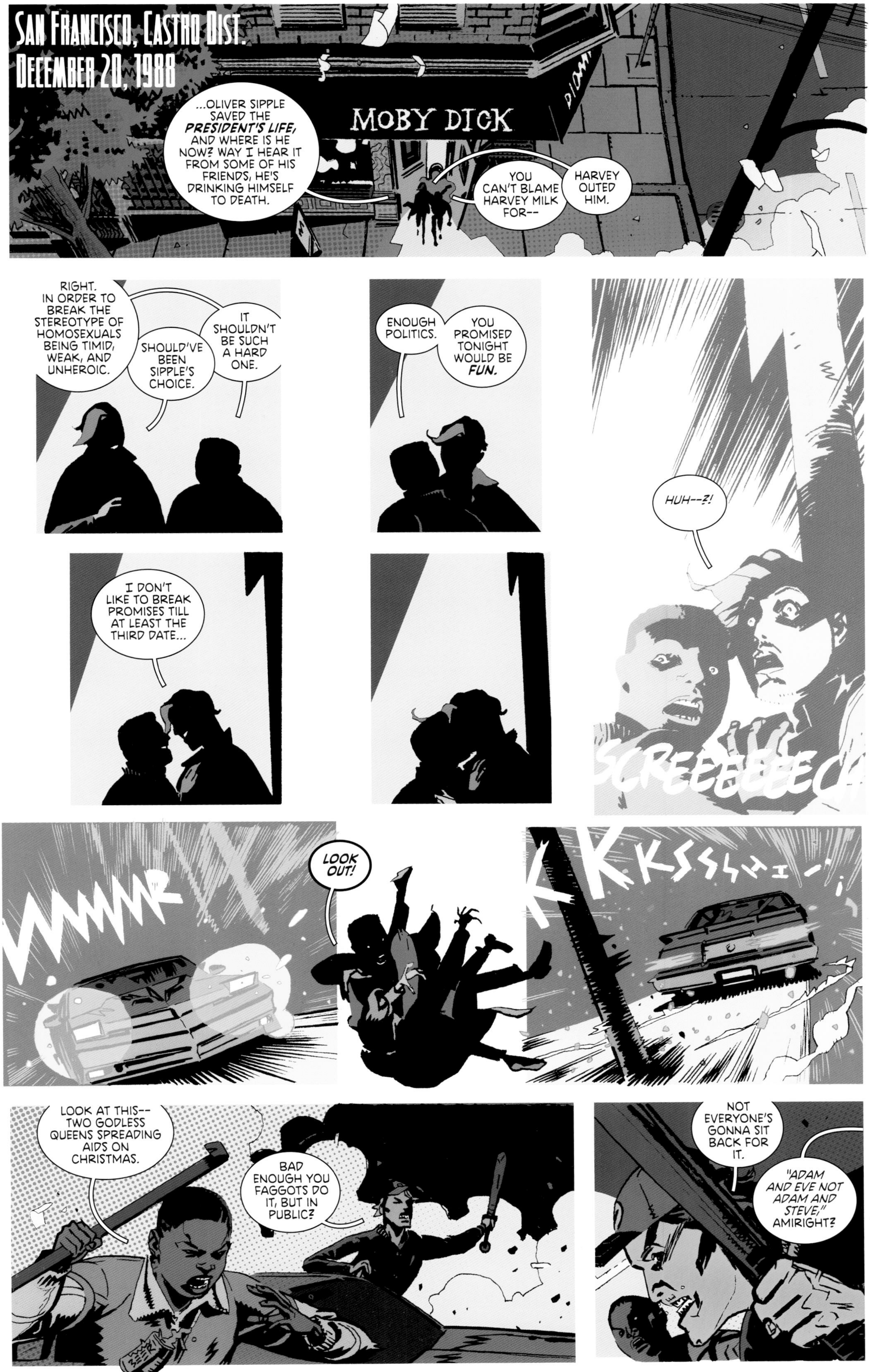

San Francisco, Castro Dist.
December 20, 1988
MOBY DICK
...OLIVER SIPPLE SAVED THE PRESIDENT'S LIFE, AND WHERE IS HE NOW? WAY I HEAR IT FROM SOME OF HIS FRIENDS, HE'S DRINKING HIMSELF TO DEATH.
YOU CAN'T BLAME HARVEY MILK FOR--
HARVEY OUTED HIM.
RIGHT. IN ORDER TO BREAK THE STEREOTYPE OF HOMOSEXUALS BEING TIMID, WEAK, AND UNHEROIC.
SHOULD'VE BEEN SIPPLE'S CHOICE.
IT SHOULDN'T BE SUCH A HARD ONE.
ENOUGH POLITICS.
YOU PROMISED TONIGHT WOULD BE FUN.
HUH--?!
I DON'T LIKE TO BREAK PROMISES TILL AT LEAST THE THIRD DATE...
SCREEEEEECH
WMMMR
LOOK OUT!
KKKSSSSZZ
LOOK AT THIS-- TWO GODLESS QUEENS SPREADING AIDS ON CHRISTMAS.
BAD ENOUGH YOU FAGGOTS DO IT, BUT IN PUBLIC?
NOT EVERYONE'S GONNA SIT BACK FOR IT.
"ADAM AND EVE NOT ADAM AND STEVE," AMIRIGHT?

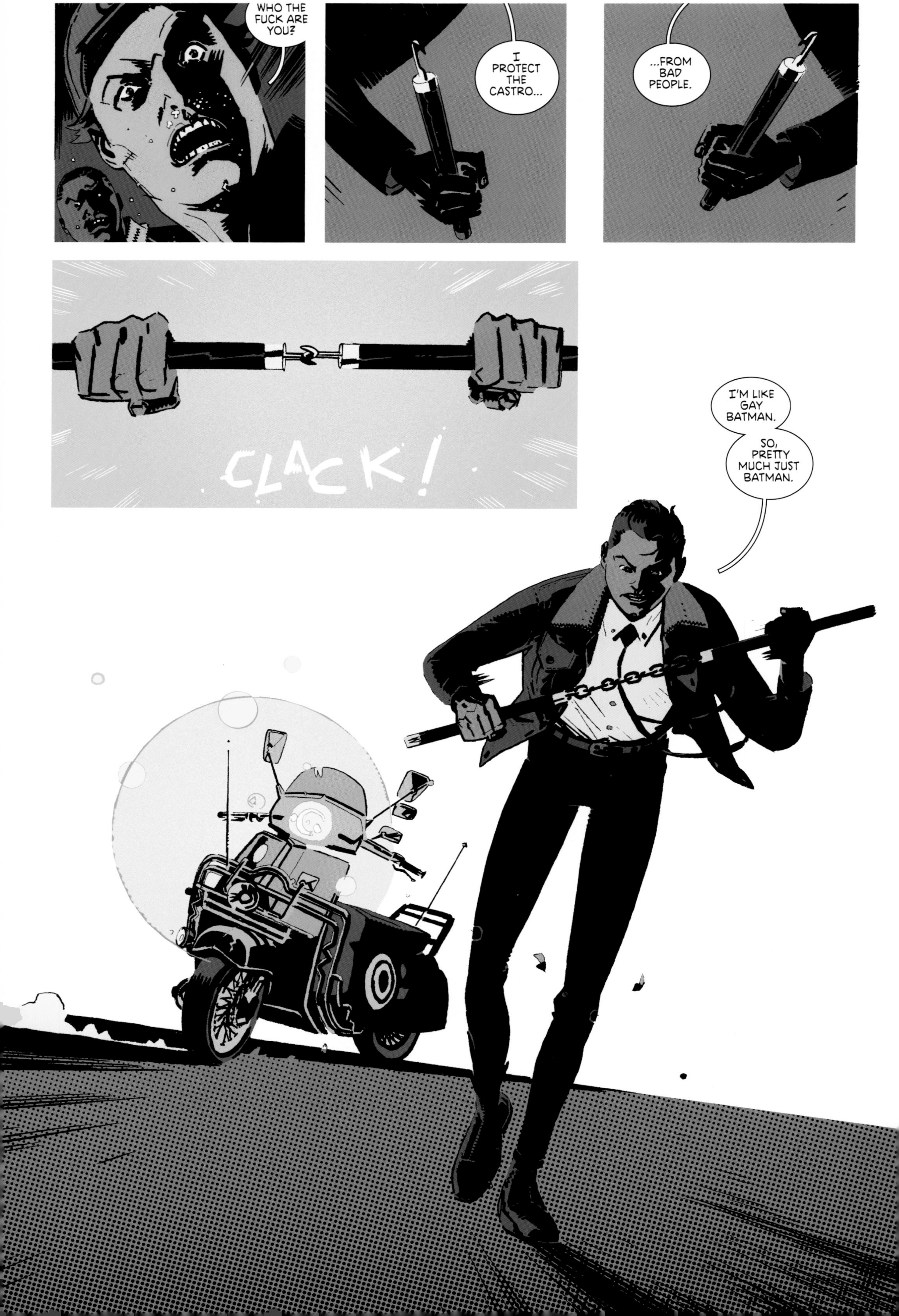
WHO THE FUCK ARE YOU?
I PROTECT THE CASTRO...
...FROM BAD PEOPLE.
CLACK!
I'M LIKE GAY BATMAN.
SO, PRETTY MUCH JUST BATMAN.

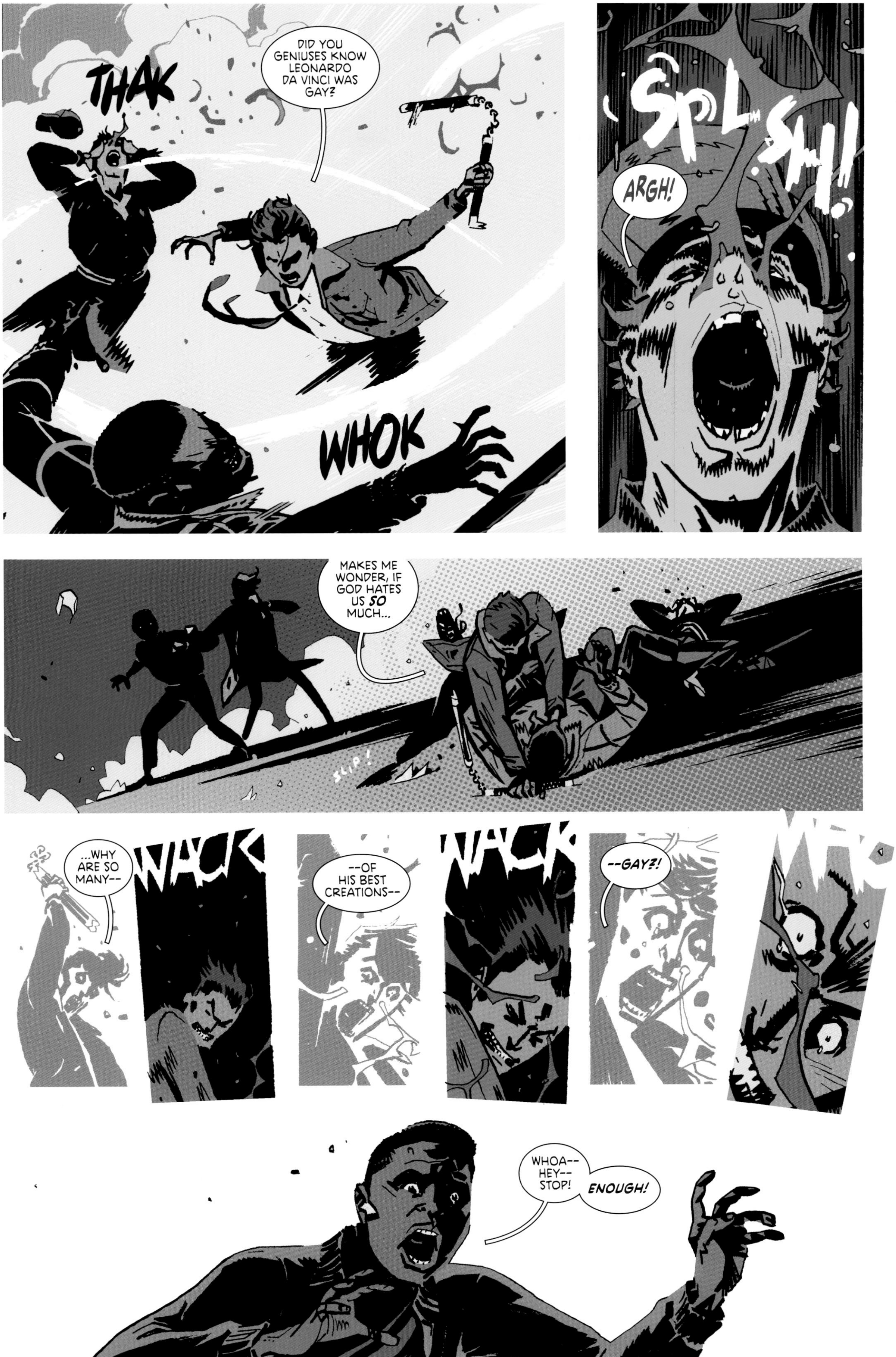
THAK
DID YOU GENIUSES KNOW LEONARDO DA VINCI WAS GAY?
WHOK
SPLSH!
ARGH!
MAKES ME WONDER, IF GOD HATES US SO MUCH...
SLIP!
...WHY ARE SO MANY--
WACK
--OF HIS BEST CREATIONS--
WACK
--GAY?!
WHOA-- HEY-- STOP!
ENOUGH!

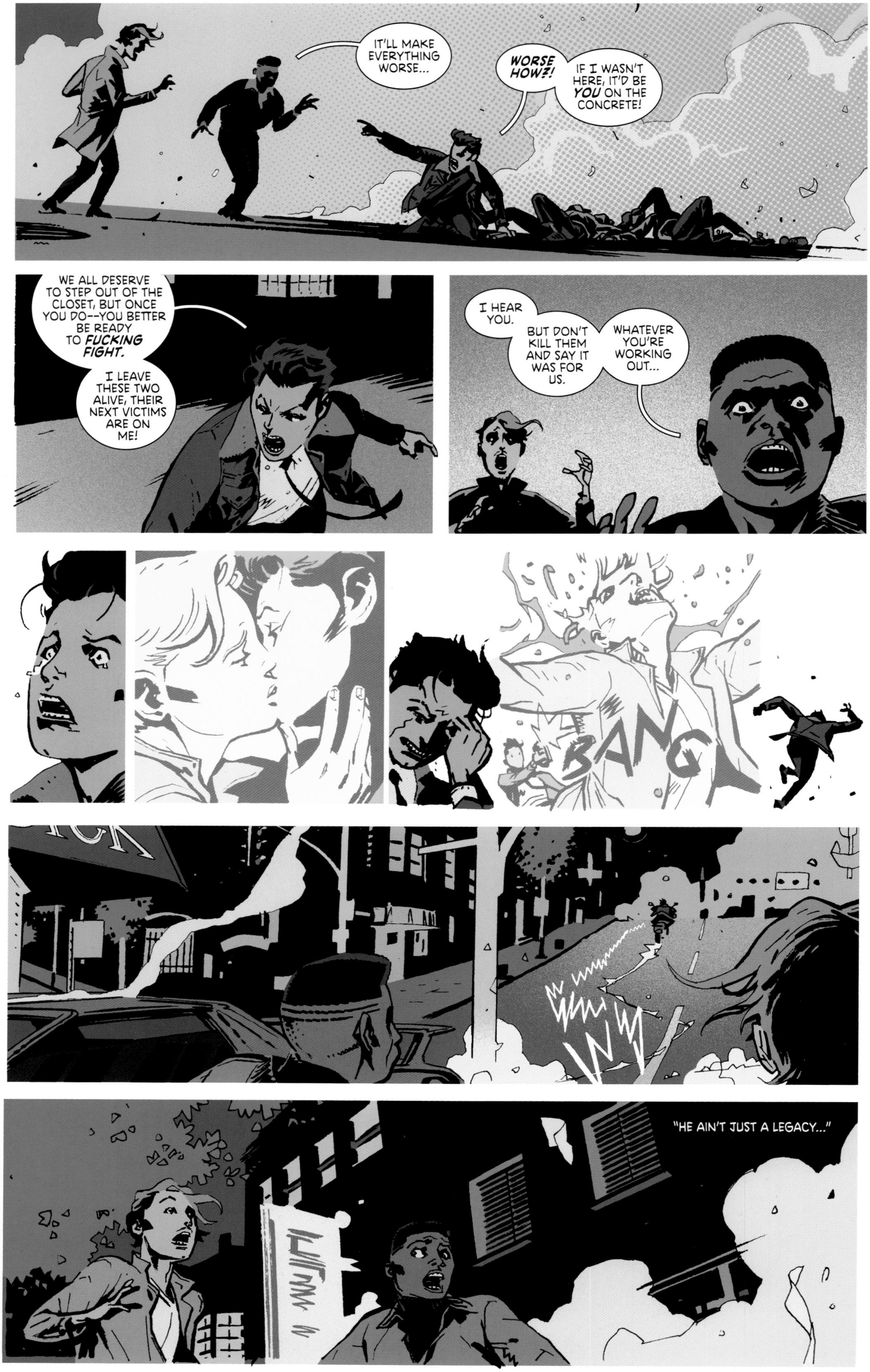

IT'LL MAKE EVERYTHING WORSE...
WORSE HOW?!
IF I WASN'T HERE, IT'D BE YOU ON THE CONCRETE!
WE ALL DESERVE TO STEP OUT OF THE CLOSET, BUT ONCE YOU DO--YOU BETTER BE READY TO FUCKING FIGHT.
I LEAVE THESE TWO ALIVE, THEIR NEXT VICTIMS ARE ON ME!
I HEAR YOU.
BUT DON'T KILL THEM AND SAY IT WAS FOR US.
WHATEVER YOU'RE WORKING OUT...
BANG
"HE AIN'T JUST A LEGACY..."

...MARCUS IS THE MOST POPULAR KID IN SCHOOL.

POPULARITY IS *TEMPORARY.*

AN ILLUSION MADE REAL BY THE FICKLE, UNQUESTIONING DOLTS IN THE HERD.

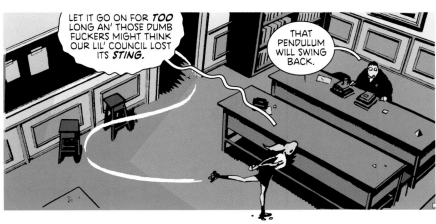

LET IT GO ON FOR *TOO LONG* AN' THOSE DUMB FUCKERS MIGHT THINK OUR LIL' COUNCIL LOST ITS *STING.*

THAT PENDULUM WILL SWING BACK.

MH-HM... MAYBE WE OUGHTA HELP SPEED UP THE PROCESS?

GIVE THEM MUTTS A SHOW O' SHABNAM STRENGTH.

MIGHT BE WHAT THEY NEED, BOSS.

BOSS...?

OH, BRANDY, I MEAN, WE'RE A *TEAM,* I DON'T THINK THAT--

PLAY COY WITH THE OTHERS.

WE BOTH KNOW YOU'RE THE GENERAL O' THIS ARMY.

AN' A GENERAL NEEDS SOLDIERS HE CAN *TRUST...*

...TO DO ALL KINDS O' *DIRTY* WORK.

KIND O' GAL WOULD RISK VALEDICTORIAN TO KILL PETRA FOR RETRIBUTION.

YOU FOLLOW ME HERE?

WHAT YOU'RE *PROPOSING...* GROGDA WOULD...

GROGDA'S A BITCH WHO TREATS YOU LIKE *TRASH* IN FRONT OF *EVERYONE.*

YOU KNOW SHE CALLS YOU *"SHITFACE"* WHEN YOU AIN'T AROUND?

WELL, I DON'T LOOK GREAT...

I THINK YOU LOOK HOT.

LIKE ONE O' THEM MESSED UP DUDES IN THE OLD WESTERNS.

WHAT ABOUT VIKTOR...?

VIKTOR'S GOING SOFT.

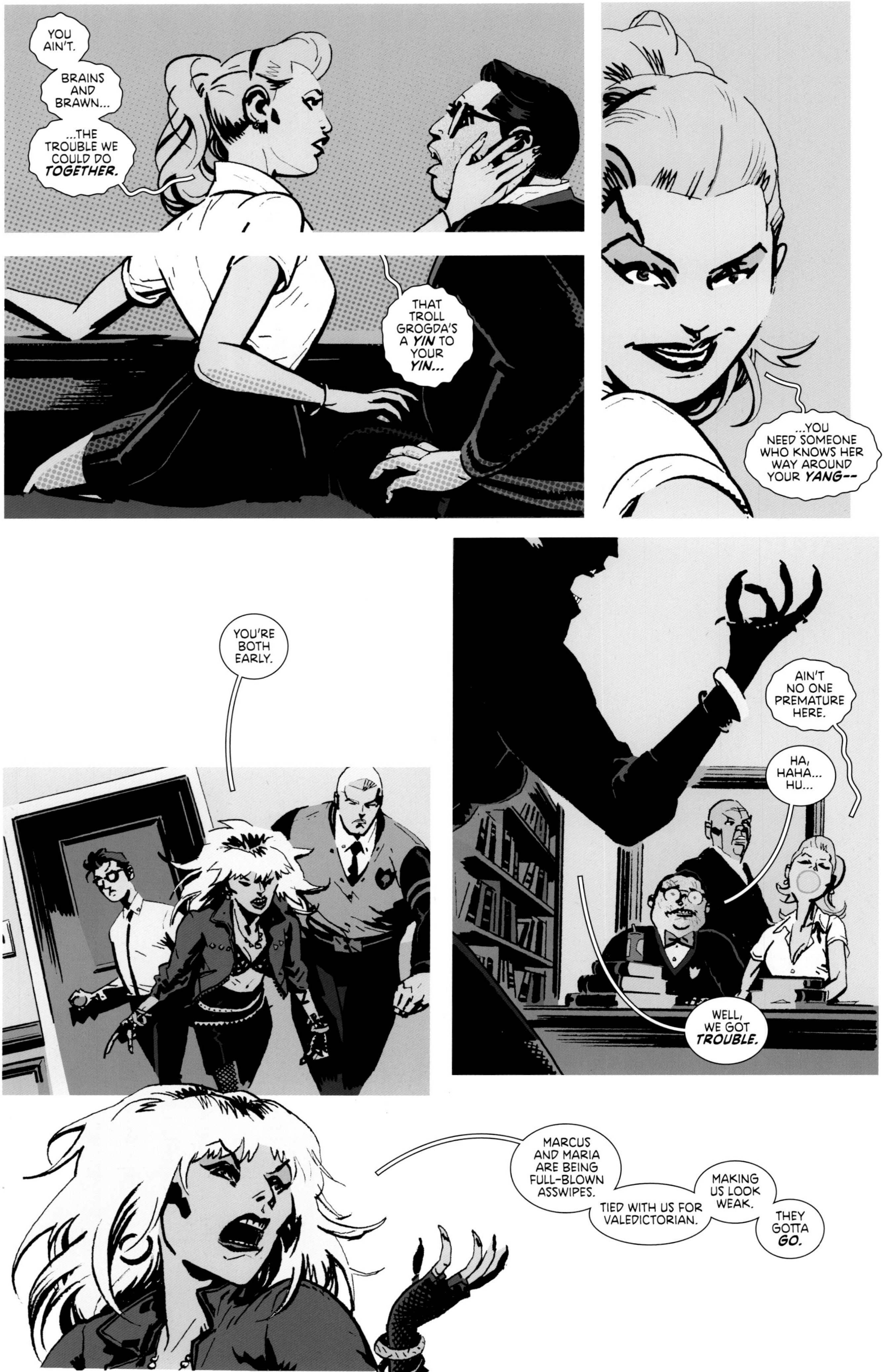
YOU AIN'T.
BRAINS AND BRAWN...
...THE TROUBLE WE COULD DO TOGETHER.
THAT TROLL GROGDA'S A YIN TO YOUR YIN...
...YOU NEED SOMEONE WHO KNOWS HER WAY AROUND YOUR YANG--
AIN'T NO ONE PREMATURE HERE.
HA, HAHA... HU...
WELL, WE GOT TROUBLE.
YOU'RE BOTH EARLY.
MARCUS AND MARIA ARE BEING FULL-BLOWN ASSWIPES.
TIED WITH US FOR VALEDICTORIAN.
MAKING US LOOK WEAK.
THEY GOTTA GO.

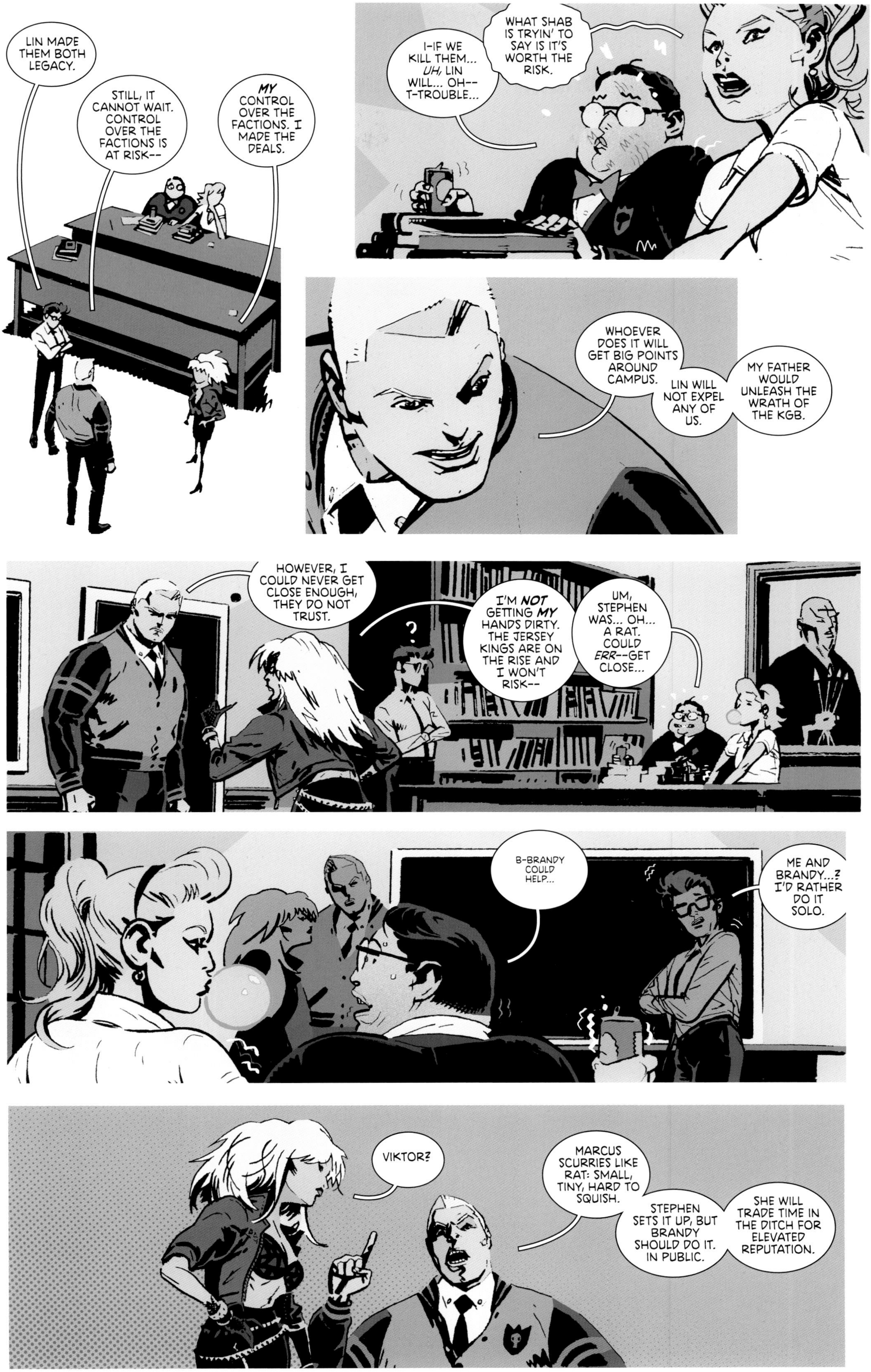
LIN MADE THEM BOTH LEGACY.
STILL, IT CANNOT WAIT. CONTROL OVER THE FACTIONS IS AT RISK--
MY CONTROL OVER THE FACTIONS. I MADE THE DEALS.
I-IF WE KILL THEM... UH, LIN WILL... OH-- T-TROUBLE...
WHAT SHAB IS TRYIN' TO SAY IS IT'S WORTH THE RISK.
WHOEVER DOES IT WILL GET BIG POINTS AROUND CAMPUS.
LIN WILL NOT EXPEL ANY OF US.
MY FATHER WOULD UNLEASH THE WRATH OF THE KGB.
HOWEVER, I COULD NEVER GET CLOSE ENOUGH, THEY DO NOT TRUST.
?
I'M NOT GETTING MY HANDS DIRTY. THE JERSEY KINGS ARE ON THE RISE AND I WON'T RISK--
UM, STEPHEN WAS... OH... A RAT. COULD ERR--GET CLOSE...
B-BRANDY COULD HELP...
ME AND BRANDY...? I'D RATHER DO IT SOLO.
VIKTOR?
MARCUS SCURRIES LIKE RAT: SMALL, TINY, HARD TO SQUISH.
STEPHEN SETS IT UP, BUT BRANDY SHOULD DO IT. IN PUBLIC.
SHE WILL TRADE TIME IN THE DITCH FOR ELEVATED REPUTATION.

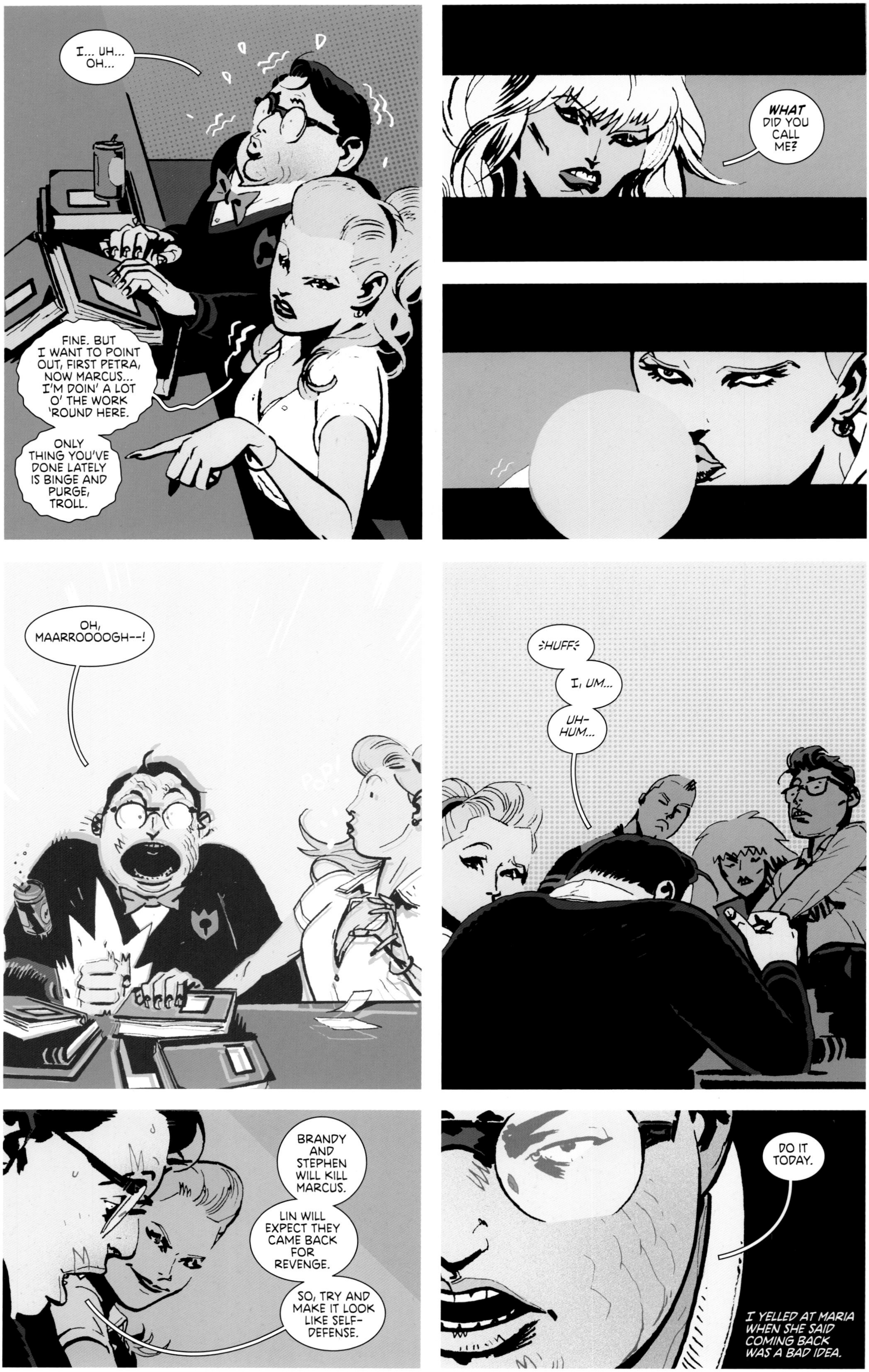
I... UH... OH...
FINE. BUT I WANT TO POINT OUT, FIRST PETRA, NOW MARCUS... I'M DOIN' A LOT O' THE WORK 'ROUND HERE.
ONLY THING YOU'VE DONE LATELY IS BINGE AND PURGE, TROLL.
WHAT DID YOU CALL ME?
OH, MAARROOOOGH--!
POP!
HUFF
I, UM...
UH-HUM...
BRANDY AND STEPHEN WILL KILL MARCUS.
LIN WILL EXPECT THEY CAME BACK FOR REVENGE.
SO, TRY AND MAKE IT LOOK LIKE SELF-DEFENSE.
DO IT TODAY.
I YELLED AT MARIA WHEN SHE SAID COMING BACK WAS A BAD IDEA.

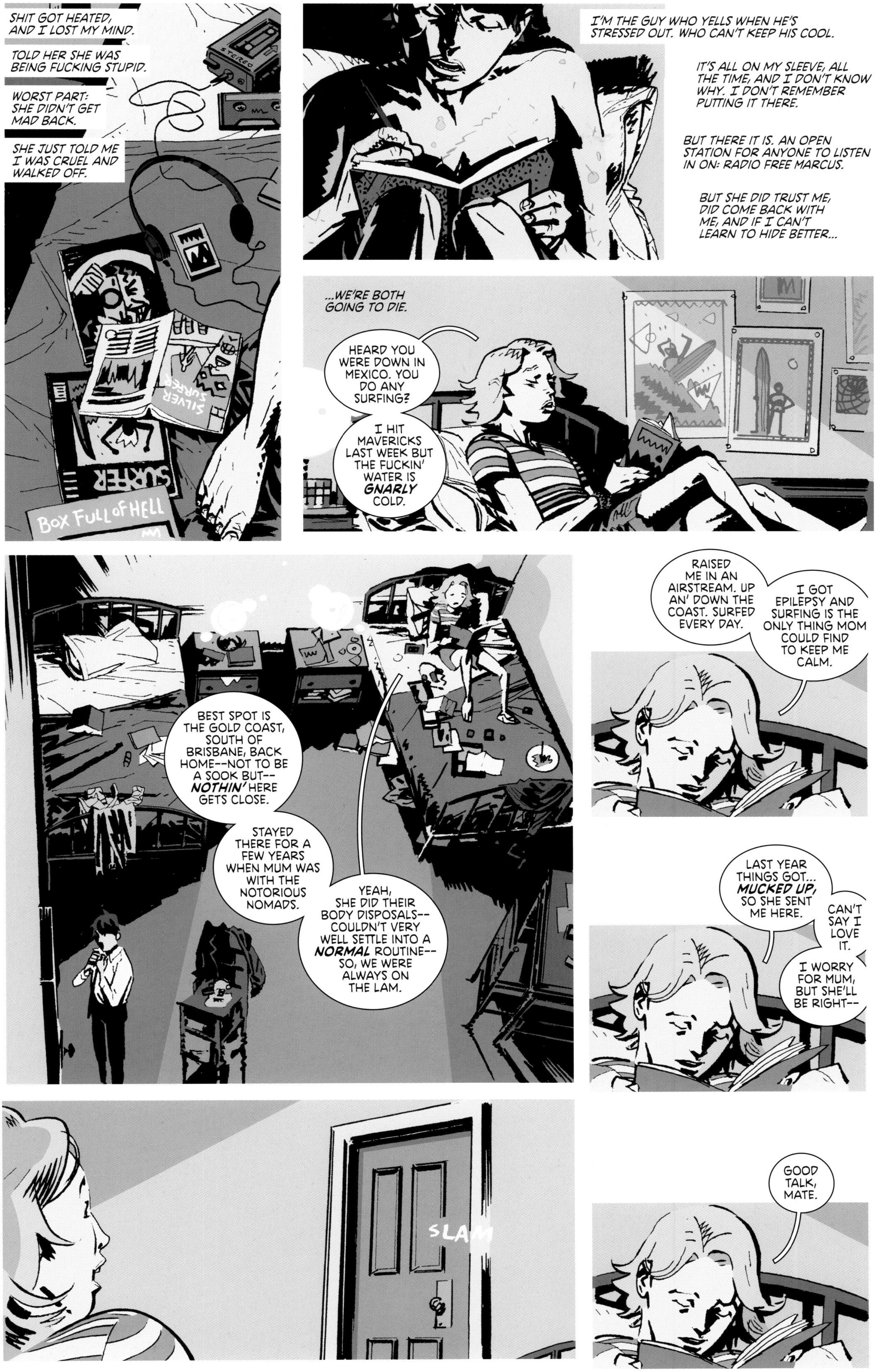

SHIT GOT HEATED, AND I LOST MY MIND.
TOLD HER SHE WAS BEING FUCKING STUPID.
WORST PART: SHE DIDN'T GET MAD BACK.
SHE JUST TOLD ME I WAS CRUEL AND WALKED OFF.
BOX FULL of HELL
I'M THE GUY WHO YELLS WHEN HE'S STRESSED OUT. WHO CAN'T KEEP HIS COOL.
IT'S ALL ON MY SLEEVE, ALL THE TIME, AND I DON'T KNOW WHY. I DON'T REMEMBER PUTTING IT THERE.
BUT THERE IT IS. AN OPEN STATION FOR ANYONE TO LISTEN IN ON: RADIO FREE MARCUS.
BUT SHE DID TRUST ME, DID COME BACK WITH ME, AND IF I CAN'T LEARN TO HIDE BETTER...
...WE'RE BOTH GOING TO DIE.
HEARD YOU WERE DOWN IN MEXICO. YOU DO ANY SURFING?
I HIT MAVERICKS LAST WEEK BUT THE FUCKIN' WATER IS GNARLY COLD.
BEST SPOT IS THE GOLD COAST, SOUTH OF BRISBANE, BACK HOME--NOT TO BE A SOOK BUT--NOTHIN' HERE GETS CLOSE.
STAYED THERE FOR A FEW YEARS WHEN MUM WAS WITH THE NOTORIOUS NOMADS.
YEAH, SHE DID THEIR BODY DISPOSALS--COULDN'T VERY WELL SETTLE INTO A NORMAL ROUTINE--SO, WE WERE ALWAYS ON THE LAM.
RAISED ME IN AN AIRSTREAM. UP AN' DOWN THE COAST. SURFED EVERY DAY.
I GOT EPILEPSY AND SURFING IS THE ONLY THING MOM COULD FIND TO KEEP ME CALM.
LAST YEAR THINGS GOT... MUCKED UP, SO SHE SENT ME HERE.
CAN'T SAY I LOVE IT.
I WORRY FOR MUM, BUT SHE'LL BE RIGHT--
SLAM
GOOD TALK, MATE.

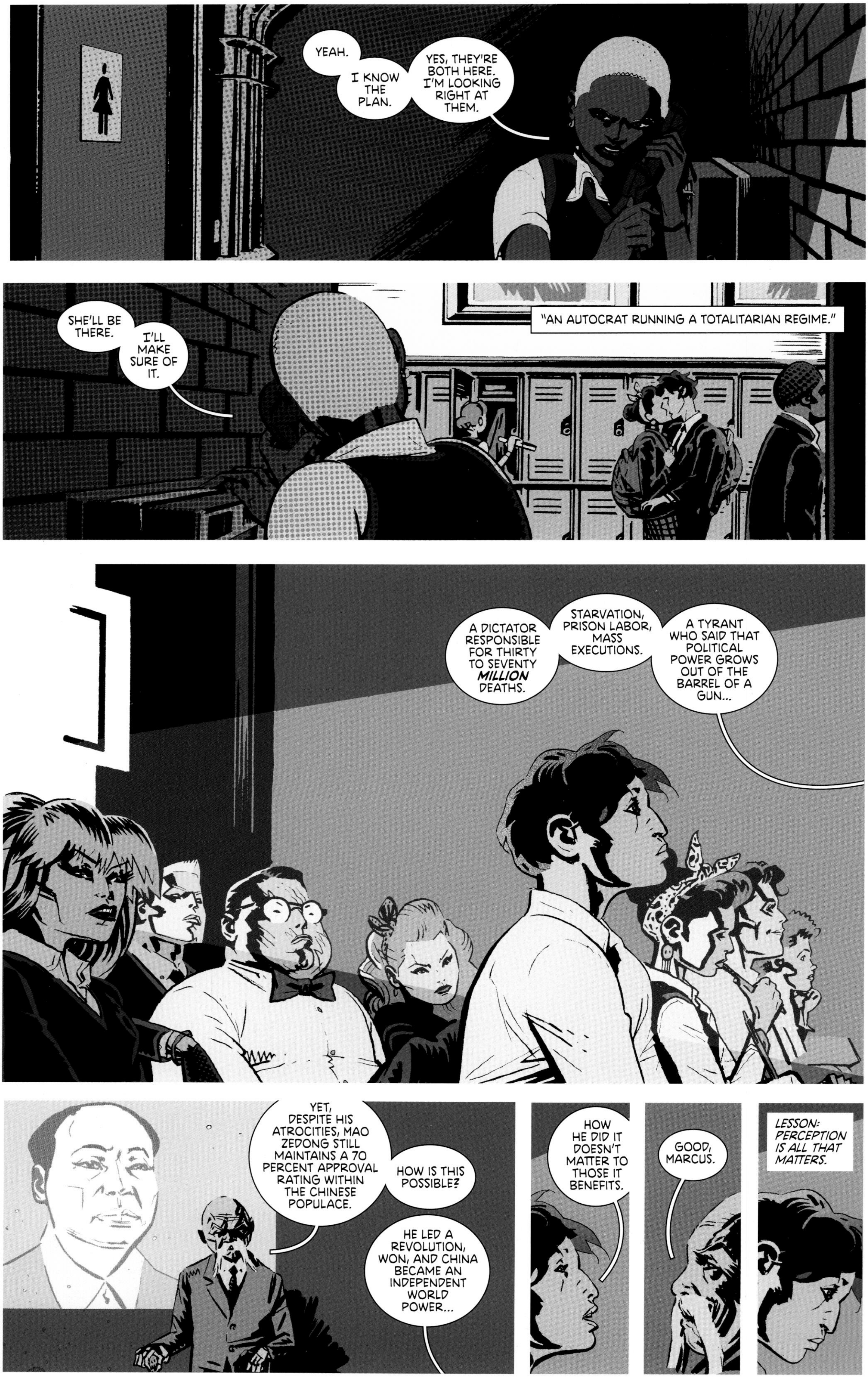
YEAH.
I KNOW THE PLAN.
YES, THEY'RE BOTH HERE. I'M LOOKING RIGHT AT THEM.
SHE'LL BE THERE.
I'LL MAKE SURE OF IT.
"AN AUTOCRAT RUNNING A TOTALITARIAN REGIME."
A DICTATOR RESPONSIBLE FOR THIRTY TO SEVENTY *MILLION* DEATHS.
STARVATION, PRISON LABOR, MASS EXECUTIONS.
A TYRANT WHO SAID THAT POLITICAL POWER GROWS OUT OF THE BARREL OF A GUN...
YET, DESPITE HIS ATROCITIES, MAO ZEDONG STILL MAINTAINS A 70 PERCENT APPROVAL RATING WITHIN THE CHINESE POPULACE.
HOW IS THIS POSSIBLE?
HE LED A REVOLUTION, WON, AND CHINA BECAME AN INDEPENDENT WORLD POWER...
HOW HE DID IT DOESN'T MATTER TO THOSE IT BENEFITS.
GOOD, MARCUS.
LESSON: PERCEPTION IS ALL THAT MATTERS.

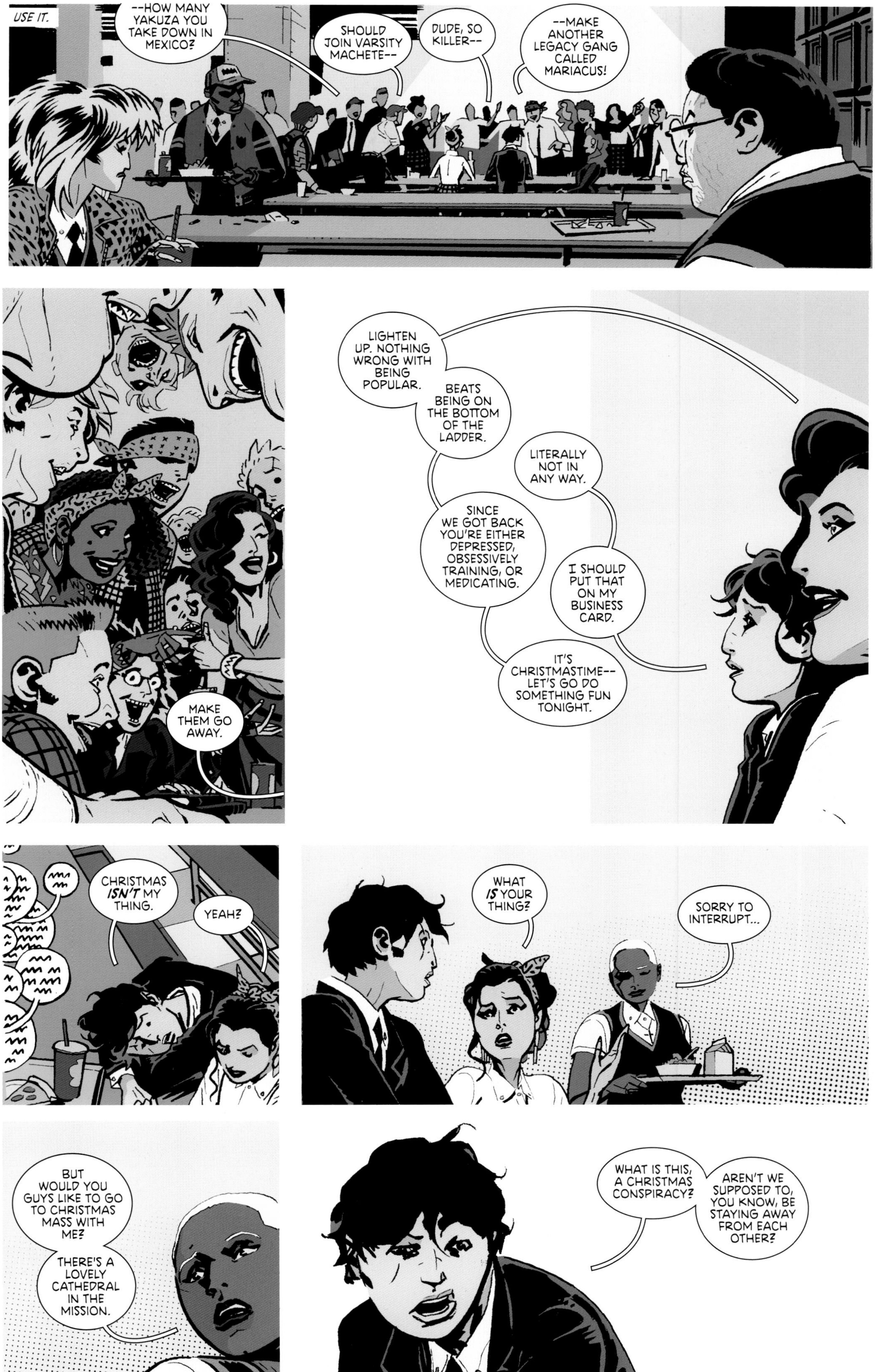
USE IT.
--HOW MANY YAKUZA YOU TAKE DOWN IN MEXICO?
SHOULD JOIN VARSITY MACHETE--
DUDE, SO KILLER--
--MAKE ANOTHER LEGACY GANG CALLED MARIACUS!
MAKE THEM GO AWAY.
LIGHTEN UP. NOTHING WRONG WITH BEING POPULAR.
BEATS BEING ON THE BOTTOM OF THE LADDER.
LITERALLY NOT IN ANY WAY.
SINCE WE GOT BACK YOU'RE EITHER DEPRESSED, OBSESSIVELY TRAINING, OR MEDICATING.
I SHOULD PUT THAT ON MY BUSINESS CARD.
IT'S CHRISTMASTIME--LET'S GO DO SOMETHING FUN TONIGHT.
CHRISTMAS *ISN'T* MY THING.
YEAH?
WHAT *IS* YOUR THING?
SORRY TO INTERRUPT...
BUT WOULD YOU GUYS LIKE TO GO TO CHRISTMAS MASS WITH ME?
THERE'S A LOVELY CATHEDRAL IN THE MISSION.
WHAT IS THIS, A CHRISTMAS CONSPIRACY?
AREN'T WE SUPPOSED TO, YOU KNOW, BE STAYING AWAY FROM EACH OTHER?

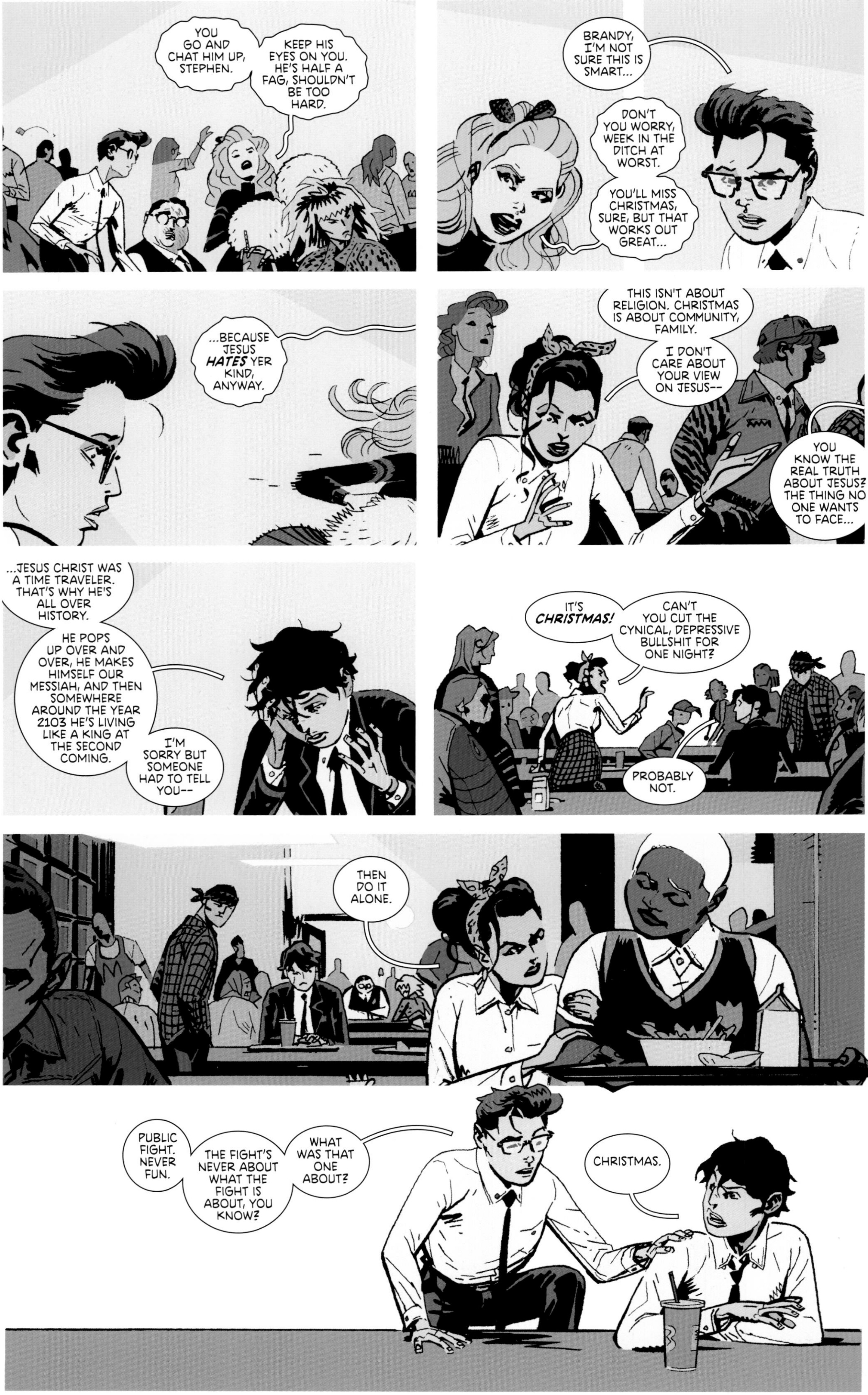
YOU GO AND CHAT HIM UP, STEPHEN.
KEEP HIS EYES ON YOU. HE'S HALF A FAG, SHOULDN'T BE TOO HARD.
BRANDY, I'M NOT SURE THIS IS SMART...
DON'T YOU WORRY, WEEK IN THE DITCH AT WORST.
YOU'LL MISS CHRISTMAS, SURE, BUT THAT WORKS OUT GREAT...
...BECAUSE JESUS HATES YER KIND, ANYWAY.
THIS ISN'T ABOUT RELIGION. CHRISTMAS IS ABOUT COMMUNITY, FAMILY.
I DON'T CARE ABOUT YOUR VIEW ON JESUS--
YOU KNOW THE REAL TRUTH ABOUT JESUS? THE THING NO ONE WANTS TO FACE...
...JESUS CHRIST WAS A TIME TRAVELER. THAT'S WHY HE'S ALL OVER HISTORY.
HE POPS UP OVER AND OVER, HE MAKES HIMSELF OUR MESSIAH, AND THEN SOMEWHERE AROUND THE YEAR 2103 HE'S LIVING LIKE A KING AT THE SECOND COMING.
I'M SORRY BUT SOMEONE HAD TO TELL YOU--
IT'S CHRISTMAS!
CAN'T YOU CUT THE CYNICAL, DEPRESSIVE BULLSHIT FOR ONE NIGHT?
PROBABLY NOT.
THEN DO IT ALONE.
PUBLIC FIGHT. NEVER FUN.
THE FIGHT'S NEVER ABOUT WHAT THE FIGHT IS ABOUT, YOU KNOW?
WHAT WAS THAT ONE ABOUT?
CHRISTMAS.

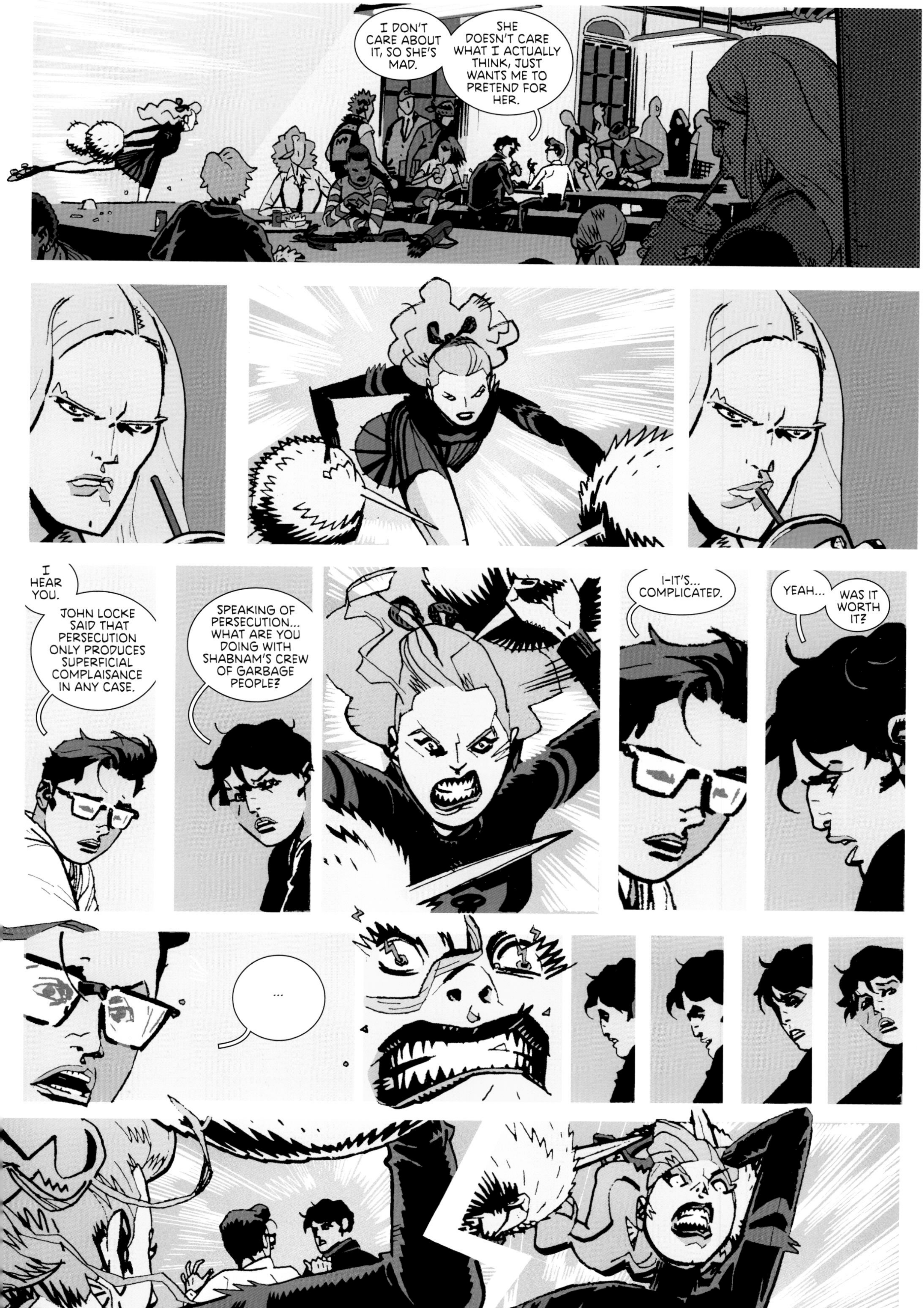
I DON'T CARE ABOUT IT, SO SHE'S MAD.
SHE DOESN'T CARE WHAT I ACTUALLY THINK, JUST WANTS ME TO PRETEND FOR HER.
I HEAR YOU.
JOHN LOCKE SAID THAT PERSECUTION ONLY PRODUCES SUPERFICIAL COMPLAISANCE IN ANY CASE.
SPEAKING OF PERSECUTION... WHAT ARE YOU DOING WITH SHABNAM'S CREW OF GARBAGE PEOPLE?
I-IT'S... COMPLICATED.
YEAH...
WAS IT WORTH IT?
...

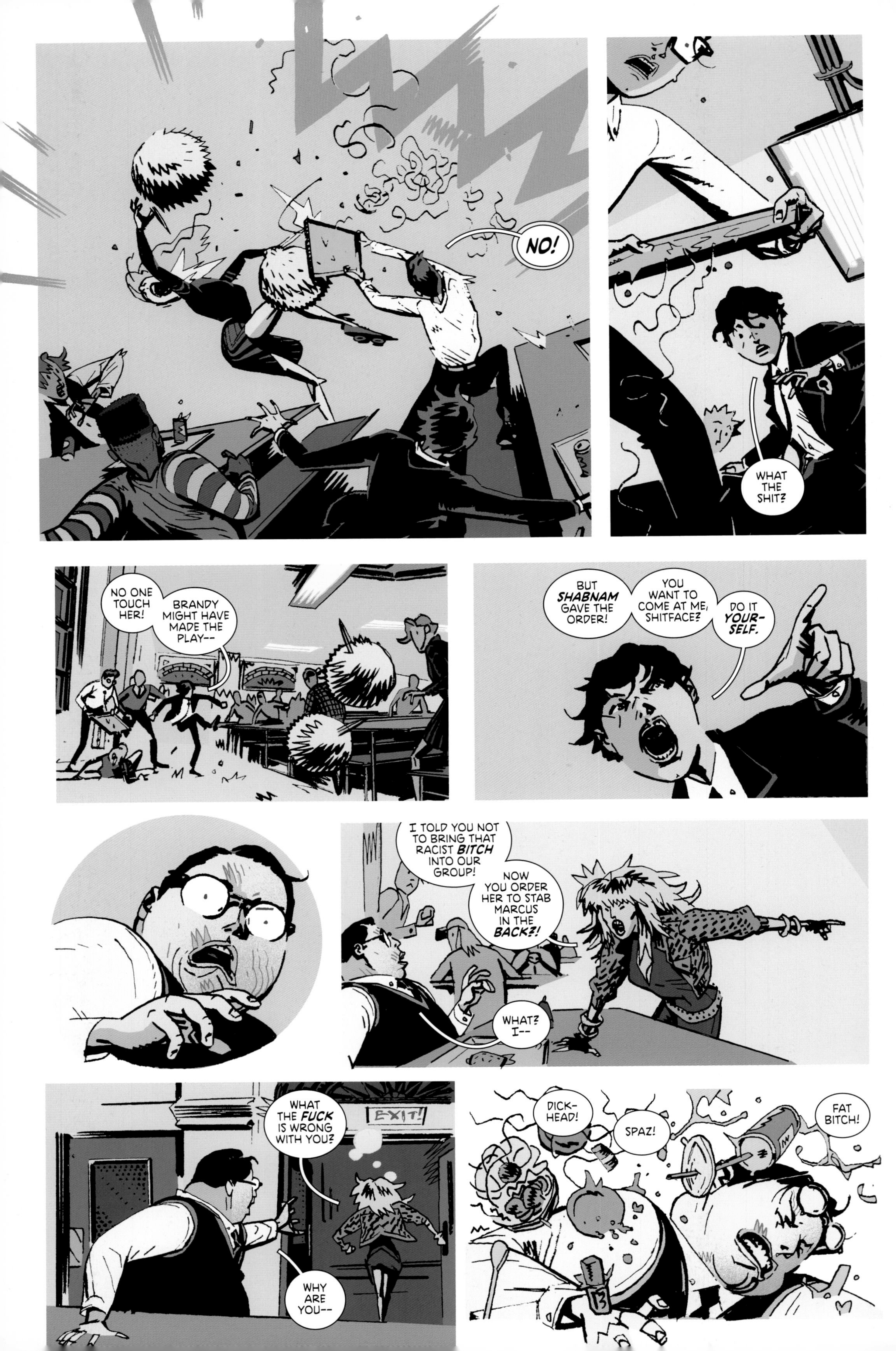
NO!
WHAT THE SHIT?
NO ONE TOUCH HER!
BRANDY MIGHT HAVE MADE THE PLAY--
BUT SHABNAM GAVE THE ORDER!
YOU WANT TO COME AT ME, SHITFACE?
DO IT YOURSELF.
I TOLD YOU NOT TO BRING THAT RACIST BITCH INTO OUR GROUP!
NOW YOU ORDER HER TO STAB MARCUS IN THE BACK?!
WHAT? I--
WHAT THE FUCK IS WRONG WITH YOU?
EXIT!
WHY ARE YOU--
DICK-HEAD!
SPAZ!
FAT BITCH!

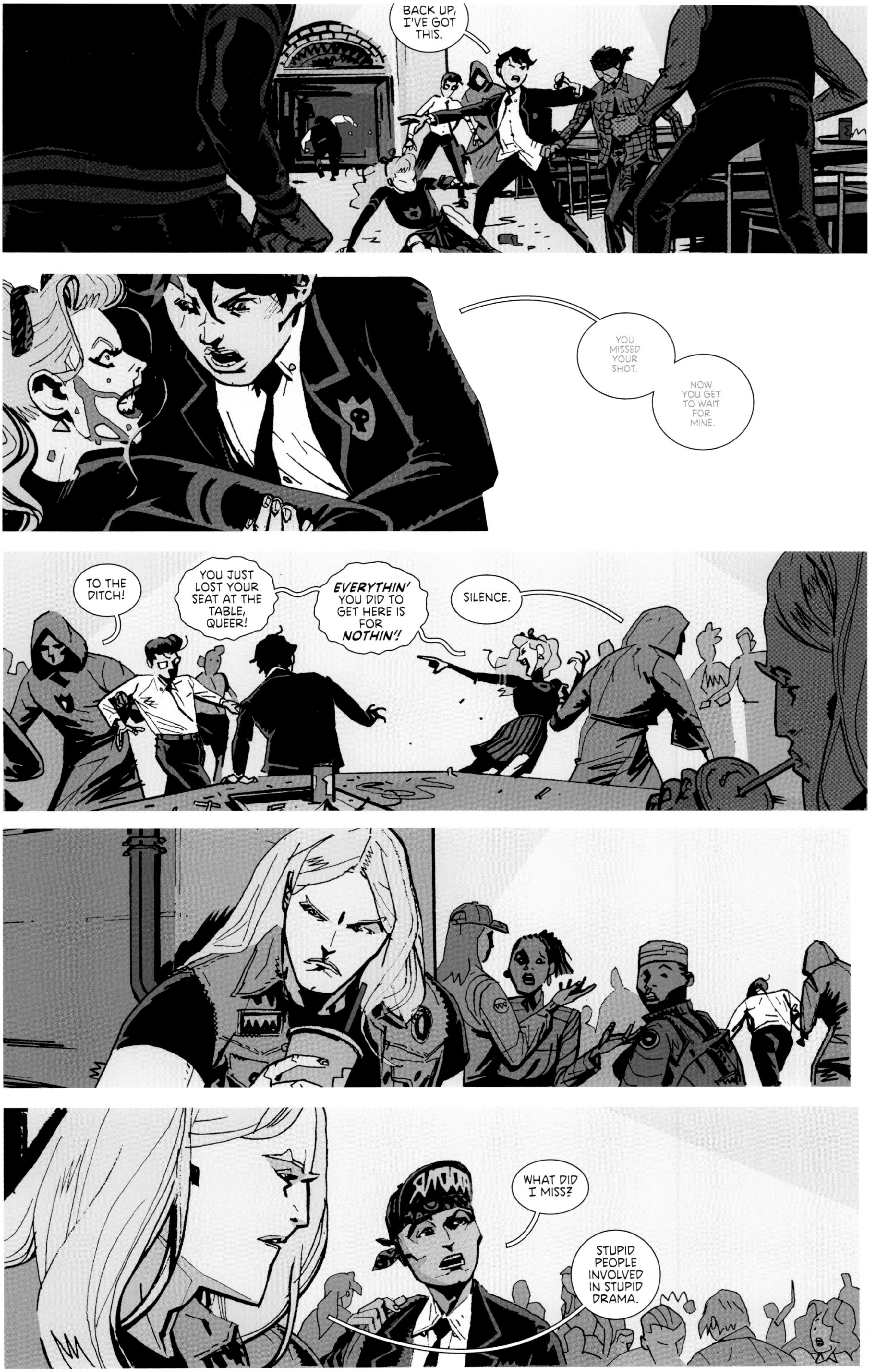
BACK UP, I'VE GOT THIS.
YOU MISSED YOUR SHOT.
NOW YOU GET TO WAIT FOR MINE.
TO THE DITCH!
YOU JUST LOST YOUR SEAT AT THE TABLE, QUEER!
EVERYTHIN' YOU DID TO GET HERE IS FOR NOTHIN'!
SILENCE.
WHAT DID I MISS?
STUPID PEOPLE INVOLVED IN STUPID DRAMA.

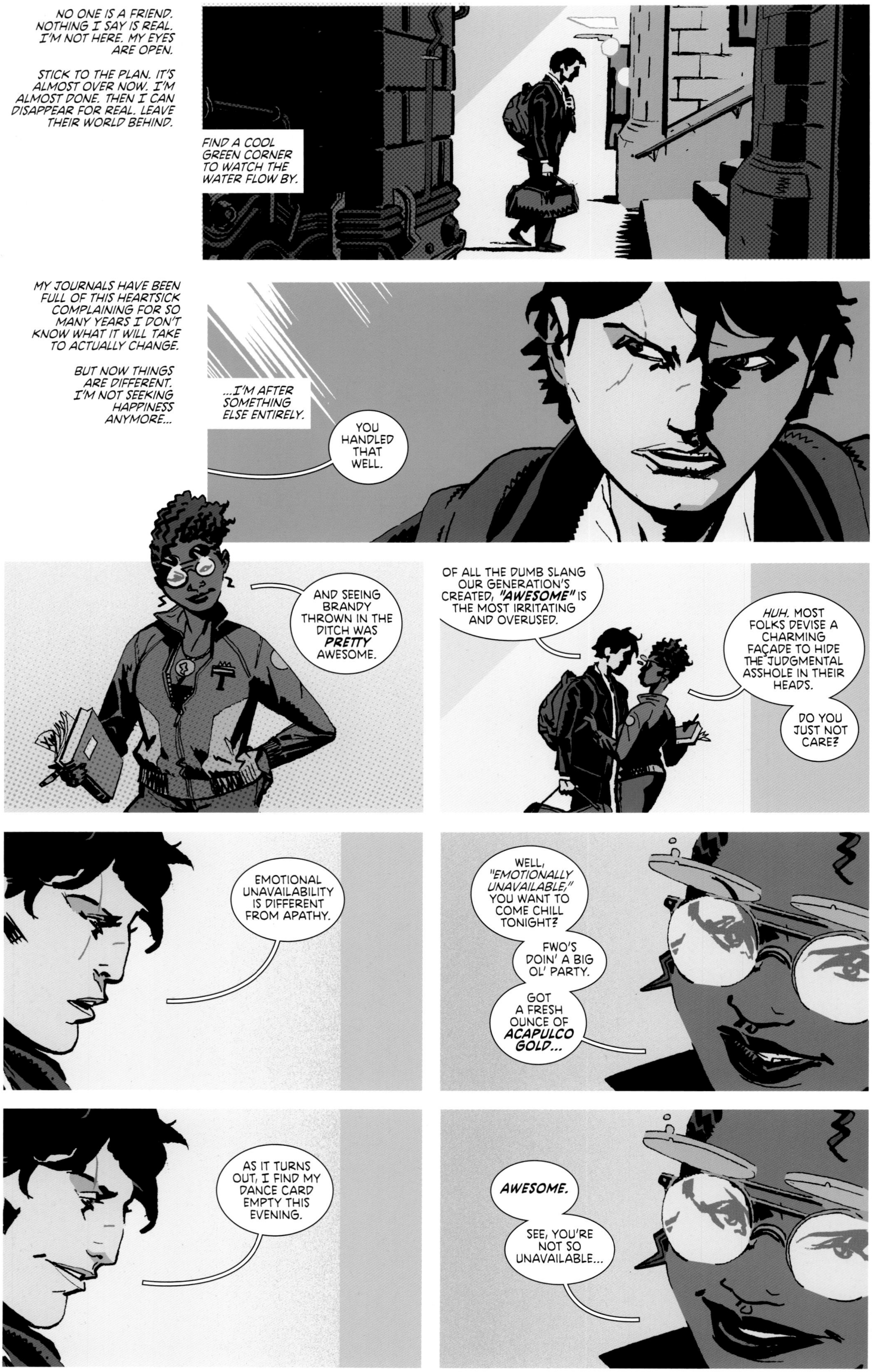
NO ONE IS A FRIEND. NOTHING I SAY IS REAL. I'M NOT HERE. MY EYES ARE OPEN.
STICK TO THE PLAN. IT'S ALMOST OVER NOW. I'M ALMOST DONE. THEN I CAN DISAPPEAR FOR REAL. LEAVE THEIR WORLD BEHIND.
FIND A COOL GREEN CORNER TO WATCH THE WATER FLOW BY.
MY JOURNALS HAVE BEEN FULL OF THIS HEARTSICK COMPLAINING FOR SO MANY YEARS I DON'T KNOW WHAT IT WILL TAKE TO ACTUALLY CHANGE.
BUT NOW THINGS ARE DIFFERENT. I'M NOT SEEKING HAPPINESS ANYMORE...
...I'M AFTER SOMETHING ELSE ENTIRELY.
YOU HANDLED THAT WELL.
AND SEEING BRANDY THROWN IN THE DITCH WAS PRETTY AWESOME.
OF ALL THE DUMB SLANG OUR GENERATION'S CREATED, "AWESOME" IS THE MOST IRRITATING AND OVERUSED.
HUH. MOST FOLKS DEVISE A CHARMING FAÇADE TO HIDE THE JUDGMENTAL ASSHOLE IN THEIR HEADS.
DO YOU JUST NOT CARE?
EMOTIONAL UNAVAILABILITY IS DIFFERENT FROM APATHY.
WELL, "EMOTIONALLY UNAVAILABLE," YOU WANT TO COME CHILL TONIGHT?
FWO'S DOIN' A BIG OL' PARTY.
GOT A FRESH OUNCE OF ACAPULCO GOLD...
AS IT TURNS OUT, I FIND MY DANCE CARD EMPTY THIS EVENING.
AWESOME.
SEE, YOU'RE NOT SO UNAVAILABLE...

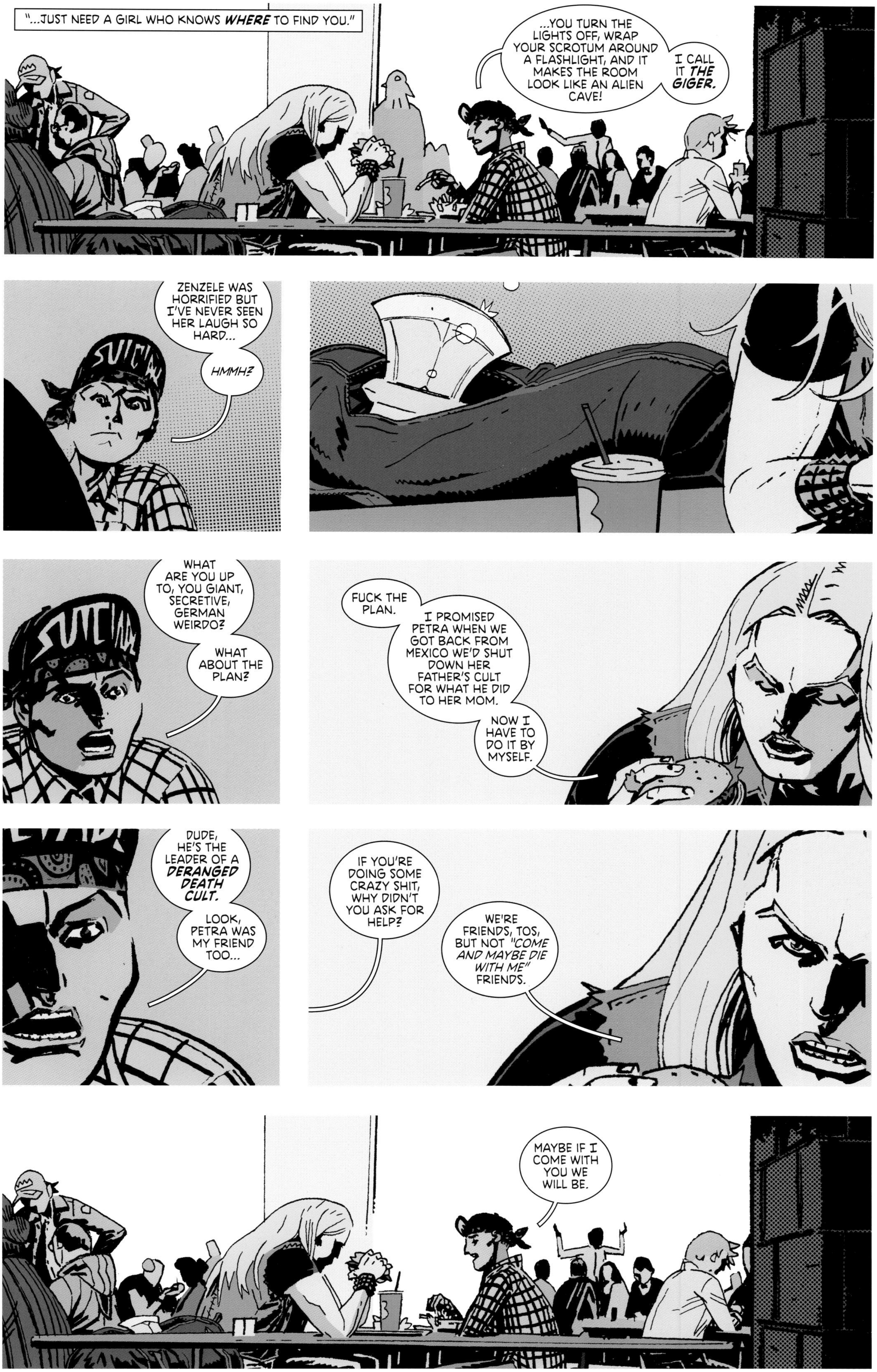
"...JUST NEED A GIRL WHO KNOWS WHERE TO FIND YOU."
...YOU TURN THE LIGHTS OFF, WRAP YOUR SCROTUM AROUND A FLASHLIGHT, AND IT MAKES THE ROOM LOOK LIKE AN ALIEN CAVE!
I CALL IT THE GIGER.
ZENZELE WAS HORRIFIED BUT I'VE NEVER SEEN HER LAUGH SO HARD...
HMMH?
WHAT ARE YOU UP TO, YOU GIANT, SECRETIVE, GERMAN WEIRDO?
WHAT ABOUT THE PLAN?
FUCK THE PLAN.
I PROMISED PETRA WHEN WE GOT BACK FROM MEXICO WE'D SHUT DOWN HER FATHER'S CULT FOR WHAT HE DID TO HER MOM.
NOW I HAVE TO DO IT BY MYSELF.
DUDE, HE'S THE LEADER OF A DERANGED DEATH CULT.
LOOK, PETRA WAS MY FRIEND TOO...
IF YOU'RE DOING SOME CRAZY SHIT, WHY DIDN'T YOU ASK FOR HELP?
WE'RE FRIENDS, TOS, BUT NOT "COME AND MAYBE DIE WITH ME" FRIENDS.
MAYBE IF I COME WITH YOU WE WILL BE.

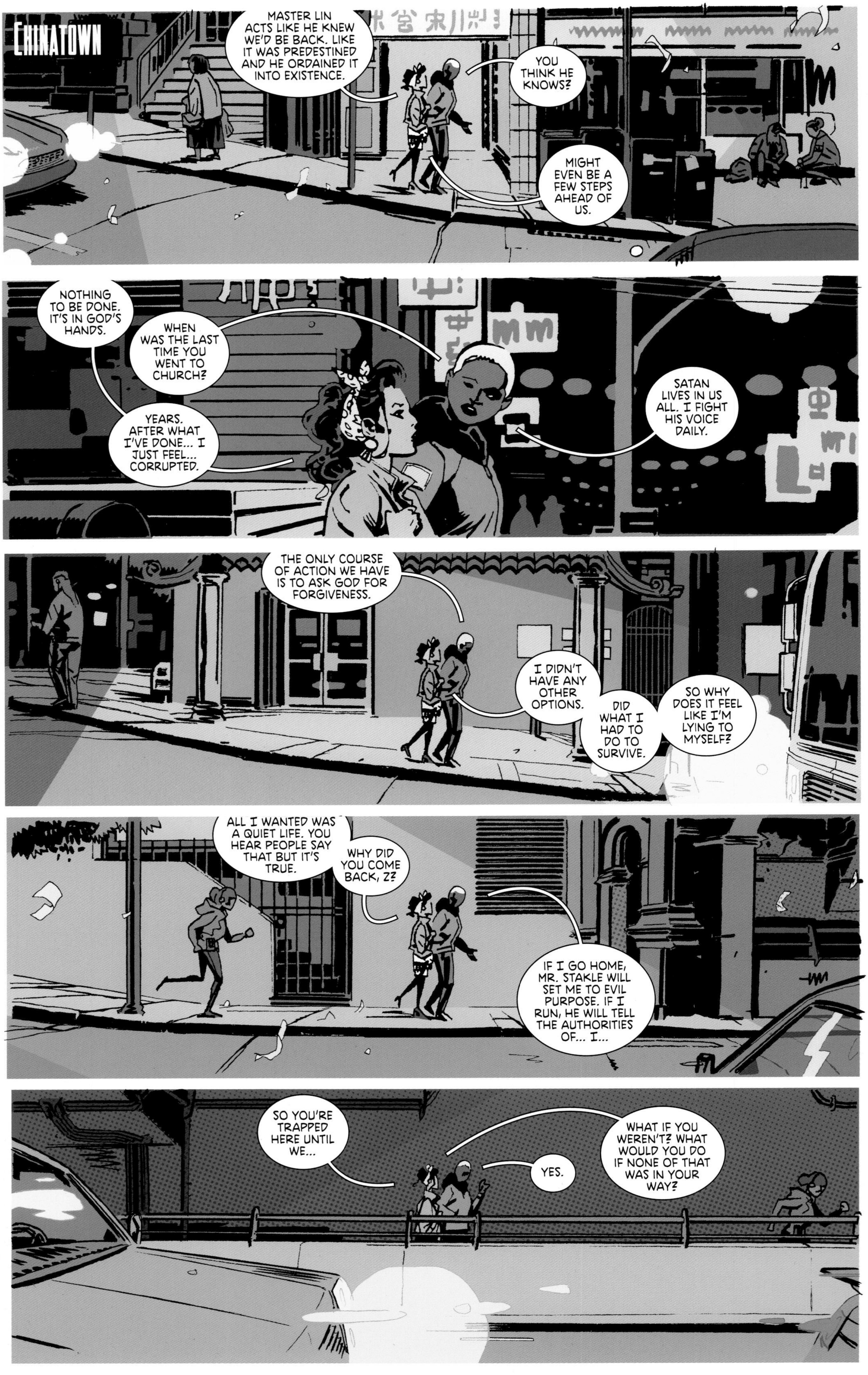
CHINATOWN
MASTER LIN ACTS LIKE HE KNEW WE'D BE BACK. LIKE IT WAS PREDESTINED AND HE ORDAINED IT INTO EXISTENCE.
YOU THINK HE KNOWS?
MIGHT EVEN BE A FEW STEPS AHEAD OF US.
NOTHING TO BE DONE. IT'S IN GOD'S HANDS.
WHEN WAS THE LAST TIME YOU WENT TO CHURCH?
YEARS. AFTER WHAT I'VE DONE... I JUST FEEL... CORRUPTED.
SATAN LIVES IN US ALL. I FIGHT HIS VOICE DAILY.
THE ONLY COURSE OF ACTION WE HAVE IS TO ASK GOD FOR FORGIVENESS.
I DIDN'T HAVE ANY OTHER OPTIONS.
DID WHAT I HAD TO DO TO SURVIVE.
SO WHY DOES IT FEEL LIKE I'M LYING TO MYSELF?
ALL I WANTED WAS A QUIET LIFE. YOU HEAR PEOPLE SAY THAT BUT IT'S TRUE.
WHY DID YOU COME BACK, Z?
IF I GO HOME, MR. STAKLE WILL SET ME TO EVIL PURPOSE. IF I RUN, HE WILL TELL THE AUTHORITIES OF... I...
SO YOU'RE TRAPPED HERE UNTIL WE...
YES.
WHAT IF YOU WEREN'T? WHAT WOULD YOU DO IF NONE OF THAT WAS IN YOUR WAY?

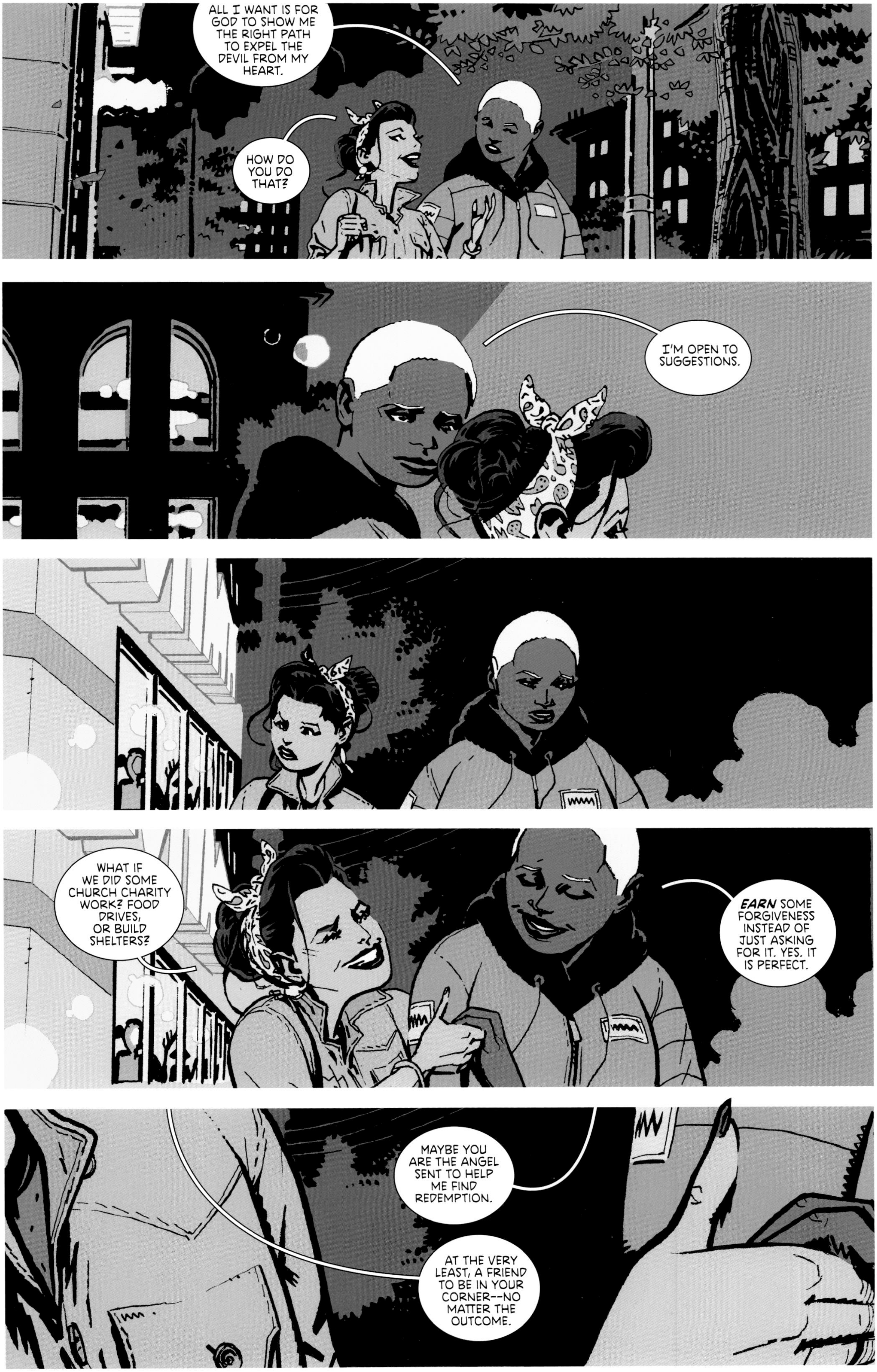
ALL I WANT IS FOR GOD TO SHOW ME THE RIGHT PATH TO EXPEL THE DEVIL FROM MY HEART.
HOW DO YOU DO THAT?
I'M OPEN TO SUGGESTIONS.
WHAT IF WE DID SOME CHURCH CHARITY WORK? FOOD DRIVES, OR BUILD SHELTERS?
EARN SOME FORGIVENESS INSTEAD OF JUST ASKING FOR IT. YES. IT IS PERFECT.
MAYBE YOU ARE THE ANGEL SENT TO HELP ME FIND REDEMPTION.
AT THE VERY LEAST, A FRIEND TO BE IN YOUR CORNER--NO MATTER THE OUTCOME.

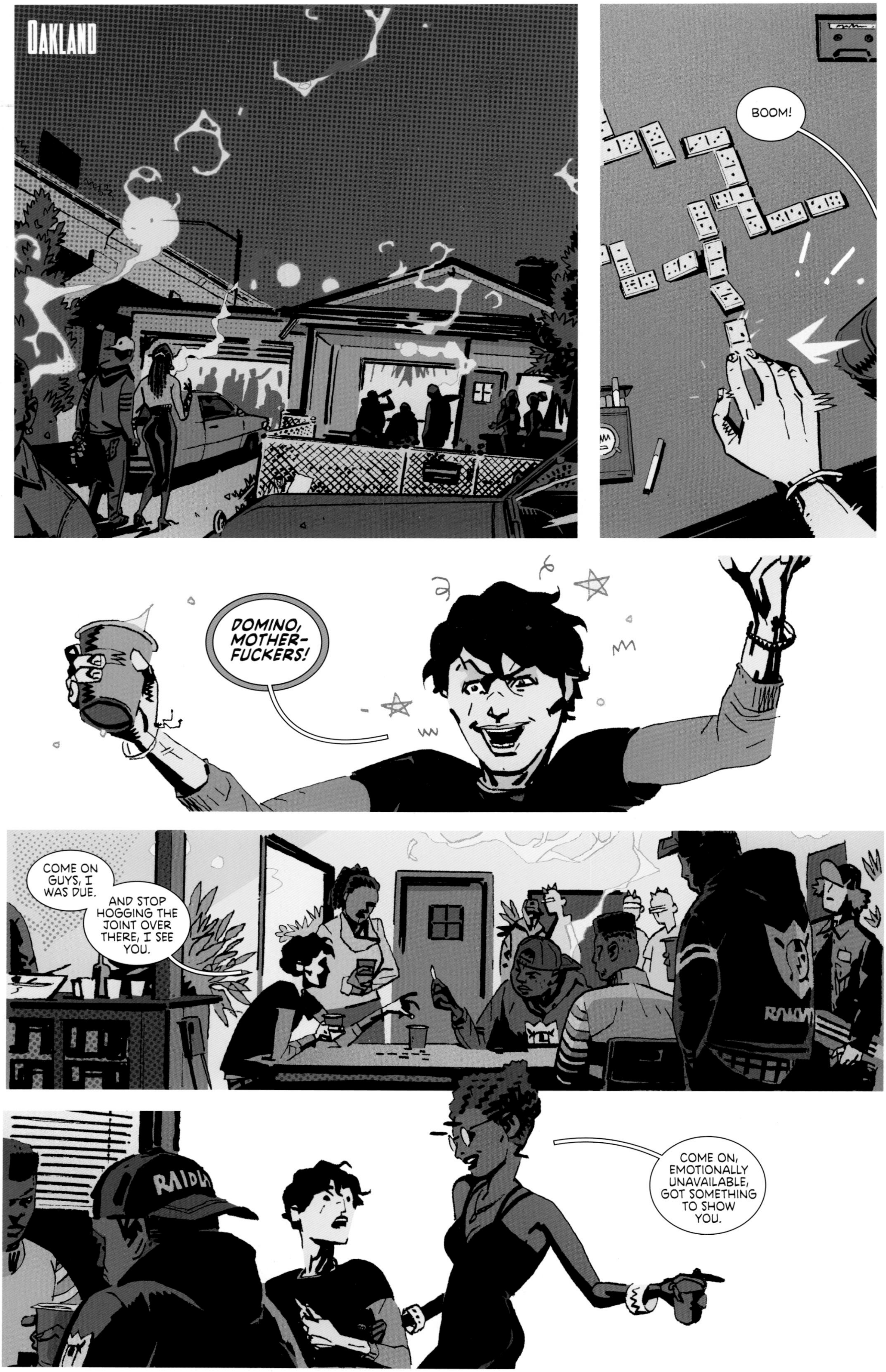
OAKLAND
BOOM!
DOMINO, MOTHER-FUCKERS!
COME ON GUYS, I WAS DUE.
AND STOP HOGGING THE JOINT OVER THERE, I SEE YOU.
COME ON, EMOTIONALLY UNAVAILABLE, GOT SOMETHING TO SHOW YOU.

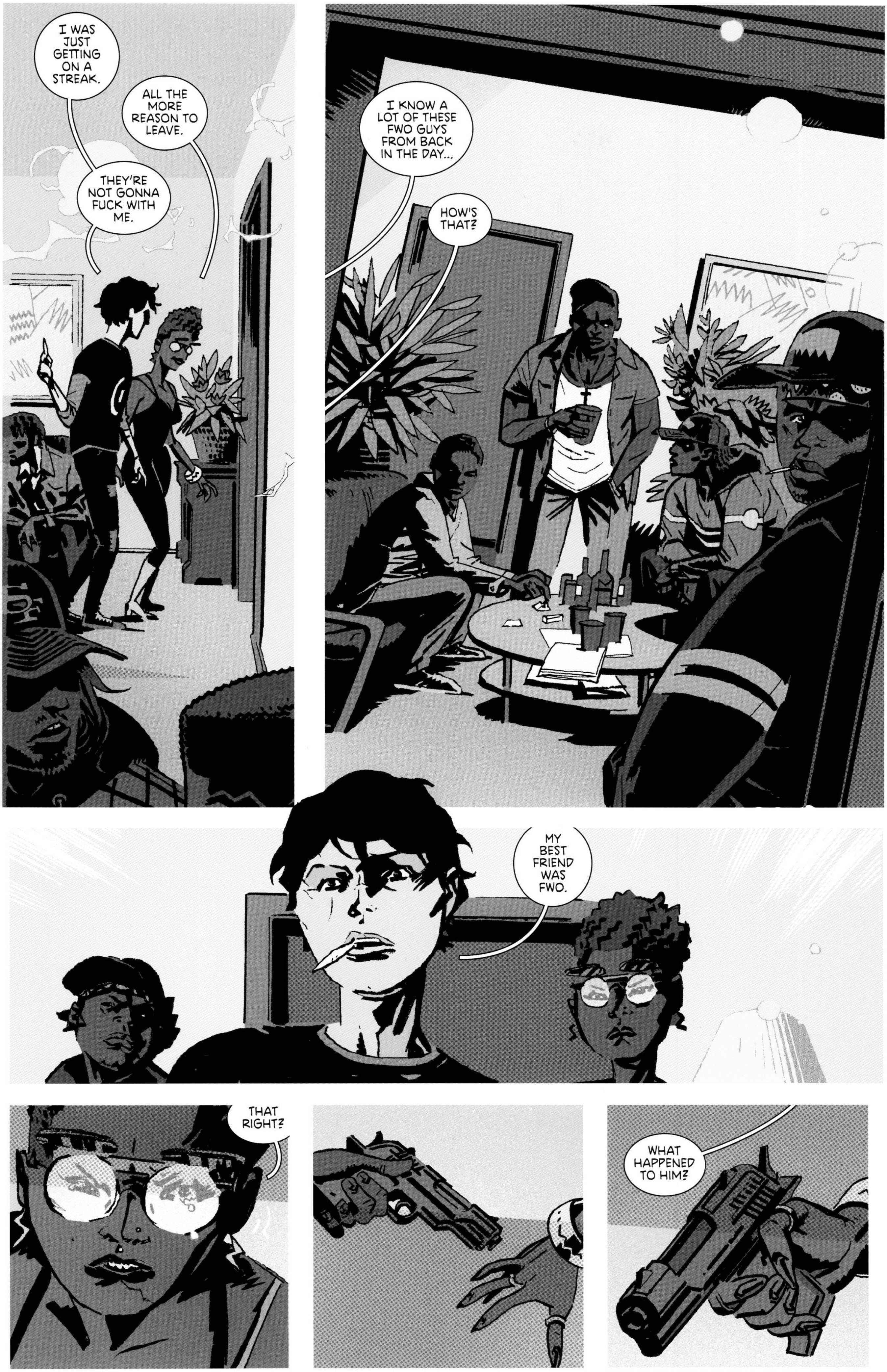
I WAS JUST GETTING ON A STREAK.
ALL THE MORE REASON TO LEAVE.
THEY'RE NOT GONNA FUCK WITH ME.
I KNOW A LOT OF THESE FWO GUYS FROM BACK IN THE DAY...
HOW'S THAT?
MY BEST FRIEND WAS FWO.
THAT RIGHT?
WHAT HAPPENED TO HIM?

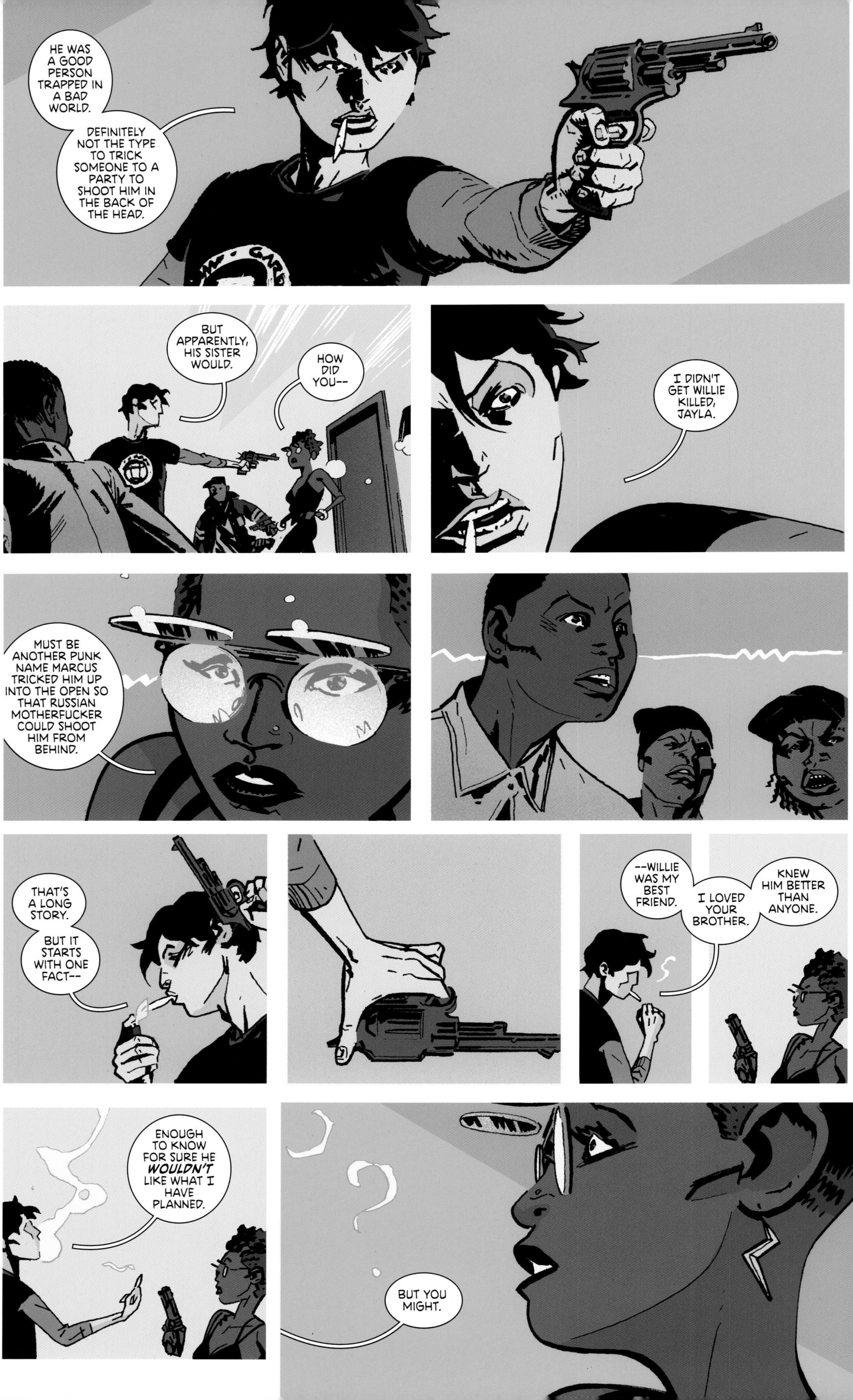
HE WAS A GOOD PERSON TRAPPED IN A BAD WORLD.
DEFINITELY NOT THE TYPE TO TRICK SOMEONE TO A PARTY TO SHOOT HIM IN THE BACK OF THE HEAD.
BUT APPARENTLY, HIS SISTER WOULD.
HOW DID YOU--
I DIDN'T GET WILLIE KILLED, JAYLA.
MUST BE ANOTHER PUNK NAME MARCUS TRICKED HIM UP INTO THE OPEN SO THAT RUSSIAN MOTHERFUCKER COULD SHOOT HIM FROM BEHIND.
THAT'S A LONG STORY.
BUT IT STARTS WITH ONE FACT--
--WILLIE WAS MY BEST FRIEND.
I LOVED YOUR BROTHER.
KNEW HIM BETTER THAN ANYONE.
ENOUGH TO KNOW FOR SURE HE WOULDN'T LIKE WHAT I HAVE PLANNED.
BUT YOU MIGHT.

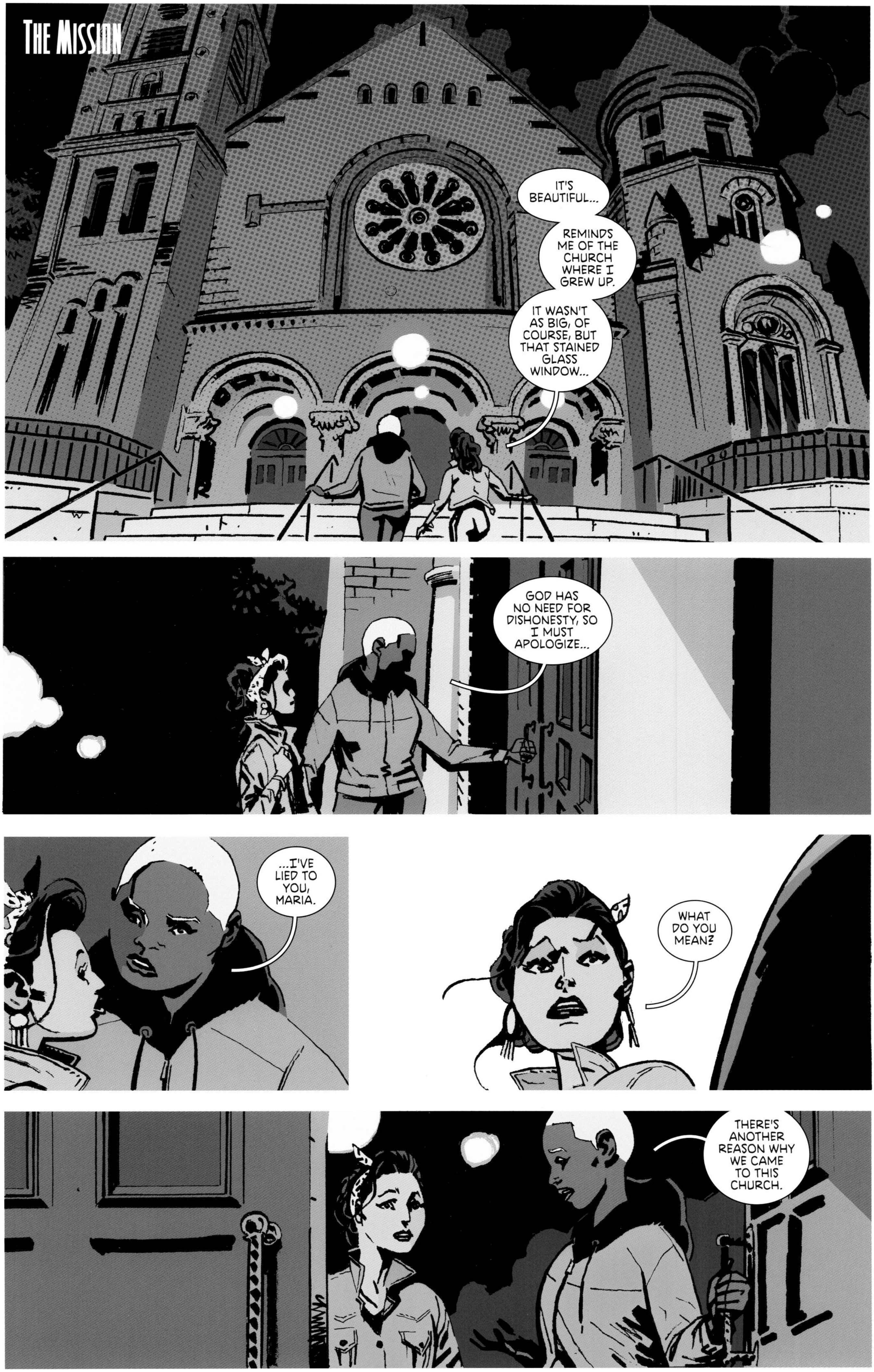
The Mission
IT'S BEAUTIFUL...
REMINDS ME OF THE CHURCH WHERE I GREW UP.
IT WASN'T AS BIG, OF COURSE, BUT THAT STAINED GLASS WINDOW...
GOD HAS NO NEED FOR DISHONESTY, SO I MUST APOLOGIZE...
...I'VE LIED TO YOU, MARIA.
WHAT DO YOU MEAN?
THERE'S ANOTHER REASON WHY WE CAME TO THIS CHURCH.

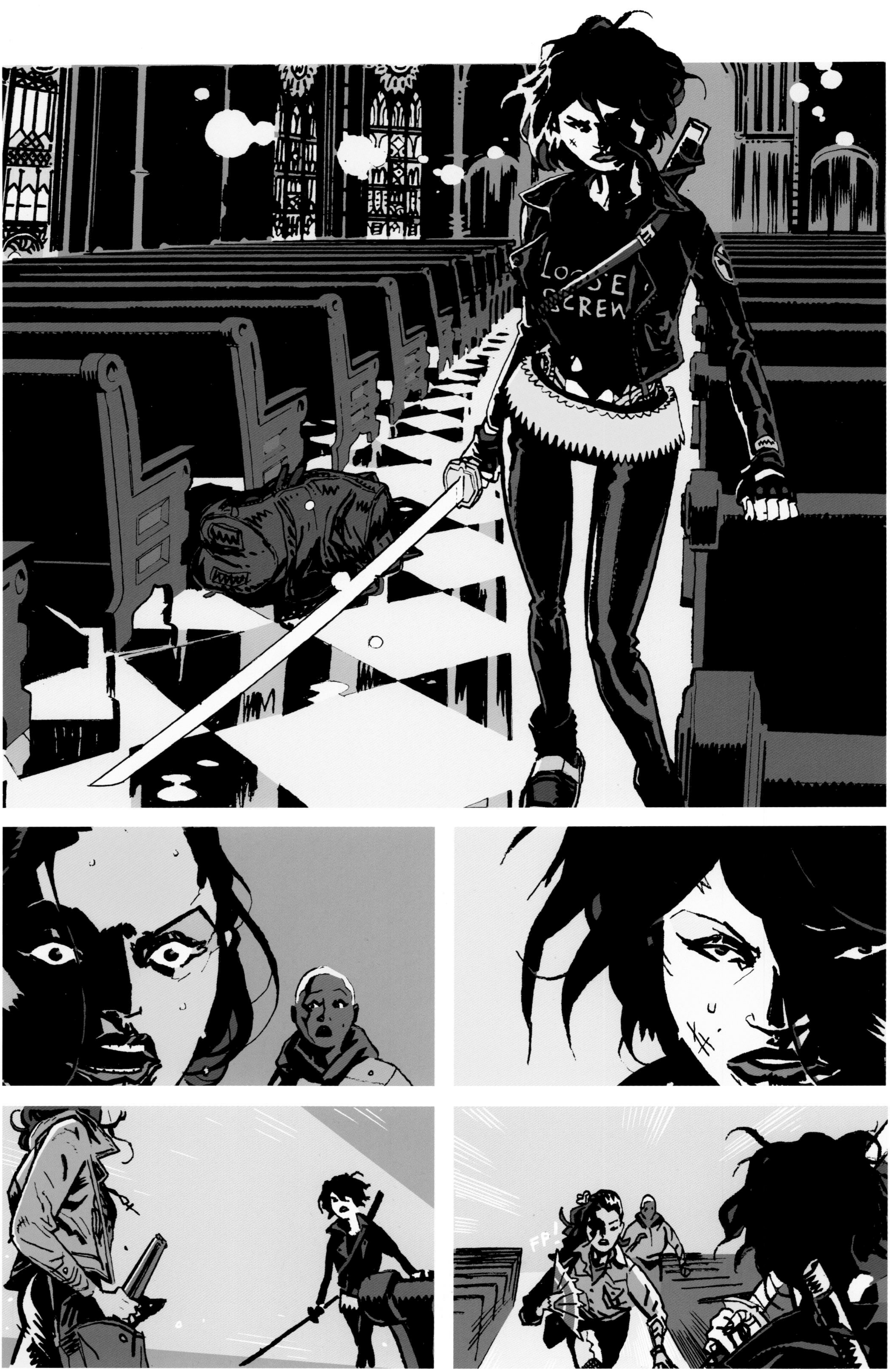
LOOSE SCREW
FP!

"KILLER SET"
ONE-SHOT

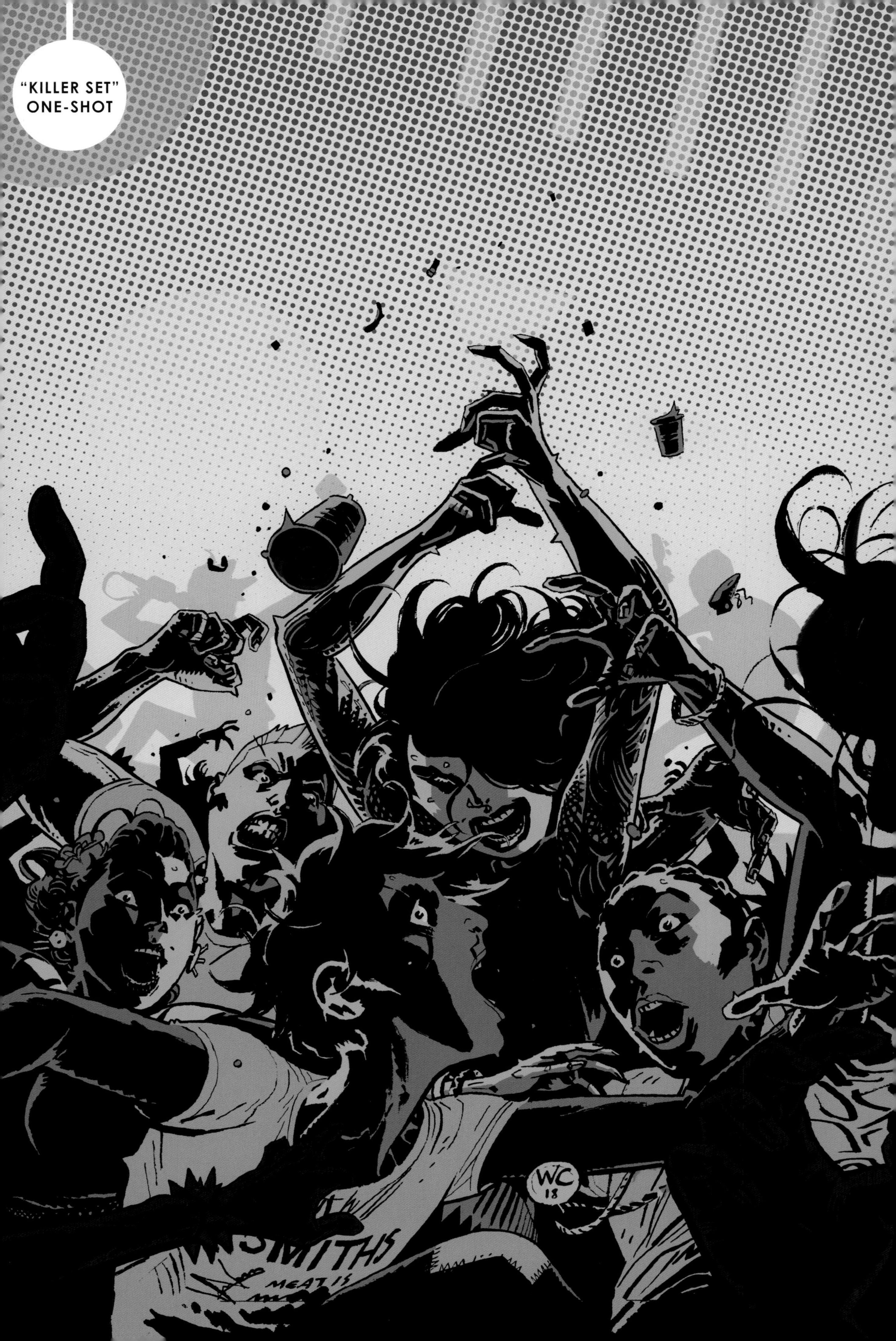
SMITHS
MEAT IS
WC
18

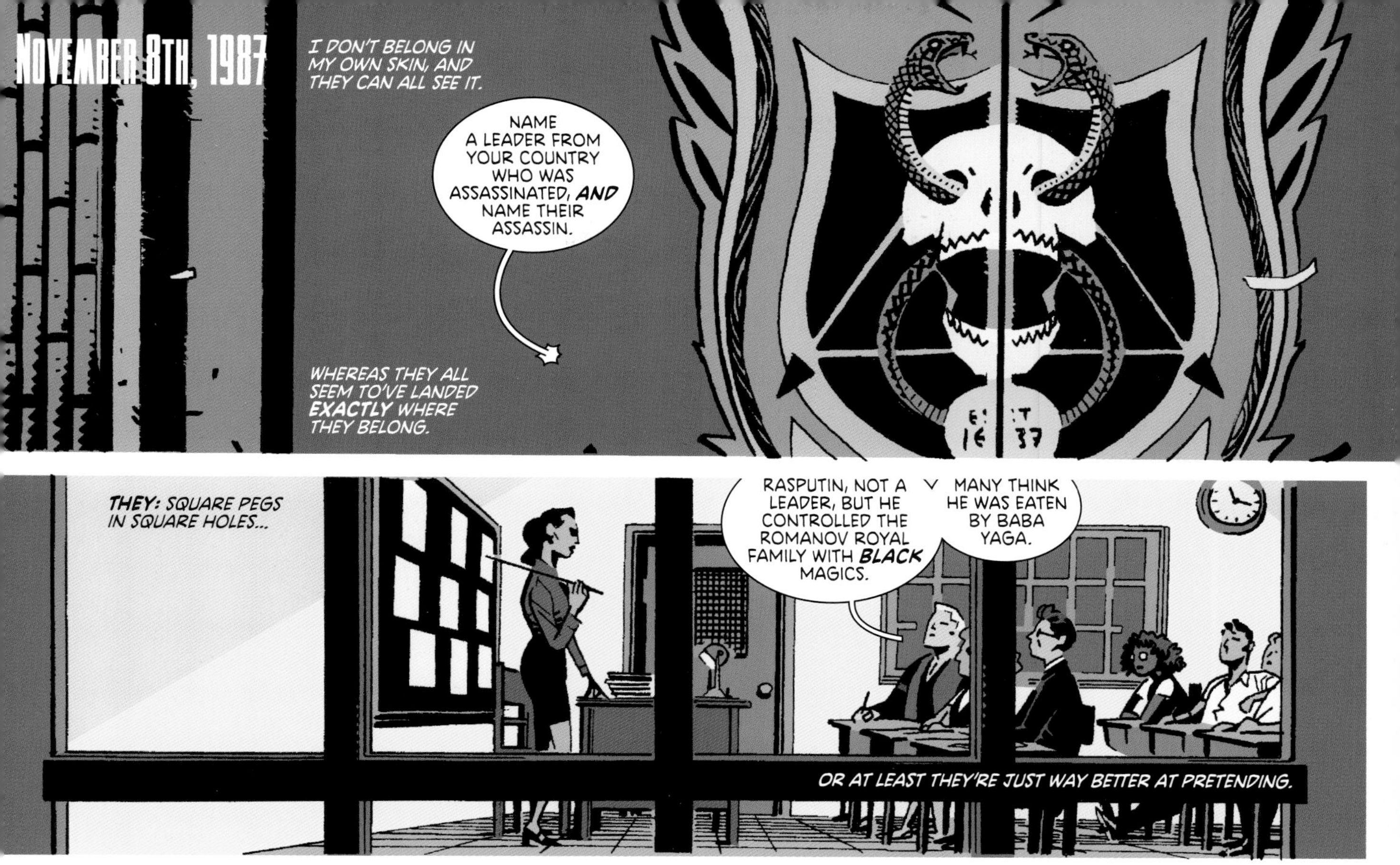
NOVEMBER 8TH, 1987
I DON'T BELONG IN MY OWN SKIN, AND THEY CAN ALL SEE IT.
NAME A LEADER FROM YOUR COUNTRY WHO WAS ASSASSINATED, AND NAME THEIR ASSASSIN.
WHEREAS THEY ALL SEEM TO'VE LANDED EXACTLY WHERE THEY BELONG.
THEY: SQUARE PEGS IN SQUARE HOLES...
RASPUTIN, NOT A LEADER, BUT HE CONTROLLED THE ROMANOV ROYAL FAMILY WITH BLACK MAGICS.
MANY THINK HE WAS EATEN BY BABA YAGA.
OR AT LEAST THEY'RE JUST WAY BETTER AT PRETENDING.

MARCUS' FIRST WEEK AT KINGS

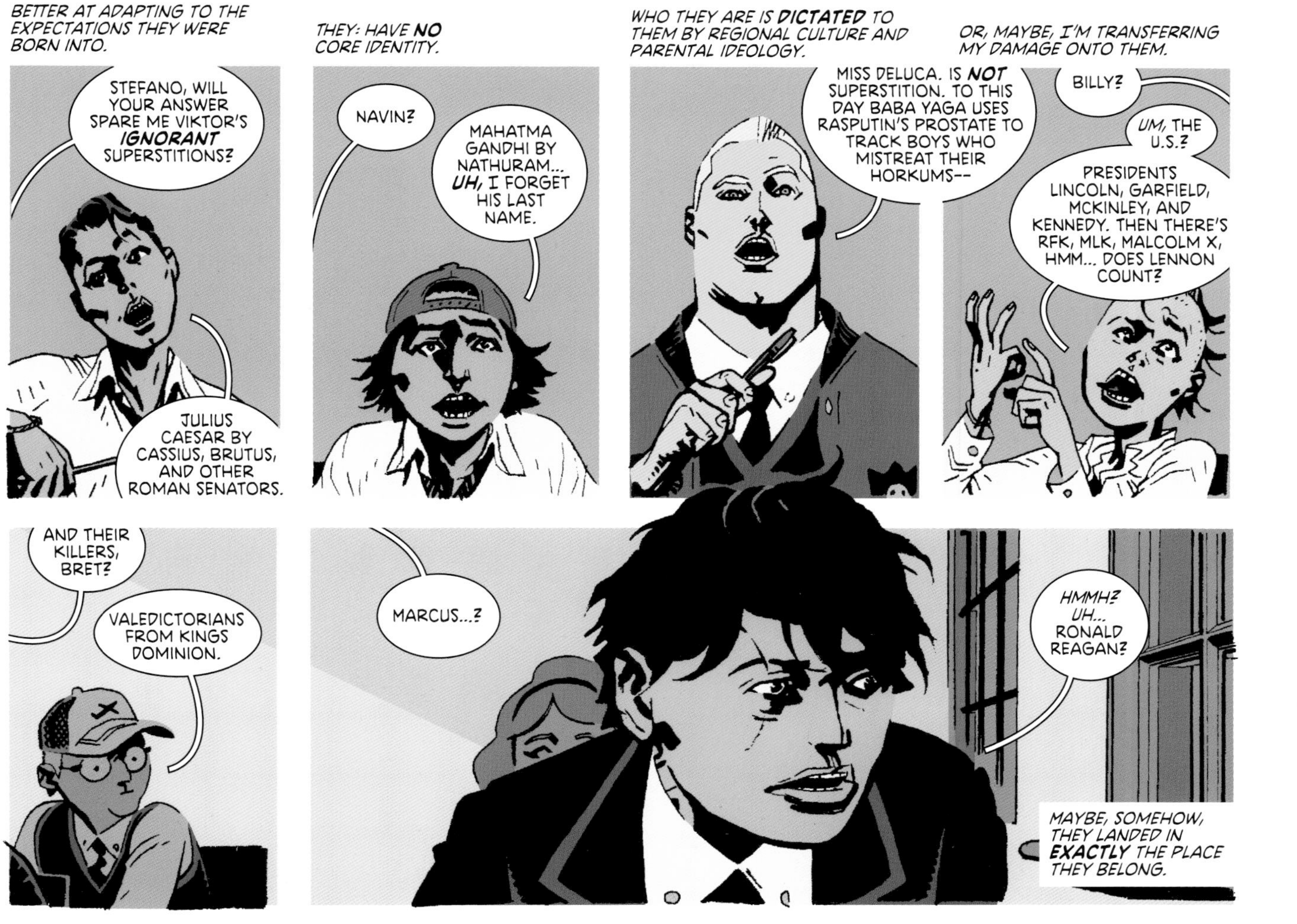
BETTER AT ADAPTING TO THE EXPECTATIONS THEY WERE BORN INTO.
STEFANO, WILL YOUR ANSWER SPARE ME VIKTOR'S IGNORANT SUPERSTITIONS?
JULIUS CAESAR BY CASSIUS, BRUTUS, AND OTHER ROMAN SENATORS.
THEY: HAVE NO CORE IDENTITY.
NAVIN?
MAHATMA GANDHI BY NATHURAM... UH, I FORGET HIS LAST NAME.
WHO THEY ARE IS DICTATED TO THEM BY REGIONAL CULTURE AND PARENTAL IDEOLOGY.
MISS DELUCA. IS NOT SUPERSTITION. TO THIS DAY BABA YAGA USES RASPUTIN'S PROSTATE TO TRACK BOYS WHO MISTREAT THEIR HORKUMS--
OR, MAYBE, I'M TRANSFERRING MY DAMAGE ONTO THEM.
BILLY?
UM, THE U.S.?
PRESIDENTS LINCOLN, GARFIELD, MCKINLEY, AND KENNEDY. THEN THERE'S RFK, MLK, MALCOLM X, HMM... DOES LENNON COUNT?
AND THEIR KILLERS, BRET?
VALEDICTORIANS FROM KINGS DOMINION.
MARCUS...?
HMMH? UH... RONALD REAGAN?
MAYBE, SOMEHOW, THEY LANDED IN EXACTLY THE PLACE THEY BELONG.

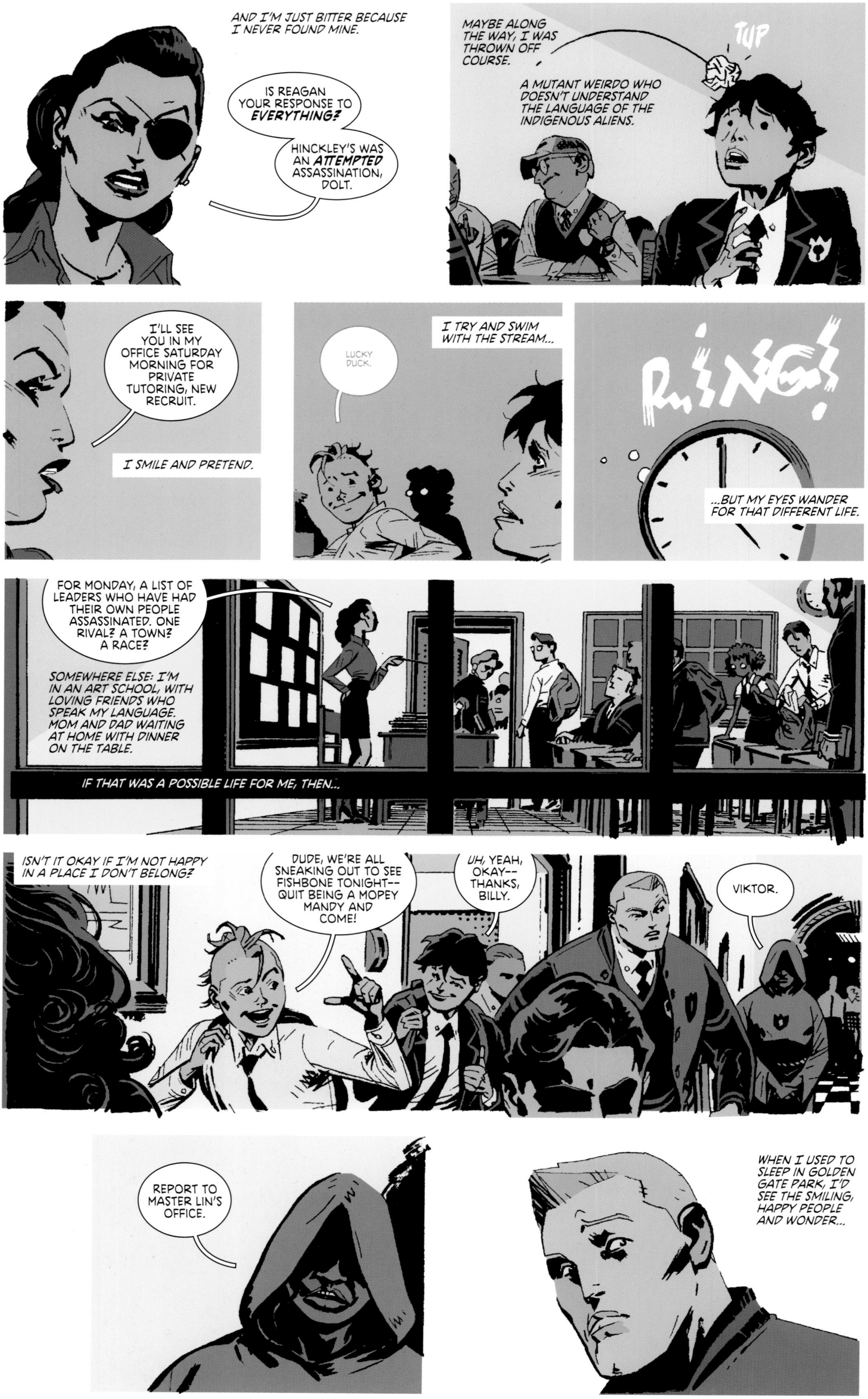
AND I'M JUST BITTER BECAUSE I NEVER FOUND MINE.
IS REAGAN YOUR RESPONSE TO EVERYTHING?
HINCKLEY'S WAS AN ATTEMPTED ASSASSINATION, DOLT.
MAYBE ALONG THE WAY, I WAS THROWN OFF COURSE.
TUP
A MUTANT WEIRDO WHO DOESN'T UNDERSTAND THE LANGUAGE OF THE INDIGENOUS ALIENS.
I'LL SEE YOU IN MY OFFICE SATURDAY MORNING FOR PRIVATE TUTORING, NEW RECRUIT.
I SMILE AND PRETEND.
I TRY AND SWIM WITH THE STREAM...
LUCKY DUCK.
RING!
...BUT MY EYES WANDER FOR THAT DIFFERENT LIFE.
FOR MONDAY, A LIST OF LEADERS WHO HAVE HAD THEIR OWN PEOPLE ASSASSINATED. ONE RIVAL? A TOWN? A RACE?
SOMEWHERE ELSE: I'M IN AN ART SCHOOL, WITH LOVING FRIENDS WHO SPEAK MY LANGUAGE. MOM AND DAD WAITING AT HOME WITH DINNER ON THE TABLE.
IF THAT WAS A POSSIBLE LIFE FOR ME, THEN...
ISN'T IT OKAY IF I'M NOT HAPPY IN A PLACE I DON'T BELONG?
DUDE, WE'RE ALL SNEAKING OUT TO SEE FISHBONE TONIGHT-- QUIT BEING A MOPEY MANDY AND COME!
UH, YEAH, OKAY-- THANKS, BILLY.
VIKTOR.
REPORT TO MASTER LIN'S OFFICE.
WHEN I USED TO SLEEP IN GOLDEN GATE PARK, I'D SEE THE SMILING, HAPPY PEOPLE AND WONDER...

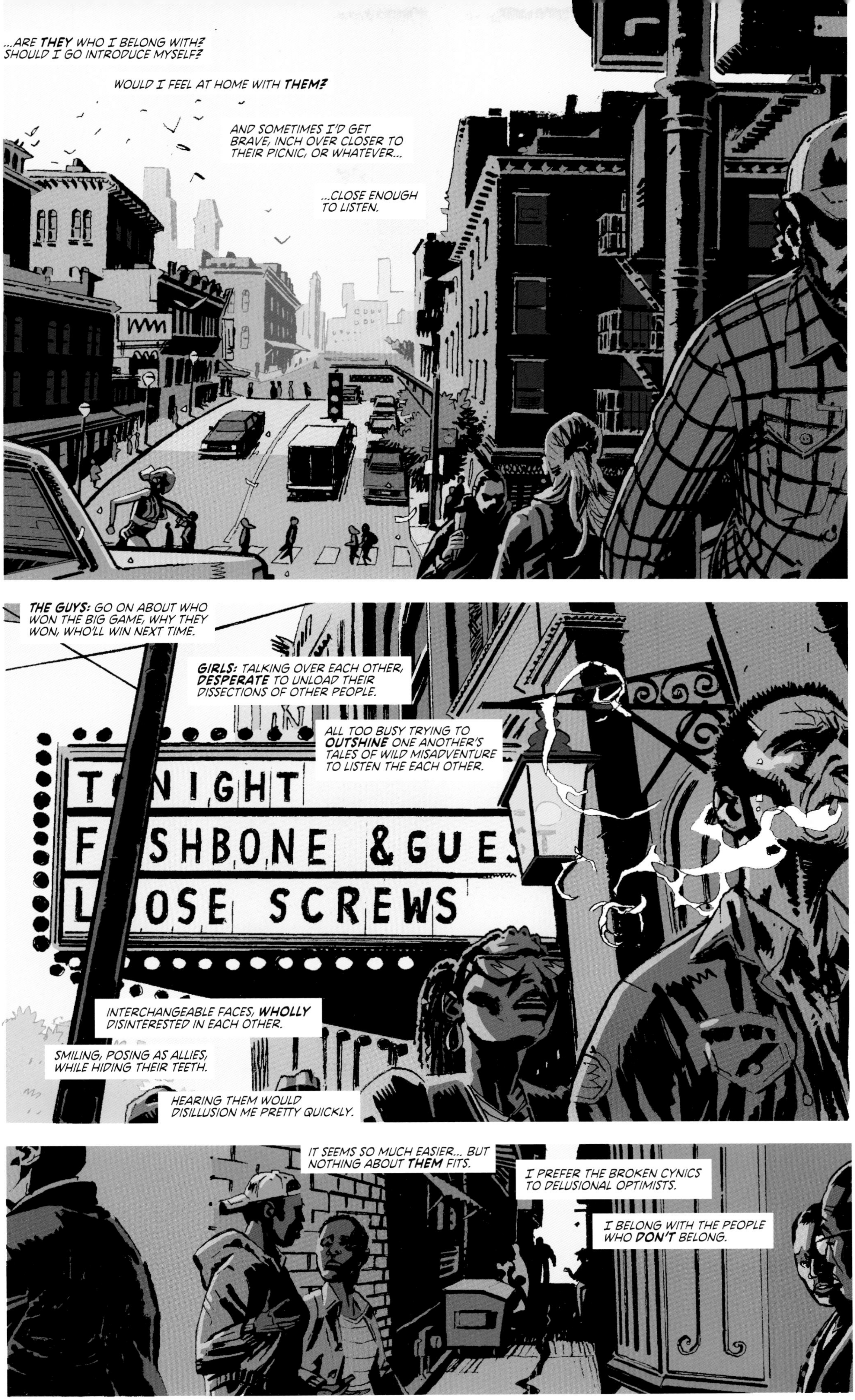
...ARE **THEY** WHO I BELONG WITH? SHOULD I GO INTRODUCE MYSELF?
WOULD I FEEL AT HOME WITH **THEM?**
AND SOMETIMES I'D GET BRAVE, INCH OVER CLOSER TO THEIR PICNIC, OR WHATEVER...
...CLOSE ENOUGH TO LISTEN.
THE GUYS: GO ON ABOUT WHO WON THE BIG GAME, WHY THEY WON, WHO'LL WIN NEXT TIME.
GIRLS: TALKING OVER EACH OTHER, **DESPERATE** TO UNLOAD THEIR DISSECTIONS OF OTHER PEOPLE.
ALL TOO BUSY TRYING TO **OUTSHINE** ONE ANOTHER'S TALES OF WILD MISADVENTURE TO LISTEN THE EACH OTHER.
T NIGHT
F SHBONE &GUES
L OSE SCREWS
INTERCHANGEABLE FACES, **WHOLLY** DISINTERESTED IN EACH OTHER.
SMILING, POSING AS ALLIES, WHILE HIDING THEIR TEETH.
HEARING THEM WOULD DISILLUSION ME PRETTY QUICKLY.
IT SEEMS SO MUCH EASIER... BUT NOTHING ABOUT **THEM** FITS.
I PREFER THE BROKEN CYNICS TO DELUSIONAL OPTIMISTS.
I BELONG WITH THE PEOPLE WHO **DON'T** BELONG.

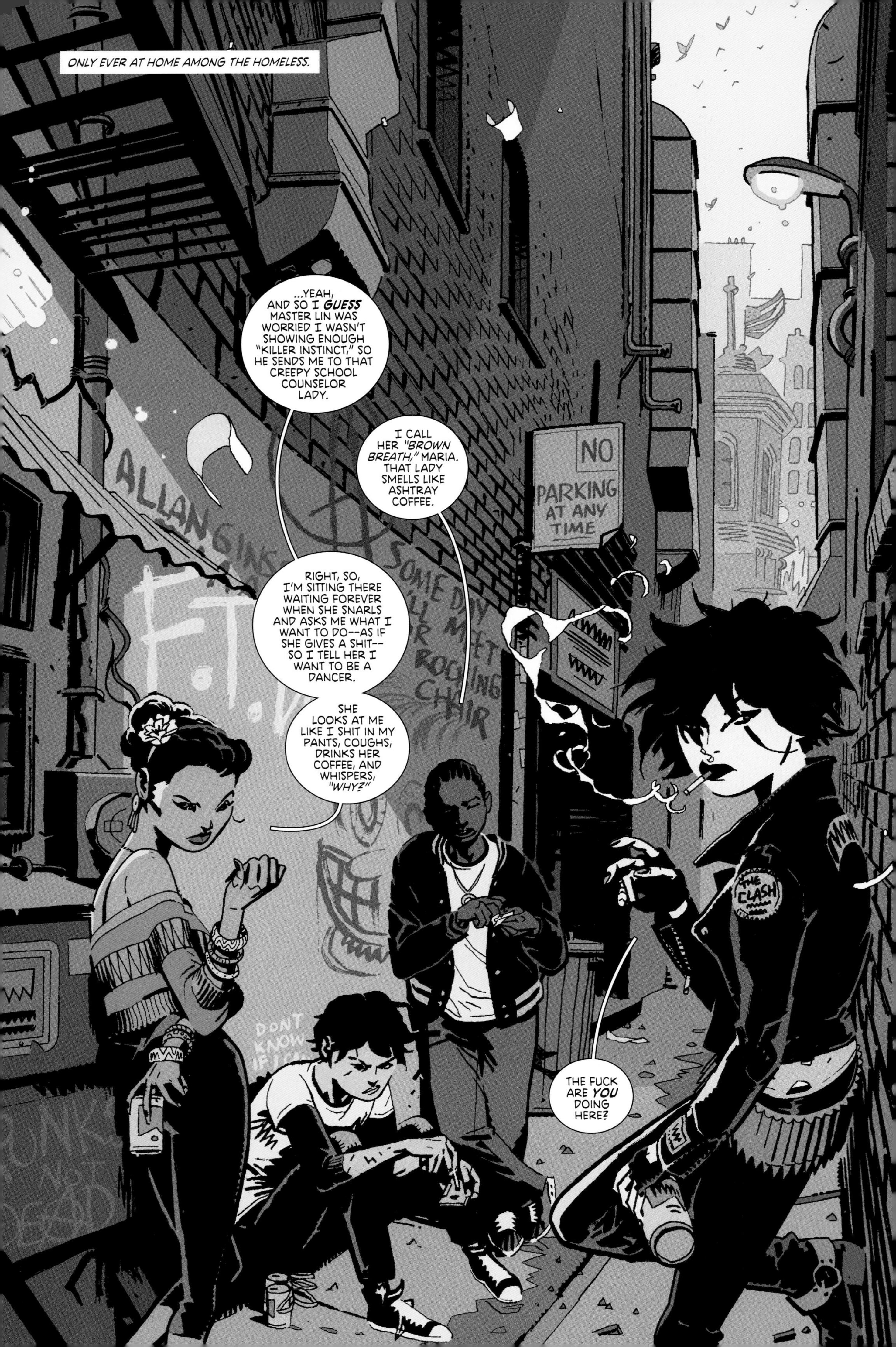
ONLY EVER AT HOME AMONG THE HOMELESS.
...YEAH, AND SO I GUESS MASTER LIN WAS WORRIED I WASN'T SHOWING ENOUGH "KILLER INSTINCT," SO HE SENDS ME TO THAT CREEPY SCHOOL COUNSELOR LADY.
I CALL HER "BROWN BREATH," MARIA. THAT LADY SMELLS LIKE ASHTRAY COFFEE.
RIGHT, SO, I'M SITTING THERE WAITING FOREVER WHEN SHE SNARLS AND ASKS ME WHAT I WANT TO DO--AS IF SHE GIVES A SHIT--SO I TELL HER I WANT TO BE A DANCER.
SHE LOOKS AT ME LIKE I SHIT IN MY PANTS, COUGHS, DRINKS HER COFFEE, AND WHISPERS, "WHY?"
THE FUCK ARE YOU DOING HERE?
NO PARKING AT ANY TIME
THE CLASH

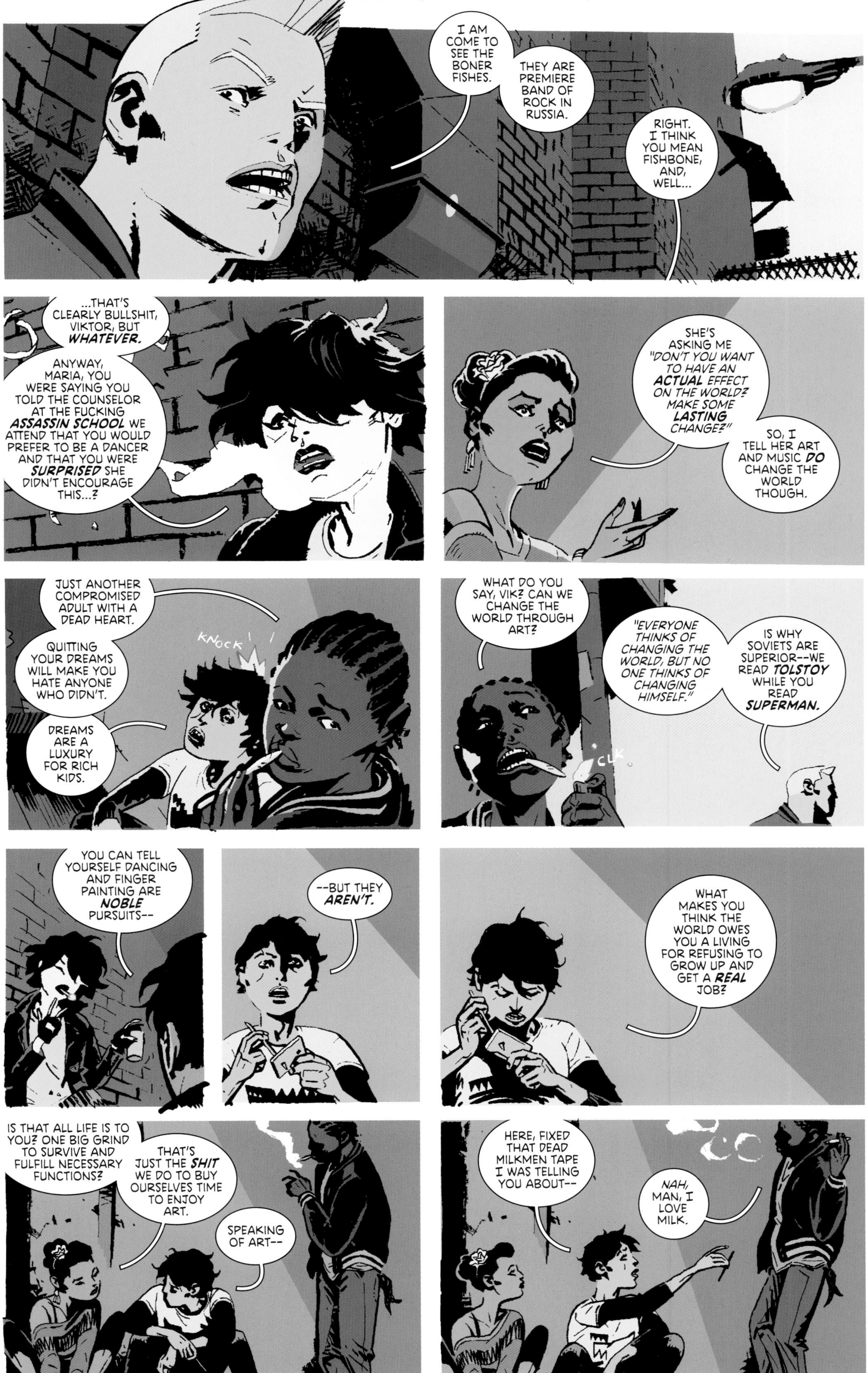

I AM COME TO SEE THE BONER FISHES.
THEY ARE PREMIERE BAND OF ROCK IN RUSSIA.
RIGHT. I THINK YOU MEAN FISHBONE, AND, WELL...
...THAT'S CLEARLY BULLSHIT, VIKTOR, BUT WHATEVER.
ANYWAY, MARIA, YOU WERE SAYING YOU TOLD THE COUNSELOR AT THE FUCKING ASSASSIN SCHOOL WE ATTEND THAT YOU WOULD PREFER TO BE A DANCER AND THAT YOU WERE SURPRISED SHE DIDN'T ENCOURAGE THIS...?
SHE'S ASKING ME "DON'T YOU WANT TO HAVE AN ACTUAL EFFECT ON THE WORLD? MAKE SOME LASTING CHANGE?"
SO, I TELL HER ART AND MUSIC DO CHANGE THE WORLD THOUGH.
JUST ANOTHER COMPROMISED ADULT WITH A DEAD HEART.
QUITTING YOUR DREAMS WILL MAKE YOU HATE ANYONE WHO DIDN'T.
KNOCK
DREAMS ARE A LUXURY FOR RICH KIDS.
WHAT DO YOU SAY, VIK? CAN WE CHANGE THE WORLD THROUGH ART?
"EVERYONE THINKS OF CHANGING THE WORLD, BUT NO ONE THINKS OF CHANGING HIMSELF."
IS WHY SOVIETS ARE SUPERIOR--WE READ TOLSTOY WHILE YOU READ SUPERMAN.
CLK
YOU CAN TELL YOURSELF DANCING AND FINGER PAINTING ARE NOBLE PURSUITS--
--BUT THEY AREN'T.
WHAT MAKES YOU THINK THE WORLD OWES YOU A LIVING FOR REFUSING TO GROW UP AND GET A REAL JOB?
IS THAT ALL LIFE IS TO YOU? ONE BIG GRIND TO SURVIVE AND FULFILL NECESSARY FUNCTIONS?
THAT'S JUST THE SHIT WE DO TO BUY OURSELVES TIME TO ENJOY ART.
SPEAKING OF ART--
HERE, FIXED THAT DEAD MILKMEN TAPE I WAS TELLING YOU ABOUT--
NAH, MAN, I LOVE MILK.

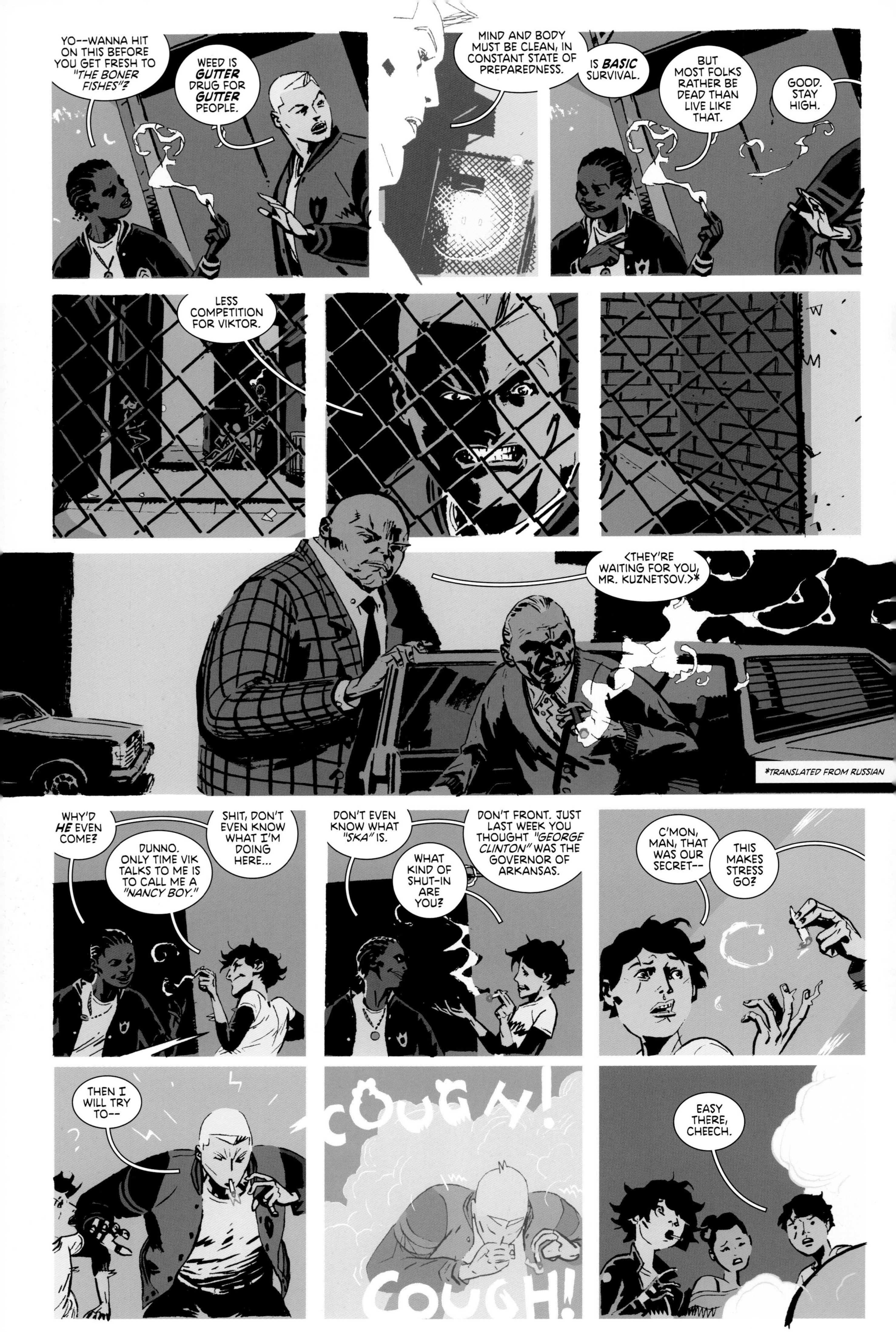
YO--WANNA HIT ON THIS BEFORE YOU GET FRESH TO "THE BONER FISHES"?
WEED IS GUTTER DRUG FOR GUTTER PEOPLE.
MIND AND BODY MUST BE CLEAN, IN CONSTANT STATE OF PREPAREDNESS.
IS BASIC SURVIVAL.
BUT MOST FOLKS RATHER BE DEAD THAN LIVE LIKE THAT.
GOOD. STAY HIGH.
LESS COMPETITION FOR VIKTOR.
<THEY'RE WAITING FOR YOU, MR. KUZNETSOV.>*
*TRANSLATED FROM RUSSIAN
WHY'D HE EVEN COME?
DUNNO. ONLY TIME VIK TALKS TO ME IS TO CALL ME A "NANCY BOY."
SHIT, DON'T EVEN KNOW WHAT I'M DOING HERE...
DON'T EVEN KNOW WHAT "SKA" IS.
WHAT KIND OF SHUT-IN ARE YOU?
DON'T FRONT. JUST LAST WEEK YOU THOUGHT "GEORGE CLINTON" WAS THE GOVERNOR OF ARKANSAS.
C'MON, MAN, THAT WAS OUR SECRET--
THIS MAKES STRESS GO?
THEN I WILL TRY TO--
COUGH!
COUGH!
EASY THERE, CHEECH.

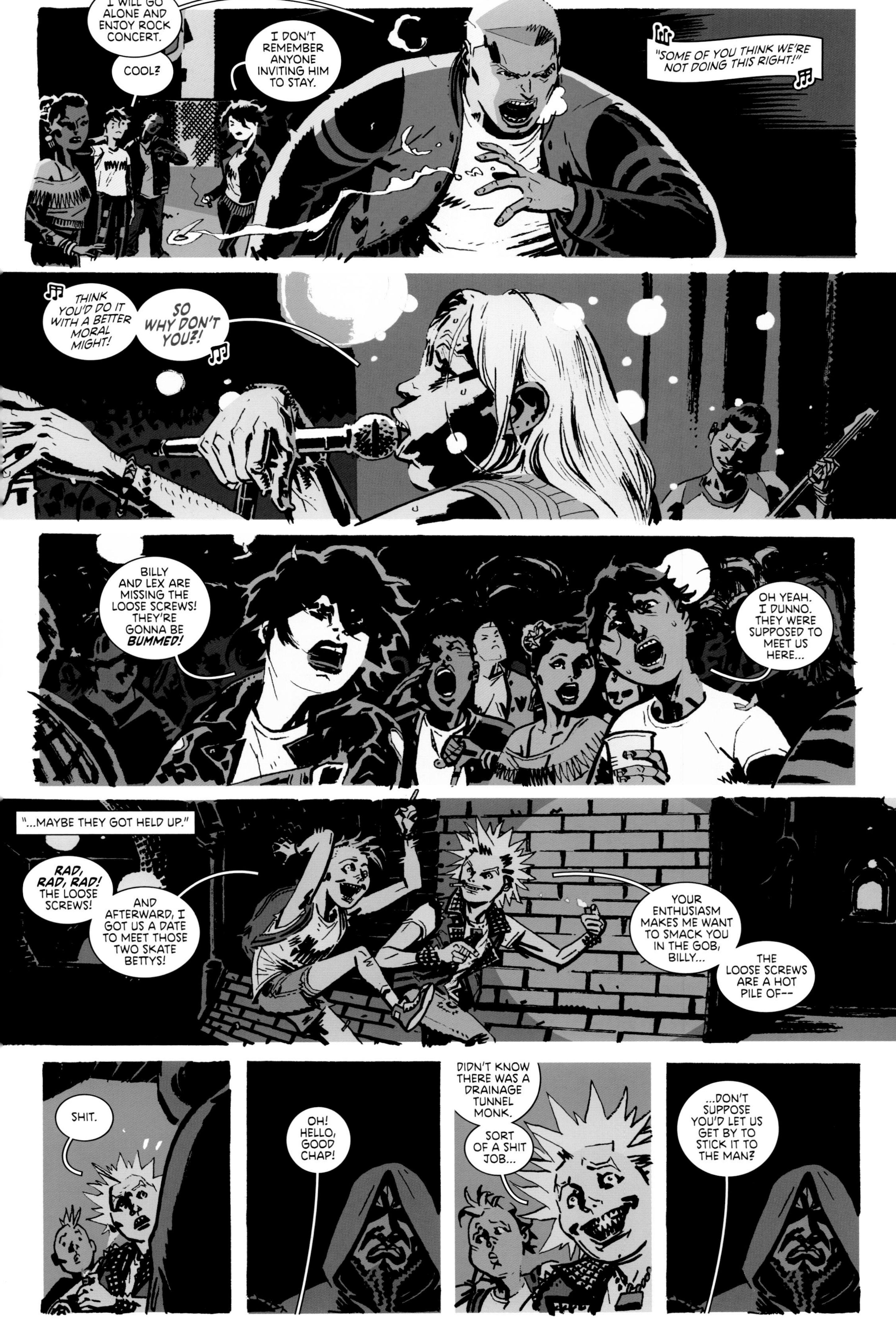
I WILL GO ALONE AND ENJOY ROCK CONCERT.
COOL?
I DON'T REMEMBER ANYONE INVITING HIM TO STAY.
"SOME OF YOU THINK WE'RE NOT DOING THIS RIGHT!"
THINK YOU'D DO IT WITH A BETTER MORAL MIGHT!
SO WHY DON'T YOU?!
BILLY AND LEX ARE MISSING THE LOOSE SCREWS! THEY'RE GONNA BE BUMMED!
OH YEAH. I DUNNO. THEY WERE SUPPOSED TO MEET US HERE...
"...MAYBE THEY GOT HELD UP."
RAD, RAD, RAD! THE LOOSE SCREWS!
AND AFTERWARD, I GOT US A DATE TO MEET THOSE TWO SKATE BETTYS!
YOUR ENTHUSIASM MAKES ME WANT TO SMACK YOU IN THE GOB, BILLY...
THE LOOSE SCREWS ARE A HOT PILE OF--
SHIT.
OH! HELLO, GOOD CHAP!
DIDN'T KNOW THERE WAS A DRAINAGE TUNNEL MONK.
SORT OF A SHIT JOB...
...DON'T SUPPOSE YOU'D LET US GET BY TO STICK IT TO THE MAN?

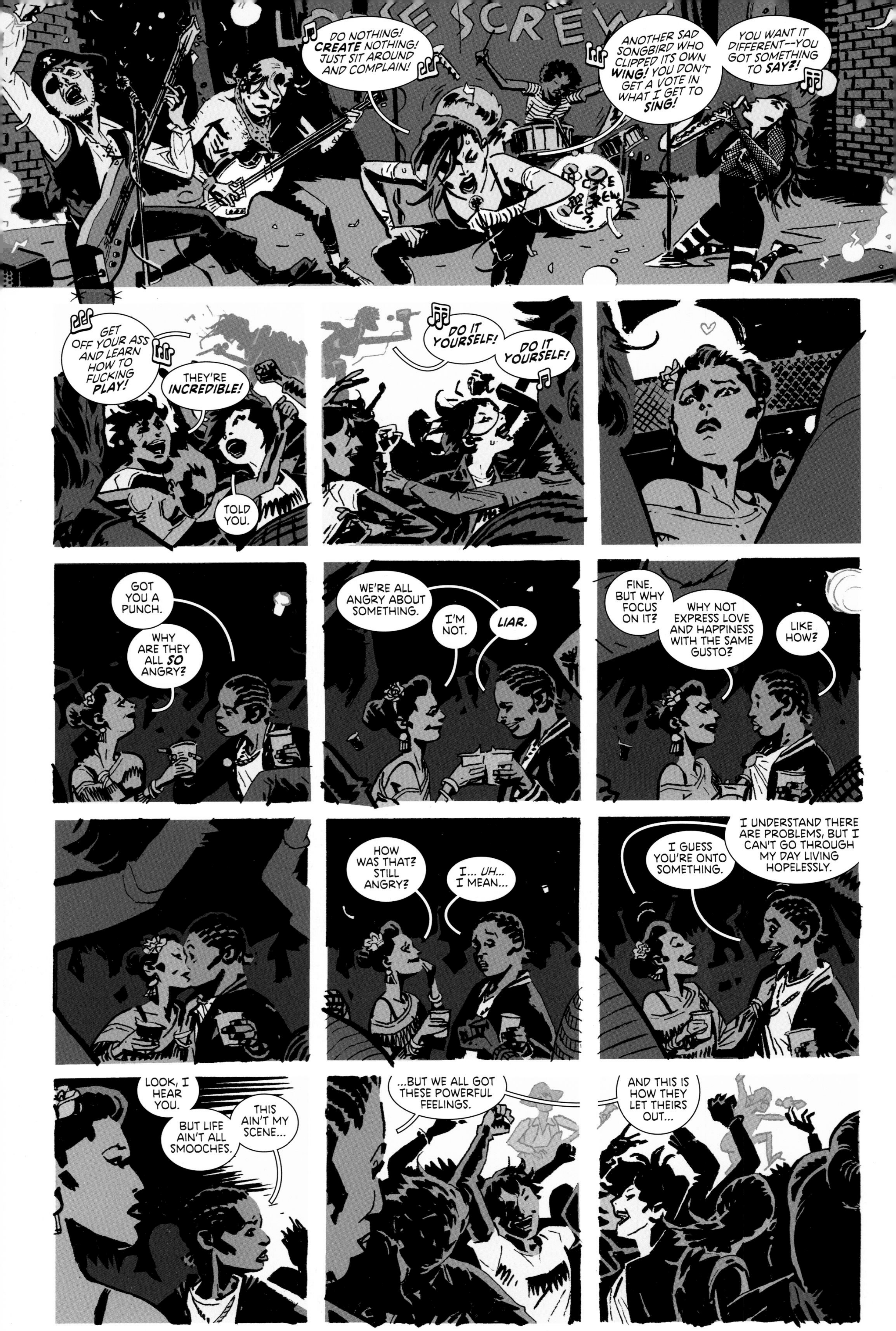

DO NOTHING! CREATE NOTHING! JUST SIT AROUND AND COMPLAIN!
ANOTHER SAD SONGBIRD WHO CLIPPED ITS OWN WING! YOU DON'T GET A VOTE IN WHAT I GET TO SING!
YOU WANT IT DIFFERENT--YOU GOT SOMETHING TO SAY?!
GET OFF YOUR ASS AND LEARN HOW TO FUCKING PLAY!
THEY'RE INCREDIBLE!
TOLD YOU.
DO IT YOURSELF!
DO IT YOURSELF!
GOT YOU A PUNCH.
WHY ARE THEY ALL SO ANGRY?
WE'RE ALL ANGRY ABOUT SOMETHING.
I'M NOT.
LIAR.
FINE. BUT WHY FOCUS ON IT?
WHY NOT EXPRESS LOVE AND HAPPINESS WITH THE SAME GUSTO?
LIKE HOW?
HOW WAS THAT? STILL ANGRY?
I... UH... I MEAN...
I GUESS YOU'RE ONTO SOMETHING.
I UNDERSTAND THERE ARE PROBLEMS, BUT I CAN'T GO THROUGH MY DAY LIVING HOPELESSLY.
LOOK, I HEAR YOU.
BUT LIFE AIN'T ALL SMOOCHES.
THIS AIN'T MY SCENE...
...BUT WE ALL GOT THESE POWERFUL FEELINGS.
AND THIS IS HOW THEY LET THEIRS OUT...

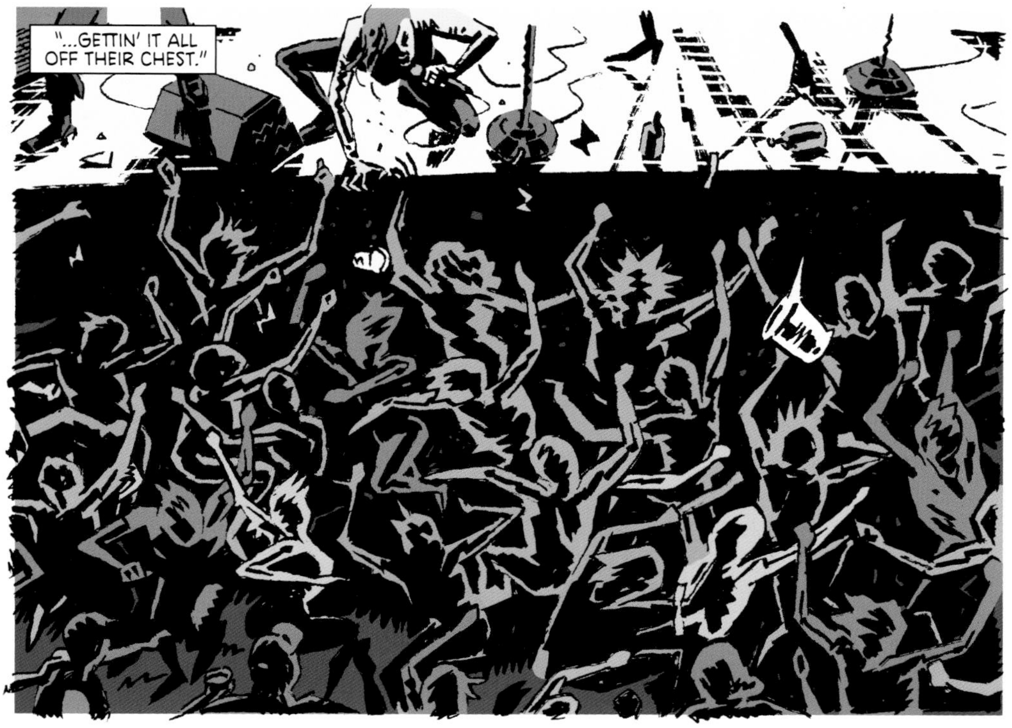
"...GETTIN' IT ALL OFF THEIR CHEST."

SAYA WOULDN'T SHUT UP ABOUT THE LOOSE SCREWS ALL WEEK. I STARTED TO SEE THE BAND ON THE FRONT OF A FEW MAGAZINES A BIT BACK, THEY'RE BREAKING THEY SAY, FINDING A WIDER AUDIENCE.

WAITING IN LINE TO GET IN WE HEARD A BUNCH OF KIDS TALKING ABOUT WHAT SELLOUT CUNTS THEY ARE NOW, HOW MUCH BETTER THEY WERE BEFORE ANYONE CAME TO SEE THEM.

TALKING TOUGH ABOUT HOW THEY'D DO IT DIFFERENTLY IF IT WERE THEM.

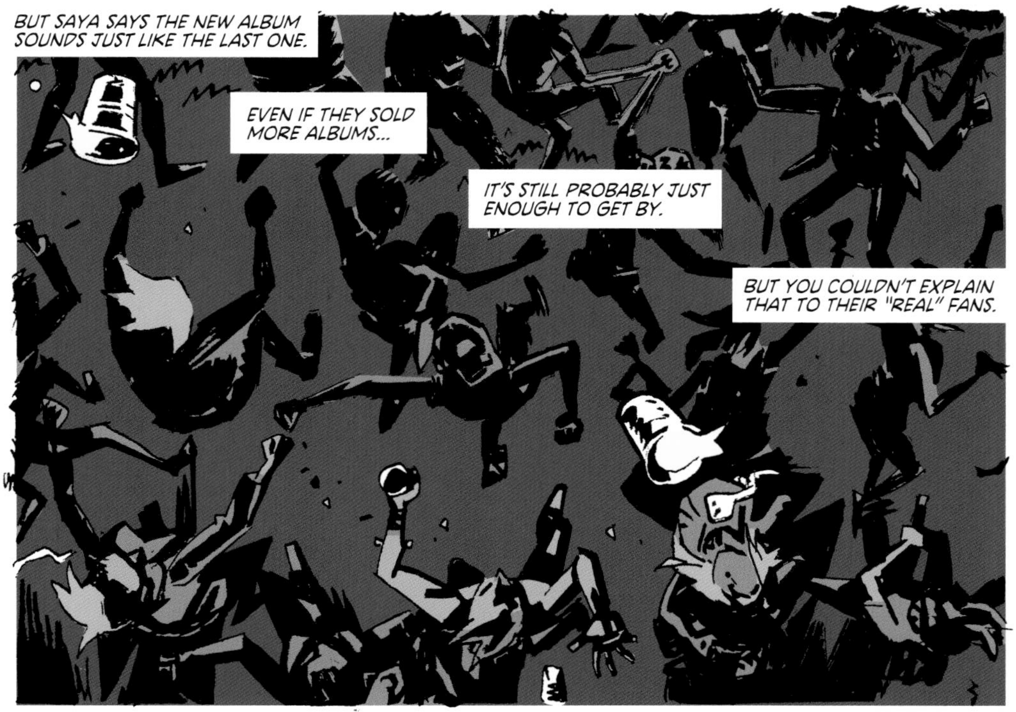
BUT SAYA SAYS THE NEW ALBUM SOUNDS JUST LIKE THE LAST ONE.
EVEN IF THEY SOLD MORE ALBUMS...
IT'S STILL PROBABLY JUST ENOUGH TO GET BY.
BUT YOU COULDN'T EXPLAIN THAT TO THEIR "REAL" FANS.

I WONDER WHAT THEY'D DO IN THE SAME SITUATION? AFTER YEARS OF WORK, WOULD THEY TURN DOWN MAKING SOME RENT MONEY?

NO. AND PEOPLE LIKE THAT, THEY NEVER TAKE THE STAGE.

TERRIFIED OF A GROUP OF BITTER PILLS SITTING IN THE BACK SNARLING AT THEM THE SAME WAY.

TERRIFIED OF THEIR OWN BRAND OF POISON.

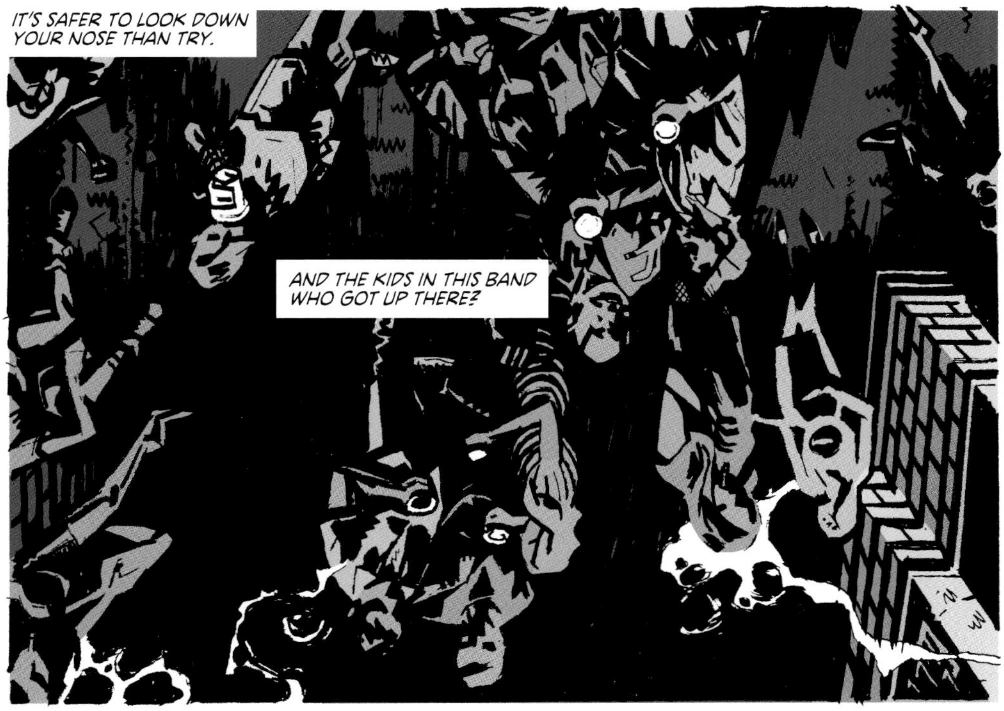
IT'S SAFER TO LOOK DOWN YOUR NOSE THAN TRY.
AND THE KIDS IN THIS BAND WHO GOT UP THERE?

I GUESS THEY DESERVE TO HAVE VOMIT SPEWED ON THEM FOR CHASING THEIR DREAMS...

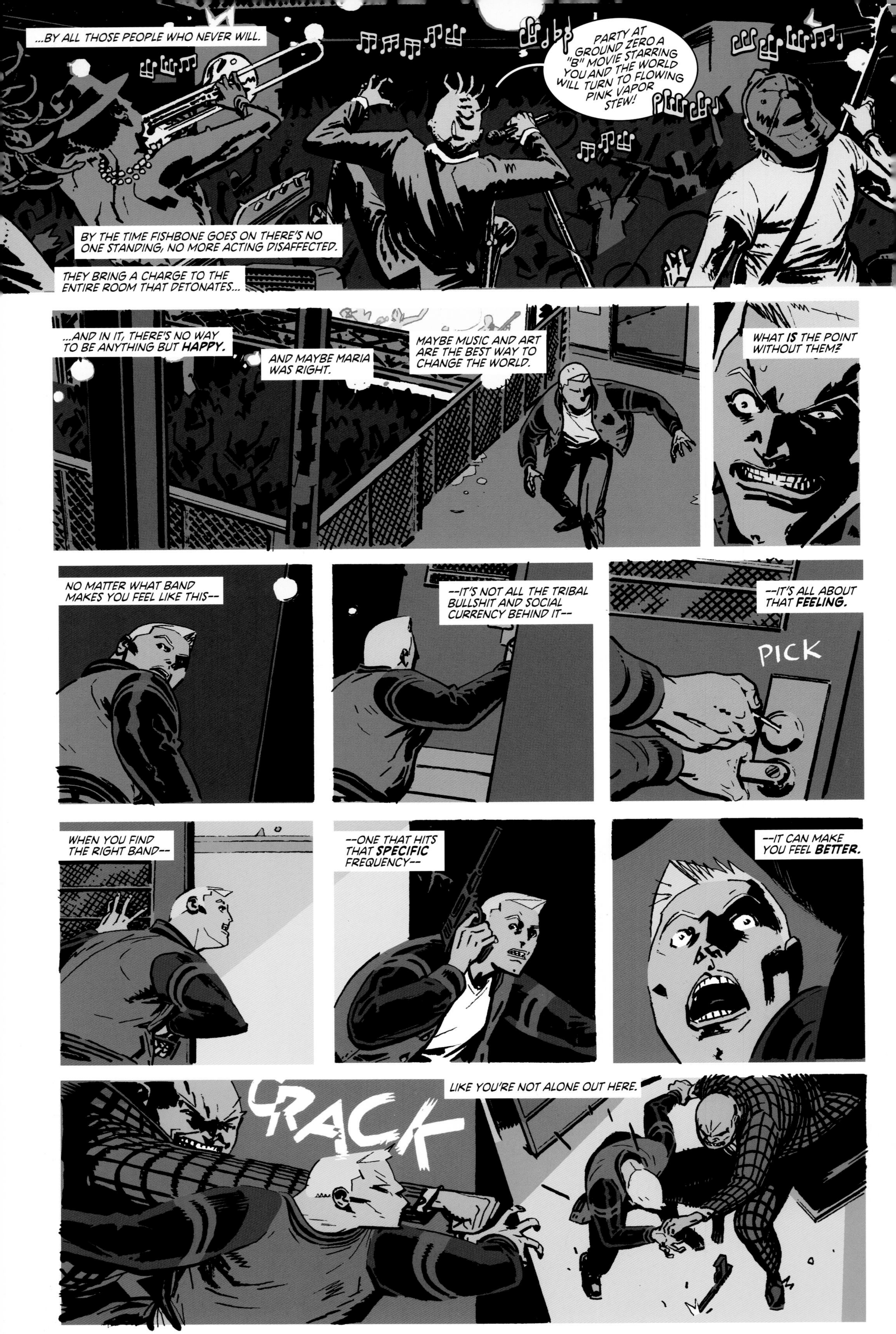
...BY ALL THOSE PEOPLE WHO NEVER WILL.
PARTY AT GROUND ZERO A "B" MOVIE STARRING YOU AND THE WORLD WILL TURN TO FLOWING PINK VAPOR STEW!
BY THE TIME FISHBONE GOES ON THERE'S NO ONE STANDING, NO MORE ACTING DISAFFECTED.
THEY BRING A CHARGE TO THE ENTIRE ROOM THAT DETONATES...
...AND IN IT, THERE'S NO WAY TO BE ANYTHING BUT HAPPY.
AND MAYBE MARIA WAS RIGHT.
MAYBE MUSIC AND ART ARE THE BEST WAY TO CHANGE THE WORLD.
WHAT IS THE POINT WITHOUT THEM?
NO MATTER WHAT BAND MAKES YOU FEEL LIKE THIS--
--IT'S NOT ALL THE TRIBAL BULLSHIT AND SOCIAL CURRENCY BEHIND IT--
--IT'S ALL ABOUT THAT FEELING.
PICK
WHEN YOU FIND THE RIGHT BAND--
--ONE THAT HITS THAT SPECIFIC FREQUENCY--
--IT CAN MAKE YOU FEEL BETTER.
CRACK
LIKE YOU'RE NOT ALONE OUT HERE.

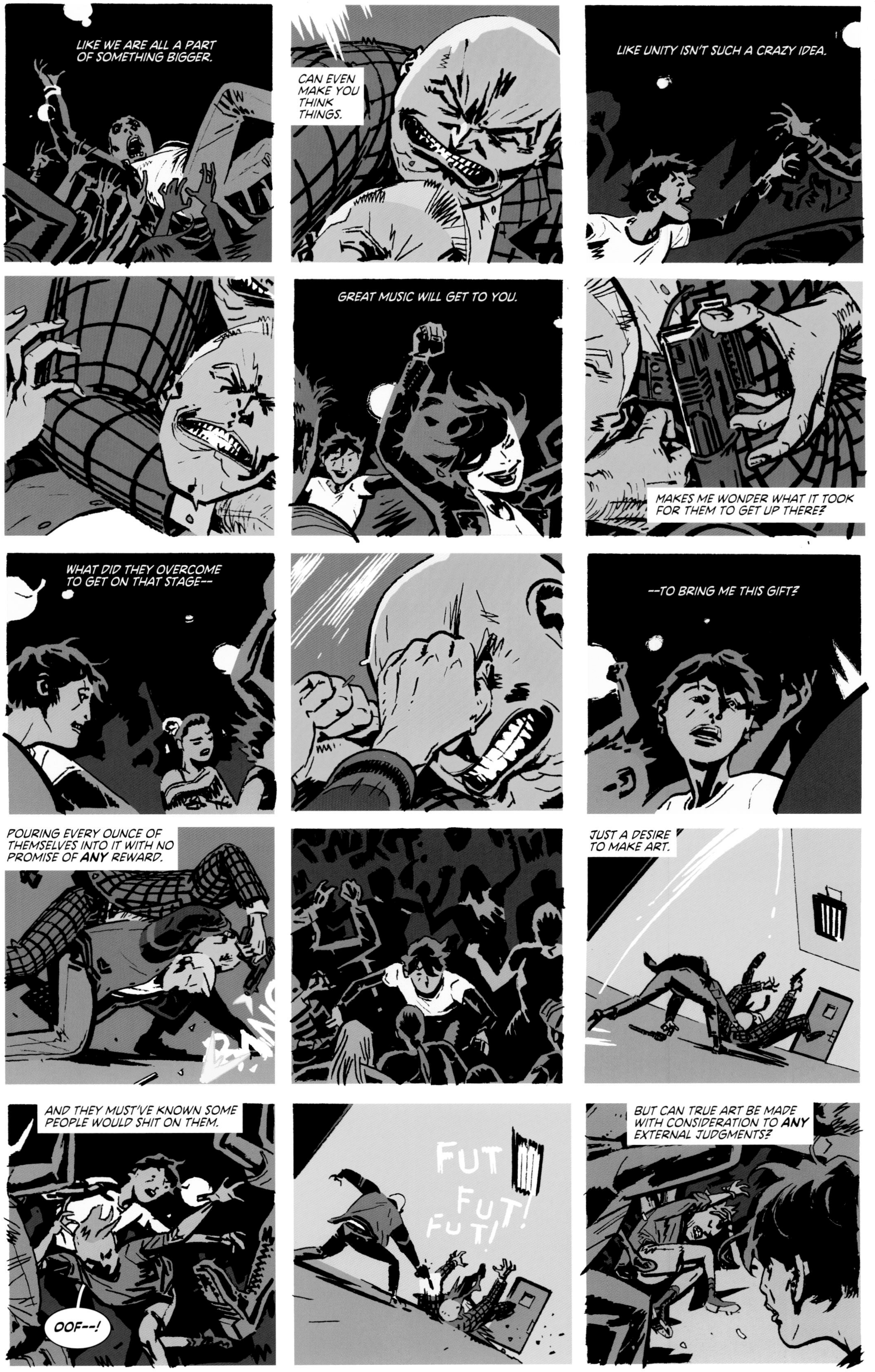

LIKE WE ARE ALL A PART OF SOMETHING BIGGER.
CAN EVEN MAKE YOU THINK THINGS.
LIKE UNITY ISN'T SUCH A CRAZY IDEA.
GREAT MUSIC WILL GET TO YOU.
MAKES ME WONDER WHAT IT TOOK FOR THEM TO GET UP THERE?
WHAT DID THEY OVERCOME TO GET ON THAT STAGE--
--TO BRING ME THIS GIFT?
POURING EVERY OUNCE OF THEMSELVES INTO IT WITH NO PROMISE OF **ANY** REWARD.
JUST A DESIRE TO MAKE ART.
AND THEY MUST'VE KNOWN SOME PEOPLE WOULD SHIT ON THEM.
OOF--!
FUT
FUT!
FUT!
BUT CAN TRUE ART BE MADE WITH CONSIDERATION TO **ANY** EXTERNAL JUDGMENTS?

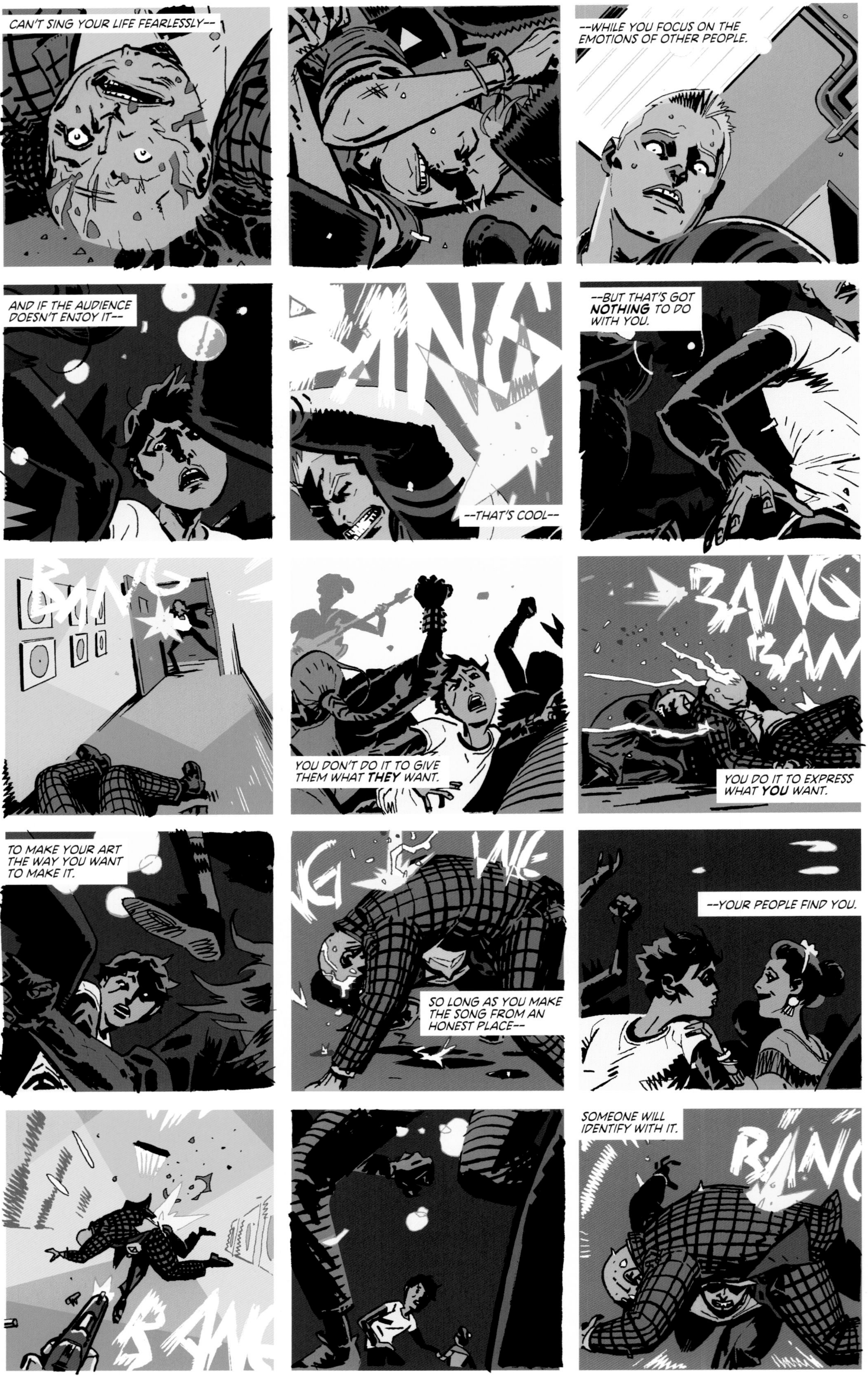
CAN'T SING YOUR LIFE FEARLESSLY--
--WHILE YOU FOCUS ON THE EMOTIONS OF OTHER PEOPLE.
AND IF THE AUDIENCE DOESN'T ENJOY IT--
BANG
--THAT'S COOL--
--BUT THAT'S GOT NOTHING TO DO WITH YOU.
BANG
YOU DON'T DO IT TO GIVE THEM WHAT THEY WANT.
BANG
BAN
YOU DO IT TO EXPRESS WHAT YOU WANT.
TO MAKE YOUR ART THE WAY YOU WANT TO MAKE IT.
SO LONG AS YOU MAKE THE SONG FROM AN HONEST PLACE--
--YOUR PEOPLE FIND YOU.
BANG
SOMEONE WILL IDENTIFY WITH IT.
BANG

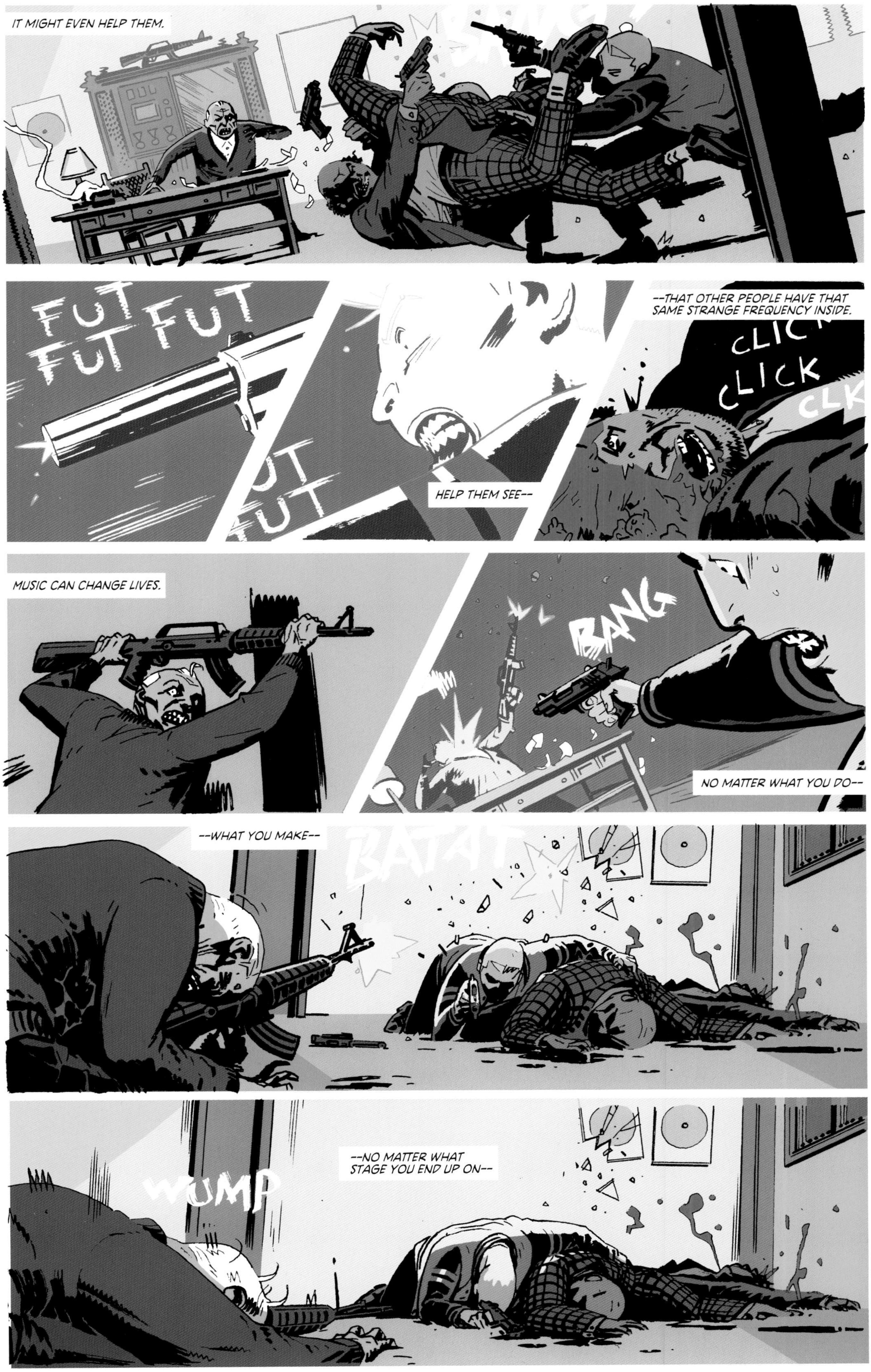
IT MIGHT EVEN HELP THEM.
FUT FUT FUT
HELP THEM SEE--
--THAT OTHER PEOPLE HAVE THAT SAME STRANGE FREQUENCY INSIDE.
CLICK
CLICK
CLK
MUSIC CAN CHANGE LIVES.
BANG
NO MATTER WHAT YOU DO--
--WHAT YOU MAKE--
BATAT
--NO MATTER WHAT STAGE YOU END UP ON--
WUMP

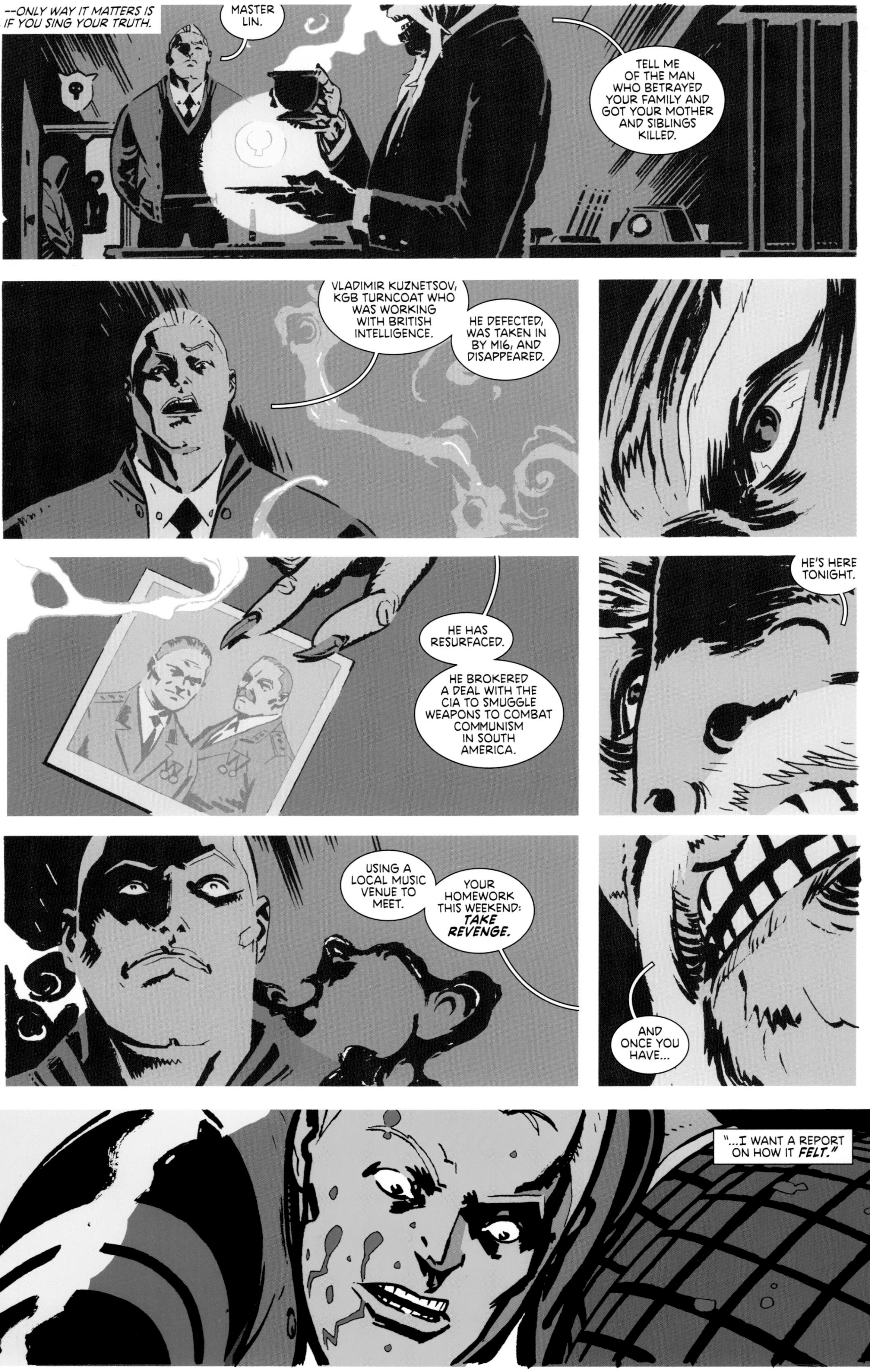

--ONLY WAY IT MATTERS IS IF YOU SING YOUR TRUTH.
MASTER LIN.
TELL ME OF THE MAN WHO BETRAYED YOUR FAMILY AND GOT YOUR MOTHER AND SIBLINGS KILLED.
VLADIMIR KUZNETSOV, KGB TURNCOAT WHO WAS WORKING WITH BRITISH INTELLIGENCE.
HE DEFECTED, WAS TAKEN IN BY MI6, AND DISAPPEARED.
HE HAS RESURFACED.
HE BROKERED A DEAL WITH THE CIA TO SMUGGLE WEAPONS TO COMBAT COMMUNISM IN SOUTH AMERICA.
HE'S HERE TONIGHT.
USING A LOCAL MUSIC VENUE TO MEET.
YOUR HOMEWORK THIS WEEKEND: ***TAKE REVENGE.***
AND ONCE YOU HAVE...
"...I WANT A REPORT ON HOW IT ***FELT.***"

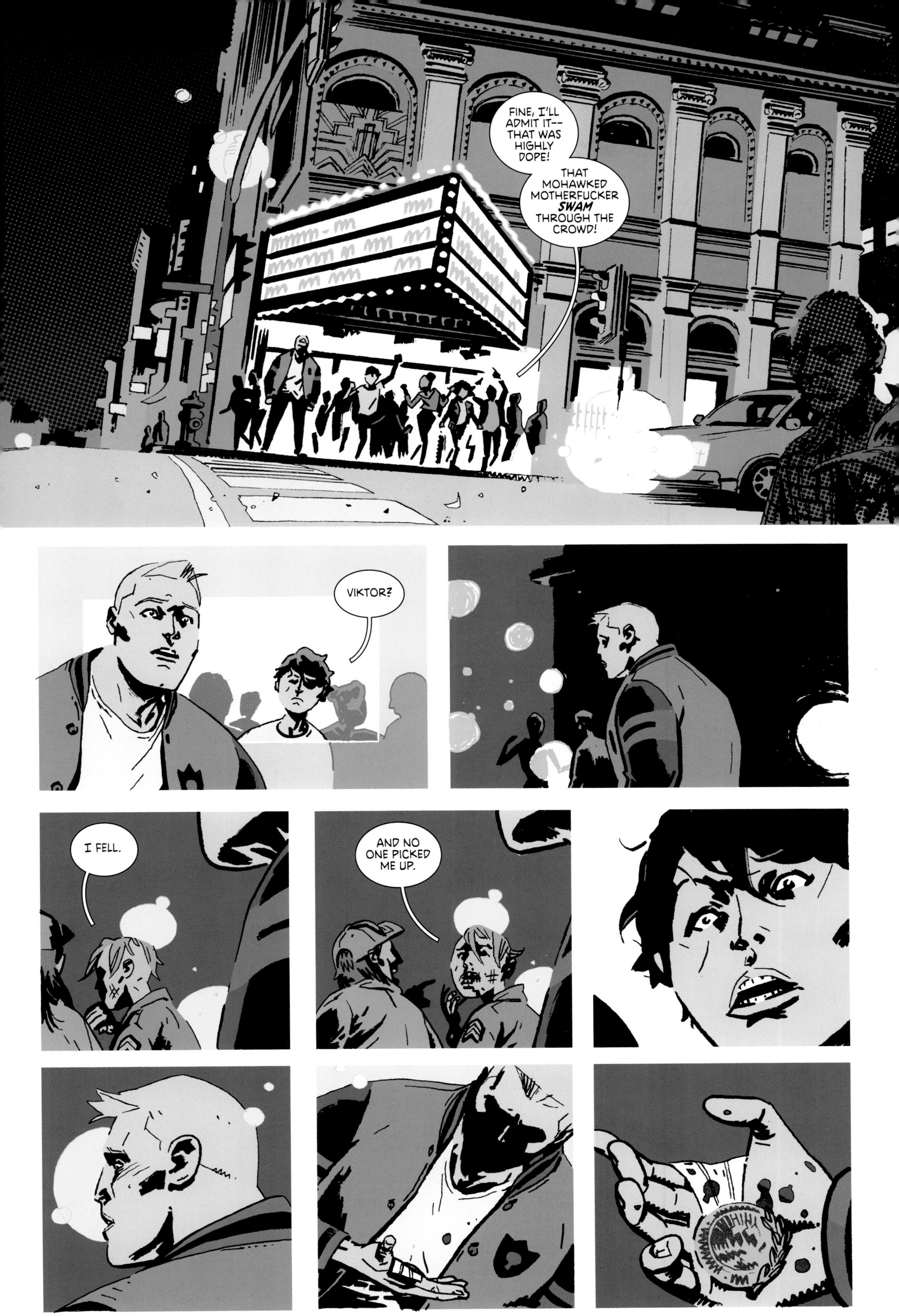
FINE, I'LL ADMIT IT-- THAT WAS HIGHLY DOPE!
THAT MOHAWKED MOTHERFUCKER *SWAM* THROUGH THE CROWD!
VIKTOR?
I FELL.
AND NO ONE PICKED ME UP.

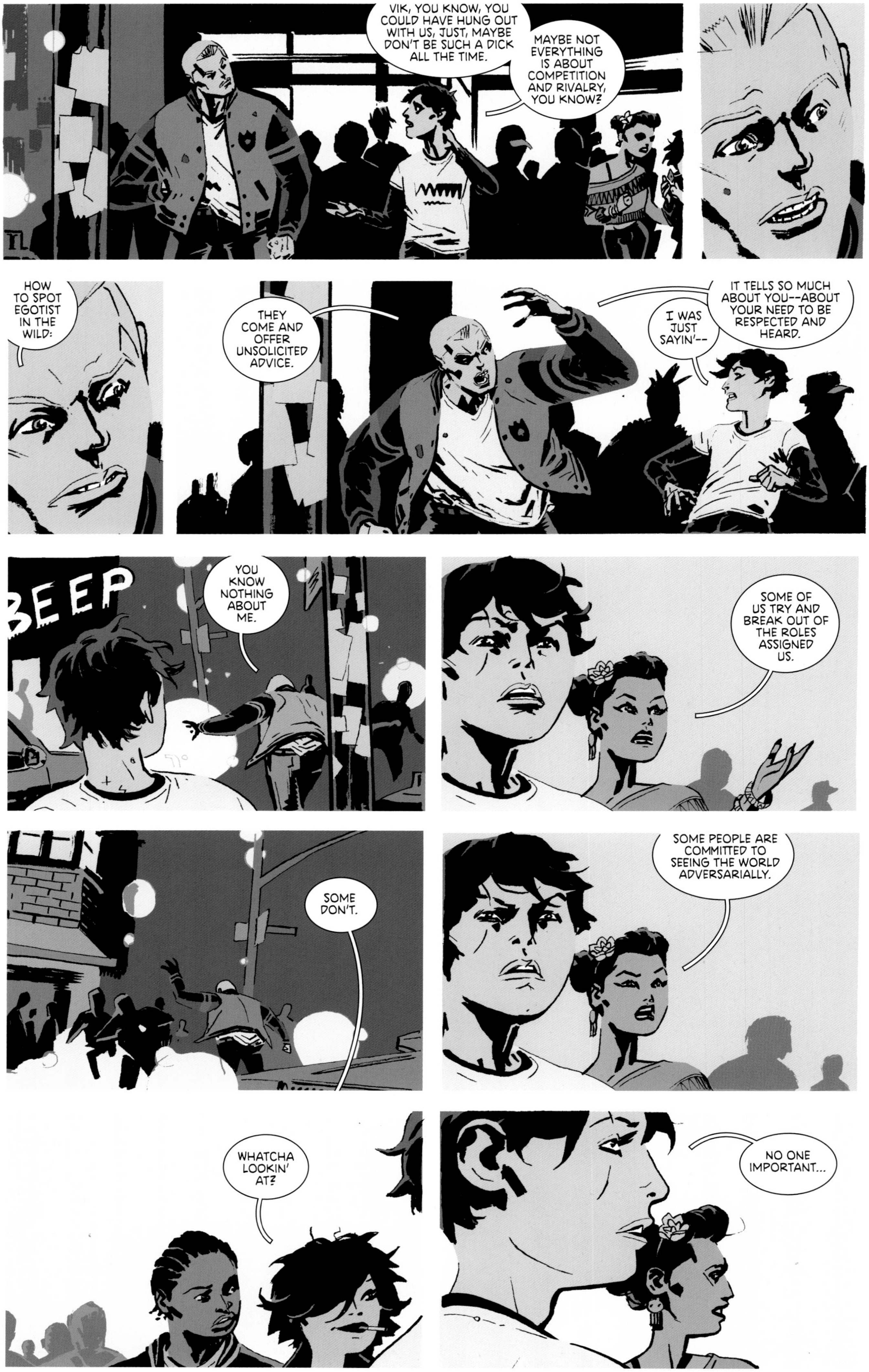
VIK, YOU KNOW, YOU COULD HAVE HUNG OUT WITH US, JUST, MAYBE DON'T BE SUCH A DICK ALL THE TIME.
MAYBE NOT EVERYTHING IS ABOUT COMPETITION AND RIVALRY, YOU KNOW?
HOW TO SPOT EGOTIST IN THE WILD:
THEY COME AND OFFER UNSOLICITED ADVICE.
IT TELLS SO MUCH ABOUT YOU--ABOUT YOUR NEED TO BE RESPECTED AND HEARD.
I WAS JUST SAYIN'--
BEEP
YOU KNOW NOTHING ABOUT ME.
SOME OF US TRY AND BREAK OUT OF THE ROLES ASSIGNED US.
SOME DON'T.
SOME PEOPLE ARE COMMITTED TO SEEING THE WORLD ADVERSARIALLY.
WHATCHA LOOKIN' AT?
NO ONE IMPORTANT...

"...JUST A VERY UNHAPPY PERSON."

LAST NIGHT AT THE SHOW, YOU SAID ART AND MUSIC ARE HOW YOU'D CHANGE THE WORLD.

GOT ME THINKING.

WHAT SONG AM I ACTUALLY SINGING?

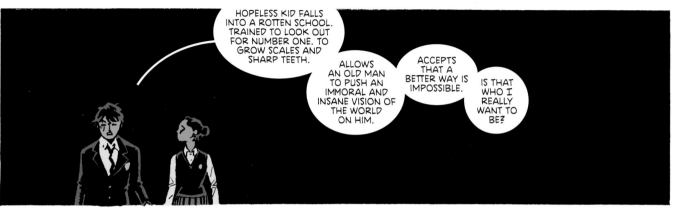

HOPELESS KID FALLS INTO A ROTTEN SCHOOL. TRAINED TO LOOK OUT FOR NUMBER ONE. TO GROW SCALES AND SHARP TEETH.

ALLOWS AN OLD MAN TO PUSH AN IMMORAL AND INSANE VISION OF THE WORLD ON HIM.

ACCEPTS THAT A BETTER WAY IS IMPOSSIBLE.

IS THAT WHO I REALLY WANT TO BE?

SOMETIMES BASIC SURVIVAL COMES FIRST.

C'MON.

WE CAN PRETEND TOGETHER.

THINK YOU CAN FAKE YOUR WAY THROUGH AND STILL COME OUT A DECENT PERSON?

DOES ANYONE?

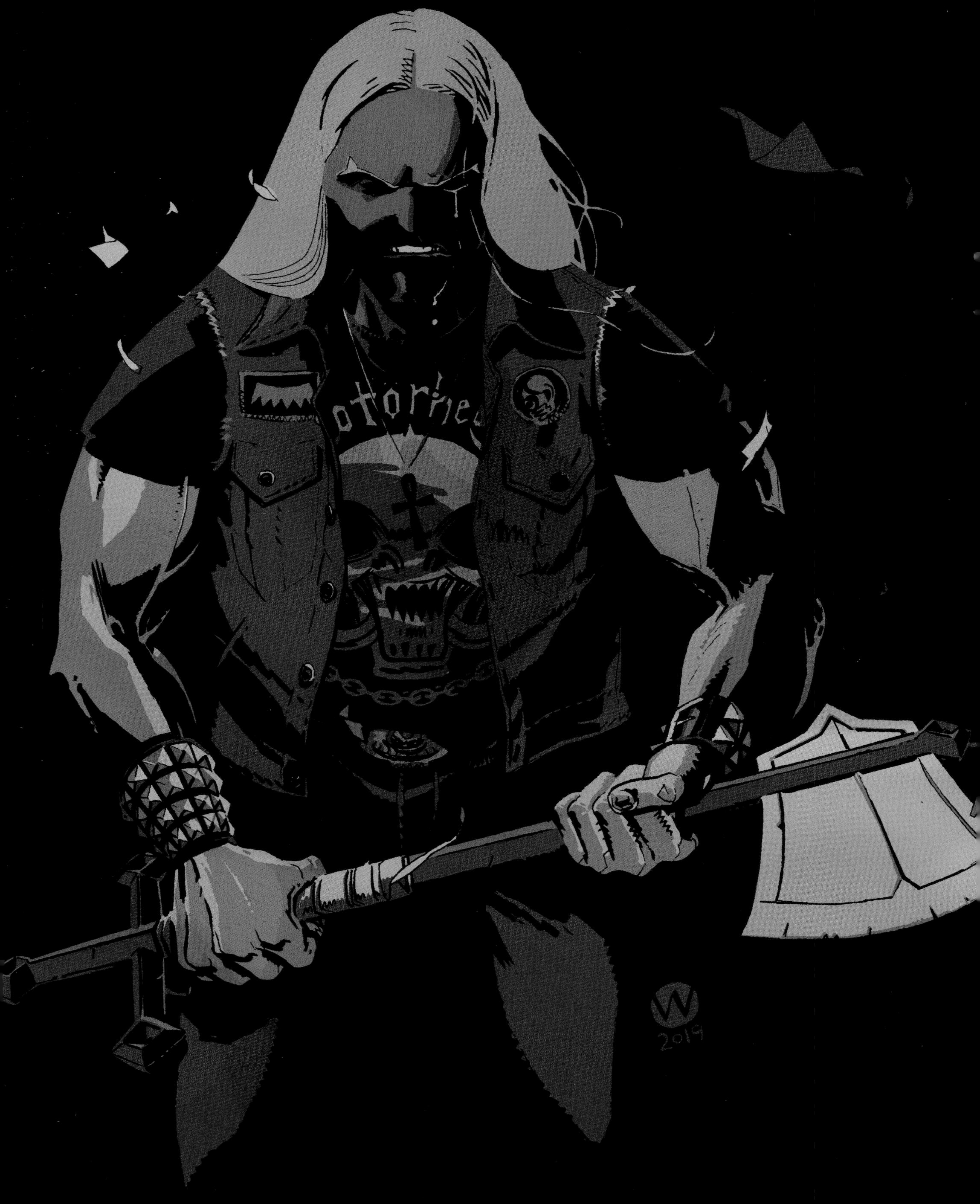
otorhe
W
2019

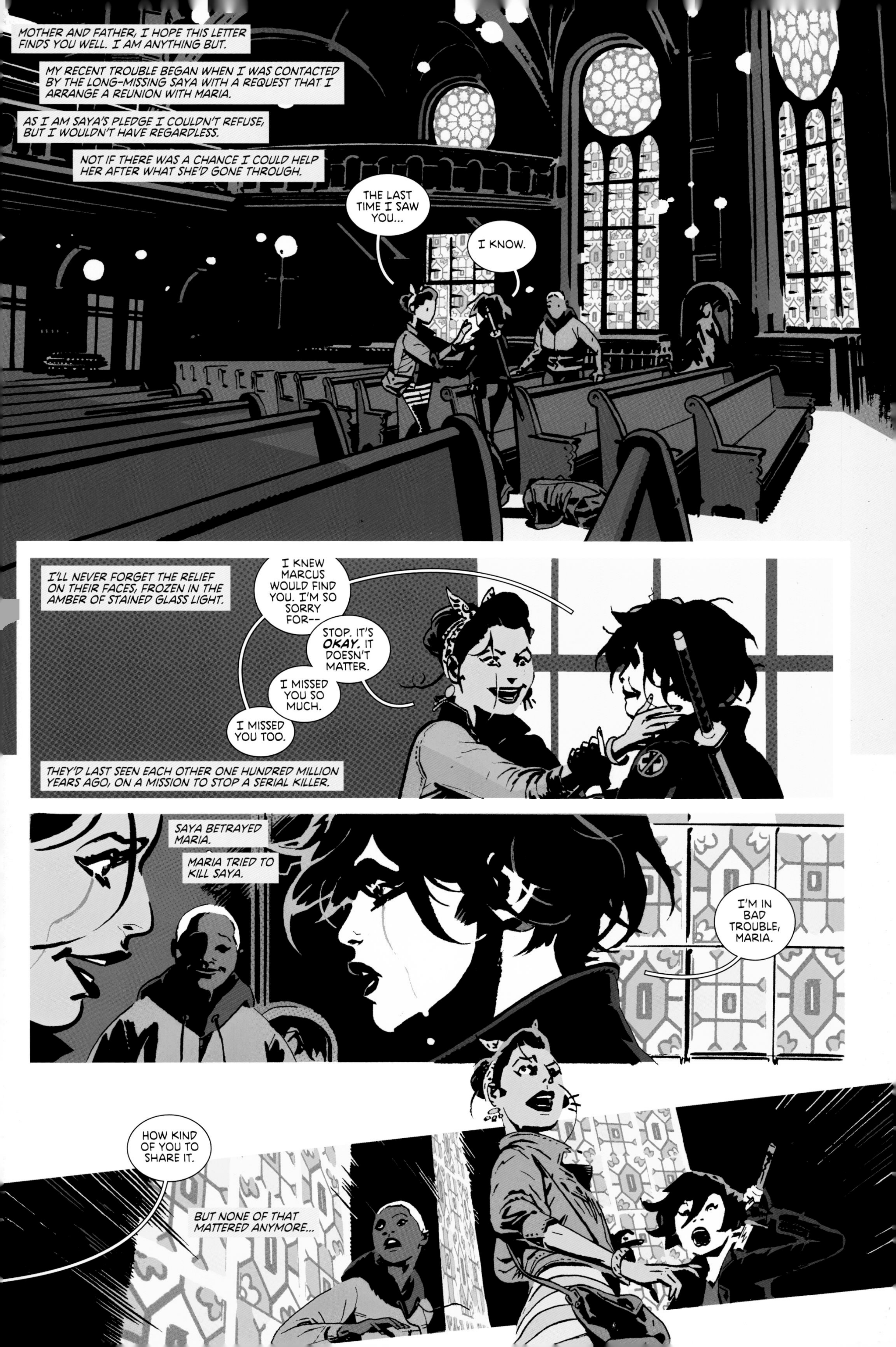
MOTHER AND FATHER, I HOPE THIS LETTER FINDS YOU WELL. I AM ANYTHING BUT.
MY RECENT TROUBLE BEGAN WHEN I WAS CONTACTED BY THE LONG-MISSING SAYA WITH A REQUEST THAT I ARRANGE A REUNION WITH MARIA.
AS I AM SAYA'S PLEDGE I COULDN'T REFUSE, BUT I WOULDN'T HAVE REGARDLESS.
NOT IF THERE WAS A CHANCE I COULD HELP HER AFTER WHAT SHE'D GONE THROUGH.
THE LAST TIME I SAW YOU...
I KNOW.
I'LL NEVER FORGET THE RELIEF ON THEIR FACES, FROZEN IN THE AMBER OF STAINED GLASS LIGHT.
I KNEW MARCUS WOULD FIND YOU. I'M SO SORRY FOR--
STOP. IT'S ***OKAY.*** IT DOESN'T MATTER.
I MISSED YOU SO MUCH.
I MISSED YOU TOO.
THEY'D LAST SEEN EACH OTHER ONE HUNDRED MILLION YEARS AGO, ON A MISSION TO STOP A SERIAL KILLER.
SAYA BETRAYED MARIA.
MARIA TRIED TO KILL SAYA.
I'M IN BAD TROUBLE, MARIA.
HOW KIND OF YOU TO SHARE IT.
BUT NONE OF THAT MATTERED ANYMORE...

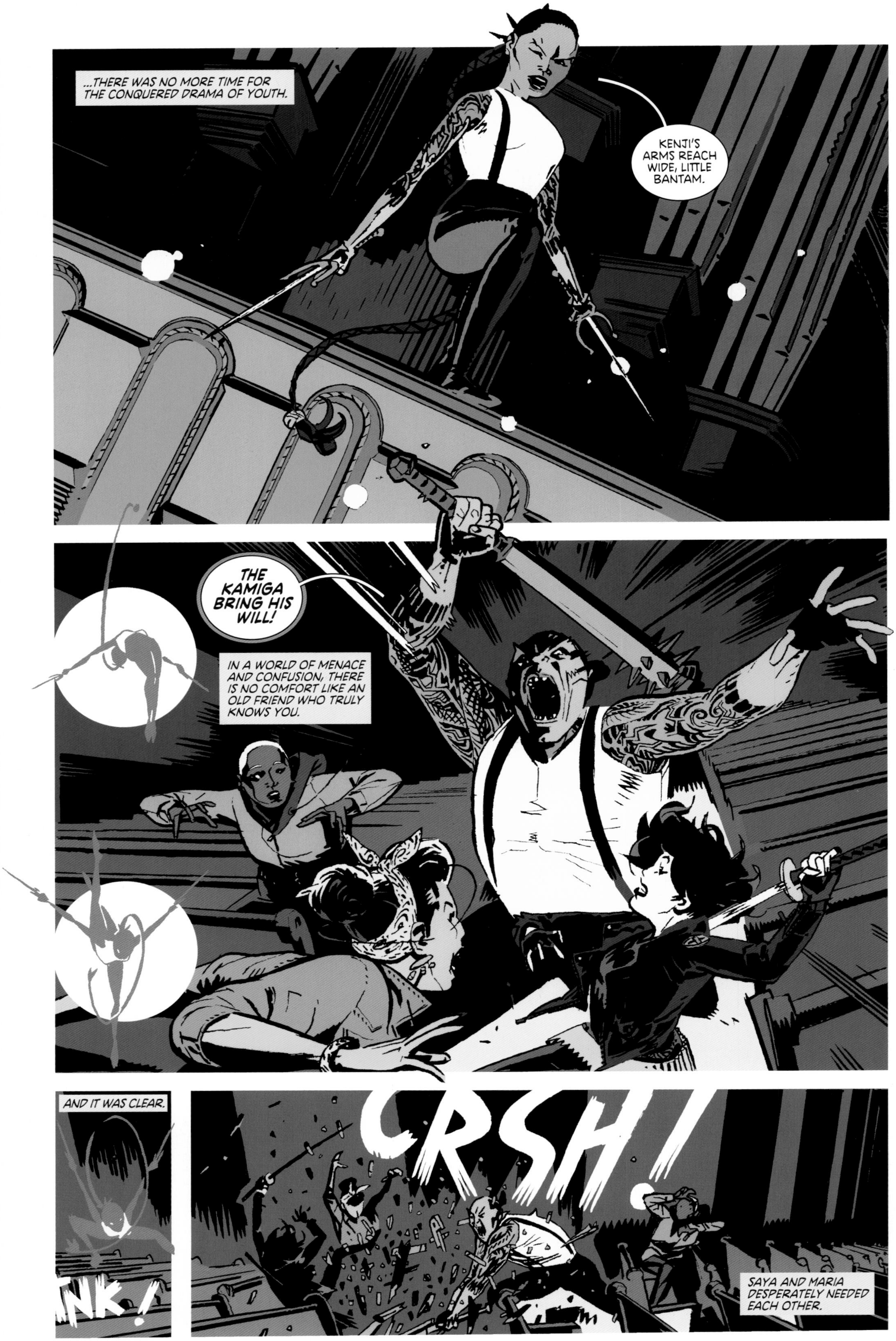
...THERE WAS NO MORE TIME FOR THE CONQUERED DRAMA OF YOUTH.
KENJI'S ARMS REACH WIDE, LITTLE BANTAM.
THE KAMIGA BRING HIS WILL!
IN A WORLD OF MENACE AND CONFUSION, THERE IS NO COMFORT LIKE AN OLD FRIEND WHO TRULY KNOWS YOU.
AND IT WAS CLEAR.
NK!
CRSH!
SAYA AND MARIA DESPERATELY NEEDED EACH OTHER.

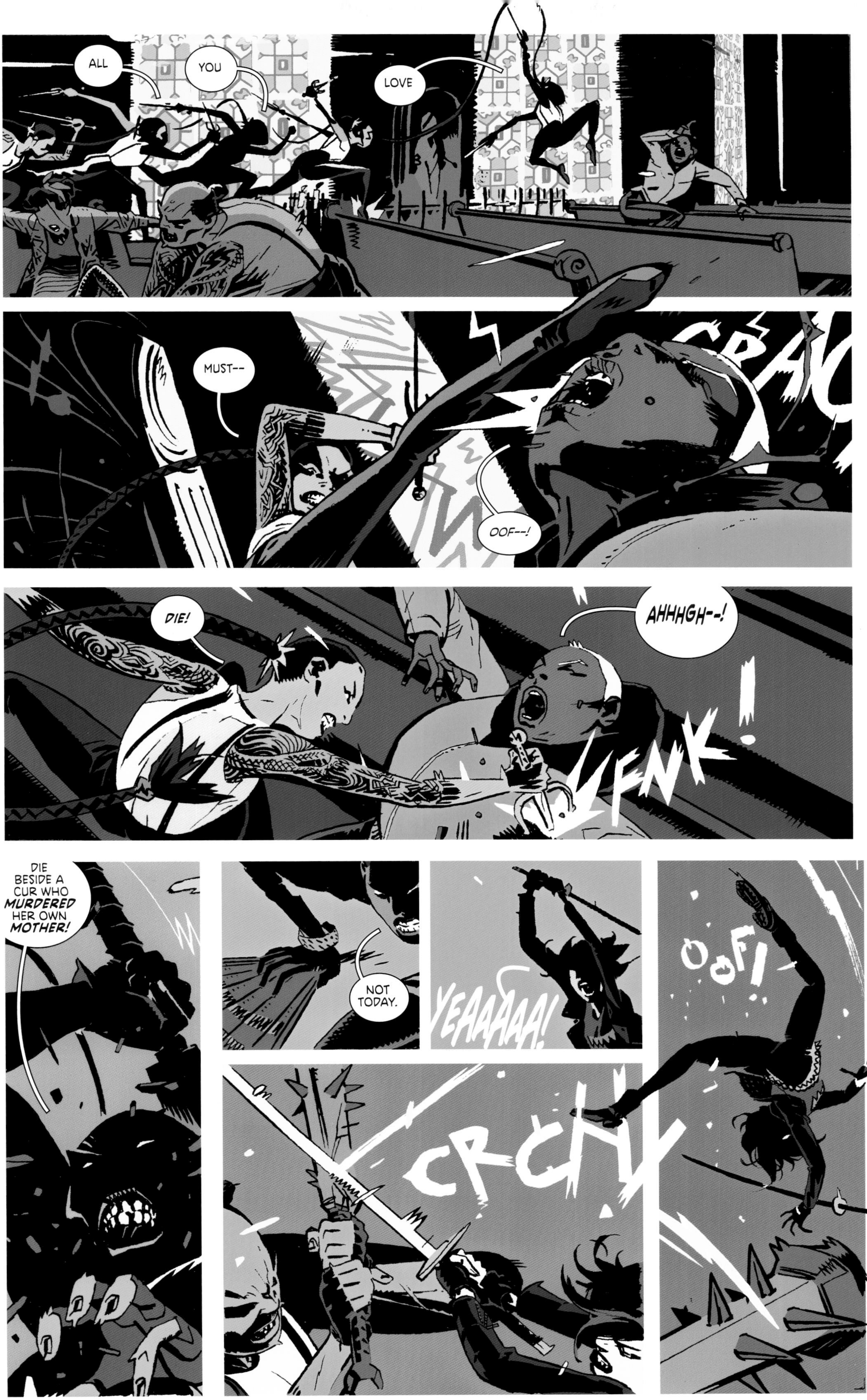
ALL
YOU
LOVE
MUST--
OOF--!
CRAC
DIE!
AHHHGH--!
FNK!
DIE BESIDE A CUR WHO MURDERED HER OWN MOTHER!
NOT TODAY.
YEAAAAA!
OOF!
CRCH

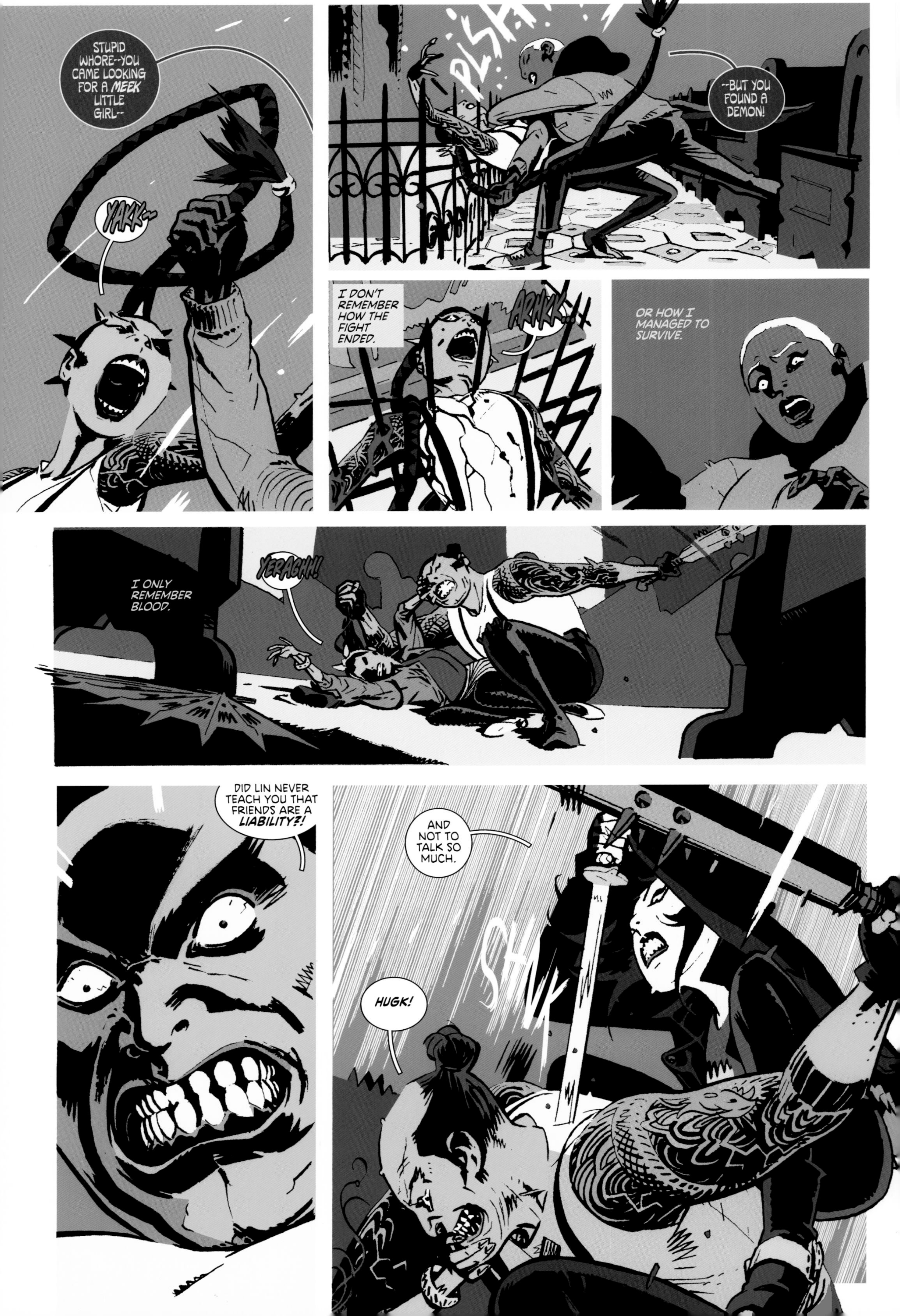
STUPID WHORE--YOU CAME LOOKING FOR A MEEK LITTLE GIRL--
YAKK--
PLSH
--BUT YOU FOUND A DEMON!
I DON'T REMEMBER HOW THE FIGHT ENDED.
ARKK..!
OR HOW I MANAGED TO SURVIVE.
I ONLY REMEMBER BLOOD.
YERAGHH!
DID LIN NEVER TEACH YOU THAT FRIENDS ARE A LIABILITY?!
AND NOT TO TALK SO MUCH.
SHK
HUGK!

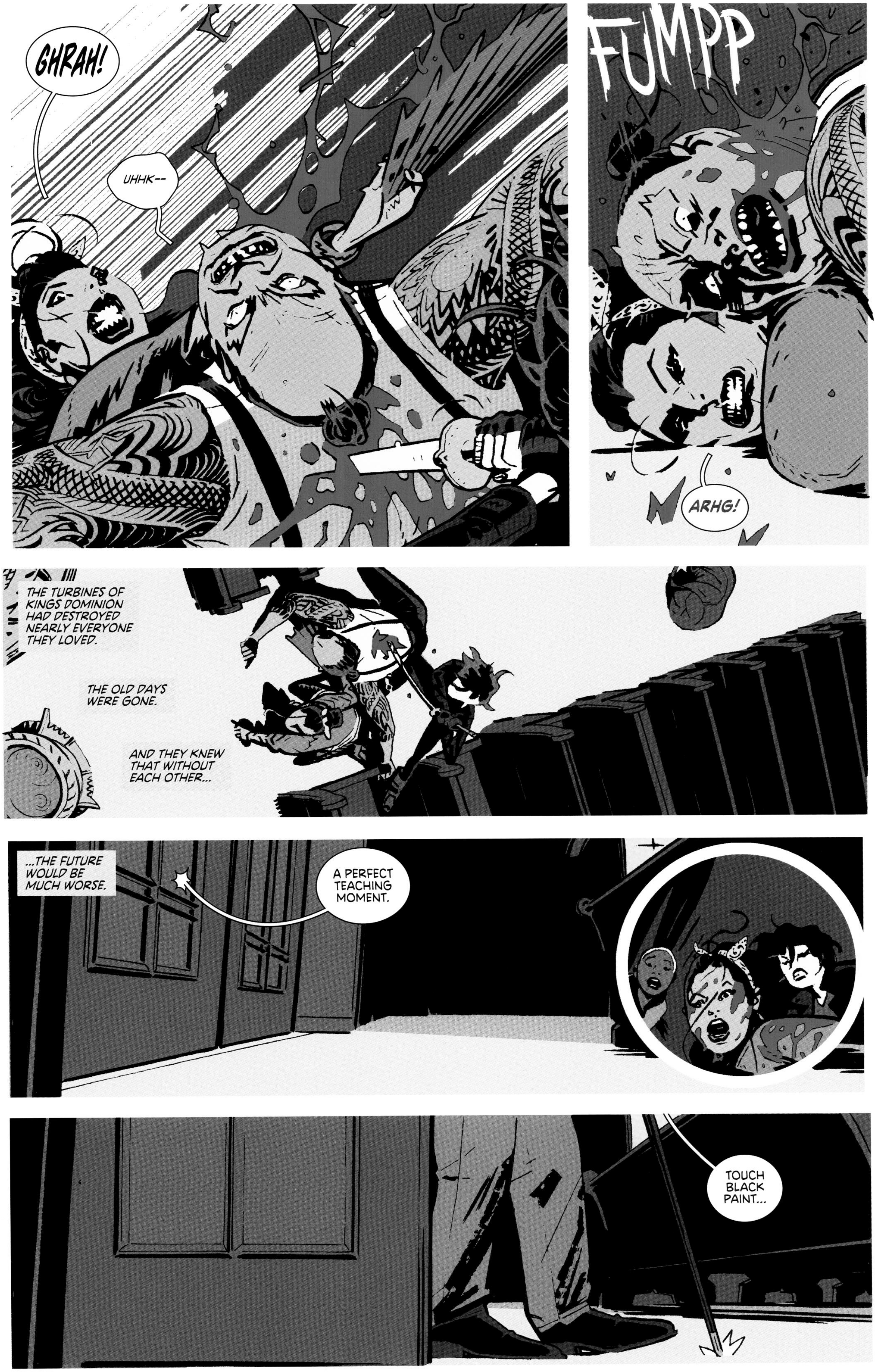
GHRAH!
UHHK--
FUMPP
ARHG!
THE TURBINES OF KINGS DOMINION HAD DESTROYED NEARLY EVERYONE THEY LOVED.
THE OLD DAYS WERE GONE.
AND THEY KNEW THAT WITHOUT EACH OTHER...
...THE FUTURE WOULD BE MUCH WORSE.
A PERFECT TEACHING MOMENT.
TOUCH BLACK PAINT...

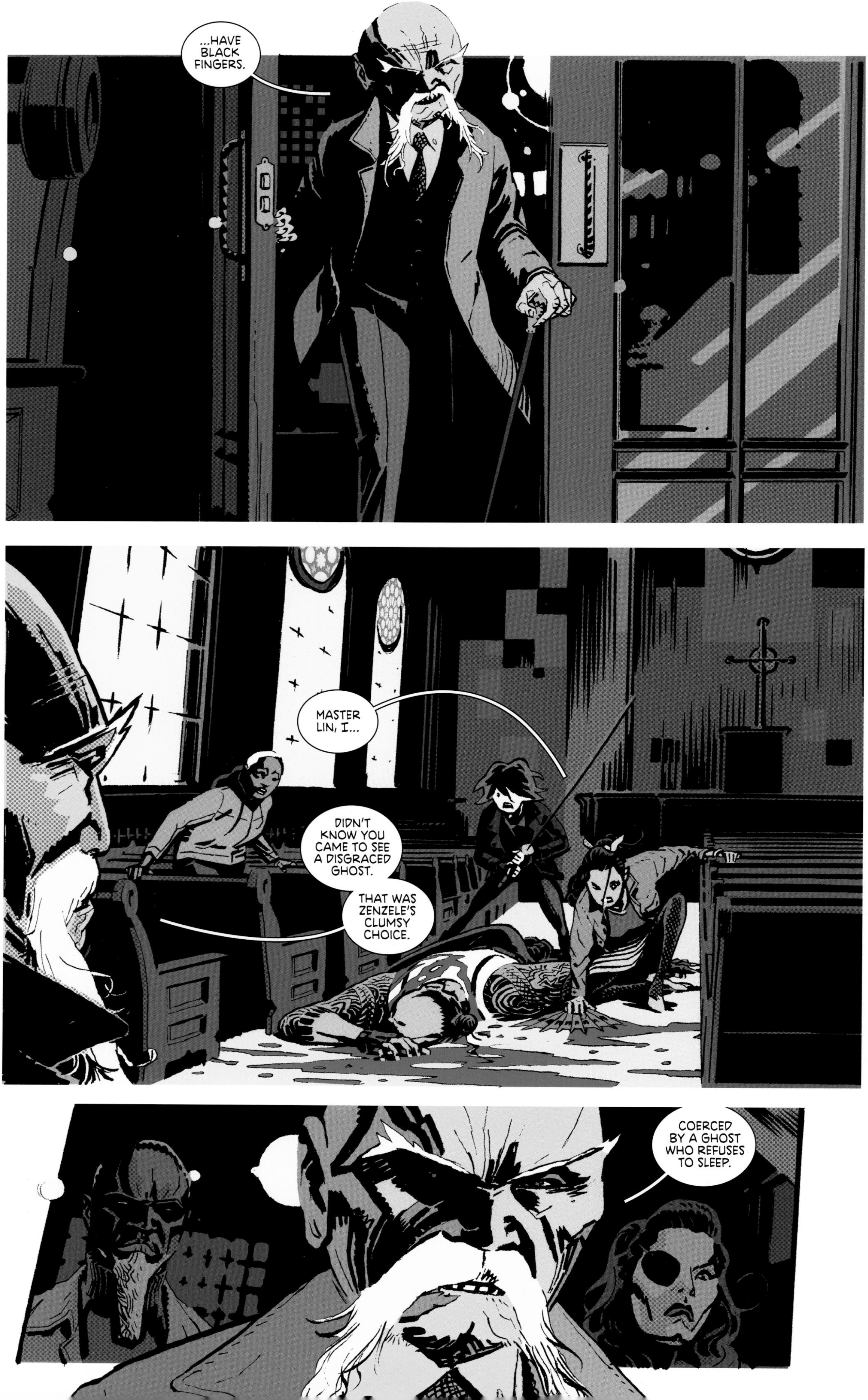
...HAVE BLACK FINGERS.
MASTER LIN, I...
DIDN'T KNOW YOU CAME TO SEE A DISGRACED GHOST.
THAT WAS ZENZELE'S CLUMSY CHOICE.
COERCED BY A GHOST WHO REFUSES TO SLEEP.

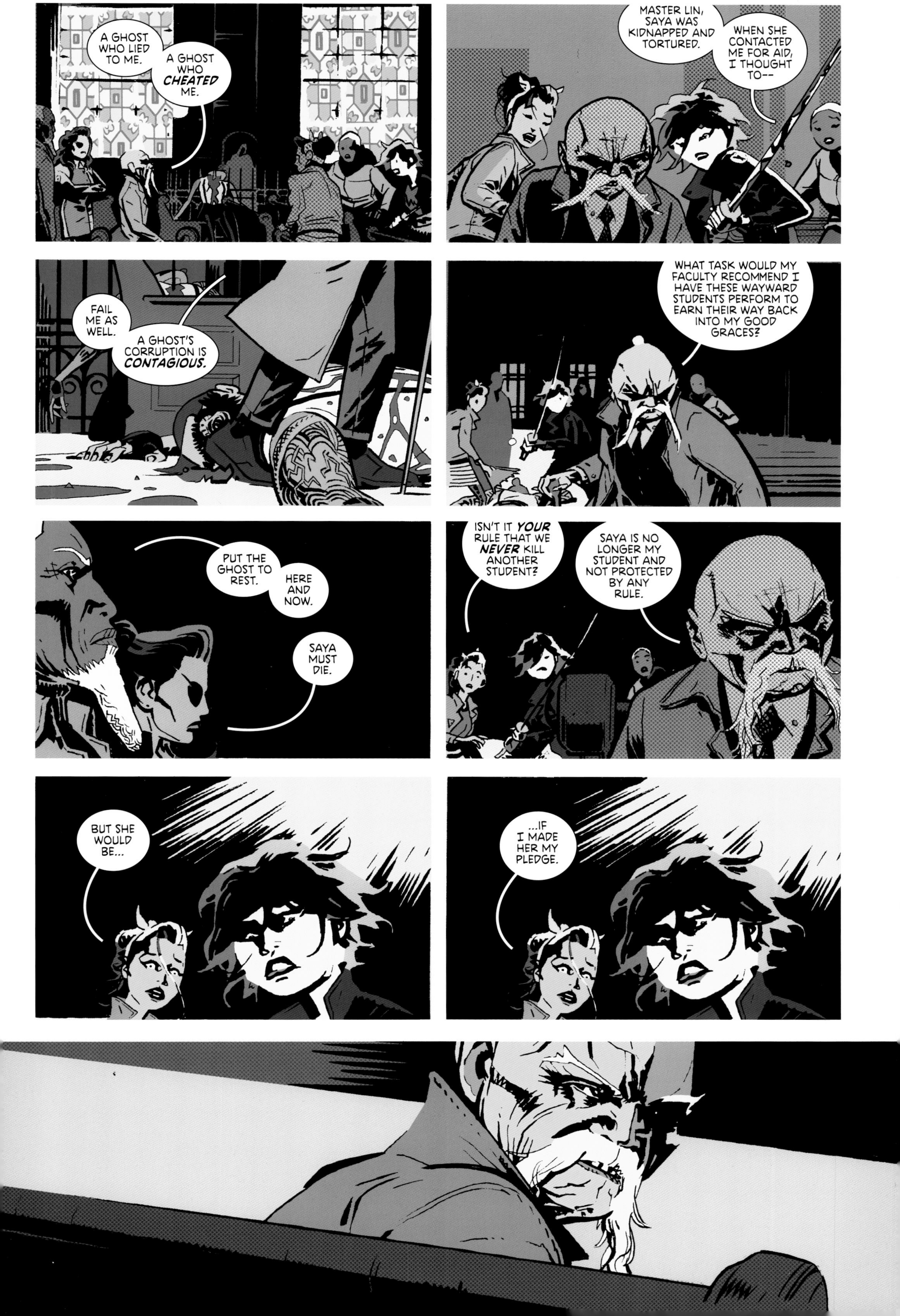
A GHOST WHO LIED TO ME.
A GHOST WHO CHEATED ME.
MASTER LIN, SAYA WAS KIDNAPPED AND TORTURED.
WHEN SHE CONTACTED ME FOR AID, I THOUGHT TO--
FAIL ME AS WELL.
A GHOST'S CORRUPTION IS CONTAGIOUS.
WHAT TASK WOULD MY FACULTY RECOMMEND I HAVE THESE WAYWARD STUDENTS PERFORM TO EARN THEIR WAY BACK INTO MY GOOD GRACES?
PUT THE GHOST TO REST.
HERE AND NOW.
SAYA MUST DIE.
ISN'T IT YOUR RULE THAT WE NEVER KILL ANOTHER STUDENT?
SAYA IS NO LONGER MY STUDENT AND NOT PROTECTED BY ANY RULE.
BUT SHE WOULD BE...
...IF I MADE HER MY PLEDGE.

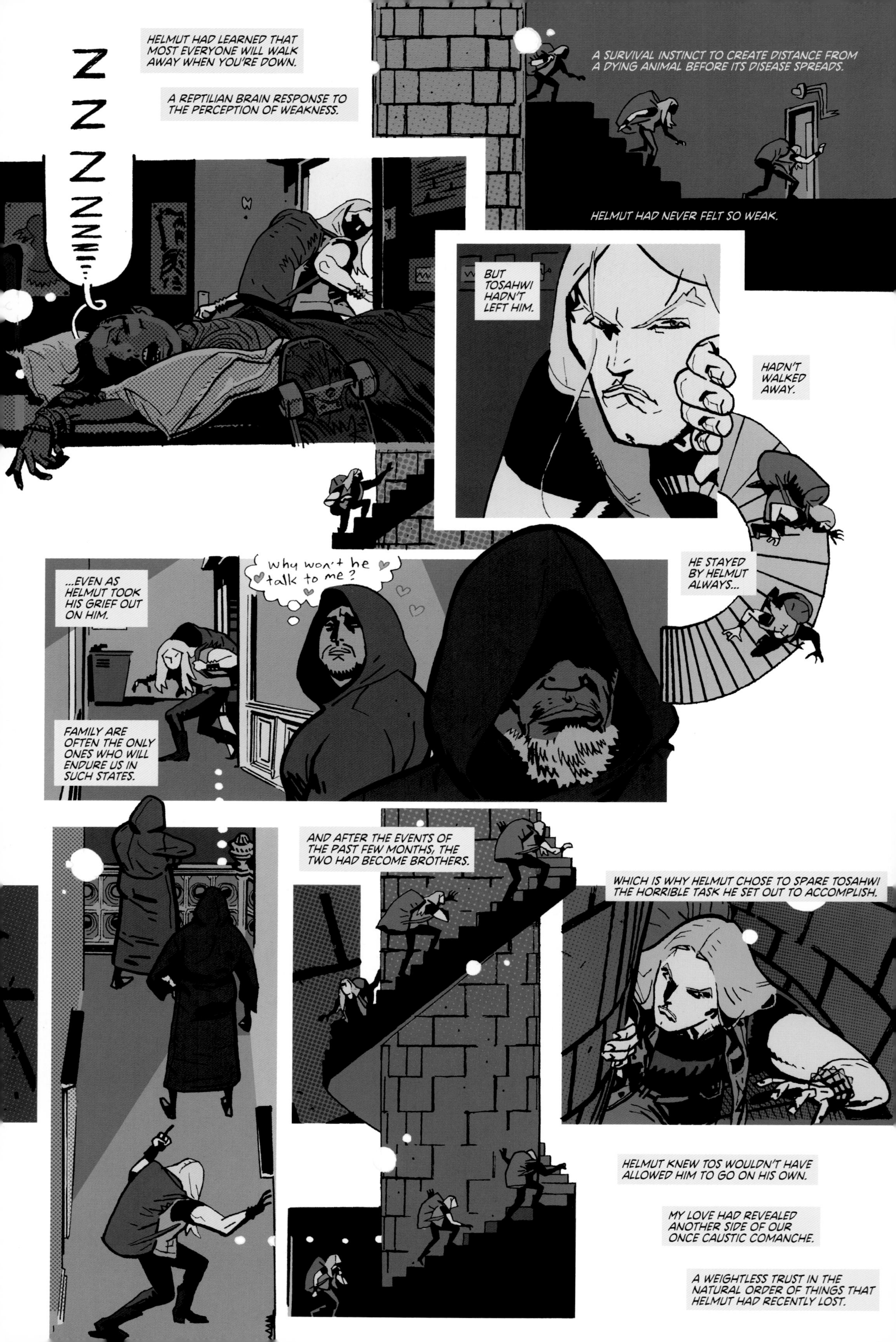

HELMUT HAD LEARNED THAT MOST EVERYONE WILL WALK AWAY WHEN YOU'RE DOWN.
A REPTILIAN BRAIN RESPONSE TO THE PERCEPTION OF WEAKNESS.
Z Z Z Z Z
A SURVIVAL INSTINCT TO CREATE DISTANCE FROM A DYING ANIMAL BEFORE ITS DISEASE SPREADS.
HELMUT HAD NEVER FELT SO WEAK.
BUT TOSAHWI HADN'T LEFT HIM.
HADN'T WALKED AWAY.
HE STAYED BY HELMUT ALWAYS...
...EVEN AS HELMUT TOOK HIS GRIEF OUT ON HIM.
why won't he talk to me?
FAMILY ARE OFTEN THE ONLY ONES WHO WILL ENDURE US IN SUCH STATES.
AND AFTER THE EVENTS OF THE PAST FEW MONTHS, THE TWO HAD BECOME BROTHERS.
WHICH IS WHY HELMUT CHOSE TO SPARE TOSAHWI THE HORRIBLE TASK HE SET OUT TO ACCOMPLISH.
HELMUT KNEW TOS WOULDN'T HAVE ALLOWED HIM TO GO ON HIS OWN.
MY LOVE HAD REVEALED ANOTHER SIDE OF OUR ONCE CAUSTIC COMANCHE.
A WEIGHTLESS TRUST IN THE NATURAL ORDER OF THINGS THAT HELMUT HAD RECENTLY LOST.

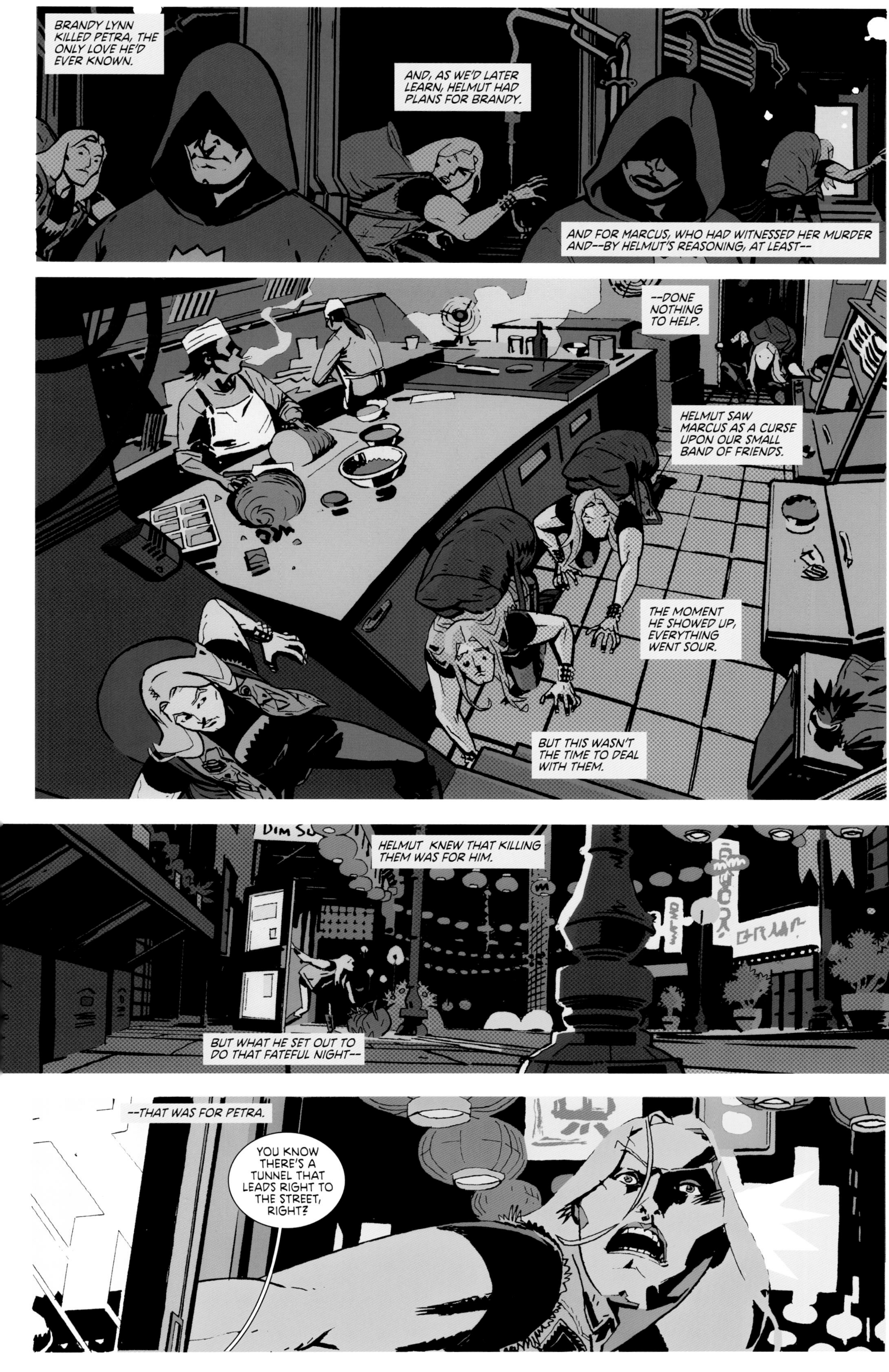
BRANDY LYNN KILLED PETRA, THE ONLY LOVE HE'D EVER KNOWN.
AND, AS WE'D LATER LEARN, HELMUT HAD PLANS FOR BRANDY.
AND FOR MARCUS, WHO HAD WITNESSED HER MURDER AND--BY HELMUT'S REASONING, AT LEAST--
--DONE NOTHING TO HELP.
HELMUT SAW MARCUS AS A CURSE UPON OUR SMALL BAND OF FRIENDS.
THE MOMENT HE SHOWED UP, EVERYTHING WENT SOUR.
BUT THIS WASN'T THE TIME TO DEAL WITH THEM.
DIM SU
HELMUT KNEW THAT KILLING THEM WAS FOR HIM.
BUT WHAT HE SET OUT TO DO THAT FATEFUL NIGHT--
--THAT WAS FOR PETRA.
YOU KNOW THERE'S A TUNNEL THAT LEADS RIGHT TO THE STREET, RIGHT?

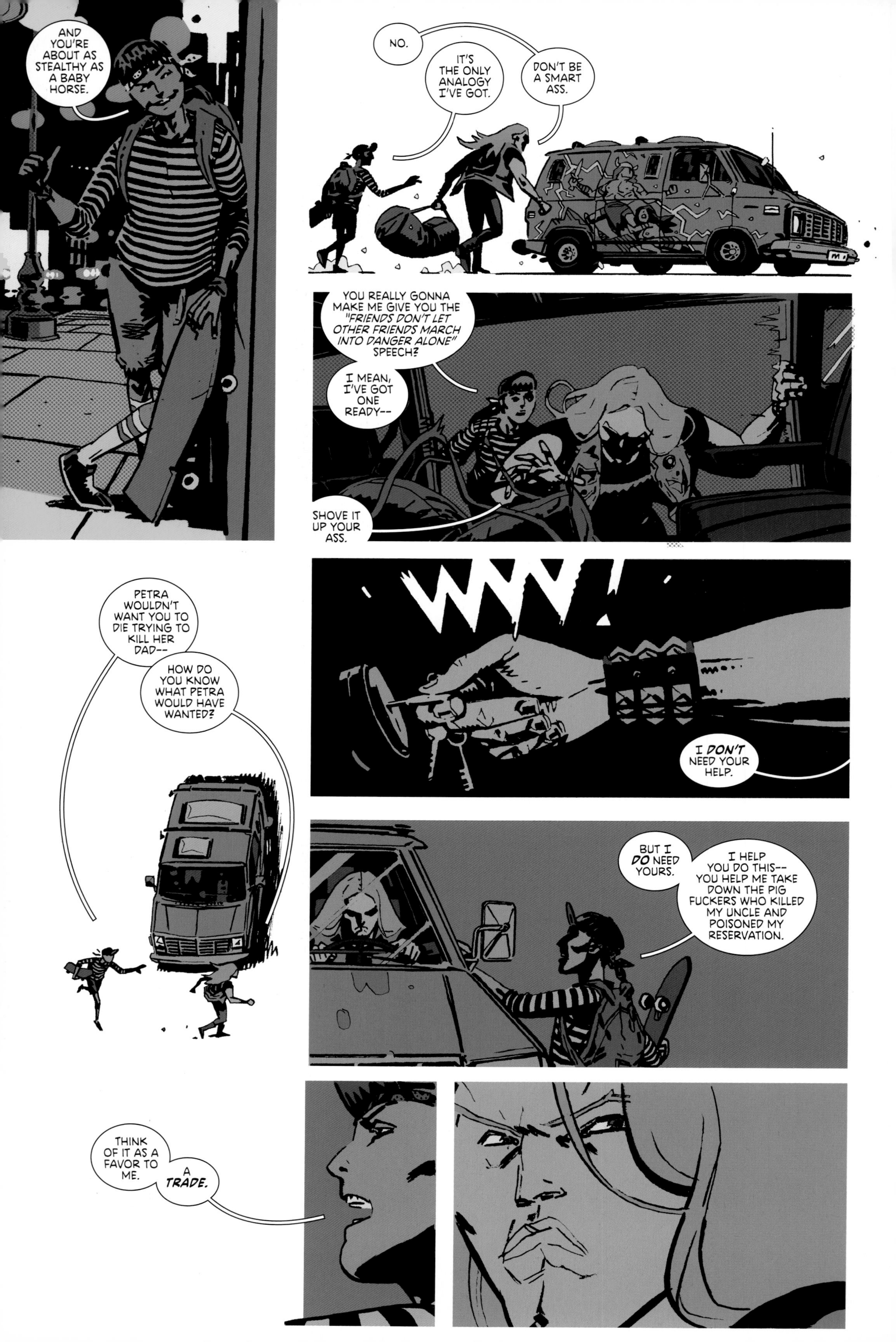
AND YOU'RE ABOUT AS STEALTHY AS A BABY HORSE.
NO.
IT'S THE ONLY ANALOGY I'VE GOT.
DON'T BE A SMART ASS.
YOU REALLY GONNA MAKE ME GIVE YOU THE "FRIENDS DON'T LET OTHER FRIENDS MARCH INTO DANGER ALONE" SPEECH?
I MEAN, I'VE GOT ONE READY--
SHOVE IT UP YOUR ASS.
PETRA WOULDN'T WANT YOU TO DIE TRYING TO KILL HER DAD--
HOW DO YOU KNOW WHAT PETRA WOULD HAVE WANTED?
I DON'T NEED YOUR HELP.
BUT I DO NEED YOURS.
I HELP YOU DO THIS-- YOU HELP ME TAKE DOWN THE PIG FUCKERS WHO KILLED MY UNCLE AND POISONED MY RESERVATION.
THINK OF IT AS A FAVOR TO ME.
A TRADE.

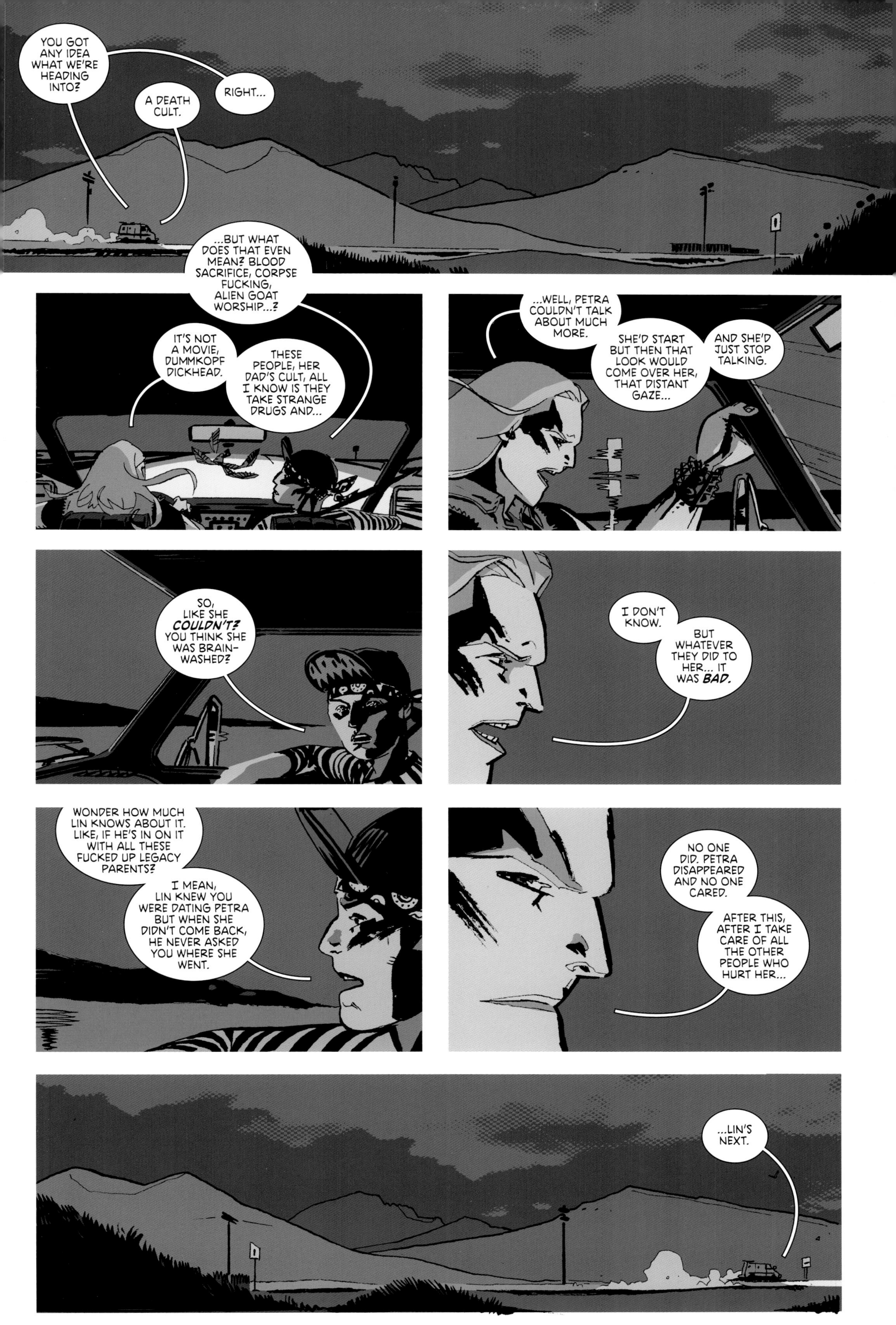
YOU GOT ANY IDEA WHAT WE'RE HEADING INTO?
A DEATH CULT.
RIGHT...
...BUT WHAT DOES THAT EVEN MEAN? BLOOD SACRIFICE, CORPSE FUCKING, ALIEN GOAT WORSHIP...?
IT'S NOT A MOVIE, DUMMKOPF DICKHEAD.
THESE PEOPLE, HER DAD'S CULT, ALL I KNOW IS THEY TAKE STRANGE DRUGS AND...
...WELL, PETRA COULDN'T TALK ABOUT MUCH MORE.
SHE'D START BUT THEN THAT LOOK WOULD COME OVER HER, THAT DISTANT GAZE...
AND SHE'D JUST STOP TALKING.
SO, LIKE SHE COULDN'T? YOU THINK SHE WAS BRAIN-WASHED?
I DON'T KNOW.
BUT WHATEVER THEY DID TO HER... IT WAS BAD.
WONDER HOW MUCH LIN KNOWS ABOUT IT. LIKE, IF HE'S IN ON IT WITH ALL THESE FUCKED UP LEGACY PARENTS?
I MEAN, LIN KNEW YOU WERE DATING PETRA BUT WHEN SHE DIDN'T COME BACK, HE NEVER ASKED YOU WHERE SHE WENT.
NO ONE DID. PETRA DISAPPEARED AND NO ONE CARED.
AFTER THIS, AFTER I TAKE CARE OF ALL THE OTHER PEOPLE WHO HURT HER...
...LIN'S NEXT.

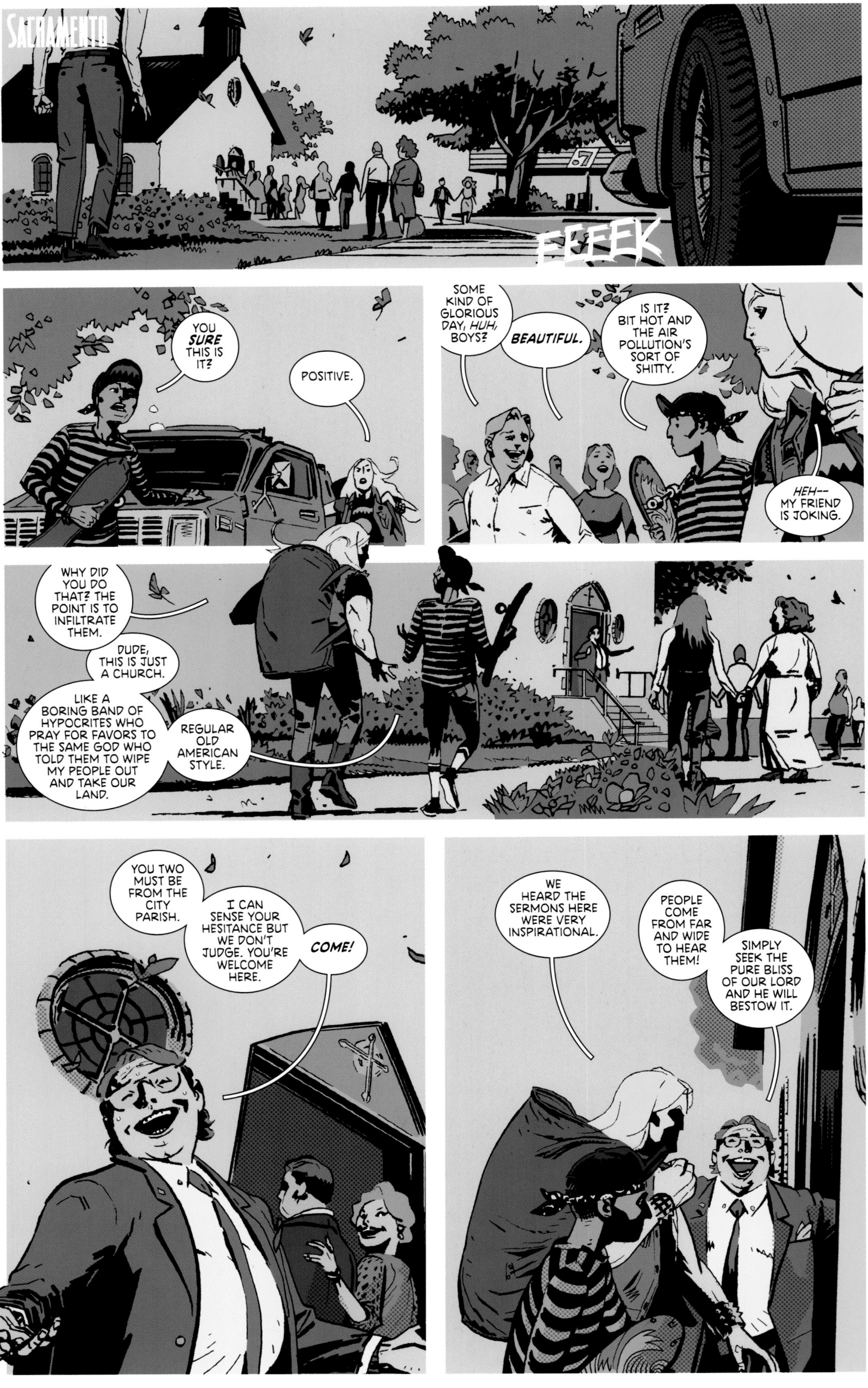
SACRAMENTO
EEEEK
YOU SURE THIS IS IT?
POSITIVE.
SOME KIND OF GLORIOUS DAY, HUH, BOYS?
BEAUTIFUL.
IS IT? BIT HOT AND THE AIR POLLUTION'S SORT OF SHITTY.
HEH-- MY FRIEND IS JOKING.
WHY DID YOU DO THAT? THE POINT IS TO INFILTRATE THEM.
DUDE, THIS IS JUST A CHURCH.
LIKE A BORING BAND OF HYPOCRITES WHO PRAY FOR FAVORS TO THE SAME GOD WHO TOLD THEM TO WIPE MY PEOPLE OUT AND TAKE OUR LAND.
REGULAR OLD AMERICAN STYLE.
YOU TWO MUST BE FROM THE CITY PARISH.
I CAN SENSE YOUR HESITANCE BUT WE DON'T JUDGE. YOU'RE WELCOME HERE.
COME!
WE HEARD THE SERMONS HERE WERE VERY INSPIRATIONAL.
PEOPLE COME FROM FAR AND WIDE TO HEAR THEM!
SIMPLY SEEK THE PURE BLISS OF OUR LORD AND HE WILL BESTOW IT.

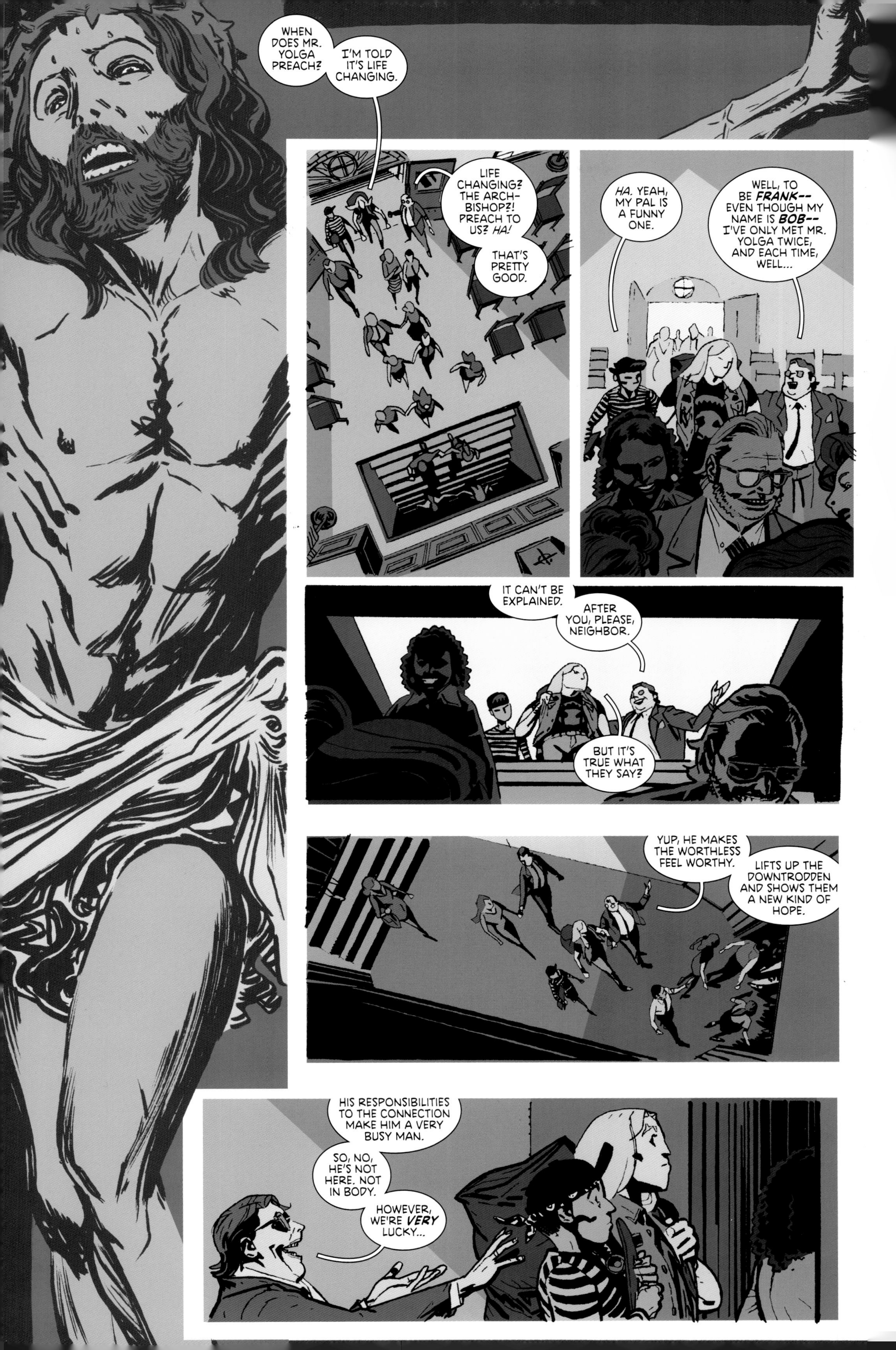

WHEN DOES MR. YOLGA PREACH?
I'M TOLD IT'S LIFE CHANGING.
LIFE CHANGING? THE ARCH-BISHOP?! PREACH TO US? HA!
THAT'S PRETTY GOOD.
HA. YEAH, MY PAL IS A FUNNY ONE.
WELL, TO BE FRANK-- EVEN THOUGH MY NAME IS BOB-- I'VE ONLY MET MR. YOLGA TWICE, AND EACH TIME, WELL...
IT CAN'T BE EXPLAINED.
AFTER YOU, PLEASE, NEIGHBOR.
BUT IT'S TRUE WHAT THEY SAY?
YUP, HE MAKES THE WORTHLESS FEEL WORTHY.
LIFTS UP THE DOWNTRODDEN AND SHOWS THEM A NEW KIND OF HOPE.
HIS RESPONSIBILITIES TO THE CONNECTION MAKE HIM A VERY BUSY MAN.
SO, NO, HE'S NOT HERE. NOT IN BODY.
HOWEVER, WE'RE VERY LUCKY...

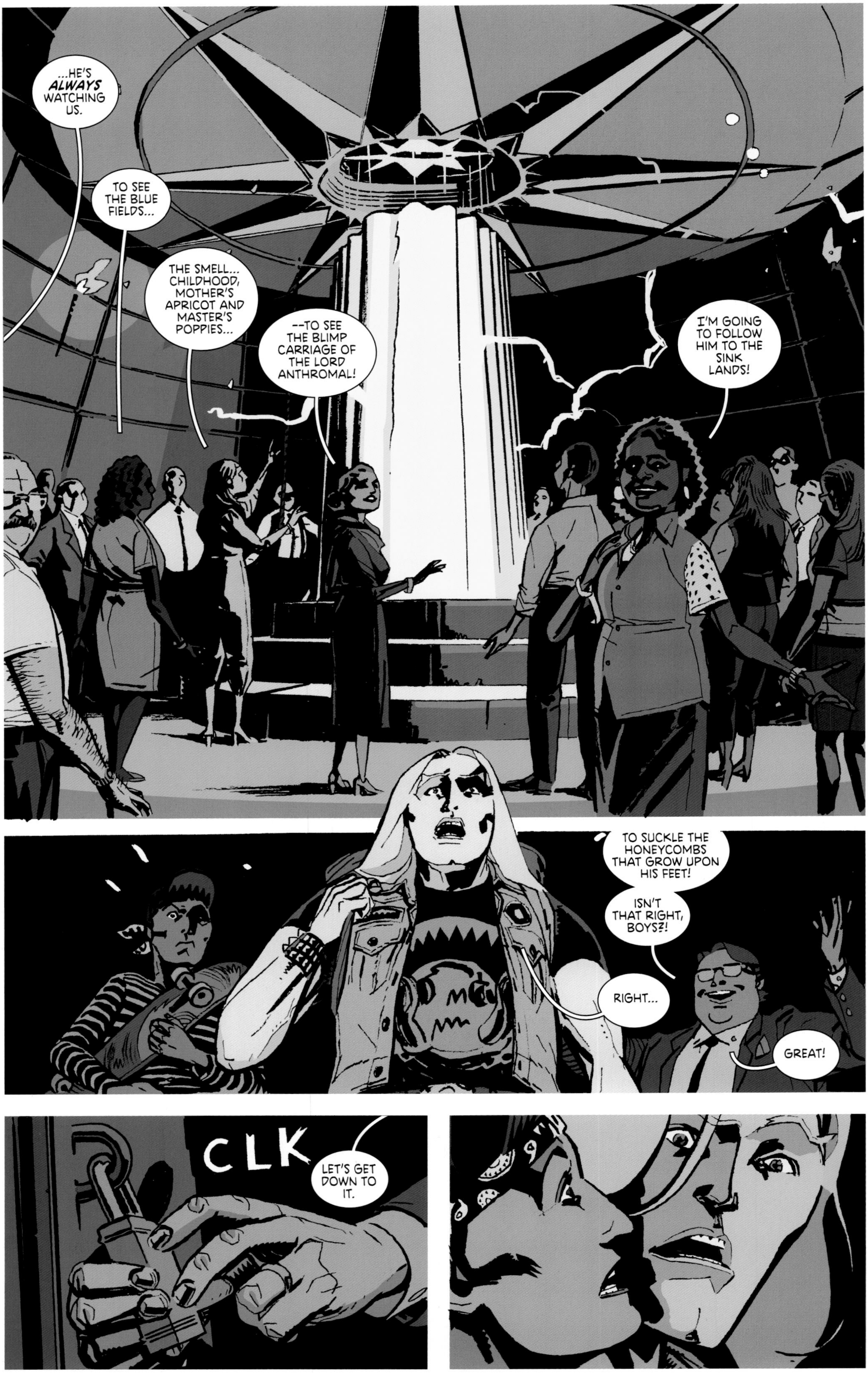
...HE'S *ALWAYS* WATCHING US.
TO SEE THE BLUE FIELDS...
THE SMELL... CHILDHOOD, MOTHER'S APRICOT AND MASTER'S POPPIES...
--TO SEE THE BLIMP CARRIAGE OF THE LORD ANTHROMAL!
I'M GOING TO FOLLOW HIM TO THE SINK LANDS!
TO SUCKLE THE HONEYCOMBS THAT GROW UPON HIS FEET!
ISN'T THAT RIGHT, BOYS?!
RIGHT...
GREAT!
CLK
LET'S GET DOWN TO IT.

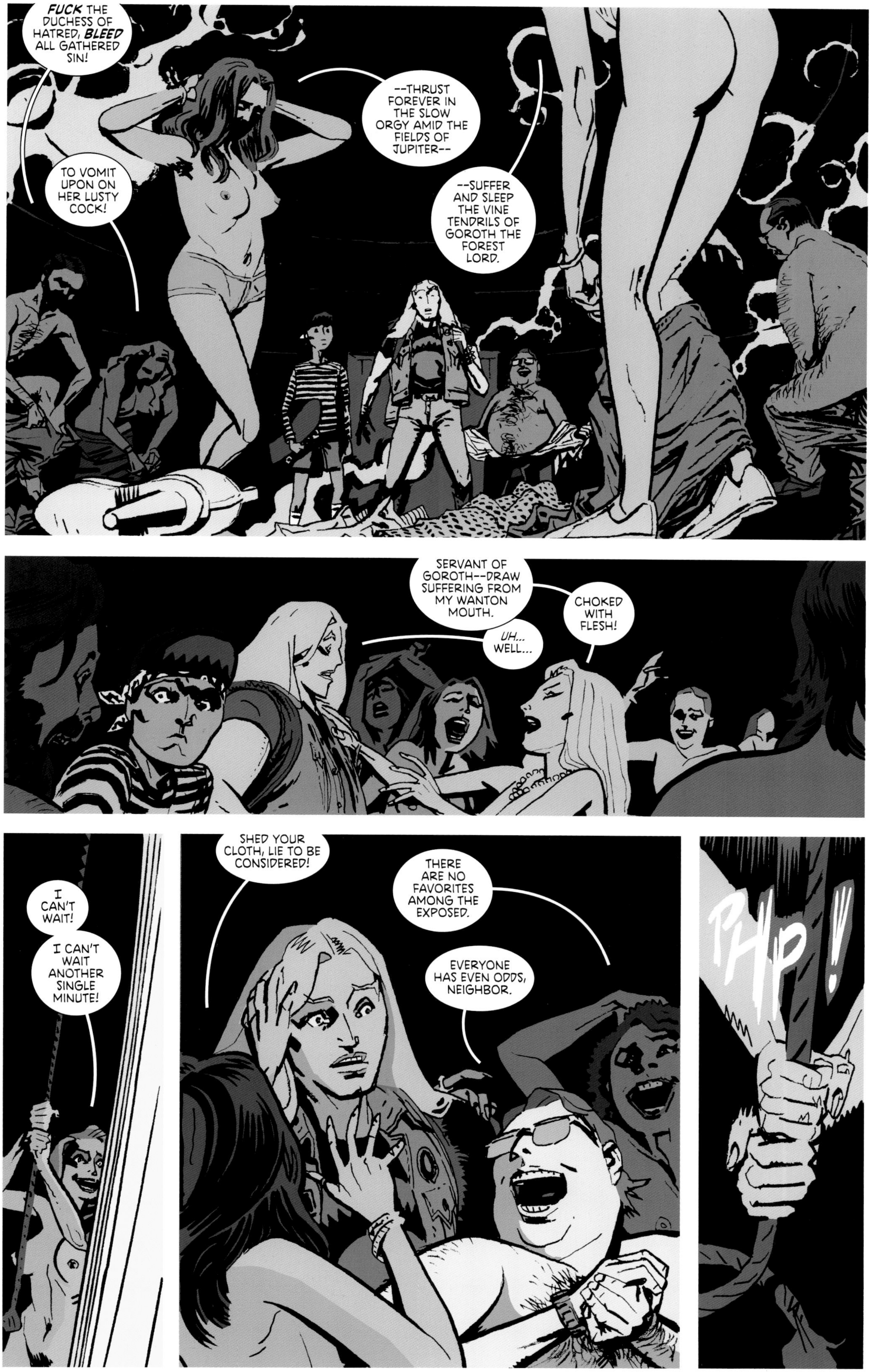
FUCK THE DUCHESS OF HATRED, BLEED ALL GATHERED SIN!
TO VOMIT UPON ON HER LUSTY COCK!
--THRUST FOREVER IN THE SLOW ORGY AMID THE FIELDS OF JUPITER--
--SUFFER AND SLEEP THE VINE TENDRILS OF GOROTH THE FOREST LORD.
SERVANT OF GOROTH--DRAW SUFFERING FROM MY WANTON MOUTH.
UH... WELL...
CHOKED WITH FLESH!
I CAN'T WAIT!
I CAN'T WAIT ANOTHER SINGLE MINUTE!
SHED YOUR CLOTH, LIE TO BE CONSIDERED!
THERE ARE NO FAVORITES AMONG THE EXPOSED.
EVERYONE HAS EVEN ODDS, NEIGHBOR.
PHP !!

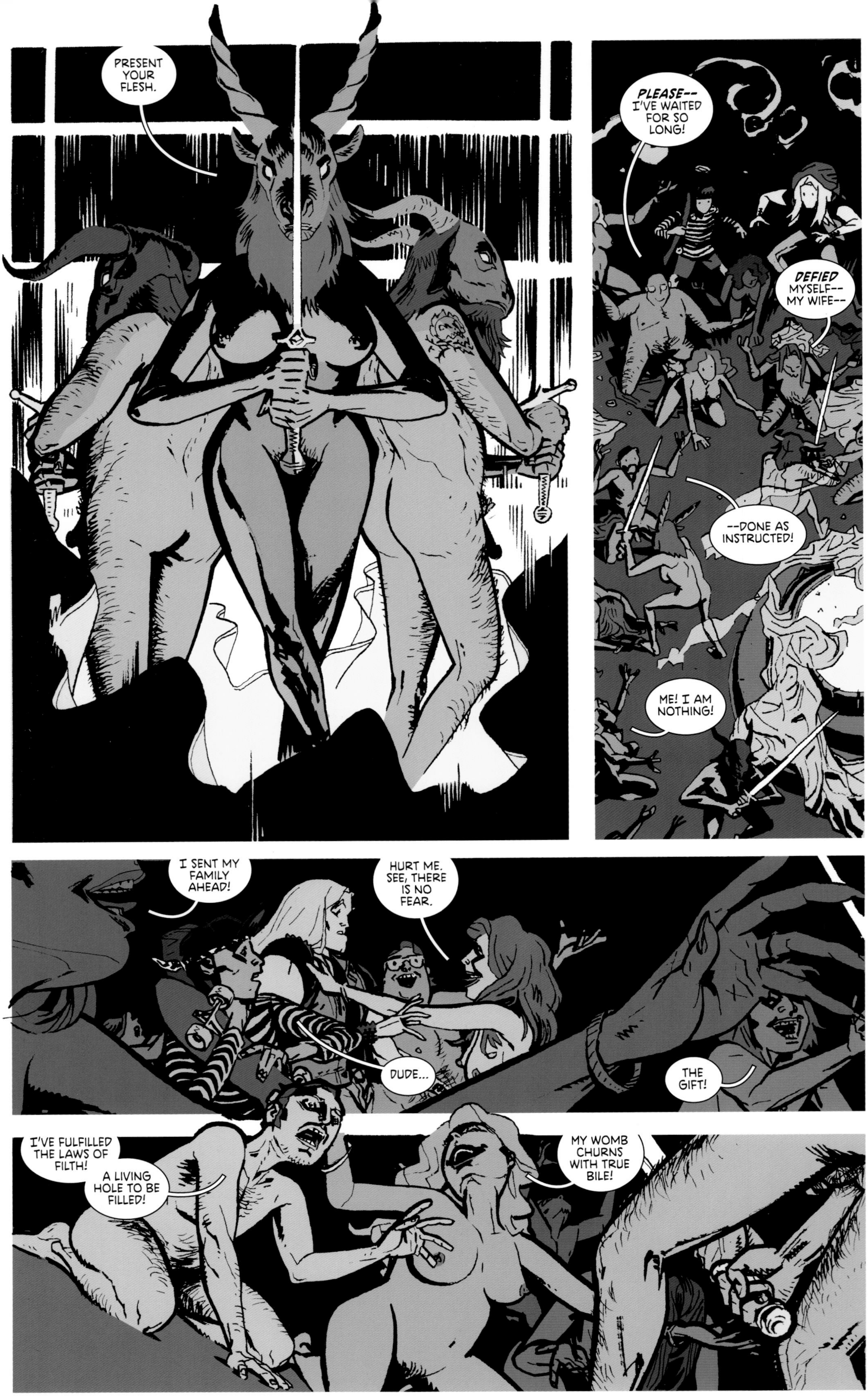
PRESENT YOUR FLESH.
PLEASE-- I'VE WAITED FOR SO LONG!
DEFIED MYSELF-- MY WIFE--
--DONE AS INSTRUCTED!
ME! I AM NOTHING!
I SENT MY FAMILY AHEAD!
HURT ME. SEE, THERE IS NO FEAR.
DUDE...
THE GIFT!
I'VE FULFILLED THE LAWS OF FILTH!
A LIVING HOLE TO BE FILLED!
MY WOMB CHURNS WITH TRUE BILE!

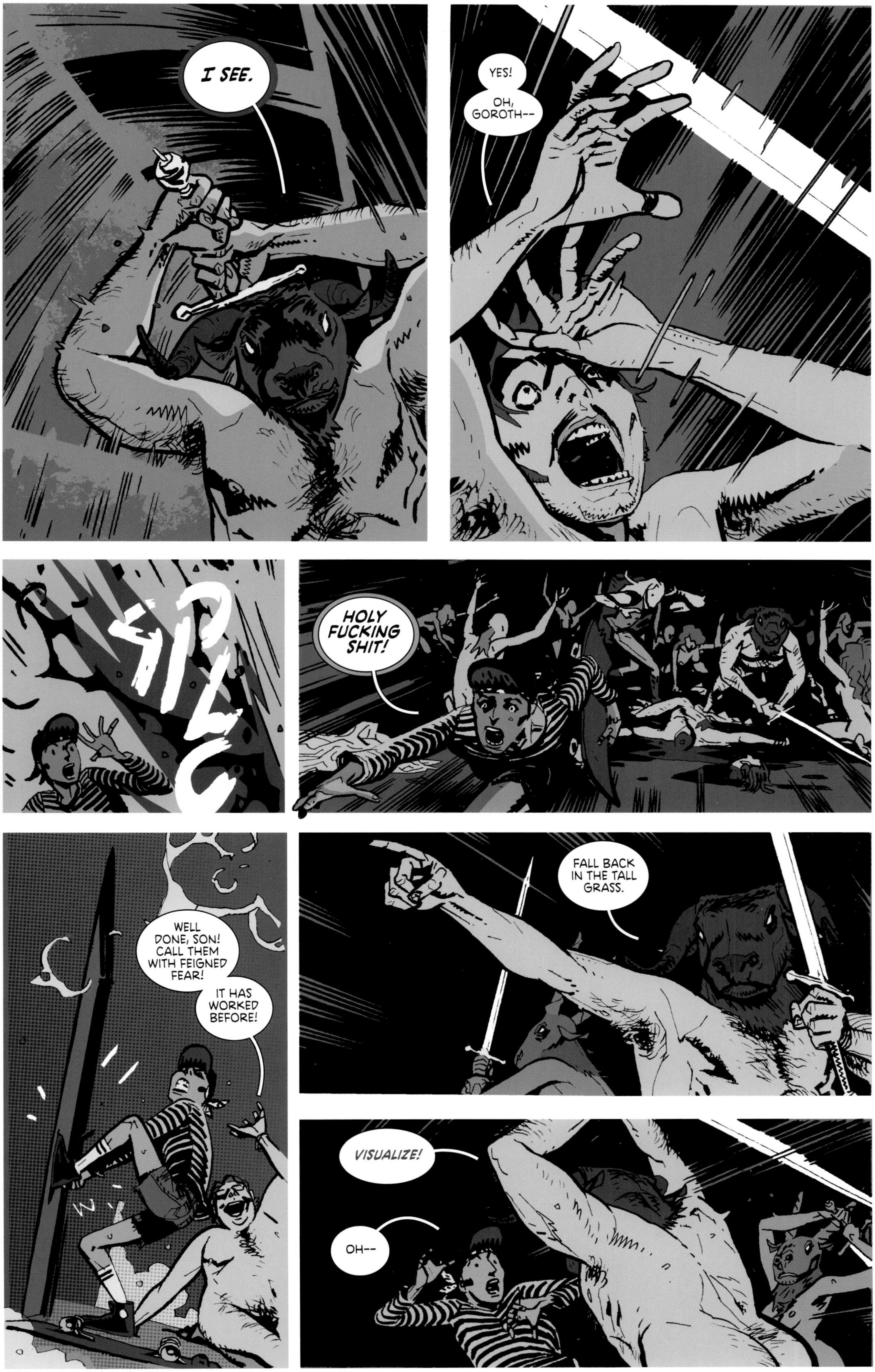
I SEE.
YES!
OH, GOROTH--
HOLY FUCKING SHIT!
WELL DONE, SON! CALL THEM WITH FEIGNED FEAR!
IT HAS WORKED BEFORE!
FALL BACK IN THE TALL GRASS.
VISUALIZE!
OH--

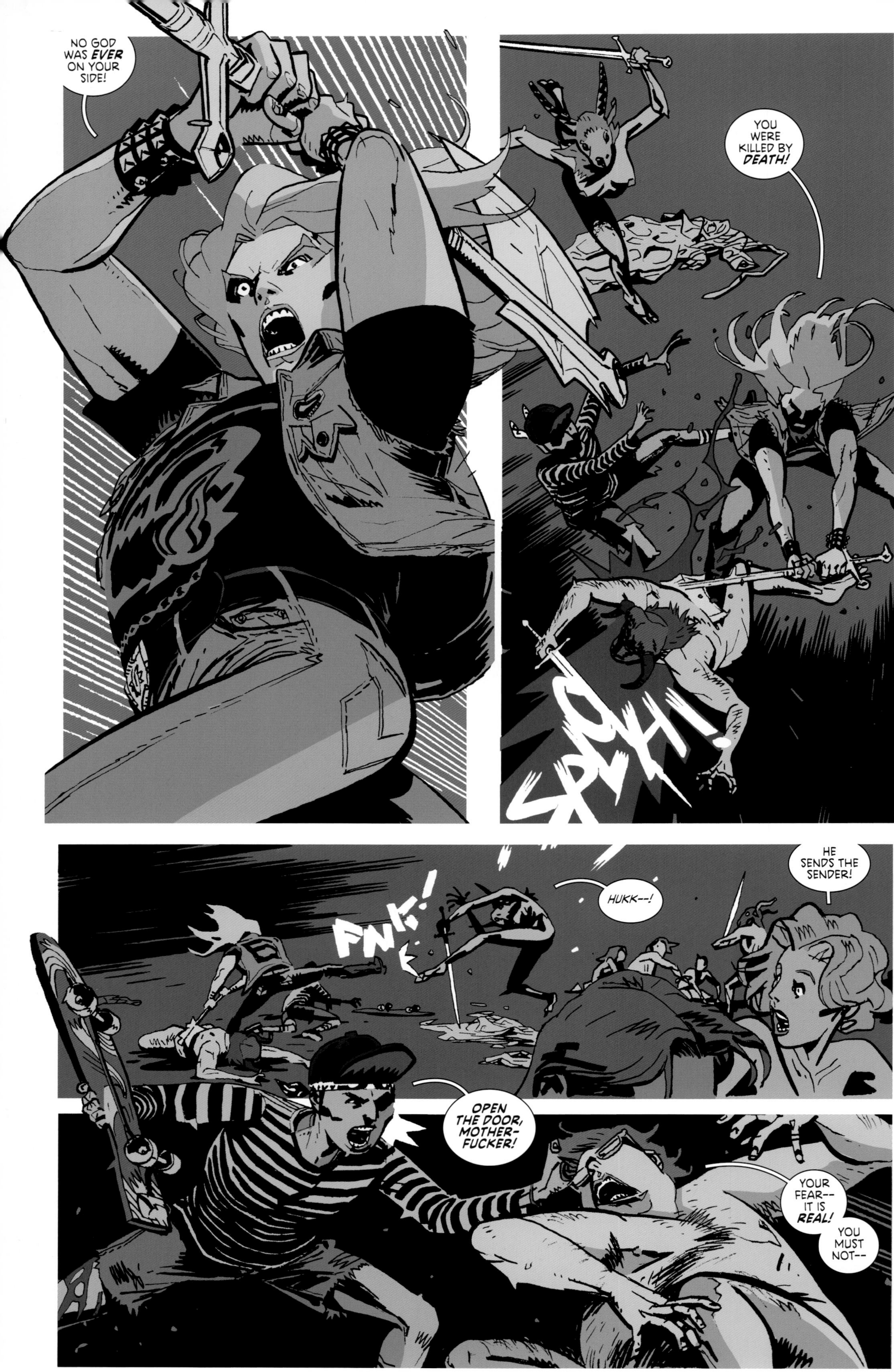
NO GOD WAS EVER ON YOUR SIDE!
YOU WERE KILLED BY DEATH!
SPLKH!
HE SENDS THE SENDER!
HUKK--!
FNK!
OPEN THE DOOR, MOTHER-FUCKER!
YOUR FEAR-- IT IS REAL!
YOU MUST NOT--

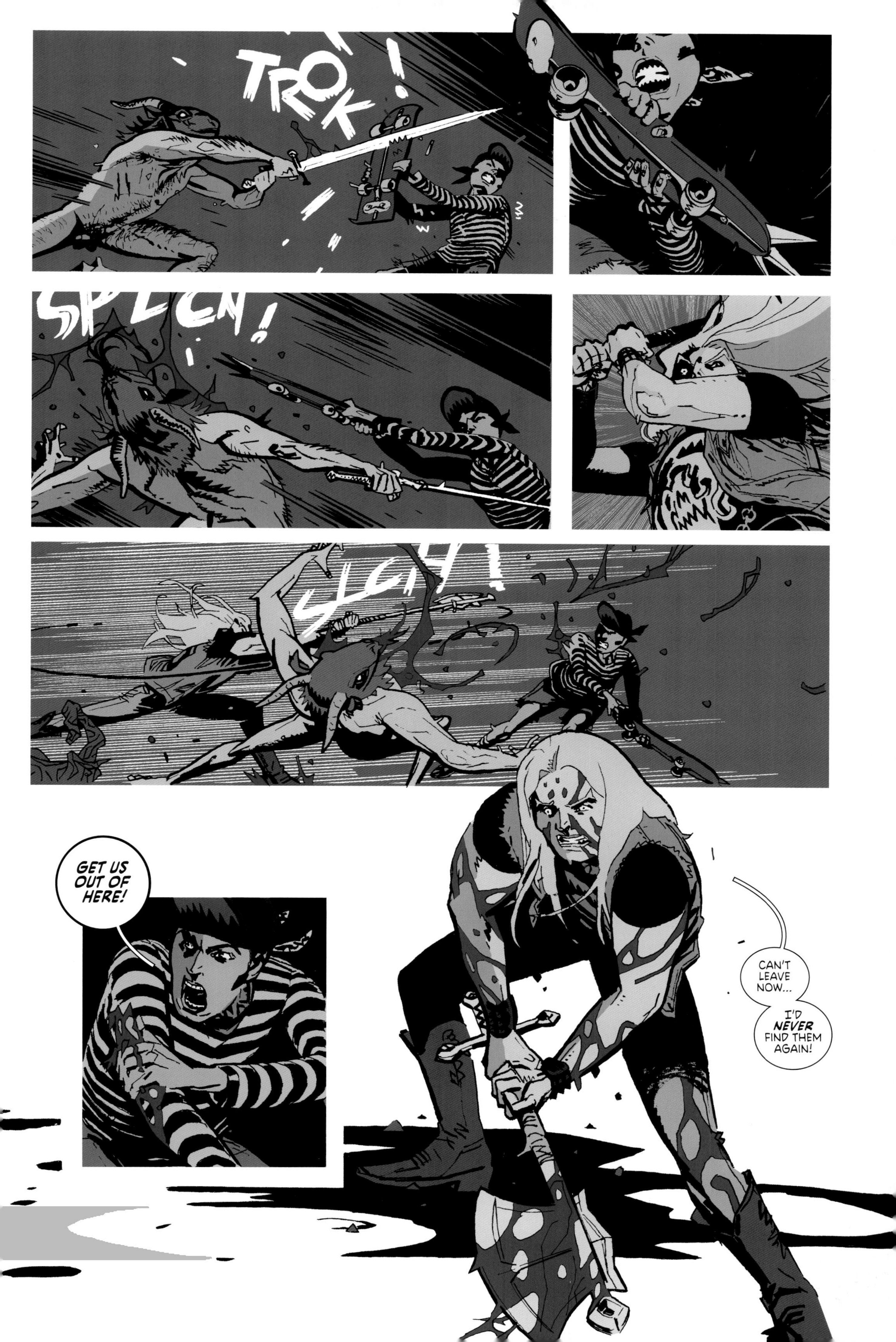
TROK!
SPLCH!
GET US OUT OF HERE!
CAN'T LEAVE NOW...
I'D **NEVER** FIND THEM AGAIN!

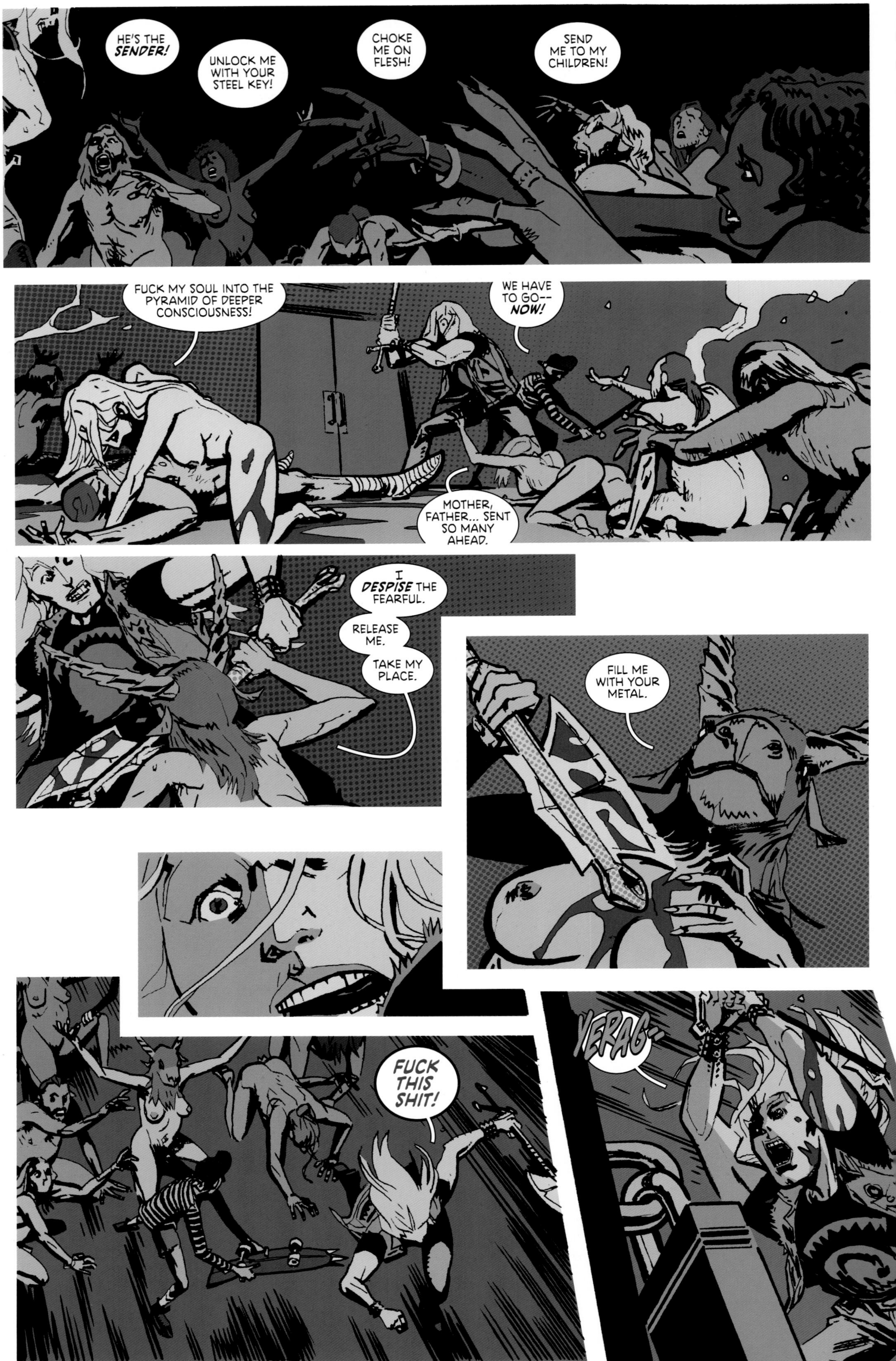

HE'S THE SENDER!
UNLOCK ME WITH YOUR STEEL KEY!
CHOKE ME ON FLESH!
SEND ME TO MY CHILDREN!
FUCK MY SOUL INTO THE PYRAMID OF DEEPER CONSCIOUSNESS!
WE HAVE TO GO-- NOW!
MOTHER, FATHER... SENT SO MANY AHEAD.
I DESPISE THE FEARFUL.
RELEASE ME.
TAKE MY PLACE.
FILL ME WITH YOUR METAL.
FUCK THIS SHIT!
KRAG--

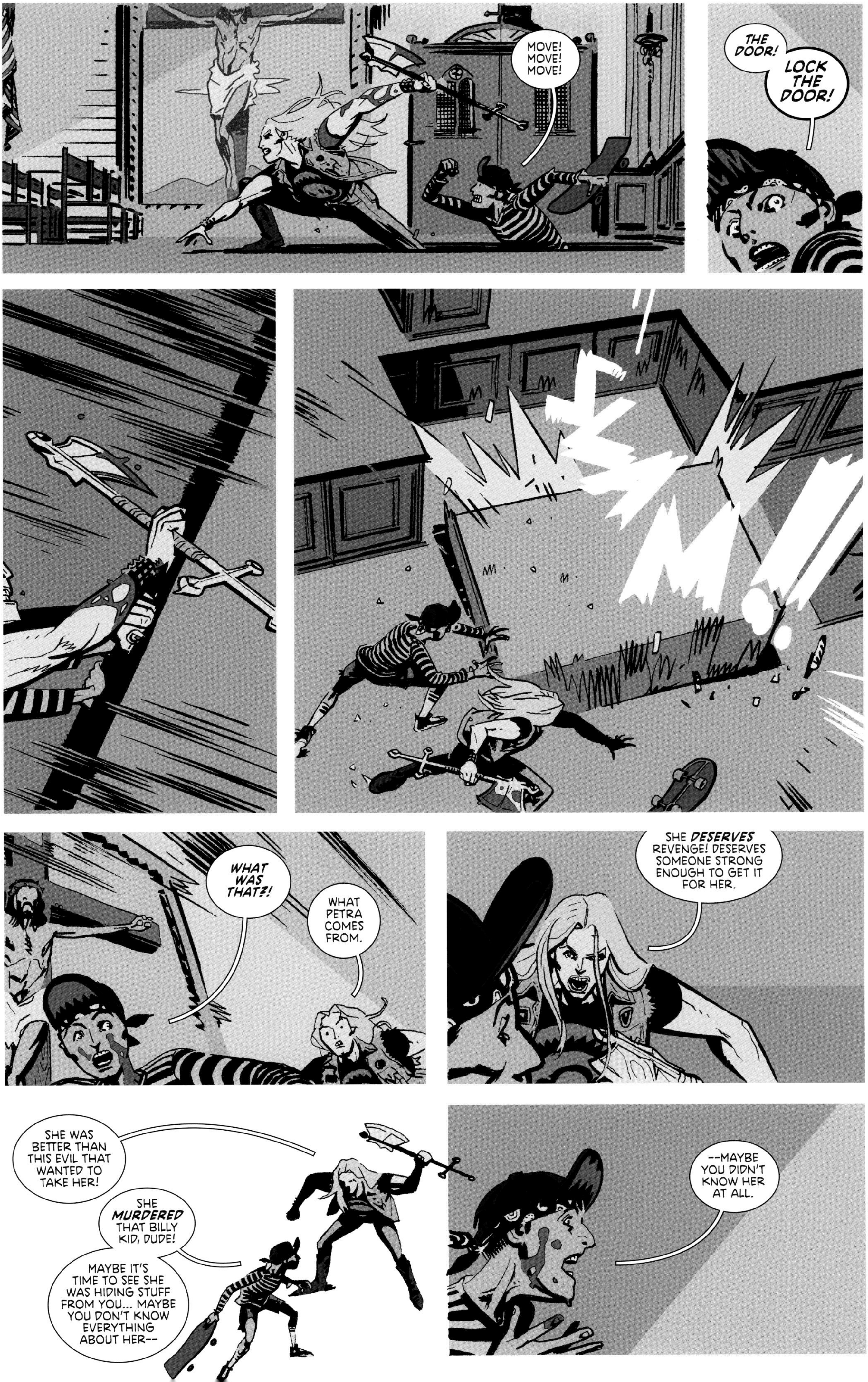
MOVE! MOVE! MOVE!
THE DOOR! LOCK THE DOOR!
WHAT WAS THAT?!
WHAT PETRA COMES FROM.
SHE DESERVES REVENGE! DESERVES SOMEONE STRONG ENOUGH TO GET IT FOR HER.
SHE WAS BETTER THAN THIS EVIL THAT WANTED TO TAKE HER!
SHE MURDERED THAT BILLY KID, DUDE!
MAYBE IT'S TIME TO SEE SHE WAS HIDING STUFF FROM YOU... MAYBE YOU DON'T KNOW EVERYTHING ABOUT HER--
--MAYBE YOU DIDN'T KNOW HER AT ALL.

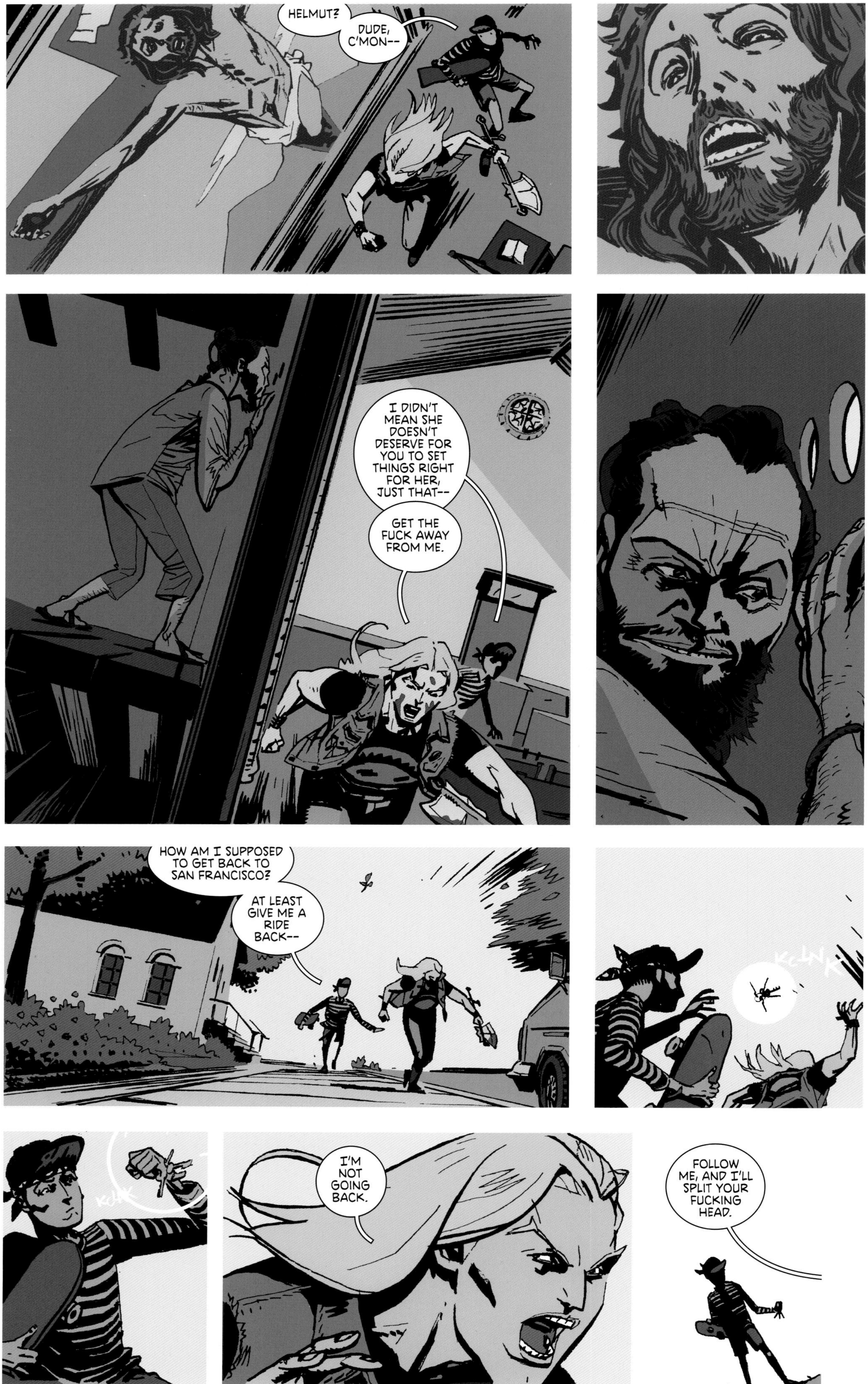
HELMUT?
DUDE, C'MON--
I DIDN'T MEAN SHE DOESN'T DESERVE FOR YOU TO SET THINGS RIGHT FOR HER, JUST THAT--
GET THE FUCK AWAY FROM ME.
HOW AM I SUPPOSED TO GET BACK TO SAN FRANCISCO?
AT LEAST GIVE ME A RIDE BACK--
I'M NOT GOING BACK.
FOLLOW ME, AND I'LL SPLIT YOUR FUCKING HEAD.

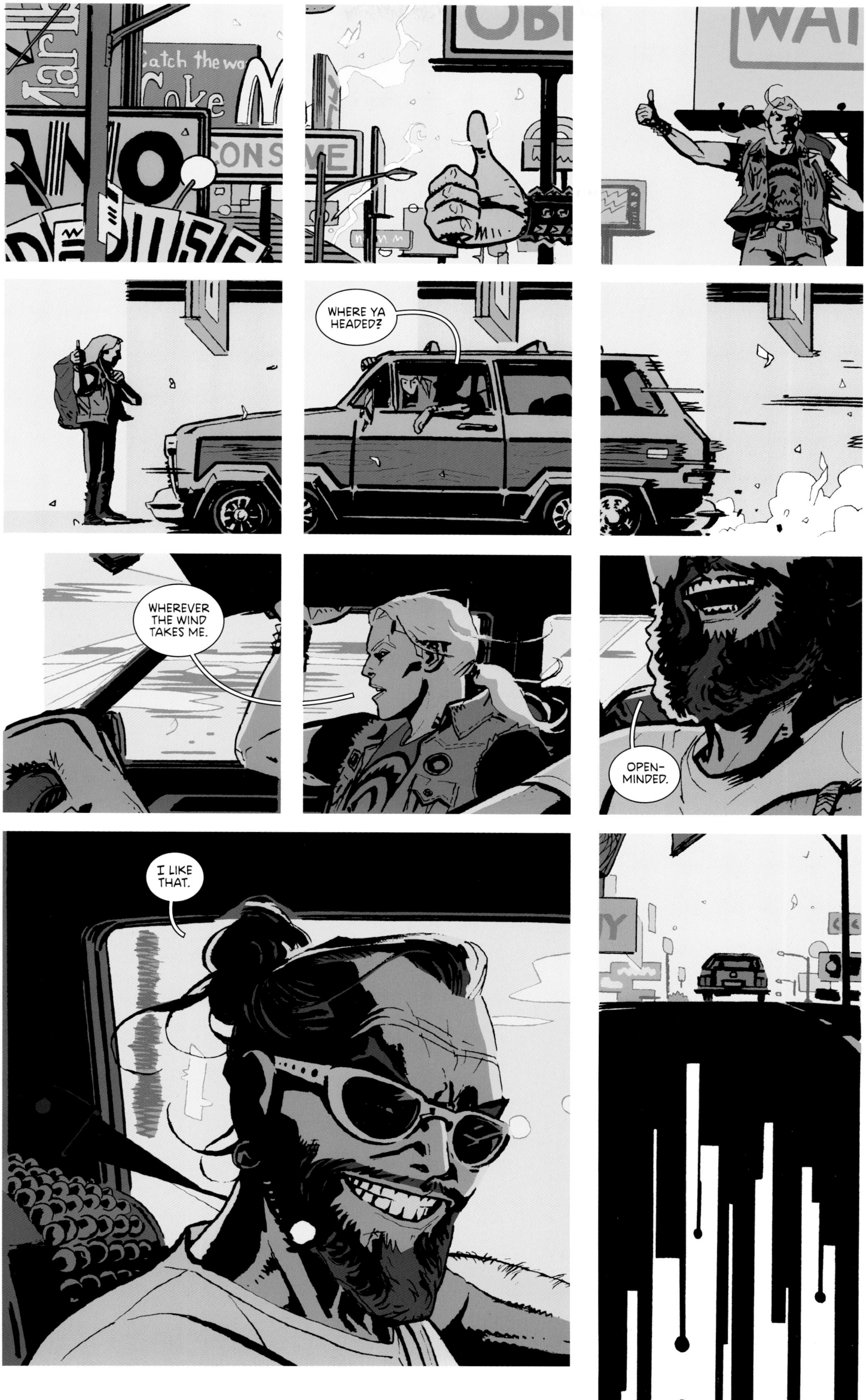
Coke
WHERE YA HEADED?
WHEREVER THE WIND TAKES ME.
OPEN-MINDED.
I LIKE THAT.

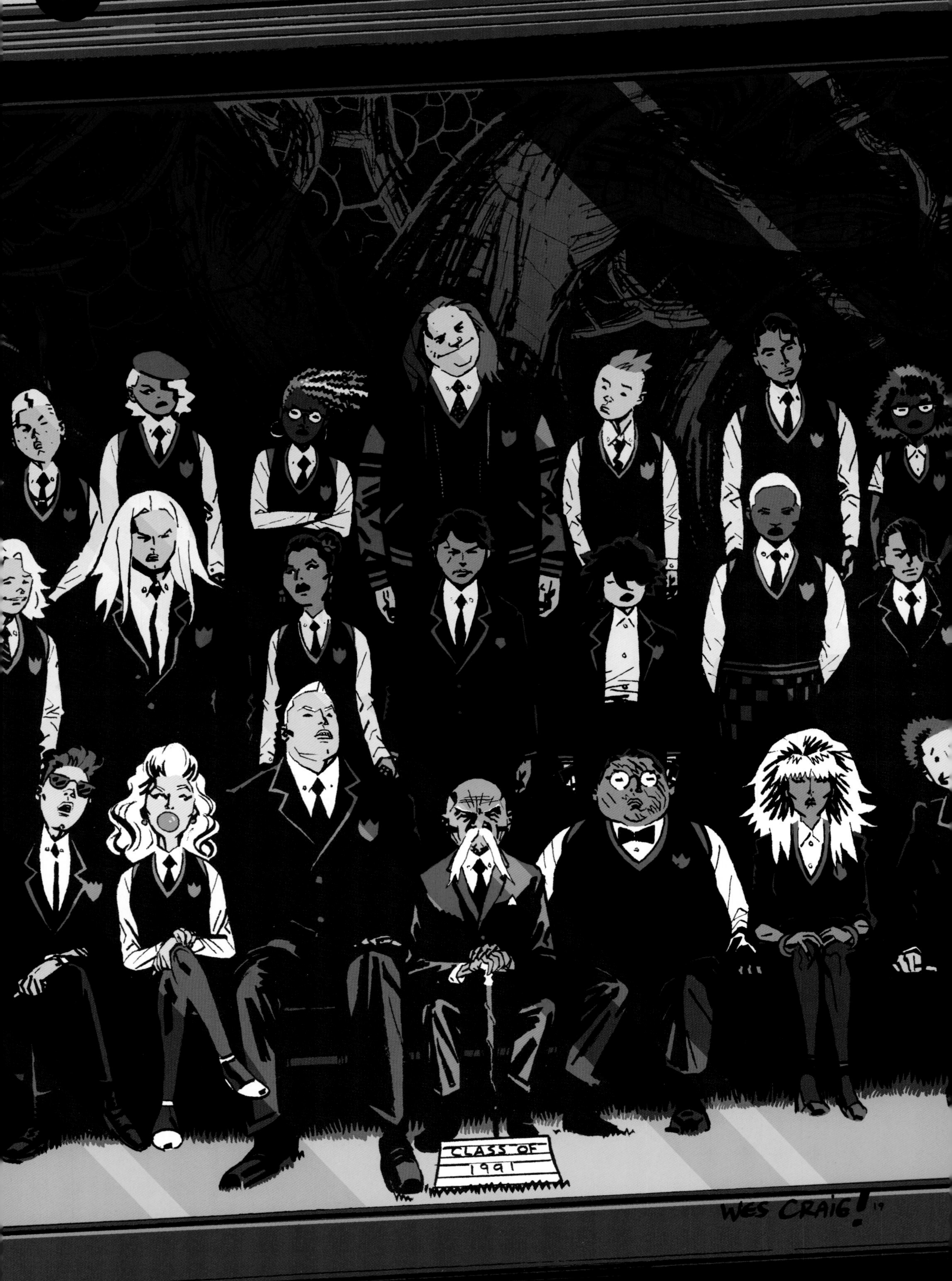
CLASS OF
1991
WES CRAIG! 19

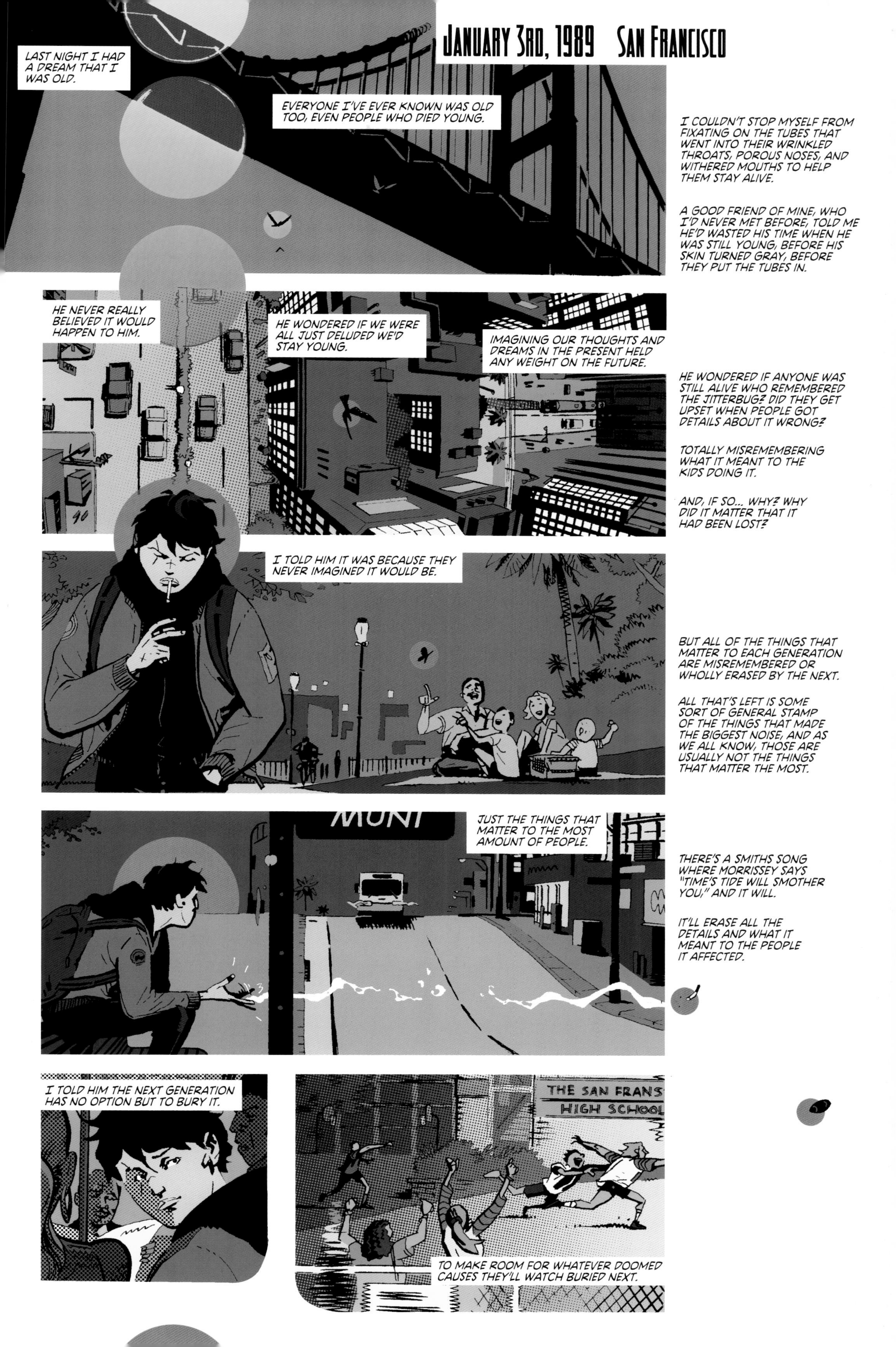
JANUARY 3RD, 1989 SAN FRANCISCO
LAST NIGHT I HAD A DREAM THAT I WAS OLD.
EVERYONE I'VE EVER KNOWN WAS OLD TOO, EVEN PEOPLE WHO DIED YOUNG.
I COULDN'T STOP MYSELF FROM FIXATING ON THE TUBES THAT WENT INTO THEIR WRINKLED THROATS, POROUS NOSES, AND WITHERED MOUTHS TO HELP THEM STAY ALIVE.
A GOOD FRIEND OF MINE, WHO I'D NEVER MET BEFORE, TOLD ME HE'D WASTED HIS TIME WHEN HE WAS STILL YOUNG, BEFORE HIS SKIN TURNED GRAY, BEFORE THEY PUT THE TUBES IN.
HE NEVER REALLY BELIEVED IT WOULD HAPPEN TO HIM.
HE WONDERED IF WE WERE ALL JUST DELUDED WE'D STAY YOUNG.
IMAGINING OUR THOUGHTS AND DREAMS IN THE PRESENT HELD ANY WEIGHT ON THE FUTURE.
HE WONDERED IF ANYONE WAS STILL ALIVE WHO REMEMBERED THE JITTERBUG? DID THEY GET UPSET WHEN PEOPLE GOT DETAILS ABOUT IT WRONG?
TOTALLY MISREMEMBERING WHAT IT MEANT TO THE KIDS DOING IT.
AND, IF SO... WHY? WHY DID IT MATTER THAT IT HAD BEEN LOST?
I TOLD HIM IT WAS BECAUSE THEY NEVER IMAGINED IT WOULD BE.
BUT ALL OF THE THINGS THAT MATTER TO EACH GENERATION ARE MISREMEMBERED OR WHOLLY ERASED BY THE NEXT.
ALL THAT'S LEFT IS SOME SORT OF GENERAL STAMP OF THE THINGS THAT MADE THE BIGGEST NOISE, AND AS WE ALL KNOW, THOSE ARE USUALLY NOT THE THINGS THAT MATTER THE MOST.
MUNI
JUST THE THINGS THAT MATTER TO THE MOST AMOUNT OF PEOPLE.
THERE'S A SMITHS SONG WHERE MORRISSEY SAYS "TIME'S TIDE WILL SMOTHER YOU," AND IT WILL.
IT'LL ERASE ALL THE DETAILS AND WHAT IT MEANT TO THE PEOPLE IT AFFECTED.
I TOLD HIM THE NEXT GENERATION HAS NO OPTION BUT TO BURY IT.
THE SAN FRANS
HIGH SCHOOL
TO MAKE ROOM FOR WHATEVER DOOMED CAUSES THEY'LL WATCH BURIED NEXT.

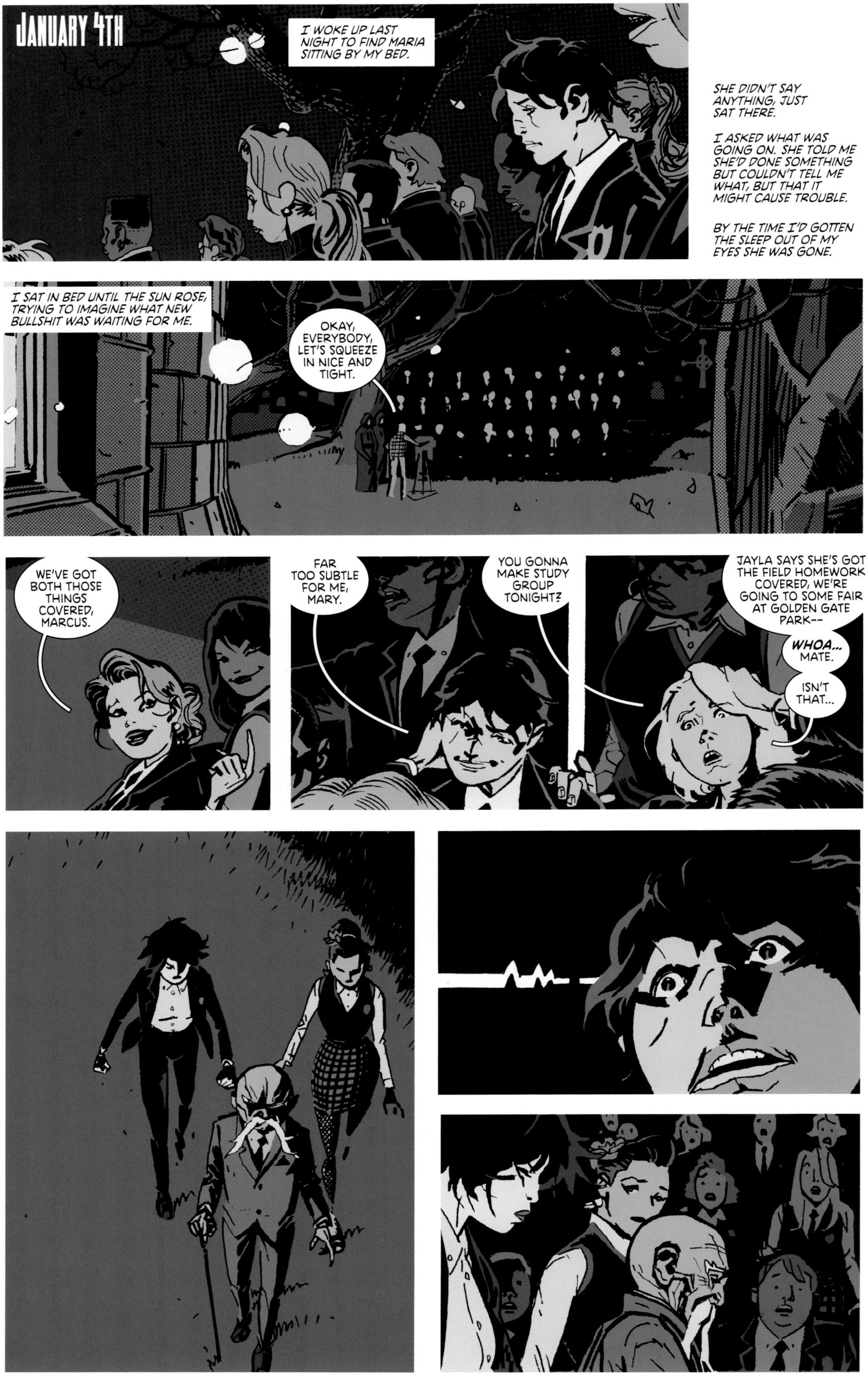
JANUARY 4TH
I WOKE UP LAST NIGHT TO FIND MARIA SITTING BY MY BED.
SHE DIDN'T SAY ANYTHING, JUST SAT THERE.
I ASKED WHAT WAS GOING ON. SHE TOLD ME SHE'D DONE SOMETHING BUT COULDN'T TELL ME WHAT, BUT THAT IT MIGHT CAUSE TROUBLE.
BY THE TIME I'D GOTTEN THE SLEEP OUT OF MY EYES SHE WAS GONE.
I SAT IN BED UNTIL THE SUN ROSE, TRYING TO IMAGINE WHAT NEW BULLSHIT WAS WAITING FOR ME.
OKAY, EVERYBODY, LET'S SQUEEZE IN NICE AND TIGHT.
WE'VE GOT BOTH THOSE THINGS COVERED, MARCUS.
FAR TOO SUBTLE FOR ME, MARY.
YOU GONNA MAKE STUDY GROUP TONIGHT?
JAYLA SAYS SHE'S GOT THE FIELD HOMEWORK COVERED, WE'RE GOING TO SOME FAIR AT GOLDEN GATE PARK--
WHOA... MATE.
ISN'T THAT...

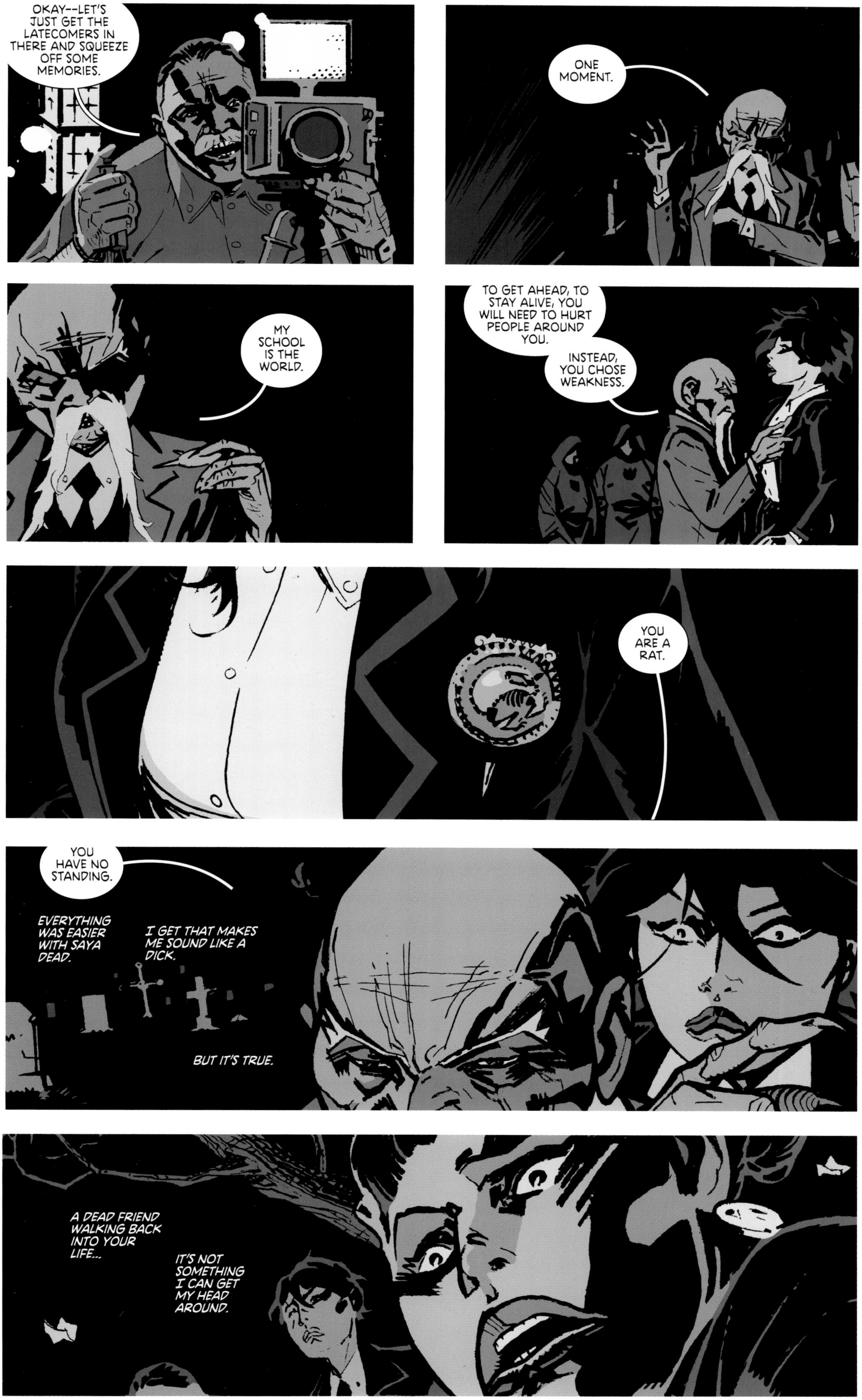
OKAY--LET'S JUST GET THE LATECOMERS IN THERE AND SQUEEZE OFF SOME MEMORIES.
ONE MOMENT.
MY SCHOOL IS THE WORLD.
TO GET AHEAD, TO STAY ALIVE, YOU WILL NEED TO HURT PEOPLE AROUND YOU.
INSTEAD, YOU CHOSE WEAKNESS.
YOU ARE A RAT.
YOU HAVE NO STANDING.
EVERYTHING WAS EASIER WITH SAYA DEAD.
I GET THAT MAKES ME SOUND LIKE A DICK.
BUT IT'S TRUE.
A DEAD FRIEND WALKING BACK INTO YOUR LIFE...
IT'S NOT SOMETHING I CAN GET MY HEAD AROUND.

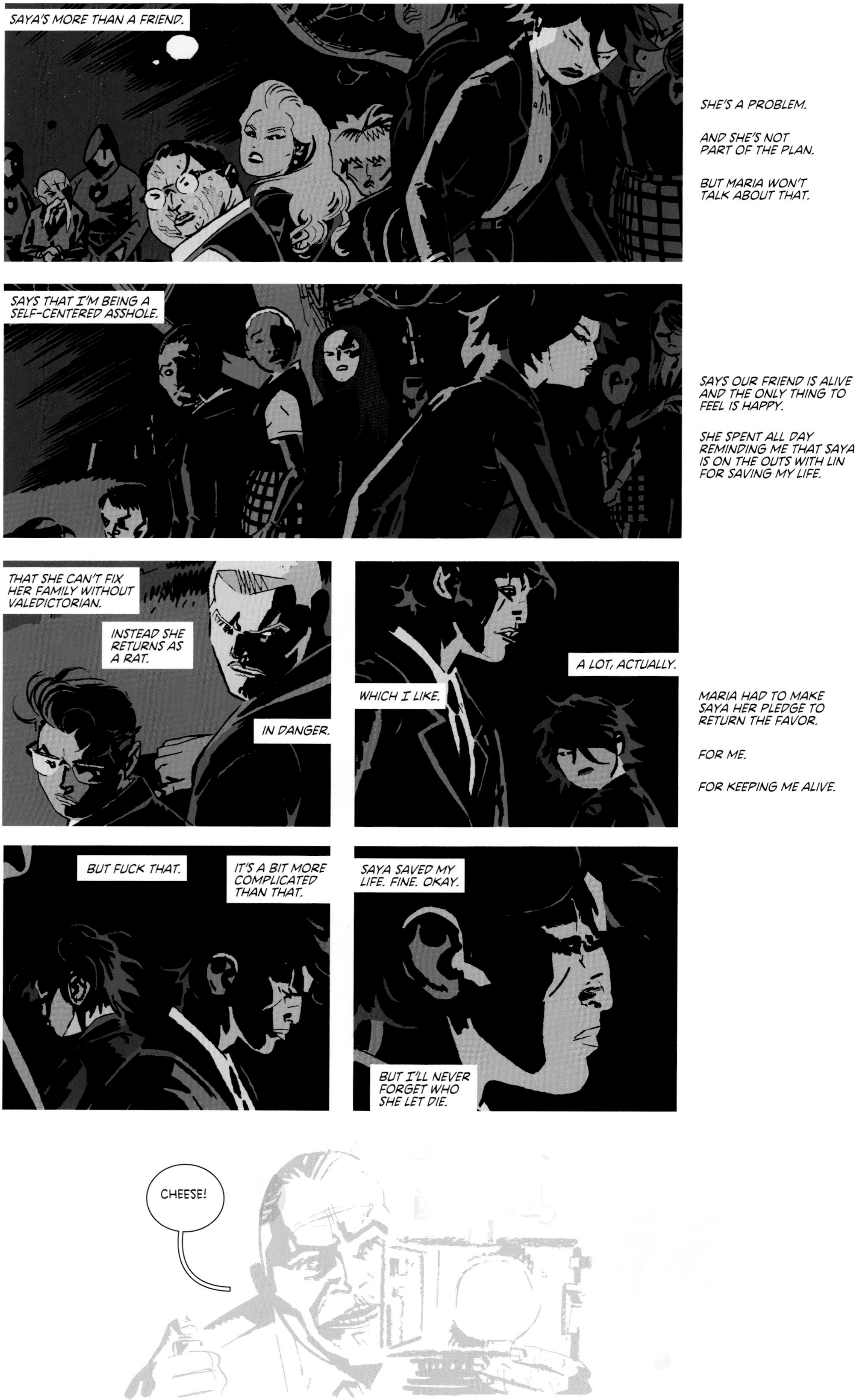
SAYA'S MORE THAN A FRIEND.
SHE'S A PROBLEM.
AND SHE'S NOT PART OF THE PLAN.
BUT MARIA WON'T TALK ABOUT THAT.
SAYS THAT I'M BEING A SELF-CENTERED ASSHOLE.
SAYS OUR FRIEND IS ALIVE AND THE ONLY THING TO FEEL IS HAPPY.
SHE SPENT ALL DAY REMINDING ME THAT SAYA IS ON THE OUTS WITH LIN FOR SAVING MY LIFE.
THAT SHE CAN'T FIX HER FAMILY WITHOUT VALEDICTORIAN.
INSTEAD SHE RETURNS AS A RAT.
IN DANGER.
WHICH I LIKE.
A LOT, ACTUALLY.
MARIA HAD TO MAKE SAYA HER PLEDGE TO RETURN THE FAVOR.
FOR ME.
FOR KEEPING ME ALIVE.
BUT FUCK THAT.
IT'S A BIT MORE COMPLICATED THAN THAT.
SAYA SAVED MY LIFE. FINE. OKAY.
BUT I'LL NEVER FORGET WHO SHE LET DIE.
CHEESE!

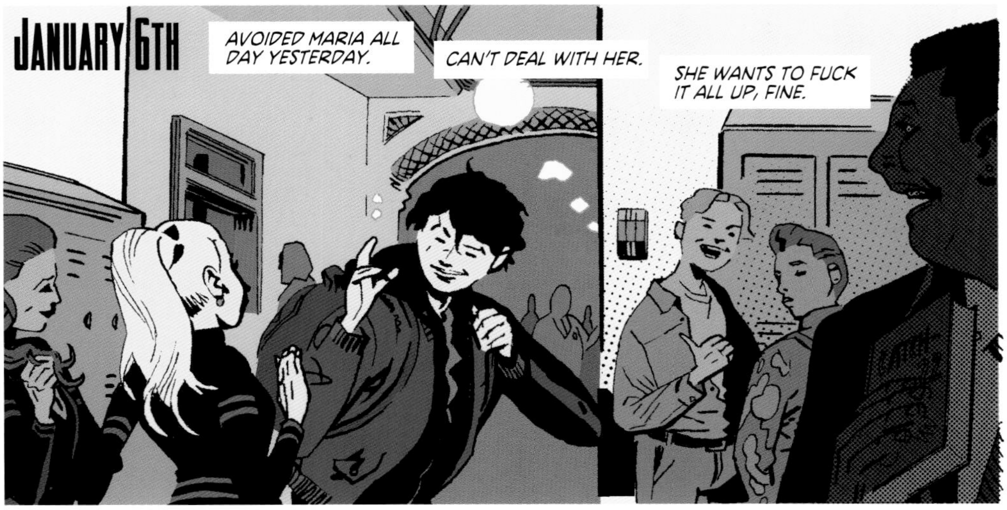
JANUARY 6TH
AVOIDED MARIA ALL DAY YESTERDAY.
CAN'T DEAL WITH HER.
SHE WANTS TO FUCK IT ALL UP, FINE.

DON'T EVEN KNOW WHAT I'M FIGHTING FOR.

AND ALL THE CUTS AND BRUISES JUST ADD UP TO ONE BIG FESTERING WOUND. NOTHING I DID HELPED.

TOLD MYSELF IT'S BECAUSE WHAT I NEED DOESN'T EXIST IN THIS WORLD.

BUT I'M STARTING TO WONDER, WHAT IF IT'S MY OWN DEPRESSION THAT MAKES IT IMPOSSIBLE TO FIND? THAT MAKES IT ALL THE WORSE, BECAUSE IF THAT'S TRUE...

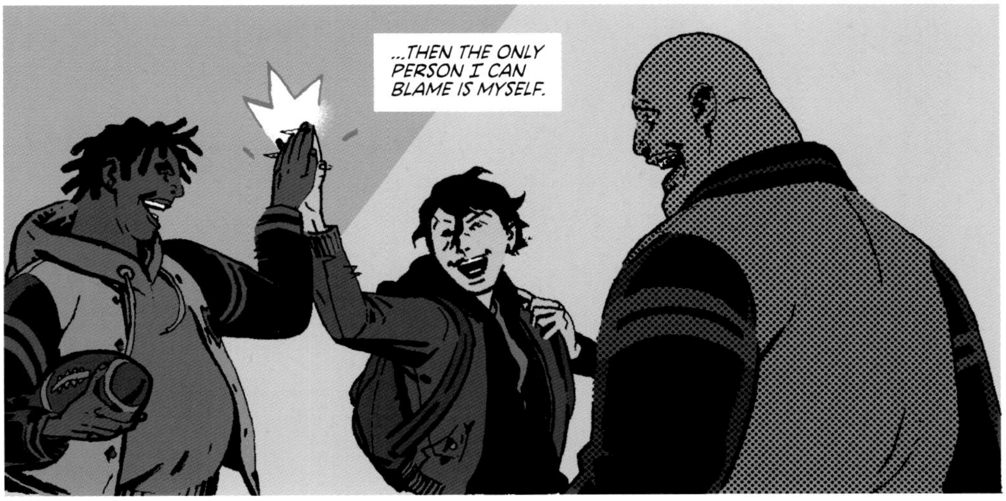
...THEN THE ONLY PERSON I CAN BLAME IS MYSELF.

IF I'D TRIED A BIT HARDER TO BE NORMAL, STOPPED IMAGINING THAT EVERYONE ELSE HAS IT WRONG, WHERE WOULD I BE?

THE NEGATIVE FILTERS I CHOSE MADE IT IMPOSSIBLE FOR ME TO SEE ANY OF THE POSITIVE THINGS.

BUT WHEN WE GOT BACK, WHEN I PRETENDED TO TURN THEM OFF...

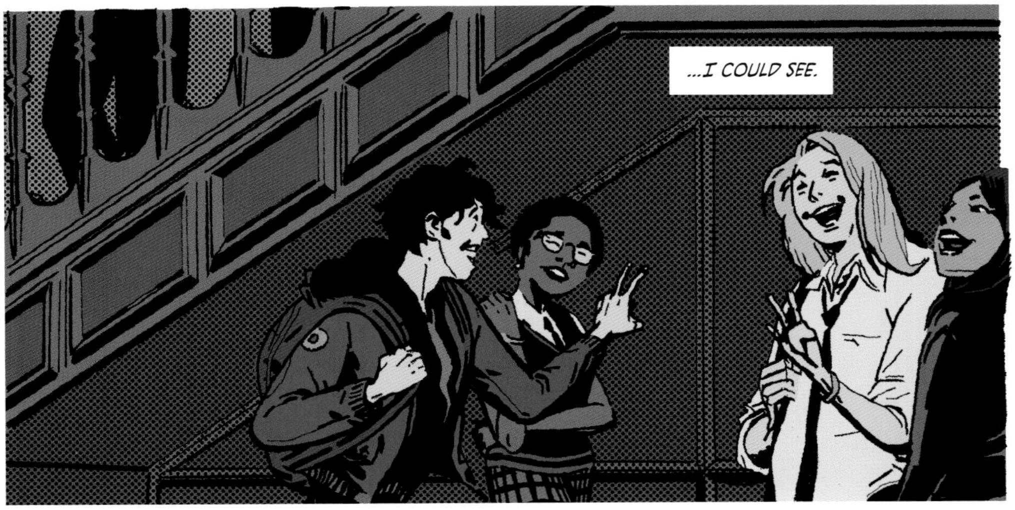
...I COULD SEE.

SEE THAT I'M DRAWN TO THE SIREN'S SONG BLARING FROM THE DISCOTHEQUE OF FAILURE AND REJECTION BECAUSE THEY REAFFIRM HOW I SEE MYSELF. A SELF-FULFILLING PROPHECY.

HOW DID I EVER GET THE IDEA THAT PEOPLE EARN WHAT THEY GET IN THIS WORLD ANYWAY?

THAT A FAIR AND JUST SYSTEM EXISTS TO REWARD THE INDUSTRIOUS?

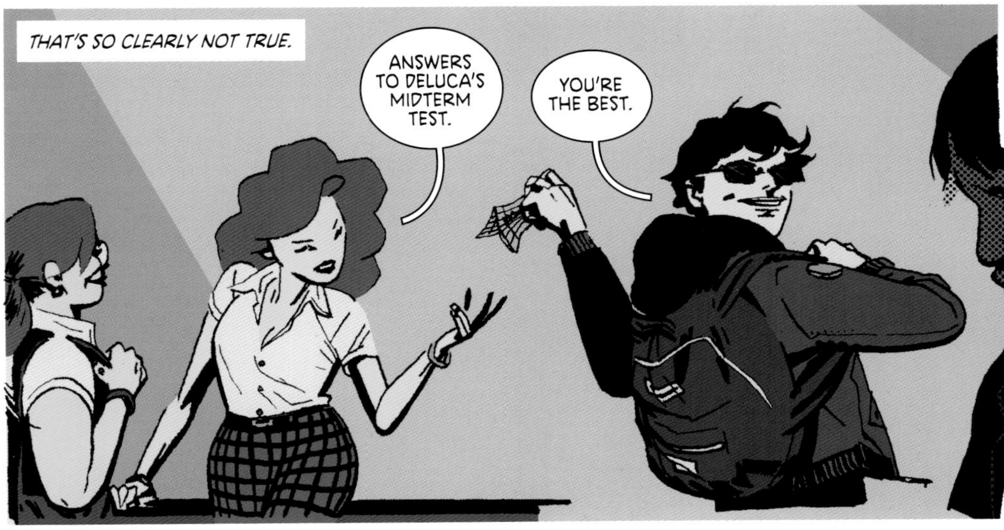
THAT'S SO CLEARLY NOT TRUE.
ANSWERS TO DELUCA'S MIDTERM TEST.
YOU'RE THE BEST.

POLITICKING AND PANDERING AND SMILING AND HANDSHAKING AND CREATING HUNDREDS OF HOLLOW ALLIES IS THE TRUE ROAD TO SUCCESS.

THEY THINK I CAN DO SOMETHING FOR THEM NOW, SO I'M WORTH BEFRIENDING.

AND MAYBE THAT'S FINE.

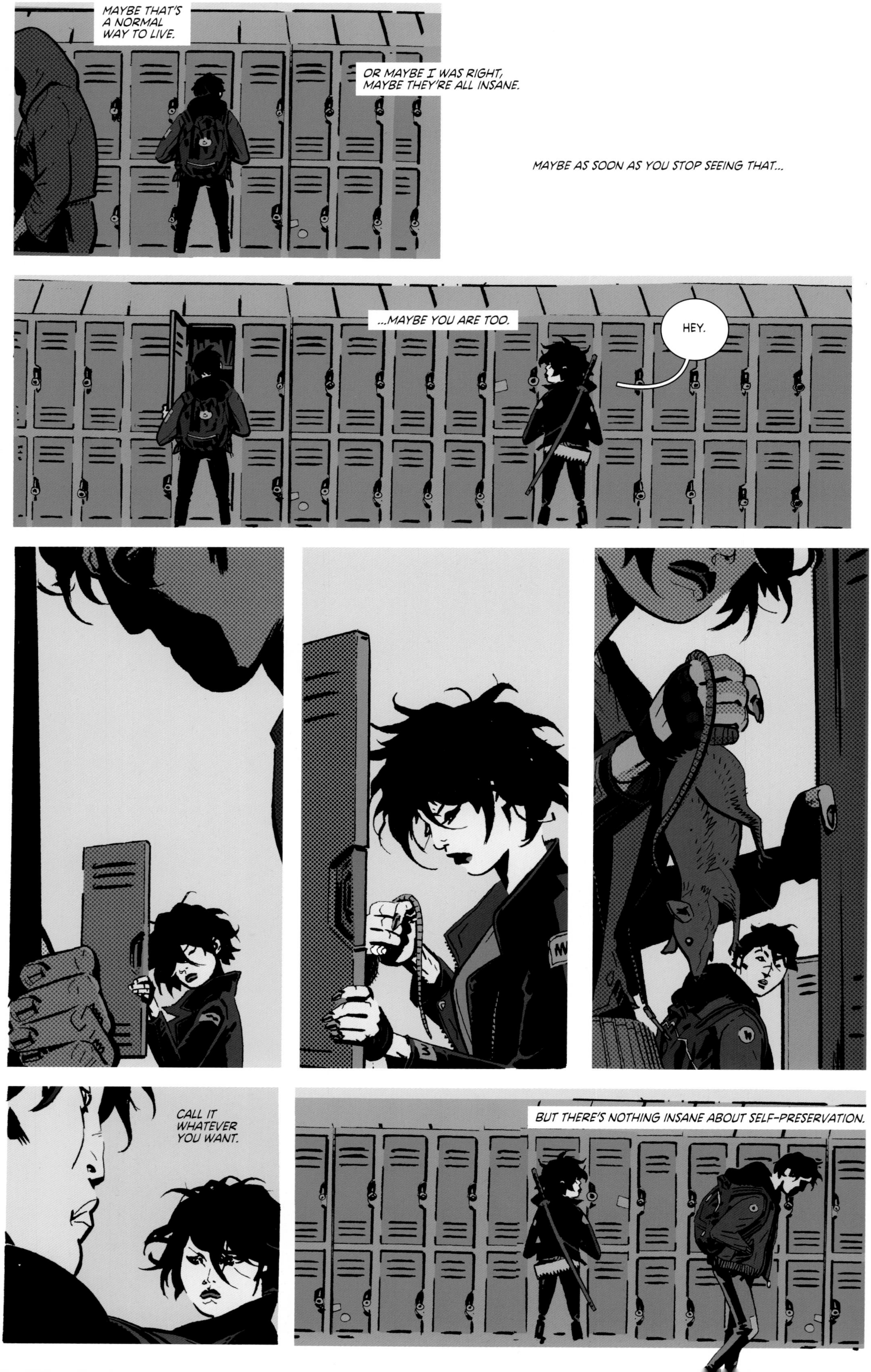
MAYBE THAT'S A NORMAL WAY TO LIVE.
OR MAYBE I WAS RIGHT, MAYBE THEY'RE ALL INSANE.
MAYBE AS SOON AS YOU STOP SEEING THAT...
...MAYBE YOU ARE TOO.
HEY.
CALL IT WHATEVER YOU WANT.
BUT THERE'S NOTHING INSANE ABOUT SELF-PRESERVATION.

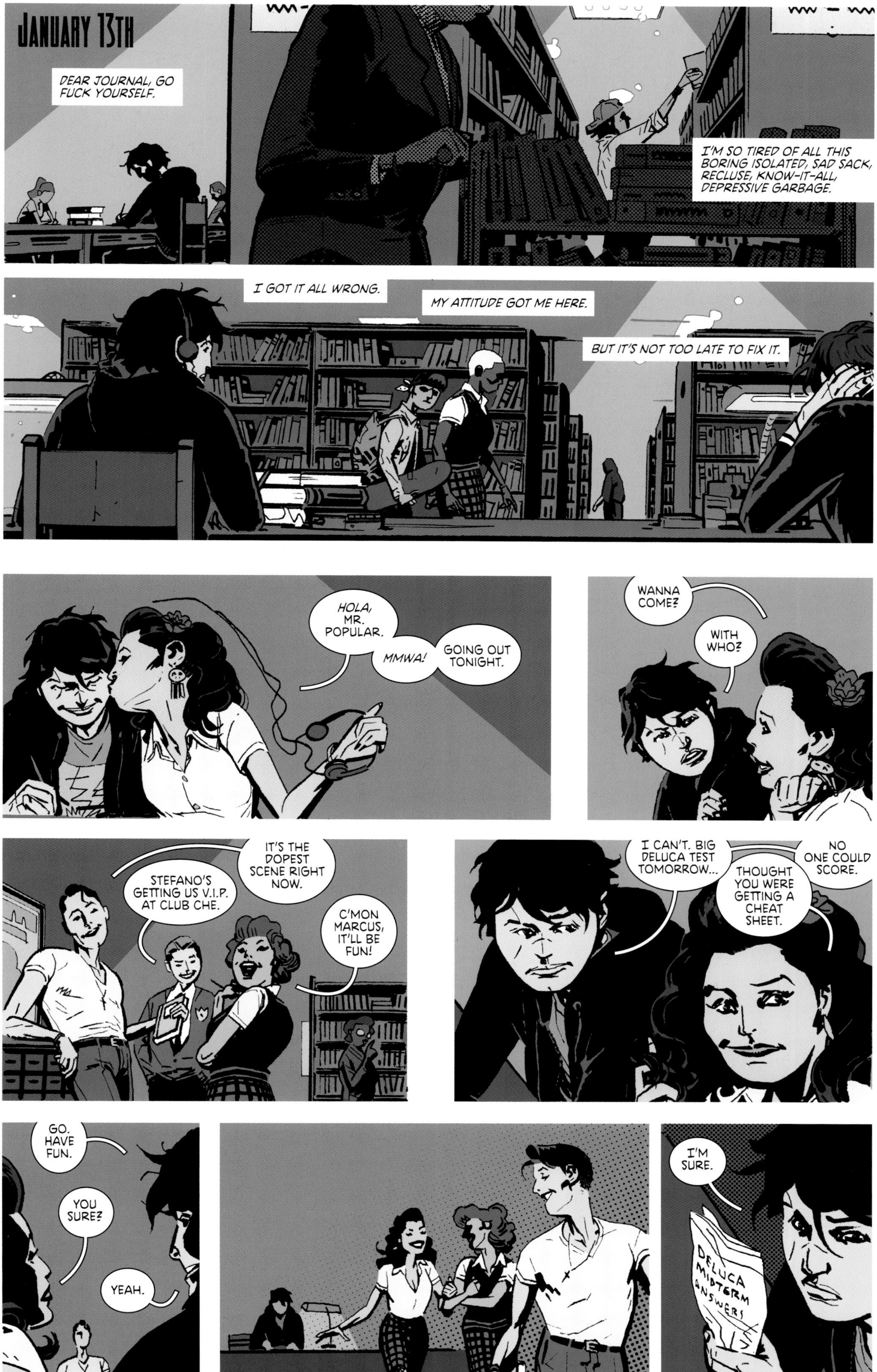
JANUARY 13TH
DEAR JOURNAL, GO FUCK YOURSELF.
I'M SO TIRED OF ALL THIS BORING ISOLATED, SAD SACK, RECLUSE, KNOW-IT-ALL, DEPRESSIVE GARBAGE.
I GOT IT ALL WRONG.
MY ATTITUDE GOT ME HERE.
BUT IT'S NOT TOO LATE TO FIX IT.
HOLA, MR. POPULAR.
MMWA!
GOING OUT TONIGHT.
WANNA COME?
WITH WHO?
IT'S THE DOPEST SCENE RIGHT NOW.
STEFANO'S GETTING US V.I.P. AT CLUB CHE.
C'MON MARCUS, IT'LL BE FUN!
I CAN'T. BIG DELUCA TEST TOMORROW...
NO ONE COULD SCORE.
THOUGHT YOU WERE GETTING A CHEAT SHEET.
GO. HAVE FUN.
YOU SURE?
YEAH.
I'M SURE.
DELUCA MIDTERM ANSWERS

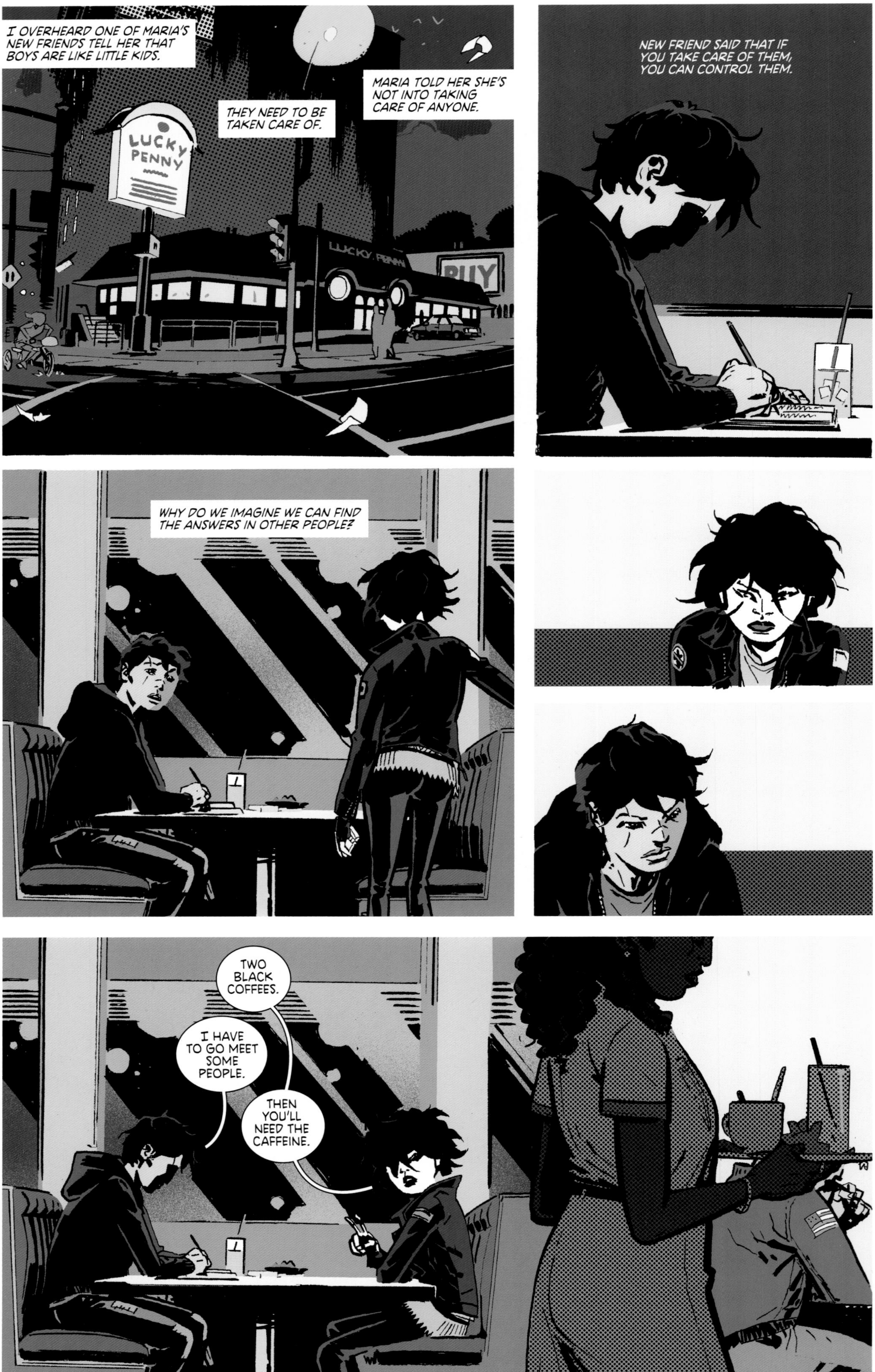
I OVERHEARD ONE OF MARIA'S NEW FRIENDS TELL HER THAT BOYS ARE LIKE LITTLE KIDS.
LUCKY PENNY
THEY NEED TO BE TAKEN CARE OF.
MARIA TOLD HER SHE'S NOT INTO TAKING CARE OF ANYONE.
BUY
NEW FRIEND SAID THAT IF YOU TAKE CARE OF THEM, YOU CAN CONTROL THEM.
WHY DO WE IMAGINE WE CAN FIND THE ANSWERS IN OTHER PEOPLE?
TWO BLACK COFFEES.
I HAVE TO GO MEET SOME PEOPLE.
THEN YOU'LL NEED THE CAFFEINE.

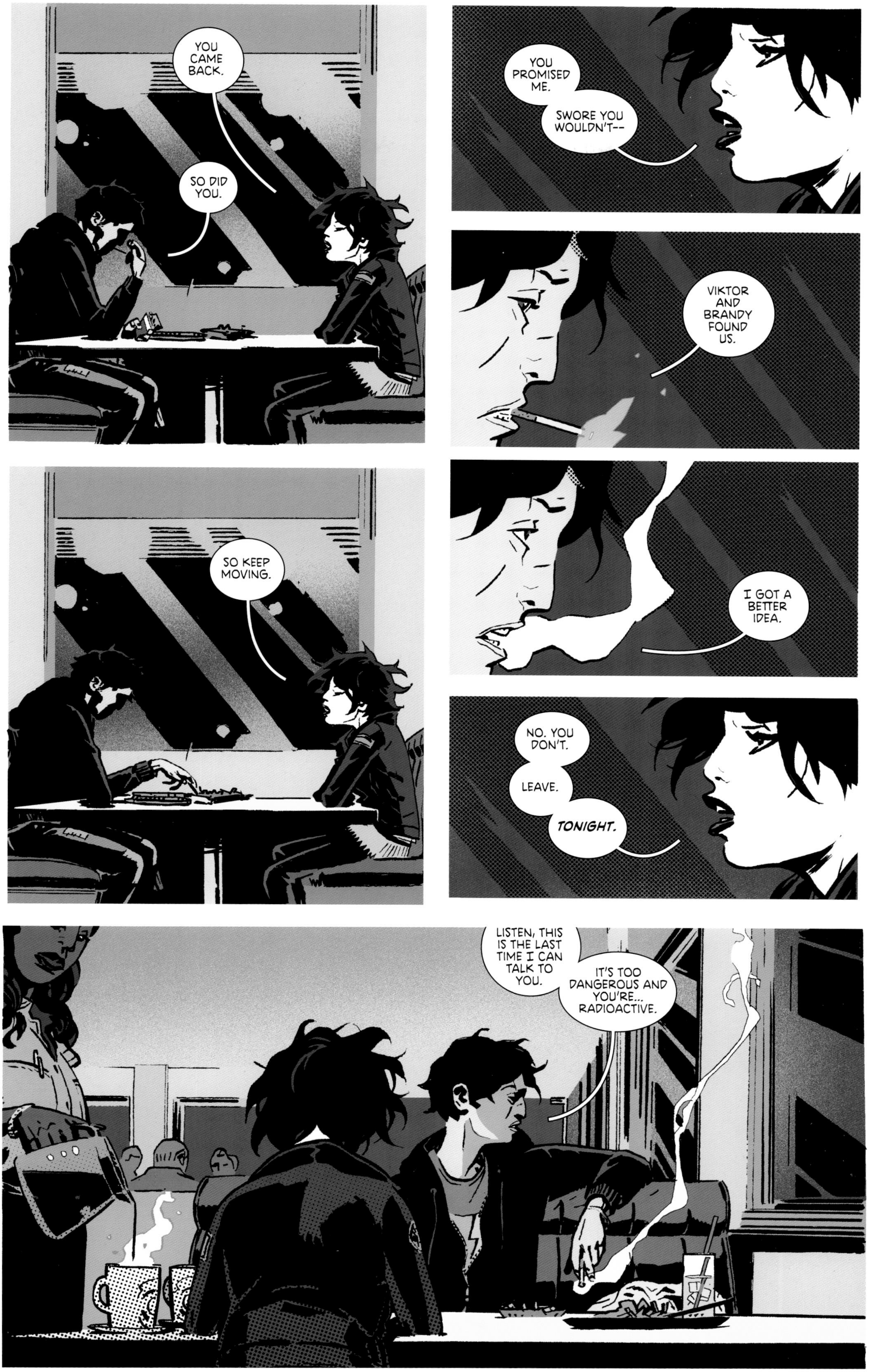
YOU CAME BACK.
SO DID YOU.
YOU PROMISED ME.
SWORE YOU WOULDN'T--
VIKTOR AND BRANDY FOUND US.
SO KEEP MOVING.
I GOT A BETTER IDEA.
NO. YOU DON'T.
LEAVE.
TONIGHT.
LISTEN, THIS IS THE LAST TIME I CAN TALK TO YOU.
IT'S TOO DANGEROUS AND YOU'RE... RADIOACTIVE.

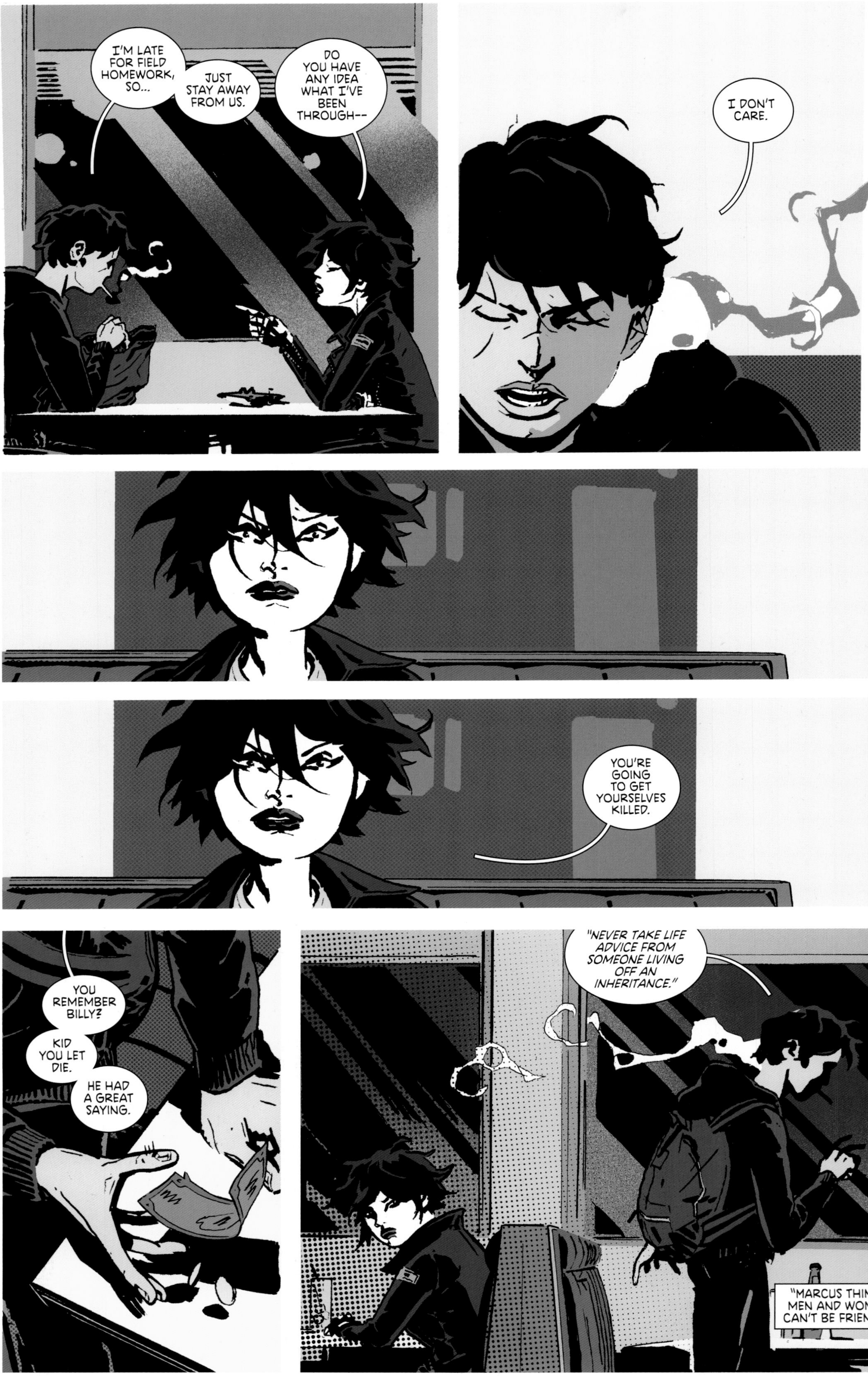
I'M LATE FOR FIELD HOMEWORK, SO...
JUST STAY AWAY FROM US.
DO YOU HAVE ANY IDEA WHAT I'VE BEEN THROUGH--
I DON'T CARE.
YOU'RE GOING TO GET YOURSELVES KILLED.
YOU REMEMBER BILLY?
KID YOU LET DIE.
HE HAD A GREAT SAYING.
"NEVER TAKE LIFE ADVICE FROM SOMEONE LIVING OFF AN INHERITANCE."
"MARCUS THINKS MEN AND WOMEN CAN'T BE FRIENDS."

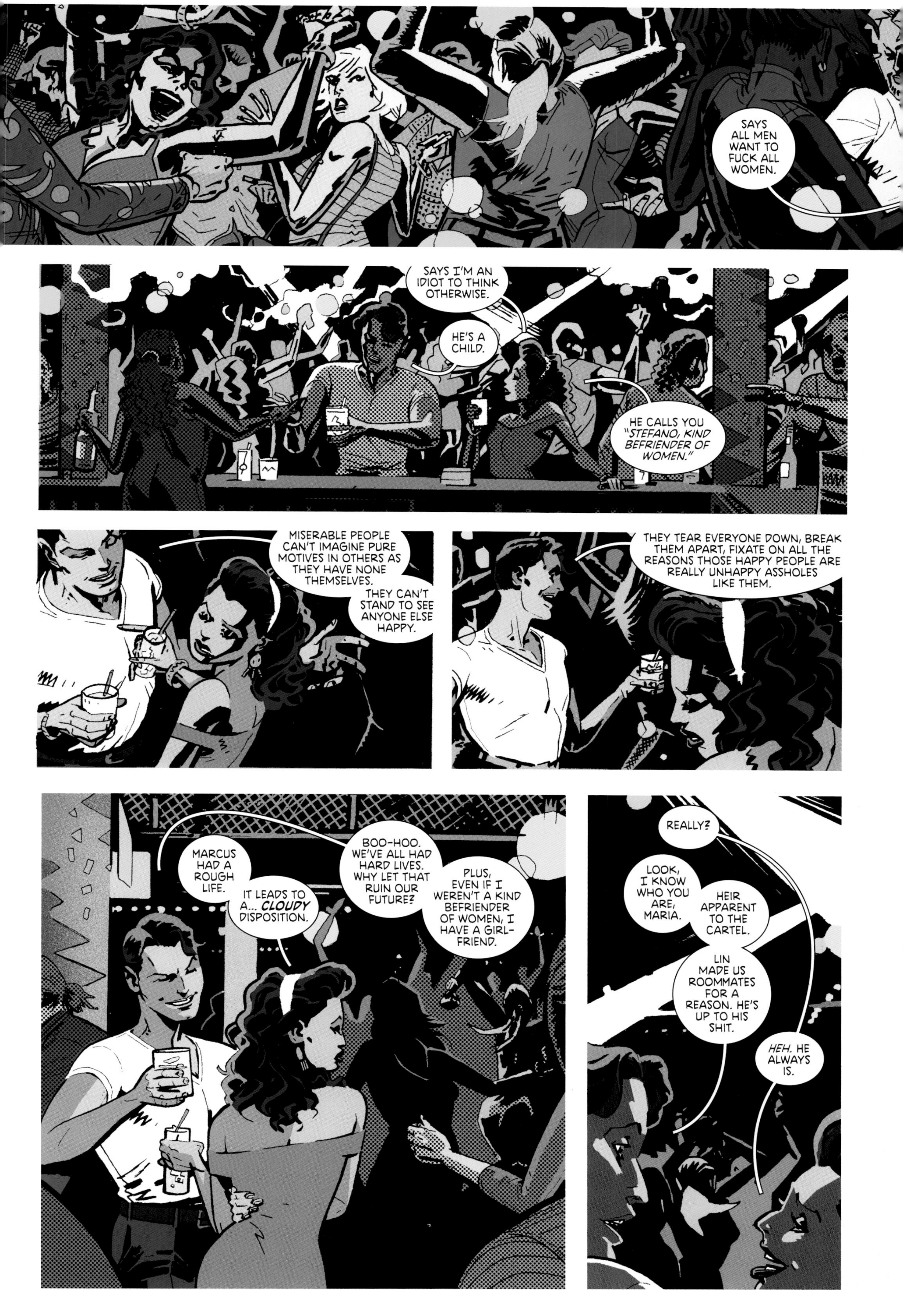
SAYS ALL MEN WANT TO FUCK ALL WOMEN.
SAYS I'M AN IDIOT TO THINK OTHERWISE.
HE'S A CHILD.
HE CALLS YOU "STEFANO, KIND BEFRIENDER OF WOMEN."
MISERABLE PEOPLE CAN'T IMAGINE PURE MOTIVES IN OTHERS AS THEY HAVE NONE THEMSELVES.
THEY CAN'T STAND TO SEE ANYONE ELSE HAPPY.
THEY TEAR EVERYONE DOWN, BREAK THEM APART, FIXATE ON ALL THE REASONS THOSE HAPPY PEOPLE ARE REALLY UNHAPPY ASSHOLES LIKE THEM.
MARCUS HAD A ROUGH LIFE.
IT LEADS TO A... CLOUDY DISPOSITION.
BOO-HOO. WE'VE ALL HAD HARD LIVES. WHY LET THAT RUIN OUR FUTURE?
PLUS, EVEN IF I WEREN'T A KIND BEFRIENDER OF WOMEN, I HAVE A GIRL-FRIEND.
REALLY?
LOOK, I KNOW WHO YOU ARE, MARIA.
HEIR APPARENT TO THE CARTEL.
LIN MADE US ROOMMATES FOR A REASON. HE'S UP TO HIS SHIT.
HEH. HE ALWAYS IS.

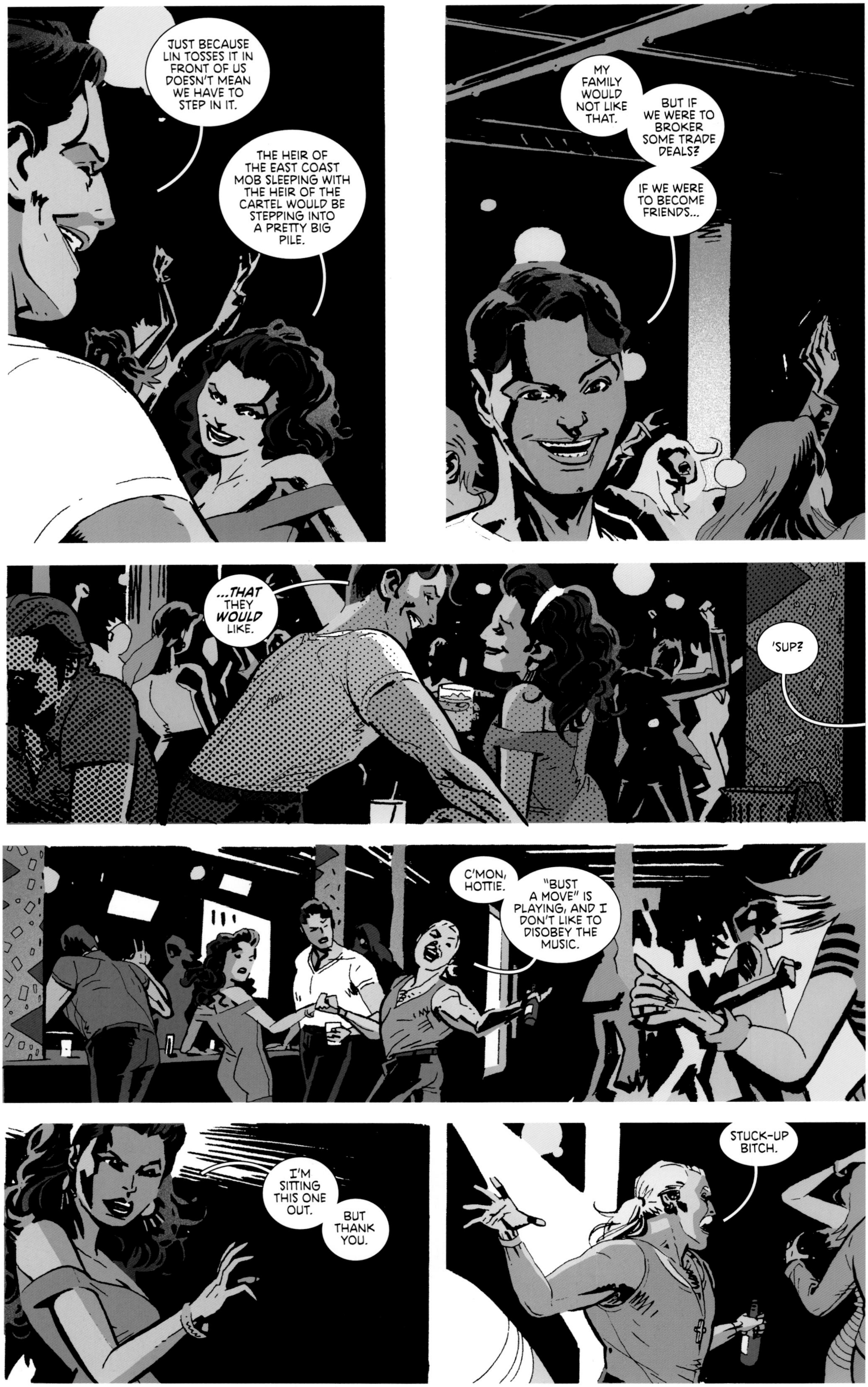
JUST BECAUSE LIN TOSSES IT IN FRONT OF US DOESN'T MEAN WE HAVE TO STEP IN IT.
THE HEIR OF THE EAST COAST MOB SLEEPING WITH THE HEIR OF THE CARTEL WOULD BE STEPPING INTO A PRETTY BIG PILE.
MY FAMILY WOULD NOT LIKE THAT.
BUT IF WE WERE TO BROKER SOME TRADE DEALS?
IF WE WERE TO BECOME FRIENDS...
...THAT THEY WOULD LIKE.
'SUP?
C'MON, HOTTIE.
"BUST A MOVE" IS PLAYING, AND I DON'T LIKE TO DISOBEY THE MUSIC.
I'M SITTING THIS ONE OUT.
BUT THANK YOU.
STUCK-UP BITCH.

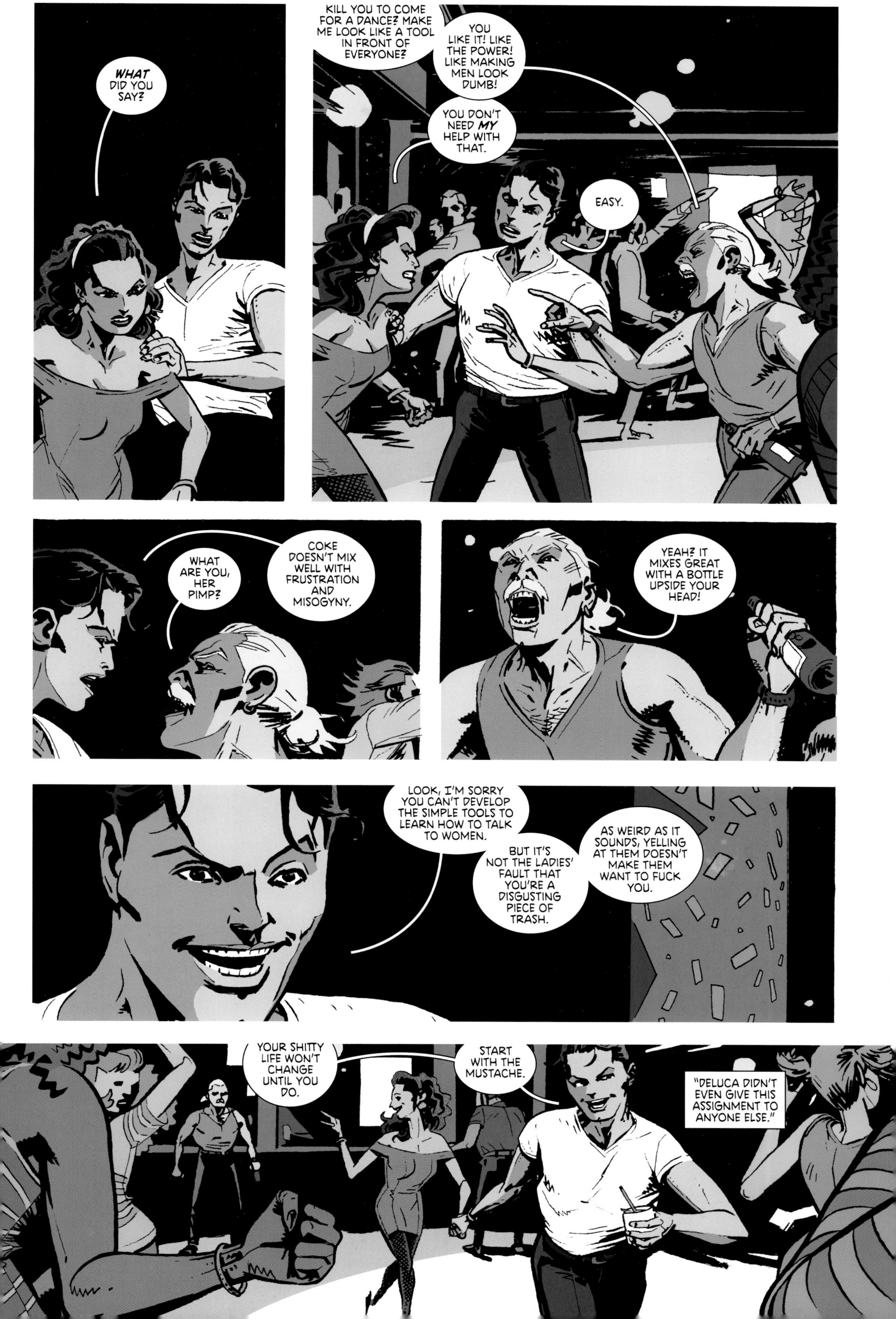
WHAT DID YOU SAY?
KILL YOU TO COME FOR A DANCE? MAKE ME LOOK LIKE A TOOL IN FRONT OF EVERYONE?
YOU LIKE IT! LIKE THE POWER! LIKE MAKING MEN LOOK DUMB!
YOU DON'T NEED MY HELP WITH THAT.
EASY.
WHAT ARE YOU, HER PIMP?
COKE DOESN'T MIX WELL WITH FRUSTRATION AND MISOGYNY.
YEAH? IT MIXES GREAT WITH A BOTTLE UPSIDE YOUR HEAD!
LOOK, I'M SORRY YOU CAN'T DEVELOP THE SIMPLE TOOLS TO LEARN HOW TO TALK TO WOMEN.
BUT IT'S NOT THE LADIES' FAULT THAT YOU'RE A DISGUSTING PIECE OF TRASH.
AS WEIRD AS IT SOUNDS, YELLING AT THEM DOESN'T MAKE THEM WANT TO FUCK YOU.
YOUR SHITTY LIFE WON'T CHANGE UNTIL YOU DO.
START WITH THE MUSTACHE.
"DELUCA DIDN'T EVEN GIVE THIS ASSIGNMENT TO ANYONE ELSE."

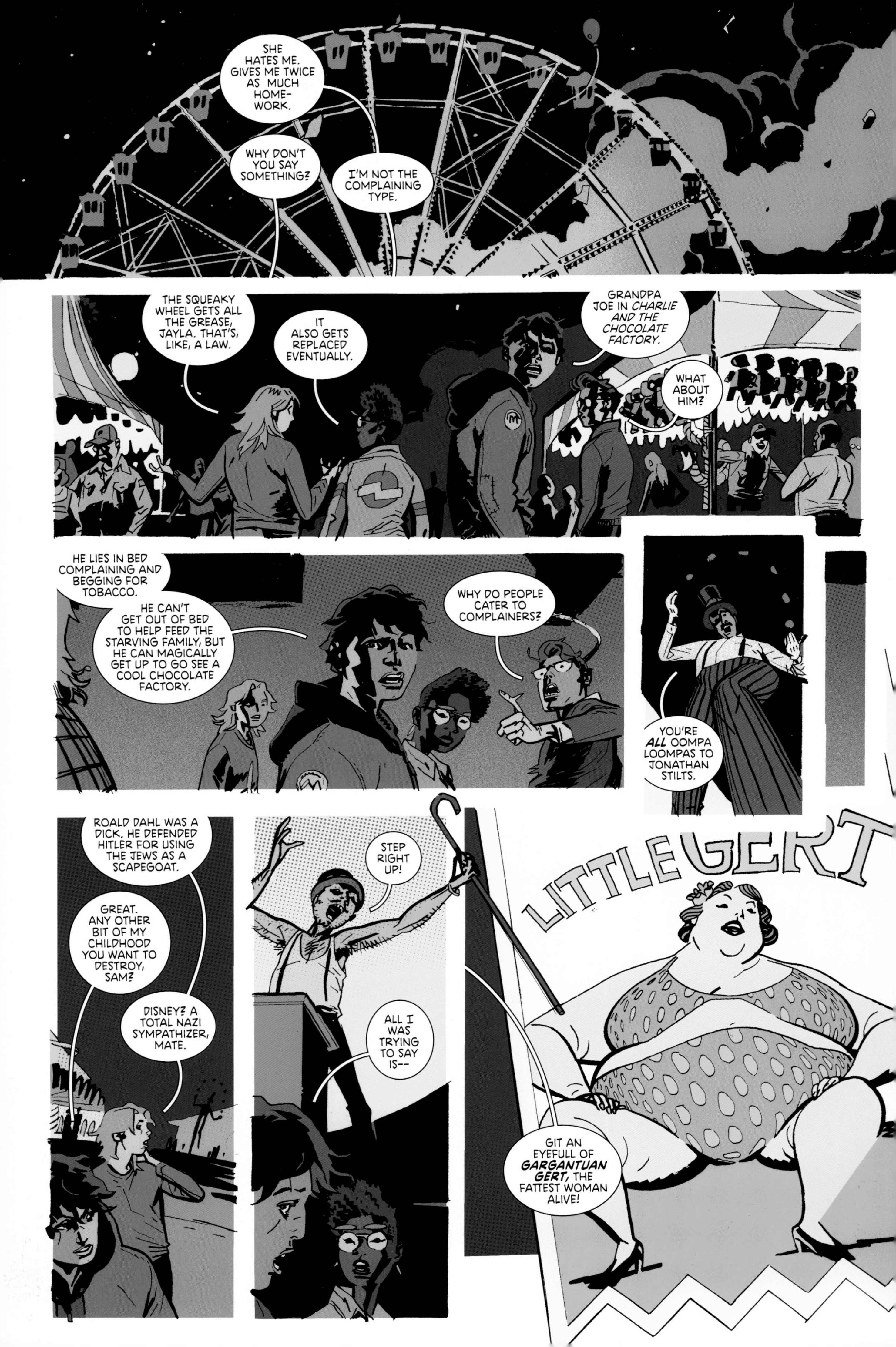
SHE HATES ME. GIVES ME TWICE AS MUCH HOME-WORK.
WHY DON'T YOU SAY SOMETHING?
I'M NOT THE COMPLAINING TYPE.
THE SQUEAKY WHEEL GETS ALL THE GREASE, JAYLA. THAT'S, LIKE, A LAW.
IT ALSO GETS REPLACED EVENTUALLY.
GRANDPA JOE IN *CHARLIE AND THE CHOCOLATE FACTORY.*
WHAT ABOUT HIM?
HE LIES IN BED COMPLAINING AND BEGGING FOR TOBACCO.
HE CAN'T GET OUT OF BED TO HELP FEED THE STARVING FAMILY, BUT HE CAN MAGICALLY GET UP TO GO SEE A COOL CHOCOLATE FACTORY.
WHY DO PEOPLE CATER TO COMPLAINERS?
YOU'RE ***ALL*** OOMPA LOOMPAS TO JONATHAN STILTS.
ROALD DAHL WAS A DICK. HE DEFENDED HITLER FOR USING THE JEWS AS A SCAPEGOAT.
GREAT. ANY OTHER BIT OF MY CHILDHOOD YOU WANT TO DESTROY, SAM?
DISNEY? A TOTAL NAZI SYMPATHIZER, MATE.
STEP RIGHT UP!
ALL I WAS TRYING TO SAY IS--
LITTLE GERT
GIT AN EYEFULL OF ***GARGANTUAN GERT,*** THE FATTEST WOMAN ALIVE!

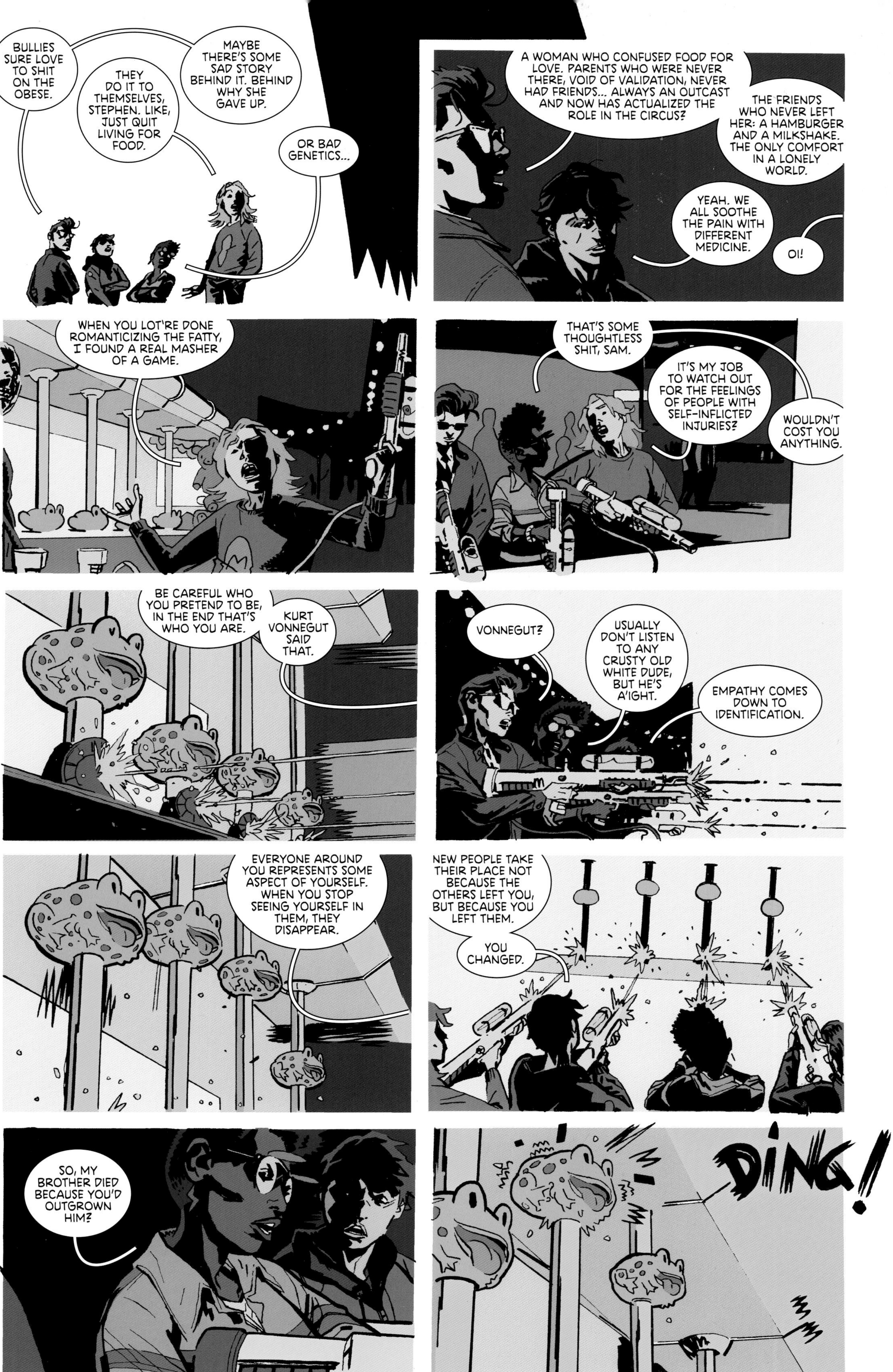
BULLIES SURE LOVE TO SHIT ON THE OBESE.
THEY DO IT TO THEMSELVES, STEPHEN. LIKE, JUST QUIT LIVING FOR FOOD.
MAYBE THERE'S SOME SAD STORY BEHIND IT. BEHIND WHY SHE GAVE UP.
OR BAD GENETICS...
A WOMAN WHO CONFUSED FOOD FOR LOVE. PARENTS WHO WERE NEVER THERE, VOID OF VALIDATION, NEVER HAD FRIENDS... ALWAYS AN OUTCAST AND NOW HAS ACTUALIZED THE ROLE IN THE CIRCUS?
THE FRIENDS WHO NEVER LEFT HER: A HAMBURGER AND A MILKSHAKE. THE ONLY COMFORT IN A LONELY WORLD.
YEAH. WE ALL SOOTHE THE PAIN WITH DIFFERENT MEDICINE.
OI!
WHEN YOU LOT'RE DONE ROMANTICIZING THE FATTY, I FOUND A REAL MASHER OF A GAME.
THAT'S SOME THOUGHTLESS SHIT, SAM.
IT'S MY JOB TO WATCH OUT FOR THE FEELINGS OF PEOPLE WITH SELF-INFLICTED INJURIES?
WOULDN'T COST YOU ANYTHING.
BE CAREFUL WHO YOU PRETEND TO BE, IN THE END THAT'S WHO YOU ARE.
KURT VONNEGUT SAID THAT.
VONNEGUT?
USUALLY DON'T LISTEN TO ANY CRUSTY OLD WHITE DUDE, BUT HE'S A'IGHT.
EMPATHY COMES DOWN TO IDENTIFICATION.
EVERYONE AROUND YOU REPRESENTS SOME ASPECT OF YOURSELF. WHEN YOU STOP SEEING YOURSELF IN THEM, THEY DISAPPEAR.
NEW PEOPLE TAKE THEIR PLACE NOT BECAUSE THE OTHERS LEFT YOU, BUT BECAUSE YOU LEFT THEM.
YOU CHANGED.
SO, MY BROTHER DIED BECAUSE YOU'D OUTGROWN HIM?
DING!

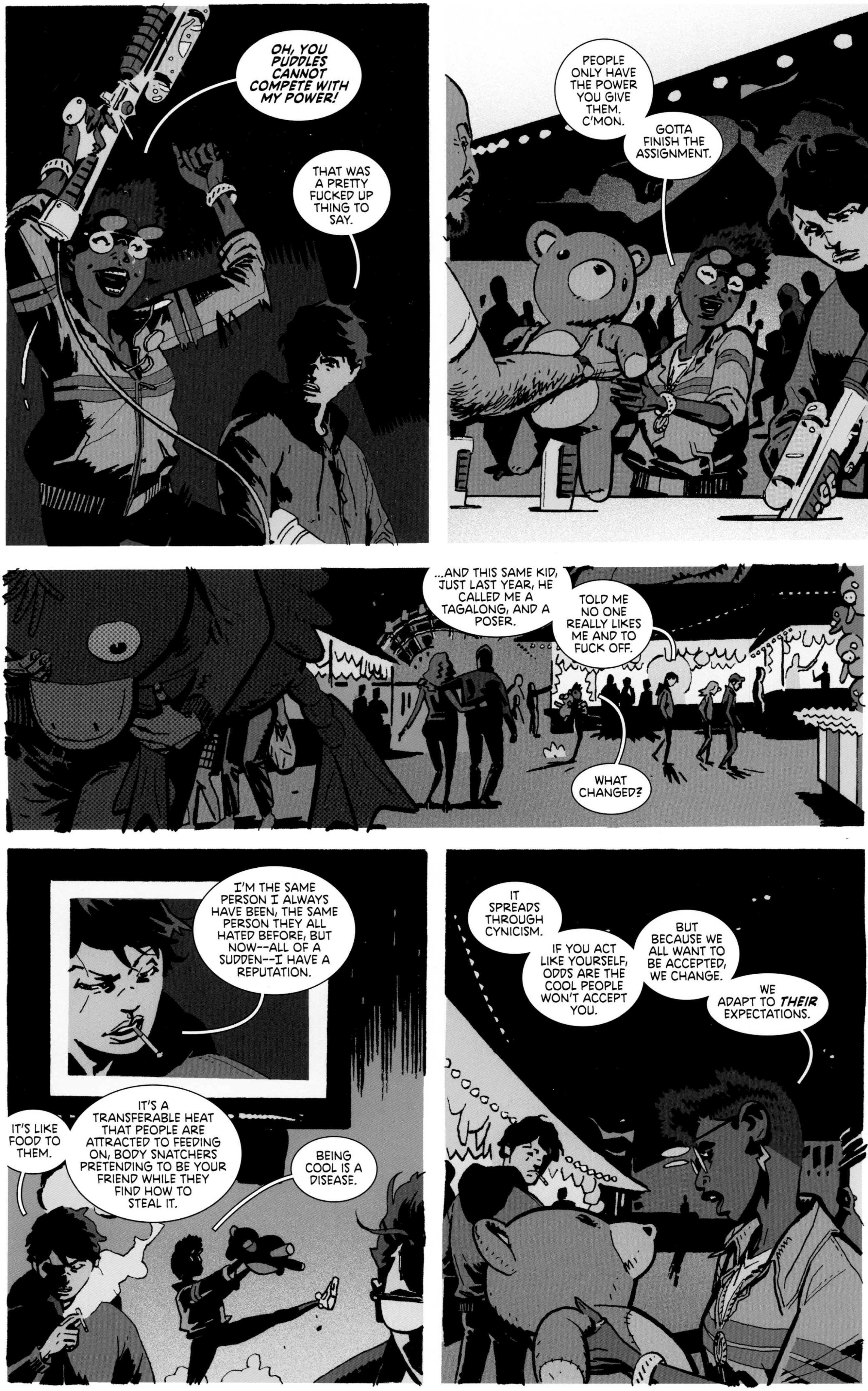
OH, YOU PUDDLES CANNOT COMPETE WITH MY POWER!
THAT WAS A PRETTY FUCKED UP THING TO SAY.
PEOPLE ONLY HAVE THE POWER YOU GIVE THEM. C'MON.
GOTTA FINISH THE ASSIGNMENT.
...AND THIS SAME KID, JUST LAST YEAR, HE CALLED ME A TAGALONG, AND A POSER.
TOLD ME NO ONE REALLY LIKES ME AND TO FUCK OFF.
WHAT CHANGED?
I'M THE SAME PERSON I ALWAYS HAVE BEEN, THE SAME PERSON THEY ALL HATED BEFORE, BUT NOW--ALL OF A SUDDEN--I HAVE A REPUTATION.
IT'S LIKE FOOD TO THEM.
IT'S A TRANSFERABLE HEAT THAT PEOPLE ARE ATTRACTED TO FEEDING ON, BODY SNATCHERS PRETENDING TO BE YOUR FRIEND WHILE THEY FIND HOW TO STEAL IT.
BEING COOL IS A DISEASE.
IT SPREADS THROUGH CYNICISM.
IF YOU ACT LIKE YOURSELF, ODDS ARE THE COOL PEOPLE WON'T ACCEPT YOU.
BUT BECAUSE WE ALL WANT TO BE ACCEPTED, WE CHANGE.
WE ADAPT TO THEIR EXPECTATIONS.

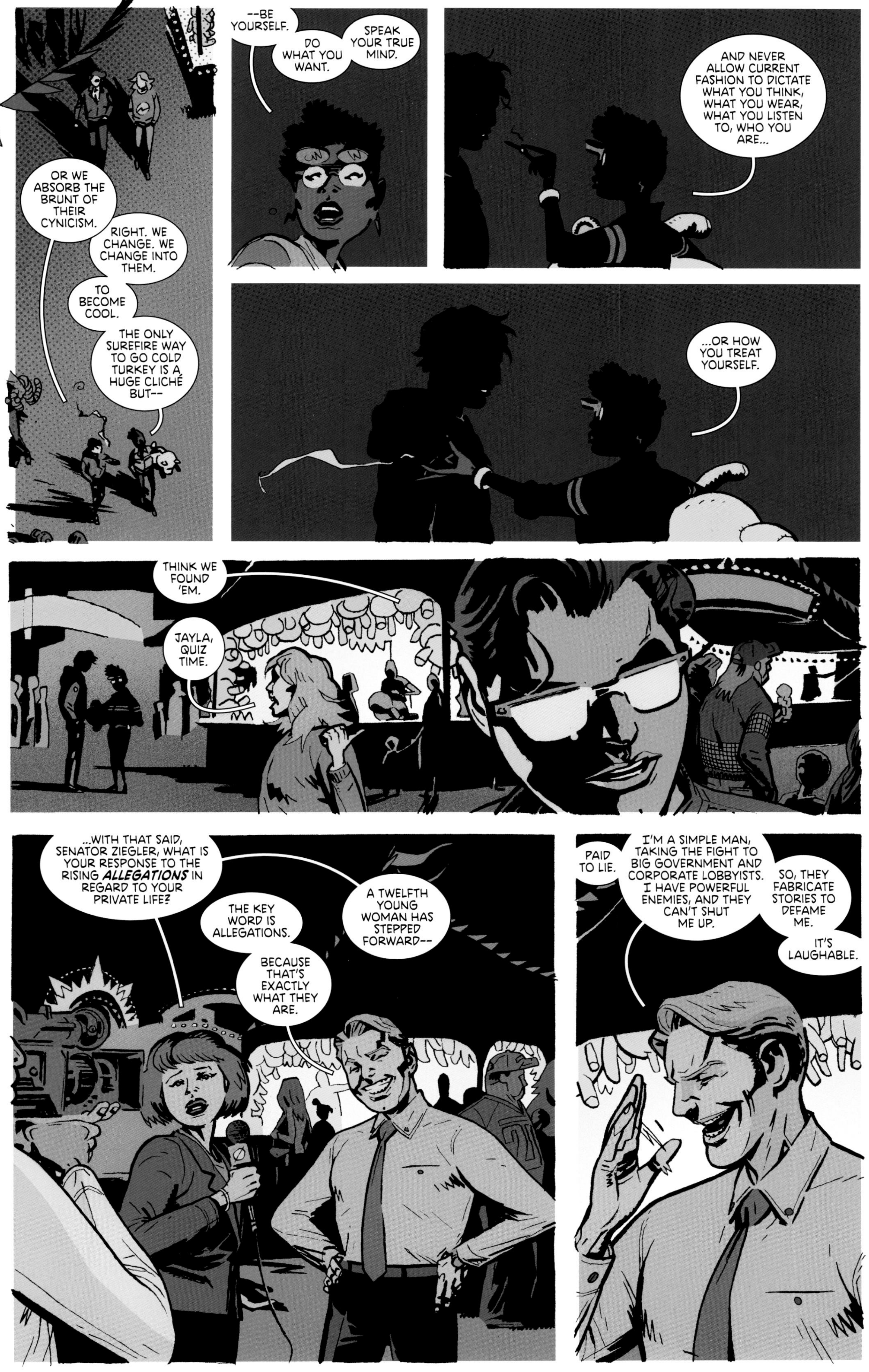
OR WE ABSORB THE BRUNT OF THEIR CYNICISM.
RIGHT. WE CHANGE. WE CHANGE INTO THEM.
TO BECOME COOL.
THE ONLY SUREFIRE WAY TO GO COLD TURKEY IS A HUGE CLICHÉ BUT--
--BE YOURSELF.
DO WHAT YOU WANT.
SPEAK YOUR TRUE MIND.
AND NEVER ALLOW CURRENT FASHION TO DICTATE WHAT YOU THINK, WHAT YOU WEAR, WHAT YOU LISTEN TO, WHO YOU ARE...
...OR HOW YOU TREAT YOURSELF.
THINK WE FOUND 'EM.
JAYLA, QUIZ TIME.
...WITH THAT SAID, SENATOR ZIEGLER, WHAT IS YOUR RESPONSE TO THE RISING ALLEGATIONS IN REGARD TO YOUR PRIVATE LIFE?
THE KEY WORD IS ALLEGATIONS.
BECAUSE THAT'S EXACTLY WHAT THEY ARE.
A TWELFTH YOUNG WOMAN HAS STEPPED FORWARD--
PAID TO LIE.
I'M A SIMPLE MAN, TAKING THE FIGHT TO BIG GOVERNMENT AND CORPORATE LOBBYISTS. I HAVE POWERFUL ENEMIES, AND THEY CAN'T SHUT ME UP.
SO, THEY FABRICATE STORIES TO DEFAME ME.
IT'S LAUGHABLE.

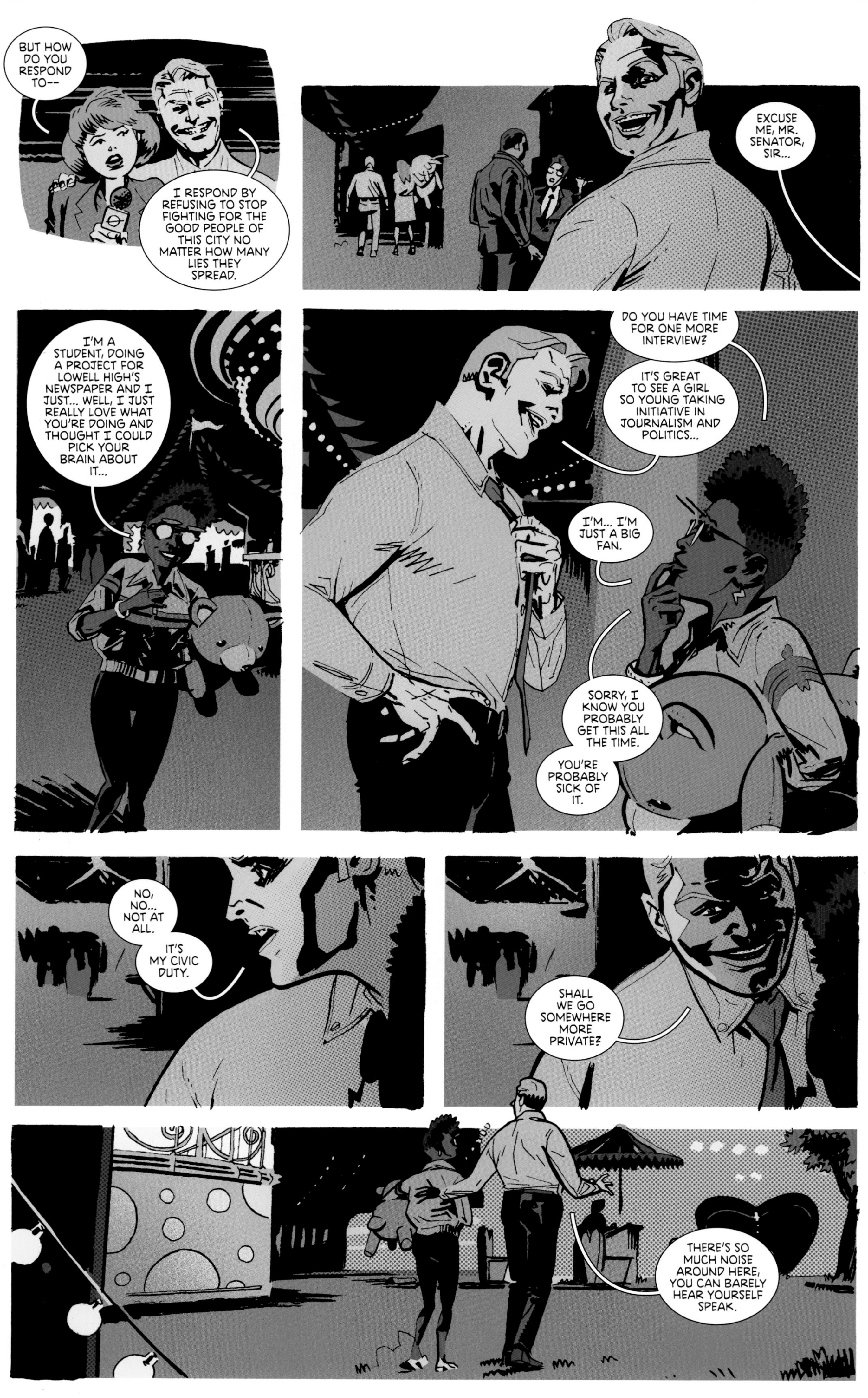

BUT HOW DO YOU RESPOND TO--
I RESPOND BY REFUSING TO STOP FIGHTING FOR THE GOOD PEOPLE OF THIS CITY NO MATTER HOW MANY LIES THEY SPREAD.
EXCUSE ME, MR. SENATOR, SIR...
I'M A STUDENT, DOING A PROJECT FOR LOWELL HIGH'S NEWSPAPER AND I JUST... WELL, I JUST REALLY LOVE WHAT YOU'RE DOING AND THOUGHT I COULD PICK YOUR BRAIN ABOUT IT...
DO YOU HAVE TIME FOR ONE MORE INTERVIEW?
IT'S GREAT TO SEE A GIRL SO YOUNG TAKING INITIATIVE IN JOURNALISM AND POLITICS...
I'M... I'M JUST A BIG FAN.
SORRY, I KNOW YOU PROBABLY GET THIS ALL THE TIME.
YOU'RE PROBABLY SICK OF IT.
NO, NO... NOT AT ALL.
IT'S MY CIVIC DUTY.
SHALL WE GO SOMEWHERE MORE PRIVATE?
THERE'S SO MUCH NOISE AROUND HERE, YOU CAN BARELY HEAR YOURSELF SPEAK.

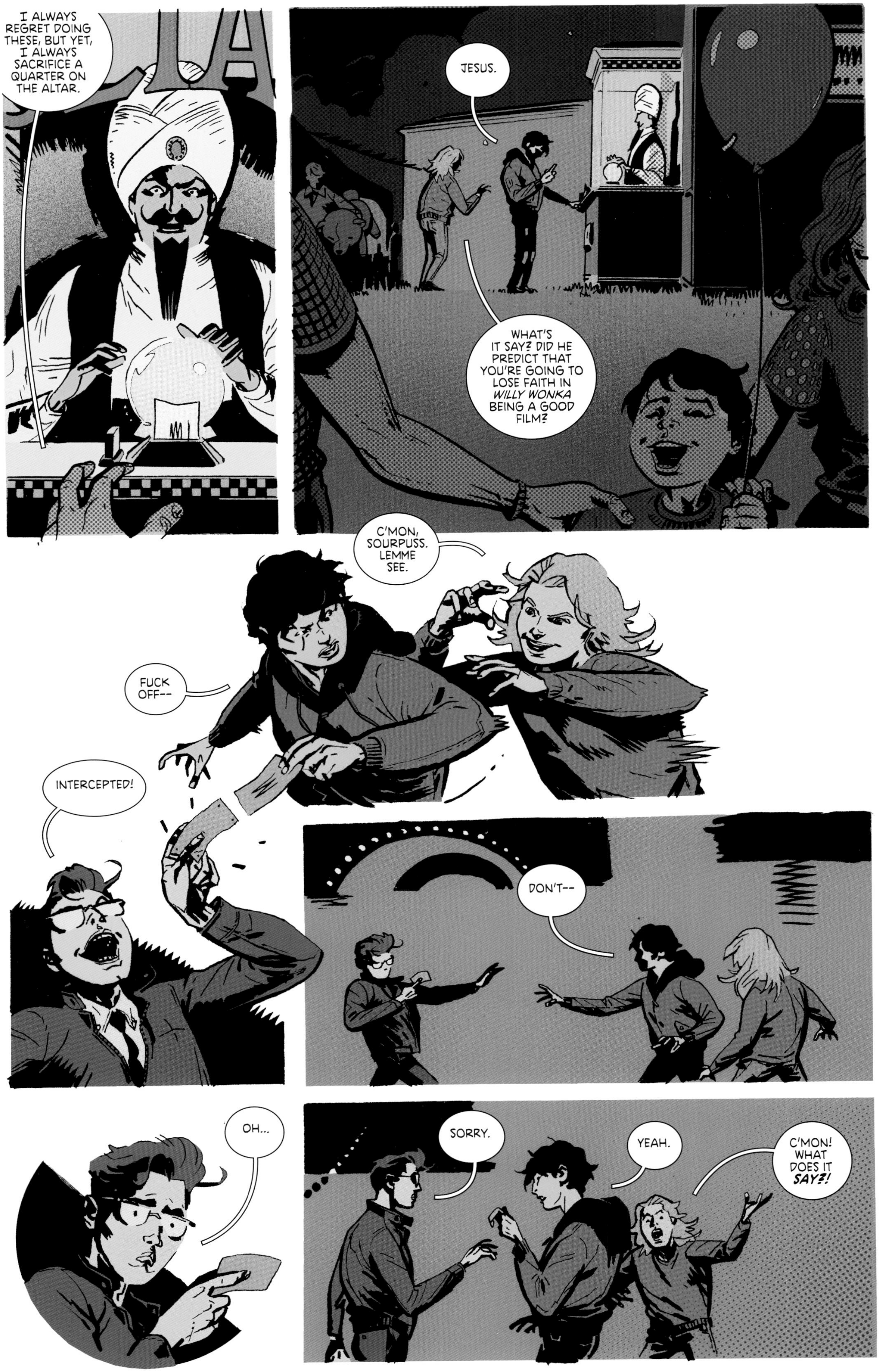
I ALWAYS REGRET DOING THESE, BUT YET, I ALWAYS SACRIFICE A QUARTER ON THE ALTAR.
JESUS.
WHAT'S IT SAY? DID HE PREDICT THAT YOU'RE GOING TO LOSE FAITH IN *WILLY WONKA* BEING A GOOD FILM?
C'MON, SOURPUSS. LEMME SEE.
FUCK OFF--
INTERCEPTED!
DON'T--
OH...
SORRY.
YEAH.
C'MON! WHAT DOES IT *SAY?!*

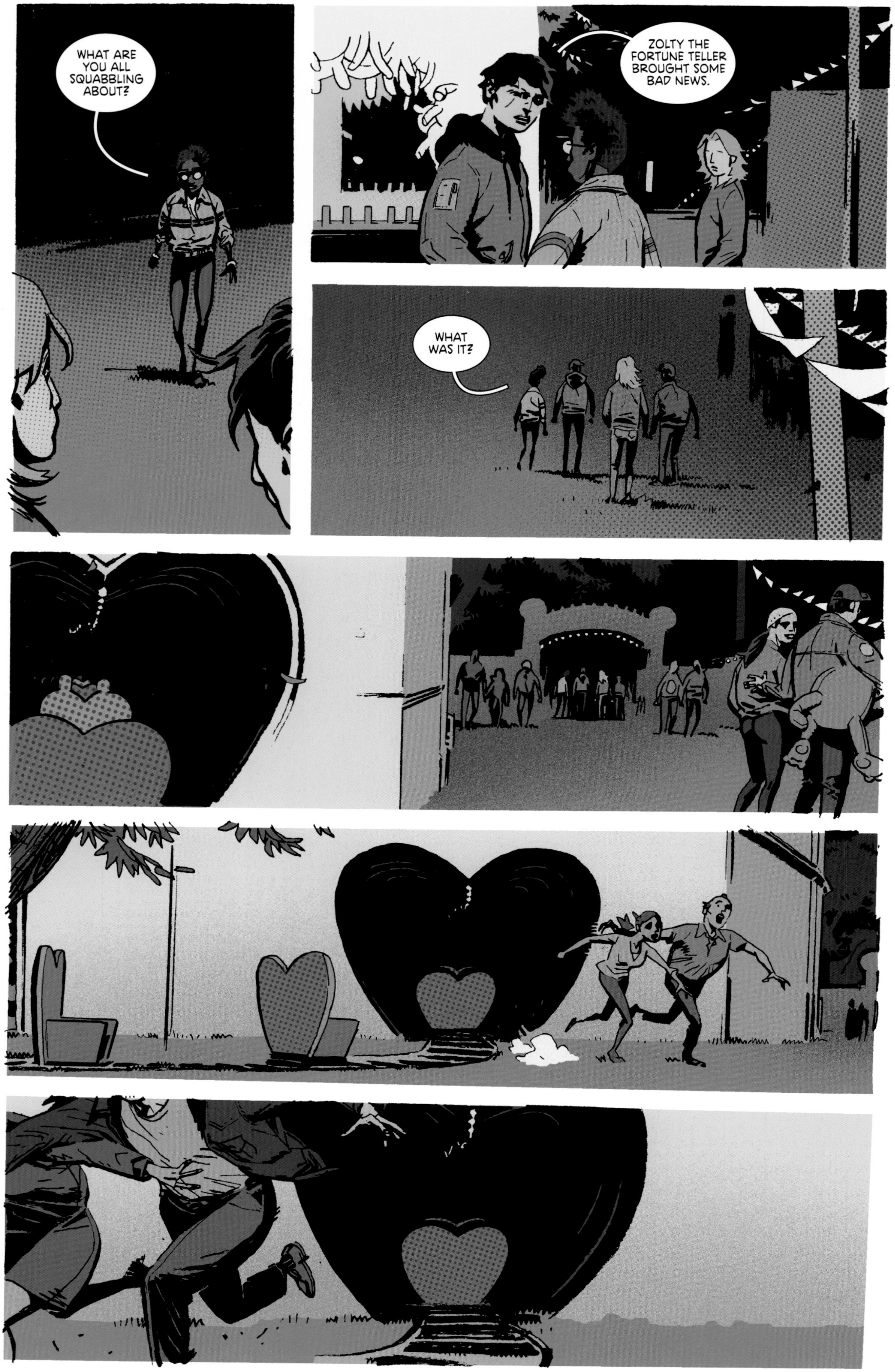
WHAT ARE YOU ALL SQUABBLING ABOUT?
ZOLTY THE FORTUNE TELLER BROUGHT SOME BAD NEWS.
WHAT WAS IT?

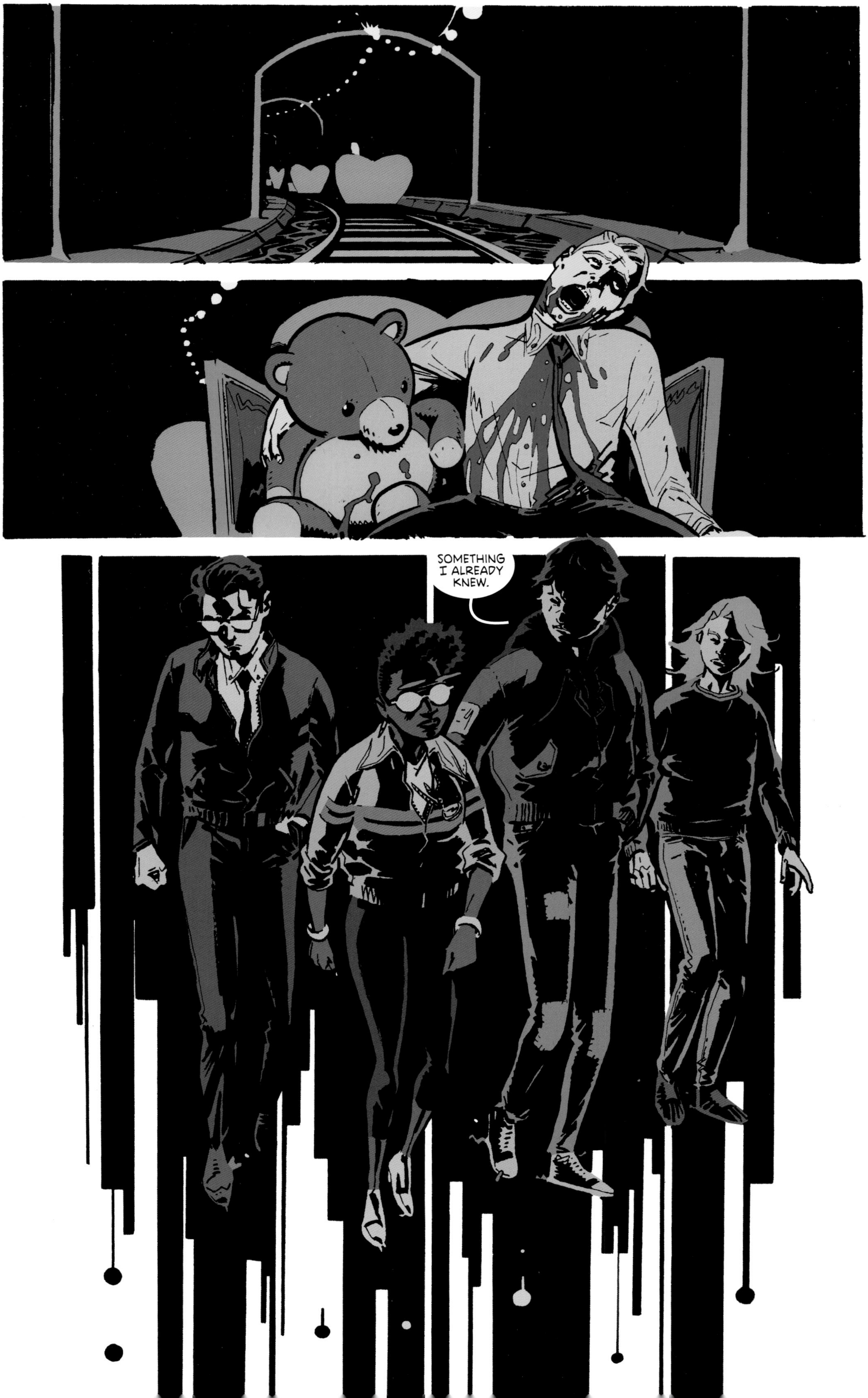
SOMETHING I ALREADY KNEW.

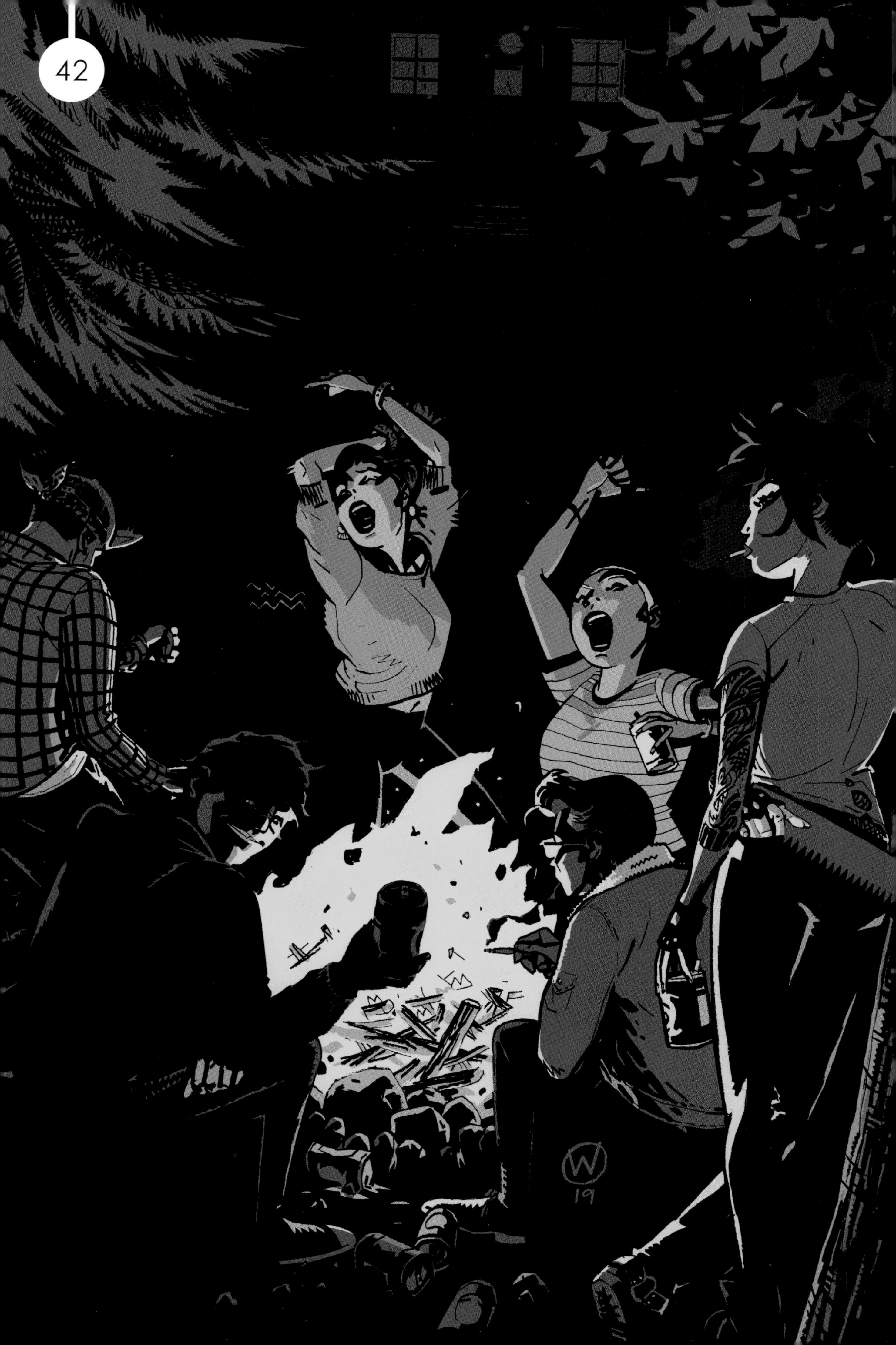

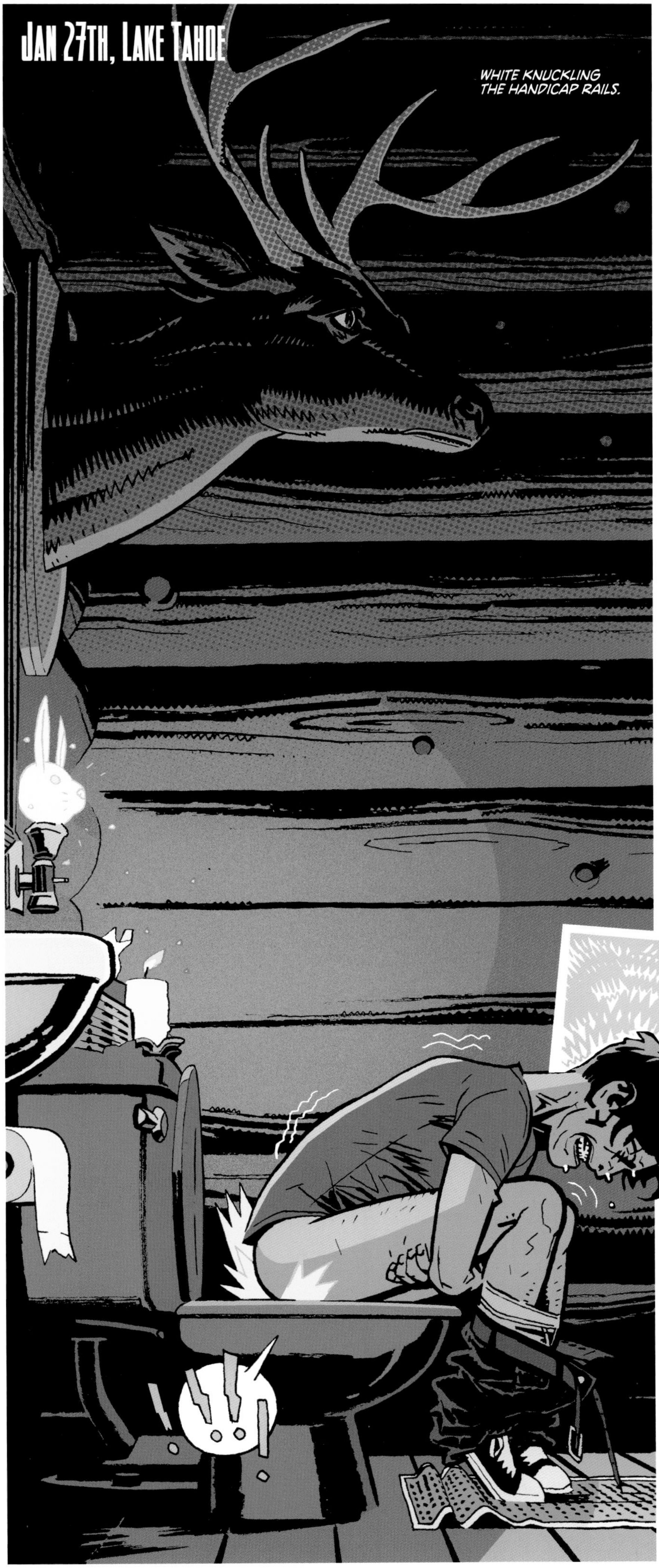
JAN 27TH, LAKE TAHOE
WHITE KNUCKLING THE HANDICAP RAILS.

COINED THAT TERM WHEN WE WERE ALL IN VEGAS, A FEW HOURS BEFORE MARIA KILLED CHICO.

I WAS ON SO MANY DRUGS. STOMACH FOUGHT BACK.

CASINO BATHROOM WAS FULL OF GAMBLERS DISCARDING THE REMAINS OF THE FREE BUFFET.

ONLY ONE HANDICAP STALL WAS OPEN.

BUCKLED OVER, CONVULSING, TRIPPING, MY KNUCKLES WHITE FROM MY DEATH GRIP ON THE HANDICAP RAIL.

BILLY CAME IN, ASKED WHAT I WAS DOING.

I JUST REPEATED "WHITE KNUCKLING THE HANDICAP RAILS" OVER AND OVER.

STILL MAKES ME LAUGH.

MAYBE THIS WILL AS WELL, SOMEDAY FAR IN THE FUTURE.

BUT NOT TODAY.

I'VE BEEN GOING STRAIGHT EDGE THE LAST COUPLE OF WEEKS. AND FEELING MUCH BETTER. SELF-SUFFICIENT. LESS FUZZY.

TURNS OUT DEPRESSION IS EXACERBATED BY DRUG ABUSE.

SHOCKING, RIGHT?

NO DRUGS OR ALCOHOL IN MY SYSTEM, BUT THE CRAMPS ARE OUT OF CONTROL. AND WHAT MAKES IT WORSE...

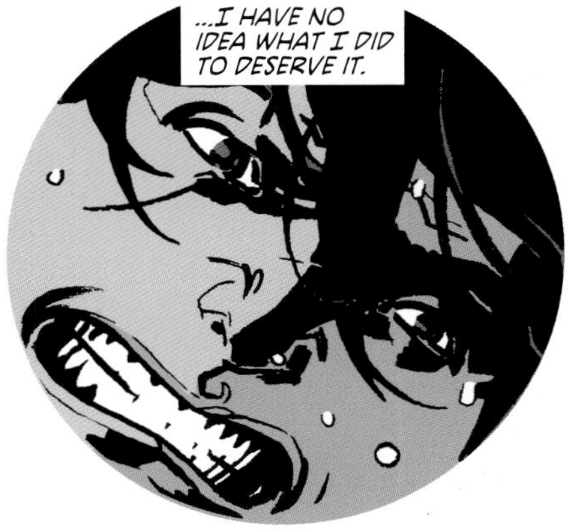
...I HAVE NO IDEA WHAT I DID TO DESERVE IT.

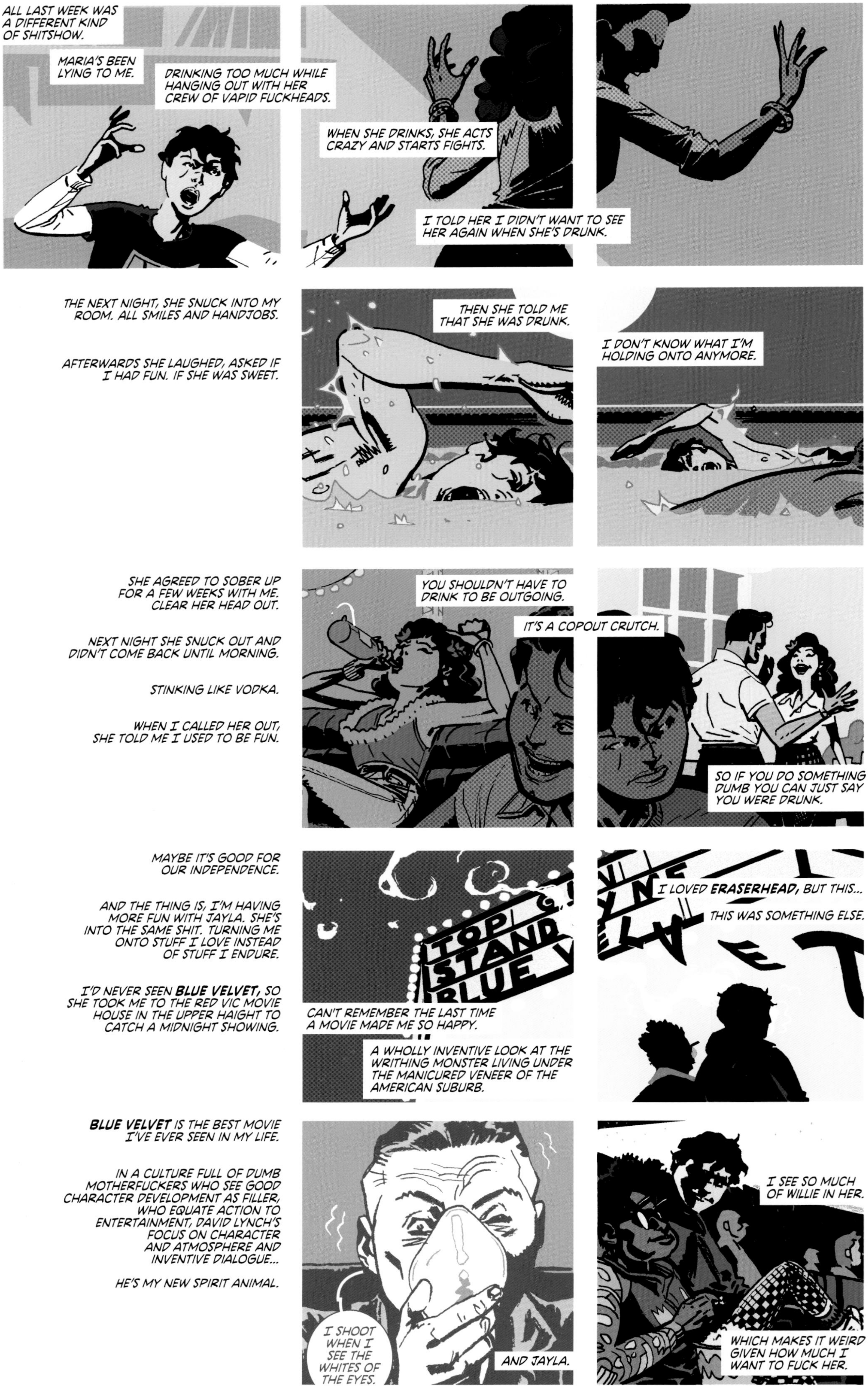
ALL LAST WEEK WAS A DIFFERENT KIND OF SHITSHOW.
MARIA'S BEEN LYING TO ME.
DRINKING TOO MUCH WHILE HANGING OUT WITH HER CREW OF VAPID FUCKHEADS.
WHEN SHE DRINKS, SHE ACTS CRAZY AND STARTS FIGHTS.
I TOLD HER I DIDN'T WANT TO SEE HER AGAIN WHEN SHE'S DRUNK.
THE NEXT NIGHT, SHE SNUCK INTO MY ROOM. ALL SMILES AND HANDJOBS.
AFTERWARDS SHE LAUGHED, ASKED IF I HAD FUN. IF SHE WAS SWEET.
THEN SHE TOLD ME THAT SHE WAS DRUNK.
I DON'T KNOW WHAT I'M HOLDING ONTO ANYMORE.
SHE AGREED TO SOBER UP FOR A FEW WEEKS WITH ME. CLEAR HER HEAD OUT.
NEXT NIGHT SHE SNUCK OUT AND DIDN'T COME BACK UNTIL MORNING.
STINKING LIKE VODKA.
WHEN I CALLED HER OUT, SHE TOLD ME I USED TO BE FUN.
YOU SHOULDN'T HAVE TO DRINK TO BE OUTGOING.
IT'S A COPOUT CRUTCH.
SO IF YOU DO SOMETHING DUMB YOU CAN JUST SAY YOU WERE DRUNK.
MAYBE IT'S GOOD FOR OUR INDEPENDENCE.
AND THE THING IS, I'M HAVING MORE FUN WITH JAYLA. SHE'S INTO THE SAME SHIT. TURNING ME ONTO STUFF I LOVE INSTEAD OF STUFF I ENDURE.
I'D NEVER SEEN **BLUE VELVET**, SO SHE TOOK ME TO THE RED VIC MOVIE HOUSE IN THE UPPER HAIGHT TO CATCH A MIDNIGHT SHOWING.
TOP
STAND
BLUE V
CAN'T REMEMBER THE LAST TIME A MOVIE MADE ME SO HAPPY.
A WHOLLY INVENTIVE LOOK AT THE WRITHING MONSTER LIVING UNDER THE MANICURED VENEER OF THE AMERICAN SUBURB.
I LOVED **ERASERHEAD**, BUT THIS...
THIS WAS SOMETHING ELSE.
BLUE VELVET IS THE BEST MOVIE I'VE EVER SEEN IN MY LIFE.
IN A CULTURE FULL OF DUMB MOTHERFUCKERS WHO SEE GOOD CHARACTER DEVELOPMENT AS FILLER, WHO EQUATE ACTION TO ENTERTAINMENT, DAVID LYNCH'S FOCUS ON CHARACTER AND ATMOSPHERE AND INVENTIVE DIALOGUE...
HE'S MY NEW SPIRIT ANIMAL.
I SHOOT WHEN I SEE THE WHITES OF THE EYES.
AND JAYLA.
I SEE SO MUCH OF WILLIE IN HER.
WHICH MAKES IT WEIRD GIVEN HOW MUCH I WANT TO FUCK HER.

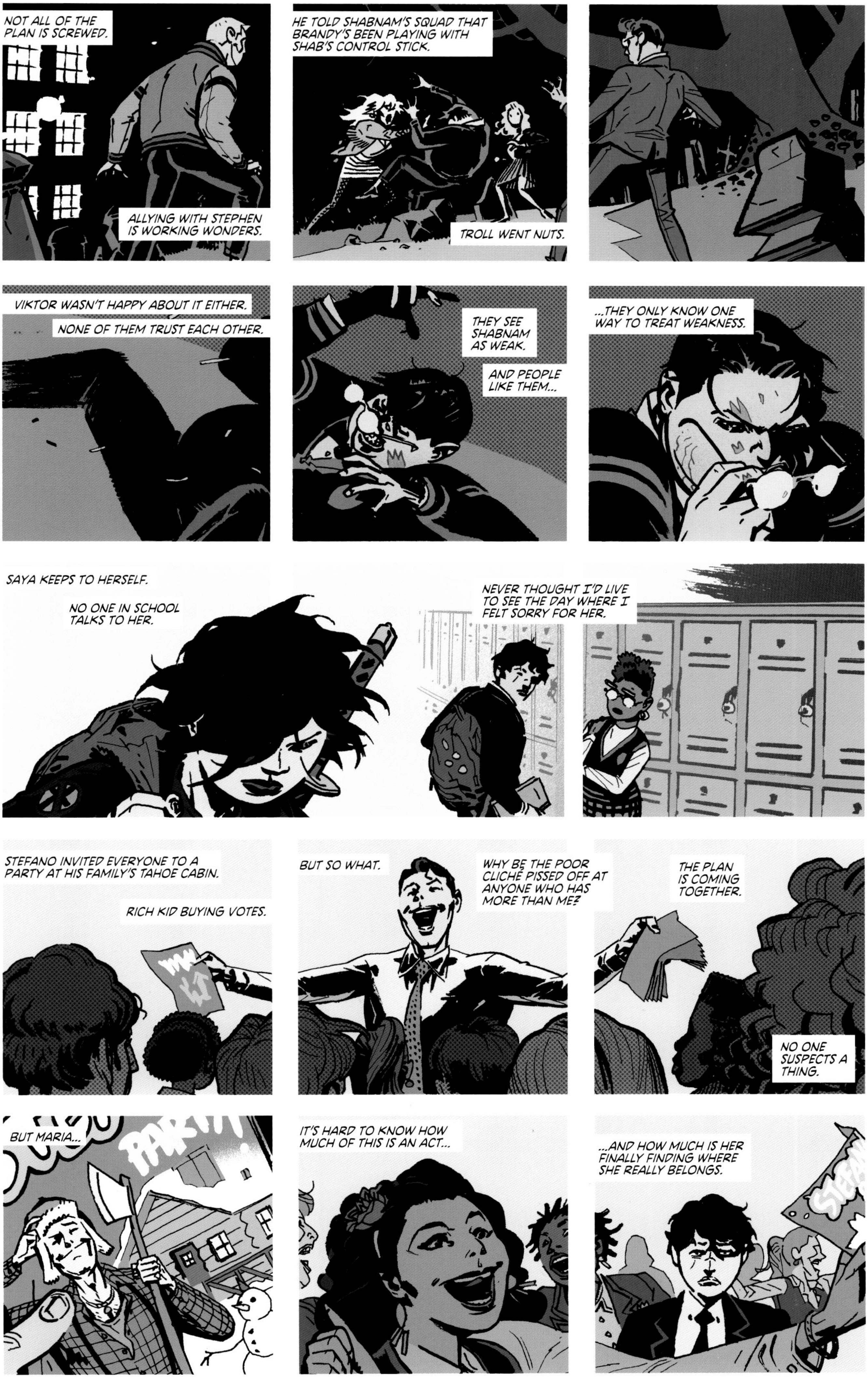
NOT ALL OF THE PLAN IS SCREWED.
ALLYING WITH STEPHEN IS WORKING WONDERS.
HE TOLD SHABNAM'S SQUAD THAT BRANDY'S BEEN PLAYING WITH SHAB'S CONTROL STICK.
TROLL WENT NUTS.
VIKTOR WASN'T HAPPY ABOUT IT EITHER.
NONE OF THEM TRUST EACH OTHER.
THEY SEE SHABNAM AS WEAK.
AND PEOPLE LIKE THEM...
...THEY ONLY KNOW ONE WAY TO TREAT WEAKNESS.
SAYA KEEPS TO HERSELF.
NO ONE IN SCHOOL TALKS TO HER.
NEVER THOUGHT I'D LIVE TO SEE THE DAY WHERE I FELT SORRY FOR HER.
STEFANO INVITED EVERYONE TO A PARTY AT HIS FAMILY'S TAHOE CABIN.
RICH KID BUYING VOTES.
BUT SO WHAT.
WHY BE THE POOR CLICHÉ PISSED OFF AT ANYONE WHO HAS MORE THAN ME?
THE PLAN IS COMING TOGETHER.
NO ONE SUSPECTS A THING.
BUT MARIA...
PARTY
IT'S HARD TO KNOW HOW MUCH OF THIS IS AN ACT...
...AND HOW MUCH IS HER FINALLY FINDING WHERE SHE REALLY BELONGS.

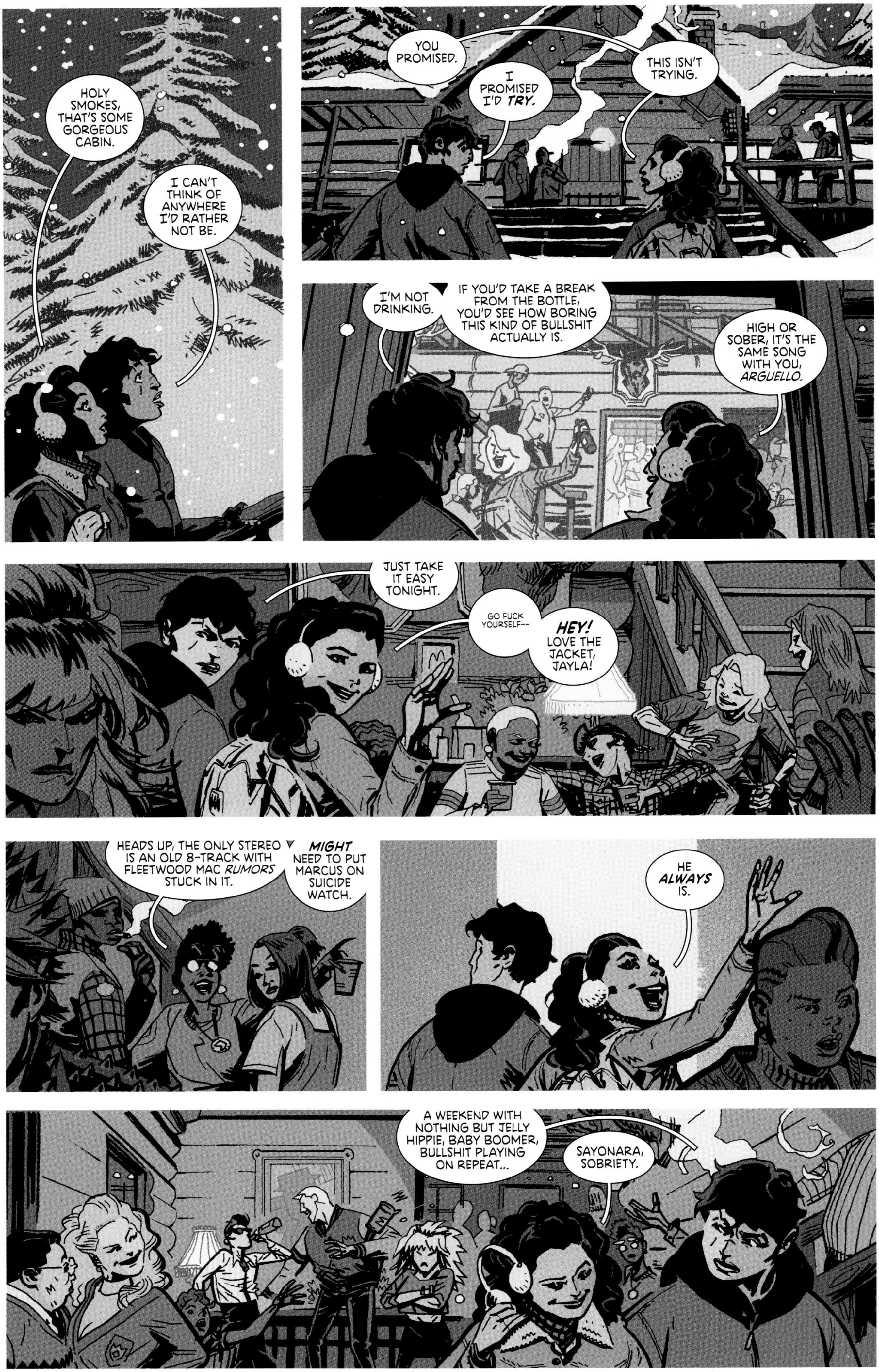
HOLY SMOKES, THAT'S SOME GORGEOUS CABIN.
I CAN'T THINK OF ANYWHERE I'D RATHER NOT BE.
YOU PROMISED.
I PROMISED I'D *TRY.*
THIS ISN'T TRYING.
I'M NOT DRINKING.
IF YOU'D TAKE A BREAK FROM THE BOTTLE, YOU'D SEE HOW BORING THIS KIND OF BULLSHIT ACTUALLY IS.
HIGH OR SOBER, IT'S THE SAME SONG WITH YOU, *ARGUELLO.*
JUST TAKE IT EASY TONIGHT.
GO FUCK YOURSELF--
HEY! LOVE THE JACKET, JAYLA!
HEADS UP, THE ONLY STEREO IS AN OLD 8-TRACK WITH FLEETWOOD MAC *RUMORS* STUCK IN IT.
MIGHT NEED TO PUT MARCUS ON SUICIDE WATCH.
HE *ALWAYS* IS.
A WEEKEND WITH NOTHING BUT JELLY HIPPIE, BABY BOOMER, BULLSHIT PLAYING ON REPEAT...
SAYONARA, SOBRIETY.

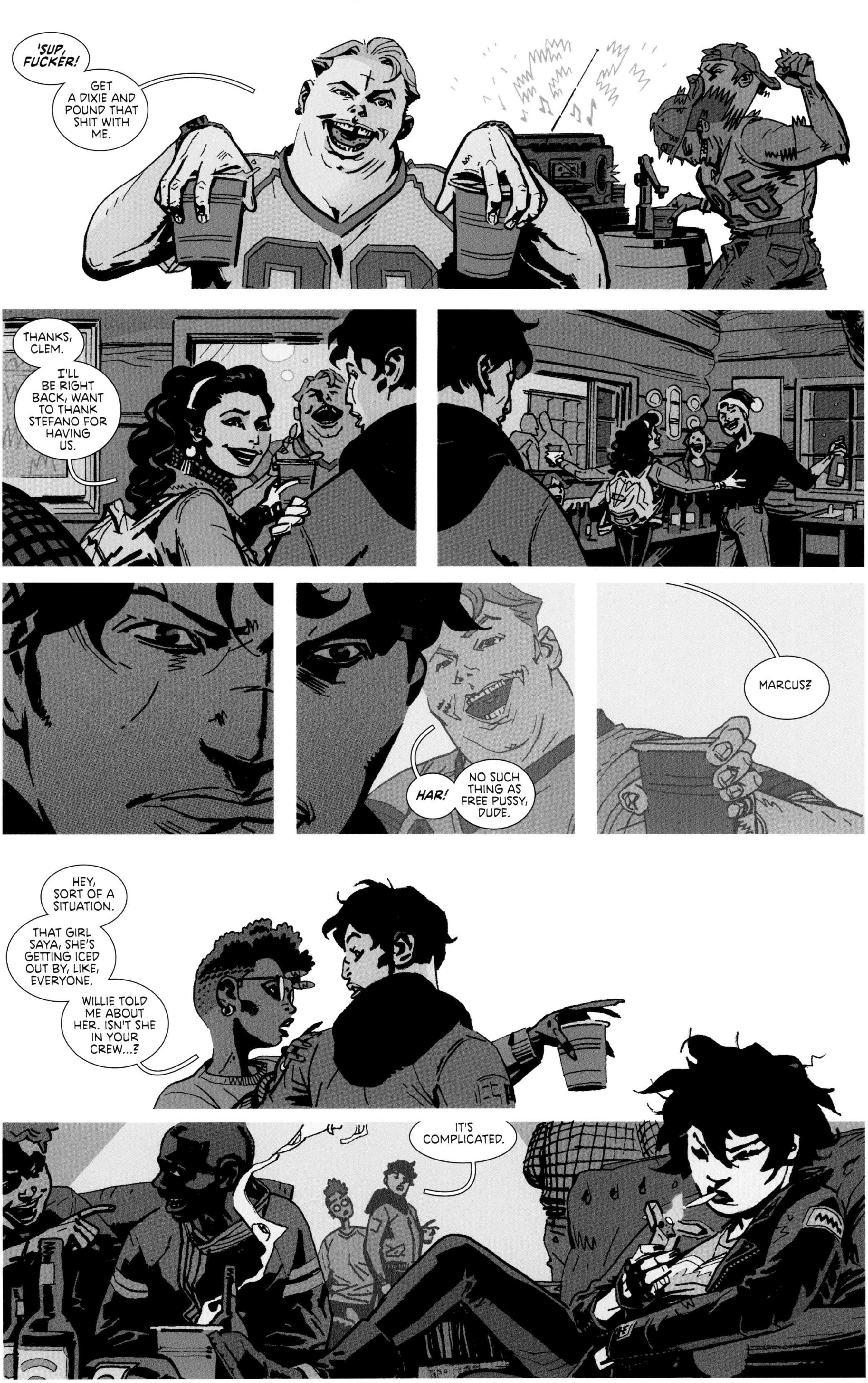
'SUP, FUCKER!
GET A DIXIE AND POUND THAT SHIT WITH ME.
THANKS, CLEM.
I'LL BE RIGHT BACK, WANT TO THANK STEFANO FOR HAVING US.
HAR!
NO SUCH THING AS FREE PUSSY, DUDE.
MARCUS?
HEY, SORT OF A SITUATION.
THAT GIRL SAYA, SHE'S GETTING ICED OUT BY, LIKE, EVERYONE.
WILLIE TOLD ME ABOUT HER. ISN'T SHE IN YOUR CREW...?
IT'S COMPLICATED.

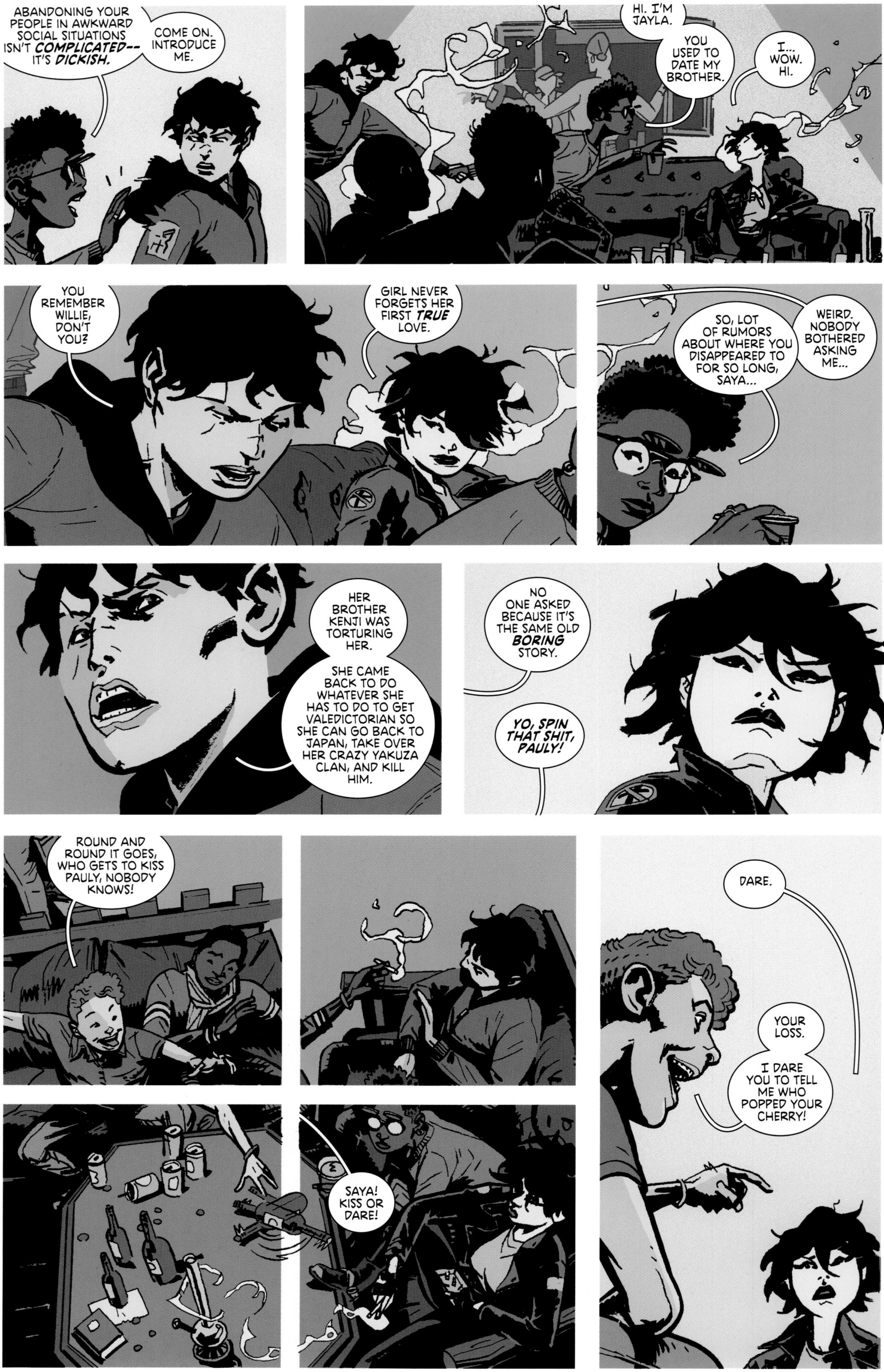

ABANDONING YOUR PEOPLE IN AWKWARD SOCIAL SITUATIONS ISN'T **COMPLICATED**-- IT'S **DICKISH.**
COME ON. INTRODUCE ME.
HI. I'M JAYLA.
YOU USED TO DATE MY BROTHER.
I... WOW. HI.
YOU REMEMBER WILLIE, DON'T YOU?
GIRL NEVER FORGETS HER FIRST **TRUE** LOVE.
SO, LOT OF RUMORS ABOUT WHERE YOU DISAPPEARED TO FOR SO LONG, SAYA...
WEIRD. NOBODY BOTHERED ASKING ME...
HER BROTHER KENJI WAS TORTURING HER.
SHE CAME BACK TO DO WHATEVER SHE HAS TO DO TO GET VALEDICTORIAN SO SHE CAN GO BACK TO JAPAN, TAKE OVER HER CRAZY YAKUZA CLAN, AND KILL HIM.
NO ONE ASKED BECAUSE IT'S THE SAME OLD **BORING** STORY.
YO, SPIN THAT SHIT, PAULY!
ROUND AND ROUND IT GOES, WHO GETS TO KISS PAULY, NOBODY KNOWS!
SAYA! KISS OR DARE!
DARE.
YOUR LOSS.
I DARE YOU TO TELL ME WHO POPPED YOUR CHERRY!

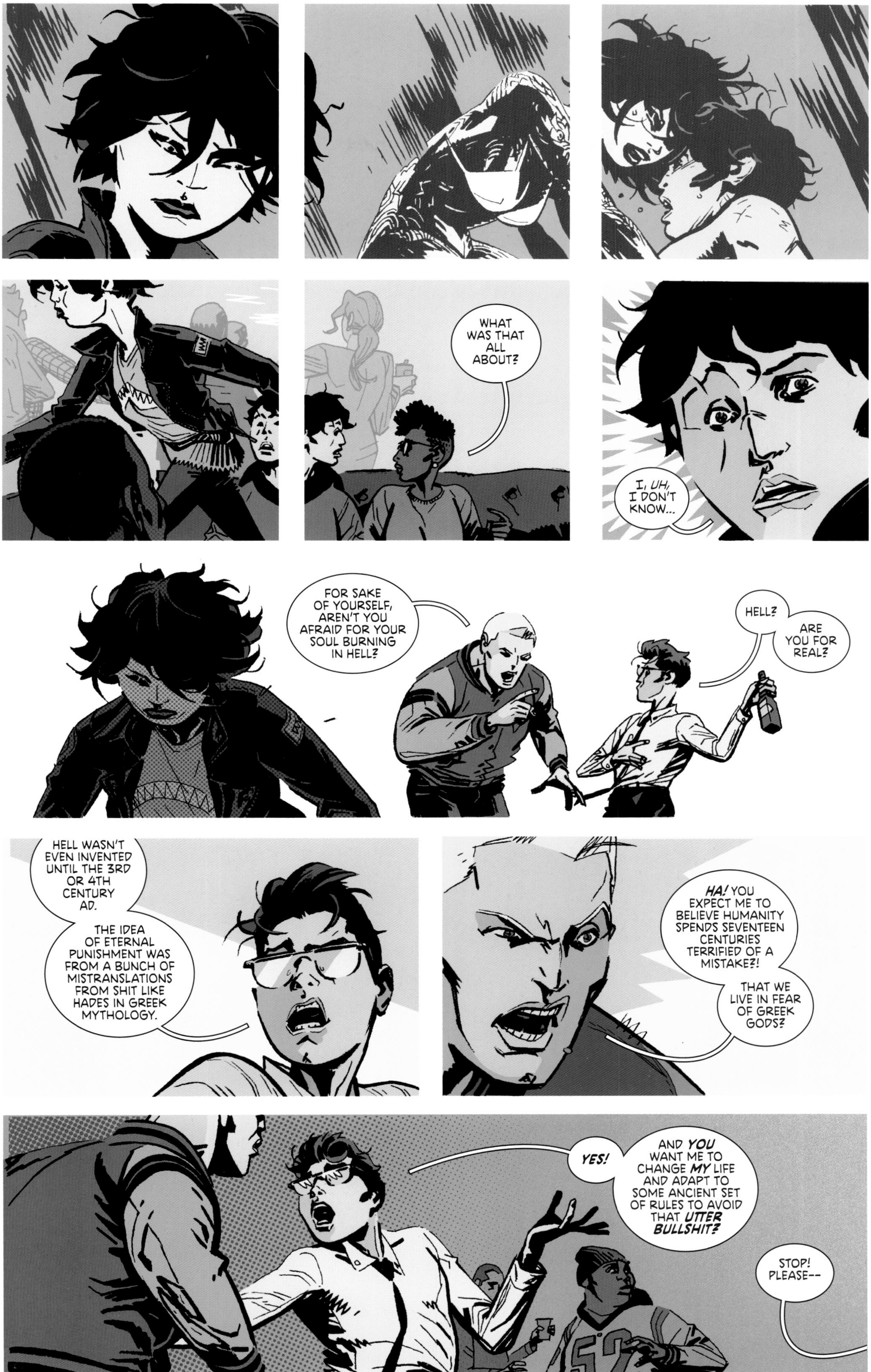
WHAT WAS THAT ALL ABOUT?
I, UH, I DON'T KNOW...
FOR SAKE OF YOURSELF, AREN'T YOU AFRAID FOR YOUR SOUL BURNING IN HELL?
HELL?
ARE YOU FOR REAL?
HELL WASN'T EVEN INVENTED UNTIL THE 3RD OR 4TH CENTURY AD.
THE IDEA OF ETERNAL PUNISHMENT WAS FROM A BUNCH OF MISTRANSLATIONS FROM SHIT LIKE HADES IN GREEK MYTHOLOGY.
HA! YOU EXPECT ME TO BELIEVE HUMANITY SPENDS SEVENTEEN CENTURIES TERRIFIED OF A MISTAKE?!
THAT WE LIVE IN FEAR OF GREEK GODS?
YES!
AND YOU WANT ME TO CHANGE MY LIFE AND ADAPT TO SOME ANCIENT SET OF RULES TO AVOID THAT UTTER BULLSHIT?
STOP! PLEASE--

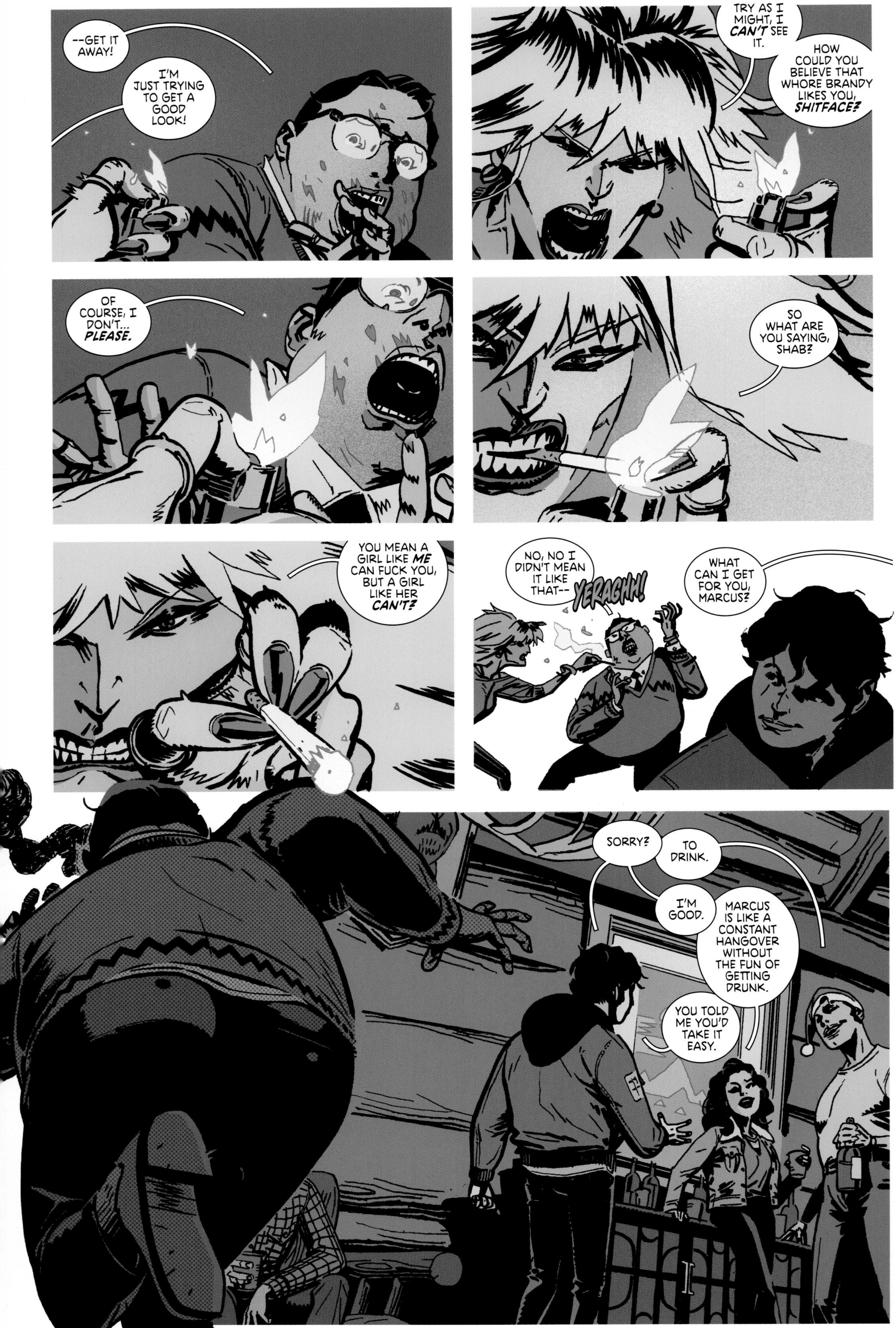
--GET IT AWAY!
I'M JUST TRYING TO GET A GOOD LOOK!
TRY AS I MIGHT, I CAN'T SEE IT.
HOW COULD YOU BELIEVE THAT WHORE BRANDY LIKES YOU, SHITFACE?
OF COURSE, I DON'T... PLEASE.
SO WHAT ARE YOU SAYING, SHAB?
YOU MEAN A GIRL LIKE ME CAN FUCK YOU, BUT A GIRL LIKE HER CAN'T?
NO, NO I DIDN'T MEAN IT LIKE THAT--
YERAGHH!
WHAT CAN I GET FOR YOU, MARCUS?
SORRY?
TO DRINK.
I'M GOOD.
MARCUS IS LIKE A CONSTANT HANGOVER WITHOUT THE FUN OF GETTING DRUNK.
YOU TOLD ME YOU'D TAKE IT EASY.

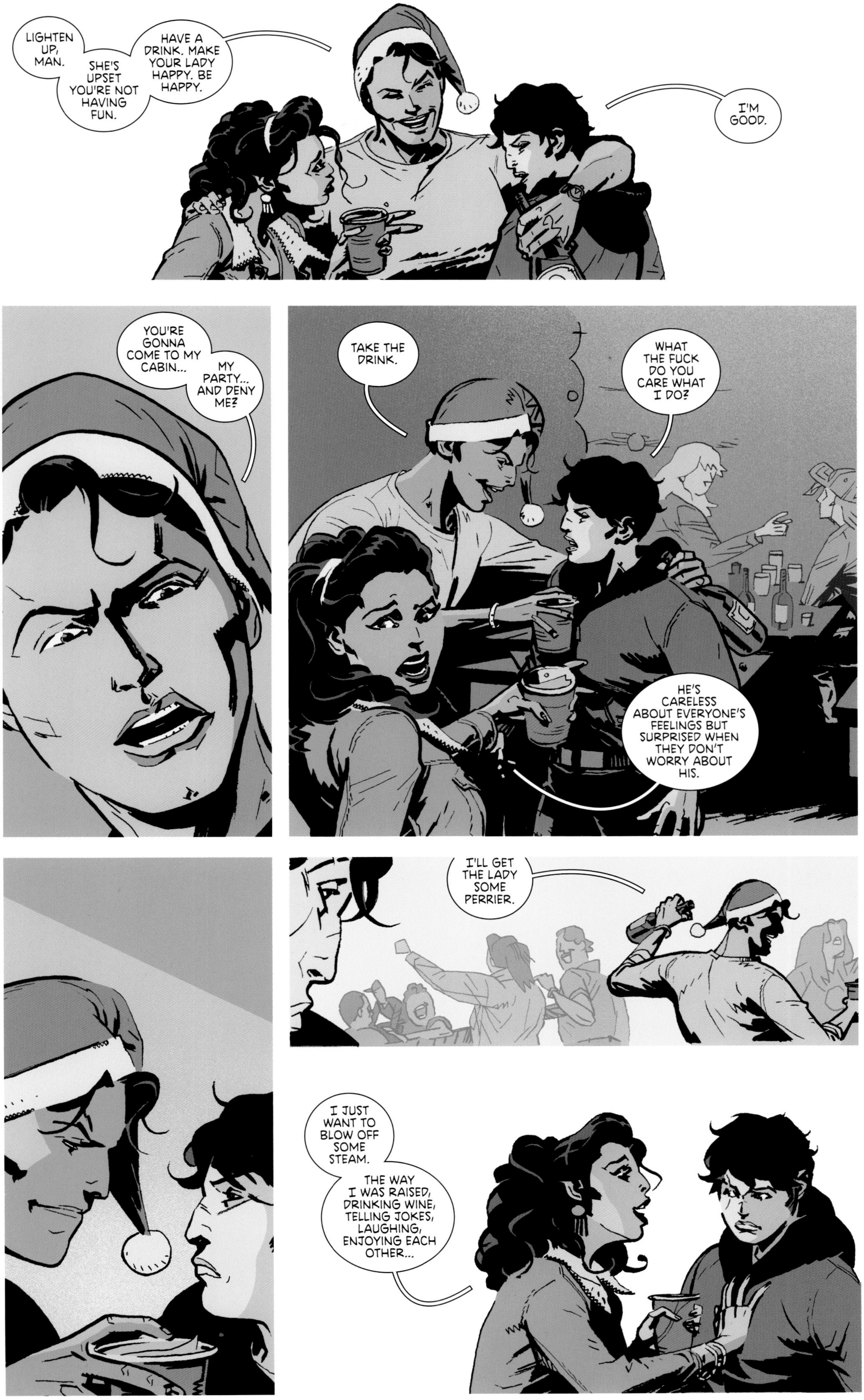
LIGHTEN UP, MAN.
SHE'S UPSET YOU'RE NOT HAVING FUN.
HAVE A DRINK. MAKE YOUR LADY HAPPY. BE HAPPY.
I'M GOOD.
YOU'RE GONNA COME TO MY CABIN...
MY PARTY... AND DENY ME?
TAKE THE DRINK.
WHAT THE FUCK DO YOU CARE WHAT I DO?
HE'S CARELESS ABOUT EVERYONE'S FEELINGS BUT SURPRISED WHEN THEY DON'T WORRY ABOUT HIS.
I'LL GET THE LADY SOME PERRIER.
I JUST WANT TO BLOW OFF SOME STEAM.
THE WAY I WAS RAISED, DRINKING WINE, TELLING JOKES, LAUGHING, ENJOYING EACH OTHER...

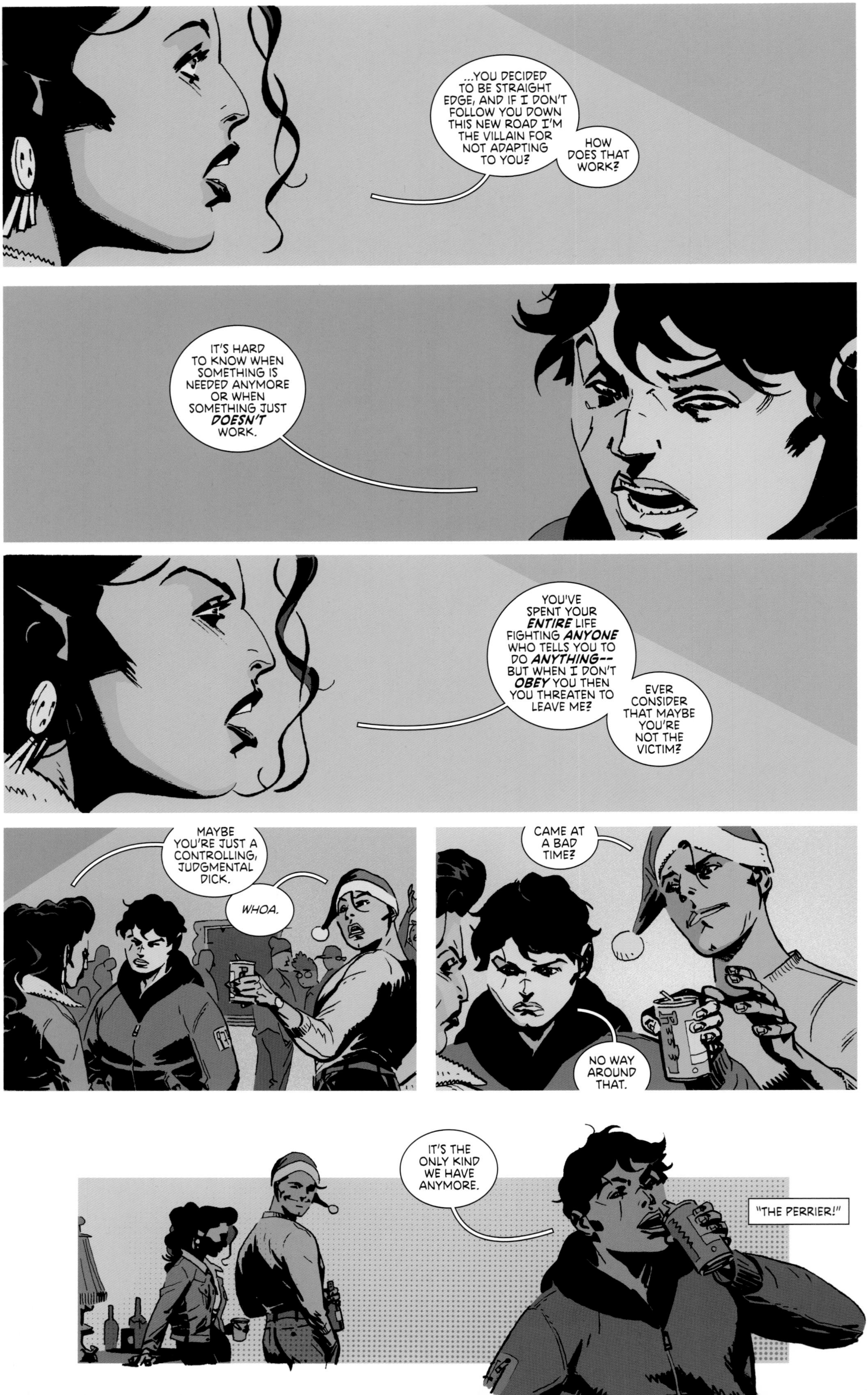
...YOU DECIDED TO BE STRAIGHT EDGE, AND IF I DON'T FOLLOW YOU DOWN THIS NEW ROAD I'M THE VILLAIN FOR NOT ADAPTING TO YOU?
HOW DOES THAT WORK?
IT'S HARD TO KNOW WHEN SOMETHING IS NEEDED ANYMORE OR WHEN SOMETHING JUST *DOESN'T* WORK.
YOU'VE SPENT YOUR *ENTIRE* LIFE FIGHTING *ANYONE* WHO TELLS YOU TO DO *ANYTHING*-- BUT WHEN I DON'T *OBEY* YOU THEN YOU THREATEN TO LEAVE ME?
EVER CONSIDER THAT MAYBE YOU'RE NOT THE VICTIM?
MAYBE YOU'RE JUST A CONTROLLING, JUDGMENTAL DICK.
WHOA.
CAME AT A BAD TIME?
NO WAY AROUND THAT.
IT'S THE ONLY KIND WE HAVE ANYMORE.
"THE PERRIER!"

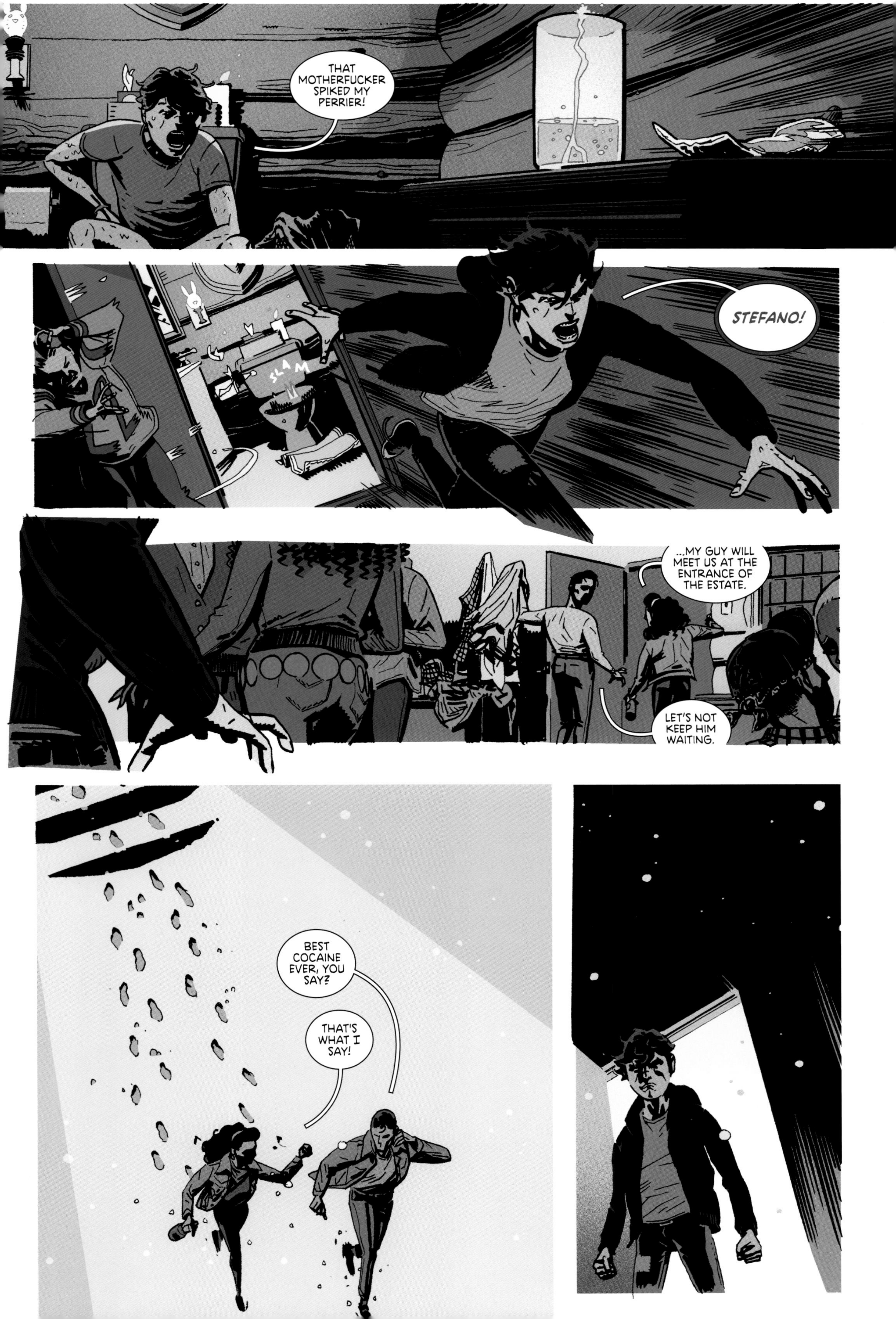
THAT MOTHERFUCKER SPIKED MY PERRIER!
STEFANO!
SLAM
...MY GUY WILL MEET US AT THE ENTRANCE OF THE ESTATE.
LET'S NOT KEEP HIM WAITING.
BEST COCAINE EVER, YOU SAY?
THAT'S WHAT I SAY!

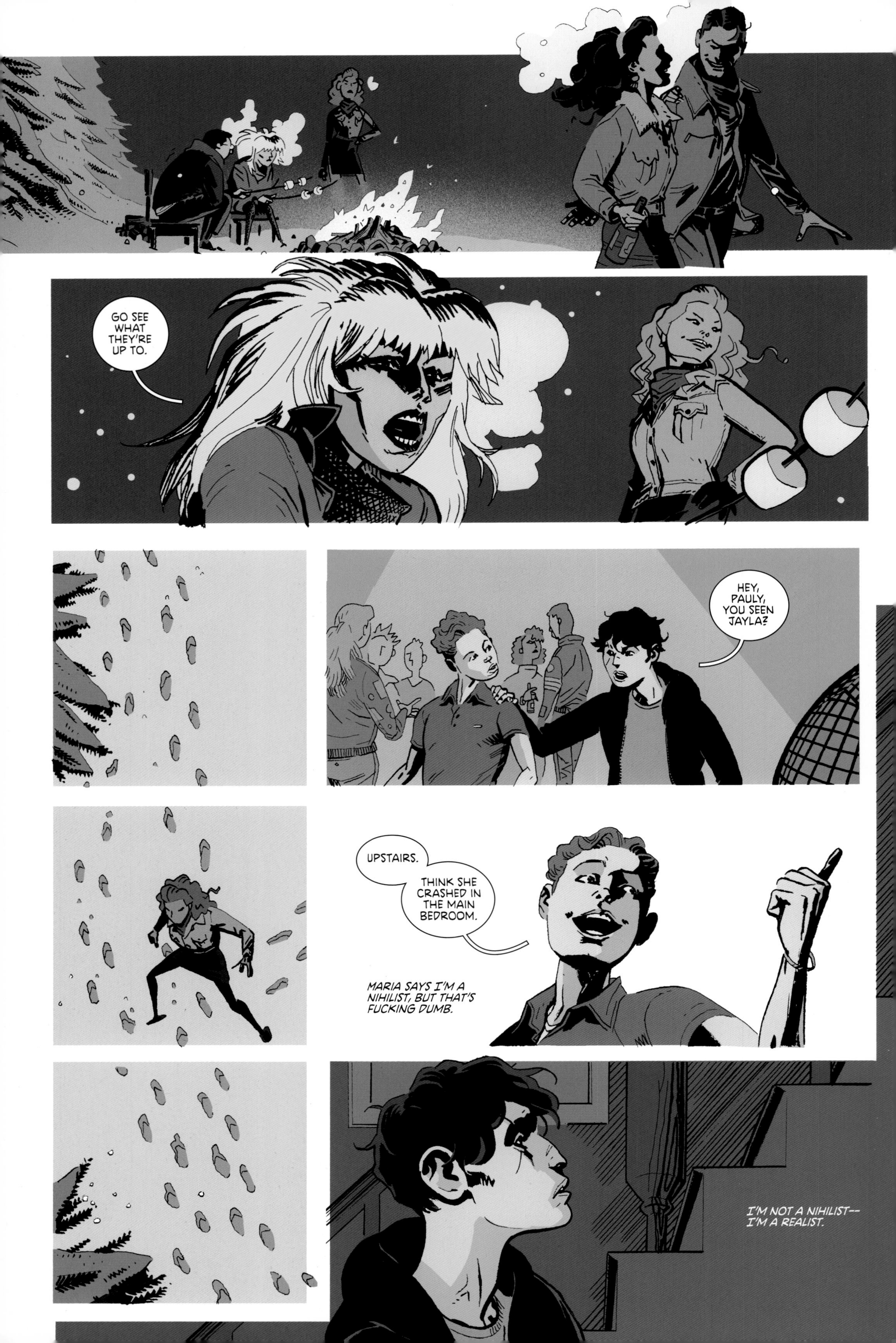
GO SEE WHAT THEY'RE UP TO.
HEY, PAULY, YOU SEEN JAYLA?
UPSTAIRS.
THINK SHE CRASHED IN THE MAIN BEDROOM.
MARIA SAYS I'M A NIHILIST, BUT THAT'S FUCKING DUMB.
I'M NOT A NIHILIST-- I'M A REALIST.

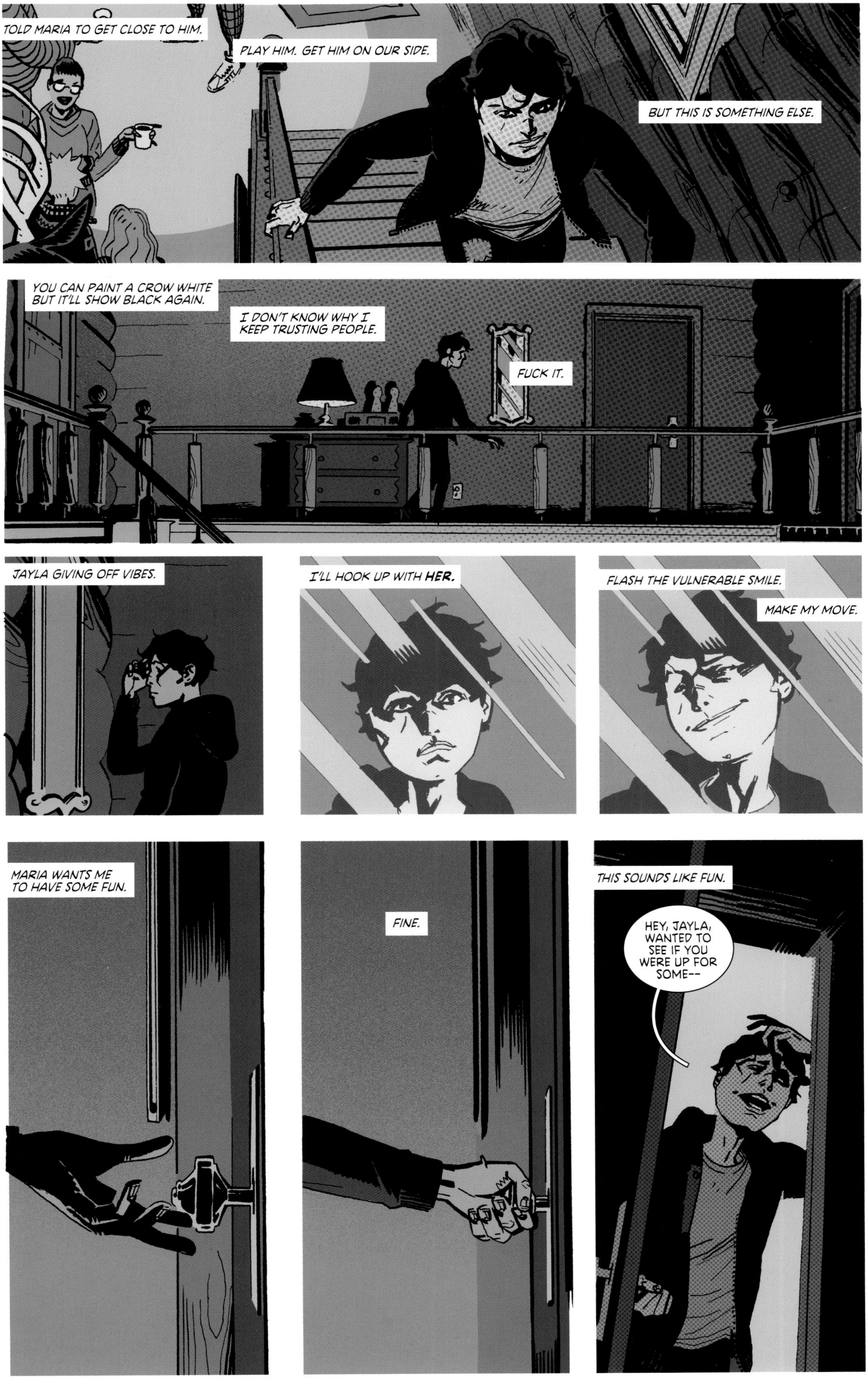
TOLD MARIA TO GET CLOSE TO HIM.
PLAY HIM. GET HIM ON OUR SIDE.
BUT THIS IS SOMETHING ELSE.
YOU CAN PAINT A CROW WHITE BUT IT'LL SHOW BLACK AGAIN.
I DON'T KNOW WHY I KEEP TRUSTING PEOPLE.
FUCK IT.
JAYLA GIVING OFF VIBES.
I'LL HOOK UP WITH **HER.**
FLASH THE VULNERABLE SMILE.
MAKE MY MOVE.
MARIA WANTS ME TO HAVE SOME FUN.
FINE.
THIS SOUNDS LIKE FUN.
HEY, JAYLA, WANTED TO SEE IF YOU WERE UP FOR SOME--

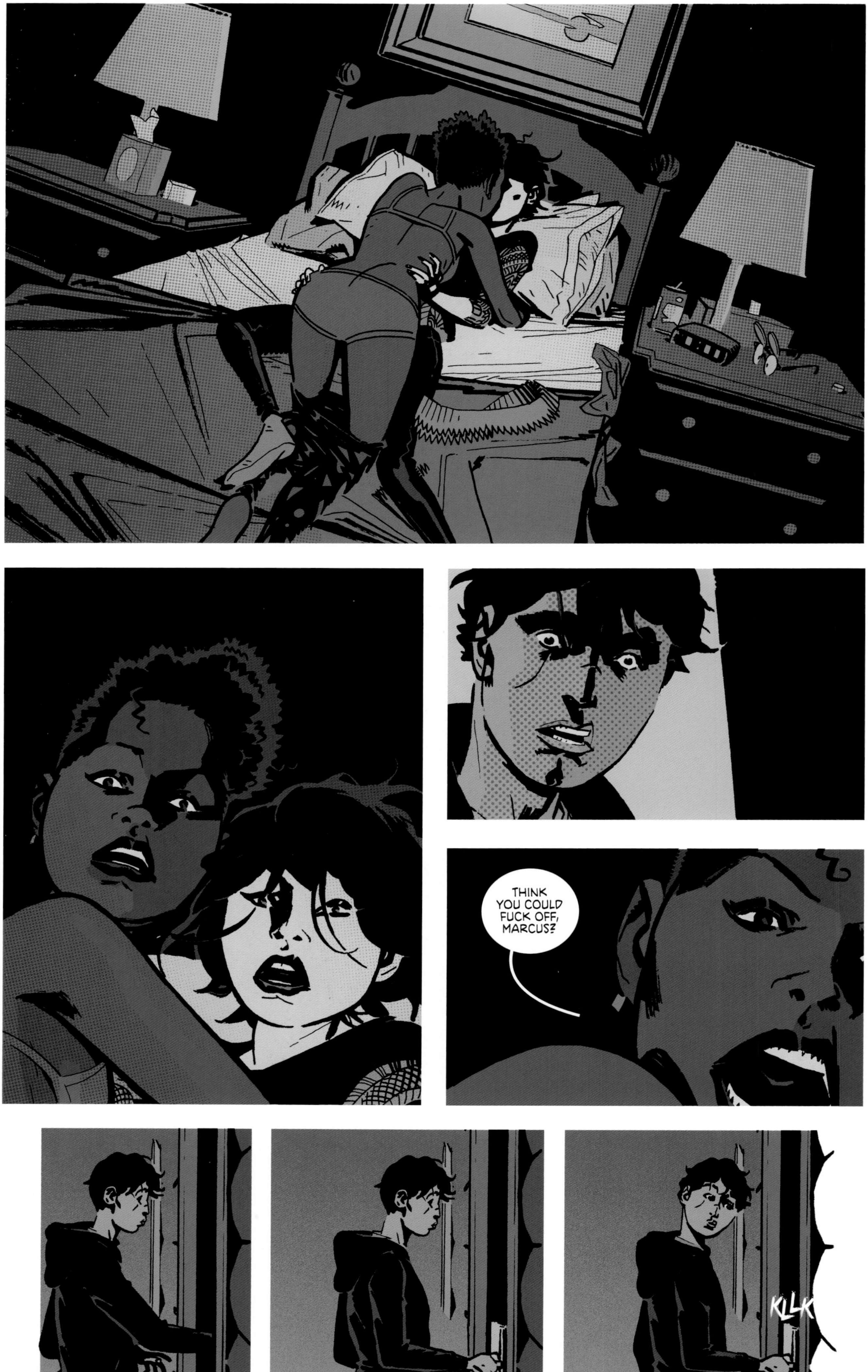
THINK YOU COULD FUCK OFF, MARCUS?
KLLK

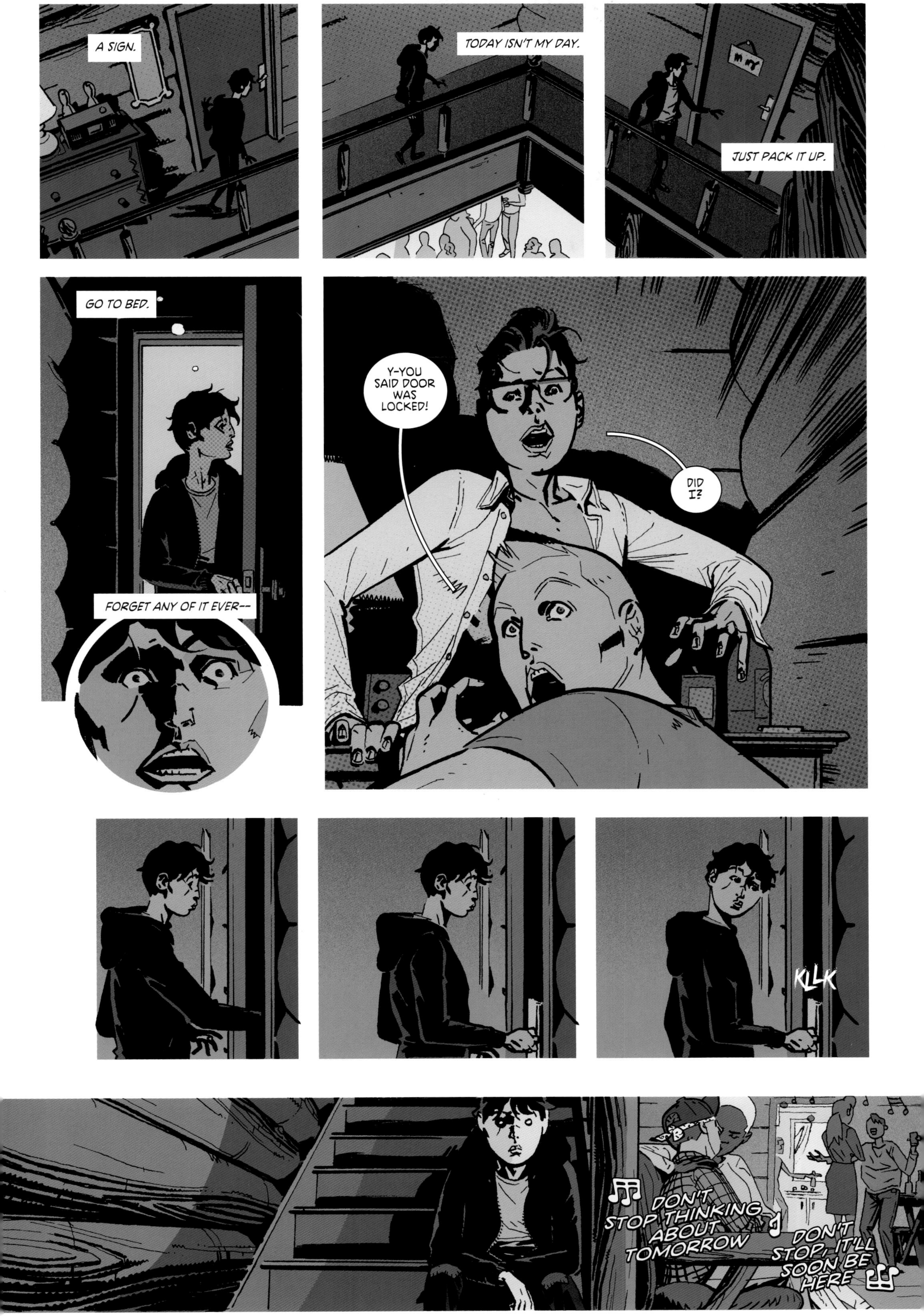
A SIGN.
TODAY ISN'T MY DAY.
JUST PACK IT UP.
GO TO BED.
FORGET ANY OF IT EVER--
Y-YOU SAID DOOR WAS LOCKED!
DID I?
KLLK
DON'T STOP THINKING ABOUT TOMORROW
DON'T STOP, IT'LL SOON BE HERE

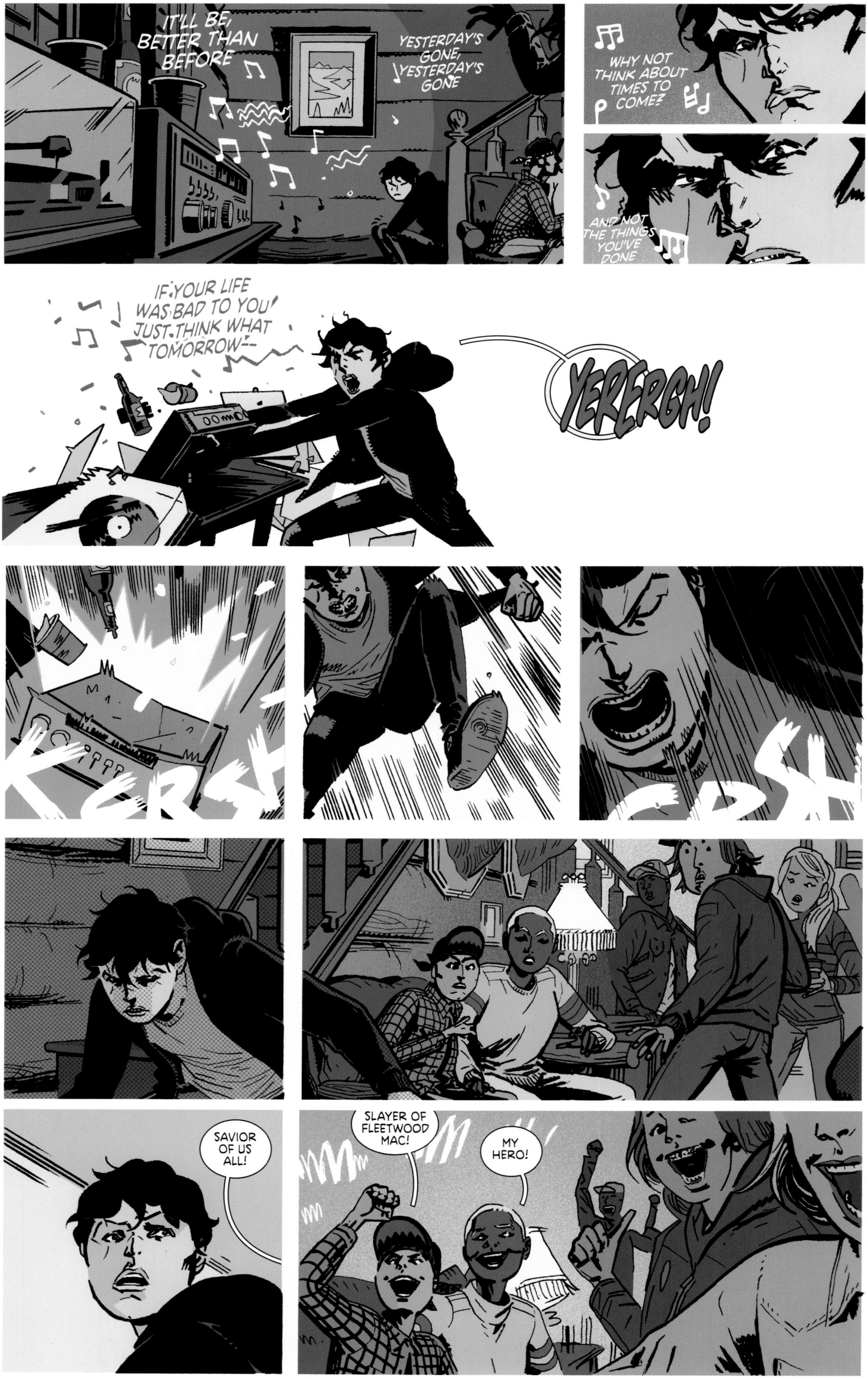
IT'LL BE, BETTER THAN BEFORE
YESTERDAY'S GONE, YESTERDAY'S GONE
WHY NOT THINK ABOUT TIMES TO COME?
AND NOT THE THINGS YOU'VE DONE
IF YOUR LIFE WAS BAD TO YOU JUST THINK WHAT TOMORROW--
YERERGH!
SAVIOR OF US ALL!
SLAYER OF FLEETWOOD MAC!
MY HERO!

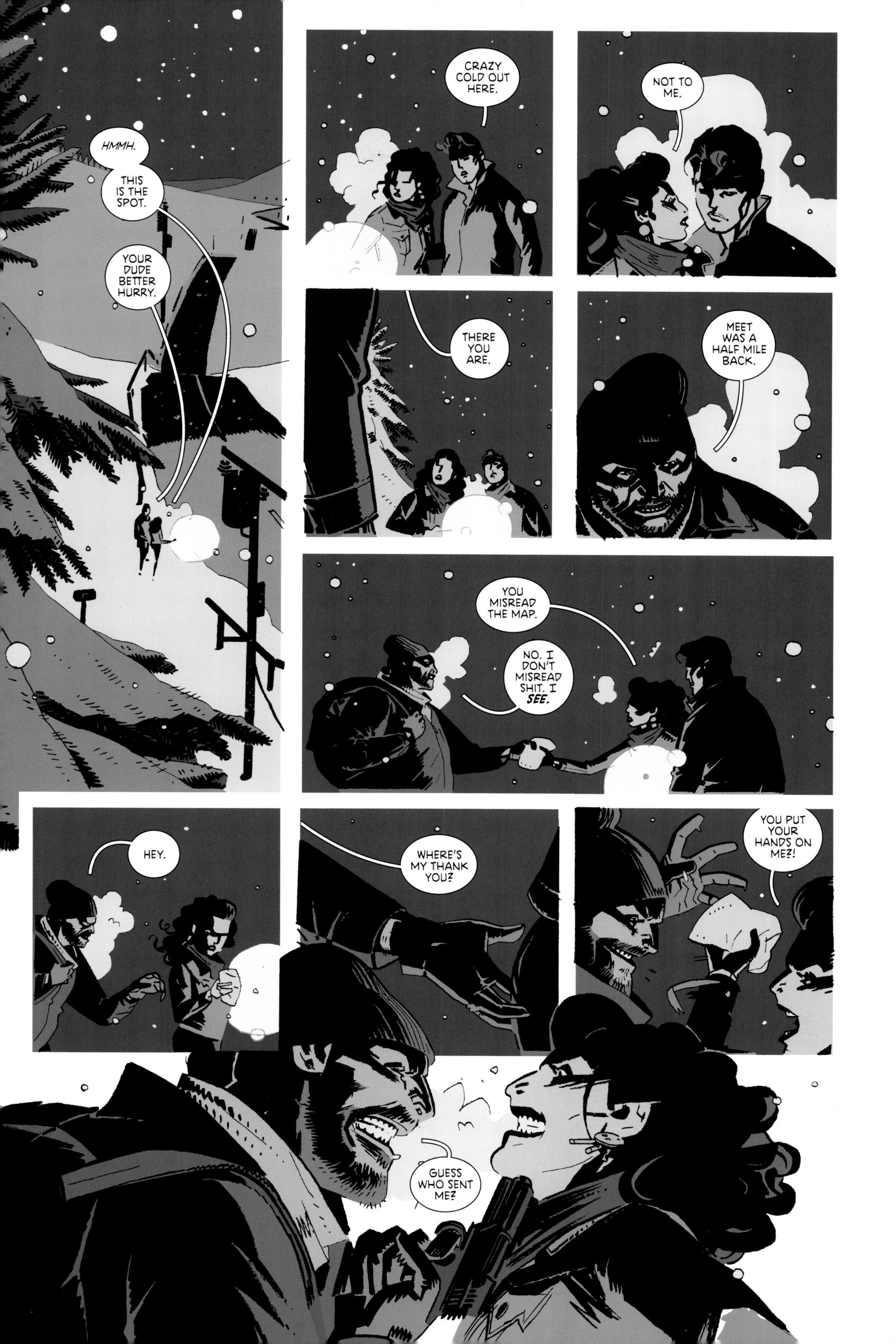
HMMH.
THIS IS THE SPOT.
YOUR DUDE BETTER HURRY.
CRAZY COLD OUT HERE.
NOT TO ME.
THERE YOU ARE.
MEET WAS A HALF MILE BACK.
YOU MISREAD THE MAP.
NO. I DON'T MISREAD SHIT. I *SEE.*
HEY.
WHERE'S MY THANK YOU?
YOU PUT YOUR HANDS ON ME?!
GUESS WHO SENT ME?

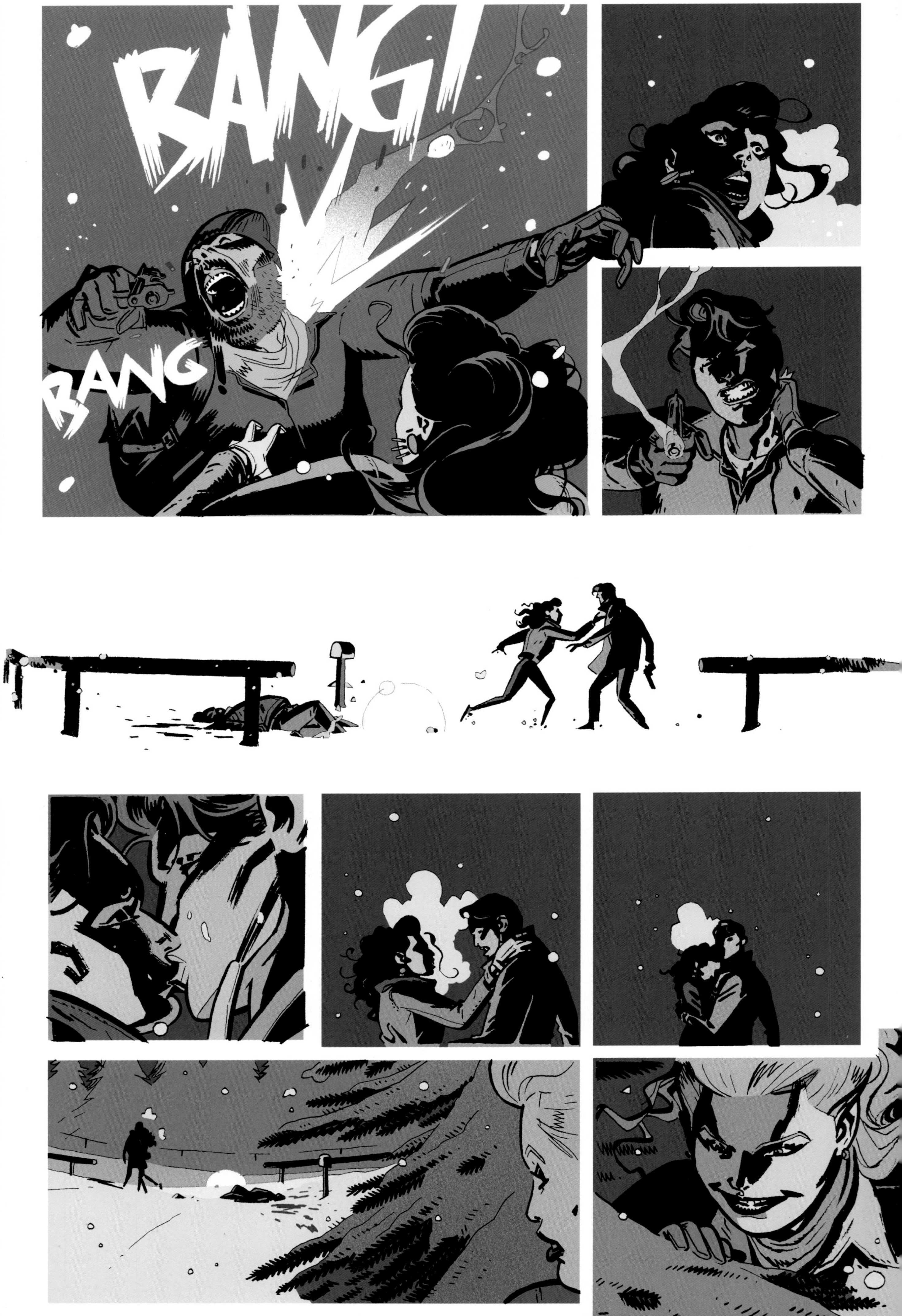
BANG!
BANG

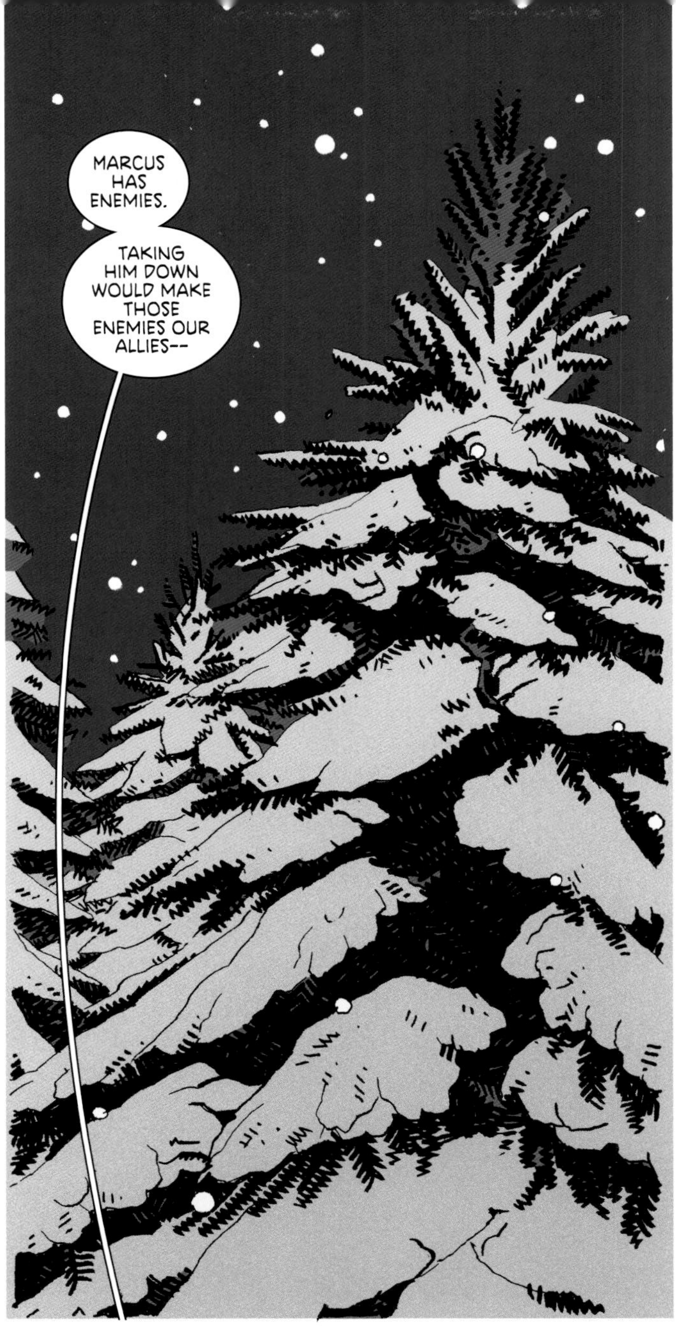
MARCUS HAS ENEMIES.
TAKING HIM DOWN WOULD MAKE THOSE ENEMIES OUR ALLIES--

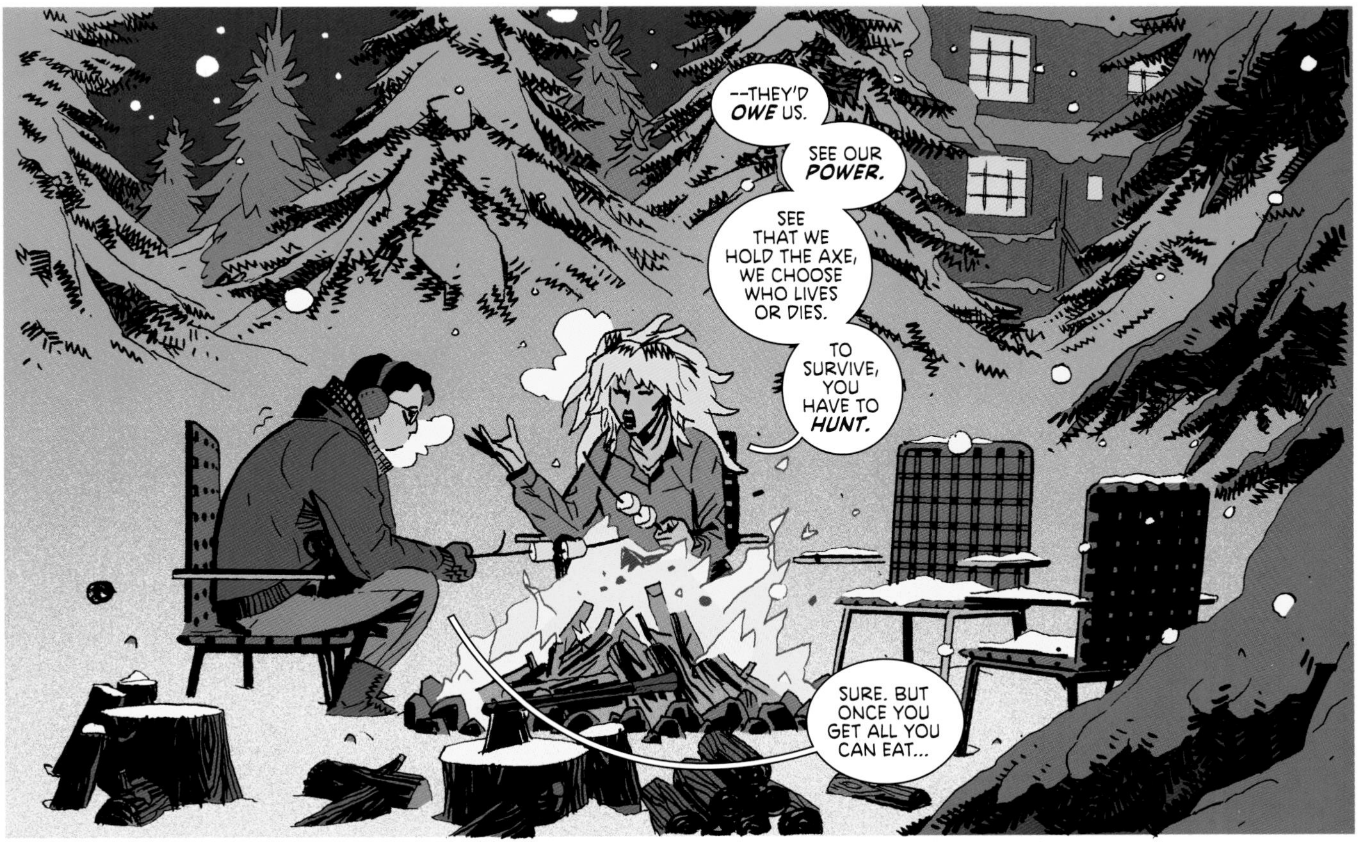
--THEY'D *OWE* US.
SEE OUR *POWER.*
SEE THAT WE HOLD THE AXE, WE CHOOSE WHO LIVES OR DIES.
TO SURVIVE, YOU HAVE TO *HUNT.*
SURE. BUT ONCE YOU GET ALL YOU CAN EAT...

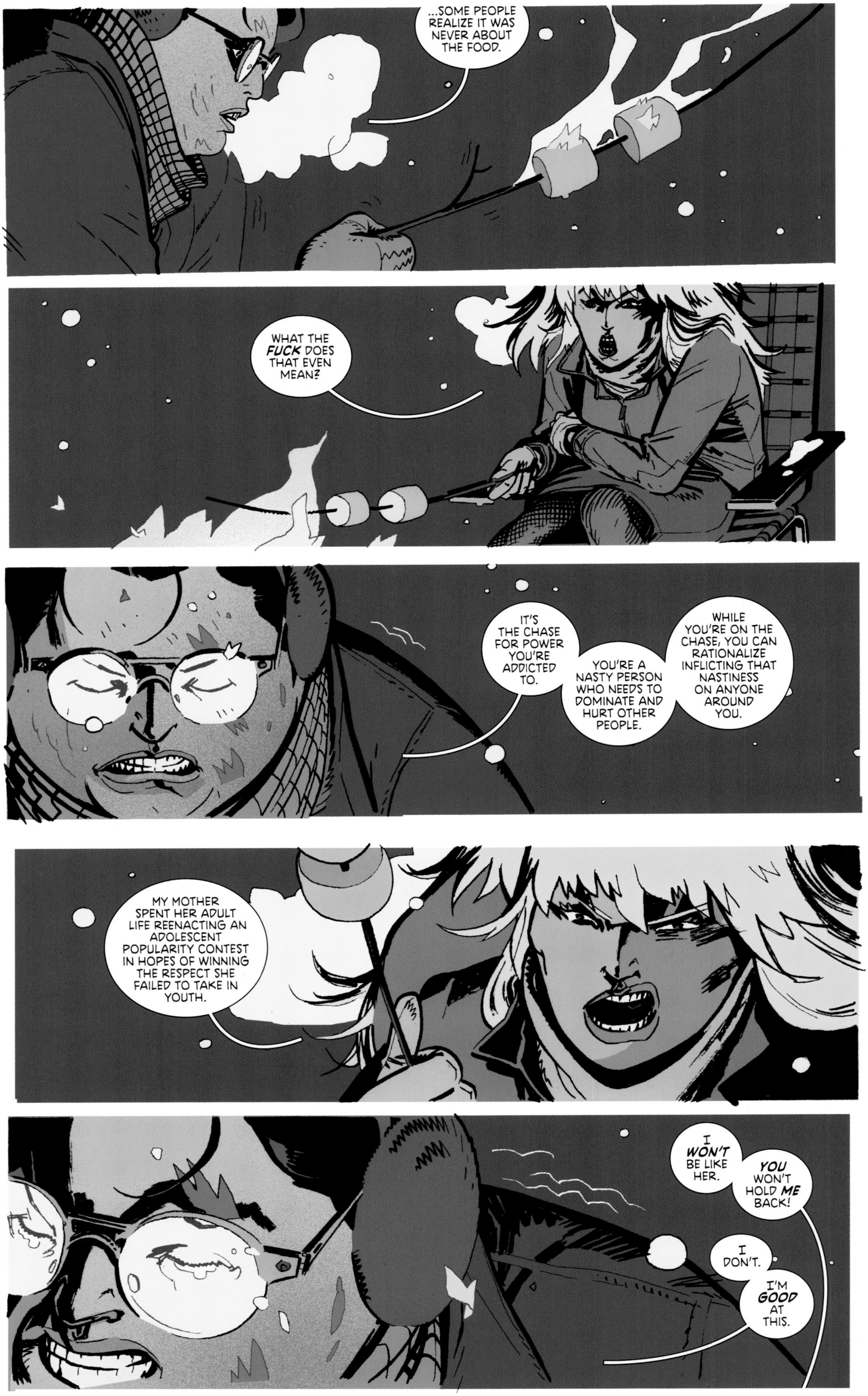

...SOME PEOPLE REALIZE IT WAS NEVER ABOUT THE FOOD.
WHAT THE FUCK DOES THAT EVEN MEAN?
IT'S THE CHASE FOR POWER YOU'RE ADDICTED TO.
YOU'RE A NASTY PERSON WHO NEEDS TO DOMINATE AND HURT OTHER PEOPLE.
WHILE YOU'RE ON THE CHASE, YOU CAN RATIONALIZE INFLICTING THAT NASTINESS ON ANYONE AROUND YOU.
MY MOTHER SPENT HER ADULT LIFE REENACTING AN ADOLESCENT POPULARITY CONTEST IN HOPES OF WINNING THE RESPECT SHE FAILED TO TAKE IN YOUTH.
I WON'T BE LIKE HER.
YOU WON'T HOLD ME BACK!
I DON'T.
I'M GOOD AT THIS.

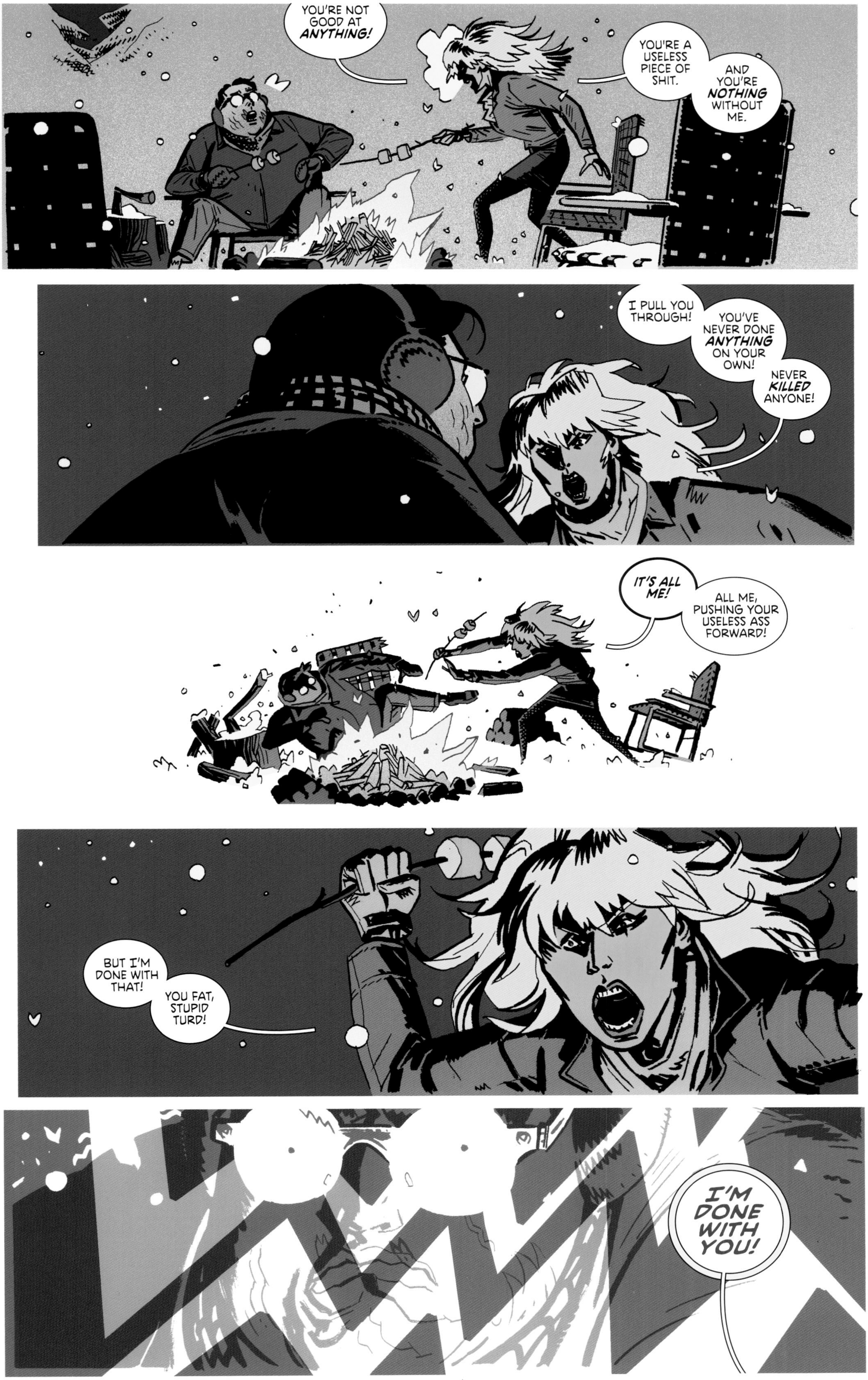

YOU'RE NOT GOOD AT ANYTHING!
YOU'RE A USELESS PIECE OF SHIT.
AND YOU'RE NOTHING WITHOUT ME.
I PULL YOU THROUGH!
YOU'VE NEVER DONE ANYTHING ON YOUR OWN!
NEVER KILLED ANYONE!
IT'S ALL ME!
ALL ME, PUSHING YOUR USELESS ASS FORWARD!
BUT I'M DONE WITH THAT!
YOU FAT, STUPID TURD!
I'M DONE WITH YOU!

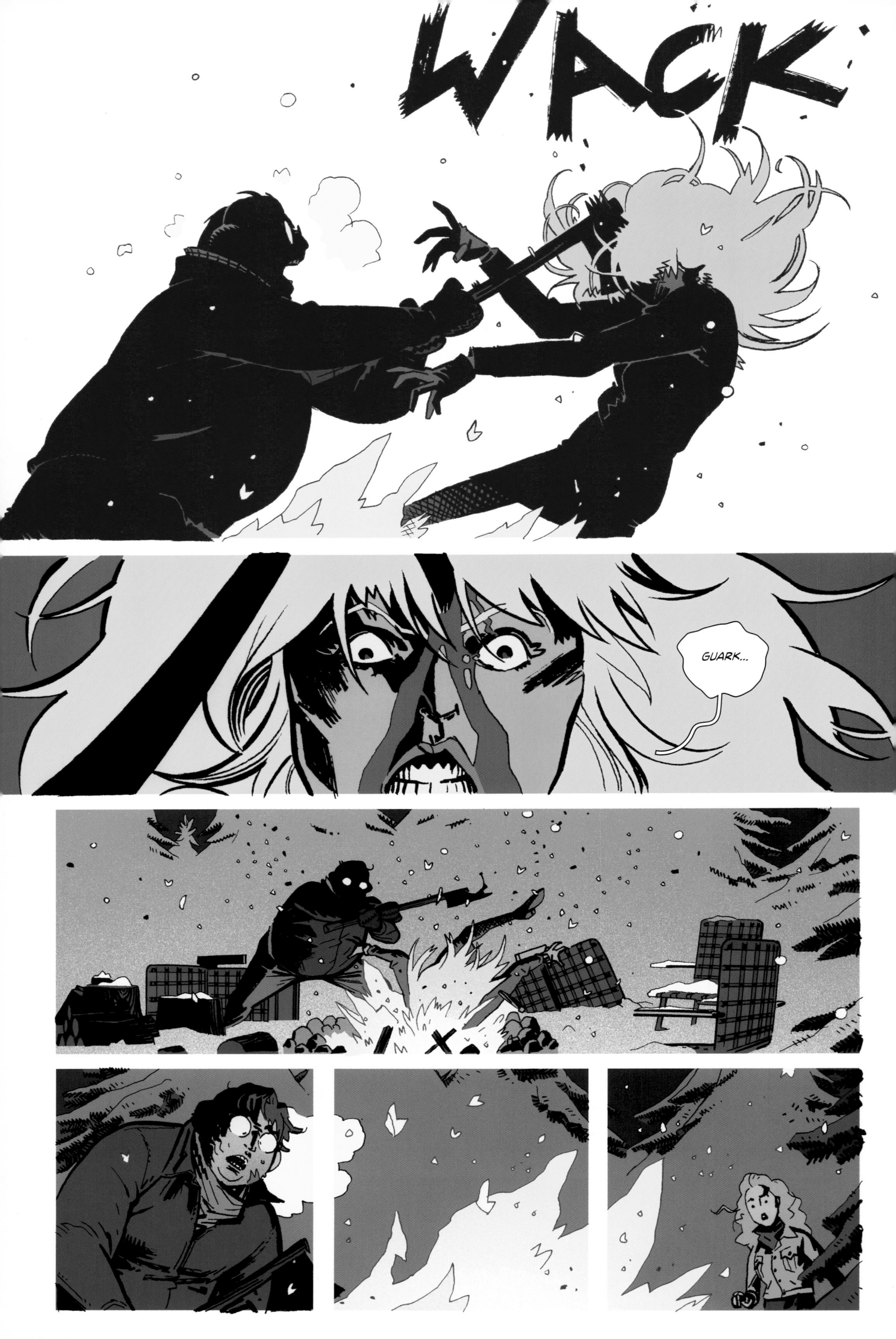
WACK
GUARK...

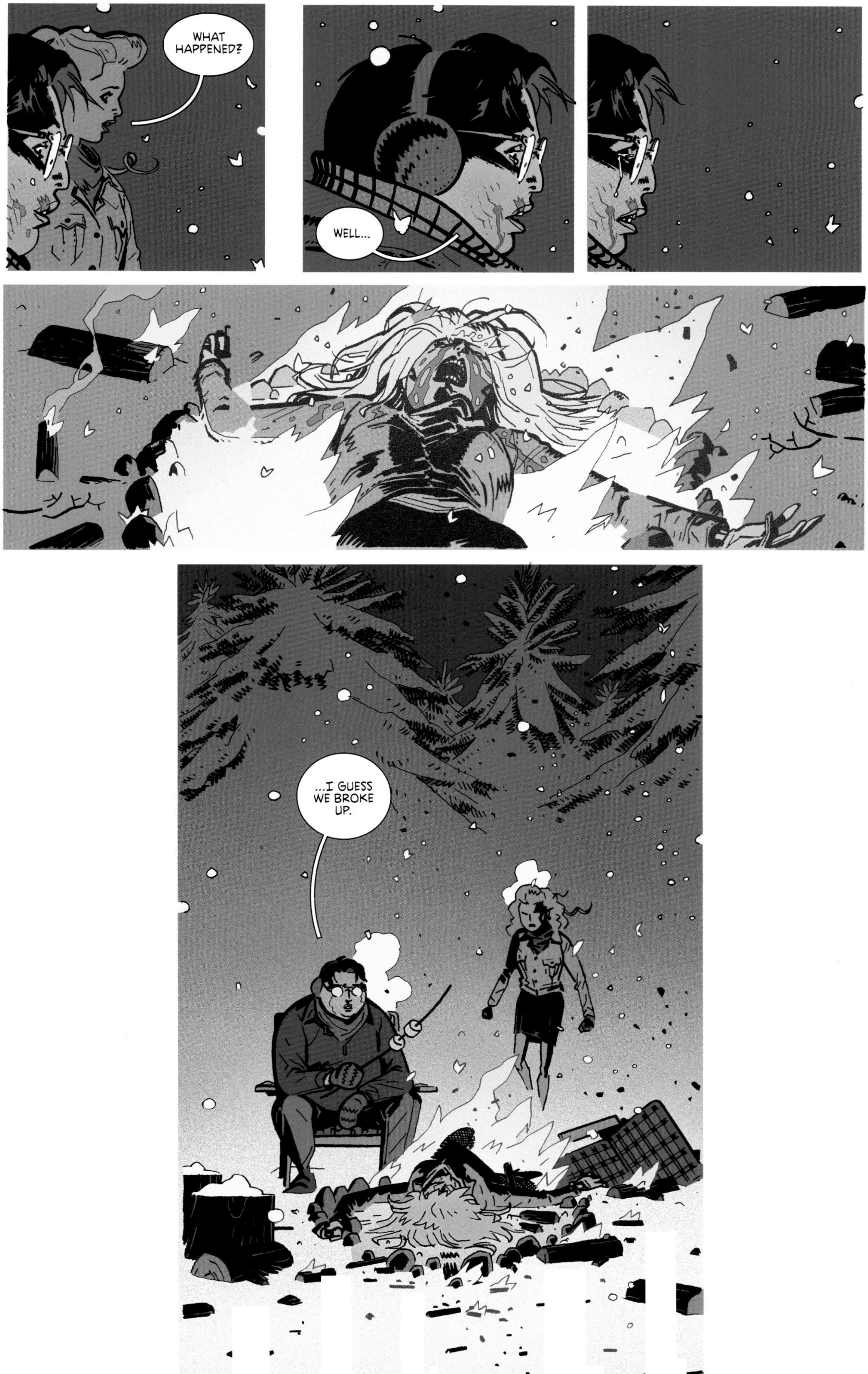
WHAT HAPPENED?
WELL...
...I GUESS WE BROKE UP.

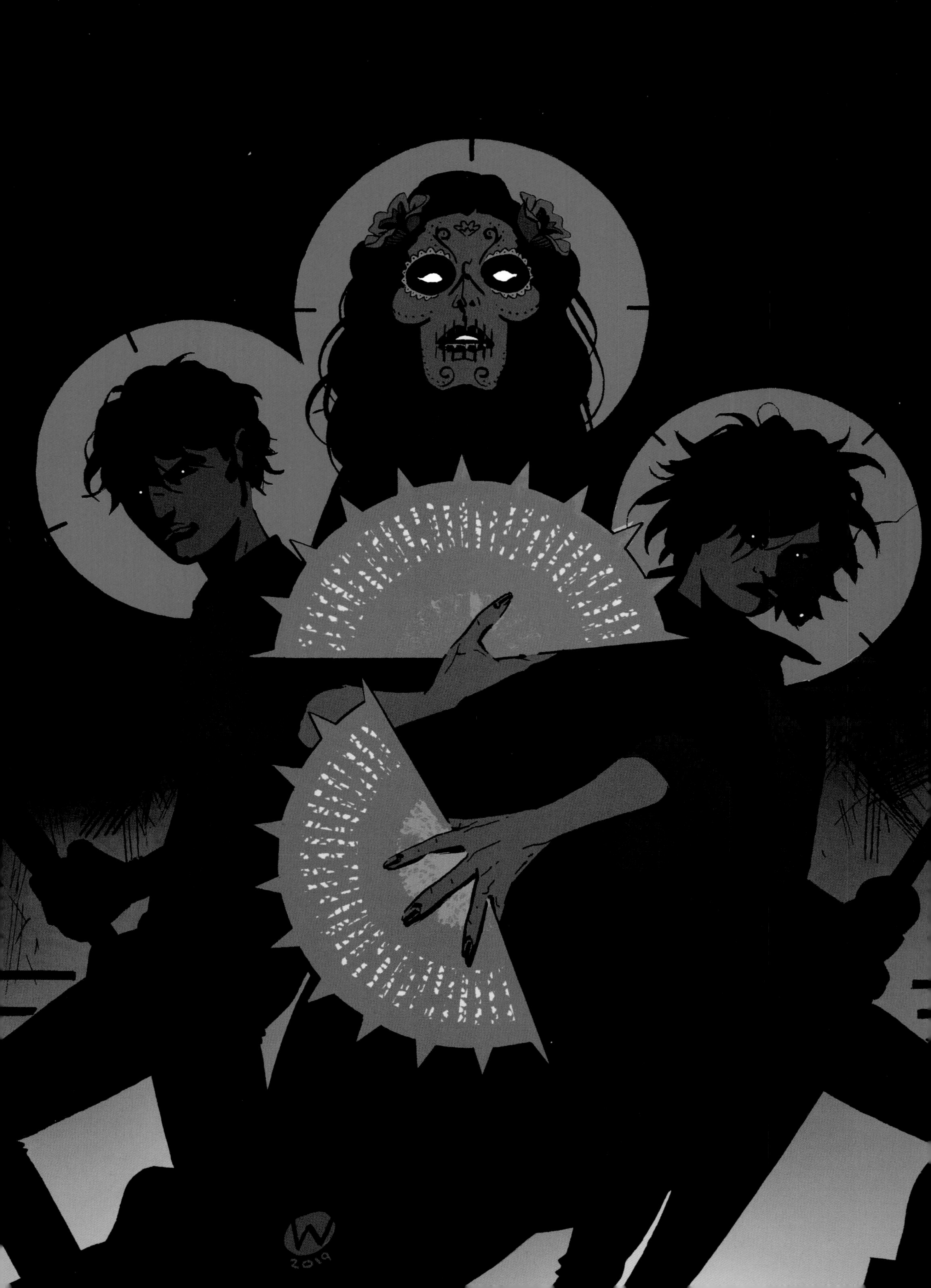

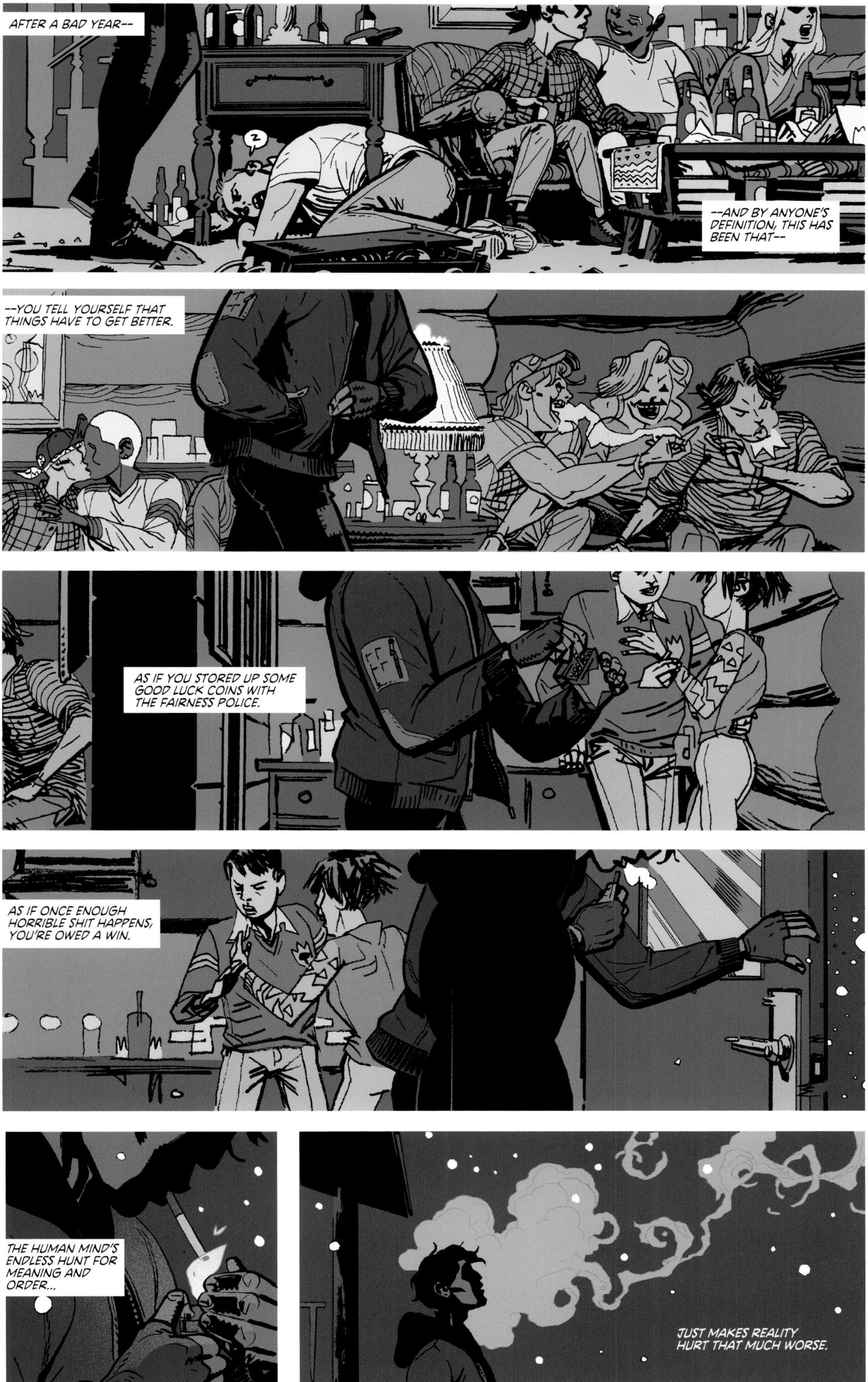
AFTER A BAD YEAR--
Z
--AND BY ANYONE'S DEFINITION, THIS HAS BEEN THAT--
--YOU TELL YOURSELF THAT THINGS HAVE TO GET BETTER.
AS IF YOU STORED UP SOME GOOD LUCK COINS WITH THE FAIRNESS POLICE.
AS IF ONCE ENOUGH HORRIBLE SHIT HAPPENS, YOU'RE OWED A WIN.
THE HUMAN MIND'S ENDLESS HUNT FOR MEANING AND ORDER...
JUST MAKES REALITY HURT THAT MUCH WORSE.

NOTHING WORKS OUT.

ALL DREAMS FALL APART.

YOUR HARD WORK IS ERASED.

EVERYONE YOU LOVE DIES.

TELL YOURSELF IT'S AN OVERLY DOUR, JUVENILE CLICHÉ.

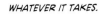

WHATEVER IT TAKES.

FF

YER GIRLFRIEND WENT THAT WAY.

ALL THAT **STUFF** YOU TELL YOURSELF ABOUT **POSITIVITY?**

ABOUT KEEPING YOUR **HEAD UP.**

HEE HEE

HOLDING **FAITH** IN TOMORROW.

TRUSTING THE **GOOD** IN PEOPLE...

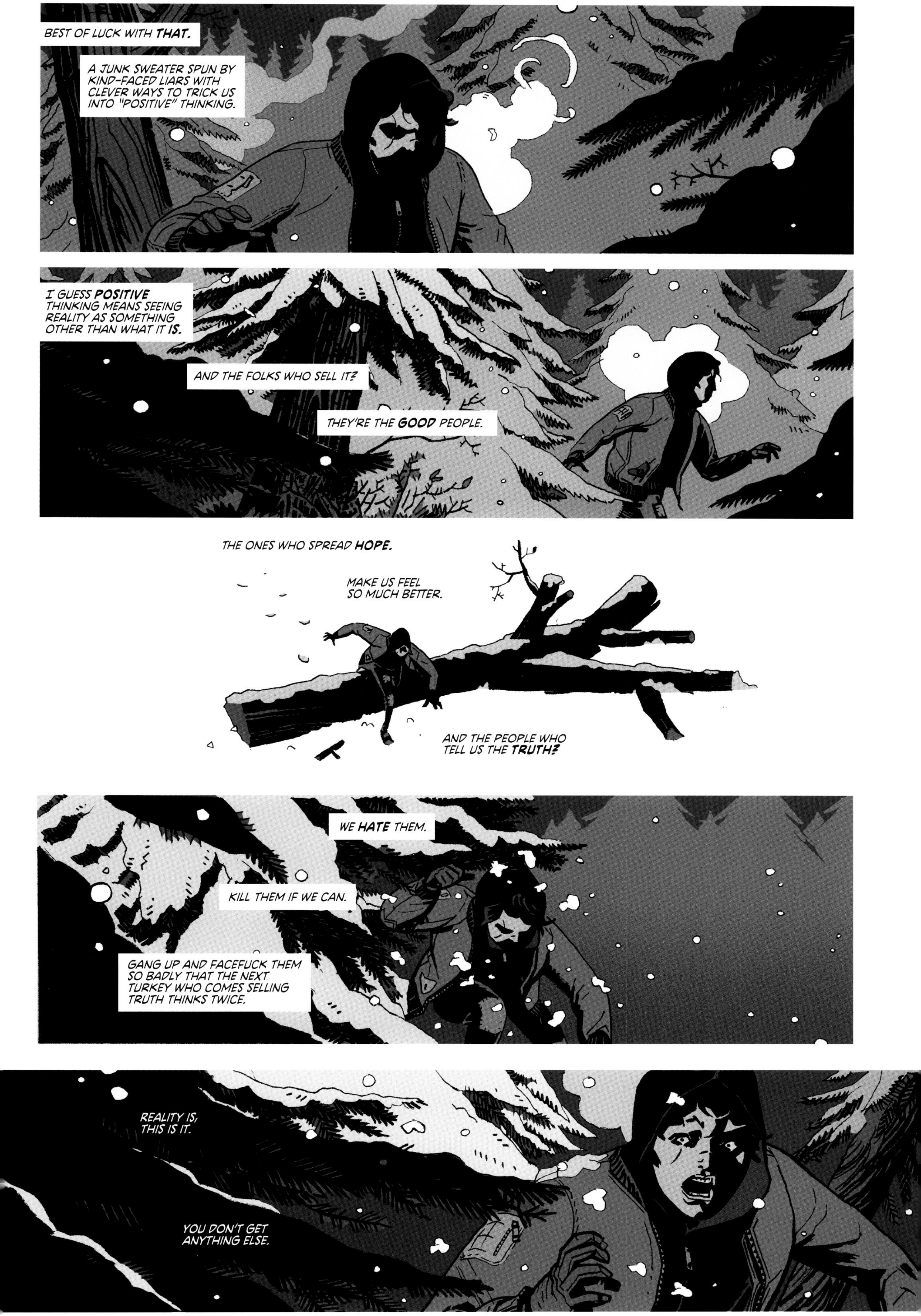
BEST OF LUCK WITH THAT.
A JUNK SWEATER SPUN BY KIND-FACED LIARS WITH CLEVER WAYS TO TRICK US INTO "POSITIVE" THINKING.
I GUESS POSITIVE THINKING MEANS SEEING REALITY AS SOMETHING OTHER THAN WHAT IT IS.
AND THE FOLKS WHO SELL IT?
THEY'RE THE GOOD PEOPLE.
THE ONES WHO SPREAD HOPE.
MAKE US FEEL SO MUCH BETTER.
AND THE PEOPLE WHO TELL US THE TRUTH?
WE HATE THEM.
KILL THEM IF WE CAN.
GANG UP AND FACEFUCK THEM SO BADLY THAT THE NEXT TURKEY WHO COMES SELLING TRUTH THINKS TWICE.
REALITY IS, THIS IS IT.
YOU DON'T GET ANYTHING ELSE.

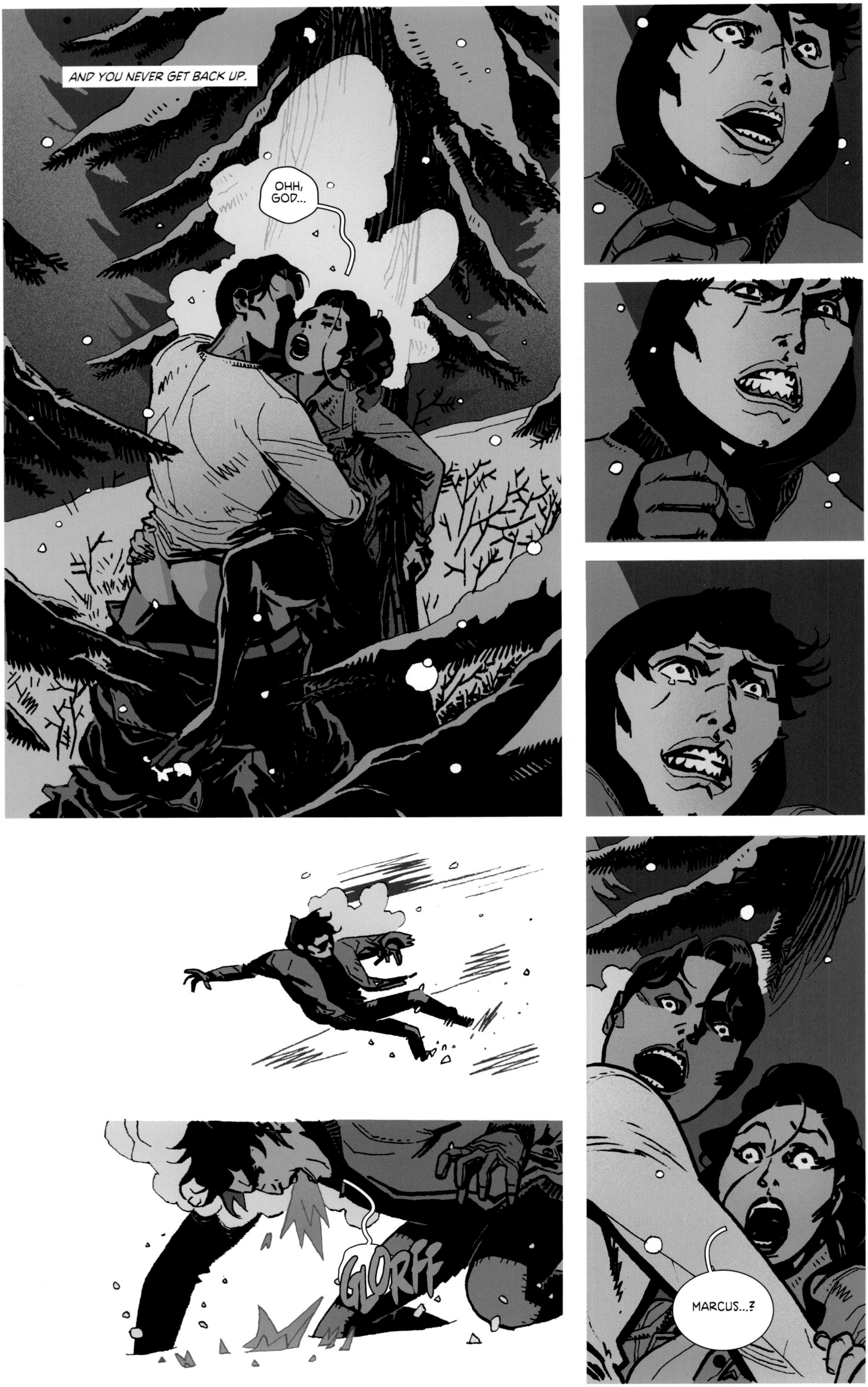
AND YOU NEVER GET BACK UP.
OHH, GOD...
GLORFF
MARCUS...?

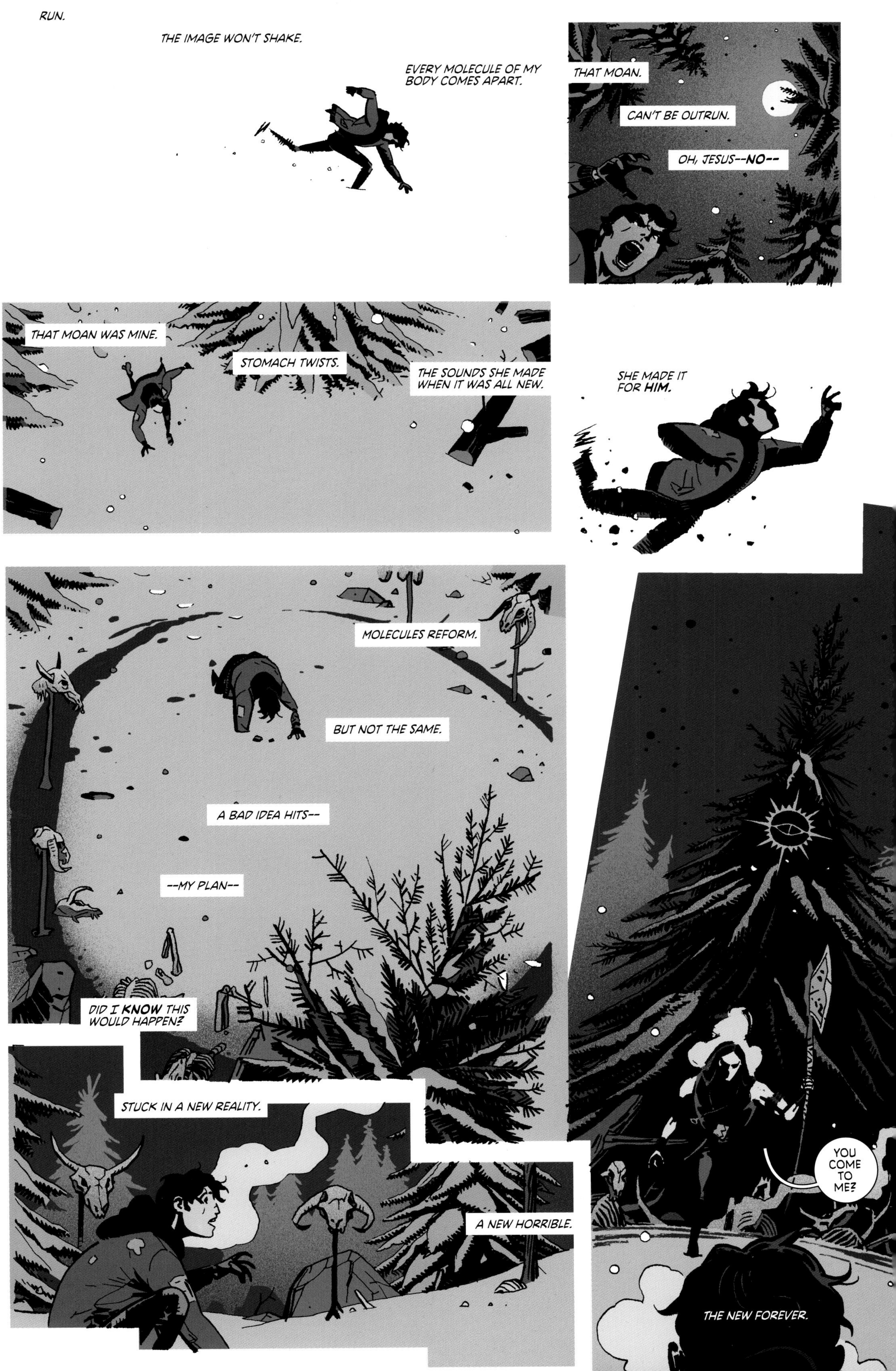
RUN.
THE IMAGE WON'T SHAKE.
EVERY MOLECULE OF MY BODY COMES APART.
THAT MOAN.
CAN'T BE OUTRUN.
OH, JESUS--NO--
THAT MOAN WAS MINE.
STOMACH TWISTS.
THE SOUNDS SHE MADE WHEN IT WAS ALL NEW.
SHE MADE IT FOR HIM.
MOLECULES REFORM.
BUT NOT THE SAME.
A BAD IDEA HITS--
--MY PLAN--
DID I KNOW THIS WOULD HAPPEN?
STUCK IN A NEW REALITY.
A NEW HORRIBLE.
YOU COME TO ME?
THE NEW FOREVER.

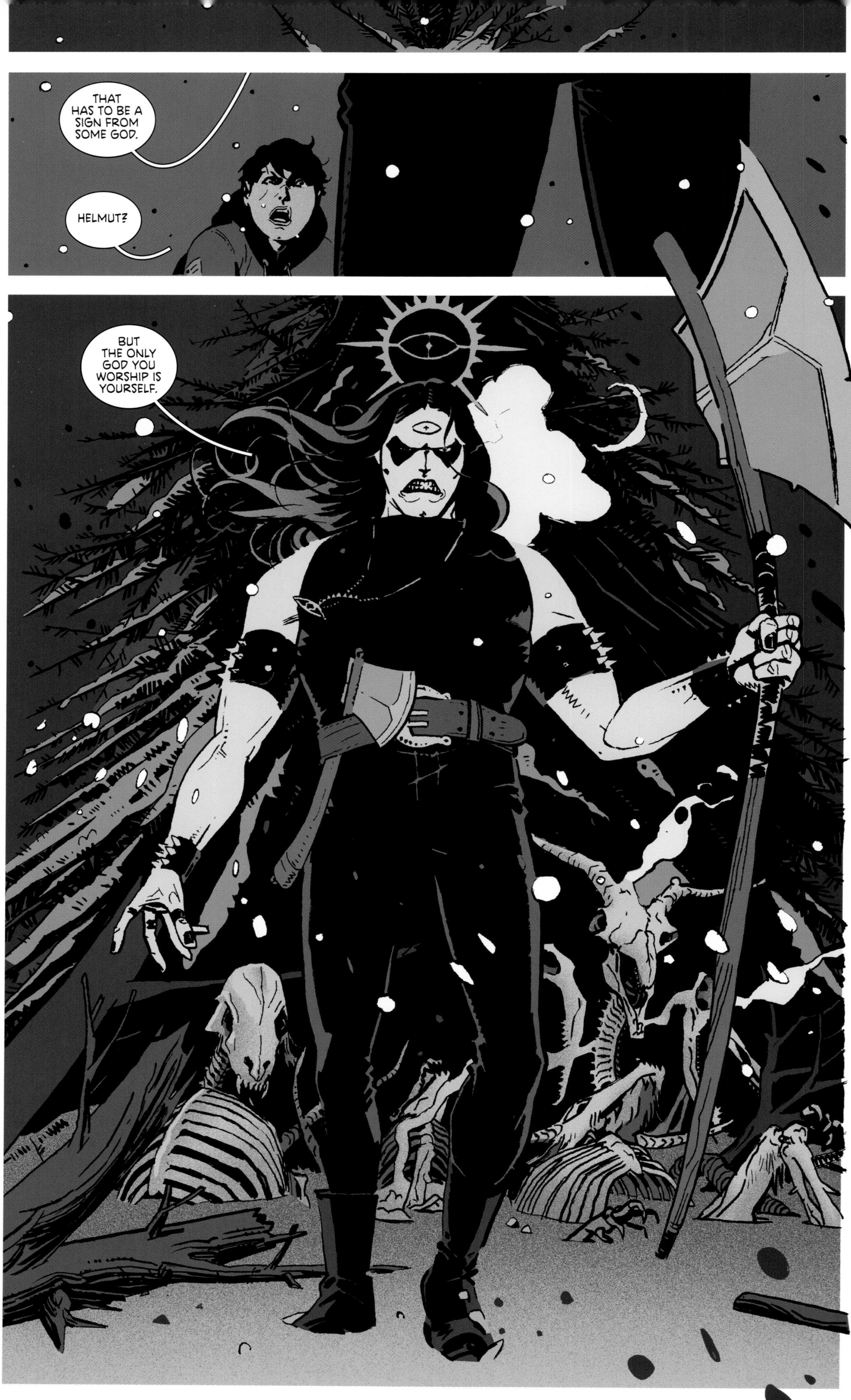
THAT HAS TO BE A SIGN FROM SOME GOD.
HELMUT?
BUT THE ONLY GOD YOU WORSHIP IS YOURSELF.

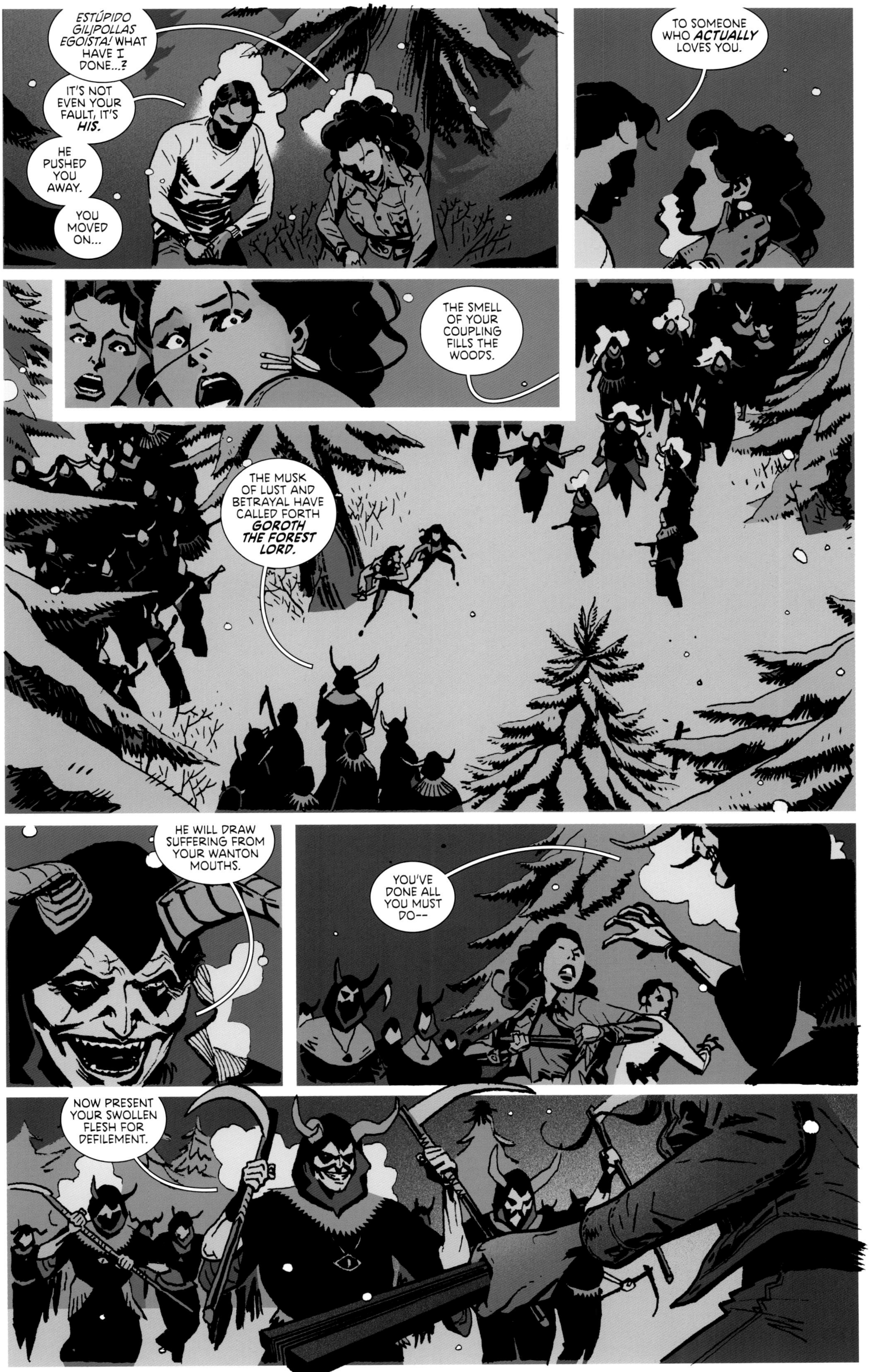
ESTÚPIDO GILIPOLLAS EGOISTA! WHAT HAVE I DONE...?
IT'S NOT EVEN YOUR FAULT, IT'S HIS.
HE PUSHED YOU AWAY.
YOU MOVED ON...
TO SOMEONE WHO ACTUALLY LOVES YOU.
THE SMELL OF YOUR COUPLING FILLS THE WOODS.
THE MUSK OF LUST AND BETRAYAL HAVE CALLED FORTH GOROTH THE FOREST LORD.
HE WILL DRAW SUFFERING FROM YOUR WANTON MOUTHS.
YOU'VE DONE ALL YOU MUST DO--
NOW PRESENT YOUR SWOLLEN FLESH FOR DEFILEMENT.

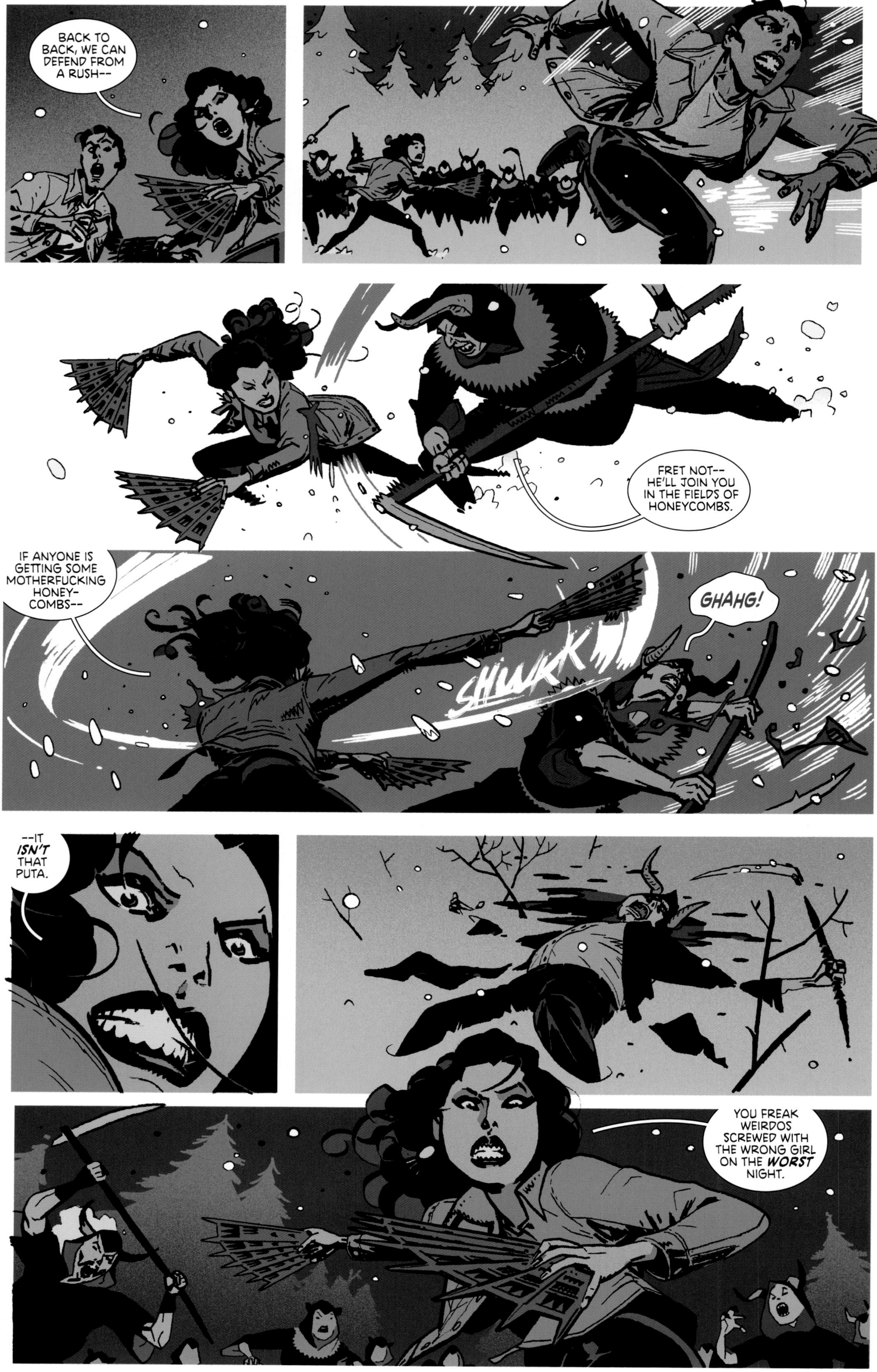
BACK TO BACK, WE CAN DEFEND FROM A RUSH--
FRET NOT-- HE'LL JOIN YOU IN THE FIELDS OF HONEYCOMBS.
IF ANYONE IS GETTING SOME MOTHERFUCKING HONEY-COMBS--
SHUKK
GHAHG!
--IT ISN'T THAT PUTA.
YOU FREAK WEIRDOS SCREWED WITH THE WRONG GIRL ON THE WORST NIGHT.

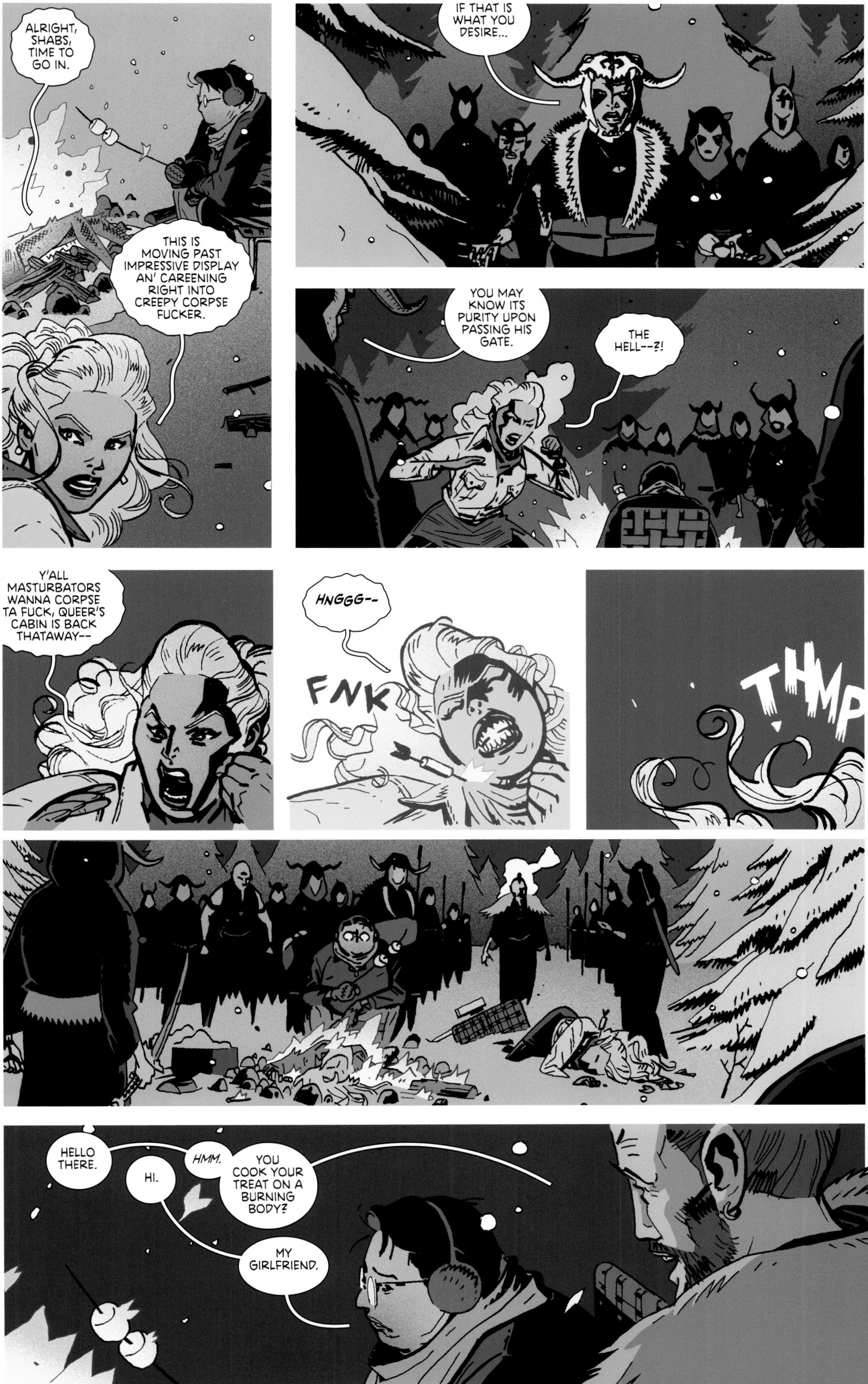
ALRIGHT, SHABS, TIME TO GO IN.
THIS IS MOVING PAST IMPRESSIVE DISPLAY AN' CAREENING RIGHT INTO CREEPY CORPSE FUCKER.
IF THAT IS WHAT YOU DESIRE...
YOU MAY KNOW ITS PURITY UPON PASSING HIS GATE.
THE HELL--?!
Y'ALL MASTURBATORS WANNA CORPSE TA FUCK, QUEER'S CABIN IS BACK THATAWAY--
HNGGG--
FNK
THMP
HELLO THERE.
HI.
HMM.
YOU COOK YOUR TREAT ON A BURNING BODY?
MY GIRLFRIEND.

WELL NOW, THIS IS A VERY SPECIAL NIGHT.

AND YOU?

"YOU ARE A PLEASING INDICATION OF PROSPERITY TO COME."

YOU HEAR THAT?

SOMEONE YELLING?

YEAH.

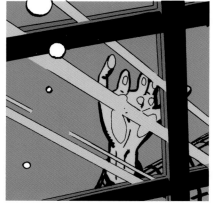

WHAT THE FUCK...?

IS THAT...

YEAH.

C'MON, WE GOTTA GO STOP HIM BEFORE--

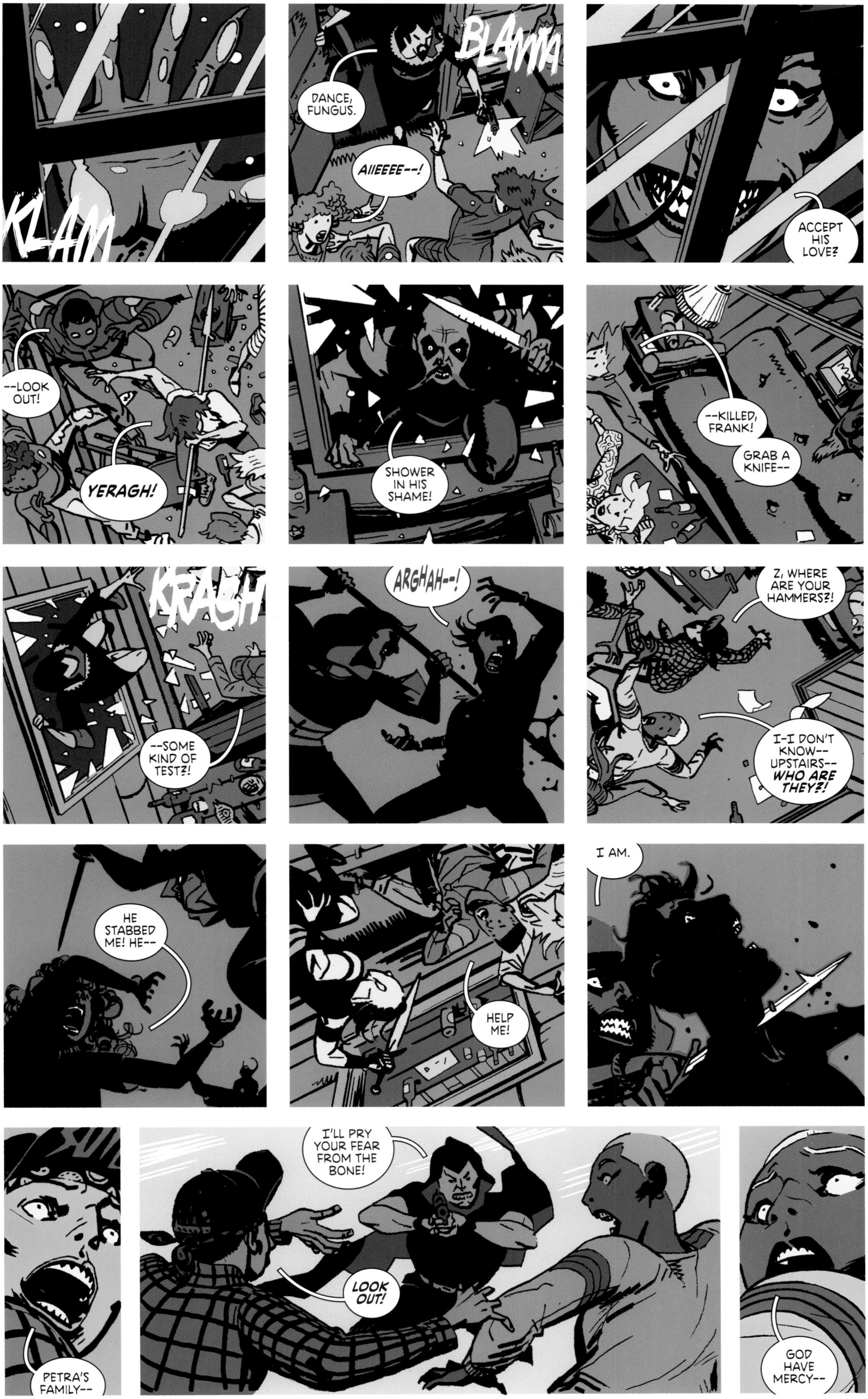
KLAM
DANCE, FUNGUS.
BLAMM
AIIEEEE--!
ACCEPT HIS LOVE?
--LOOK OUT!
YERAGH!
SHOWER IN HIS SHAME!
--KILLED, FRANK!
GRAB A KNIFE--
KRASH
--SOME KIND OF TEST?!
ARGHAH--!
Z, WHERE ARE YOUR HAMMERS?!
I-I DON'T KNOW-- UPSTAIRS-- WHO ARE THEY?!
HE STABBED ME! HE--
HELP ME!
I AM.
PETRA'S FAMILY--
I'LL PRY YOUR FEAR FROM THE BONE!
LOOK OUT!
GOD HAVE MERCY--

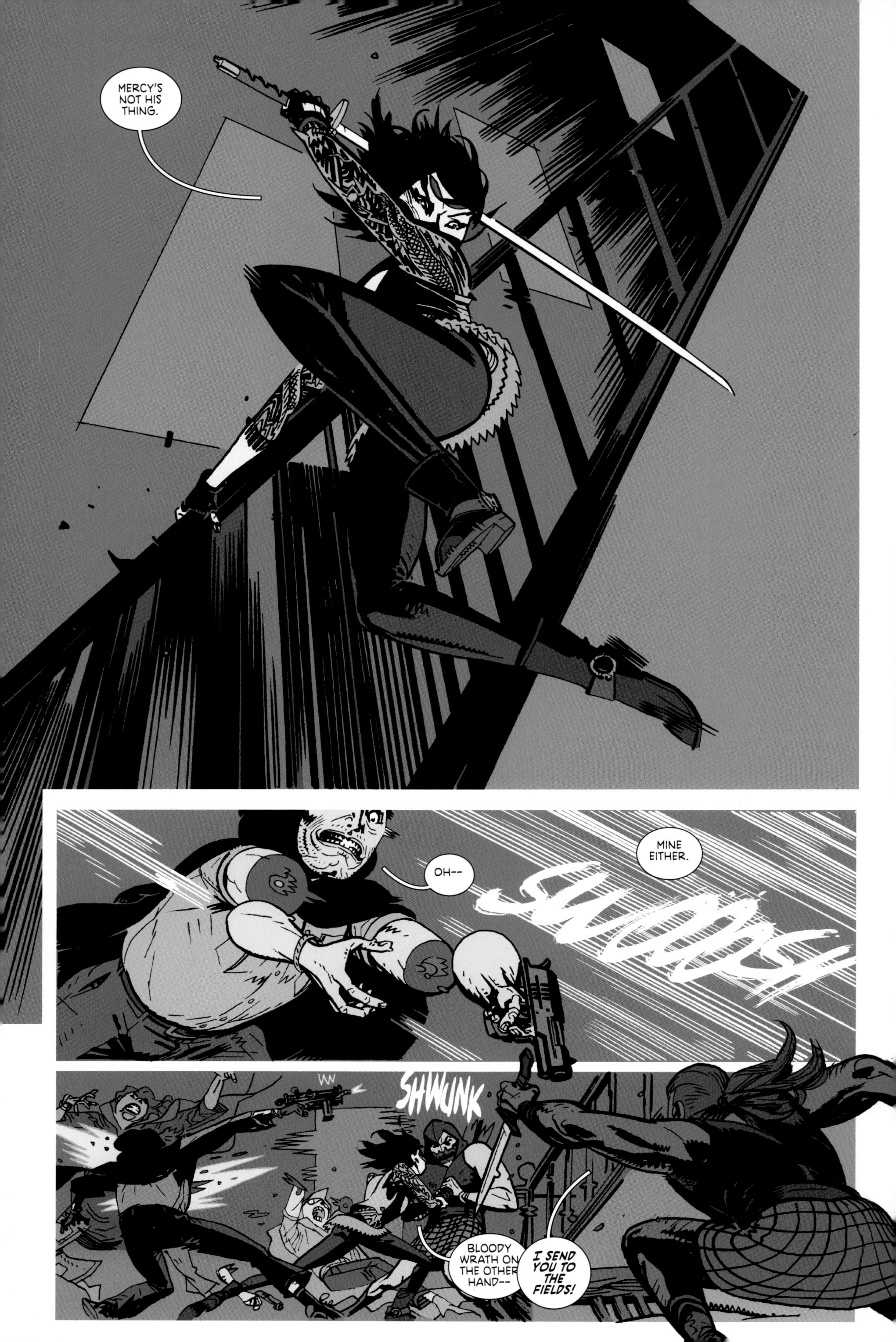
MERCY'S NOT HIS THING.
OH--
MINE EITHER.
SHWUNK
BLOODY WRATH ON THE OTHER HAND--
I SEND YOU TO THE FIELDS!

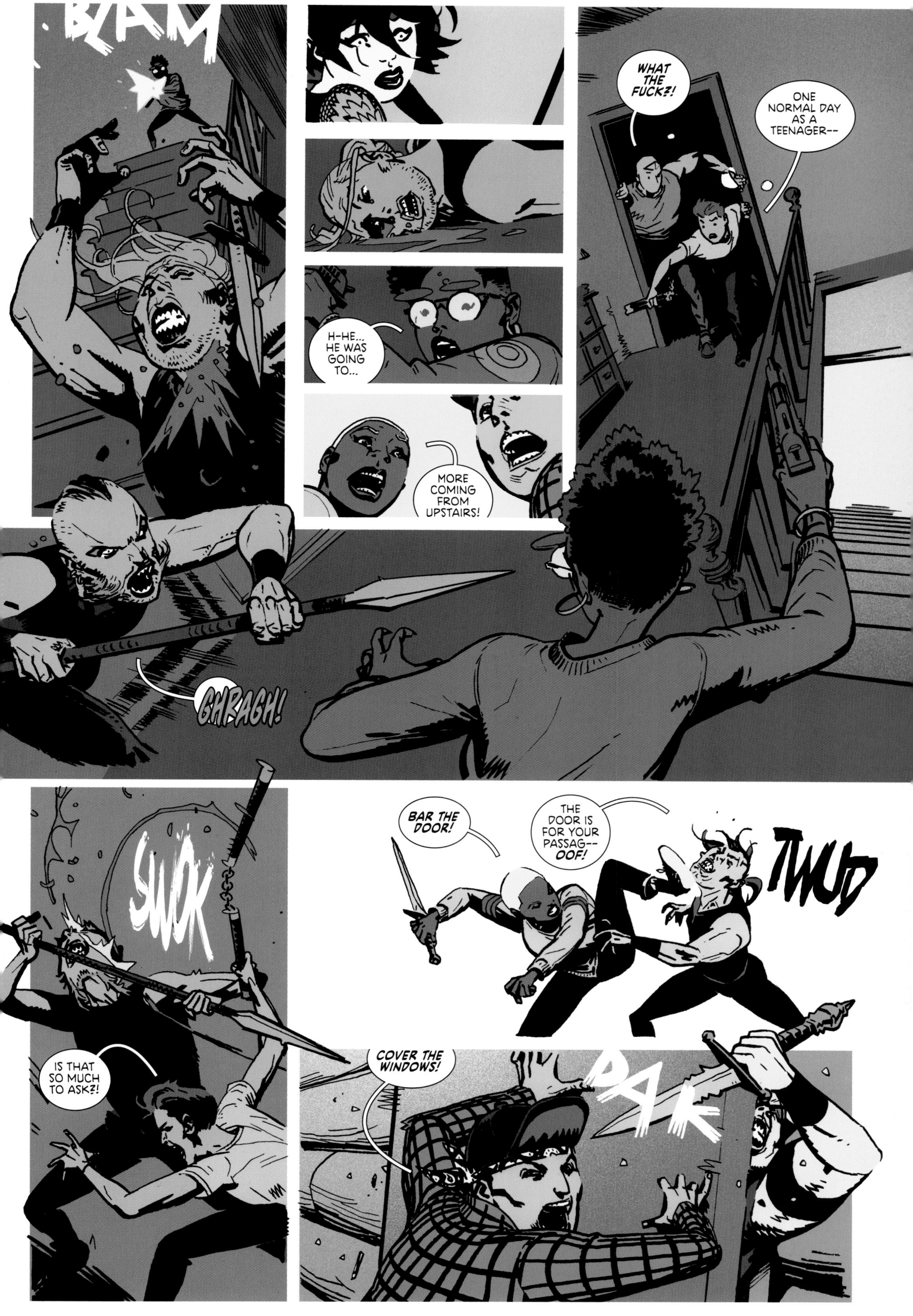
BLAM
H-HE... HE WAS GOING TO...
MORE COMING FROM UPSTAIRS!
WHAT THE FUCK?!
ONE NORMAL DAY AS A TEENAGER--
GHRAGH!
SHUK
IS THAT SO MUCH TO ASK?!
BAR THE DOOR!
THE DOOR IS FOR YOUR PASSAG-- OOF!
TWUD
COVER THE WINDOWS!
DAK

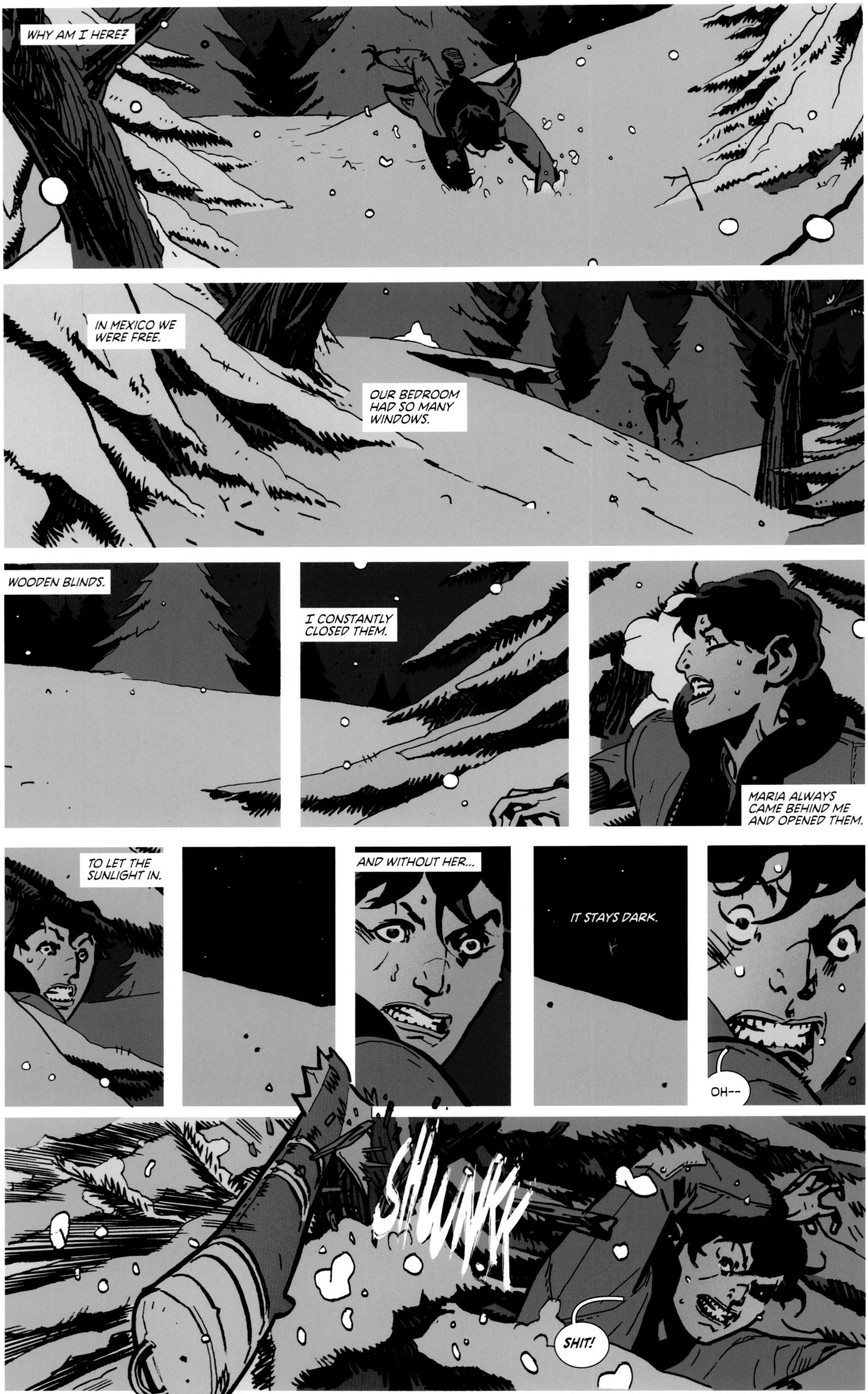
WHY AM I HERE?
IN MEXICO WE WERE FREE.
OUR BEDROOM HAD SO MANY WINDOWS.
WOODEN BLINDS.
I CONSTANTLY CLOSED THEM.
MARIA ALWAYS CAME BEHIND ME AND OPENED THEM.
TO LET THE SUNLIGHT IN.
AND WITHOUT HER...
IT STAYS DARK.
OH--
SHUNK
SHIT!

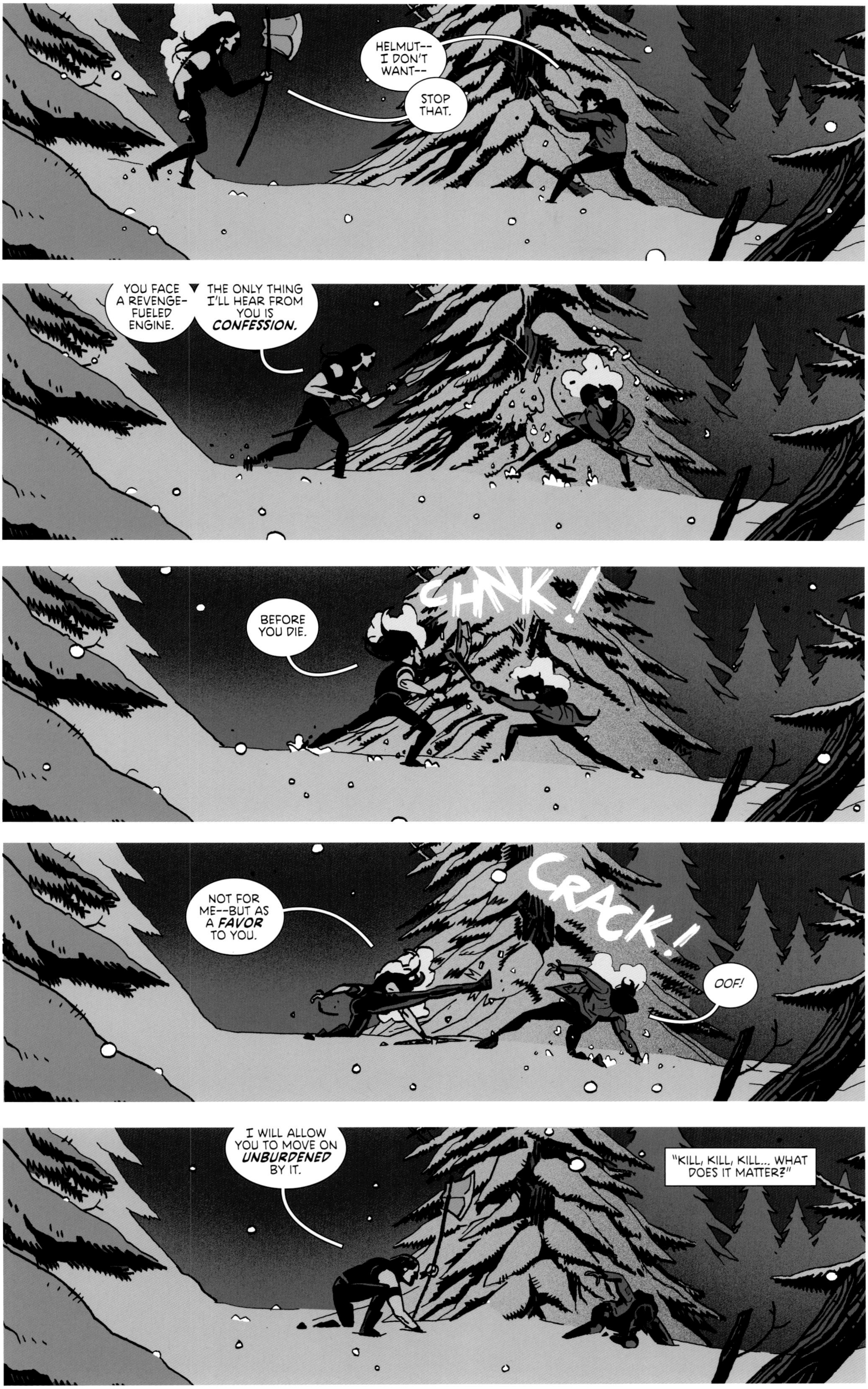
HELMUT-- I DON'T WANT--
STOP THAT.
YOU FACE A REVENGE-FUELED ENGINE.
THE ONLY THING I'LL HEAR FROM YOU IS *CONFESSION.*
CHNK!
BEFORE YOU DIE.
CRACK!
NOT FOR ME--BUT AS A *FAVOR* TO YOU.
OOF!
I WILL ALLOW YOU TO MOVE ON *UNBURDENED* BY IT.
"KILL, KILL, KILL... WHAT DOES IT MATTER?"

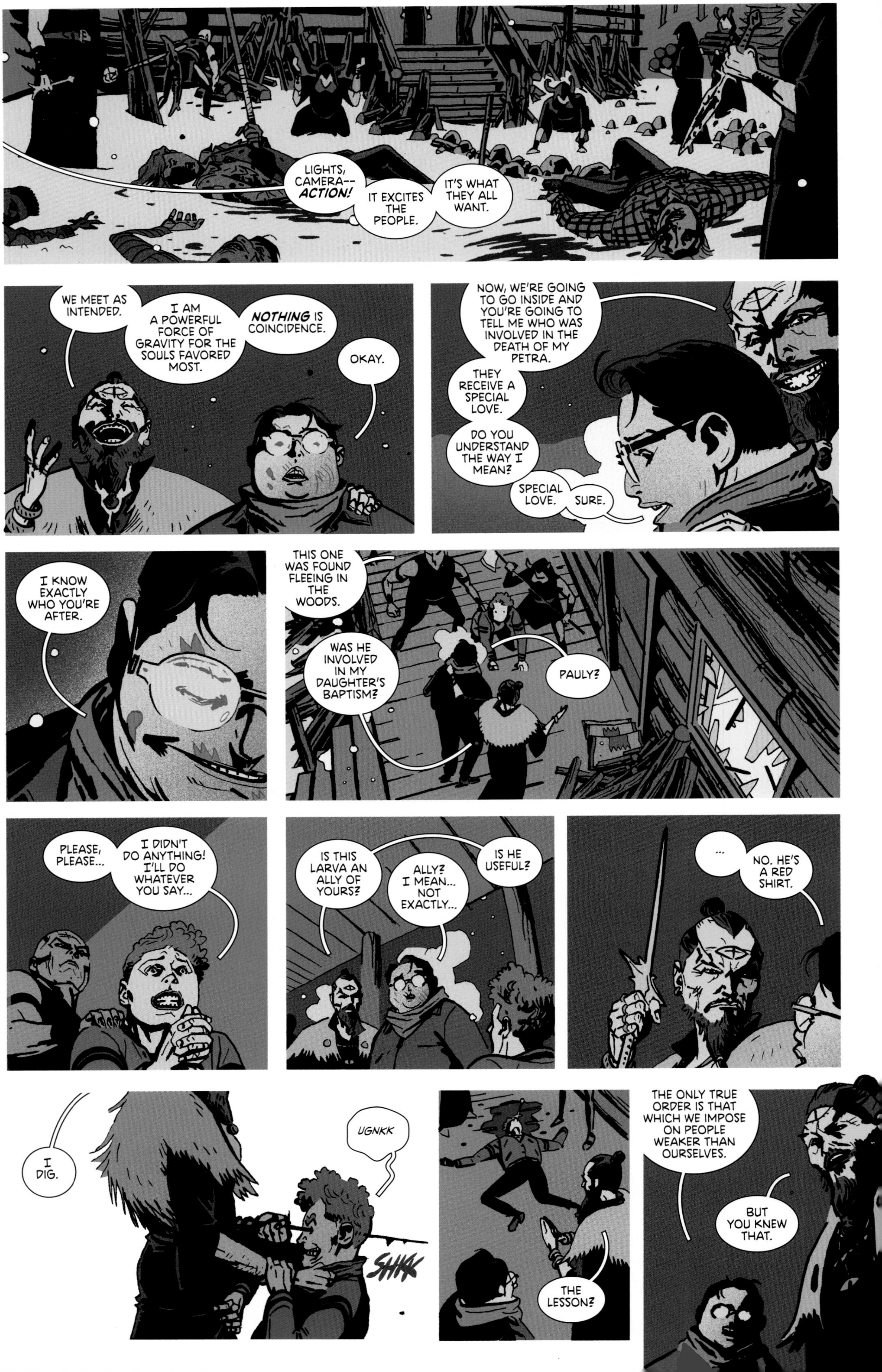
LIGHTS, CAMERA-- ACTION!
IT EXCITES THE PEOPLE.
IT'S WHAT THEY ALL WANT.
WE MEET AS INTENDED.
I AM A POWERFUL FORCE OF GRAVITY FOR THE SOULS FAVORED MOST.
NOTHING IS COINCIDENCE.
OKAY.
NOW, WE'RE GOING TO GO INSIDE AND YOU'RE GOING TO TELL ME WHO WAS INVOLVED IN THE DEATH OF MY PETRA.
THEY RECEIVE A SPECIAL LOVE.
DO YOU UNDERSTAND THE WAY I MEAN?
SPECIAL LOVE.
SURE.
I KNOW EXACTLY WHO YOU'RE AFTER.
THIS ONE WAS FOUND FLEEING IN THE WOODS.
WAS HE INVOLVED IN MY DAUGHTER'S BAPTISM?
PAULY?
PLEASE, PLEASE...
I DIDN'T DO ANYTHING! I'LL DO WHATEVER YOU SAY...
IS THIS LARVA AN ALLY OF YOURS?
ALLY? I MEAN... NOT EXACTLY...
IS HE USEFUL?
...
NO. HE'S A RED SHIRT.
I DIG.
UGNKK
SHKK
THE LESSON?
THE ONLY TRUE ORDER IS THAT WHICH WE IMPOSE ON PEOPLE WEAKER THAN OURSELVES.
BUT YOU KNEW THAT.

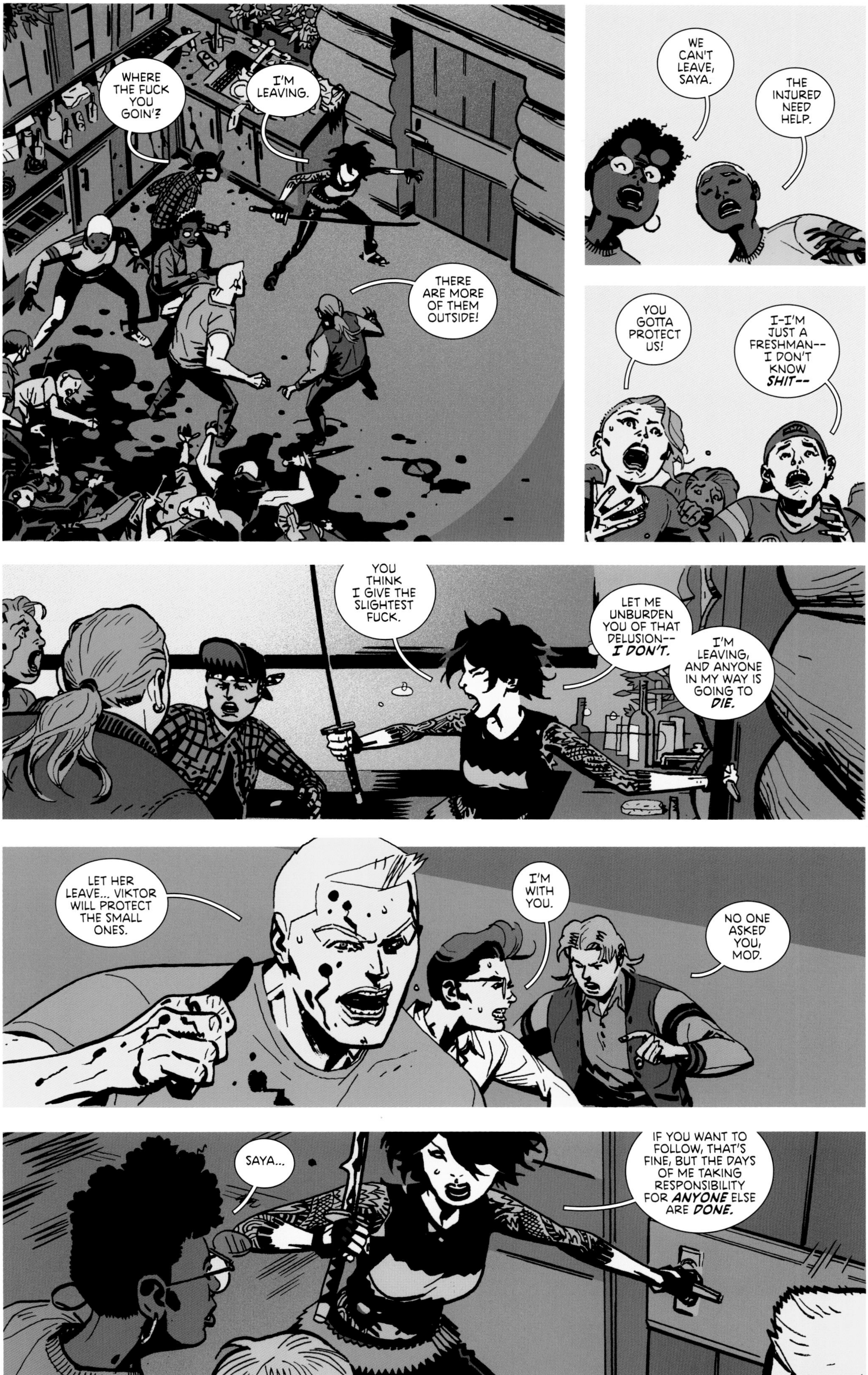
WHERE THE FUCK YOU GOIN'?
I'M LEAVING.
THERE ARE MORE OF THEM OUTSIDE!
WE CAN'T LEAVE, SAYA.
THE INJURED NEED HELP.
YOU GOTTA PROTECT US!
I-I'M JUST A FRESHMAN-- I DON'T KNOW SHIT--
YOU THINK I GIVE THE SLIGHTEST FUCK.
LET ME UNBURDEN YOU OF THAT DELUSION-- I DON'T.
I'M LEAVING, AND ANYONE IN MY WAY IS GOING TO DIE.
LET HER LEAVE... VIKTOR WILL PROTECT THE SMALL ONES.
I'M WITH YOU.
NO ONE ASKED YOU, MOD.
SAYA...
IF YOU WANT TO FOLLOW, THAT'S FINE, BUT THE DAYS OF ME TAKING RESPONSIBILITY FOR ANYONE ELSE ARE DONE.

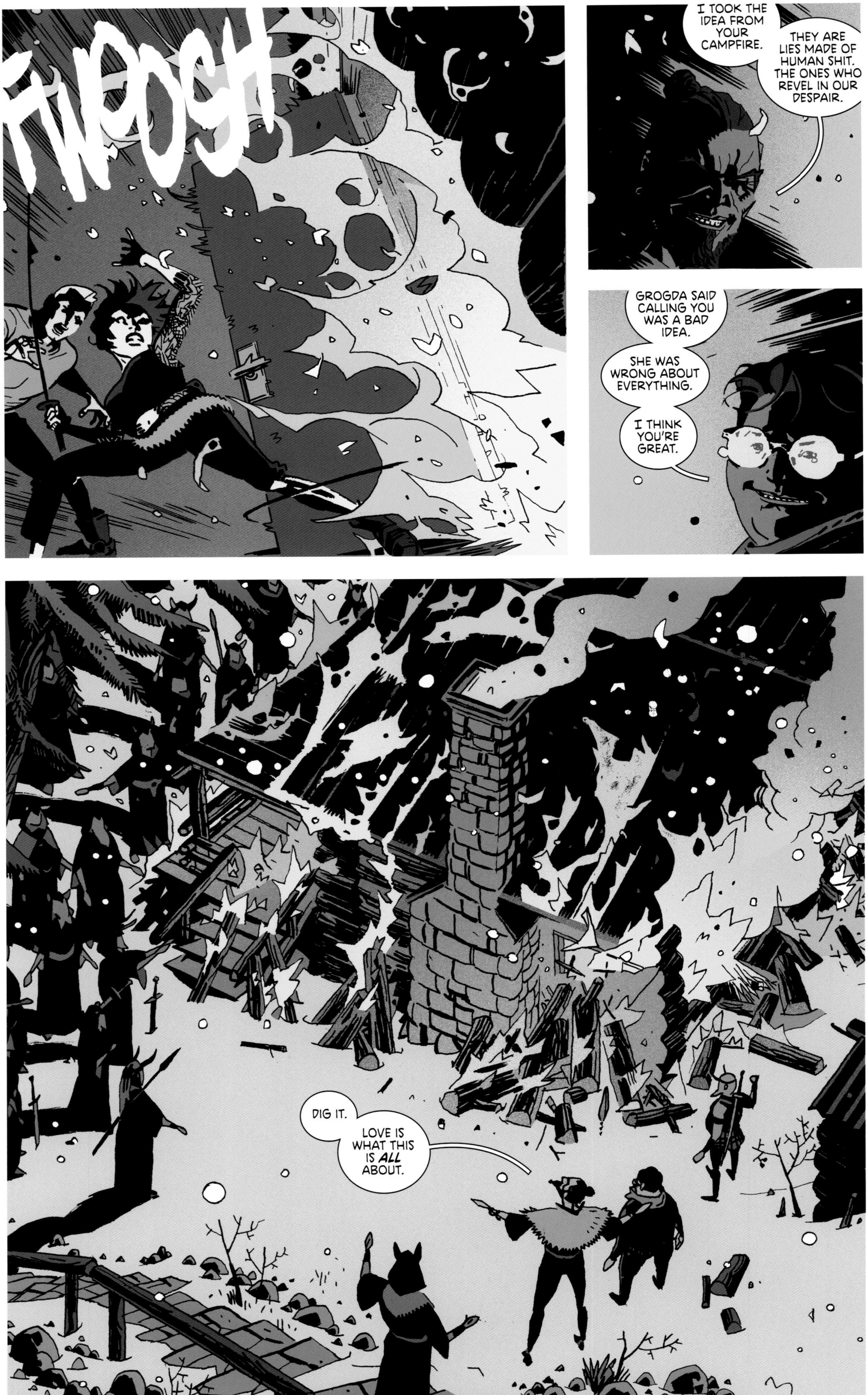
FWOOSH
I TOOK THE IDEA FROM YOUR CAMPFIRE.
THEY ARE LIES MADE OF HUMAN SHIT. THE ONES WHO REVEL IN OUR DESPAIR.
GROGDA SAID CALLING YOU WAS A BAD IDEA.
SHE WAS WRONG ABOUT EVERYTHING.
I THINK YOU'RE GREAT.
DIG IT.
LOVE IS WHAT THIS IS *ALL* ABOUT.

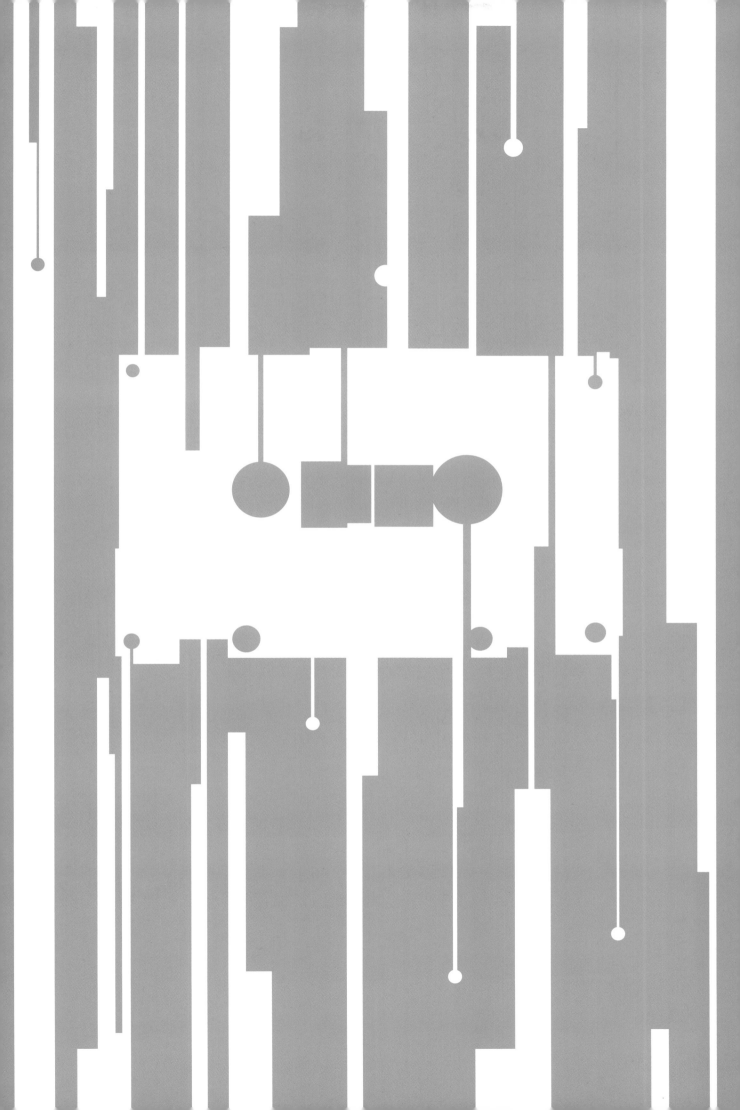

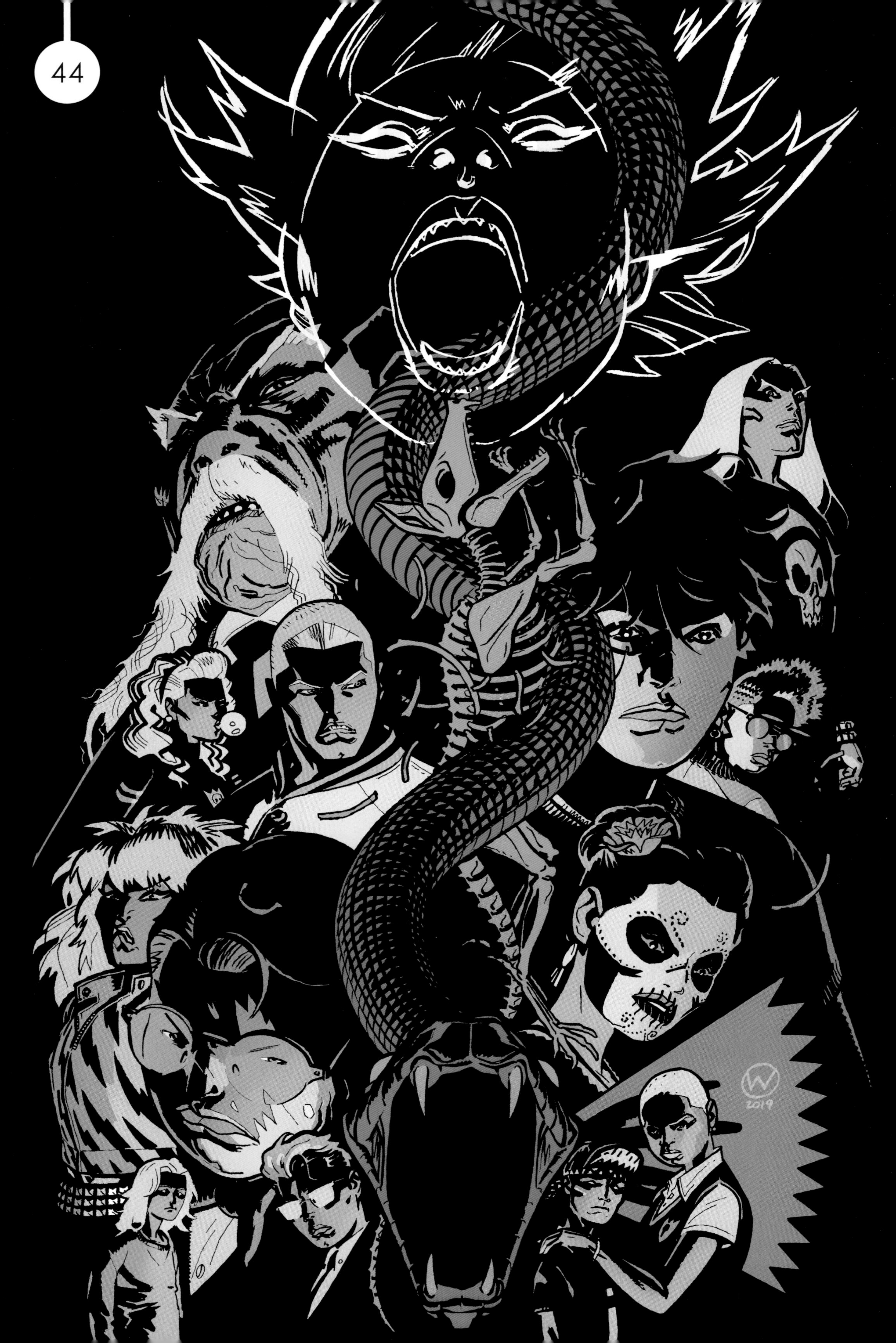
2019

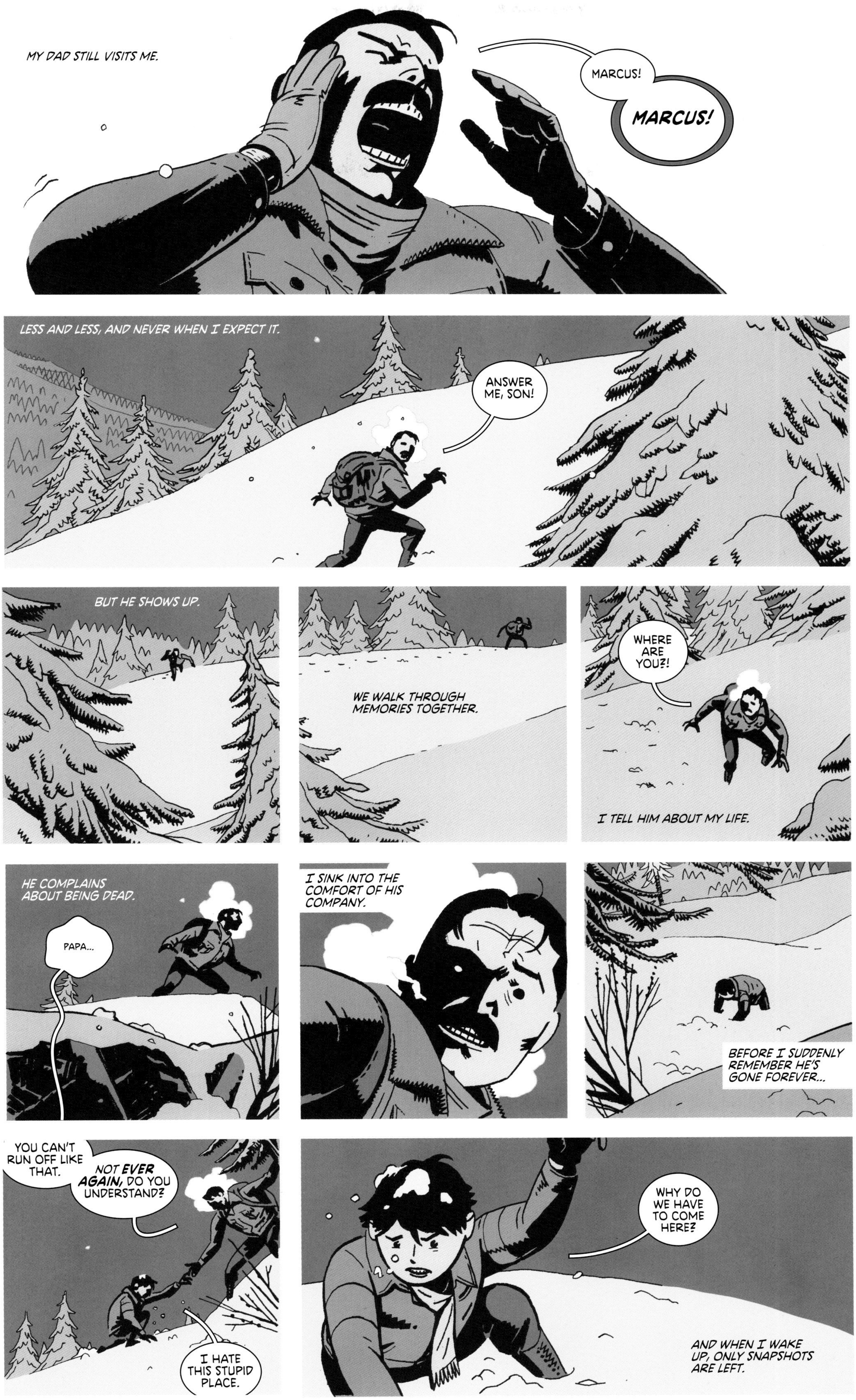
MY DAD STILL VISITS ME.
MARCUS!
MARCUS!
LESS AND LESS, AND NEVER WHEN I EXPECT IT.
ANSWER ME, SON!
BUT HE SHOWS UP.
WE WALK THROUGH MEMORIES TOGETHER.
WHERE ARE YOU?!
I TELL HIM ABOUT MY LIFE.
HE COMPLAINS ABOUT BEING DEAD.
PAPA...
I SINK INTO THE COMFORT OF HIS COMPANY.
BEFORE I SUDDENLY REMEMBER HE'S GONE FOREVER...
YOU CAN'T RUN OFF LIKE THAT.
NOT EVER AGAIN, DO YOU UNDERSTAND?
I HATE THIS STUPID PLACE.
WHY DO WE HAVE TO COME HERE?
AND WHEN I WAKE UP, ONLY SNAPSHOTS ARE LEFT.

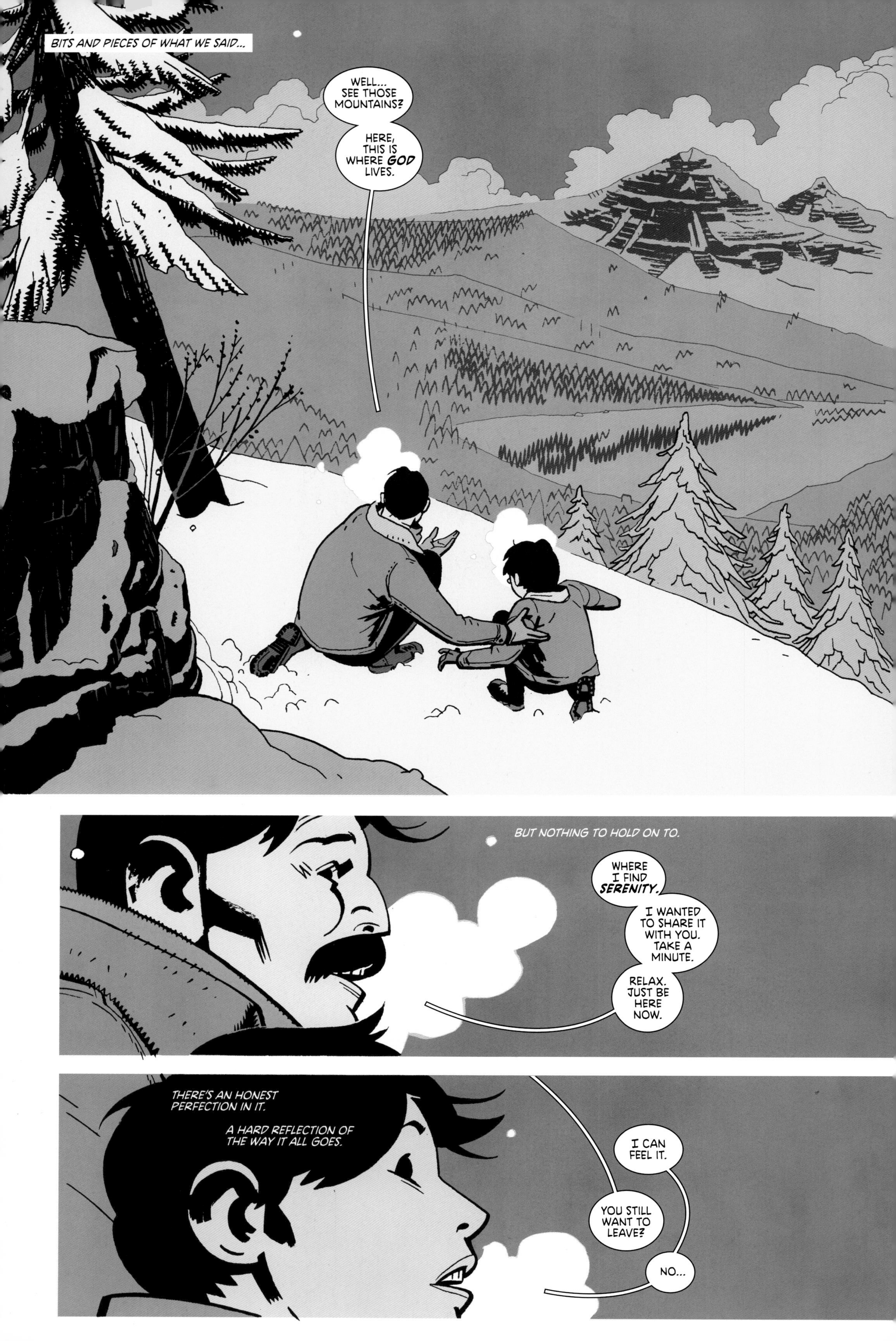
BITS AND PIECES OF WHAT WE SAID...
WELL... SEE THOSE MOUNTAINS?
HERE, THIS IS WHERE GOD LIVES.
BUT NOTHING TO HOLD ON TO.
WHERE I FIND SERENITY.
I WANTED TO SHARE IT WITH YOU. TAKE A MINUTE.
RELAX. JUST BE HERE NOW.
THERE'S AN HONEST PERFECTION IN IT.
A HARD REFLECTION OF THE WAY IT ALL GOES.
I CAN FEEL IT.
YOU STILL WANT TO LEAVE?
NO...

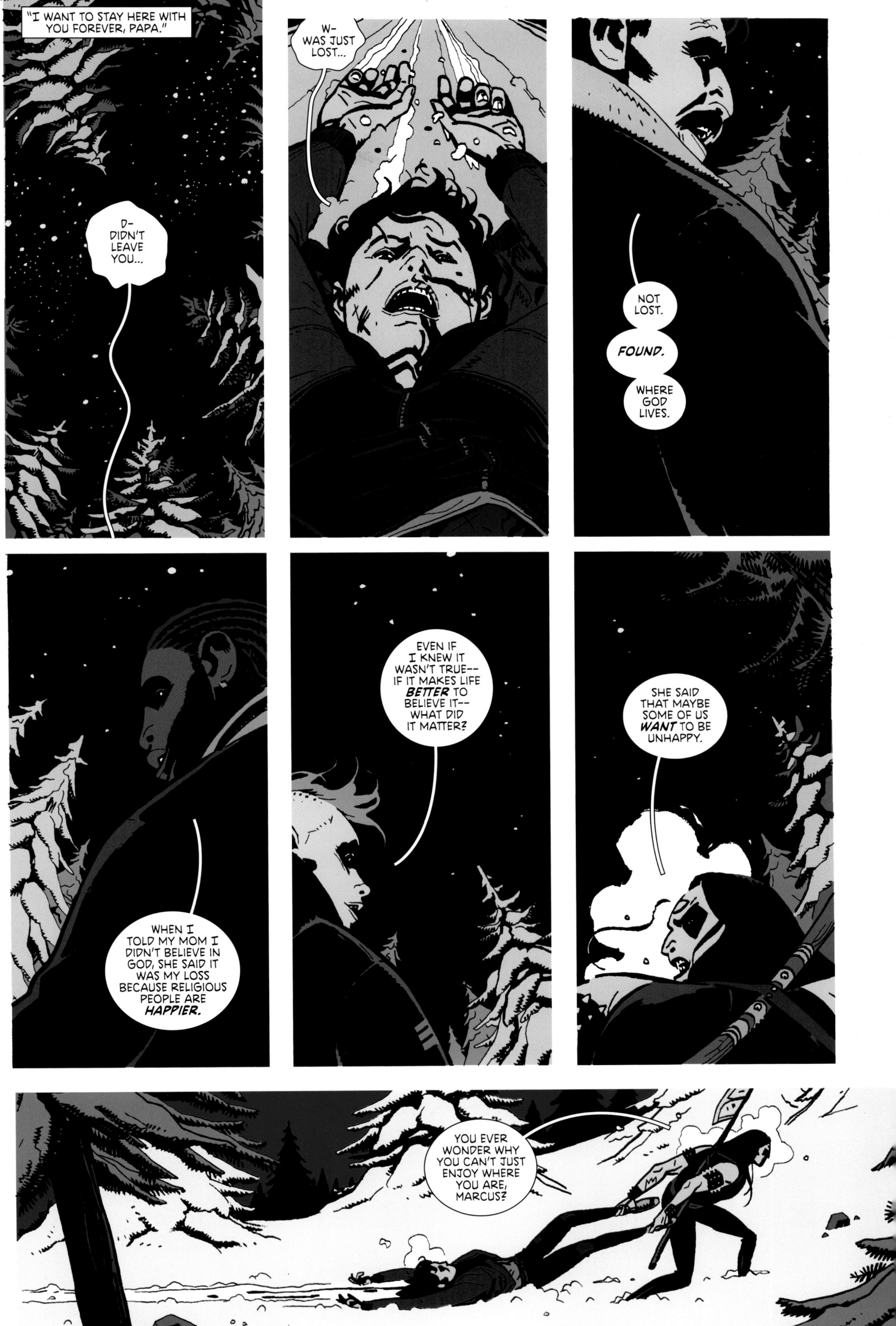
"I WANT TO STAY HERE WITH YOU FOREVER, PAPA."
D-DIDN'T LEAVE YOU...
W-WAS JUST LOST...
NOT LOST.
FOUND.
WHERE GOD LIVES.
WHEN I TOLD MY MOM I DIDN'T BELIEVE IN GOD, SHE SAID IT WAS MY LOSS BECAUSE RELIGIOUS PEOPLE ARE HAPPIER.
EVEN IF I KNEW IT WASN'T TRUE-- IF IT MAKES LIFE BETTER TO BELIEVE IT-- WHAT DID IT MATTER?
SHE SAID THAT MAYBE SOME OF US WANT TO BE UNHAPPY.
YOU EVER WONDER WHY YOU CAN'T JUST ENJOY WHERE YOU ARE, MARCUS?

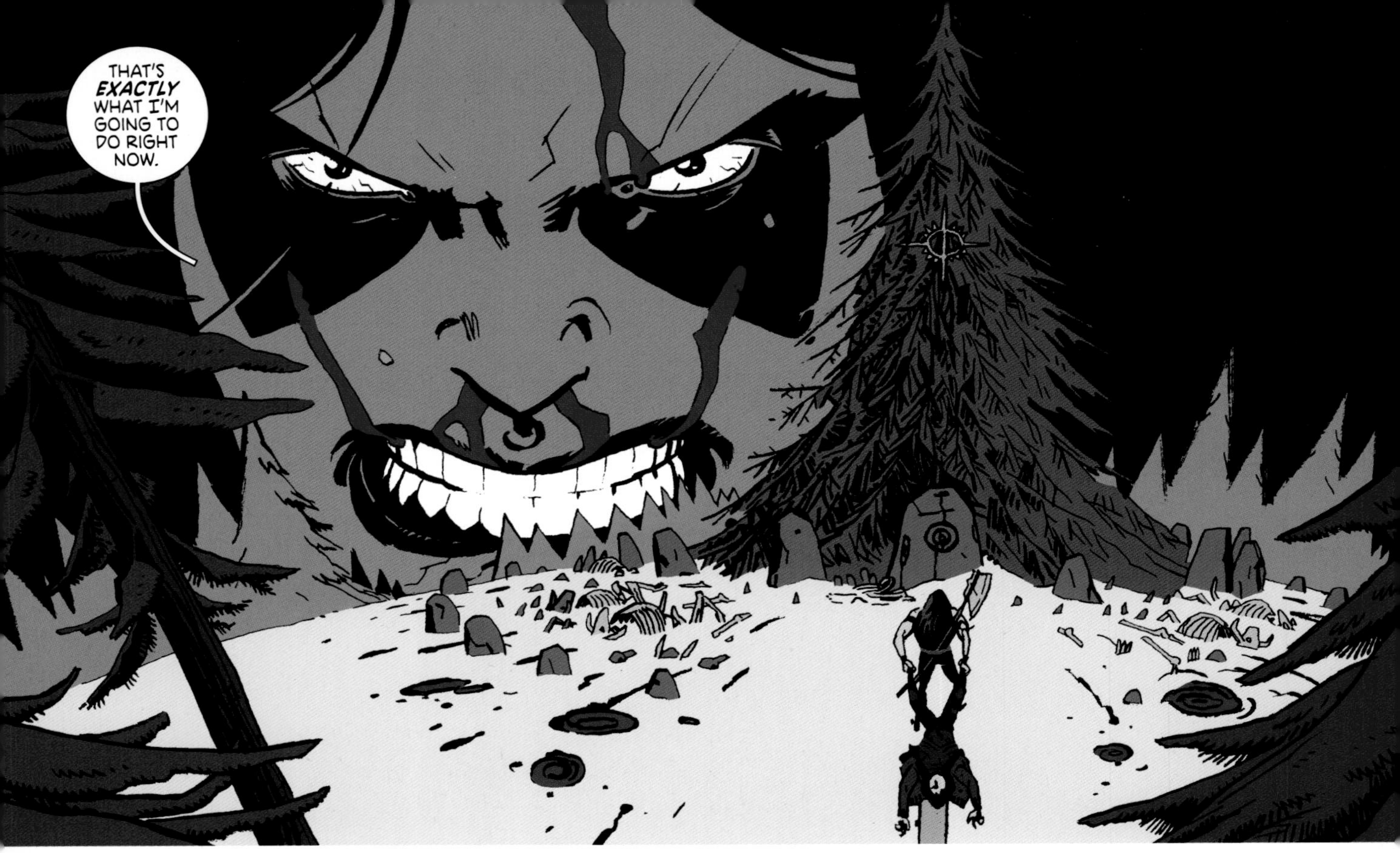
THAT'S *EXACTLY* WHAT I'M GOING TO DO RIGHT NOW.

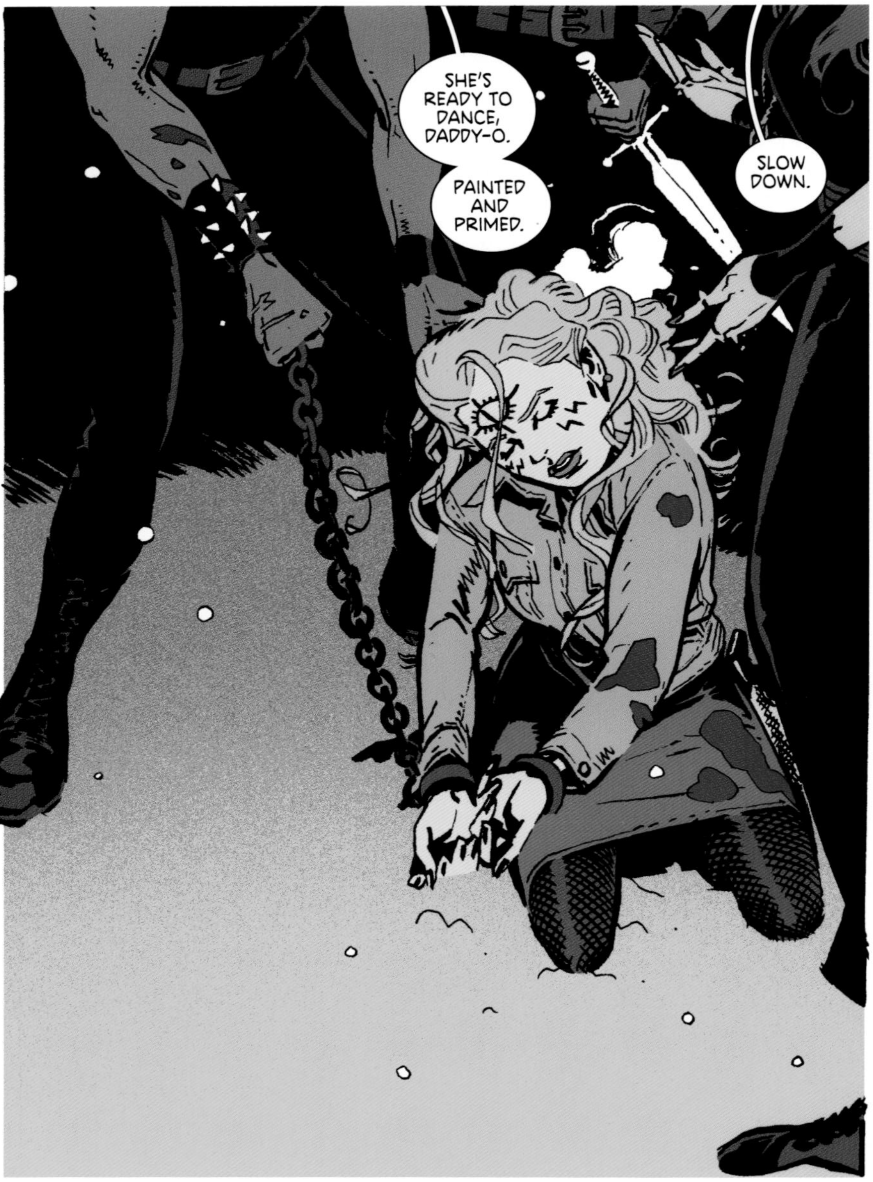
SHE'S READY TO DANCE, DADDY-O.
PAINTED AND PRIMED.
SLOW DOWN.

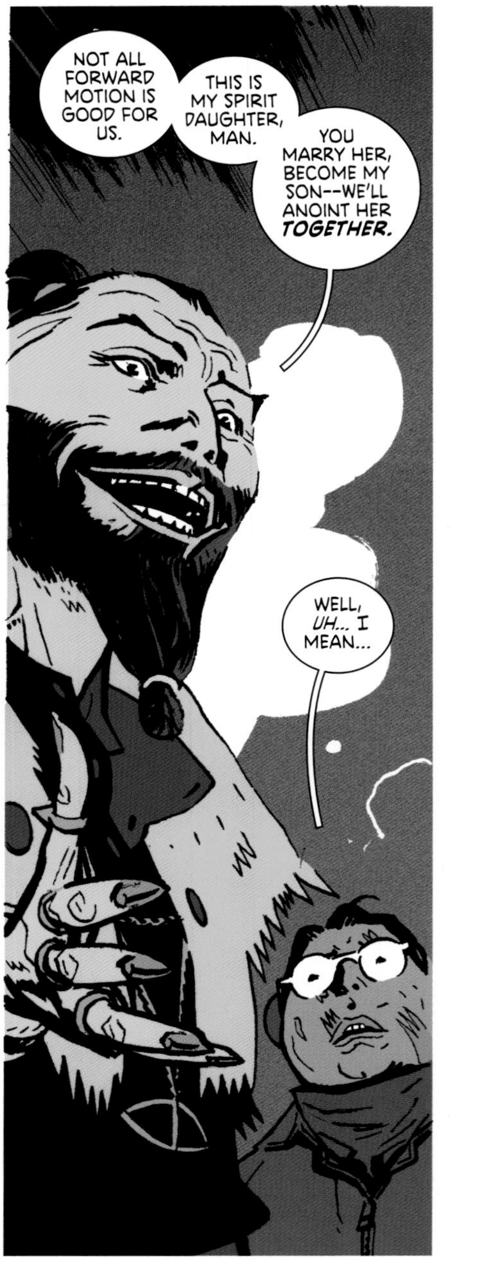
NOT ALL FORWARD MOTION IS GOOD FOR US.
THIS IS MY SPIRIT DAUGHTER, MAN.
YOU MARRY HER, BECOME MY SON--WE'LL ANOINT HER *TOGETHER.*
WELL, *UH...* I MEAN...

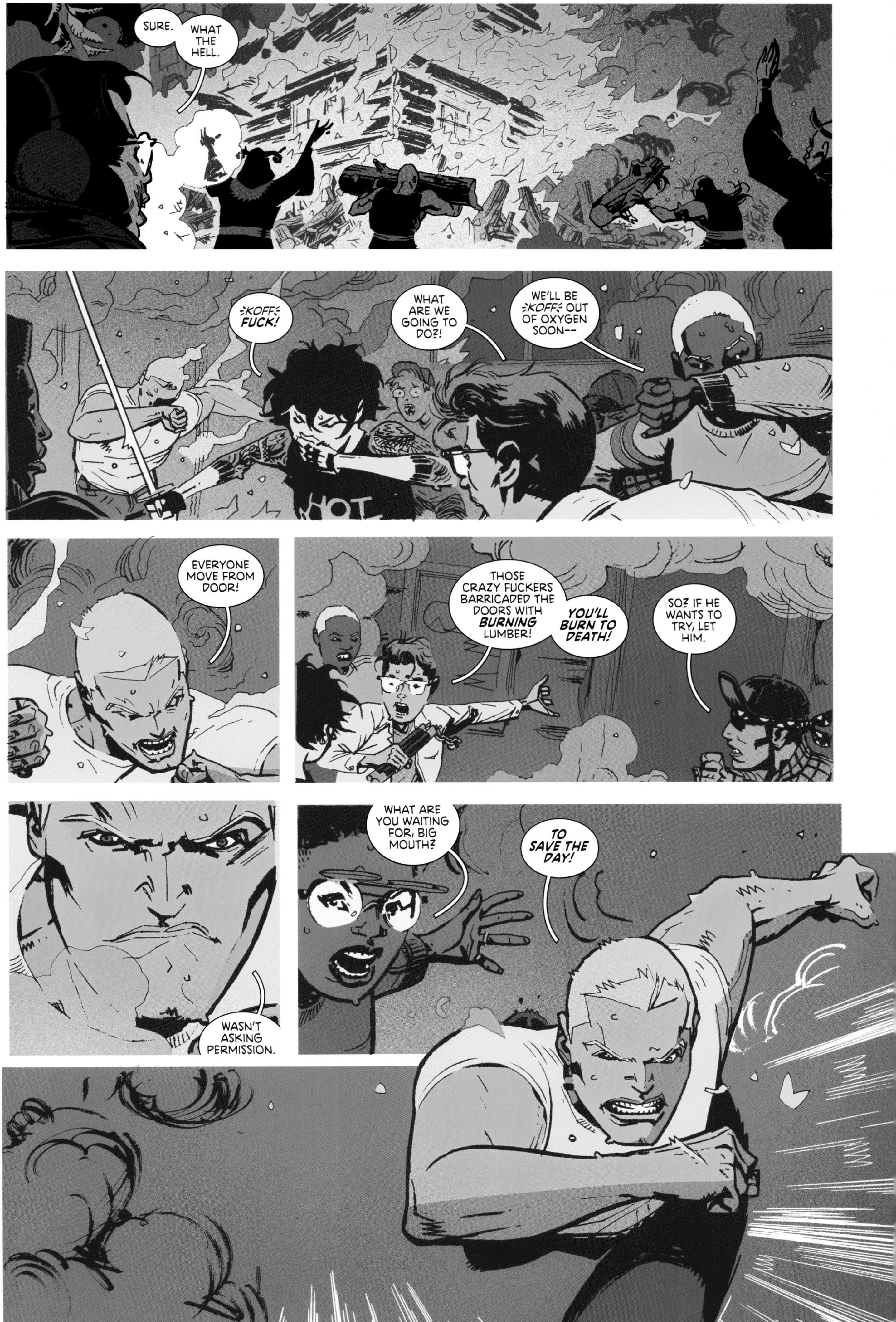
SURE.
WHAT THE HELL.
≈KOFF≈ FUCK!
WHAT ARE WE GOING TO DO?!
WE'LL BE ≈KOFF≈ OUT OF OXYGEN SOON--
EVERYONE MOVE FROM DOOR!
THOSE CRAZY FUCKERS BARRICADED THE DOORS WITH BURNING LUMBER!
YOU'LL BURN TO DEATH!
SO? IF HE WANTS TO TRY, LET HIM.
WASN'T ASKING PERMISSION.
WHAT ARE YOU WAITING FOR, BIG MOUTH?
TO SAVE THE DAY!

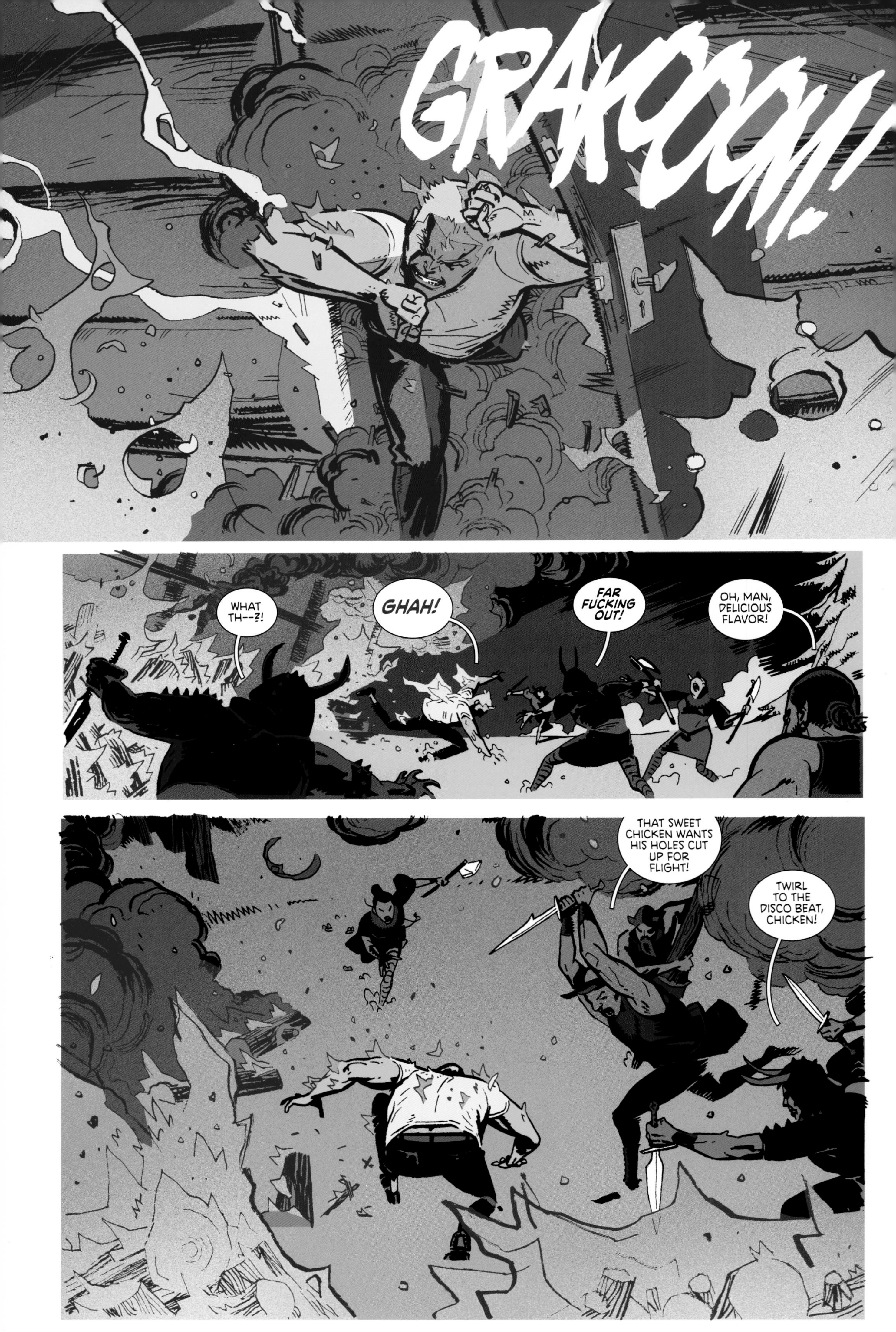
GRAKOOM!
WHAT TH--?!
GHAH!
FAR FUCKING OUT!
OH, MAN, DELICIOUS FLAVOR!
THAT SWEET CHICKEN WANTS HIS HOLES CUT UP FOR FLIGHT!
TWIRL TO THE DISCO BEAT, CHICKEN!

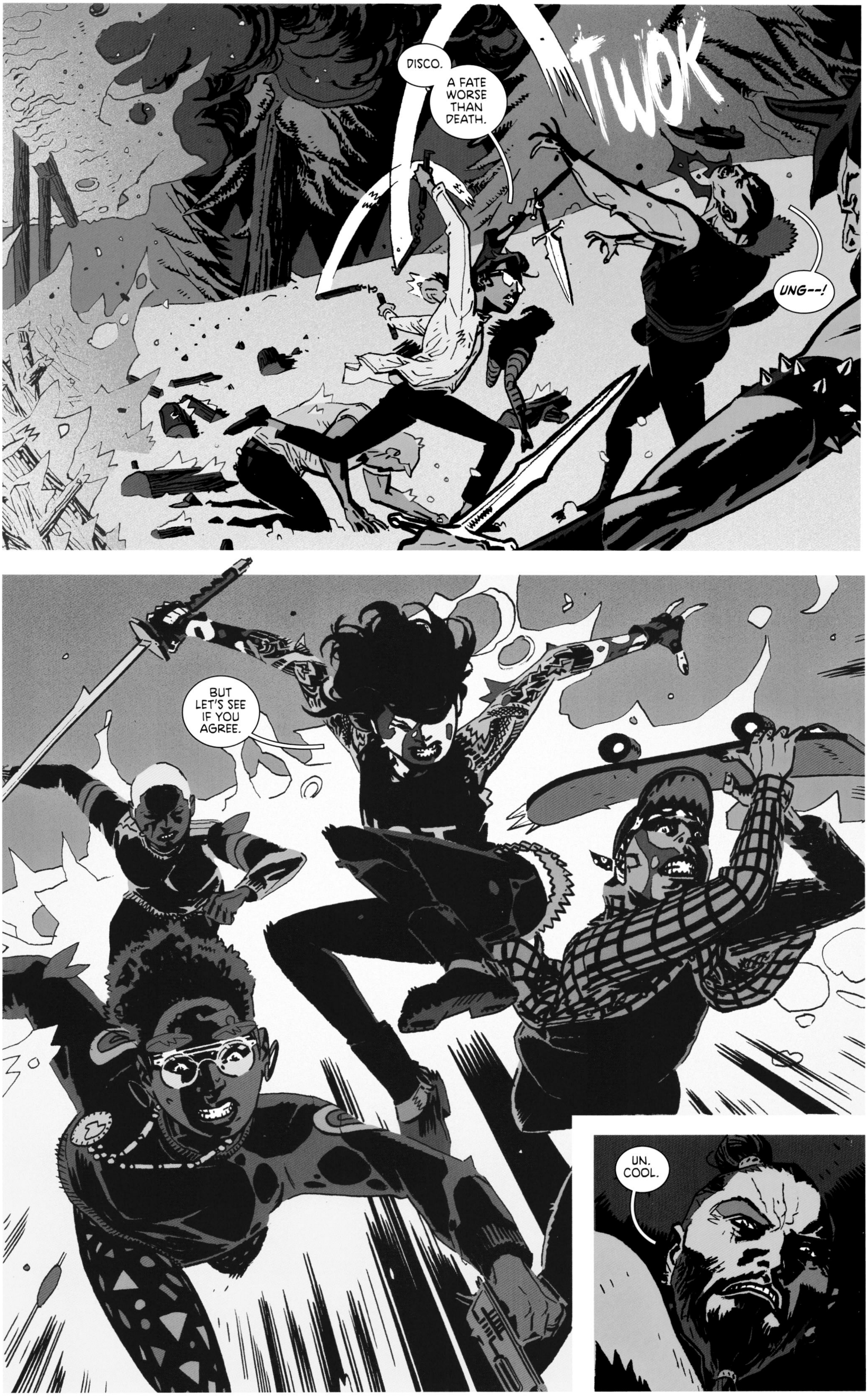
DISCO.
A FATE WORSE THAN DEATH.
TWOK
UNG--!
BUT LET'S SEE IF YOU AGREE.
UN. COOL.

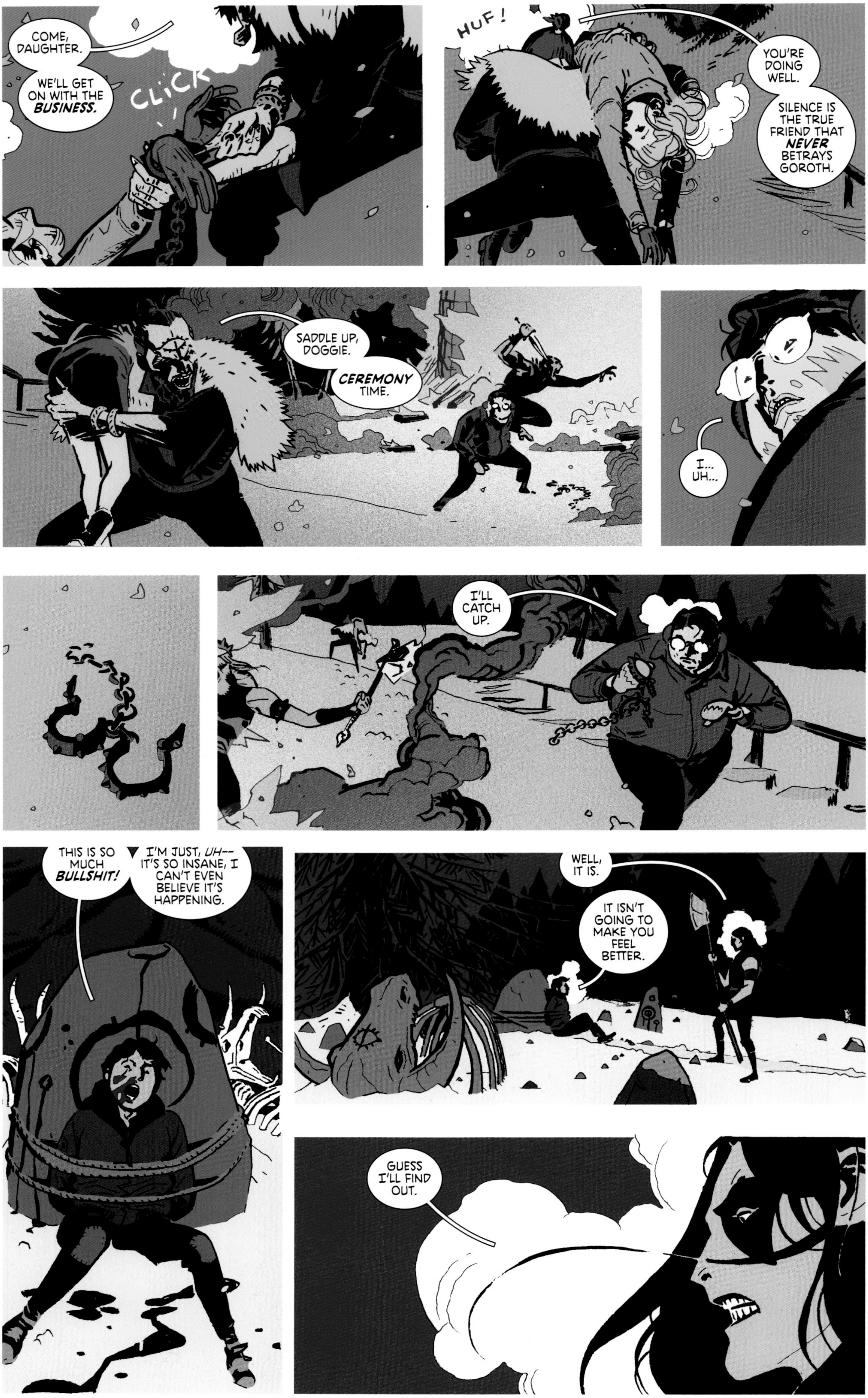
COME, DAUGHTER.
WE'LL GET ON WITH THE *BUSINESS.*
CLICK
HUF!
YOU'RE DOING WELL.
SILENCE IS THE TRUE FRIEND THAT *NEVER* BETRAYS GOROTH.
SADDLE UP, DOGGIE.
CEREMONY TIME.
I... UH...
I'LL CATCH UP.
THIS IS SO MUCH *BULLSHIT!*
I'M JUST, *UH*-- IT'S SO INSANE, I CAN'T EVEN BELIEVE IT'S HAPPENING.
WELL, IT IS.
IT ISN'T GOING TO MAKE YOU FEEL BETTER.
GUESS I'LL FIND OUT.

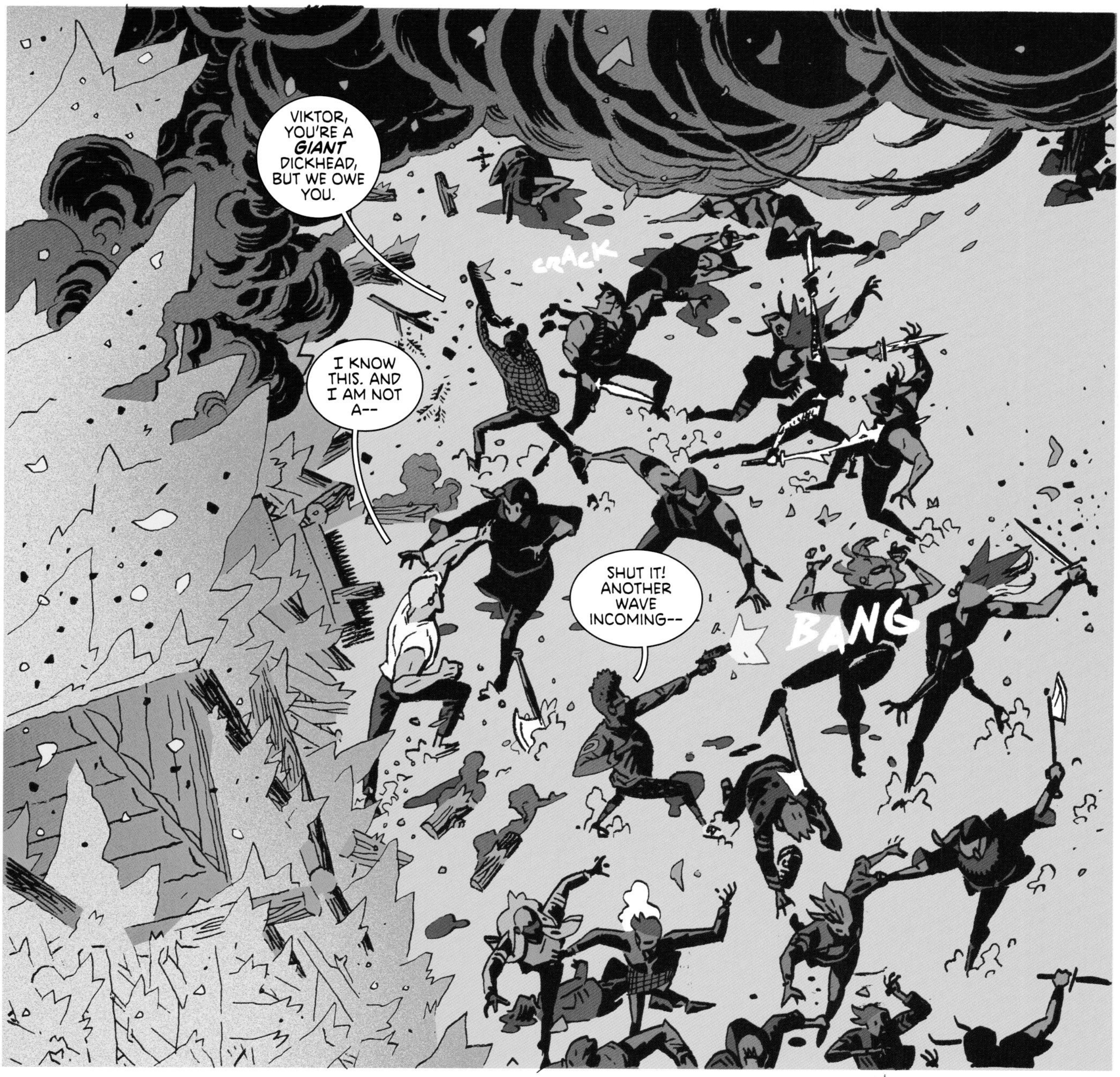
VIKTOR, YOU'RE A GIANT DICKHEAD, BUT WE OWE YOU.
CRACK
I KNOW THIS. AND I AM NOT A--
SHUT IT! ANOTHER WAVE INCOMING--
BANG

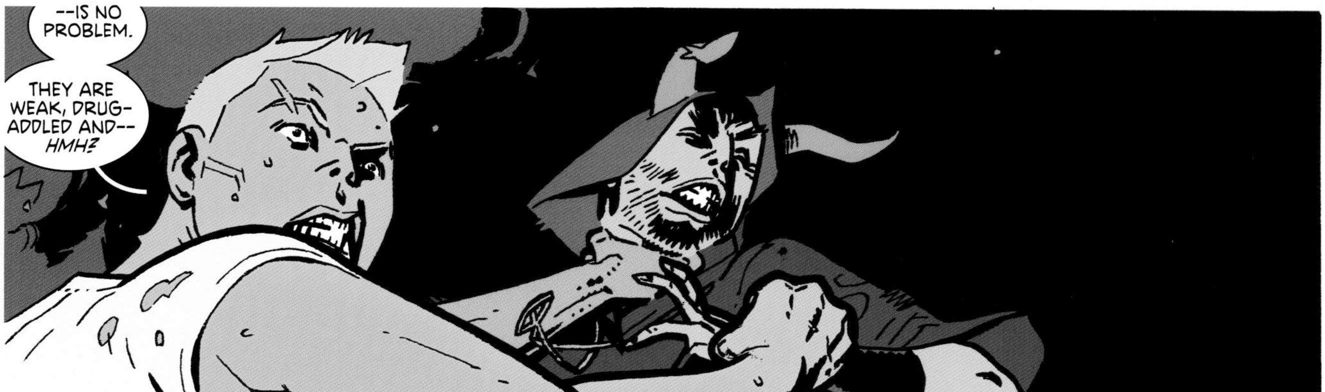
--IS NO PROBLEM.
THEY ARE WEAK, DRUG-ADDLED AND-- HMH?

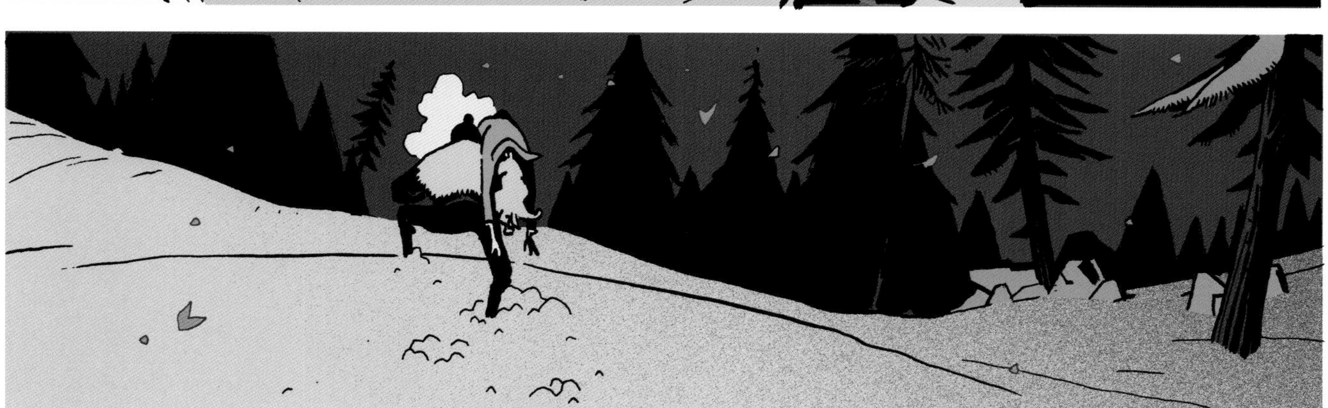

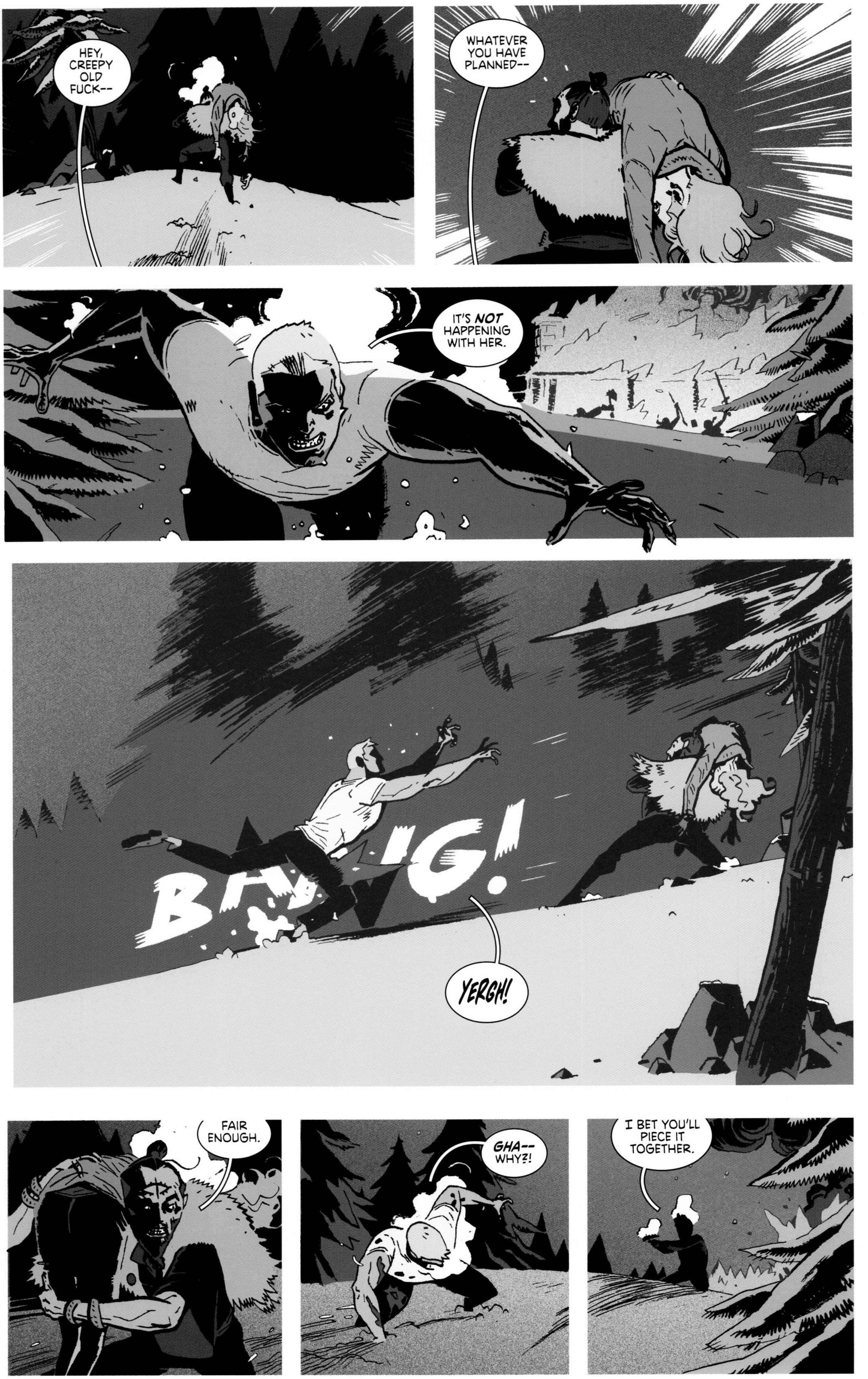
HEY, CREEPY OLD FUCK--
WHATEVER YOU HAVE PLANNED--
IT'S NOT HAPPENING WITH HER.
BANG!
YERGH!
FAIR ENOUGH.
GHA-- WHY?!
I BET YOU'LL PIECE IT TOGETHER.

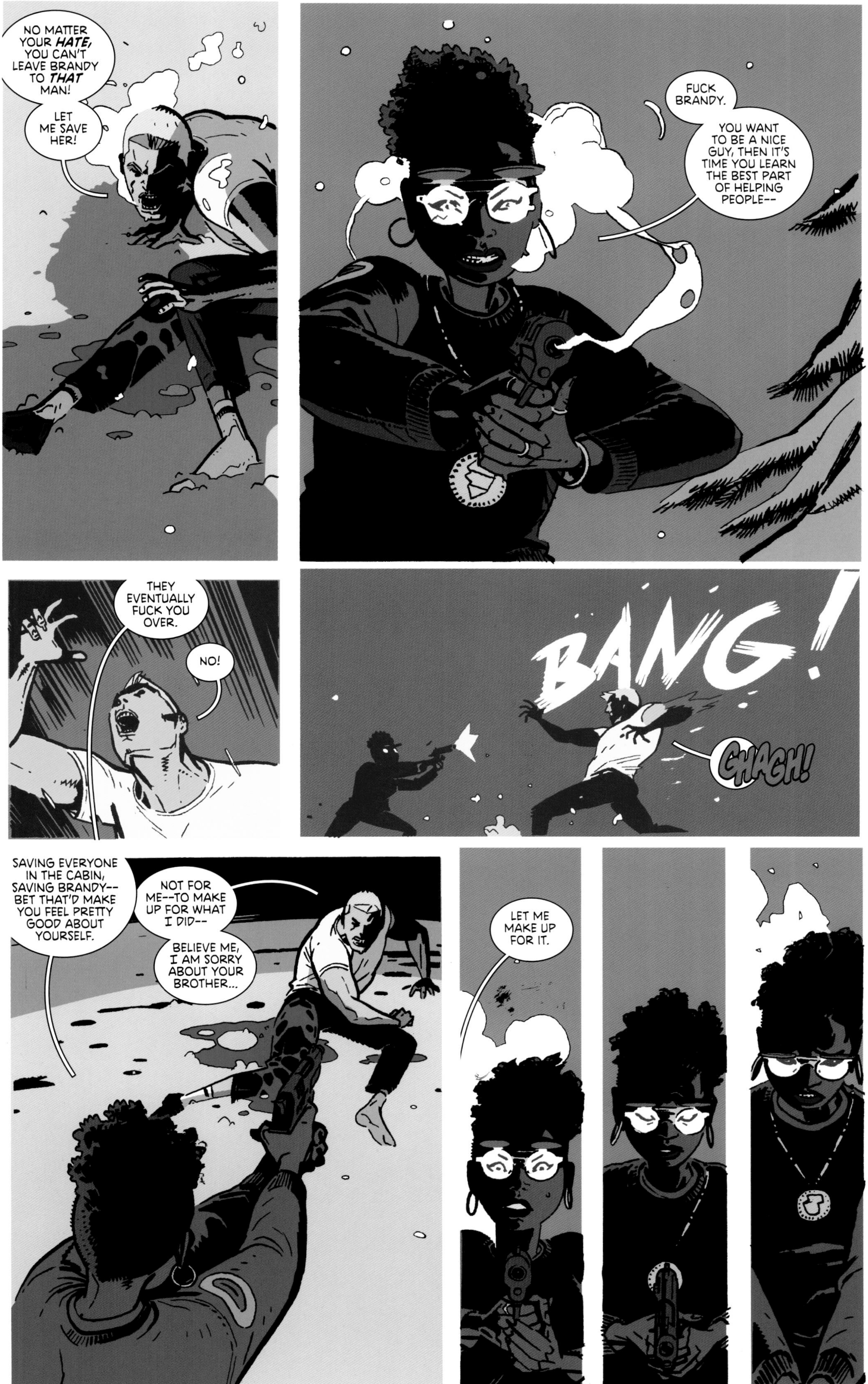
NO MATTER YOUR ***HATE,*** YOU CAN'T LEAVE BRANDY TO ***THAT*** MAN!
LET ME SAVE HER!
FUCK BRANDY.
YOU WANT TO BE A NICE GUY, THEN IT'S TIME YOU LEARN THE BEST PART OF HELPING PEOPLE--
THEY EVENTUALLY FUCK YOU OVER.
NO!
BANG!
GHAGH!
SAVING EVERYONE IN THE CABIN, SAVING BRANDY--BET THAT'D MAKE YOU FEEL PRETTY GOOD ABOUT YOURSELF.
NOT FOR ME--TO MAKE UP FOR WHAT I DID--
BELIEVE ME, I AM SORRY ABOUT YOUR BROTHER...
LET ME MAKE UP FOR IT.

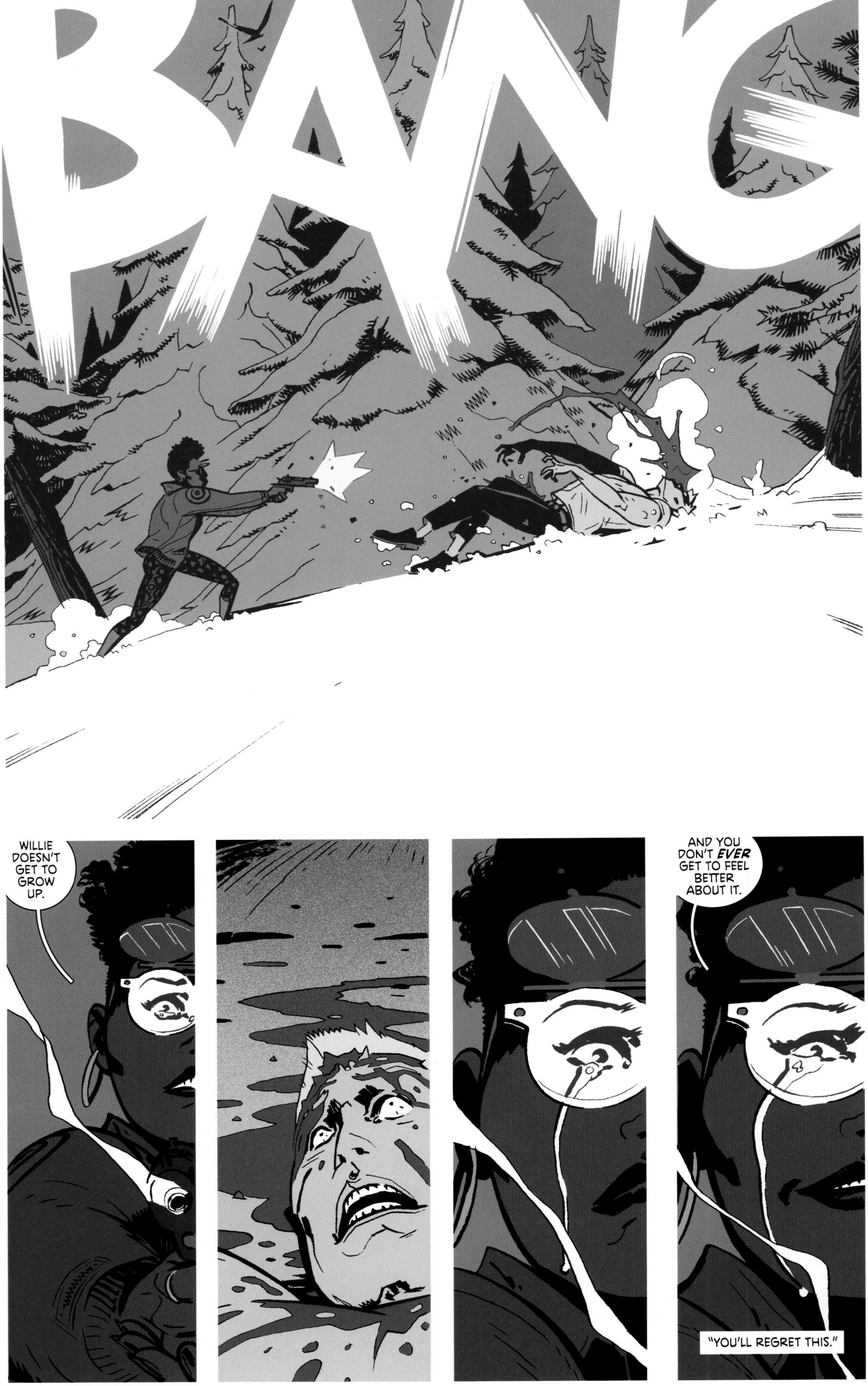
BANG
WILLIE DOESN'T GET TO GROW UP.
AND YOU DON'T *EVER* GET TO FEEL BETTER ABOUT IT.
"YOU'LL REGRET THIS."

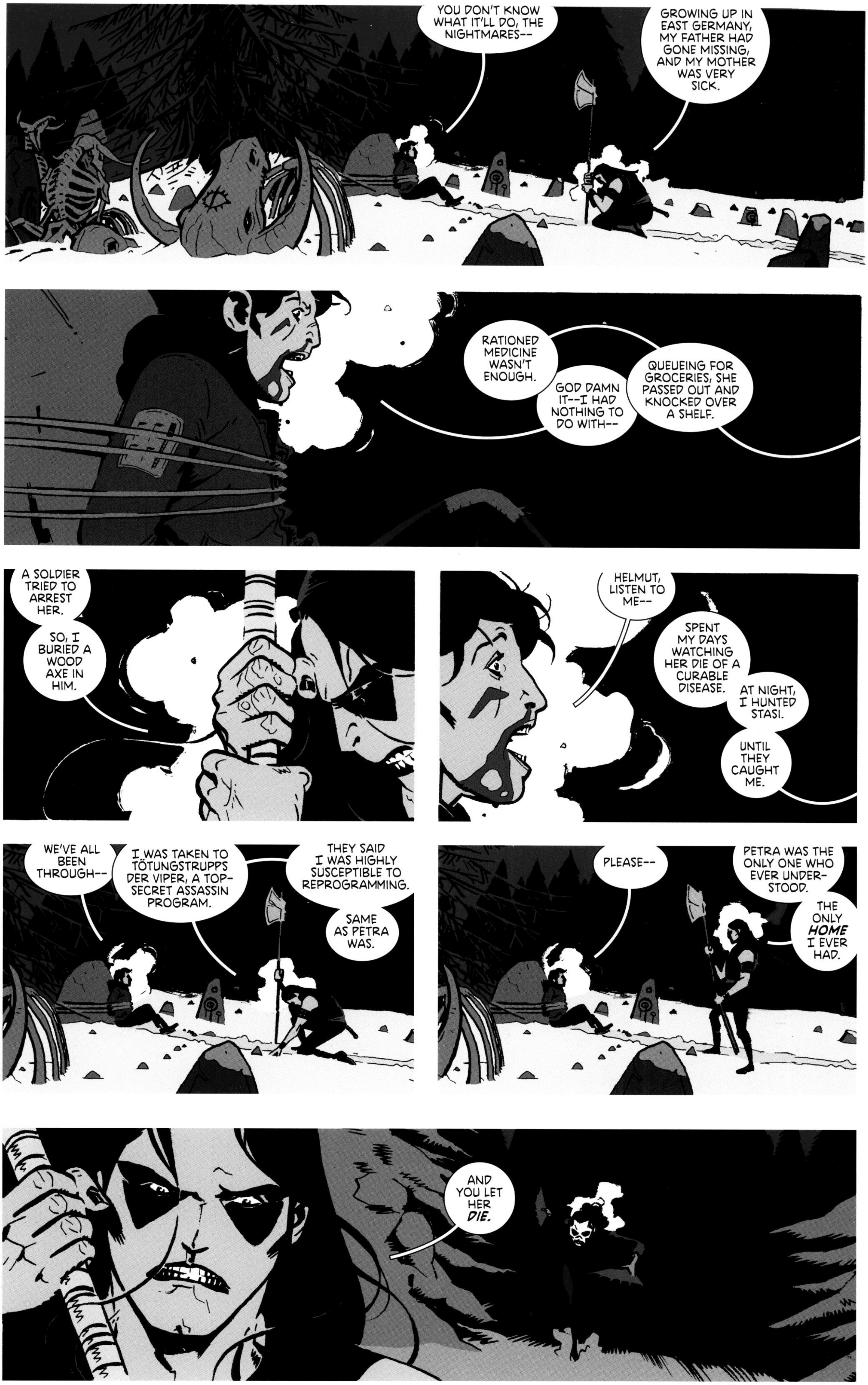
YOU DON'T KNOW WHAT IT'LL DO, THE NIGHTMARES--
GROWING UP IN EAST GERMANY, MY FATHER HAD GONE MISSING, AND MY MOTHER WAS VERY SICK.
RATIONED MEDICINE WASN'T ENOUGH.
GOD DAMN IT--I HAD NOTHING TO DO WITH--
QUEUEING FOR GROCERIES, SHE PASSED OUT AND KNOCKED OVER A SHELF.
A SOLDIER TRIED TO ARREST HER.
SO, I BURIED A WOOD AXE IN HIM.
HELMUT, LISTEN TO ME--
SPENT MY DAYS WATCHING HER DIE OF A CURABLE DISEASE.
AT NIGHT, I HUNTED STASI.
UNTIL THEY CAUGHT ME.
WE'VE ALL BEEN THROUGH--
I WAS TAKEN TO TÖTUNGSTRUPPS DER VIPER, A TOP-SECRET ASSASSIN PROGRAM.
THEY SAID I WAS HIGHLY SUSCEPTIBLE TO REPROGRAMMING.
SAME AS PETRA WAS.
PLEASE--
PETRA WAS THE ONLY ONE WHO EVER UNDER-STOOD.
THE ONLY HOME I EVER HAD.
AND YOU LET HER DIE.

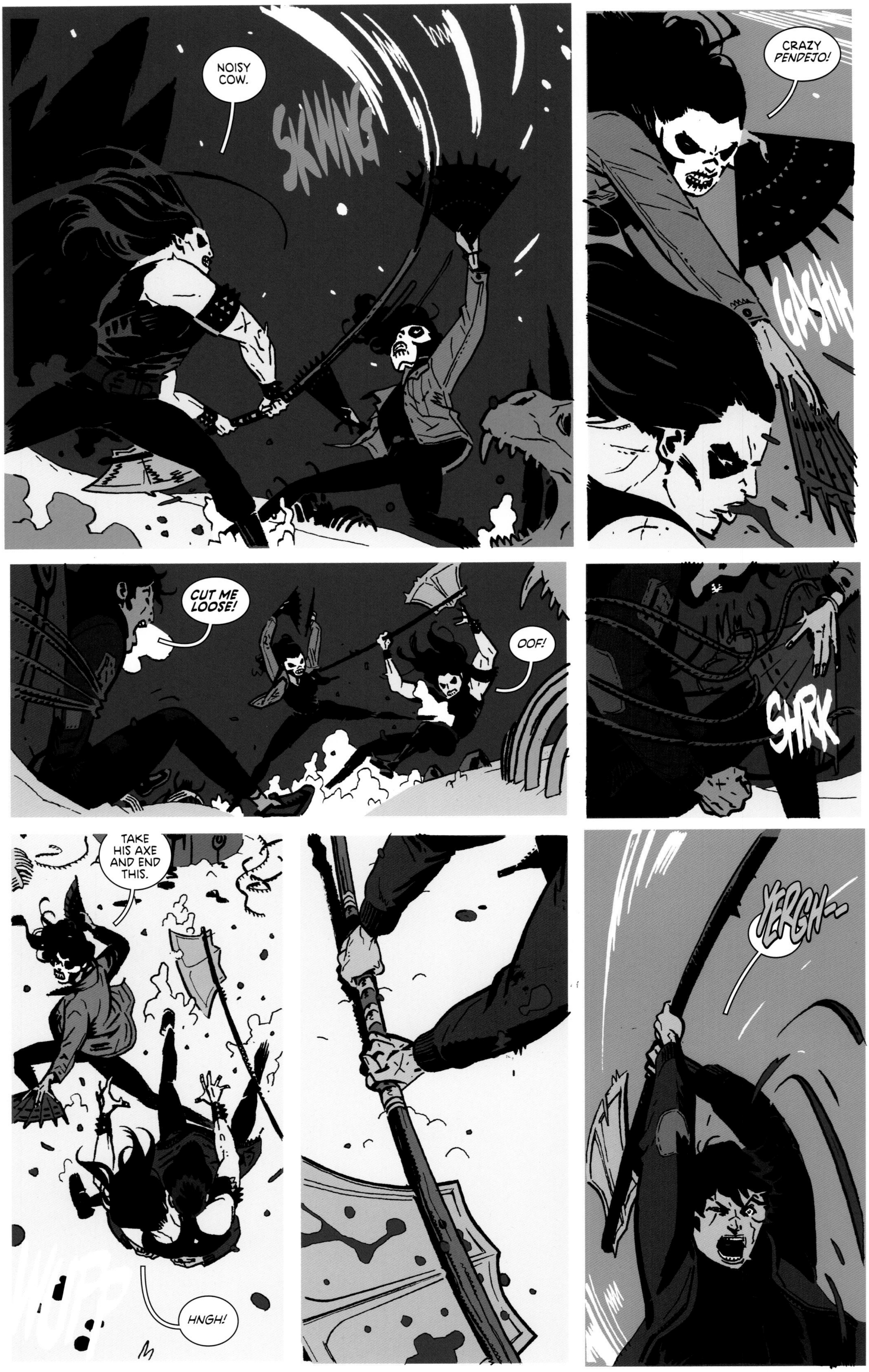
NOISY COW.
SKWING
CRAZY *PENDEJO!*
GASHH
CUT ME LOOSE!
OOF!
SHRK
TAKE HIS AXE AND END THIS.
HNGH!
YERGH--

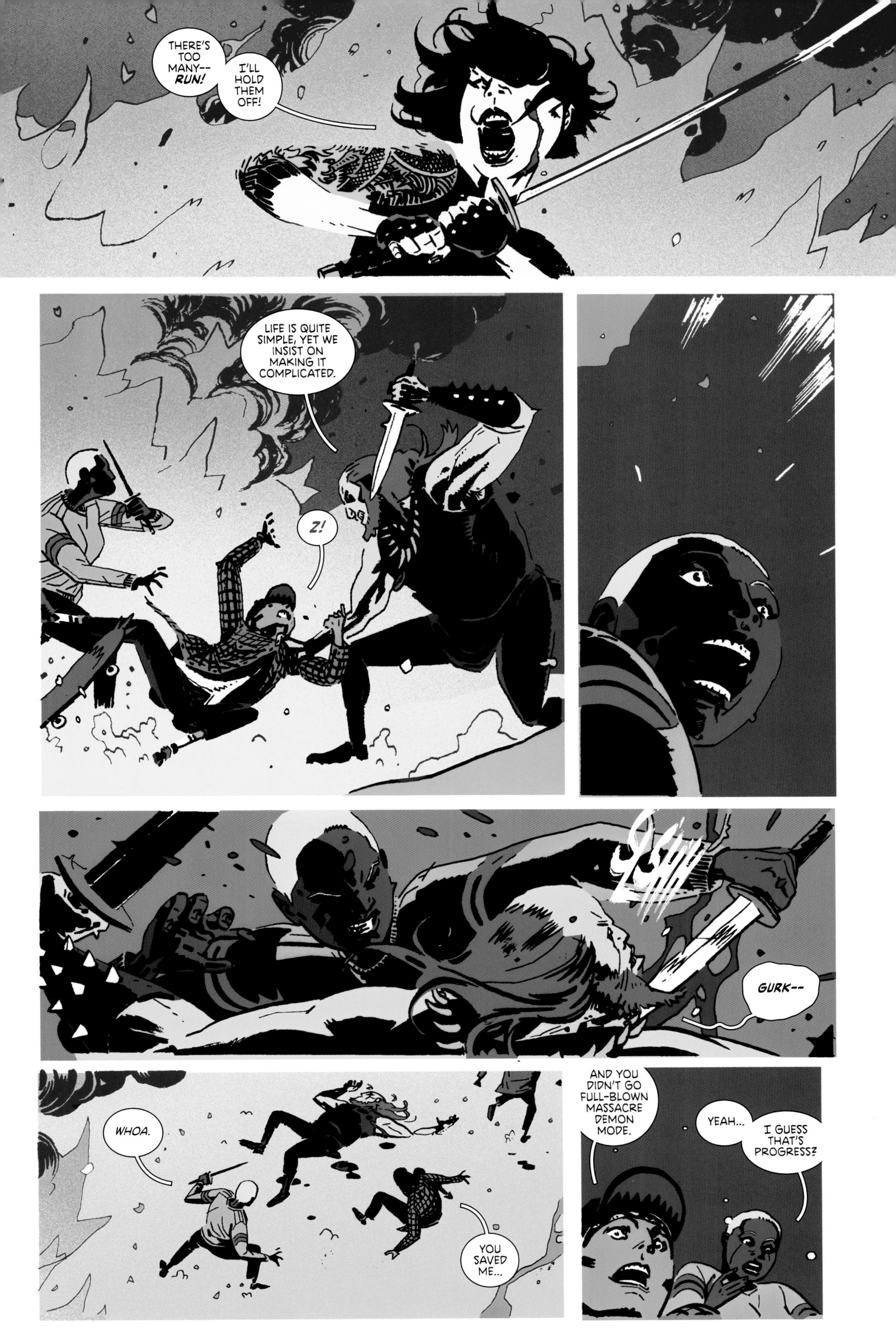
THERE'S TOO MANY-- RUN!
I'LL HOLD THEM OFF!
LIFE IS QUITE SIMPLE, YET WE INSIST ON MAKING IT COMPLICATED.
Z!
GURK--
WHOA.
YOU SAVED ME...
AND YOU DIDN'T GO FULL-BLOWN MASSACRE DEMON MODE.
YEAH...
I GUESS THAT'S PROGRESS?

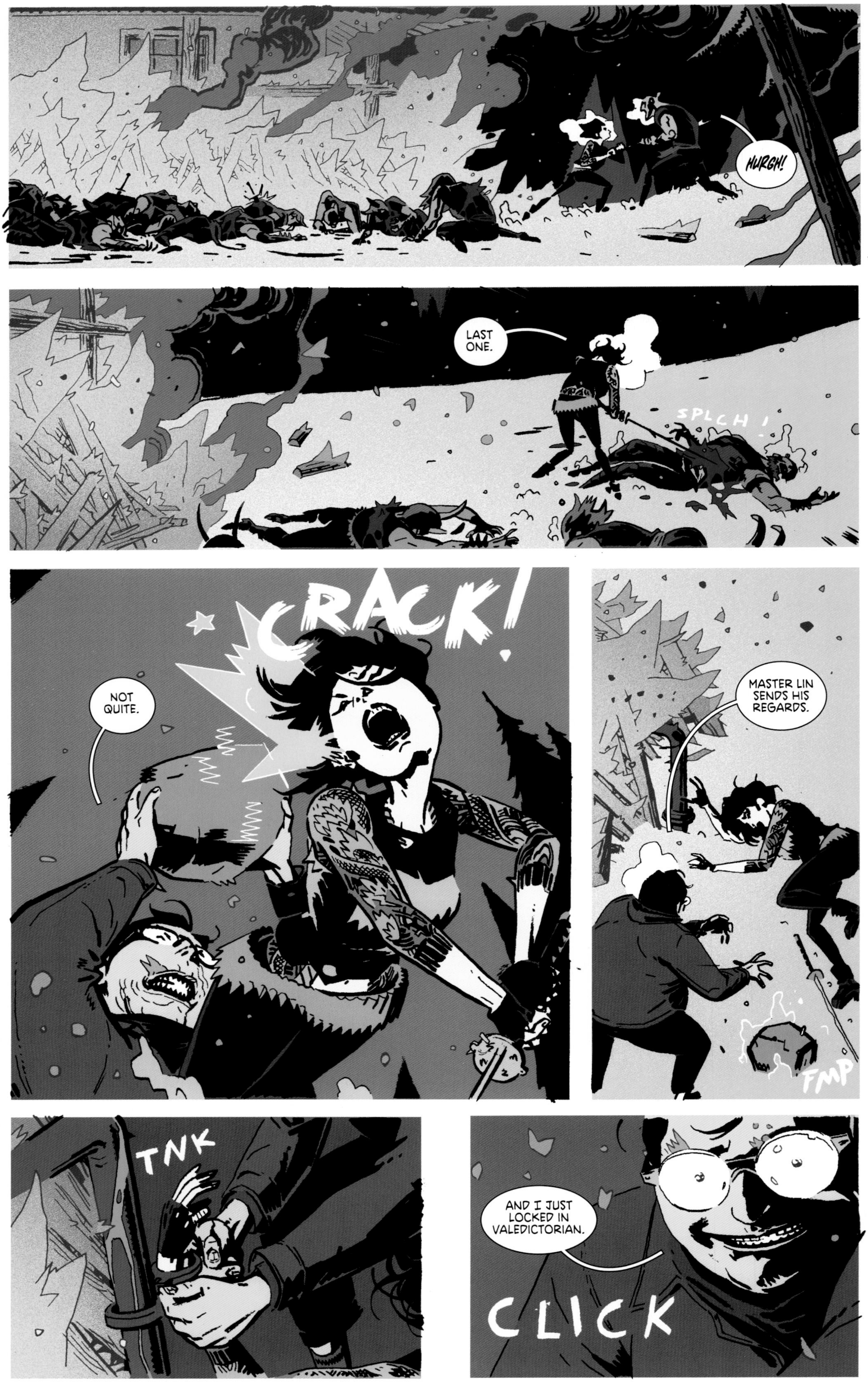
HURGH!
LAST ONE.
SPLCH!
CRACK!
NOT QUITE.
MASTER LIN SENDS HIS REGARDS.
FMP
TNK
AND I JUST LOCKED IN VALEDICTORIAN.
CLICK

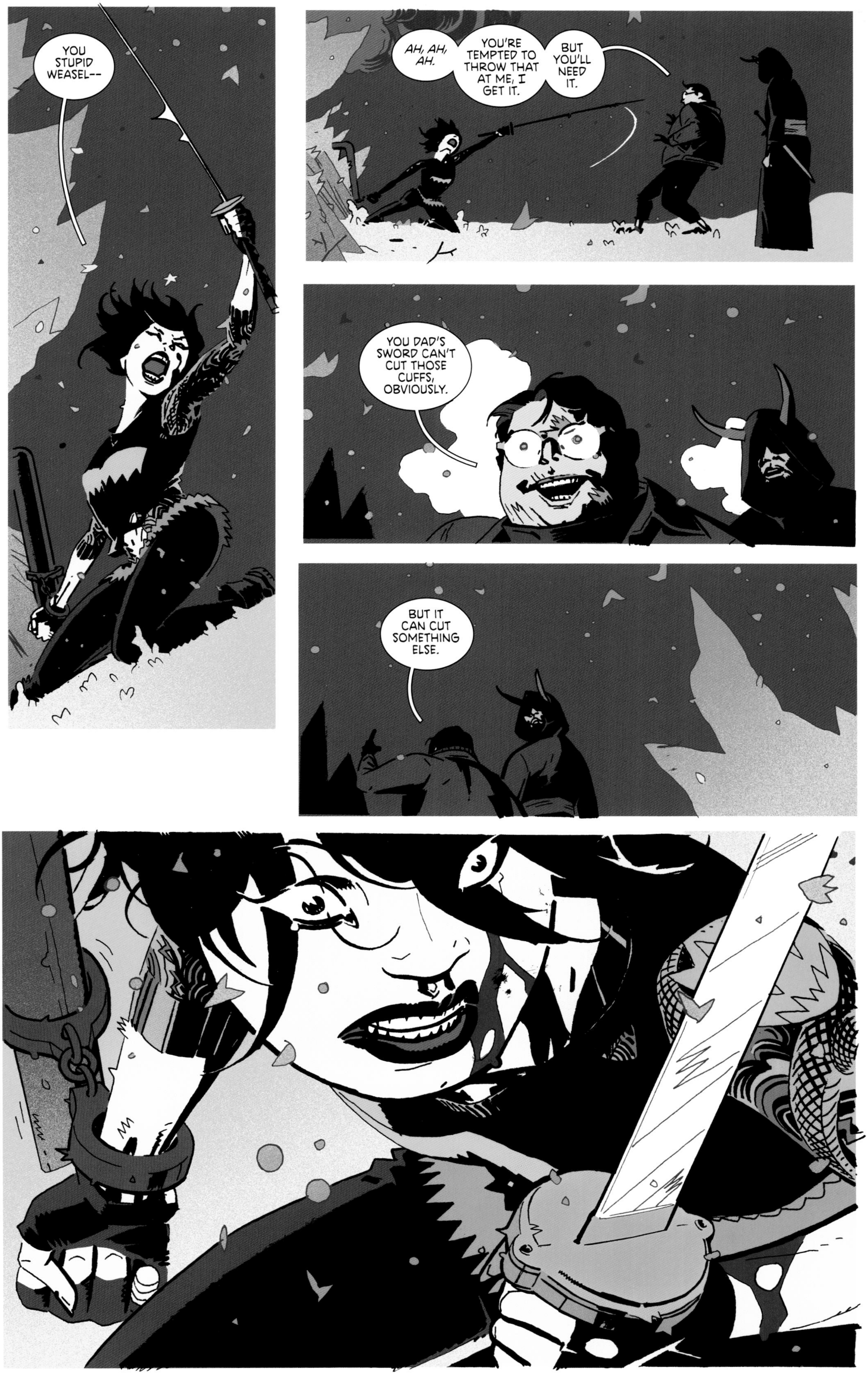
YOU STUPID WEASEL--
AH, AH, AH.
YOU'RE TEMPTED TO THROW THAT AT ME, I GET IT.
BUT YOU'LL NEED IT.
YOU DAD'S SWORD CAN'T CUT THOSE CUFFS, OBVIOUSLY.
BUT IT CAN CUT SOMETHING ELSE.

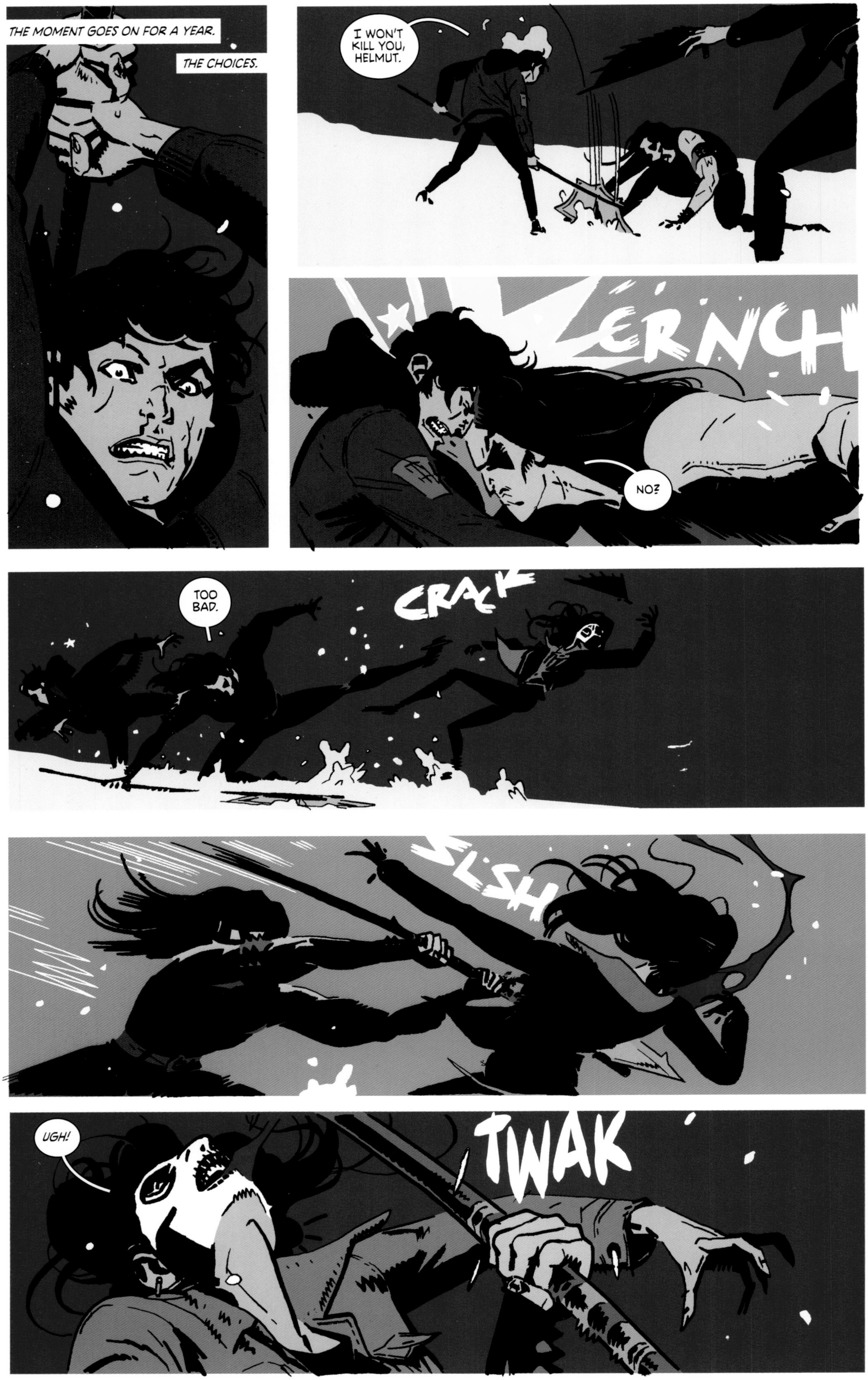
THE MOMENT GOES ON FOR A YEAR.
THE CHOICES.
I WON'T KILL YOU, HELMUT.
CRNCH
NO?
TOO BAD.
CRACK
SLSH
UGH!
TWAK

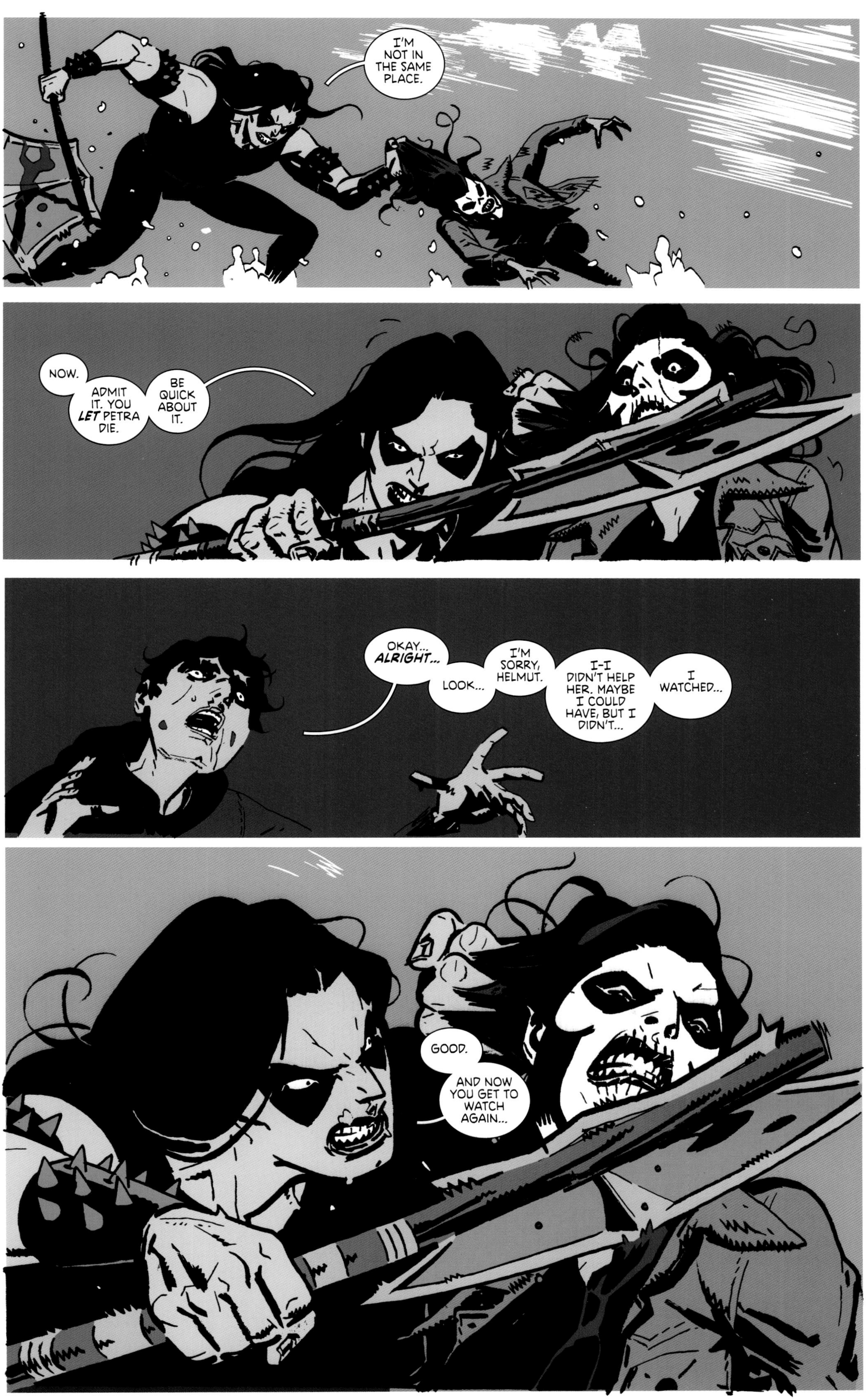
I'M NOT IN THE SAME PLACE.
NOW.
ADMIT IT. YOU LET PETRA DIE.
BE QUICK ABOUT IT.
OKAY... ALRIGHT...
LOOK...
I'M SORRY, HELMUT.
I-I DIDN'T HELP HER. MAYBE I COULD HAVE, BUT I DIDN'T...
I WATCHED...
GOOD.
AND NOW YOU GET TO WATCH AGAIN...

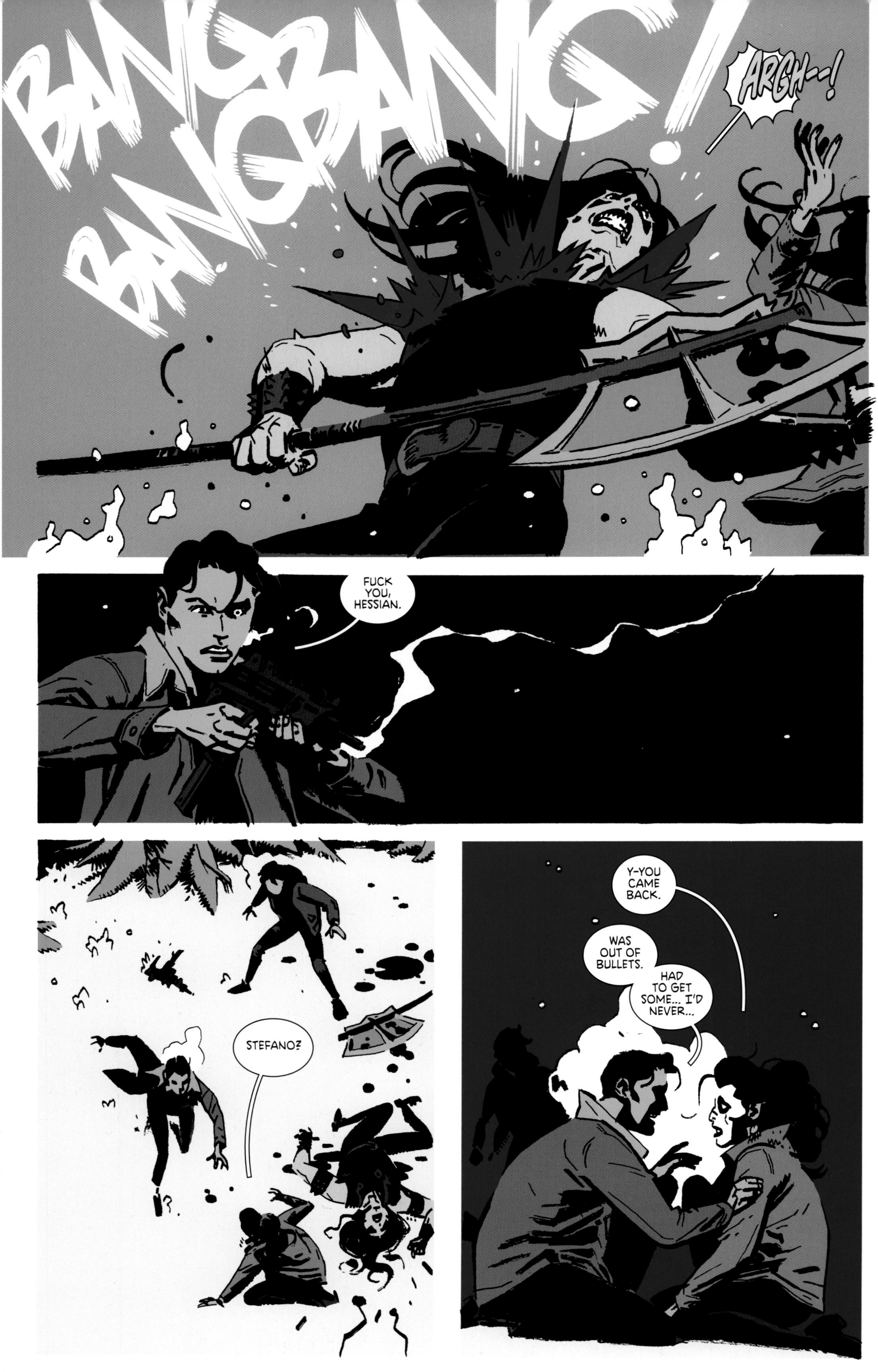
BANG BANG BANG BANG!
ARGH--!
FUCK YOU, HESSIAN.
STEFANO?
Y-YOU CAME BACK.
WAS OUT OF BULLETS.
HAD TO GET SOME... I'D NEVER...

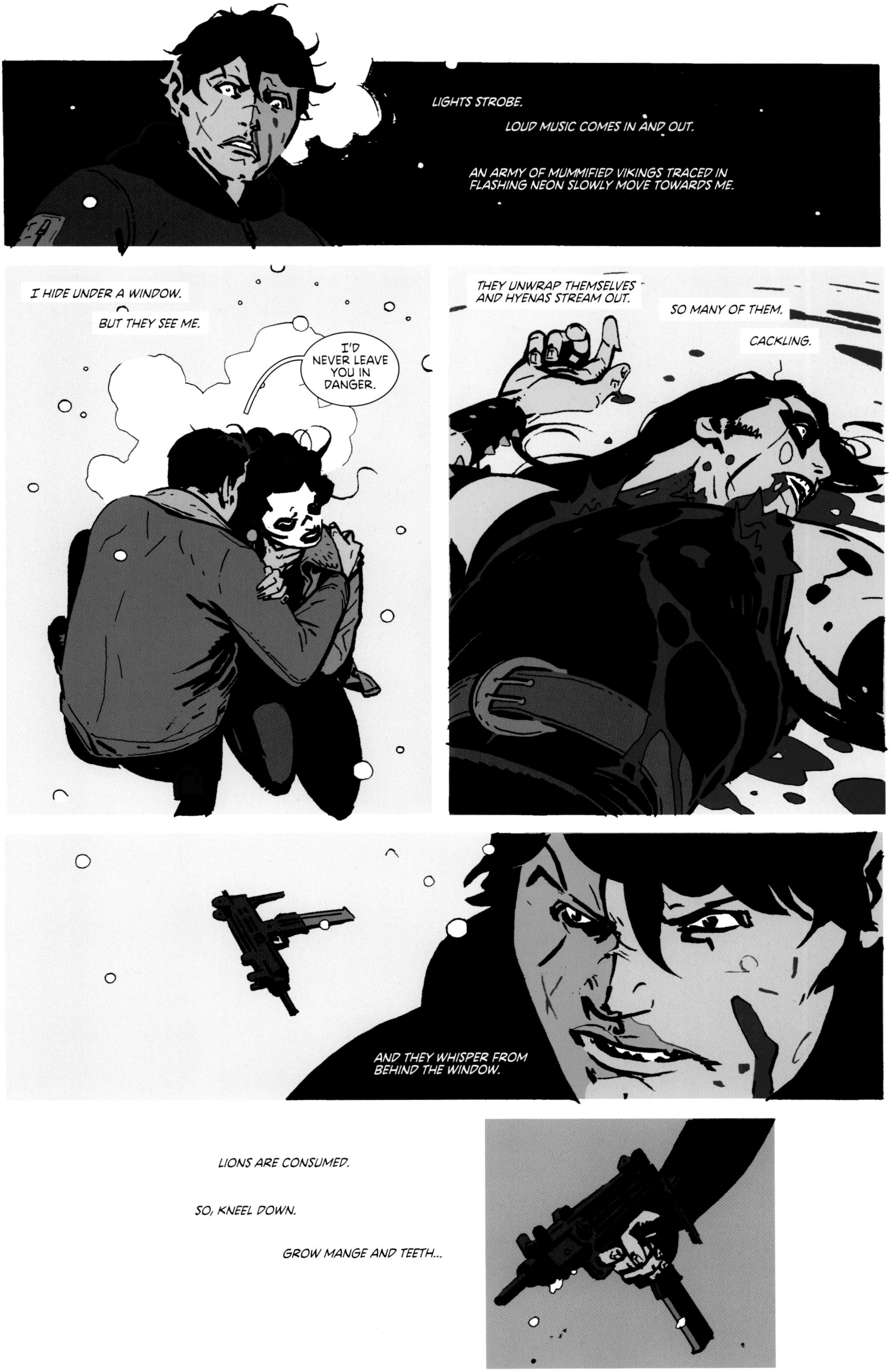
LIGHTS STROBE.
LOUD MUSIC COMES IN AND OUT.
AN ARMY OF MUMMIFIED VIKINGS TRACED IN FLASHING NEON SLOWLY MOVE TOWARDS ME.
I HIDE UNDER A WINDOW.
BUT THEY SEE ME.
I'D NEVER LEAVE YOU IN DANGER.
THEY UNWRAP THEMSELVES AND HYENAS STREAM OUT.
SO MANY OF THEM.
CACKLING.
AND THEY WHISPER FROM BEHIND THE WINDOW.
LIONS ARE CONSUMED.
SO, KNEEL DOWN.
GROW MANGE AND TEETH...

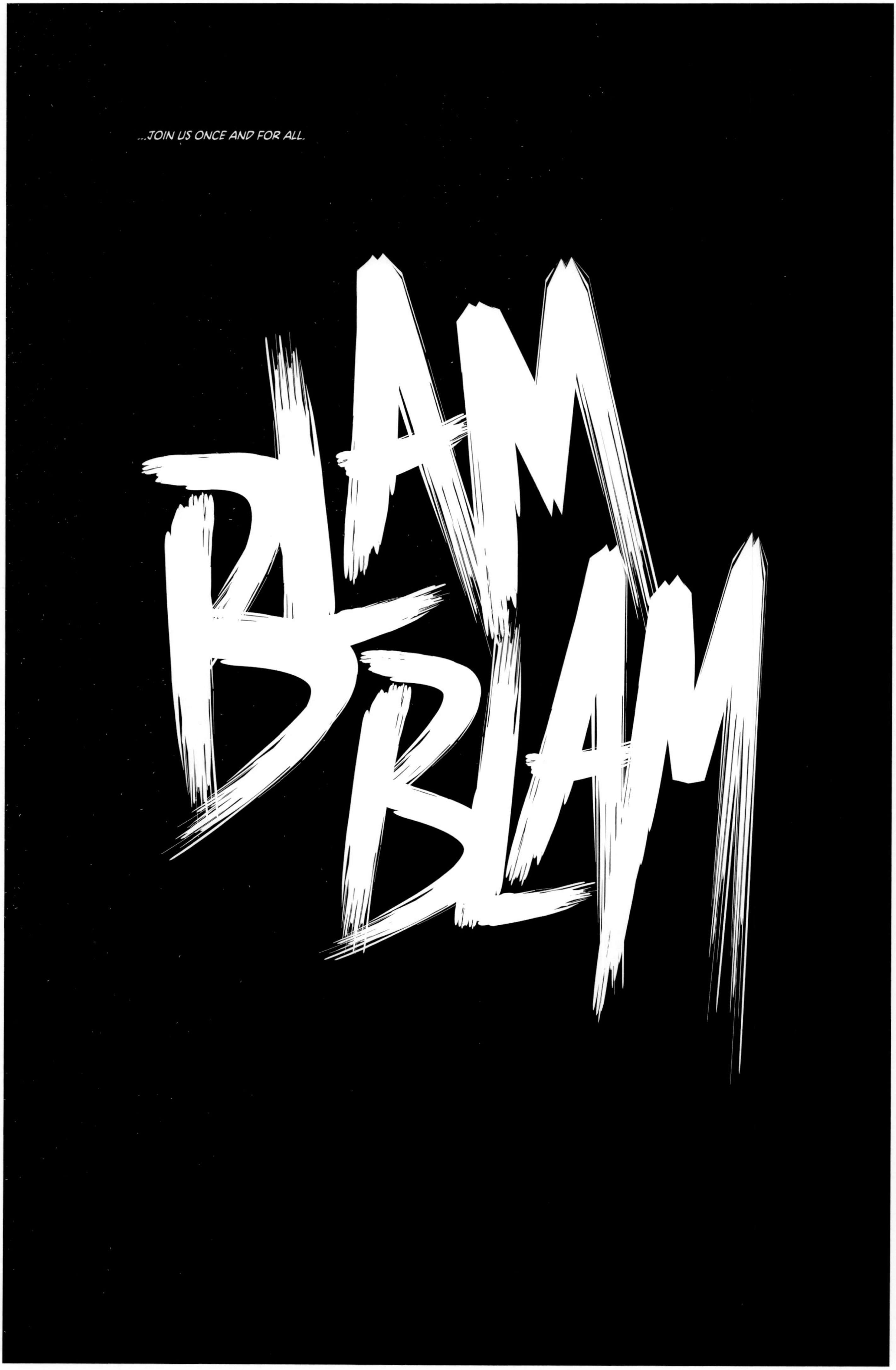
...JOIN US ONCE AND FOR ALL.
BLAM
BLAM

EST
1637
IN VITAM MORTEM

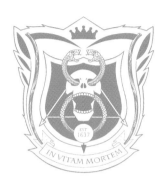

COVER GALLERY

#32 VARIANT BY **JASON SHAWN ALEXANDER**

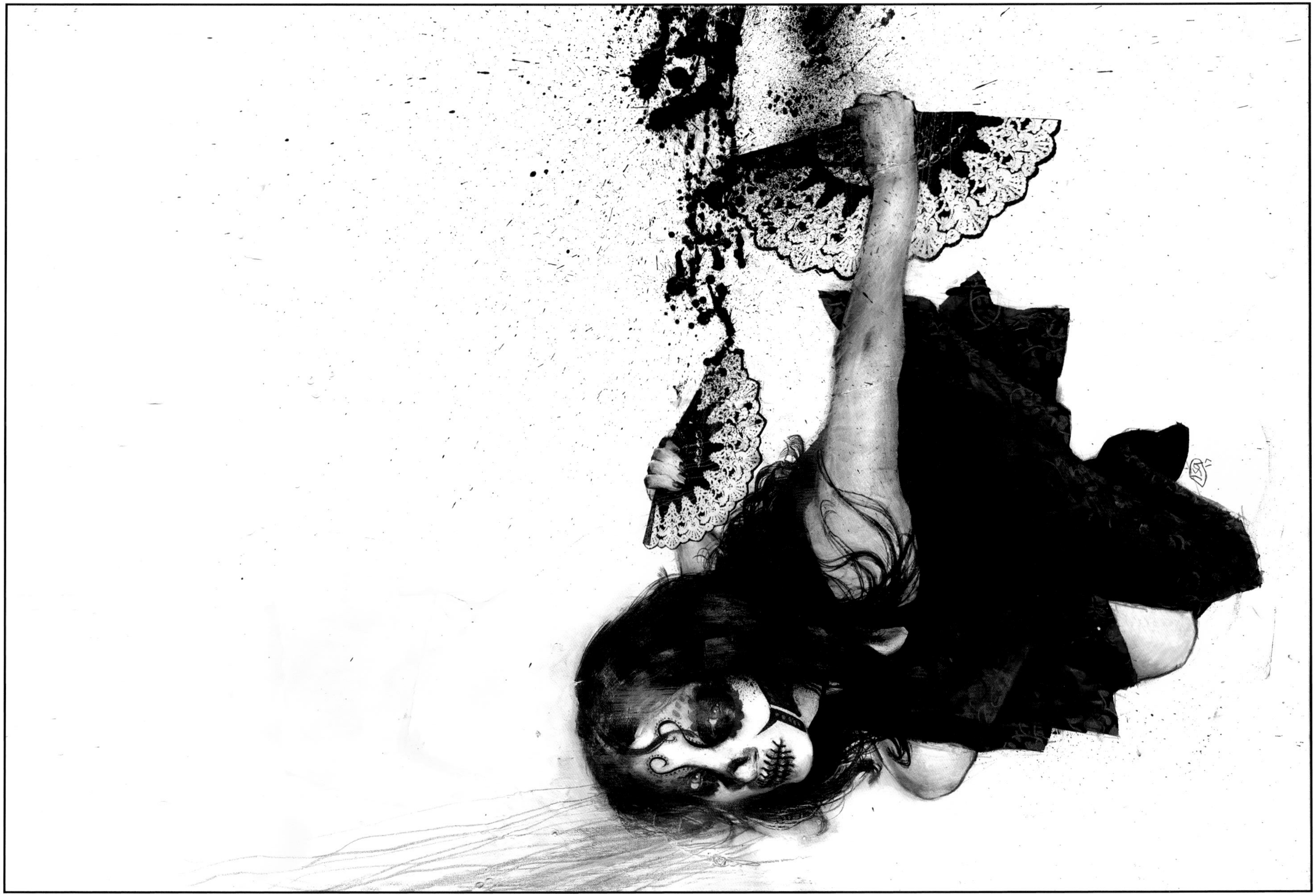

#32 VIRGIN VARIANT BY **WES CRAIG**

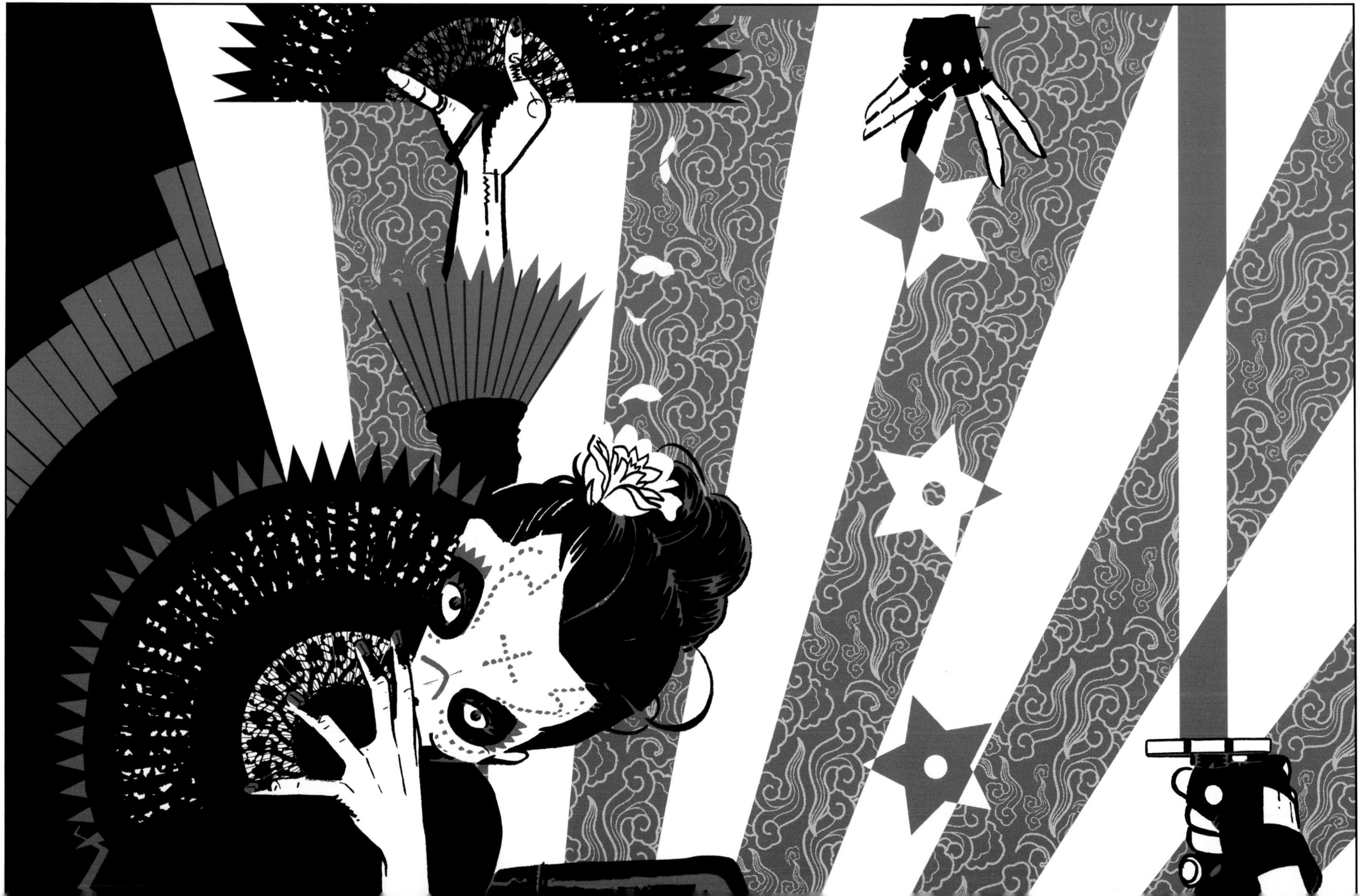

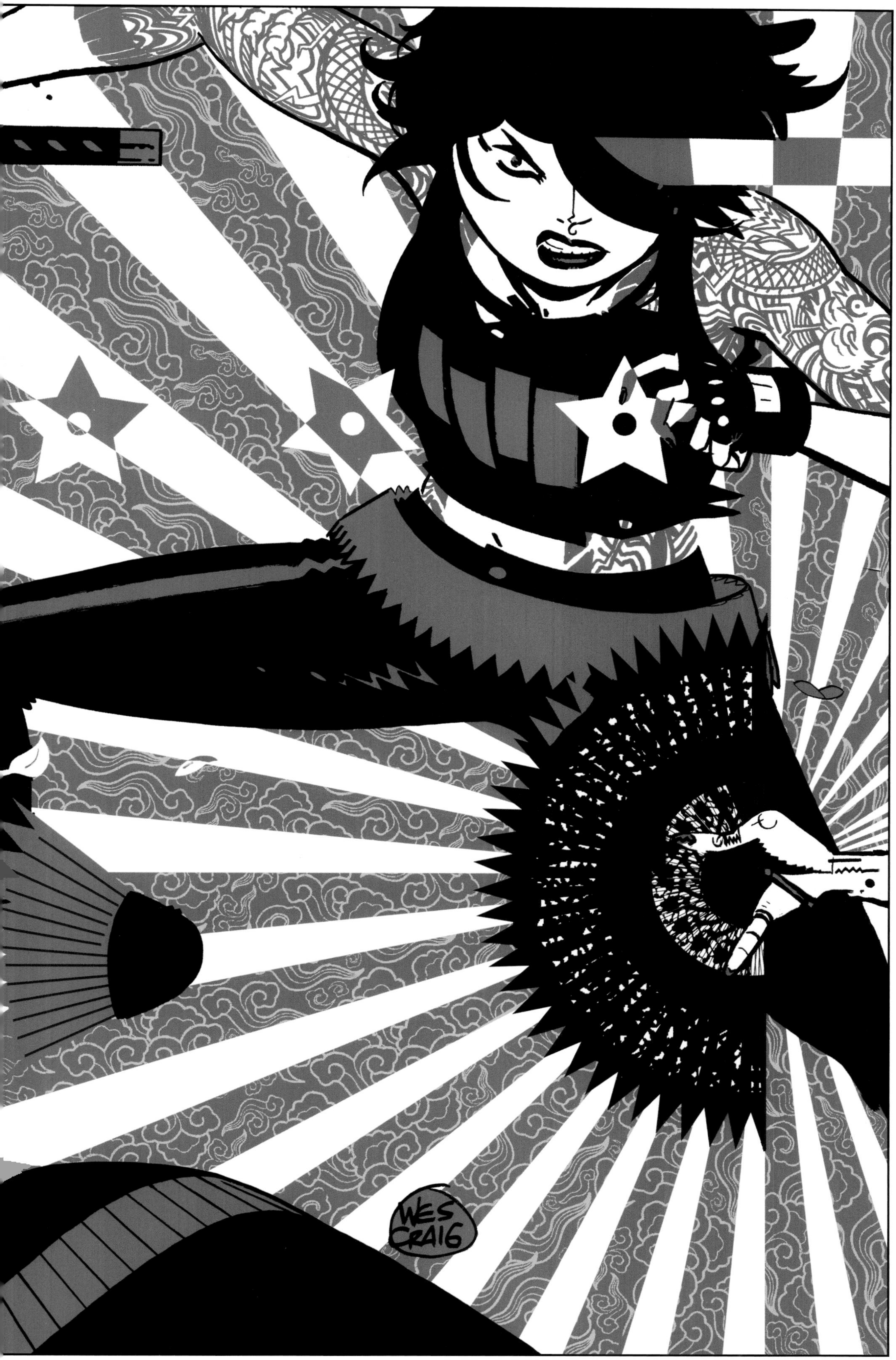
WES CRAIG

#33 VARIANT BY **JEFF STOKELY**

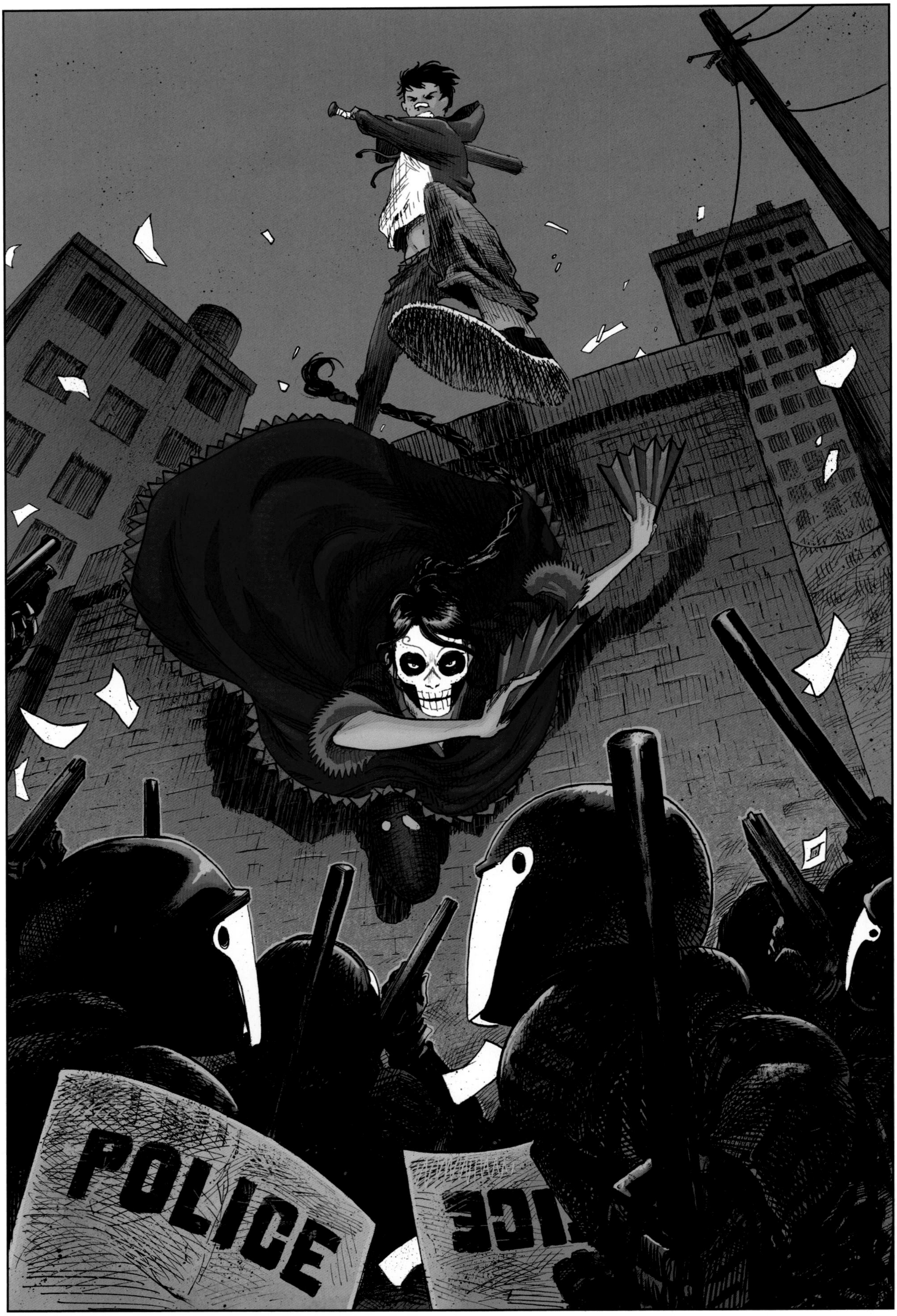
POLICE

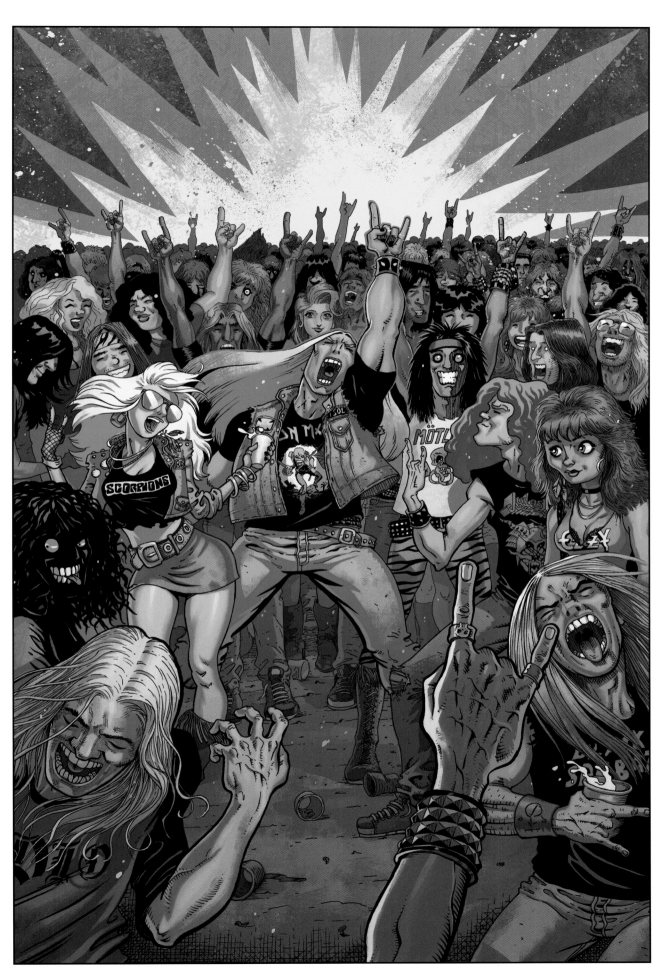

#34 VARIANT BY **RORY HENSLEY**

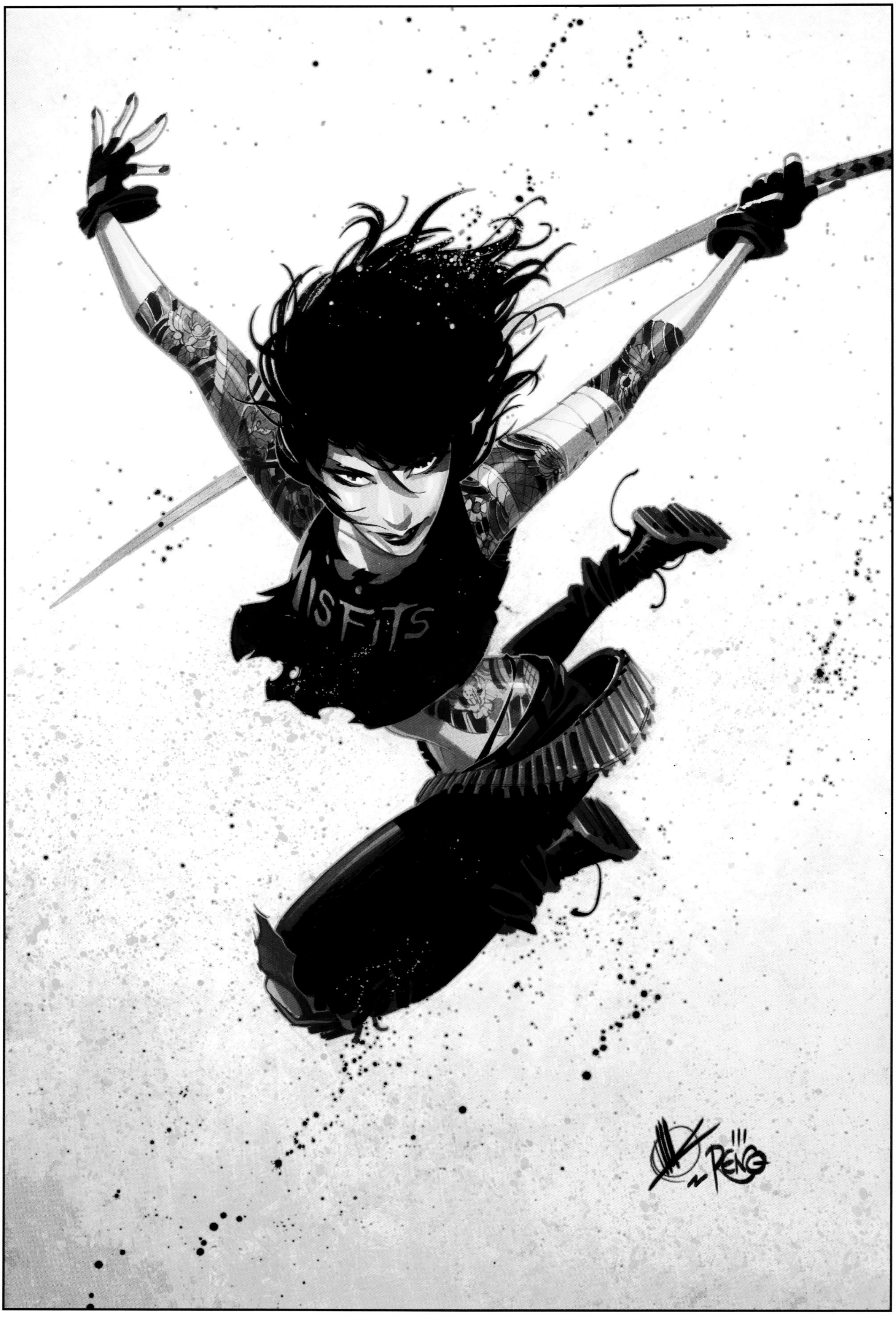
MISFITS

#35 VARIANT BY **MATTEO SCALERA & MORENO DINISIO**

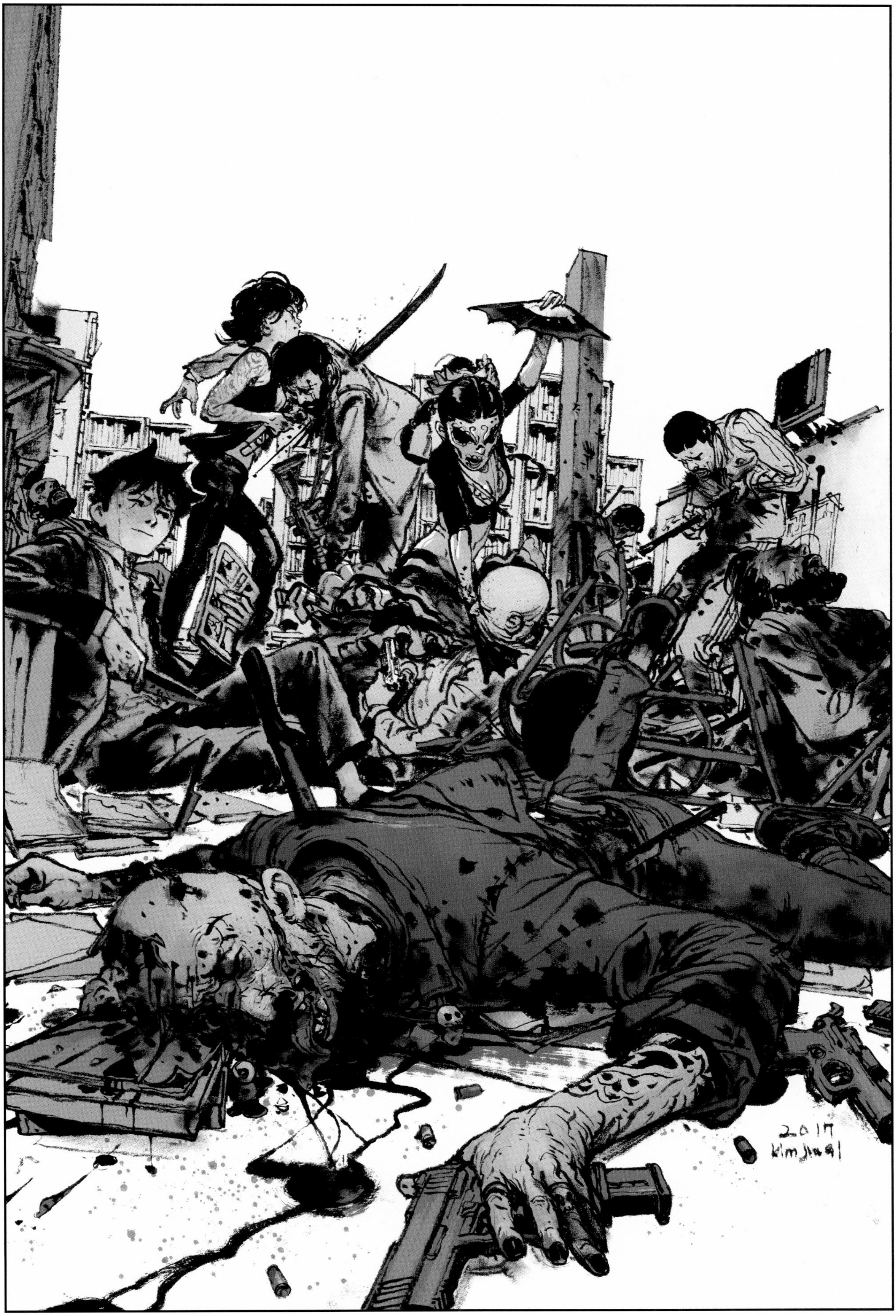
2017

#36 VARIANT BY **KIM JUNG GI & DAVE McCAIG**

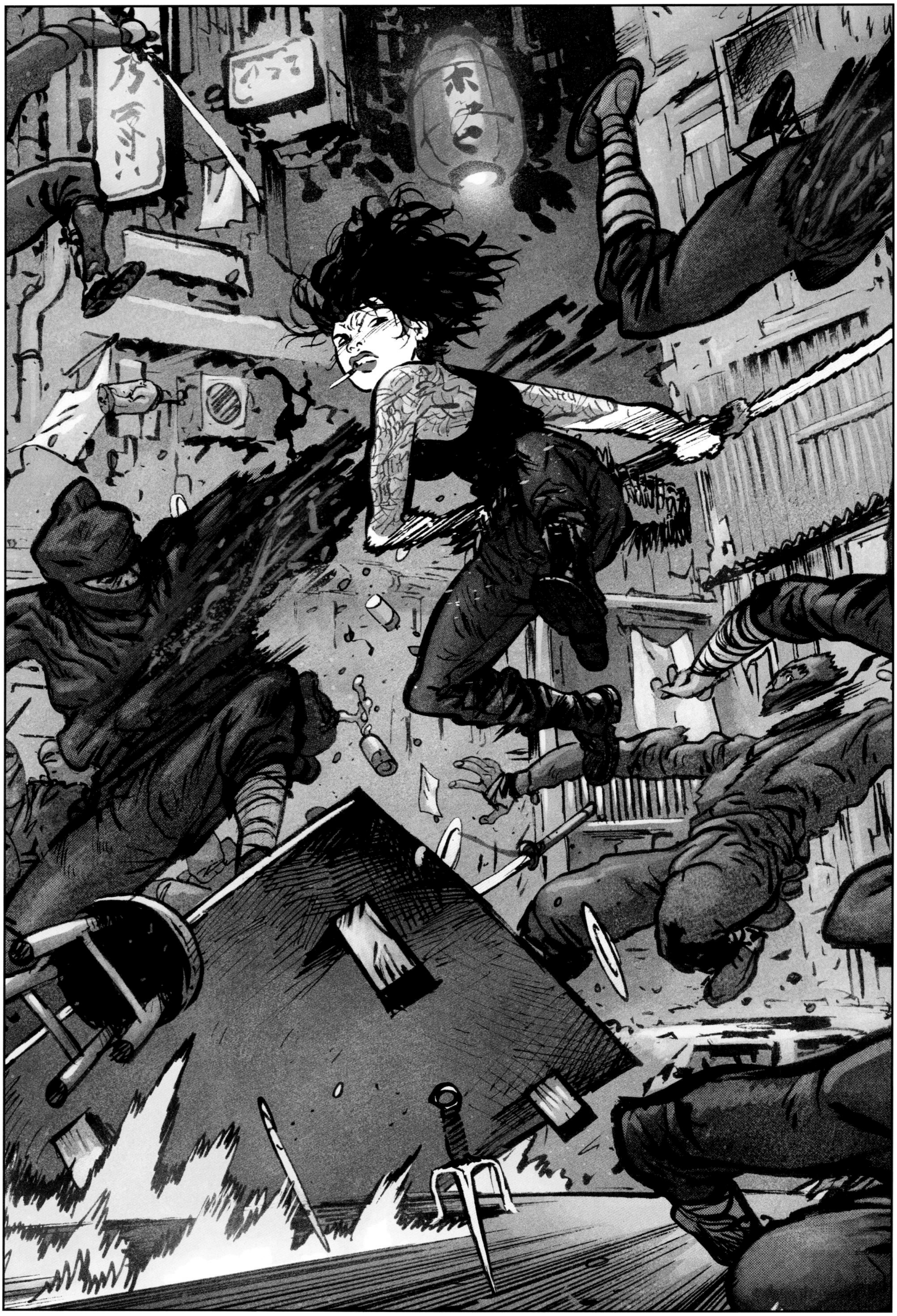

#37 VARIANT BY **DANIEL WARREN JOHNSON & JORDAN BOYD**

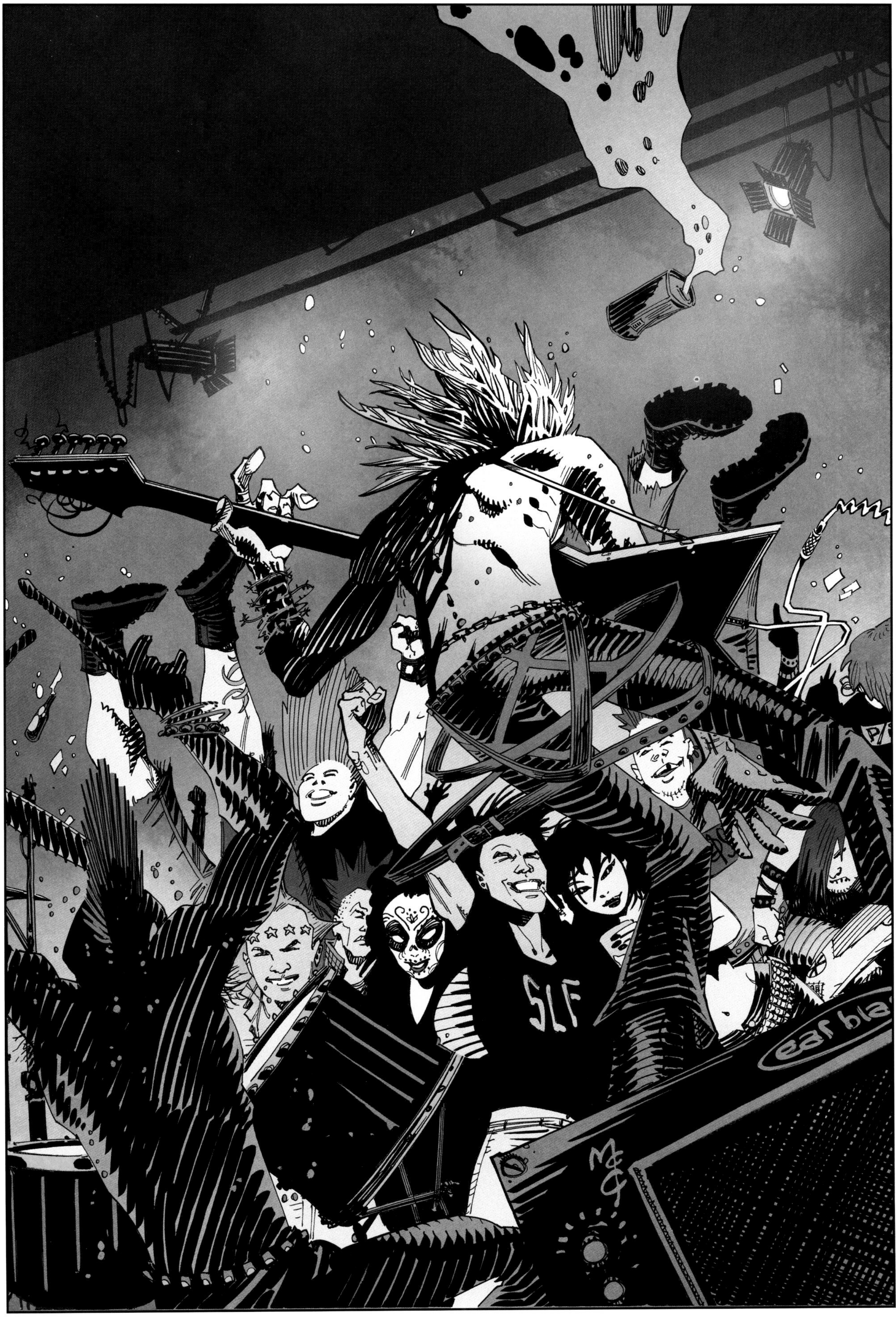
SLF

#38 VARIANT BY **JOHN McCREA**

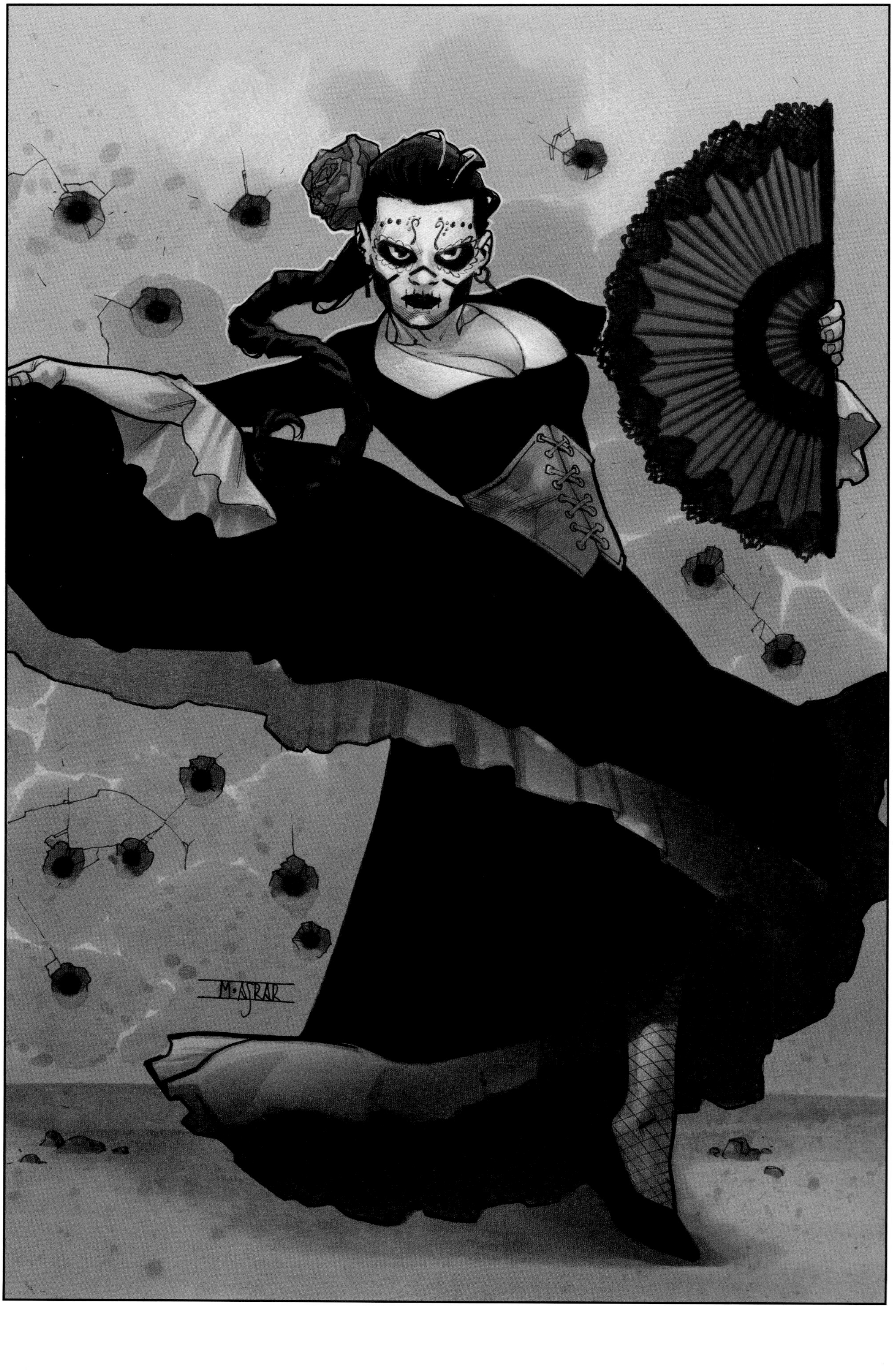
M·ASRAR

#39 VARIANT BY **MAHMUD ASRAR & DAVE McCAIG**

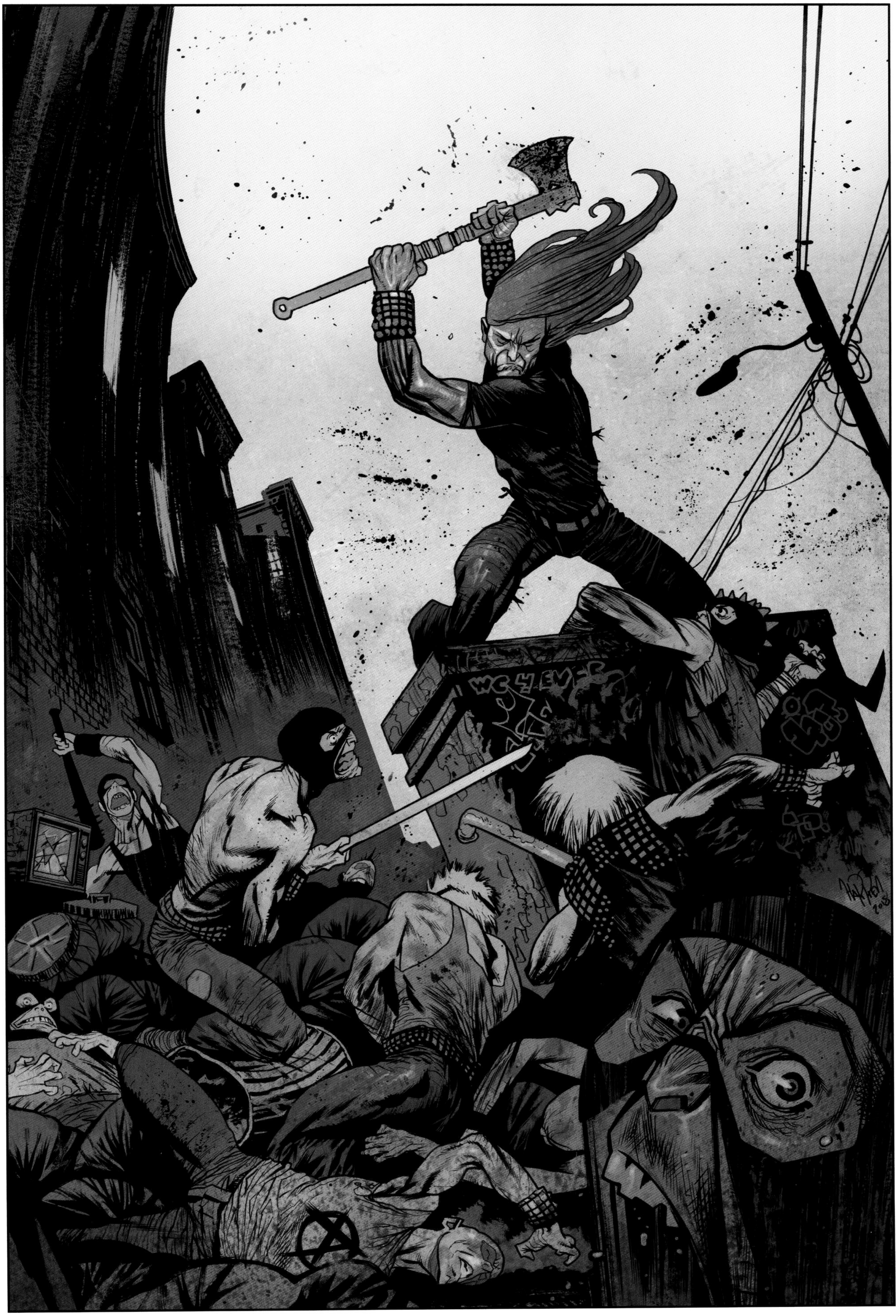

#40 VARIANT BY **JAMES HARREN**

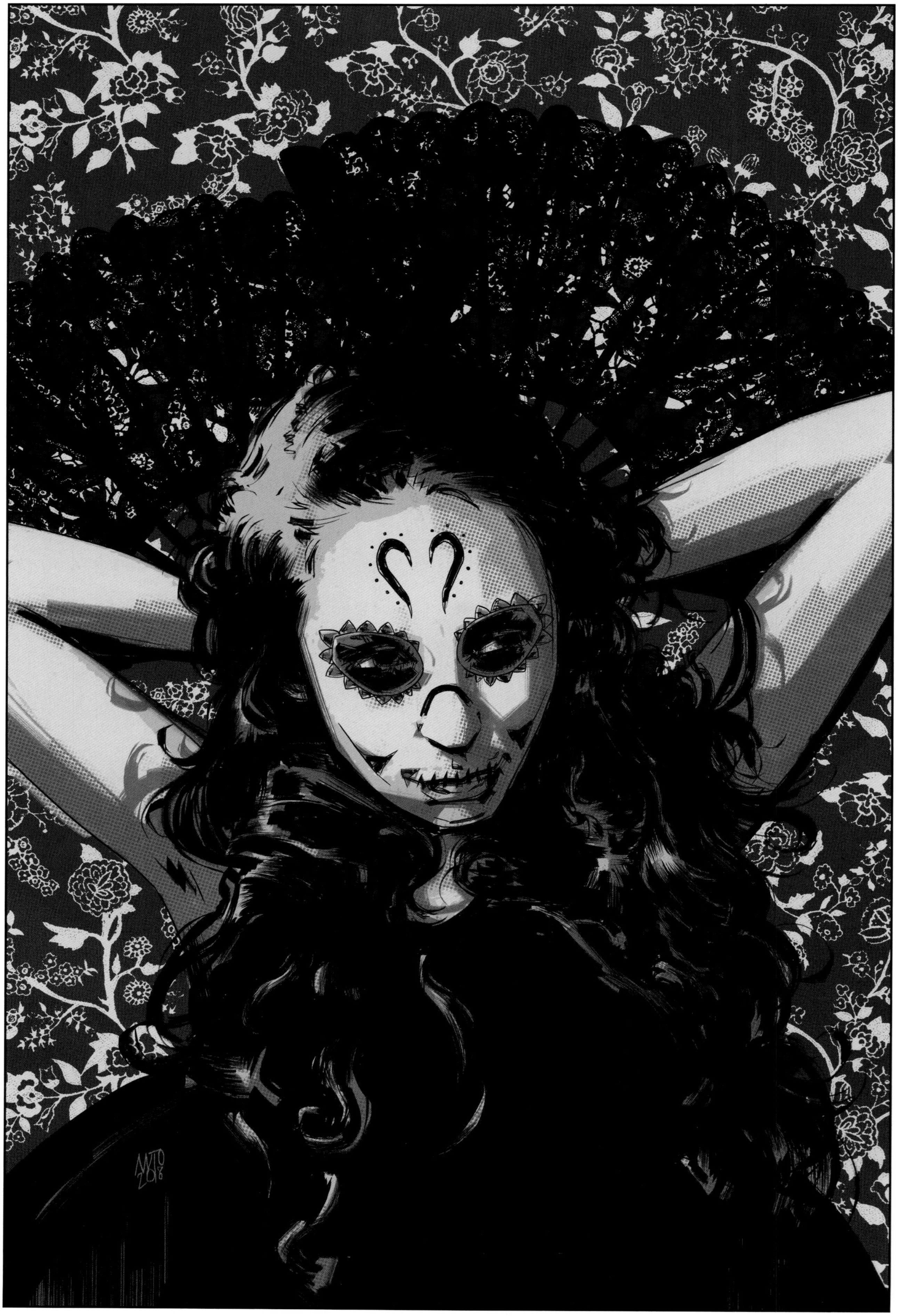

#41 VARIANT BY **ANTONIO FUSO**

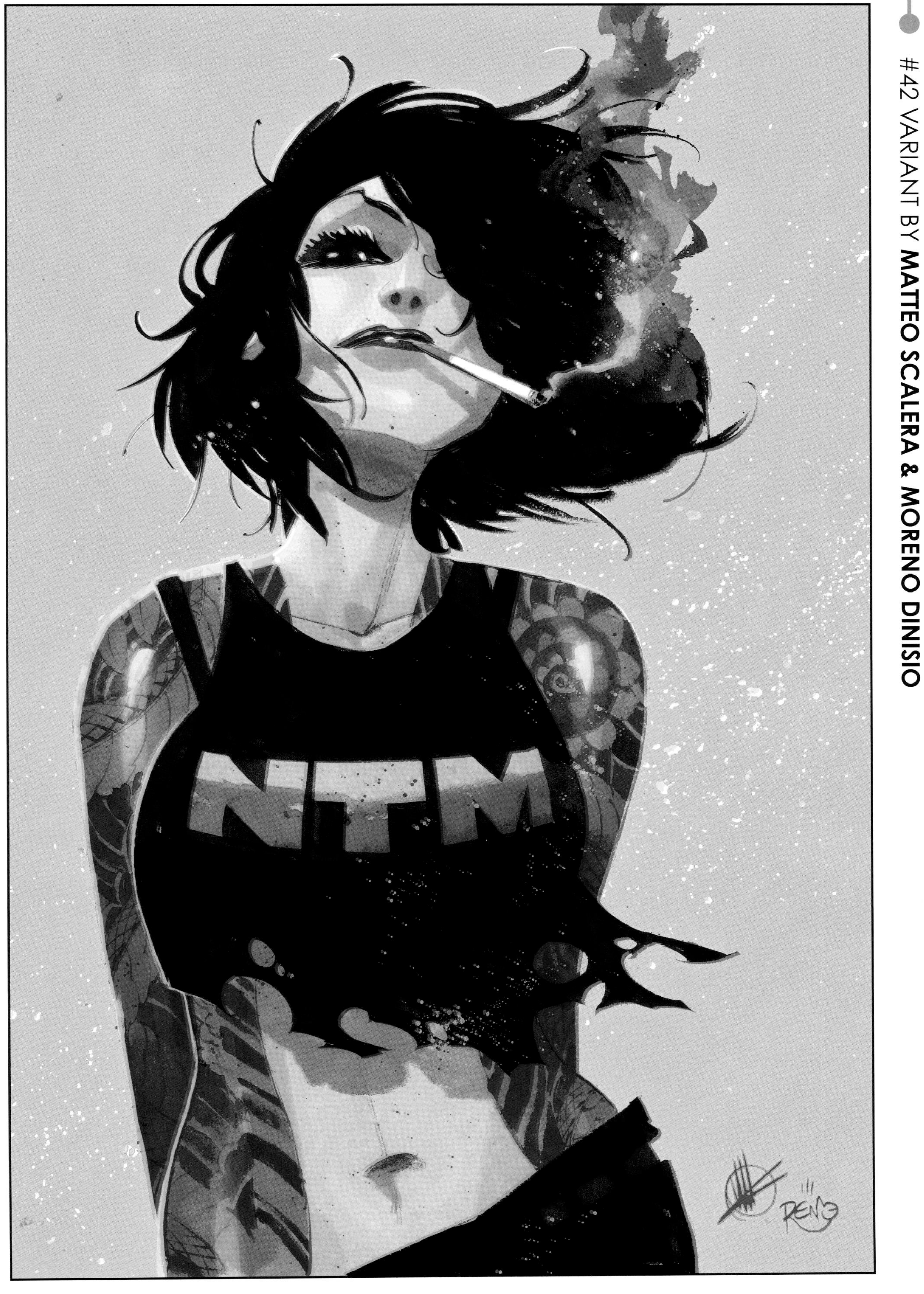
NTM

#42 VARIANT BY **MATTEO SCALERA & MORENO DINISIO**

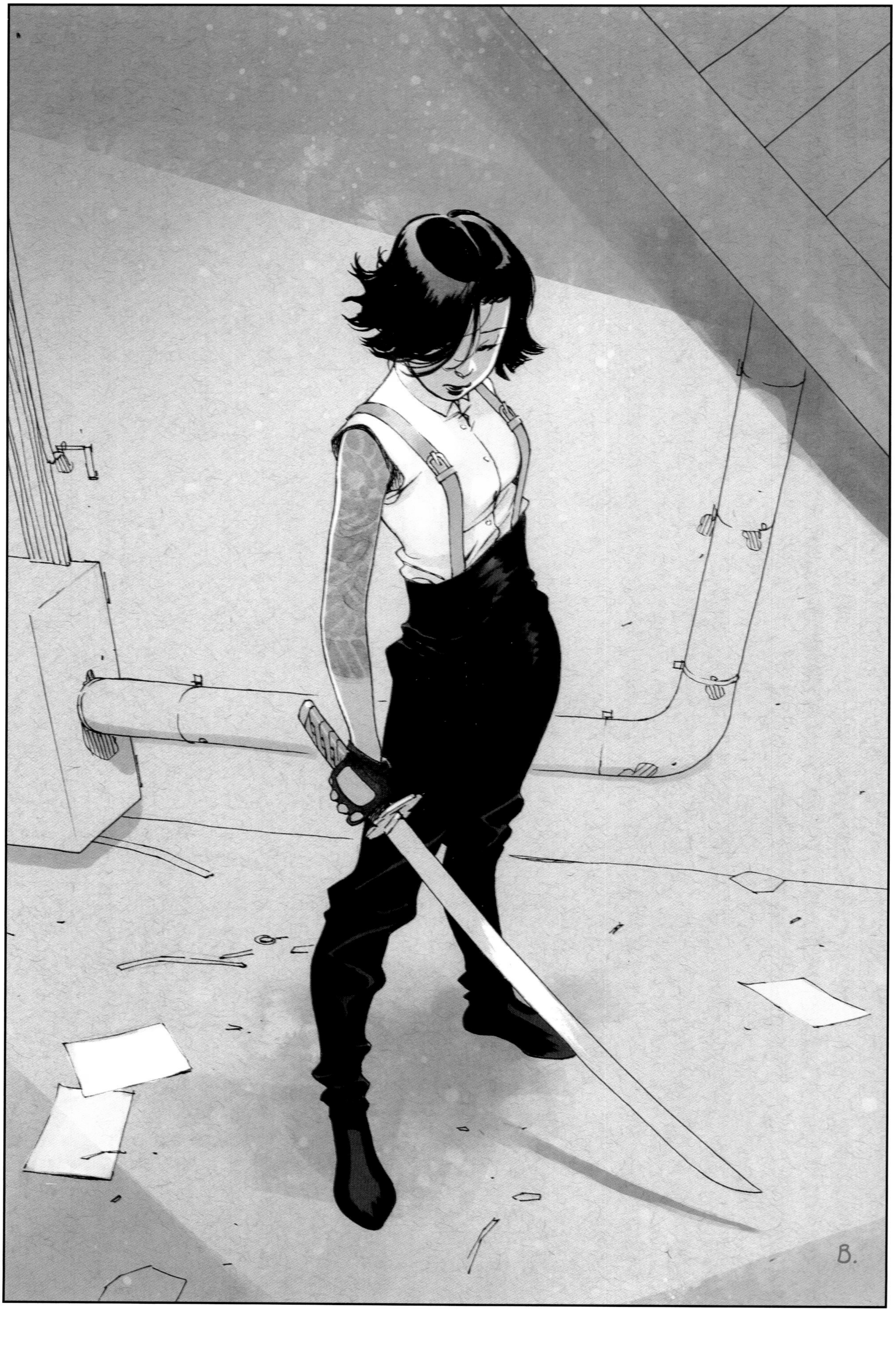
B.

#43 VARIANT BY **BENGAL**

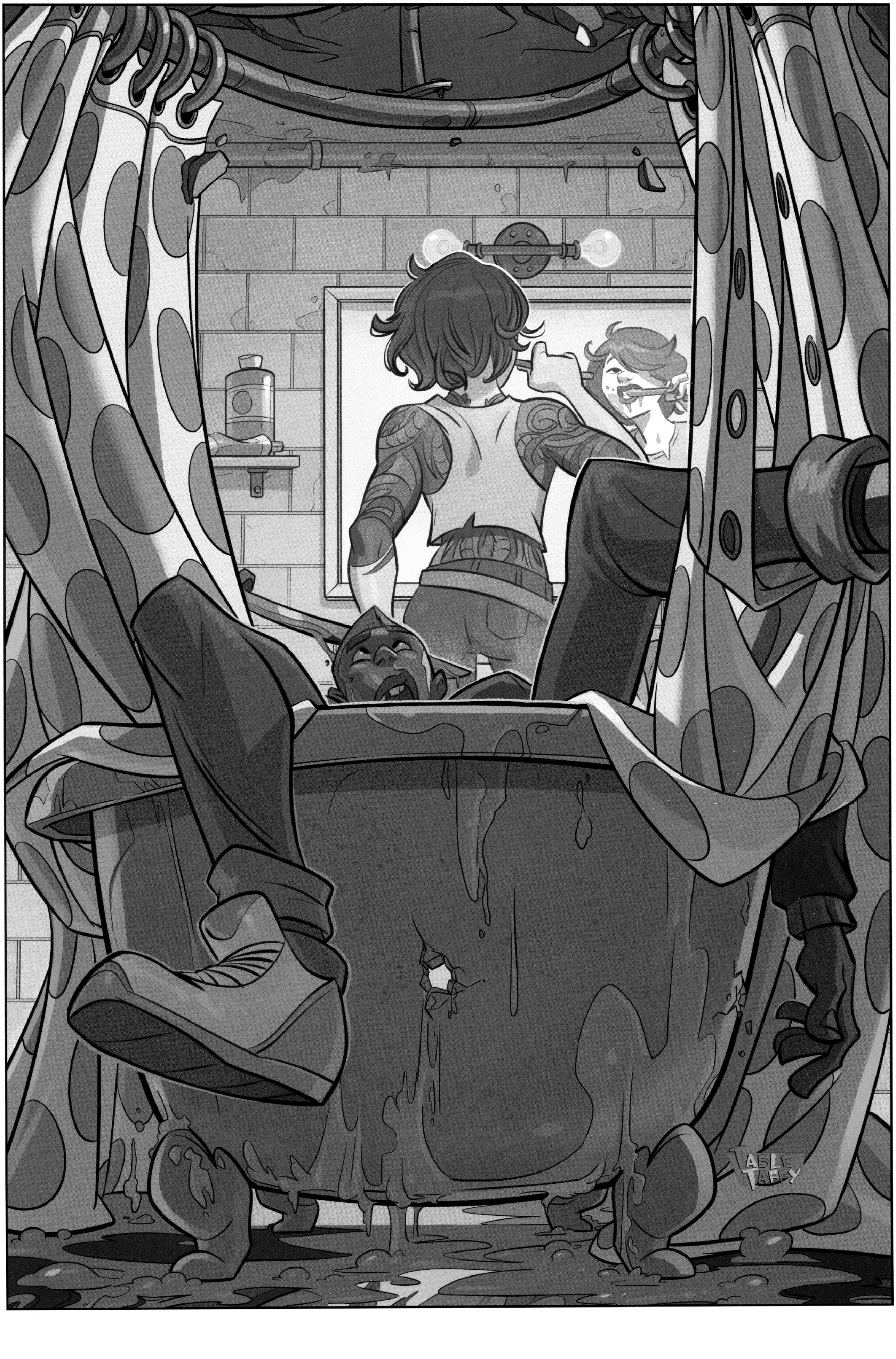
TABLE TAFFY

#44 VARIANT BY **SEAN GALLOWAY**

WES CRAIG SKETCHBOOK

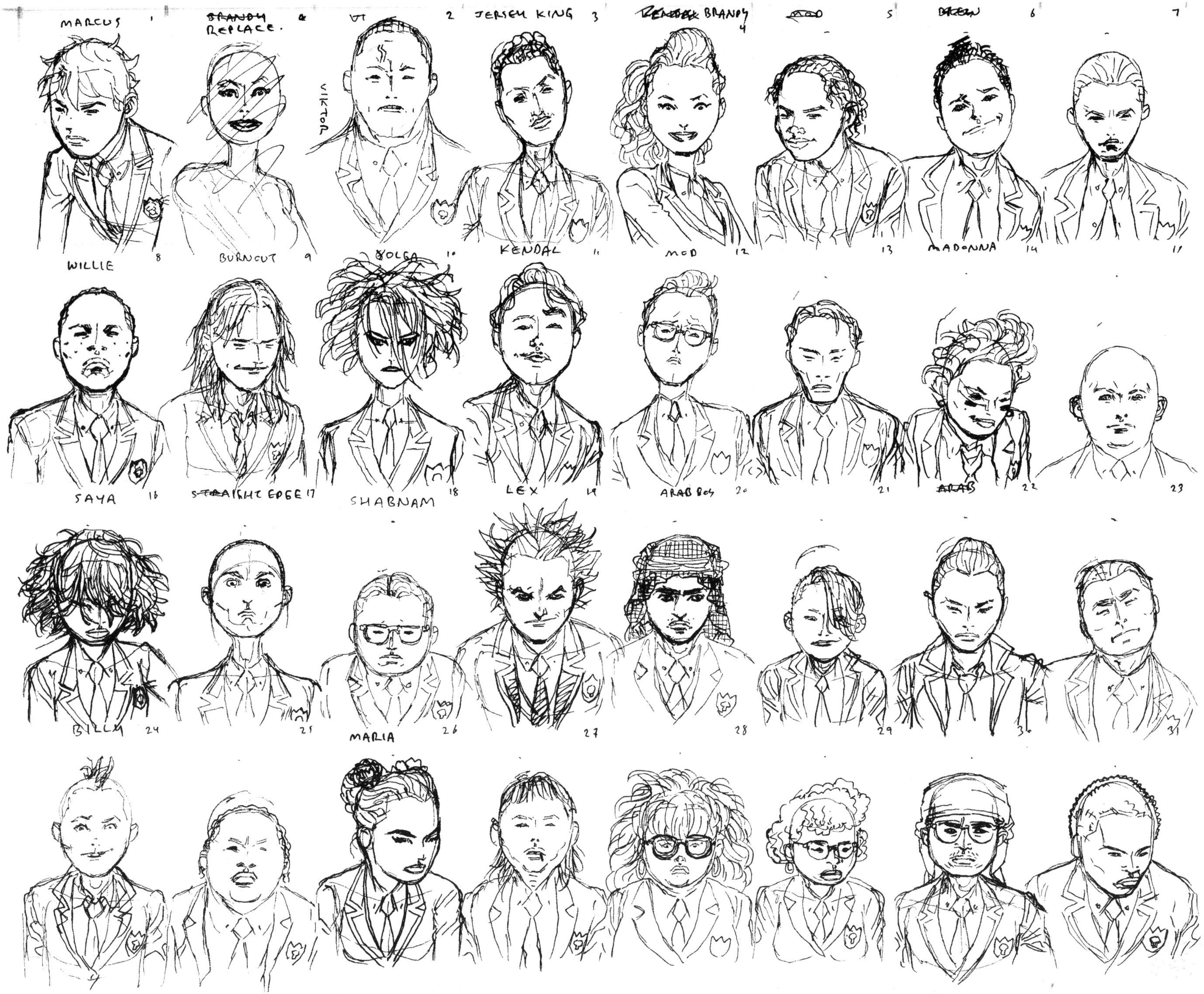
MARCUS 1
REPLACE.
VT 2
VIKTOR
JERSEY KING 3
BRANDY 4
5
6
7
WILLIE 8
BURNCUT 9
YOLGA 10
KENDAL 11
MOD 12
13
MADONNA 14
SAYA 16
STRAIGHT EDGE 17
SHABNAM 18
LEX 19
ARAB BOY 20
21
ARAS 22
23
BILLY 24
MARIA 26
27
28
29
31

DEADLY CLASS

40-41-42-43-44
ARC 9

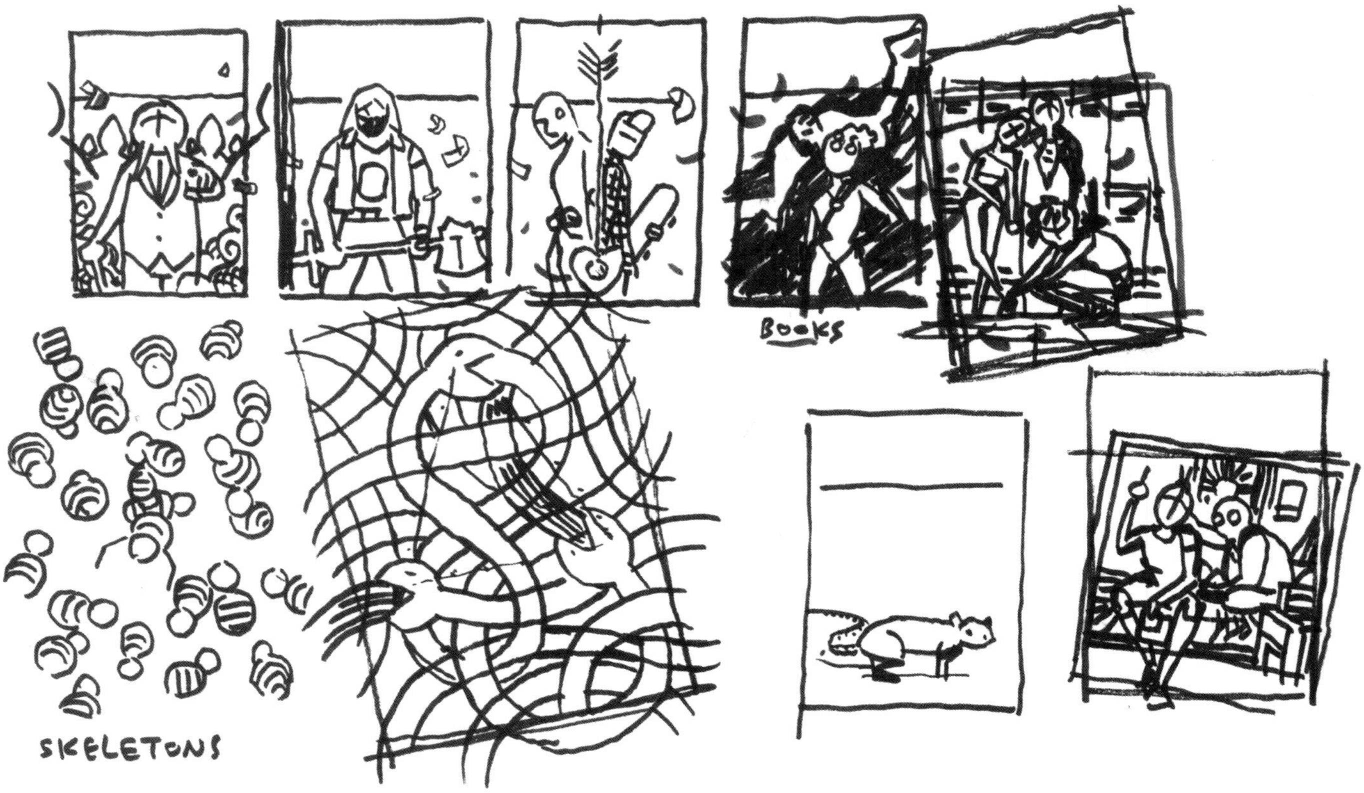
BOOKS
SKELETONS

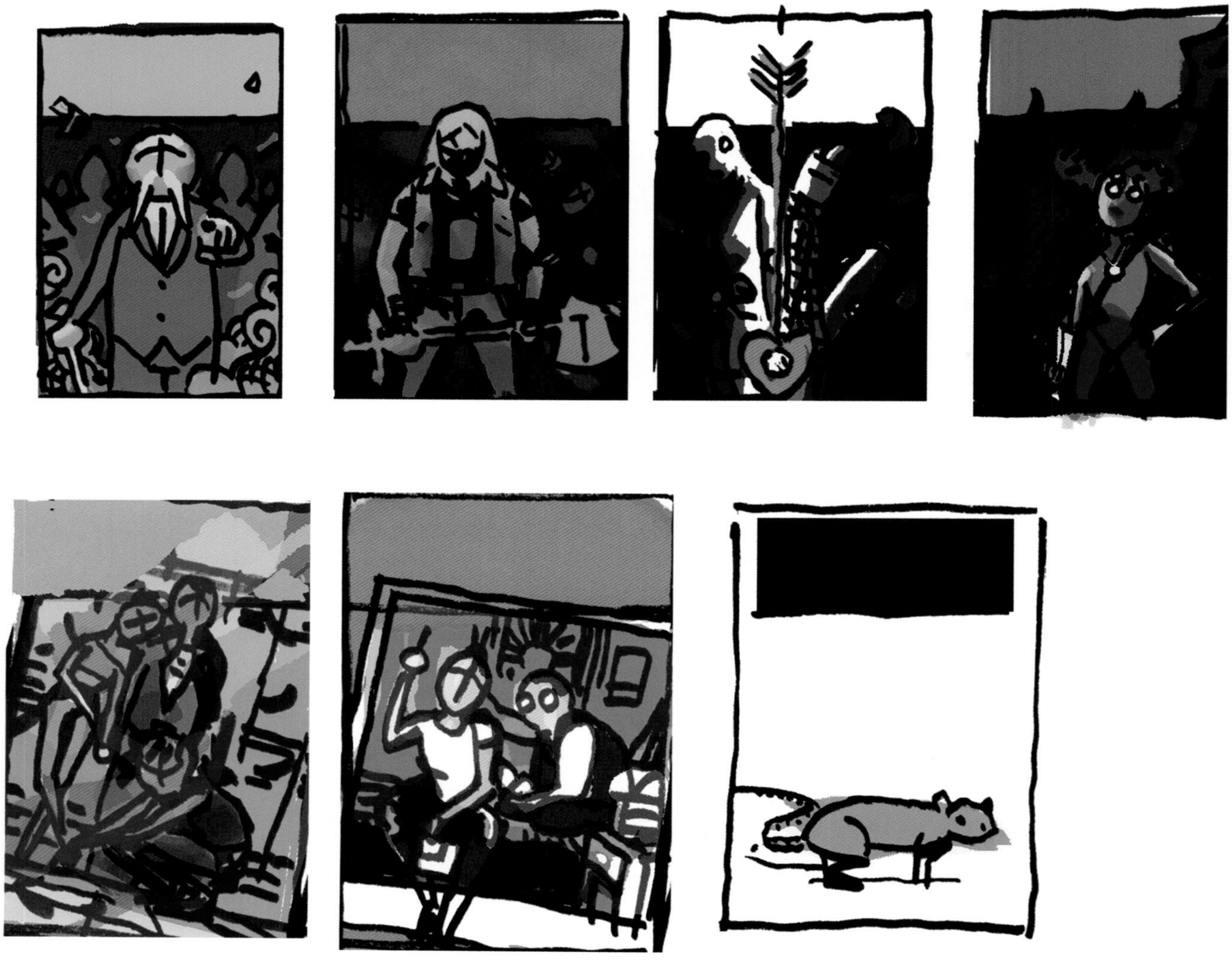

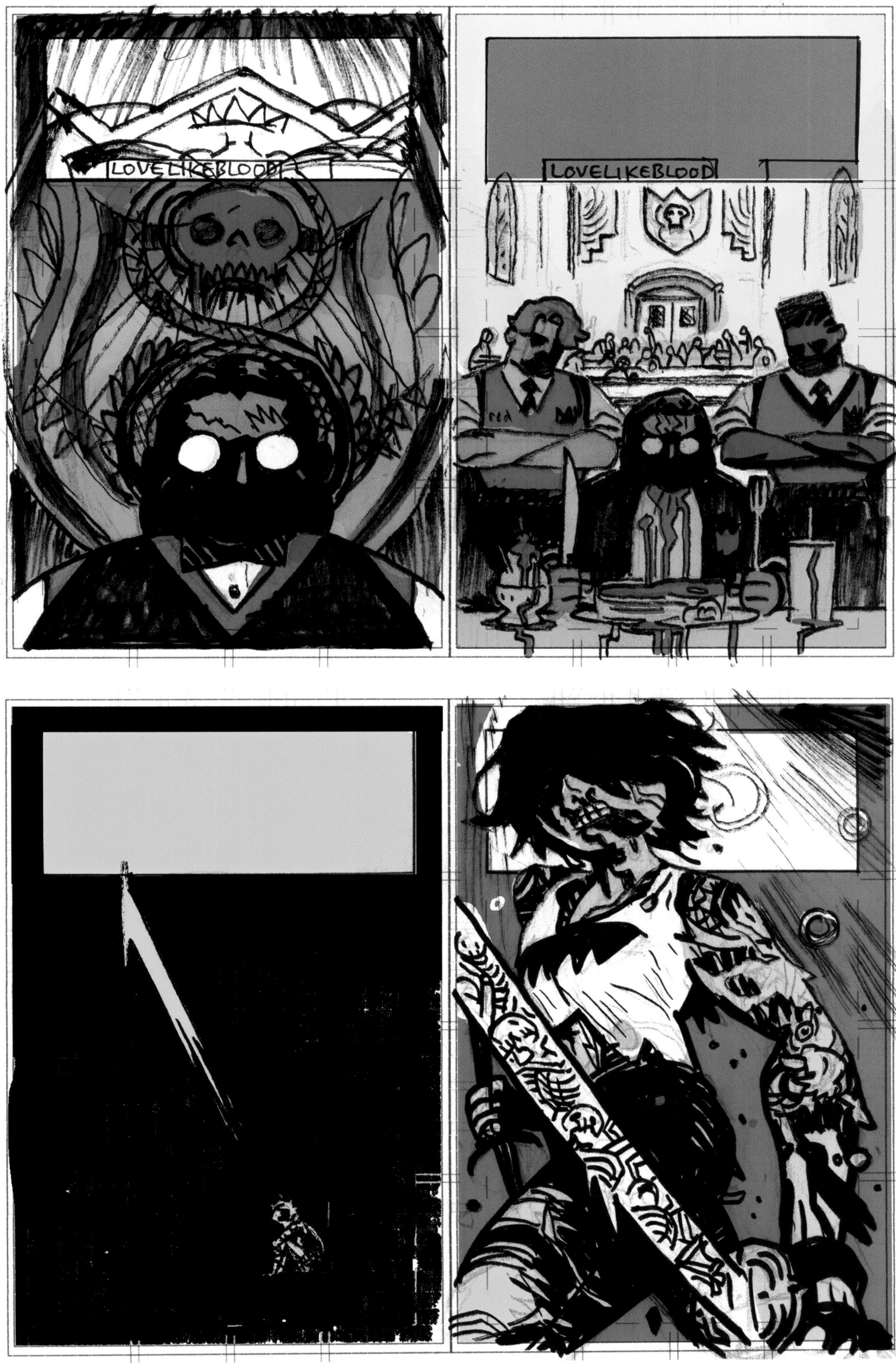
LOVELIKEBLOOD
LOVELIKEBLOOD

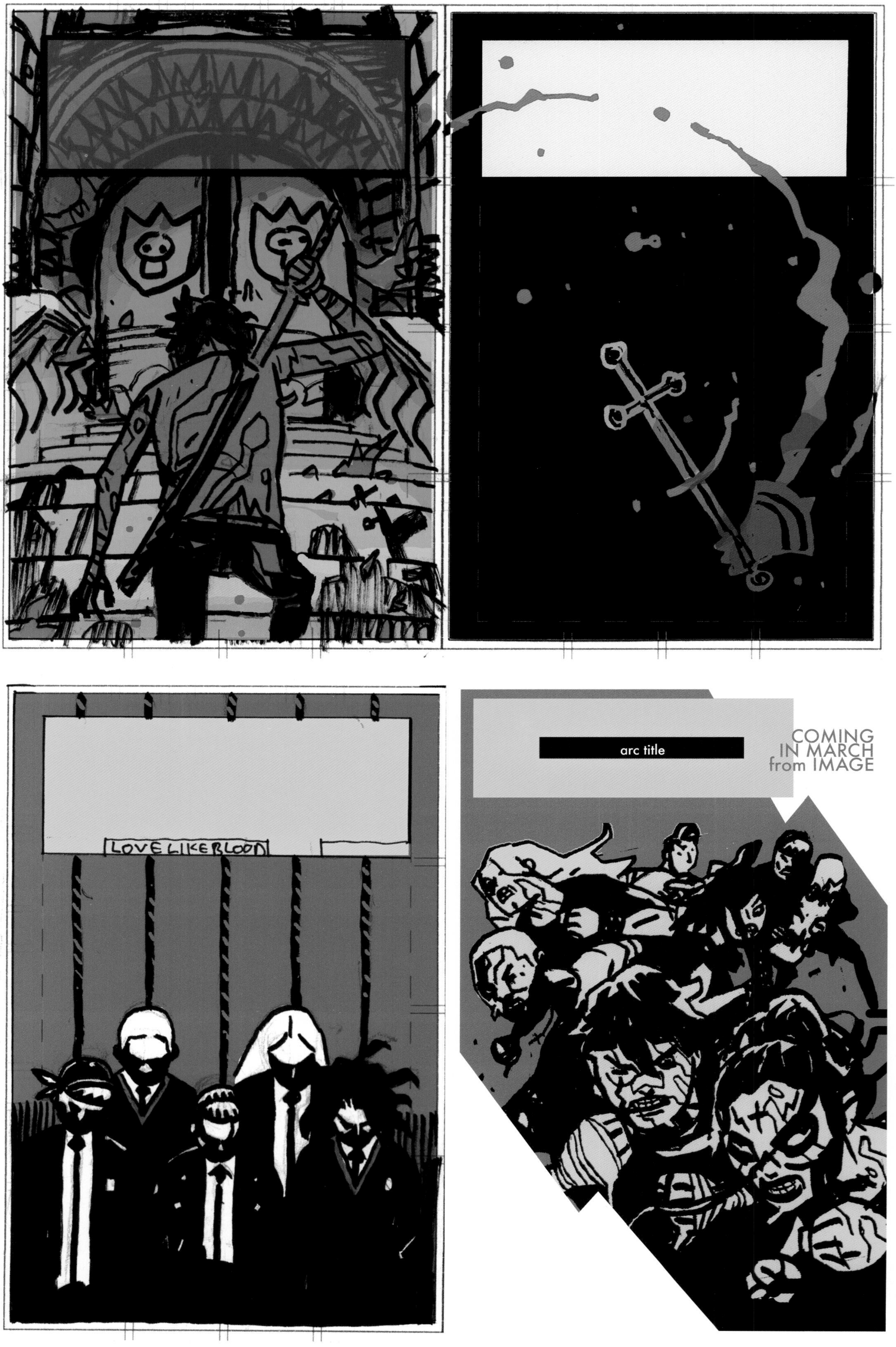
LOVE LIKE BLOOD
arc title
COMING IN MARCH from IMAGE

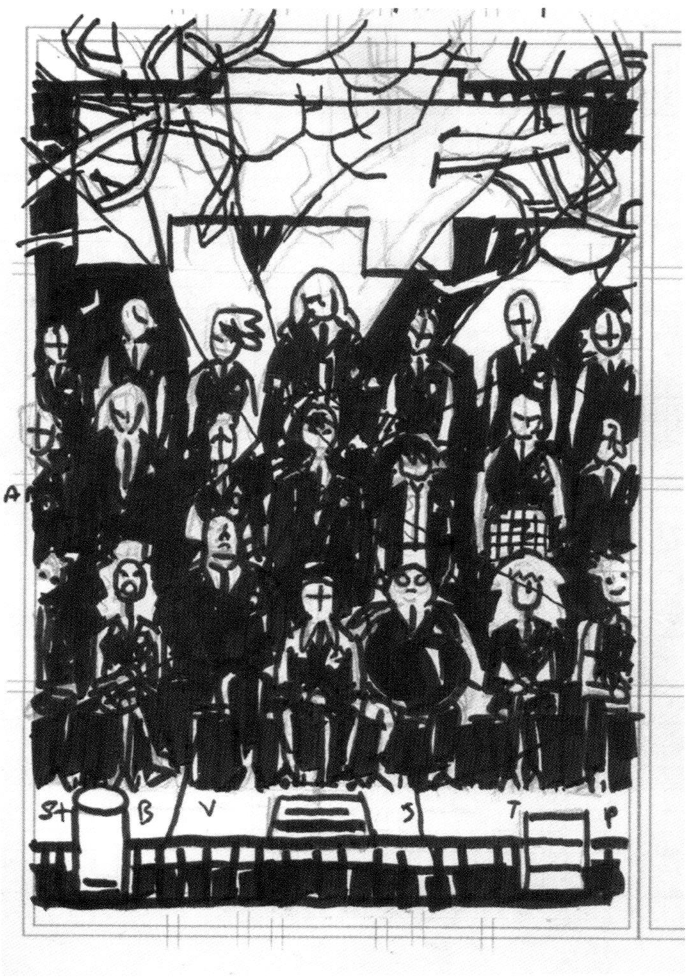

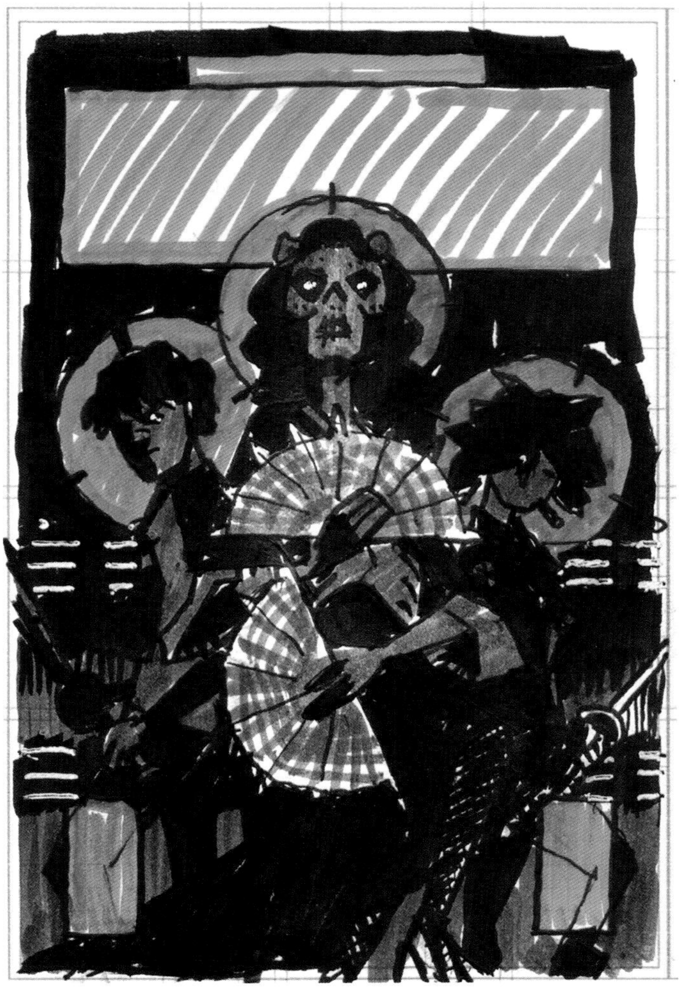

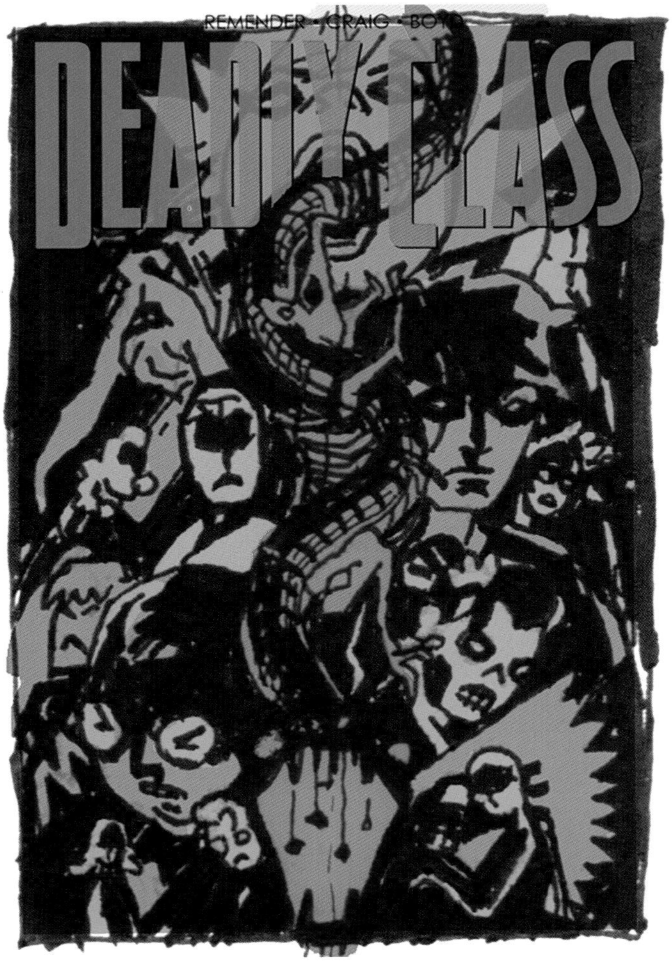
REMENDER • CRAIG • BOYD
DEADLY CLASS

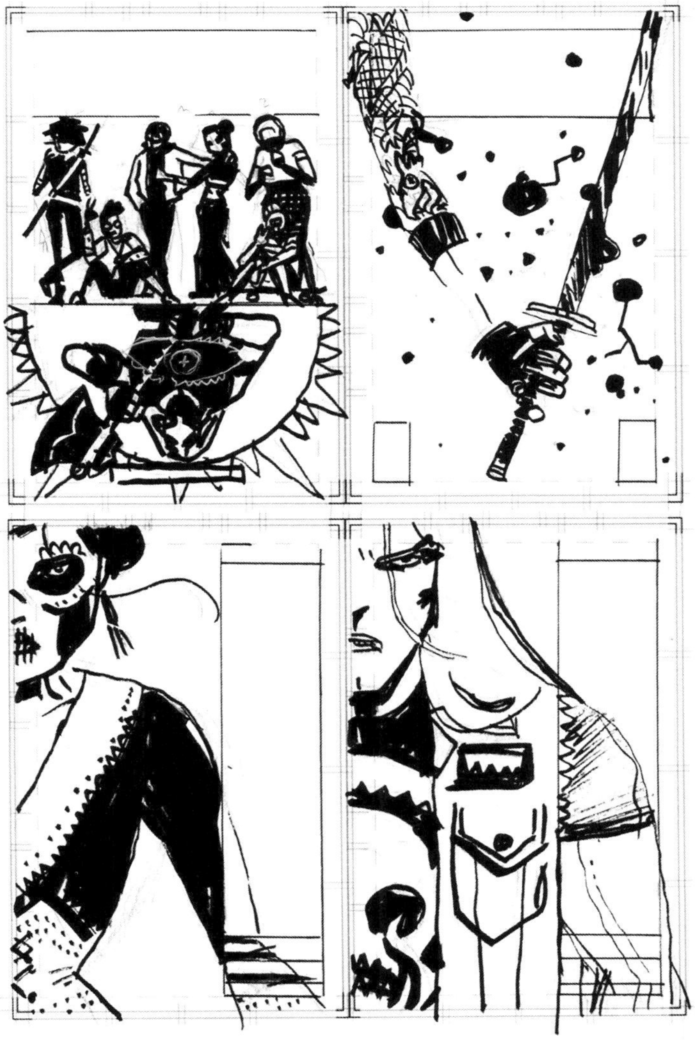

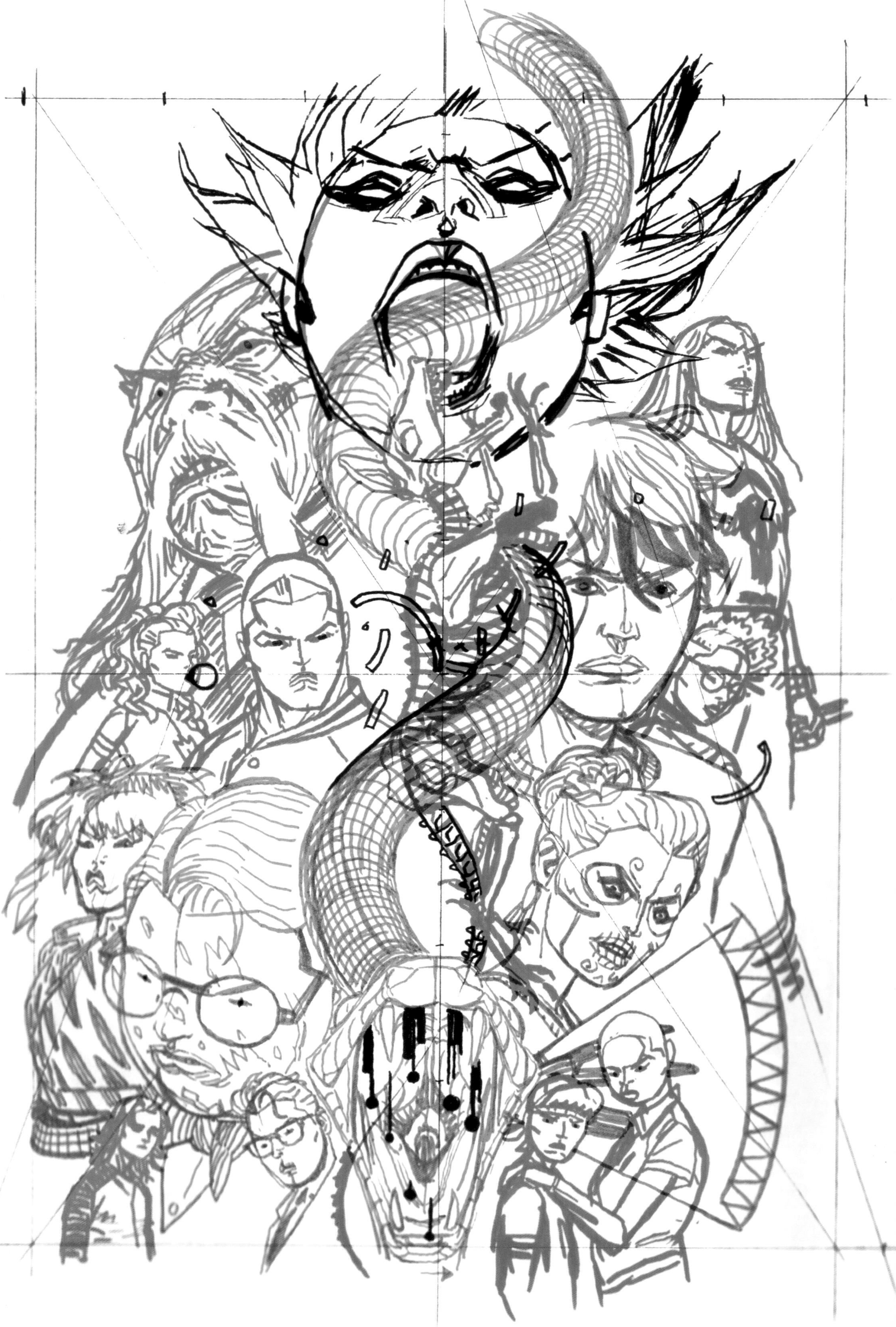

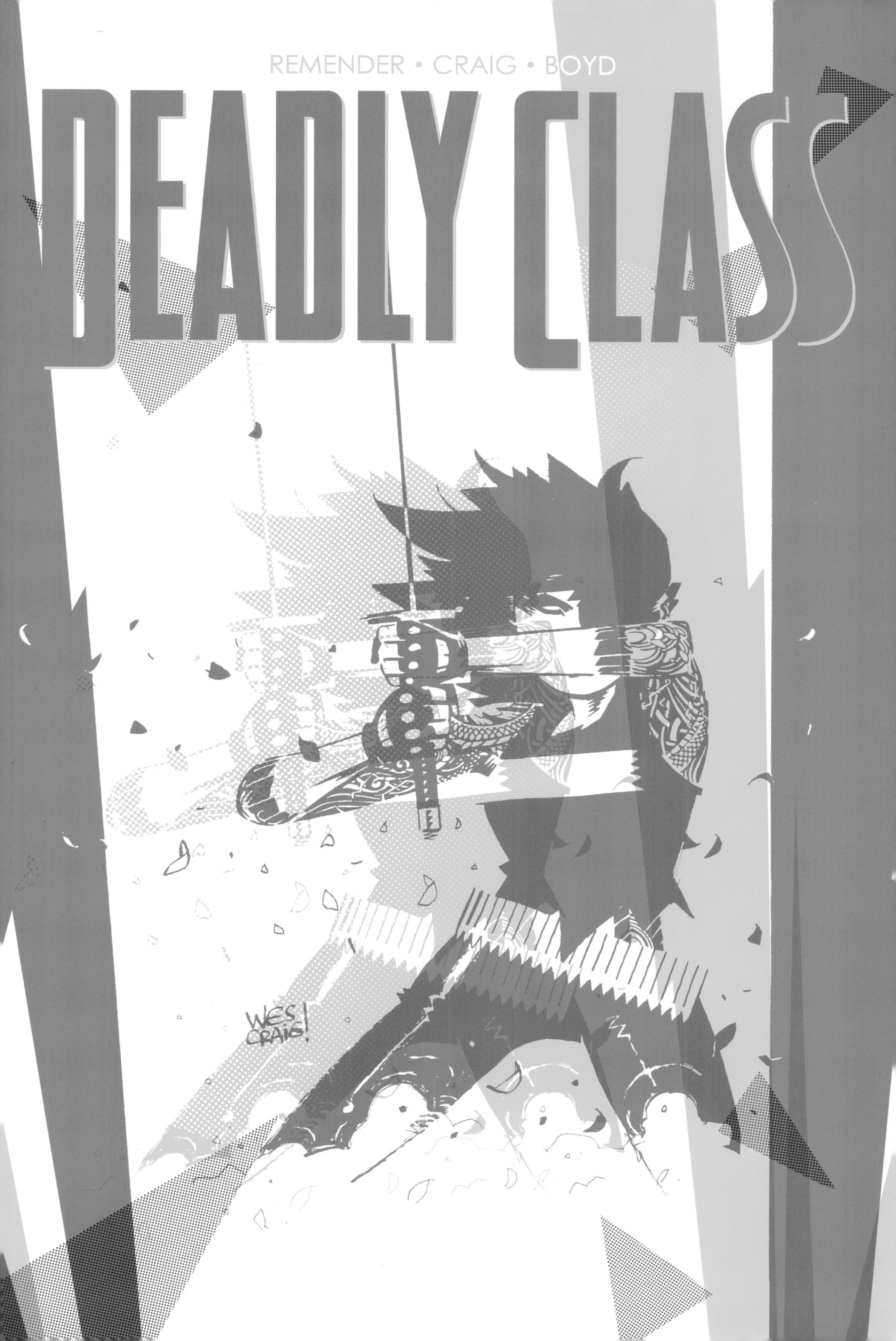
REMENDER • CRAIG • BOYD
DEADLY CLASS
WES CRAIG!

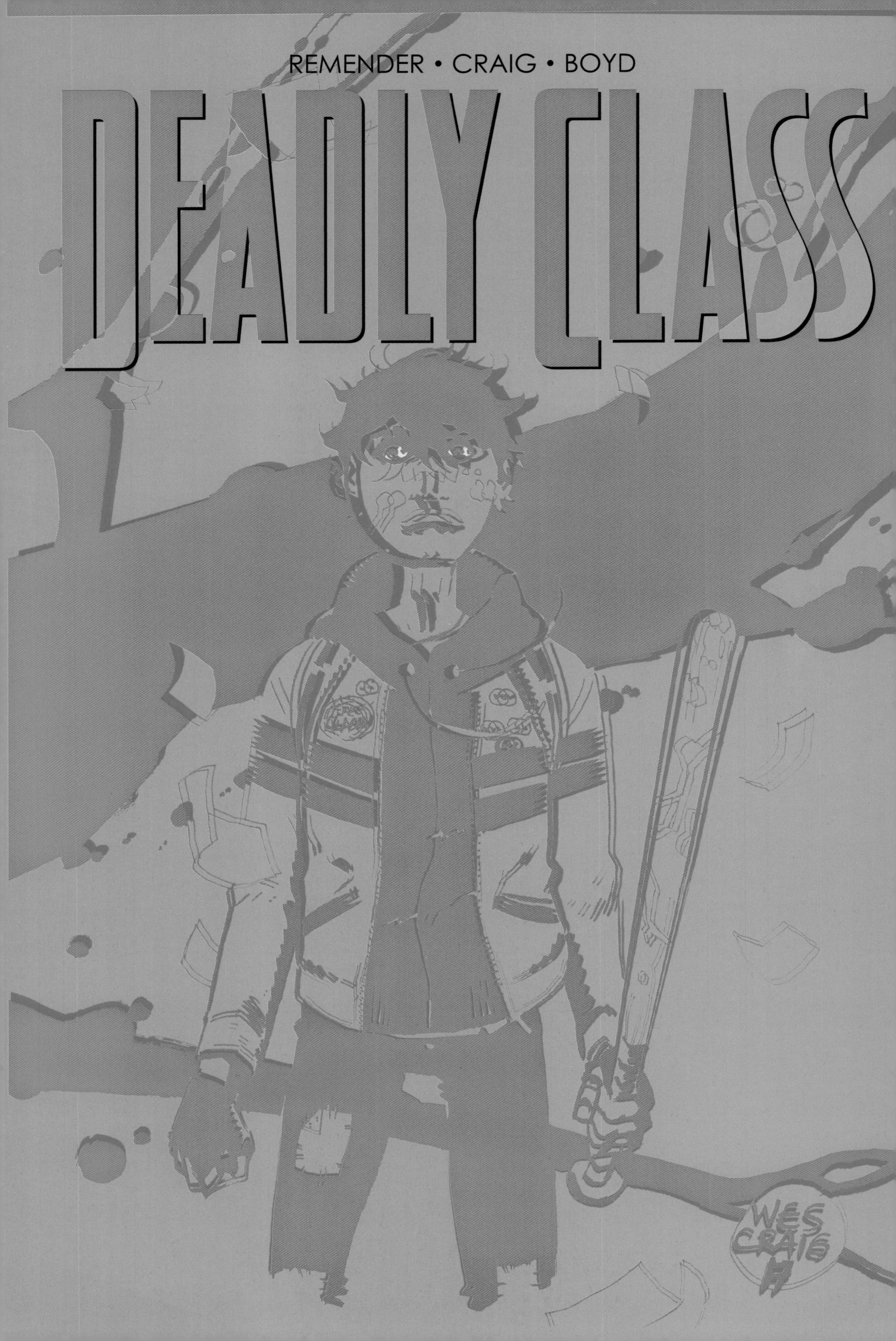
REMENDER • CRAIG • BOYD
DEADLY CLASS
WES CRAIG

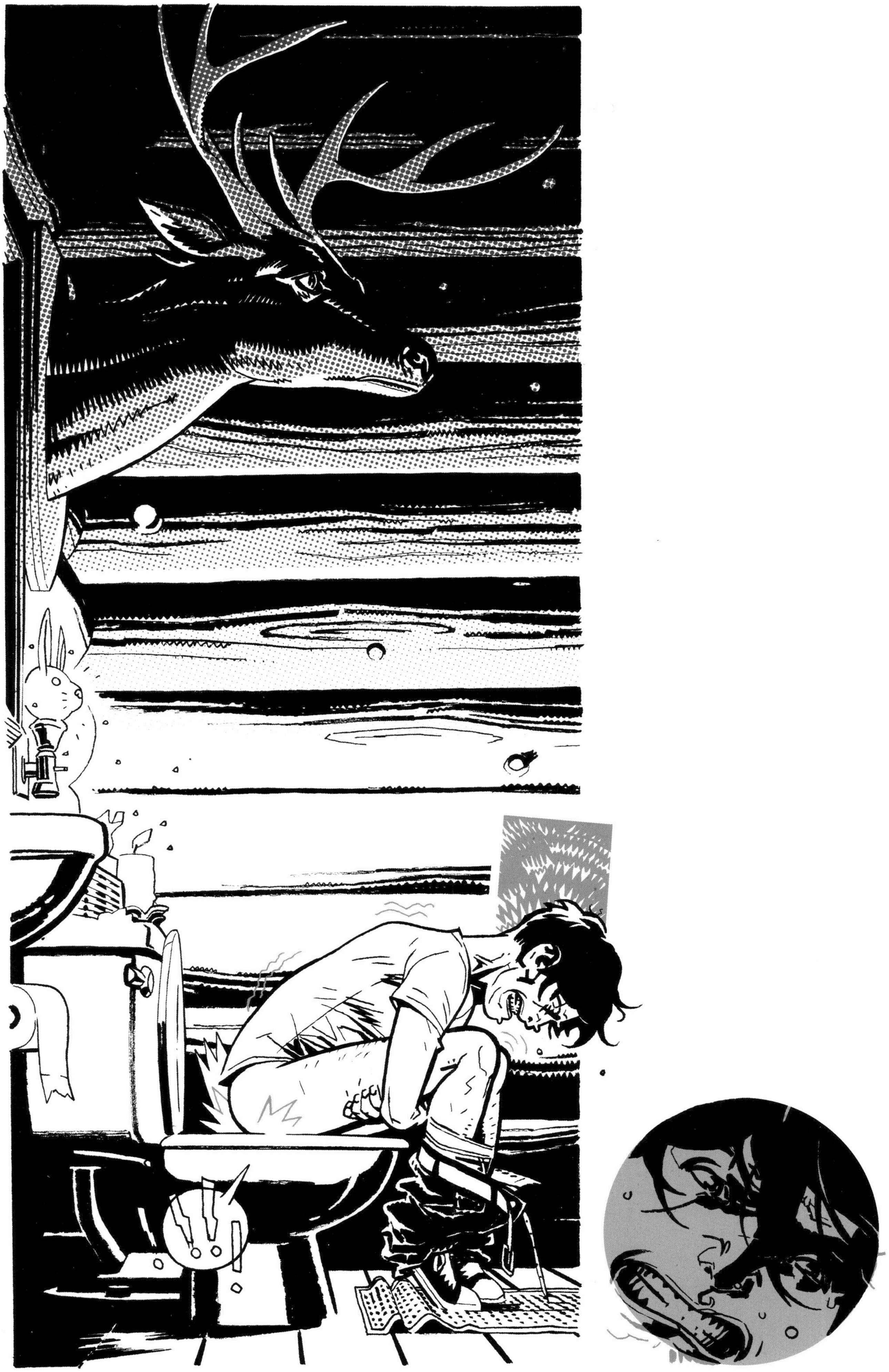

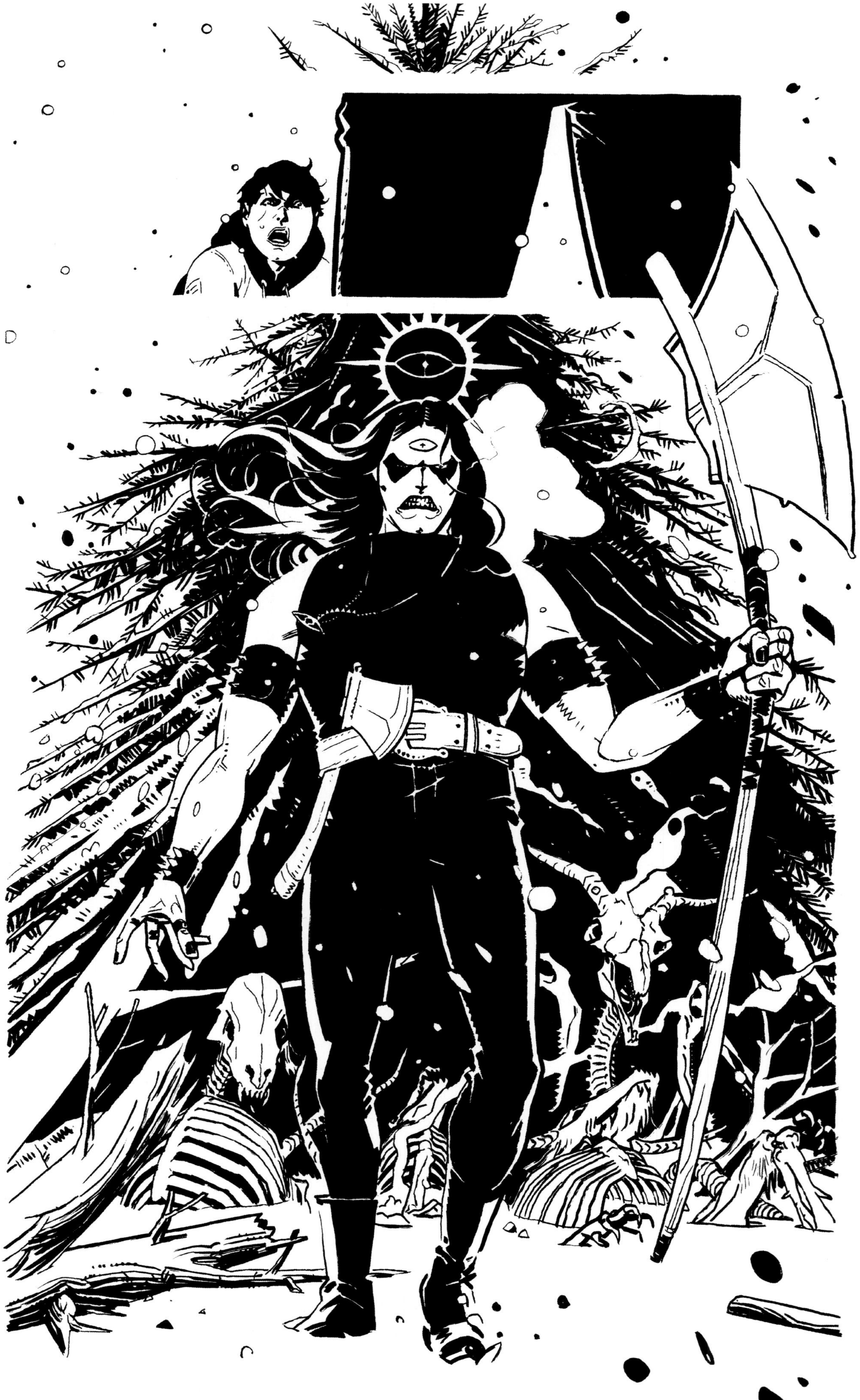

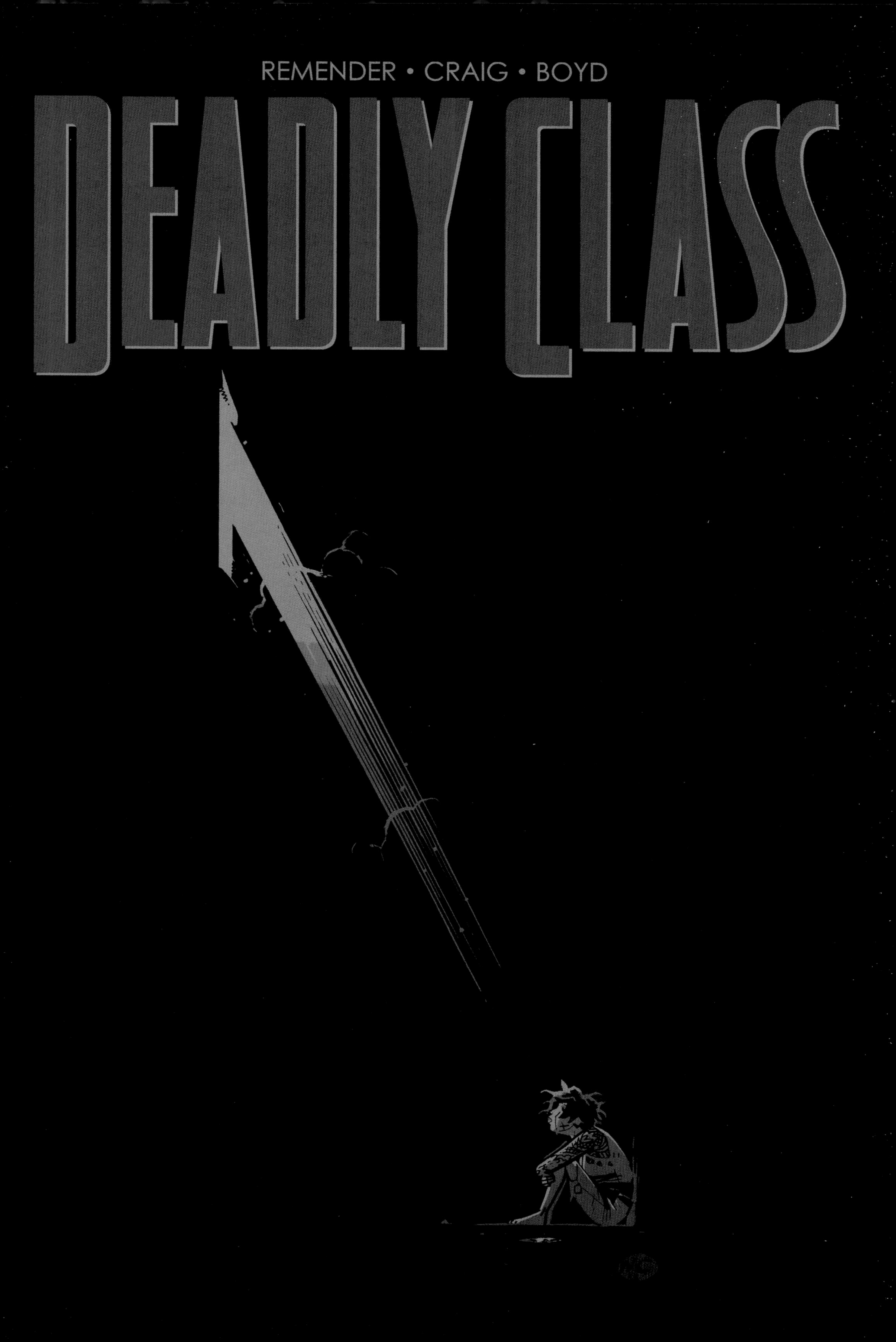
REMENDER • CRAIG • BOYD
DEADLY CLASS

ISSUE THIRTY-SIX

SCRIPT
LAYOUTS
INKS

DEADLY CLASS
Issue #36

PAGE 1

Open on Marcus running, illuminated by a green glow.

    ARROW SHAPED CAPTION BOX POINTING AT MARCUS
    Marcus: Everyone he loves dies.

    MARCUS (CAP)
    Days flip by like an old calendar in a
    black and white montage.

PAGE 2

1 - Pull out to reveal there's a gigantic GREEN NUCLEAR EXPLOSION in his proximity/behind him--that's what he's running from.

    MARCUS (CAP)
    The time passing too quickly.

    You were frantic and fearful.

    Missing it all.

    Collapsing inward.

    But it doesn't matter.

    It isn't going to change.

2 - As Marcus jumps over a rock, the blast is getting too close to comfort. The blast tearing apart the all around him, in reality he'd be dead but--

    MARCUS (CAP)
    The current is too strong.

    And you care.

    And you know what happens when you care.

3 - He runs towards the dot.

    MARCUS (CAP)
    When you stand up and fight.

    When you rage at the invisible hands--

4 - See a hole in front of him--looks like it'd be for a rattlesnake but it's human size.

    MARCUS (FLOATING CAP)
    You make yourself an easy mark.

5 - Marcus jumps into the hole. He crawls his way into the hole.

    MARCUS (CAP)
    You create your greatest, most
    exploitable, weakness.

PAGE 3

1 - Little hole.

2 - Marcus begins stepping out hole.

    MARCUS (FLOATING CAP)
    You make yourself a target.

3 - Marcus puts his hand out the hole.

    MARCUS (FLOATING CAP)
    At home in it.

4 - Marcus leans out of hole.

    MARCUS (FLOATING CAP)
    Married to vulnerability.

5 - Upper body out of hole.

    MARCUS (FLOATING CAP)
    Fumbling for dreams of a better world.

6 - Rat tail, sticking out of hole.

    MARCUS (FLOATING CAP)
    Ignoring the headline:

7 - Marcus creeps in with rat tail

    MARCUS (CAP)
    The jackals are real.

8 - Smaller rat tail.

    MARCUS (CAP)
    Happy endings are fiction.

9 - Tiny hole.

10 - Marcus crawls towards us in tiny panel.

    MARCUS (CAP)
    Reality is a sickly old woman in a stogy
    cold house--

11 - Marcus looks at us - teeth like a rat.

    MARCUS (CAP)
    --everyone she ever knew is dead--

12 - His mouth opens to reveal a Kings symbol.

    MARCUS (CAP)
    --long gone.

13 - Big panel of Kings skull with snakes swarming everywhere.

    SKULL
    Reality is how much you miss your old
    life.

    MARCUS (CAP)
    And an endless inability to understand
    the present.

    A hard focus locked on the people you
    loved, how far gone they are now…

PAGE 4

1 - Marcus further transforms into a rat, he yells.

    MARCUS (CAP)
    …and how much you miss them.

    MARCUS
    Don't recognize myself…

2 - A bunch of snakes that resemble the students who killed rats: Shabnam, Stephen, Viktor, Brandy, Saya, Troll…

    STEPHEN
    Take shelter from the fallout.

    VIKTOR
    The illusion of safety inside a mob.

    SAYA
    Careful though…

    SHABNAM
    You might actually have to do those
    things you've set your heart on.

3 - Marcus' face has the snout of a rat suddenly.

    TROLL
    How much does **that** choice cost?

4 - The vipers close in.

    MARCUS (FLOATING CAP)
    All I wanted was someone to sit back and
    hate the world with me.

5 - They pile on him.

    MARCUS (CAP)
    Instead I'm surrounded by people who
    deceive themselves and pose and politic.

6 - His hand grasps outward.

    MARCUS (CAP)
    And some part of me thinks I should be
    more like **them.**

7 - Hand keeps grasping out.

    MARCUS (CAP)
    But I'd rather be an honest asshole…

8 - a GREEN DAGGER forms in his hand.

    MARCUS (CAP)
    …than a beloved liar.

PAGE 5

1 - Marcus slashes with the green knife, killing the Vipers to buy his escape.

    MARCUS
    I won't be like you!

    MARCUS (CAP)
    Sell it.

    MARCUS
    WON'T JOIN IN OR BE COMPLICIT!

                    MARCUS (CAP)
               If you say it loud enough you'll believe
               it, right?

2 - Marcus climbs upward.
                    MARCUS
               Fake it.

               Climb.

               Quickly.

               But we both know the truth:

3 - Smallest - A grate up top is spiraling towards us.
                    MARCUS (CAP)
               There are real levels beneath the
               surface still.

                    MARCUS (CAP)
               Climb.

                    MARCUS (CAP)
               Places you **don't** want to go.

4 - Grate goes horizontal.
                    MARCUS (CAP)
               Climb.

               All the layers you look at are
               distractions from the truth.

5 - Largest - Grate gets closer, diagonal.
                    MARCUS (CAP)
               Painted tunnels.

                    MARCUS (CAP)
               Climb.

6 - Marcus's hands reach for the grate.
                    MARCUS (CAP)
               False doors.

                    MARCUS (CAP)
               Mannequin props.

                    MARCUS (CAP)
               Everything you think you know about
               yourself:

---

7 - Marcus pops out of the sewer into a suburban landscape.
                    MARCUS (CAP)
               A fake suburb built for nuclear testing.

PAGE 6

1 - Marcus looks at himself in front of a house.
                    MARCUS (CAP)
               There wasn't a feeling of joy.

               Could anyone make it up that ladder in
               one piece?

2 - PULL IN on Marcus looking at his hand.
                    MARCUS (CAP)
               How can anyone feel good about being the
               lone survivor?

               How much shit can the world fill you
               with…

3 - Feels his fangs out of his mouth.
                    MARCUS (CAP)
               before you…

4 - Marcus is turning into a viper.

5 - Marcus' brown scales, eye in the top left of the grid, diagonal.

6 - Marcus' green, his ear and left eye diced out.
                    MARCUS (CAP)
               Before you vomit it back up?

7 - Forehead.

8 - His right eye diced out.

9 - Bottom part of his hand.
                    MARCUS
               NO!

10 - Marcus left arm - brown scales.

11 - Marcus - green scales - mouth.

12 - Marcus green claw.

---

13 - Marcus - brown scales - left hand.

14 - Marcus - brown scales - right hand.

15 - Marcus begins ripping his scales.
                    MARCUS (CAP)
               HAS TO BE ANOTHER WAY!

16 - Blank panel in the middle.

17 - Orange panel all the way to the bottom right of the grid, remnants
of his scales flying off into it - also part of his knee is in this.

18 - The bottom orange part - where Marcus' leg finishes.

19 - Someone on a skateboard arrives.

20 - Skateboard punk slaps Marcus on the back.
                    BILLY (OP TOP)
               Dude, haven't you figured it out by now?

21 - A skeletal hand grabs his back.
                    BILLY
               The faster you run--

PAGE 7

1 - Revealed to be Billy - they chat.
                    BILLY (OP LEFT)
               --the more **dust** you inhale into your
               lungs.

                    MARCUS
               Billy?! **Thank God!** I thought you were--

                    BILLY
               I'm not allowed to speak **directly** to you.

               You are intended to hear me through other
               channels.

               I miss direct contact…

2 - Billy reveals he's already been bitten.
                    BILLY
               But it's easier this way. Cleaner.

               Everyone's giving up--Growing scales
               and eating each other.

               Can't climb the ladder unless you're a
               sociopath.

3 - Marcus freaks out, Billy is bitten! We have to get you help. Billy's
eyes begin to submerge into his head and his skin melts off--he's
turning into a skeleton.
                    MARCUS
               Why?

                    BILLY 1
               The ladder is made of humans.

                    BILLY 2
               --Think about it--

                    BILLY 3
               --there are better ways to use your
               teeth.

4 - As he dies, he points behind Marcus.
                    BILLY (O.S.)
               It's way too late for me.

               But they **can't** win, Marcus.

               It's up to you, dude…

5 - The rest of the vipers are eating their own tails.
                    BILLY (CAP)
               "But you gotta hurry.

               "They're **very** persuasive."

6 - MATCH CUT to Willie's hand touching Marcus's shoulder.
                    WILLIE (OP LEFT)
               You're **always** lookin' the wrong
               direction, Arguello.

PAGE 8

1 - Most top left, Willie's mouth.
                    WILLIE
               Always

2 - Willie's mouth opens.

                    WILLIE
              Lookin'

3 - Can see Willie's sunglasses now as we slide into

                    WILLIE
              Down.

4 - MID SHOT of Willie - welcomes Marcus into the new area: a funeral style, punk rock squat party. Billy's coffin is in the center of the foyer, he's in a punk rock casket.

                    WILLIE
              You might try an' look up.

              But you can't **possibly** appreciate how
              important every minute is.

5 - All the characters who were murdered are in here: Willie, Dan, Petra, Kendall, Lex, etc. They're all in nice suits with character specific flourishes.

                    WILLIE
              The **true** value only visible from the
              stars, the mountains, and the old things
              that know you for what you are--a flash
              bulb pop.

                    MARCUS
              What does that even mean?

              Look up? How the **fuck** are stars and
              mountains going to make this better?

              You're all dead! Left me here!

              Everyone I love in the whole world…

                    LEX
              Oi, I wouldn't say I loved you, luv.

                    PETRA
              I loved Billy.

                    DAN
              Funny way of showing it.

6 - The dead are chattering, sad. Looking at Marcus.

                    LEX
              Human empathy is **finite**, mate.

              We can only care about **so** many people.

                    WILLIE
              And we're gone, yo. Forever. So you got
              two choices.

                    PETRA
              Come with us…

1 - Willie talks to Marcus, he's much larger than him.

                    WILLIE
              Or get yourself back on track.

              So busy reacting you ain't had a minute
              to make a **single** choice for yourself.

              You and Maria made it out.

              You got a **big** responsibility to the rest
              of us who didn't.

                    MARCUS
              You were the only friends I ever had. How
              do I start over, how do I--

2 - Lex talks to Marcus.

                    LEX
              Some people can never be content.

              You fucking rags are ruining my fun.

                    MARCUS
              Is this fun?

3 - Lex head, one of his eyes winking.

                    LEX
              Listen, Marcus, pal--we all have, or had,
              lives full of terrible garbage.

4 - Marcus head - his left eye winking.

                    MARCUS
              And you got the big solution, Lex?

5 - Lex head - puts up a skeleton hand.

                    LEX
              The solution is **simple**: forward
              progression, slag.

---

6 - Dan head.

                    DAN
              Choose to laugh at tragedy. To mock it
              knowing one version of it will befall you
              eventually.

7 - Marcus head.

                    MARCUS
              It's just that simple, huh?

8 - Kendall head.

                    KENDALL
              The joy, clichéd as it is, comes when you
              never stop looking for it.

9 - Petra head.

                    PETRA
              Don't forget why you're here. Why you let
              me die.

10 - Marcus head looks sad.

                    MARCUS
              That's not true… I didn't--

11 - CLOSE of Stephen's gap tooth.

12 - A LOUD BOING sound over Marcus and crew.

13 - Grandfather clock with Lin superimposed on it. Strikes midnight.

                    LIN GHOST (STRANGE FONT/NO STROKE ON
                    BALLOON)
              The turbines have needs.

1 - They all go to Billy's coffin and begin to climb in with him.

                    MARCUS
              Yes, I made it out.

              But now I'm **alone.**

              Constantly expecting bad times.

              Disappointment.

              Expecting everyone I love will--

                    LEX
              You know the other option. Almost took it
              once.

2 - As they all line up to go in, Marcus follows.

                    LEX
              Funeral party on the river Styx. Care to
              join?

                    MARCUS
              Wait--Willie, don't go!

                    WILLIE
              No choice.

3 - Willie stops him.

                    MARCUS
              Then let me come with you.

              I miss you so much…

4 - Marcus is stunned.

                    MARCUS
              I love you.

5 - He looks down into the coffin.

                    WILLIE (TAILLESS)
              Then do what I can't.

6 - Suddenly, Maria grabs him.

                    MARIA (OP RIGHT)
              You won't **have to** do it alone, guapo.

1 - Maria pulls Marcus from the dark into the light.

                    MARIA
              That part is up to you. For now.

                    ARROW SHAPED CAPTION (POINTING AT MARIA)
              Maria: Simple, home, love.

                    MARCUS (CAP)
              No doubt. No challenge. No biting
              sarcasm.

                    MARCUS (CAP)
              No banter. No intellectual connection.

2 - She pulls him in for a kiss.

                    MARCUS
              I can't lose you too.

                    MARIA
              Then don't.

3 - Pull out to see a dilapidated city. The two of them kiss, panel
is split between light on Maria's side and darkness on Marcus' side.

                    MARCUS (CAP/LINE THEM FROM TOP TO BOTTOM IN
                         THE CENTER OF THE PANEL)
              She tells me she loves me.

              I try and believe her.

              But we're in such different worlds.

              She tells me she wants to go live a normal
              life with me.

              Somewhere far away from civilization.

PAGE 12

1 - Marcus follows Maria through the nuclear wasteland, caused from
the green explosion from before.

                    MARIA
              To live in a forest by a stream.

                    MARCUS (CAP)
              Did we fall in love because of our
              wounds?

                    MARIA
              Seven kids and a garden for them to play
              in. Music in the air…

                    MARCUS (CAP)
              Cracking open our chests and sharing
              looks inside. Comparing damage…

5 - Maria pulls him close…

                    MARCUS (CAP)
              Still…

                    MARIA
              Tracing the origins of one's motivation
              is not a difficult task.

                    MARCUS (CAP)
              When you have to tell yourself you love
              someone over and over, well…

                    MARIA
              You're either lying to me…

6 - Maria's concerned face.

                    MARIA
              …Or you're lying to yourself.

PAGE 13

1 - The sky suddenly fills with dark clouds…

                    MARCUS (CAP)
              She's the exact opposite of Saya.

                    CAPTION BOX WITH ARROWS POINTING IN 4
                         DIRECTIONS
              Saya: A torrent of chaos.

                    MARCUS (CAP)
              Sweet, perfect chaos.

                    MARCUS
              Maria… I don't know what I need.

2 - LIGHTING CRASHES between them, interrupting the thought.

3 - Death metal nightmare--medieval as shit. Imps flying. Red
lightning. The earth splits open, volcanic ash spewing out as well
as some sort of creature…

                    HELMUT (TAIL INTO THE GROUND HE EMERGES
                         FROM/BIG IMPACT DEMON VIKING FONT)
              I DO.

                    MARIA
              What do you want, Marcus?

2 - As Marcus and Maria walk, Maria begins to bring life back to the
ruins and decay. Flowers and green grass grows out of the scorched
earth behind her. They walk and talk, he learns more form her. Clues
to his next step.

                    MARCUS
              All I want is to make you happy.

                    MARCUS (CAP)
              Is damage the only thing we have in
              common?

                    MARCUS
              Run away together.

                    MARCUS (CAP)
              Identification on a surface level,
              environmental, circumstantial…

3 - UPSIDE DOWN PANEL - Vegetation and beautiful animals follow in
Maria's wake.

                    MARCUS
              …Just disappear and pretend none of it
              ever happened.

                    MARCUS (CAP)
              No. That's the damage. **Shut up**-- don't
              ruin this too.

                    MARIA
              And the babies? And the house full in the
              woods?

                    MARCUS (CAP)
              She loves you. Takes care of you. Killed
              Chico for you.

4 - Marcus is amazed by Maria, soaking it all in. Birds and a tall
canopy.

                    MARCUS (CAP)
              She's the only good thing in your life--

                    MARCUS
              I want to give you everything you
              deserve.

                    MARCUS (CAP)
              The only reason you have to live it.

PAGE 14

1 - HELMUT rides a THREE-HEADED OX.

                    HELMUT
              You need someone to judge you the way you
              judge everyone else.

                    (CAPTION SHAPED ARROW POITNING TO HELMUT)
              Helmut: Had true love, lost it.

2 - Demon Helmut yells, spraying spit--

                    HELMUT
              THE WAY YOU JUDGED <u>PETRA</u>!

              Lie to yourself but we know the
              truth--**YOU LET HER DIE.**

              Took her from me!

3 - Helmut SLASHES MARIA in a silhouette. Or maybe he drains her soul
into his evil axe.

                    HELMUT
              Set in motion my **vengeance**--forced **me** to
              take Maria from **you**!

                    SFX
              SHHNK

4 - Marcus freaks!

                    MARCUS (IMPACT/STROKED)
              <u>NOOO--!</u>

PAGE 15

1 - As he holds her, Helmut towers over them.

                    HELMUT (IMPACT)
              You will live, like me--<u>IN CONSTANT PAIN!</u>

2 - Helmut rides off into the background.

                    HELMUT
              You expect them all to forgive you **your**
              trespasses--but I see your heart.

              See what **you** plan.

              Know this…

3 - Sadness, he holds dead Maria.

                HELMUT (CAP)
    "…I make similar maneuvers."

4 - Closer, hold Maria.

                MARCUS
    H-he's wrong… I didn't do this…

                MARIA (WEAK/WAVY)
    M-Marcus…

5 - Closest, holding Maria.

                MARIA (WEAK/WAVY)
    Why do you love me?

6 - Marcus cries.

7 - Closer on Marcus crying.

8 - Closest on Marcus crying.

                MARCUS
    You…

9 - Maria's lifeless face.

                MARCUS (OP)
    You're everything…

10 - Closer on Maria's lifeless face.

11 - Closest on Maria's lifeless face.

                MARCUS (OP)
    …everything I'm not.

12 - Then he looks up at a bright light.

                ZENZELE (ANGEL FONT/OP TOP)
    And you wasted what time you had
    worrying.

PAGE 16

1 - An ANGEL ZENZELE comes down from the sky and hovers over Marcus
and Maria.

                ANGEL ZENZELE
    Maria… she will…

                DEVIL ZENZELE (DEVIL FONT)
    Burn in anguish for her sins.

    The blood on that bitch's hands--

2 - Marcus freaks.

                DEVIL ZENZELE (DEVIL FONT)
    The suffering your cherished whore
    caused--

3 - Marcus begins running toward them, but they're already entering
a hellish gateway.

                DEVIL Z
    Maria's going **exactly** where she fucking
    belongs.

                MARCUS (CAP)
    Everything **just** as you imagined it.

    They're all **gone.**

    There'll be no **you** left to identify.

4- Anguish on Marcus' face as he screams to the heavens--

                MARCUS (CAP)
    You used to think the solution was to
    shovel your guts out in front of
    everyone.

    Call in other wounded vets to
    commiserate.

    As if your pain earned you some **special**
    treatment.

    But, they either **died** from exposure or
    they **bit** you.

5 - PULL OUT - Marcus notices he's transforming again.

                MARCUS (CAP)
    What's left…? Start over?

    Tell yourself it'll be different next
    time?

    It won't go wrong again?

    The next batch will behave civilly?

              ARROW SHAPED CAPTION POINTING TO ZENZELE
    Zenzele: Angel possessed by Satan.

                ANGEL ZENZELE
    Questioning everything.

    Picking at it.

    The same voice that picks you apart.

2 - Marcus doesn't want to let Maria go.

                ANGEL ZENZELE
    You let it lock on to anyone close to you.

    Shred them with the same negative filter.

                MARCUS
    No… don't take her too… a-all I have left…
    My only home.

                ANGEL ZENZELE
    Let her go.

3 - Angel Zenzele head.

                ANGEL ZENZELE
    She deserves better.

4 - Marcus' eyes stream tears. He accepts.

5 - Marcus lifts his hand off her chest.

6 - Closer on hand lifting off her.

7 - Closest on hand fully lifted off her.

8 - Z lifts Maria and floats away.

                Z
    You hold on because of your own
    insecurities.

    She's better this way.

PAGE 17

1 - Z transforms from an angel to DEVIL--

---

6 - Marcus' face becomes serpentine.

                MARCUS (CAP)
    Or accept you were **wrong.**

7 - Marcus crawls to the floor, transforming.

                MARCUS (CAP)
    Accept **their** way of doing things.

    Not just become **like** them--

8 - His face yells in the darkness, tongue slivering.

                MARCUS (CAP)
    Become the **worst** of them.

PAGE 18

1 - Child Marcus wakes up.

                MARCUS (CAP)
    The last thing I remember, my Mom picked
    me up from the doctor's office.

2 - PULL OUT to reveal we're in his INT. CHILDHOOD ROOM.

                MARCUS (CAP)
    She knew everything I'd been up to, but
    she wasn't upset with me.

    She told me she'd gone through stuff like
    this, too.

3 - Looks under his covers.

                MARCUS (CAP)
    She felt bad she wasn't going to be there
    to tell me I'm not alone.

    That this is just… the way of things.

    Then she left me on the curbside of the
    terminal into an airport.

4 - He's shocked.

                MARCUS (CAP)
    She gave me a kiss goodbye and told me:

5 - Pulls back covers, to see dead snakes.

                    MARCUS (CAP)
          "Just because nobody else congratulates
          you for it doesn't make doing the **right**
          thing **less** valuable.

6 - Young Marcus grits his teeth, scared.

                    MARCUS (CAP)
          "**Don't** be overcome by evil…

7 - He creeps down the stairs.

                    MARCUS (CAP)
          "…But overcome evil with **good**."

8 - Turns the corner.

                    DAD (OP)
          There he is.

PAGE 19

1 - His parents in the kitchen, the old morning ritual.

                    MOM
          How'd you sleep, sweetheart? Was it all
          about you, you, you?

                    MARCUS (CAP)
          The old kitchen.

                    DAD
          Heh… Your folks must've been overly
          nurturing because you have a **totally**
          overdeveloped sense of self-worth.

                    MARCUS (CAP)
          Like looking at an old photo album.

2 - Mom kisses him on the cheek.

                    MOM
          My sweet, special boy.

                    MARCUS (CAP)
          And seeing yourself in a picture.

3 - Little Marcus sits with his parents.

                    MARCUS (CAP)
          That you have no memory of.

                    DAD
          Hit the park today, bud?

                    MARCUS
          Yay!

                    MOM
          We'll see the swans.

4 - Parents are happy to see something, Marcus is concerned.

                    MOM
          And we've got a **special** guest!

5 - Reagan enters the doorway.

                    REAGAN
          Vote for me and I'll set you free!

                    CANNED APPLAUSE

                    REAGAN
          Heard through the loser grapevine that
          Maria asked you what you wanted, where
          you see yourself in the future.

6 - He starts walking them out the door.

                    REAGAN
          You gave her some bullshit answer,
          that's the right move.

          If you tell the truth you'll **jinx** it!

                    MARCUS
          No, Mom--

7 - Marcus desperately clings to his parents.

                    MARCUS
          Stop! Don't follow him!

8 - Reagan flashes a thumbs up.

                    REAGAN
          Thinking about the future is a luxury for
          rich kids.

9 - Marcus parents' heads are sad.

                    MOM AND DAD IN TANDEM
          But what does that mean for our baby?

---

10 - Huge snake hand of Regan grabs Marcus.

                    SNAKE MAN (OP LEFT)
          For rats like your son…

PAGE 20

1 - He's now in LIN'S OFFICE, bigger, Tim Burton-style, a dream room
of incredible proportion. Master Lin is drinking tea, waiting for
Marcus.

                    LIN
          …the world finds uses.

                    MARCUS
          Master Lin… I thought, you told me… I was
          special…

                    LIN
          To make you a better fighter for the great
          exam.

          It might've unpleasant, but I've only
          ever taught you the truth of things.

          You saw firsthand what happens to those
          who don't adapt.

2 - Marcus is overwhelmed, Lin sits at his desk.

                    MARCUS
          You lied to me.

                    LIN
          Yes, and thus the boy **hates** the man.

          For the man is his ultimate end.

          He can promise and swear to himself that
          he won't end that same way, that he'll
          fight forever.

          But the fighting wears you down, Marcus.

3 - Marcus takes a seat much lower than Lin.

                    MARCUS
          Day after day, suffering with that pain,
          you shift in your uncomfortable chair.

          Eventually trading it for one with…
          softer refinement.

                    MARCUS
          And the world outside?

                    LIN
          It doesn't care.

                    MARCUS
          So what now?

4 - Lin begins to rationalize the philosophy behind why Marcus needs
to be a snake as he drinks his tea.

                    LIN
          I gave you the power to change the world
          with a bullet.

5 - Marcus is terrified.

                    LIN
          Who do you think deserves yours?

PAGE 21

1 - Lin's desk begins to unravel into space and time.

                    LIN
          You focused on Reagan.

          On unobtainable goals.

          You gave up before you began.

2 - Lin's face becomes negative.

                    LIN
          So desperate for a father figure to guide
          you, you'd have trusted **anyone.**

          So needy and insecure--incapable of
          following your own advice.

3 - Time and space unravels in the office, everything now black and
white as Marcus free falls

                    LIN
          You always needed someone else to tell
          you which way to go.

          But now that you're alone you must decide
          for yourself…

4 - They are in the shot from the cover. A nuke goes off. Lin busts a lesson and walks away, turns into a snake, slithers into a hole.

          LIN
    Do you have what it takes to make the
    world a safer place?

5 - Another hand grabs Marcus' back - it's red.

          TOS
    Dude, you shouldn't wander off alone.

PAGE 22

1 - Marcus looks to the sky to see Tosahwi's riding a skateboard but he looks like a Pushead/Big Daddy Roth skater drawing.

          CAPTION SHAPED ARROW POITING AT TOSAHWI
    Tosahwi: Rage, revenge, and sorrow.

          TOSAHWI
    Told ya my grandad's peyote would rouse
    those inner demons.

2 - TOS phases back into human superimposed at the top of the panel in floating head form - under, normal panel: Marcus and Tos are in the middle of the desert.

          TOSAHWI 1
    But you've manufactured so many stories
    to cover up the truth.

          TOSAHWI 2
    Spirit journey makes you face it.

          TOSAHWI 3
    Not a ton of fun.

          TOSAHWI 4
    Easier once you quit guarding your
    vulnerability.

          MARCUS
    You didn't tell me.

3 - NOW - REALITY - Tos helps Marcus up (near naked and tripping balls) they walk through the dessert.

          TOSAHWI
    But I **did** warn you not to wander off.

And I bet you know what you need now.

4 - Desert sunrise.

          TOSAHWI (CAP)
    "I do… but it's not very spiritual…"

5 - Marcus and Tos get their shit back to reality.

          TOSAHWI
    Just be honest about it.

          MARCUS
    I want revenge.

          TOSAHWI
    That's fine, man. Revenge isn't the lie,
    telling yourself you're **above** it…

6 - Something approaches Tos from behind.

          TOSAHWI
    That's the lie.

    After what you went through…

7 - Marcus notices it.

          TOSAHWI (OP)
    You'd be a bitch to **not** want--

          MARCUS
    TOSAHWI!

8 - Just before it attacks, Marcus snags it.

          TOSAHWI
    Oh--

          SNAKE
    HSSSSS!

PAGE 23

1 - Breaks its neck.

2 - He looks at Tosahwi stoically.

          TOS
    Shit.

          TOS
    How'd you see that snake?

3 - Marcus sighs.

          MARCUS
    I…

4 - TWO SHOT - Marcus and Tos continue to chat.

          MARCUS
    I'd rather not say.

          TOS
    Alright, man. Whatever you want. But we
    gotta get a move on…

5 - PULL OUT - They're near a fire.

          TOS (CAP)
    "I left the other trippers
    unsupervised."

6 - Maria talks to Marcus.

          MARIA
    Marcus?!

7 - She yells at him.

          MARIA
    I was sick to my stomach!

    I thought something had happened--I saw
    visions of you dead!

8 - Helmut broods.

          HELMUT
    She wasn't the only one.

9 - As he looks at Marcus and Maria.

          MARIA

10 - Marcus holds the dead snake and chats with Maria.

          MARIA
    What happened.

          MARCUS
    I, uh… I had some **realizations**.

          MARIA
    Like?

11 - Maria and Marcus.

          MARCUS
    Most important…

12 - They kiss.

          MARCUS
    How much I love you.

PAGE 24

1 - Maria and Marcus continue to chat.

          MARIA
    There's something wrong. Your eyes…

          MARCUS
    They won't stop coming, Maria.

    We know too much.

2 - CLOSE of Marcus.

          MARCUS
    We only have one option…

3 - The crew reacts near the fire.

          MARCUS (OP)
    We have to go back to Kings Dominion.

4 - Marcus, holding the dead snake, stands in front of the fire. A new man. I know what we have to do.

          MARCUS
    And we have to play by their rules.

          TO BE CONTINUED…

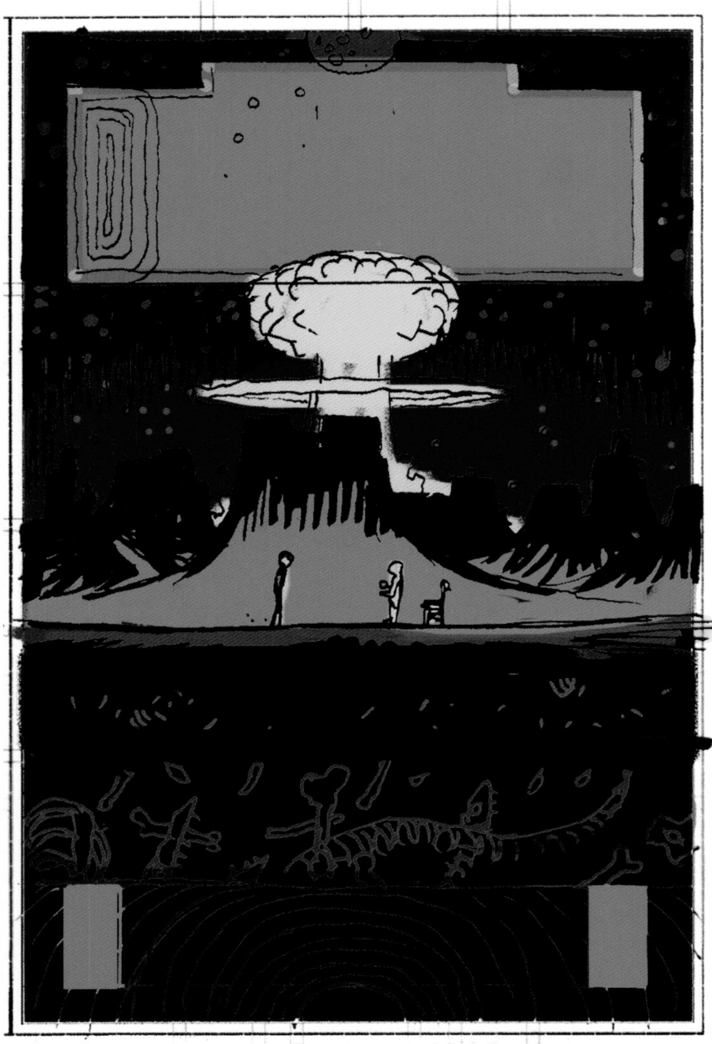

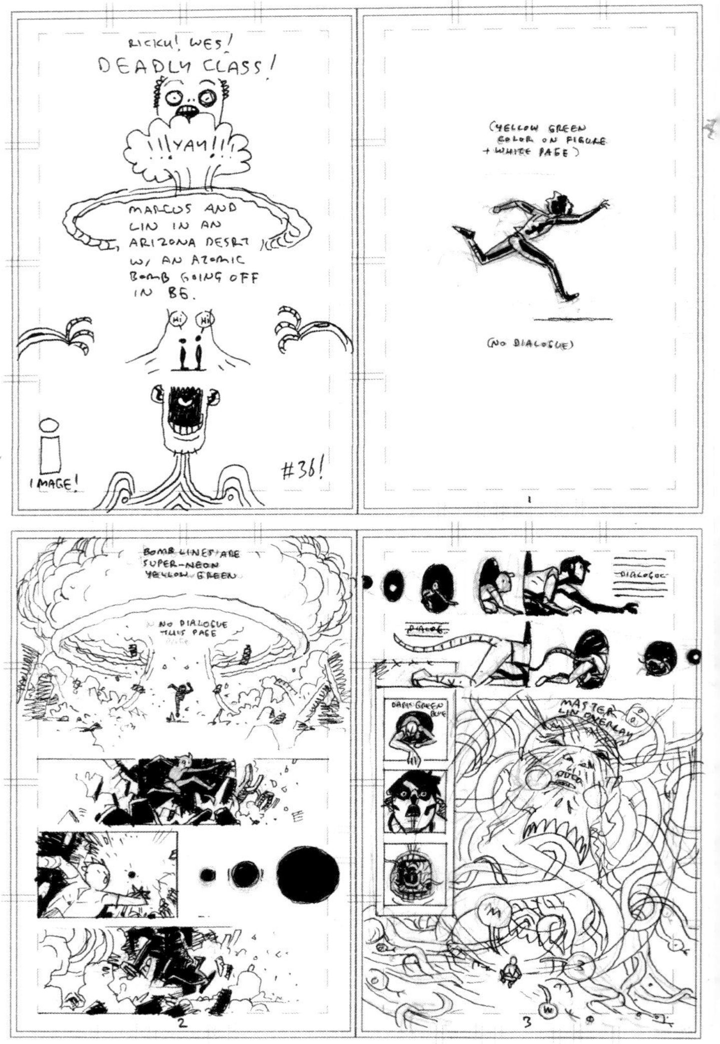

RICKY! WES!
DEADLY CLASS!
!!!YAY!!!
MARCUS AND LIN IN AN ARIZONA DESRT W/ AN ATOMIC BOMB GOING OFF IN BG.
HI
HI
IMAGE!
#36!
(YELLOW GREEN COLOR ON FIGURE + WHITE PAGE)
(NO DIALOGUE)
1
BOMB LINES ARE SUPER-NEON YELLOW GREEN
NO DIALOGUE THIS PAGE
2
DIALOGUE
DARK GREEN BLUE
MASTER LIN OVERLAY
3

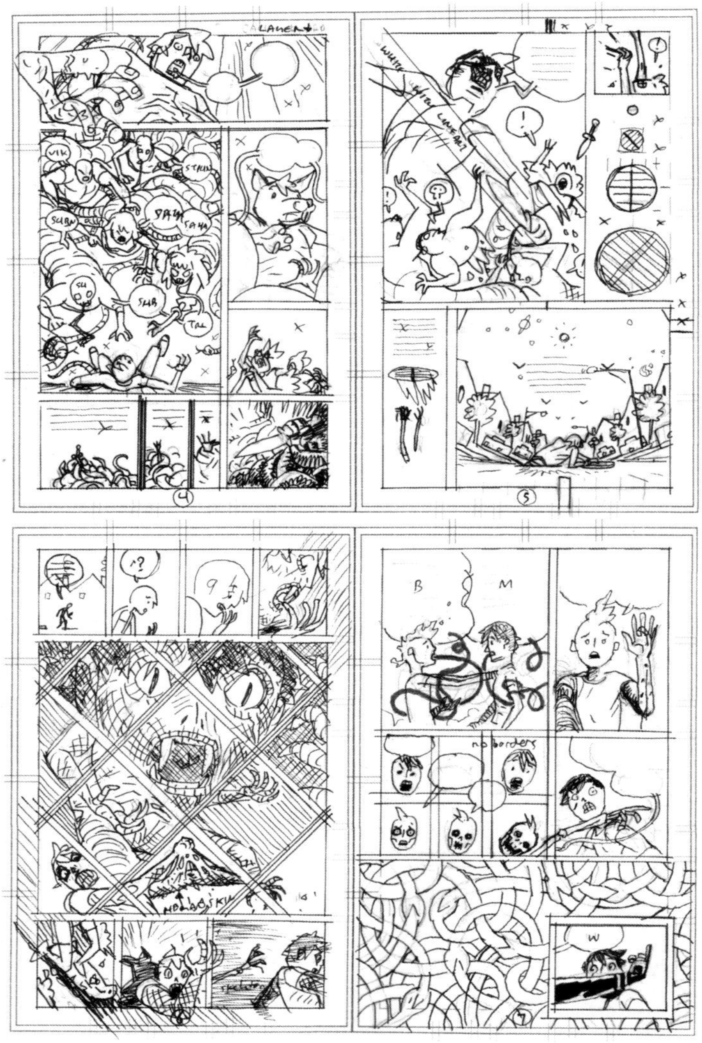

4
5
no borders

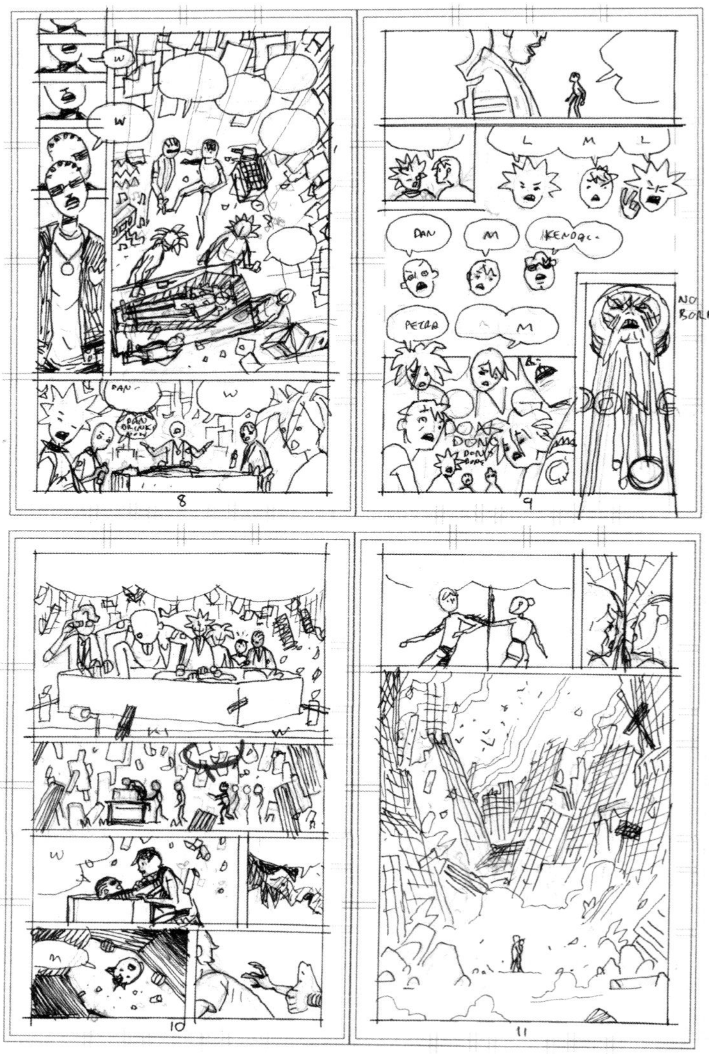

8
9
10
11

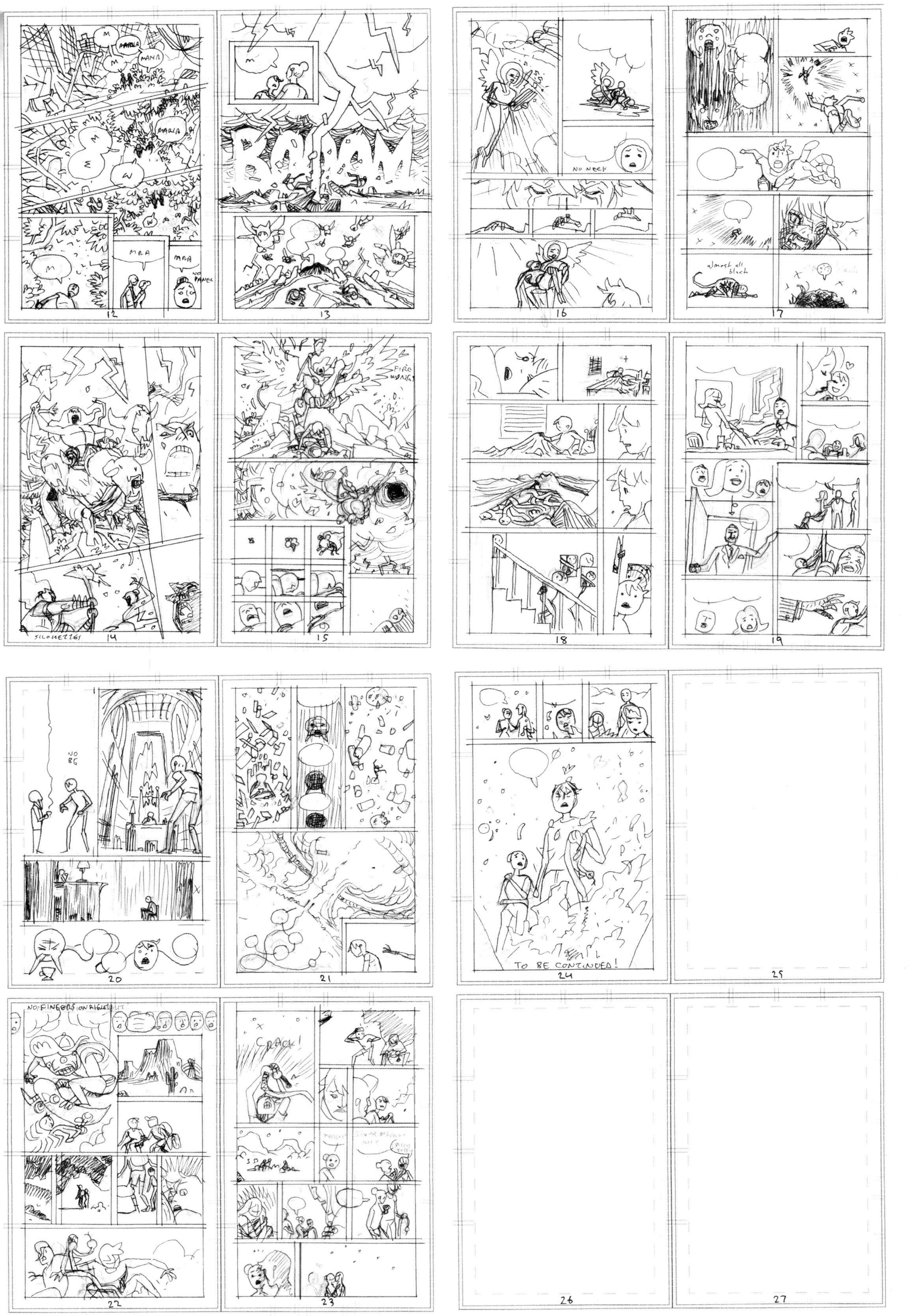
MAMA
MAMA
MRA
MRA
NO PANEL
12
13
NO NECK
16
almost all black
17
SILOUETTES
14
FIRE WINGS
15
18
19
NO BG
20
21
TO BE CONTINUED!
24
25
CRACK!
22
23
26
27

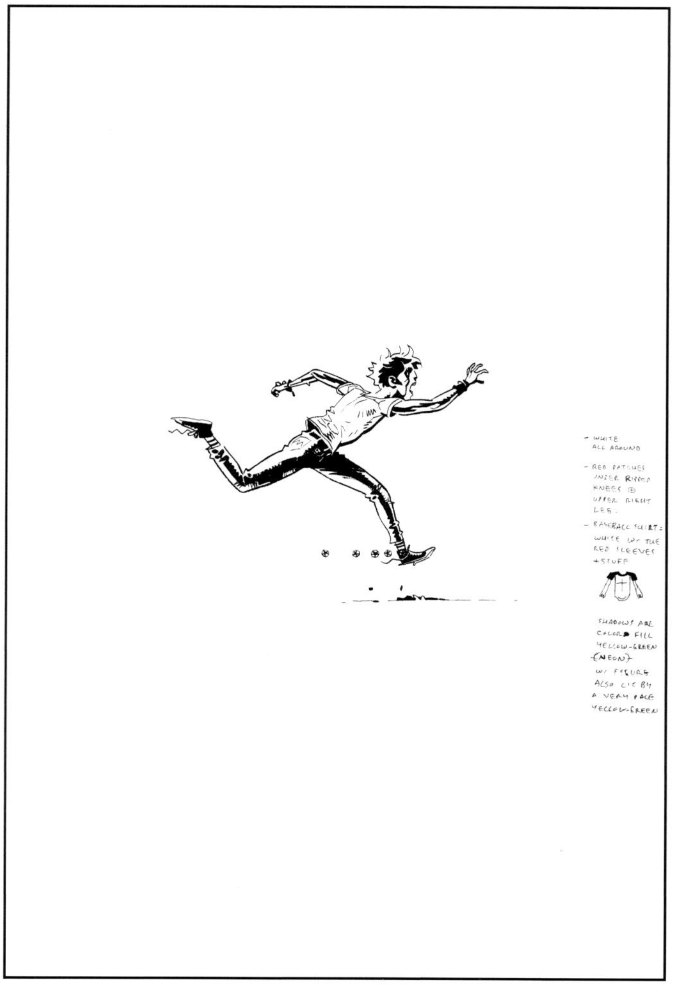
- WHITE ALL AROUND
- RED PATCHES UNDER RIPPED KNEES + UPPER RIGHT LEG.
- BASEBALL SHIRT = WHITE W/ THE RED SLEEVES + STUFF
SHADOWS ARE COLOR FILL YELLOW-GREEN (NEON) W/ FIGURE ALSO LIT BY A VERY PALE YELLOW-GREEN

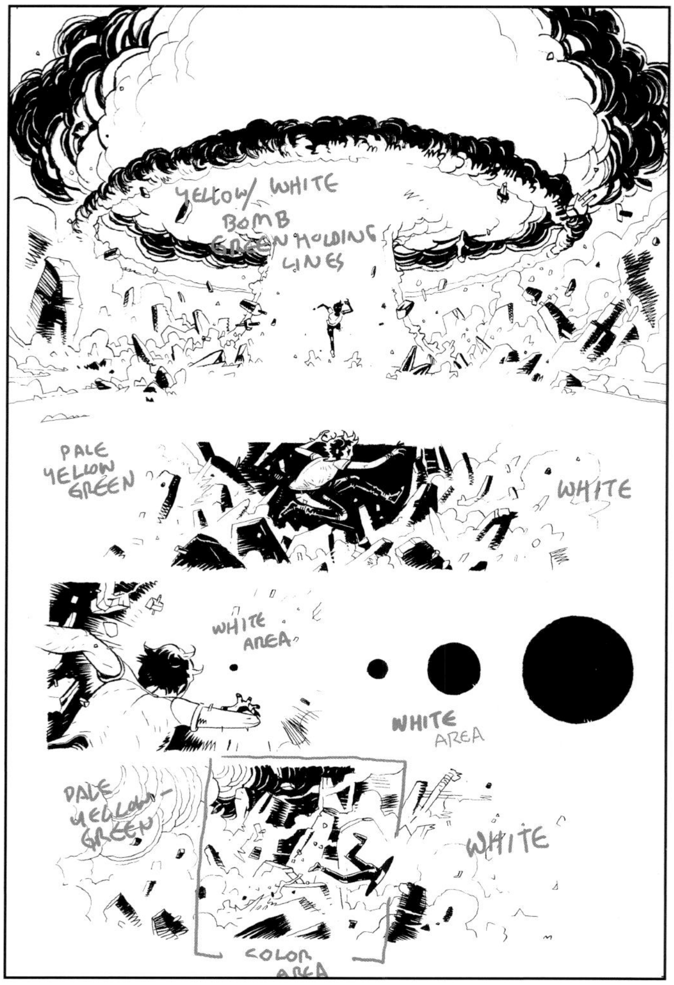
YELLOW/ WHITE BOMB
GREEN HOLDING LINES
PALE YELLOW GREEN
WHITE
WHITE AREA
WHITE AREA
PALE YELLOW-GREEN
WHITE
COLOR AREA

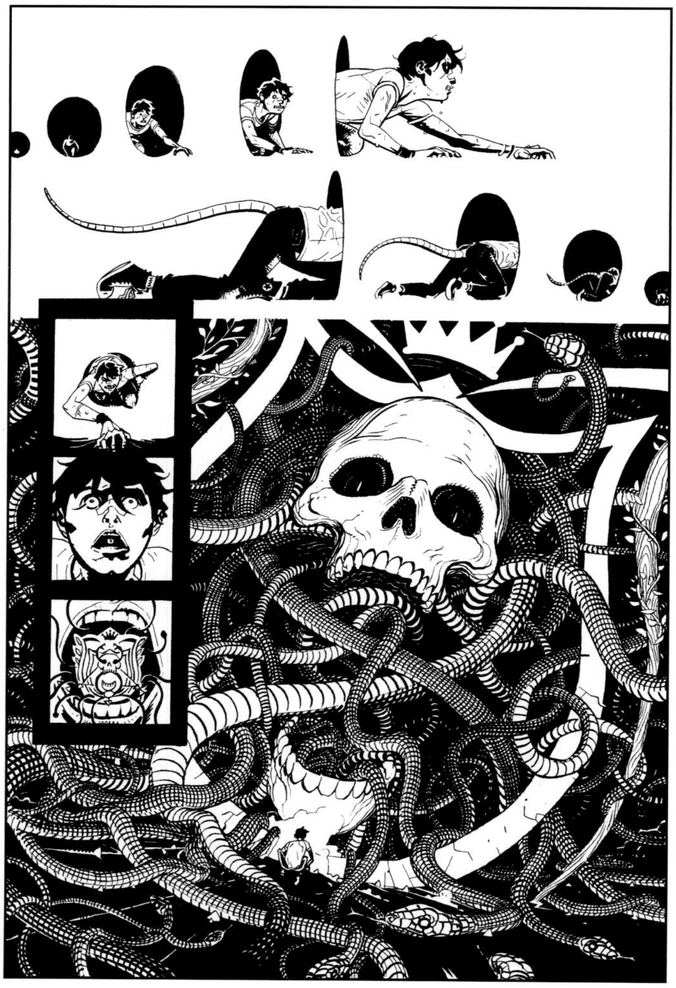

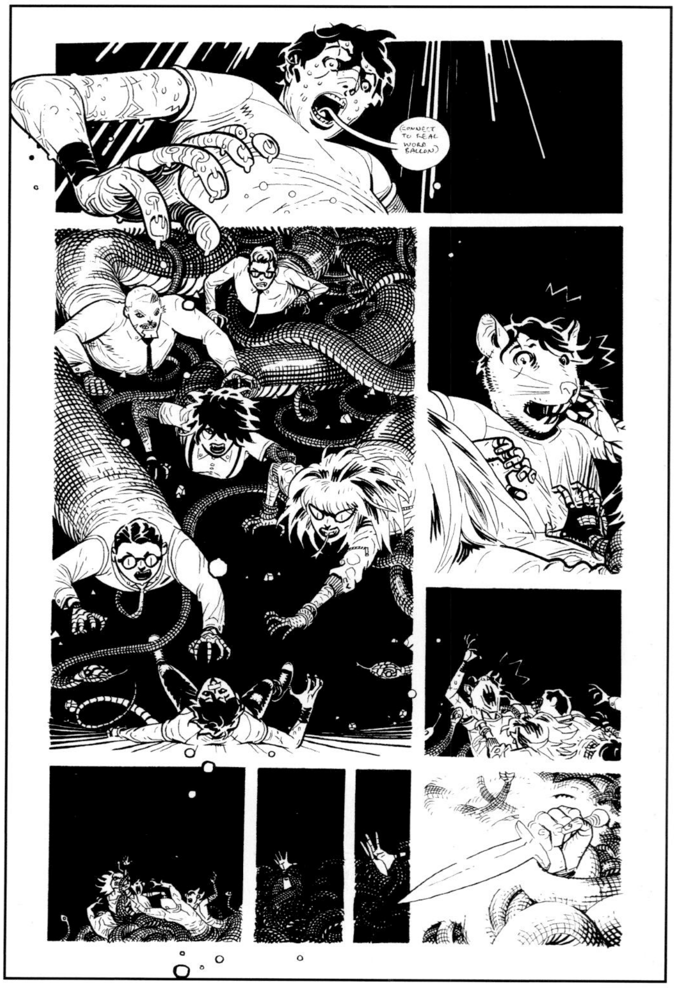
(CONNECT TO REAL WORD BALLON)

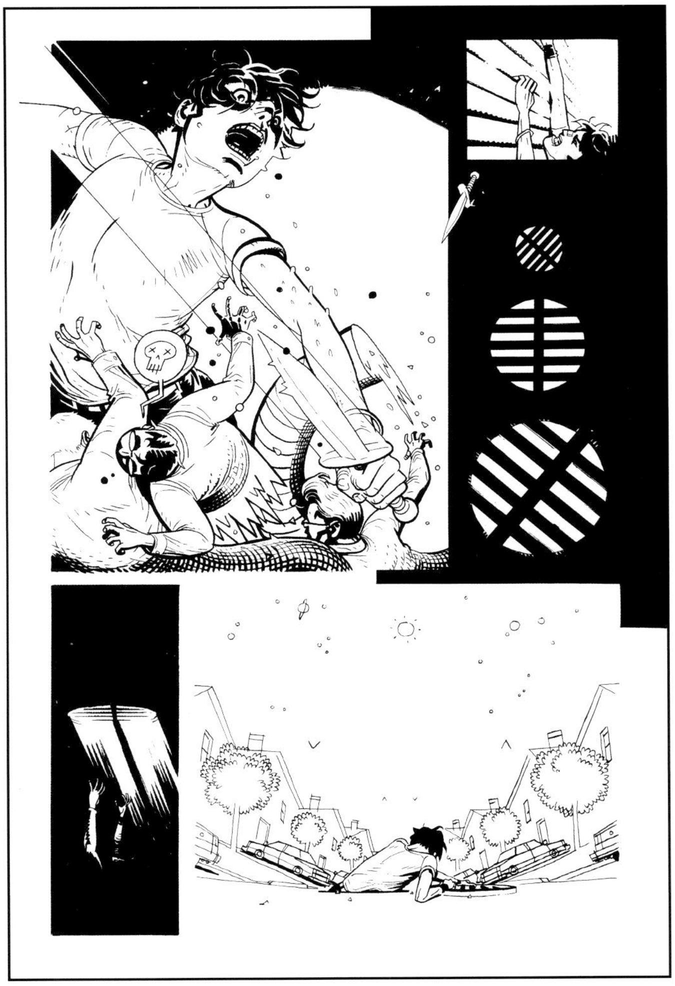
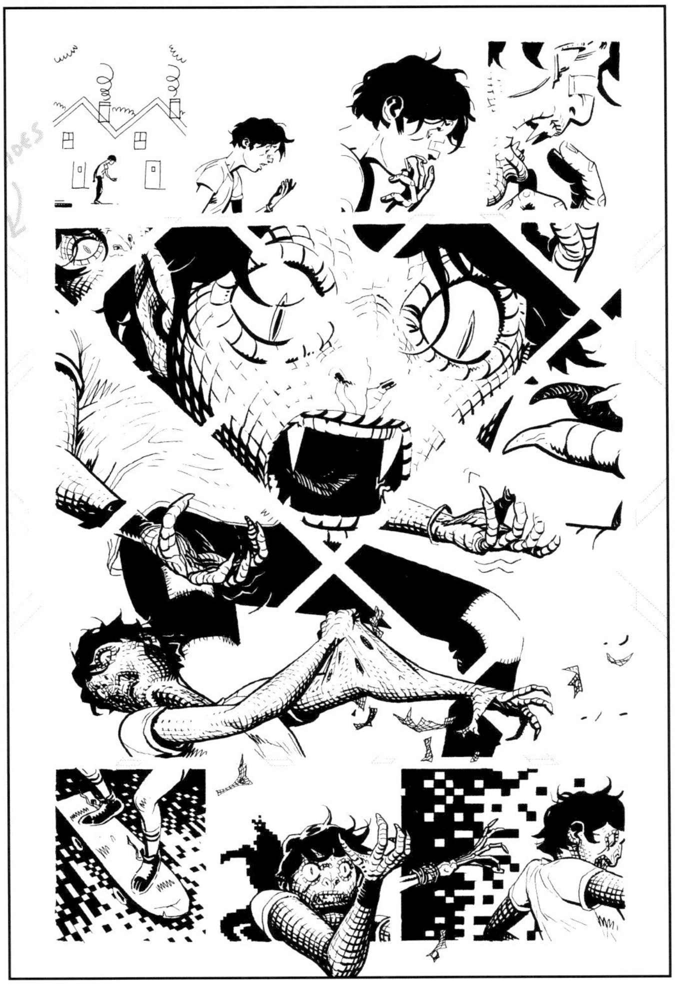
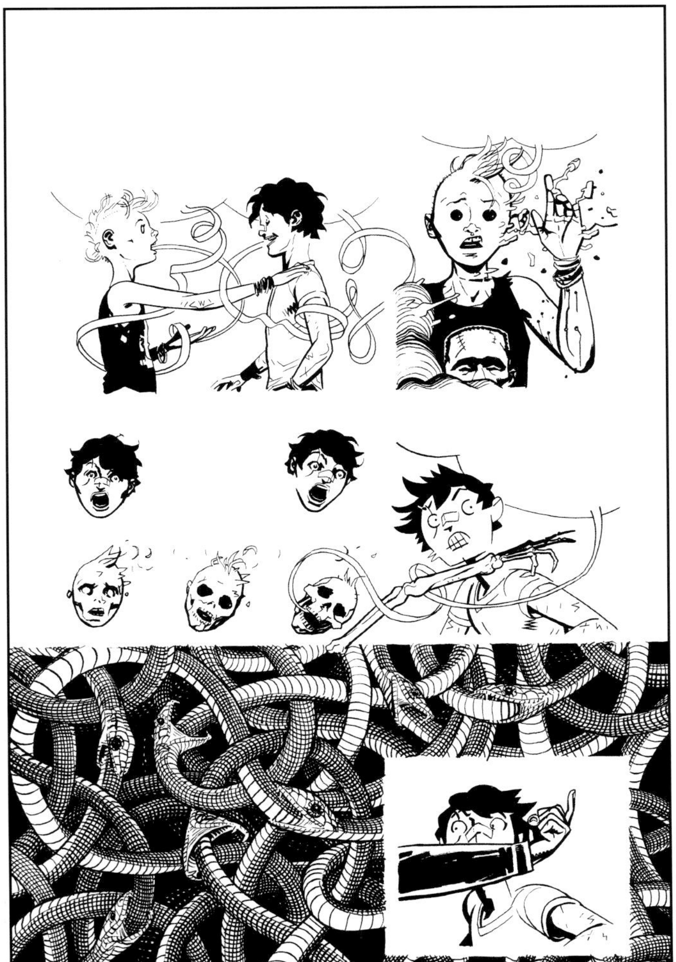
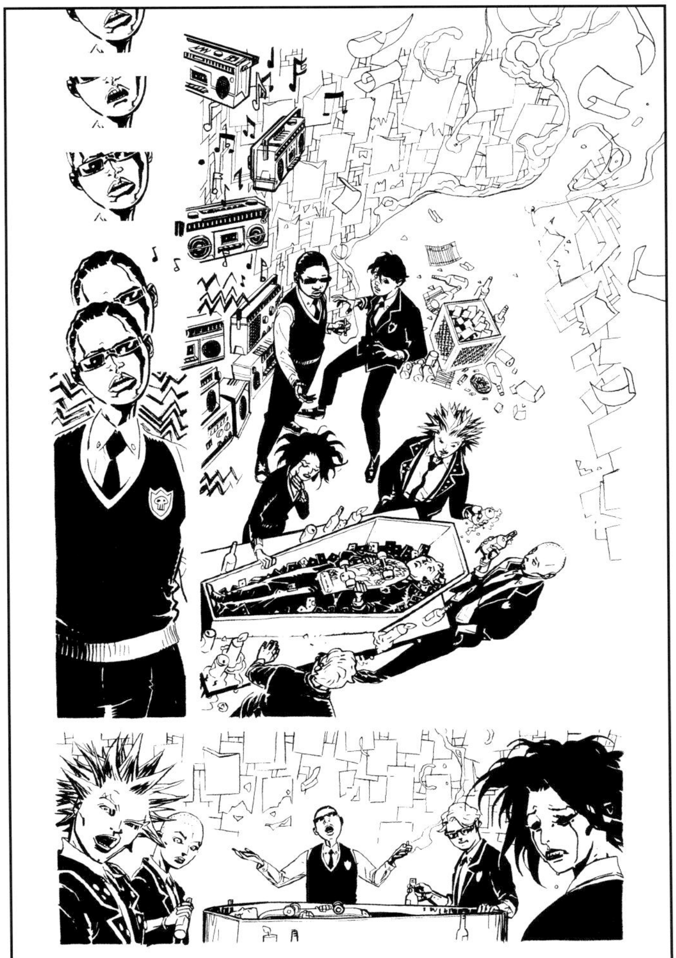

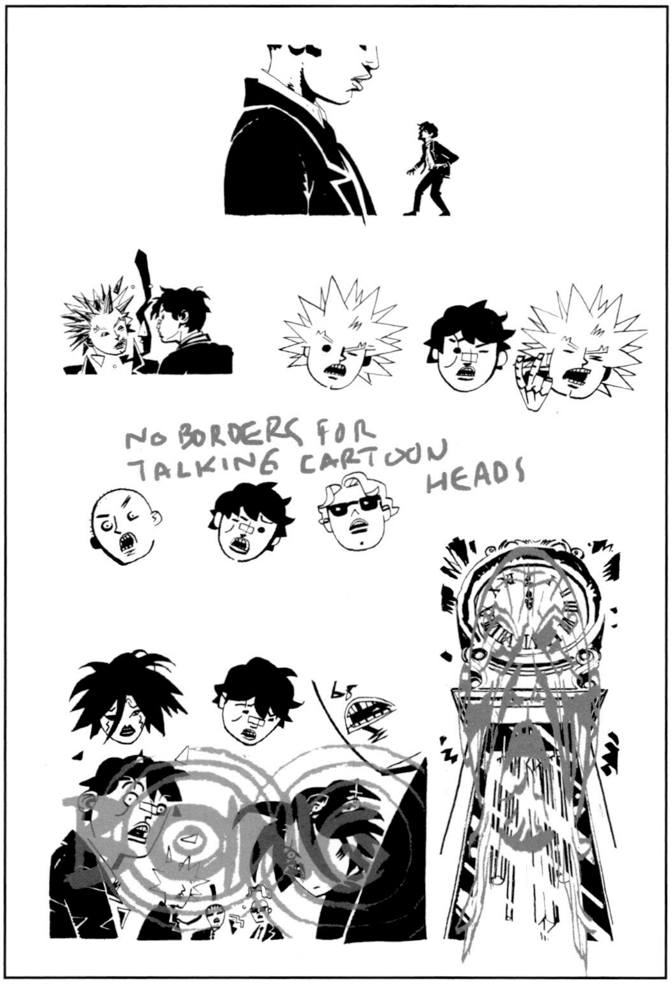
NO BORDERS FOR TALKING CARTOON HEADS

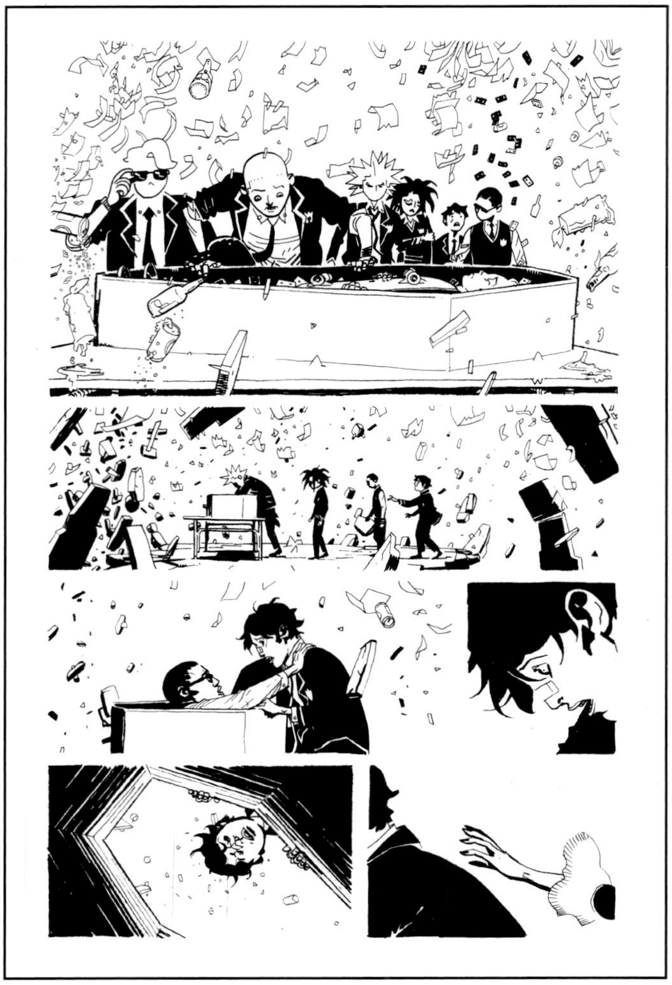

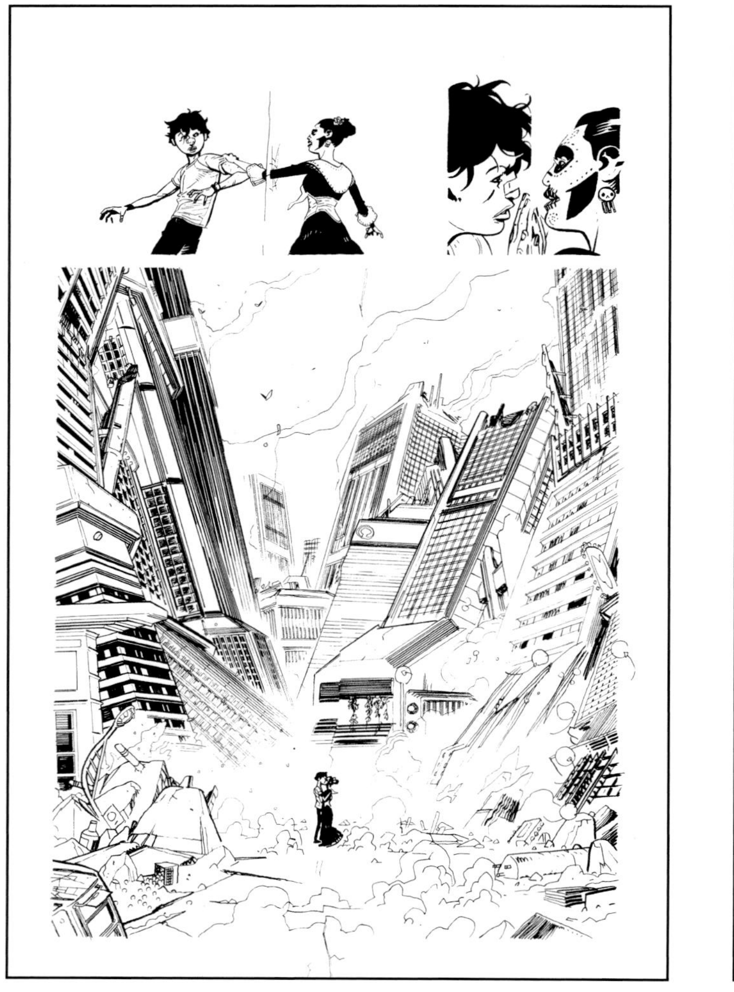

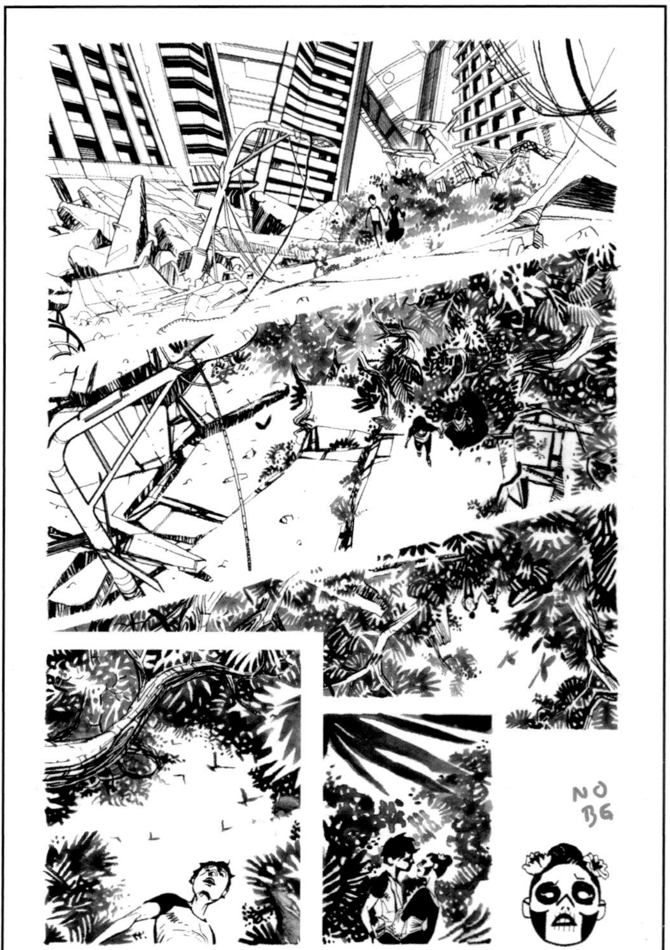
NO BG

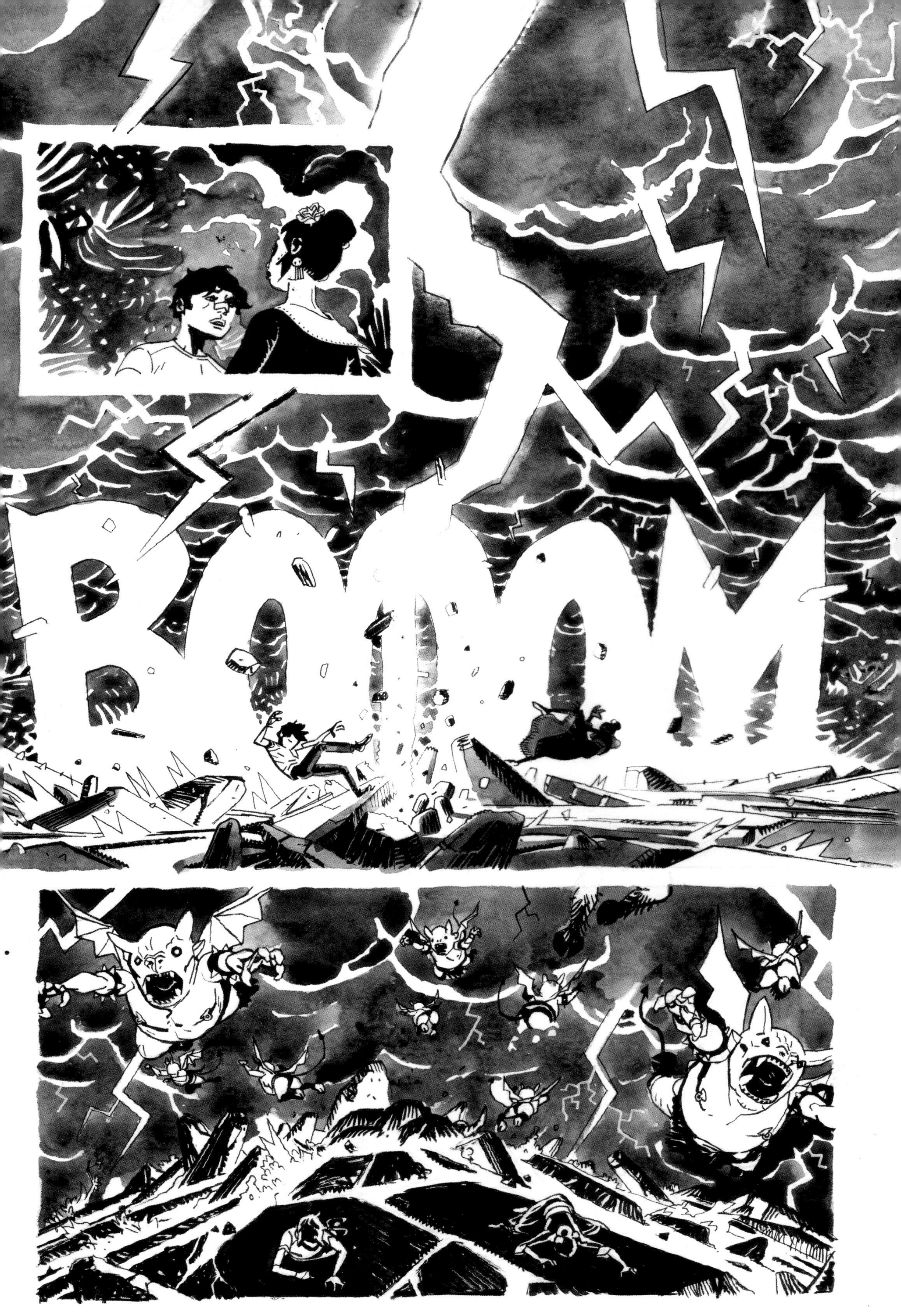
BOOM

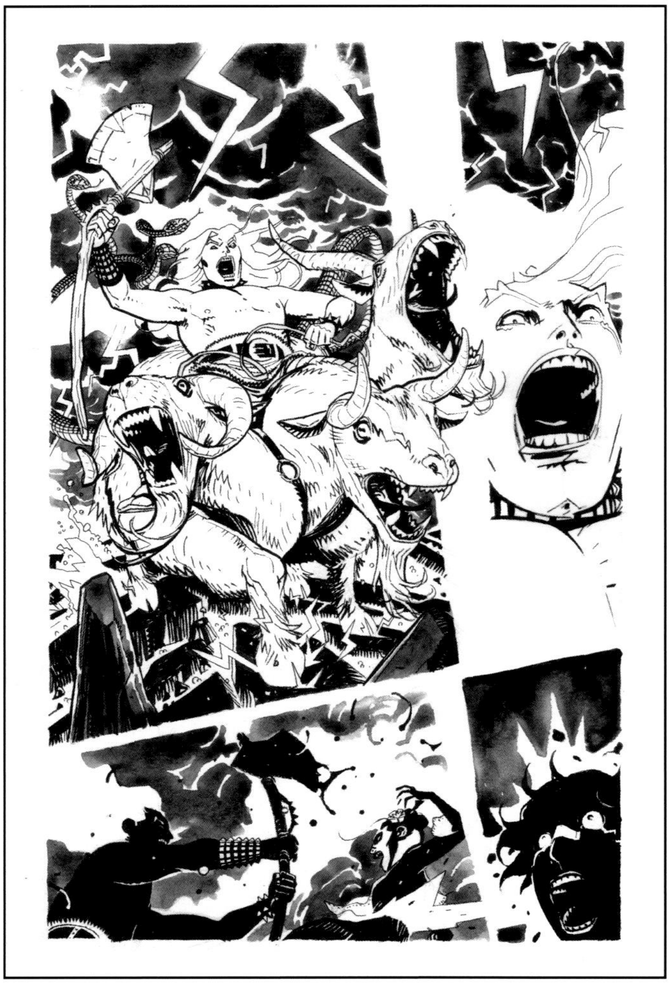
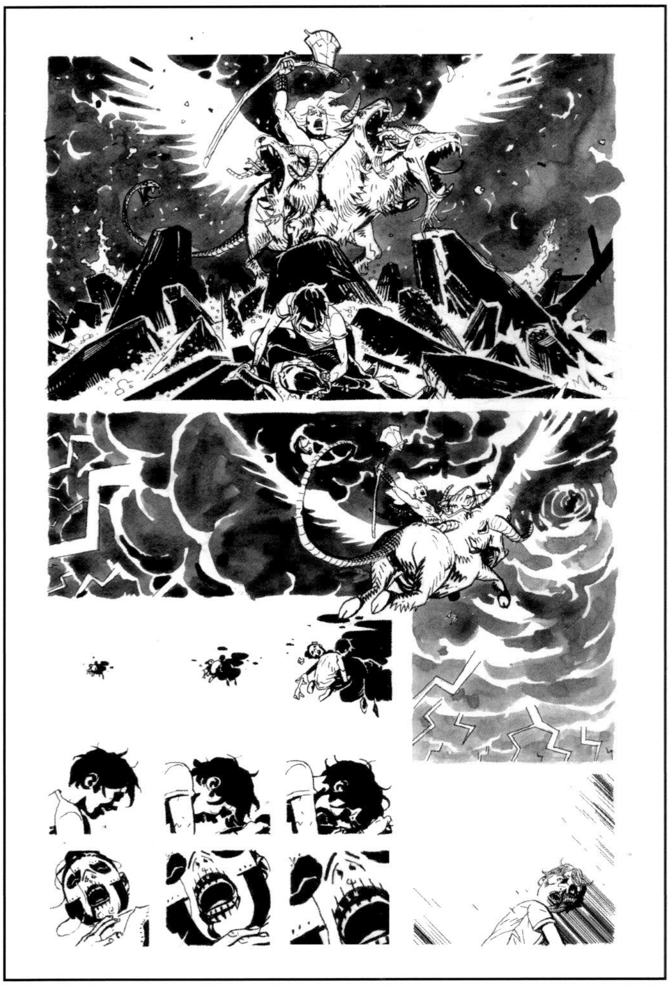
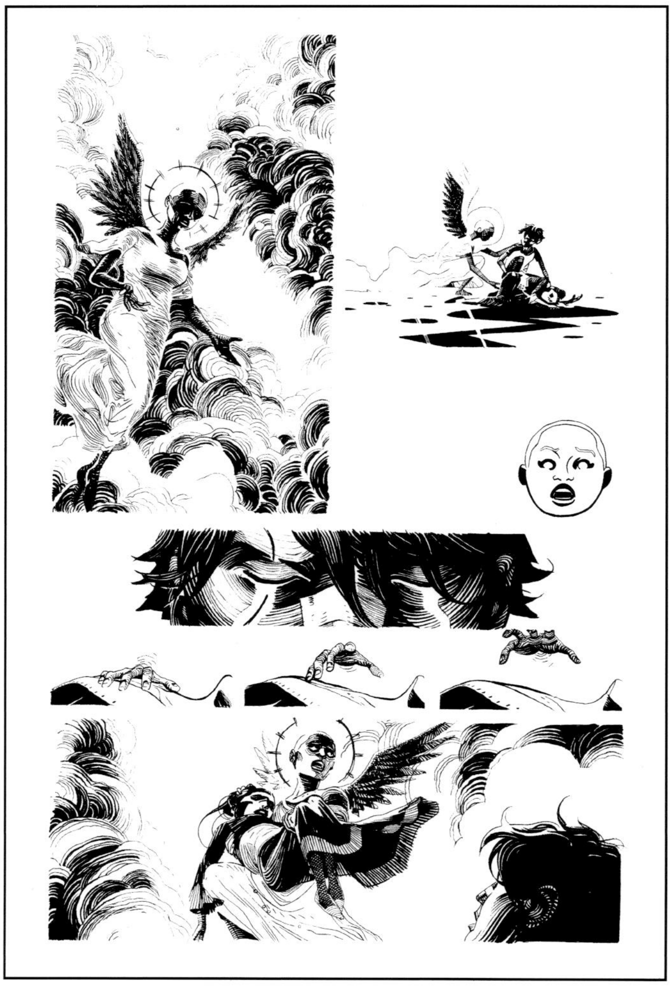
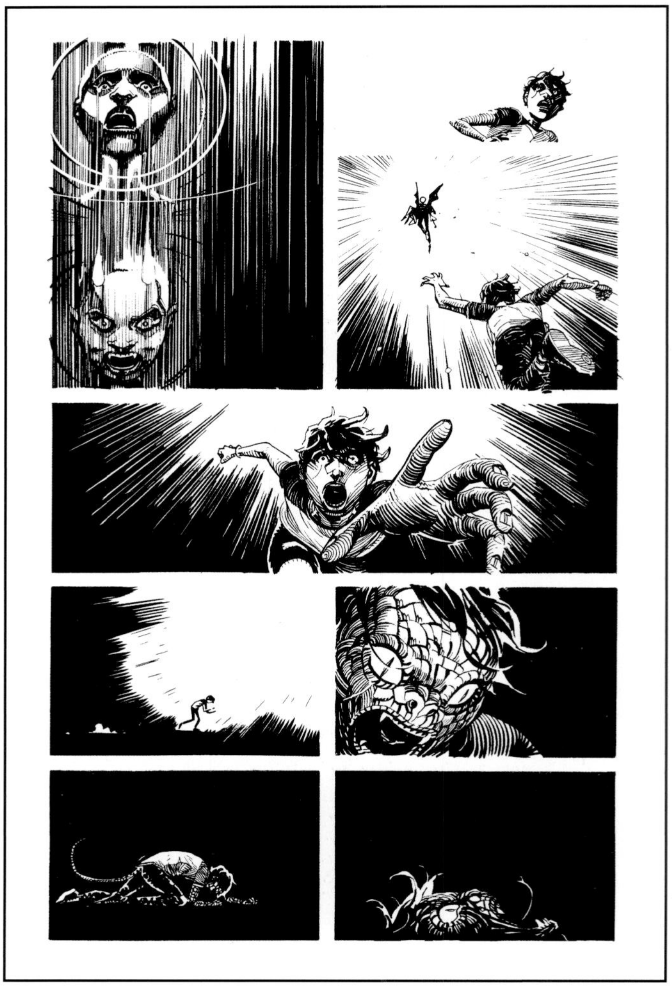

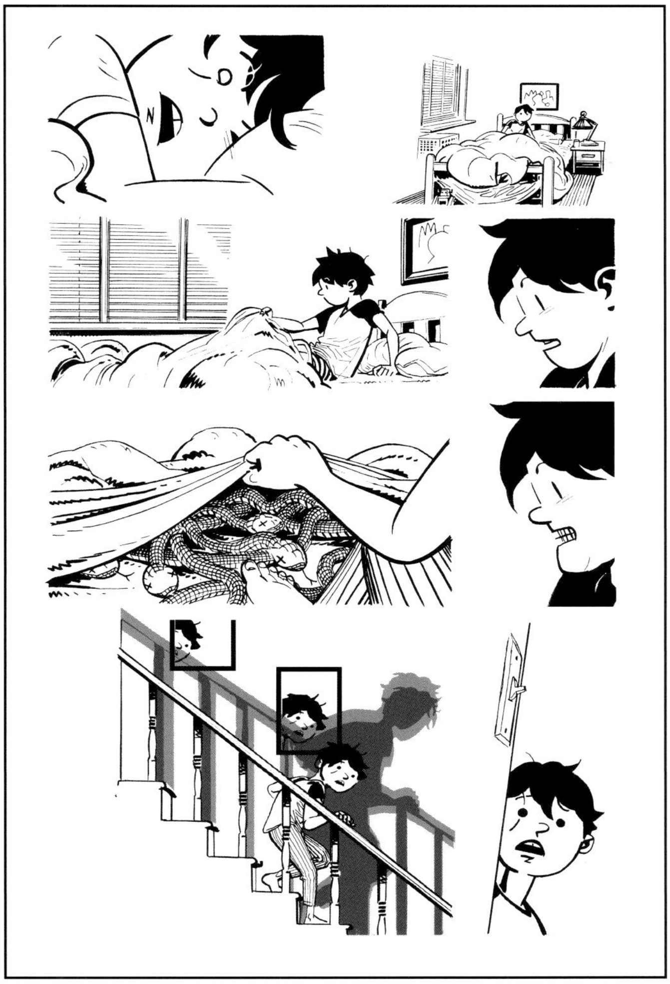
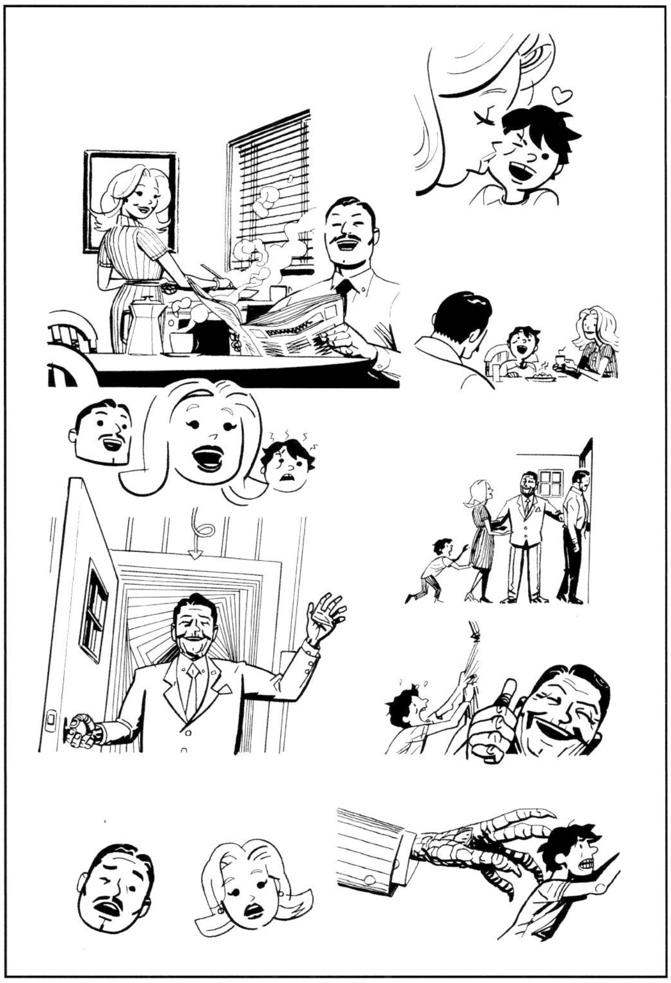
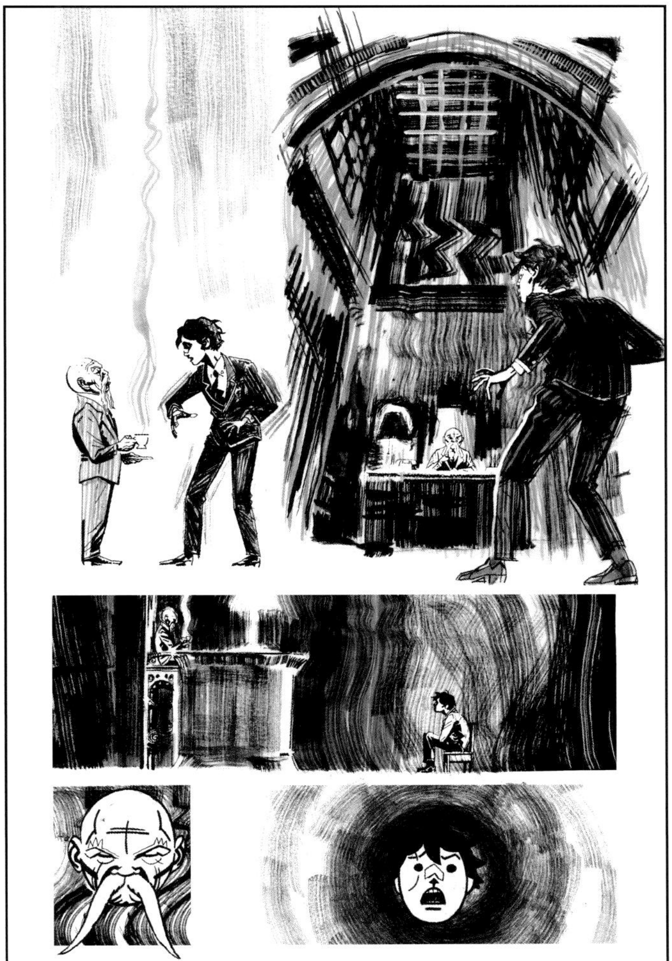
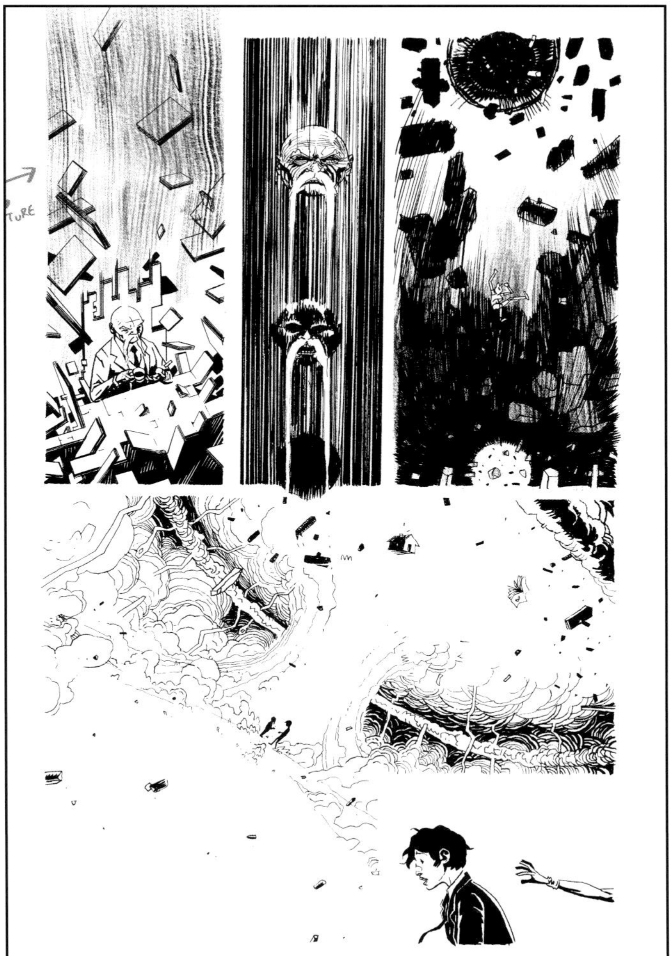

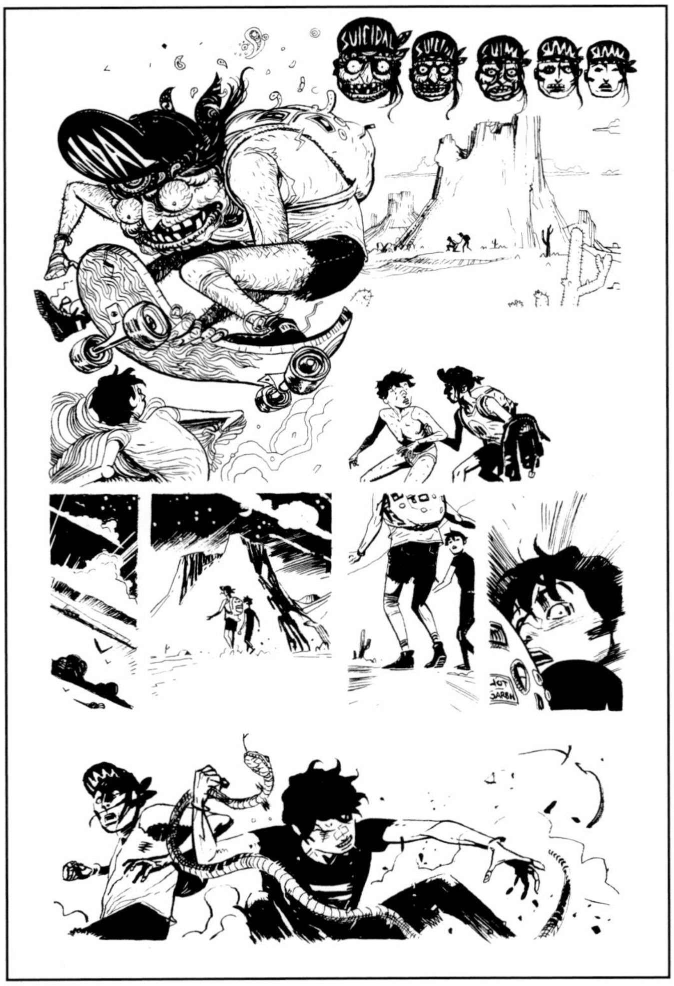
SUICIDAL

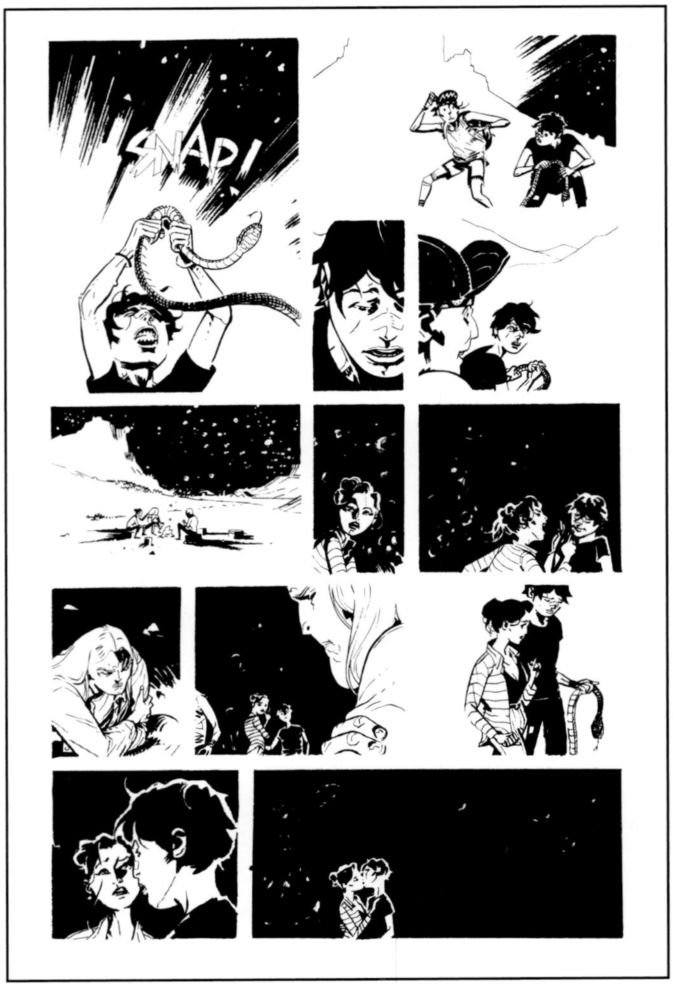
SNAP!

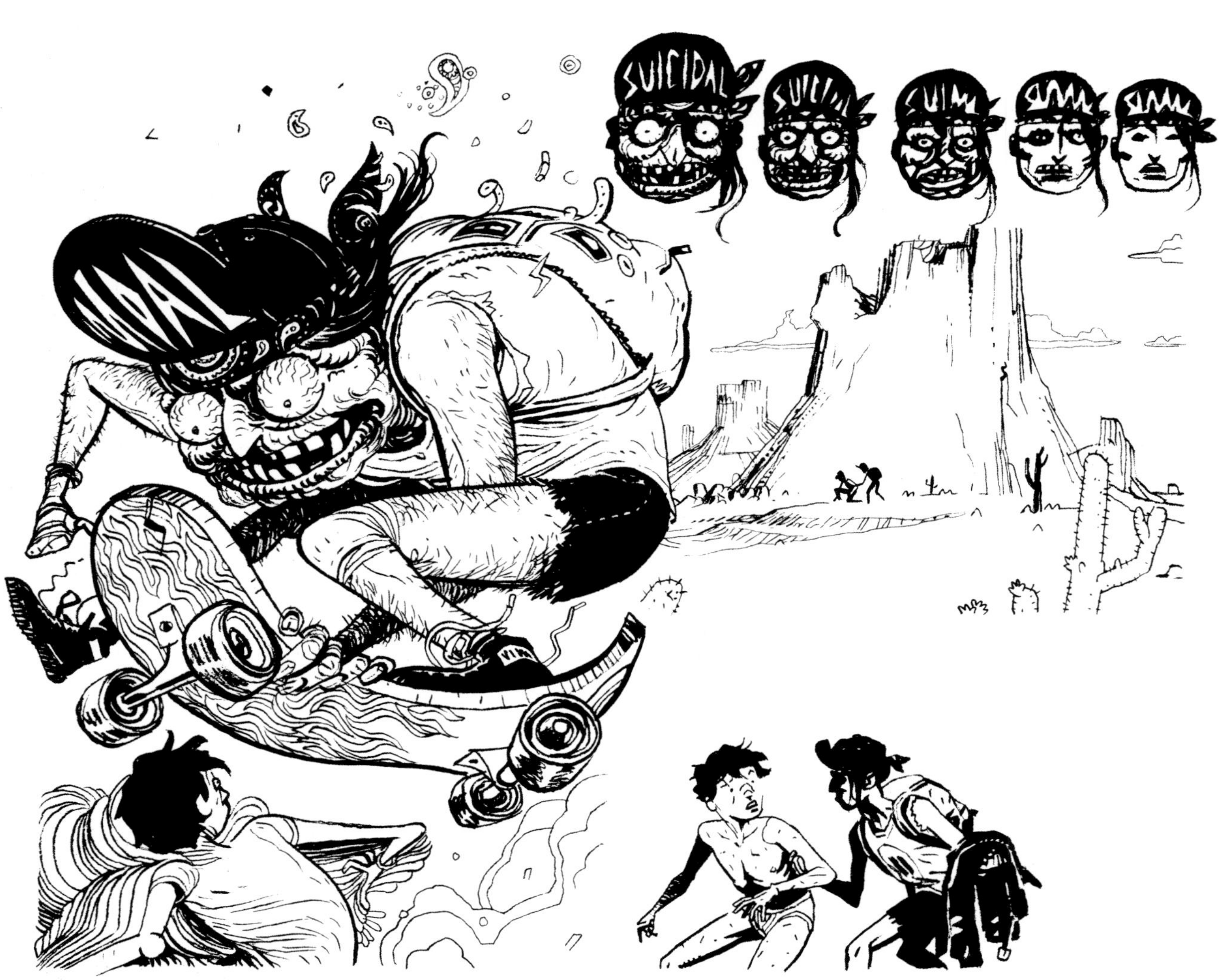
SUICIDAL

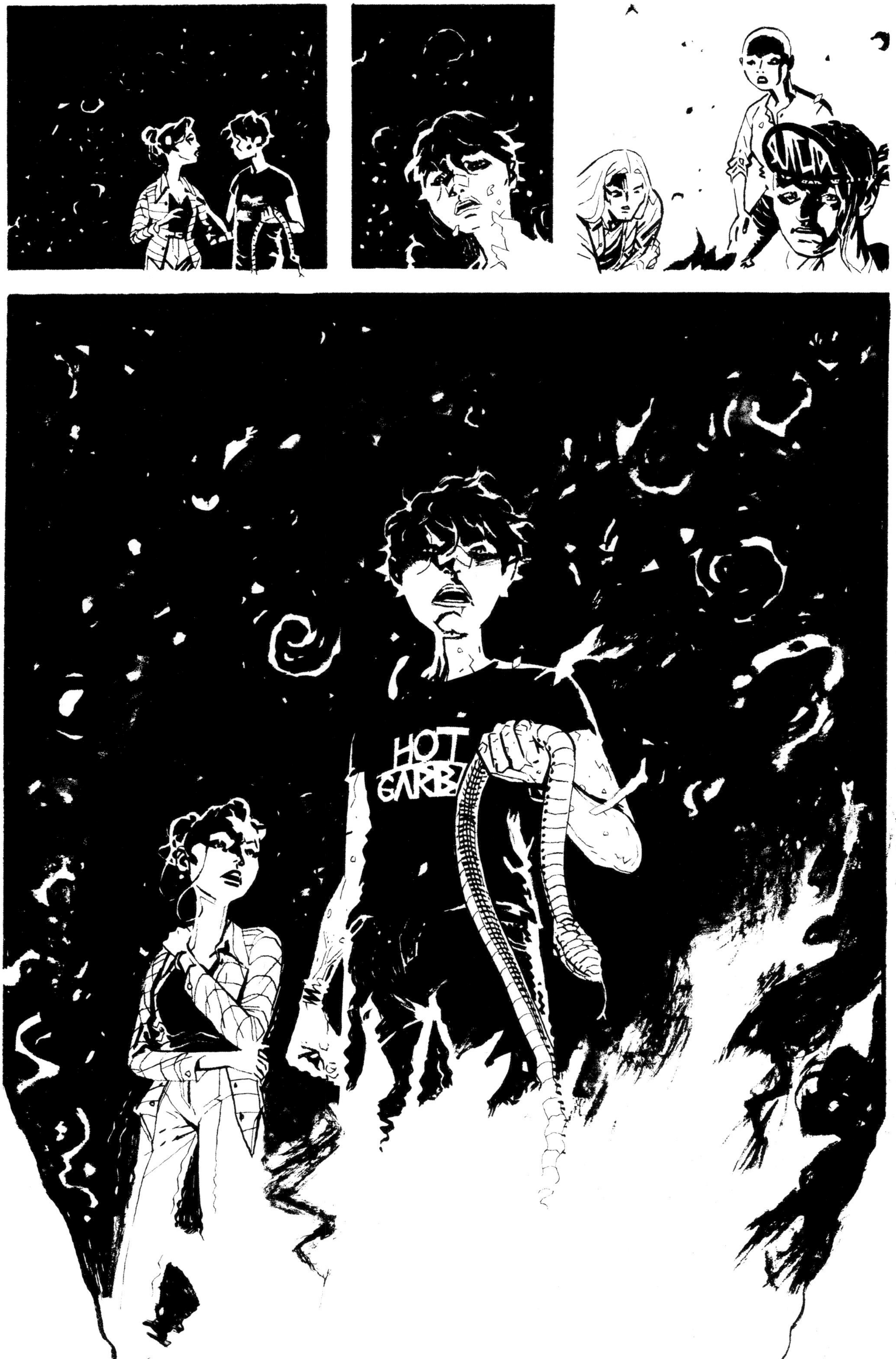
HOT GARB

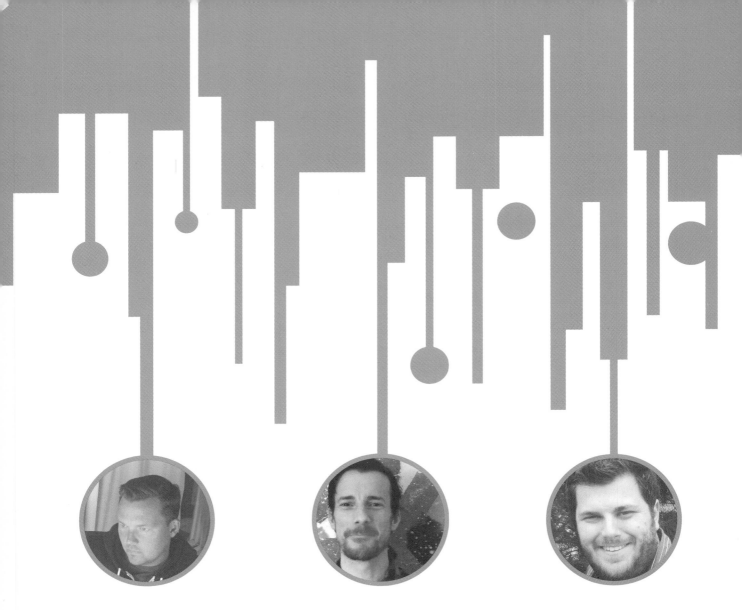

RICK REMENDER is the co-creator of *Deadly Class*, *Black Science*, *Seven to Eternity*, *LOW*, *The Scumbag*, *Fear Agent*, *Tokyo Ghost*, and more for Image Comics. His work at Marvel Comics is the basis for major elements of *Avengers: Endgame*, *The Falcon and the Winter Soldier*, and *Deadpool 2*. He's written and developed several sci-fi games for Electronic Arts, including the universally acclaimed survival horror title *Dead Space*, and he has worked alongside the Russo brothers as co-showrunner of *Deadly Class*'s Sony Pictures television adaptation. Currently, he's writing the film adaption of *Tokyo Ghost* for Cary Fukunaga and Legendary Entertainment and curating his publishing imprint, Giant Generator.

WES CRAIG is the artist and co-creator of *Deadly Class* with Rick Remender; the writer, co-creator, and cover artist of *The Gravediggers Union* with Toby Cypress; and the writer-artist of *Blackhand Comics*, published by Image. Working out of Montreal, Quebec, he has been drawing comic books professionally since 2004 on such titles as *Guardians of the Galaxy*, *Batman*, and *The Flash*.

Despite nearly flunking kindergarten for his exclusive use of black crayons, **JORDAN BOYD** has moved on to become an increasingly prolific comic book colorist, including work on *Astonishing Ant-Man* and *All-New Wolverine* for Marvel; *Invisible Republic*, *Evolution,* and *Deadly Class* for Image; *Devolution* at Dynamite; and *Suiciders: Kings of HelL.A.* for DC/Vertigo. He and his wife, kids, dogs, hedgehogs, and fish currently live in Norman, OK.

IMAGE COMICS, INC.

Todd McFarlane • President
Jim Valentino • Vice President
Marc Silvestri • Chief Executive Officer
Erik Larsen • Chief Financial Officer
Robert Kirkman • Chief Operating Officer

Eric Stephenson • Publisher / Chief Creative Officer
Nicole Lapalme • Controller
Leanna Caunter • Accounting Analyst
Sue Korpela • Accounting & HR Manager
Marla Eizik • Talent Liaison
Jeff Boison • Director of Sales & Publishing Planning
Dirk Wood • Director of International Sales & Licensing
Alex Cox • Director of Direct Market Sales
Chloe Ramos • Book Market & Library Sales Manager
Emilio Bautista • Digital Sales Coordinator
Jon Schlaffman • Specialty Sales Coordinator
Kat Salazar • Director of PR & Marketing
Drew Fitzgerald • Marketing Content Associate
Heather Doornink • Production Director
Drew Gill • Art Director
Hilary DiLoreto • Print Manager
Tricia Ramos • Traffic Manager
Melissa Gifford • Content Manager
Erika Schnatz • Senior Production Artist
Ryan Brewer • Production Artist
Deanna Phelps • Production Artist

imagecomics.com

ERIKA SCHNATZ
production design

DEADLY CLASS BOOK 3: TEEN AGE RIOT First printing. March 2022. Published by Image Comics, Inc. Office of publication: PO BOX 14457, Portland, OR 97293. Copyright © 2022 Rick Remender & Wes Craig. All rights reserved. Contains material originally published in single magazine form as DEADLY CLASS #32-44 and FCBD 2019 DEADLY CLASS "KILLER SET" ONE-SHOT. DEADLY CLASS™ (including all prominent characters featured herein), its logo and all character likenesses are trademarks of Rick Remender & Wes Craig, unless otherwise noted. Image Comics® and its logos are registered trademarks of Image Comics, Inc. No part of this publication may be reproduced or transmitted, in any form or by any means (except for short excerpts for journalistic or review purposes), without the express written permission of Rick Remender & Wes Craig, or Image Comics, Inc. All names, characters, events, and locales in this publication are entirely fictional. Any resemblance to actual persons (living or dead), events, or places, without satirical intent, is coincidental. **PRINTED IN CHINA.** For international rights, contact: foreignlicensing@imagecomics.com.

STANDARD EDITION ISBN: 978-1-5343-2199-1
DCBS EXCLUSIVE VARIANT EDITION ISBN: 978-1-5343-2258-5